THE
CURSE
ON THE
CHOSEN

by Ian Irvine

THE THREE WORLDS SERIES

THE VIEW FROM THE MIRROR QUARTET
A Shadow on the Glass
The Tower on the Rift
Dark is the Moon
The Way between the Worlds

THE WELL OF ECHOES QUARTET
Geomancer
Tetrarch
Alchymist
Chimaera

THE SONG OF THE TEARS
The Fate of the Fallen
The Curse on the Chosen

IAN IRVINE

A TALE OF THE THREE WORLDS

THE
CURSE
ON THE
CHOSEN

Volume Two of THE SONG OF THE TEARS

www.orbitbooks.net

ORBIT

First published in Australia in 2007 by Penguin Group (Australia),
a division of Pearson Australia Group Pty Ltd.
First published in Great Britain in 2006 by Orbit

Text copyright © Ian Irvine, 2007
Maps copyright © Ian Irvine, 2007

The moral right of the author has been asserted.

A CIP catalogue record for this book
is available from the British Library.

ISBN 978-1-84149-470-8

Printed and bound in Great Britain by
Clays Ltd, St Ives plc

Orbit
An imprint of
Little, Brown Book Group
100 Victoria Embankment
London EC4Y 0DY

An Hachette Livre UK Company

www.orbitbooks.net

ACKNOWLEDGEMENTS

I would like to thank my editor, Nan McNab, and my agent, Selwa Anthony, for their hard work and support over many years. Thanks to Janet Raunjak and Laura Harris at Penguin Books, and Bella Pagan and Darren Nash at Orbit Books for support, encouragement and assistance. I would like to thank everyone at Penguin Books and Orbit Books for working so hard on the ten books of this series to date, and for doing so well with them.

CONTENTS

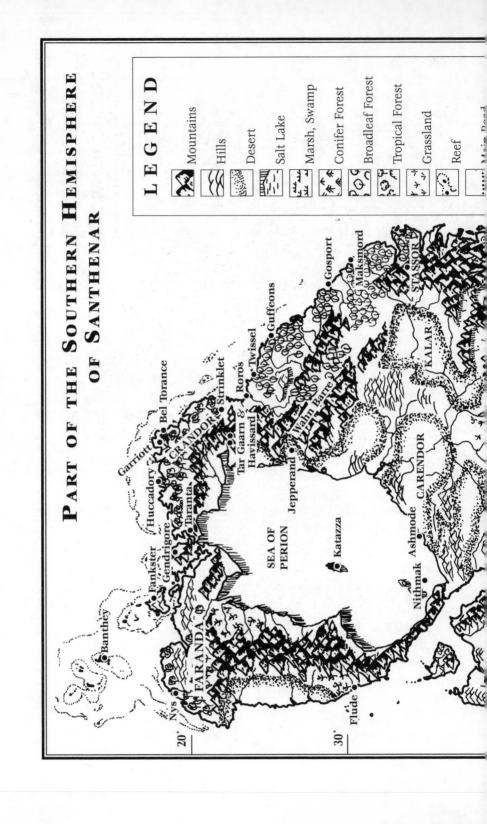

PART OF THE SOUTHERN HEMISPHERE OF SANTHENAR

LEGEND

Mountains	
Hills	
Desert	
Salt Lake	
Marsh, Swamp	
Conifer Forest	
Broadleaf Forest	
Tropical Forest	
Grassland	
Reef	
Main Road	

Banthey

Fankster

Nys

Gendrigore

FARANDA

Huccadory

Garriott

Bel Torance

CRANDOR

Strinklet

Taranta

Tar Gaarn &

Roros

Twissel

Havissard

Guffeons

Gosport

Maksmord

STASSOR

Jepperand

Wahn Barre

KALAR

SEA OF PERION

Katazza

CARENDOR

CARENDOR

Nithmak

Ashmode

Flude

20°

30°

Great Mountains

Tiksi

Tirthrax

MIRRILLADELL

Burning
Mountain

LAURALIN

Fiz Gorgo

KARAMA MALAMA
(Sea of Mists)

OOLO

HA-DROW • Ogur

LUUMA NARTA

SHAZABBA

Steppe

Noom

KARA AGEL
(Frozen Sea)

Grinding

N
E
S
W

SCALE

KILOMETERS

0 100 200 300 400 500 600 700 800 900 1000

LEAGUES

0   40   80   120   160   200

50˚

60˚

70˚

Maps by the author

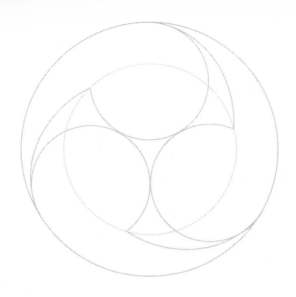

PART ONE

THE CHTHONIC FLAME

ONE

Maelys stood frozen in the centre of the cave, glaring at the rigid back of her enemy. The nightmare had come to pass. That monster, Jal-Nish Hlar, God-Emperor of all Santhenar, held her mother, aunts and her little sister Fyllis, the only family Maelys had left, in the festering dungeons of Mazurhize. Now they were going to pay for her failure; they would die in unspeakable agony for helping Nish escape his father's prison, and it had all been for nothing.

'Uurgh! Gahh!'

Xervish Flydd was on his knees, throwing up on the floor, and she blamed herself for that as well. She had pressured him to *renew* his aged, failing body, but the spell had gone wrong and the God-Emperor had appeared before Flydd could recover from the trauma. Though he now had the body of a man in middle age, he had lost his gift for the Secret Art. Without it they could not hope to escape through the sealed door into the perilous shadow realm as they had planned, then back to a distant part of Lauralin where they could hide in safety while Flydd regained his strength.

Huge, gentle Zham stood by the columns carved into the rear wall, sword in hand, but he could do nothing to save them. Neither could her friend Colm, beside him. They were also going to die.

And then there was Nish, slumped against the side wall. Maelys had once looked up to him as the Deliverer, the one man who could overthrow the tyrant God-Emperor, break his cruel grip on the world and relieve the suffering of Santhenar's downtrodden people. Nish had made that promise and all Santhenar looked to him to keep it, but he never would. Ten years in Mazurhize had broken him; he wasn't a shadow of the hero he'd once been.

Jal-Nish, secure in the power of his Profane Tear, Reaper, stood nonchalantly on the sill of the cave, at the brink of the thousand-span-high precipice of Mistmurk Mountain, gazing out. The twin bands of his platinum half-mask circled the back of his head, one high, the other low, and his good hand fondled the sorcerous quicksilver tear that hung from a chain about his neck. And well he might, for Reaper and its absent twin, Gatherer, gave him the power to control the world.

His sky palace ground its way towards them on the thigh-thick cables anchoring it to the plateau. In a few minutes it would be within reach; his Imperial Guard would come down the gangplank and all hope would be lost.

Maelys's stomach knotted at the thought of what Jal-Nish's torturers would do to her little sister, a slender, pretty, blonde-haired girl of nine – no, she would be ten now. Fyllis wasn't clever, but she possessed a gift that had saved her family several times, when the God-Emperor's scriers had come searching ruined Nifferlin Manor armed with uncanny spying devices. Jal-Nish wanted to eradicate all stray gifts for the Secret Art, and did not hesitate to kill children to ensure that he succeeded.

Her jaw was clenched so tight that her teeth hurt. A stray breeze swirled through the entrance, icing the sweat on her brow. She must save her family, whatever it took, or die trying. No, she could not die. Failure was unthinkable; she couldn't give up, even if everyone else had, but how was *she* to defeat the most powerful man in the world?

Jal-Nish had deliberately turned his back to show his utter contempt for them, and drive home their helplessness. And she *was* helpless, for Maelys was a small, demure woman, only nineteen, with no training in the warrior's arts. Moreover, she'd been brought up to be truthful, polite, gentle and respectful, and her stern aunts had taught her obedience with a leather strap. How could she hope to match wits with this cunning and merciless man; to defy his authority over them all?

She had to find a way. Jal-Nish wasn't as powerful as the world believed him to be, yet he had easily overcome everyone in this cavern. Nonetheless, he had a secret fear that someone would find the antithesis to his Profane Tears – the one thing that could nullify their power – and lead an army to overthrow him. Maelys had foolishly pressured the old, feeble Flydd to cast that terrible renewal spell upon himself in the hope that he could help her find the antithesis to the tears, and she had to answer for the consequences.

Only one person might know if the antithesis existed, and that was the Numinator, the shadowy figure who had established and controlled the former Council of Scrutators during the one hundred and fifty year war against the lyrinx. The Numinator dwelt in the Tower of a Thousand Steps, on the Island of Noom in the frozen Antarctic wastes, a thousand leagues – a year's march – to the south of here. It was an impossible distance in a world whose every ell was monitored by the God-Emperor's human, and inhuman, spies.

The sky palace crept ever closer. It was connected to the mouth of the cave by a long but narrow metal plank which swayed and flexed in the ferocious updraught rushing up the sides of the plateau. Jal-Nish watched the approach, not bothering to check on his prisoners. What if she ran and thrust him over the cliff? Any normal man would be smashed to pulp at the bottom, but Jal-Nish was not a normal man; she felt sure he could save himself with Reaper. Besides, she was no murderer; it wasn't in her to kill a man from behind, not even him.

She knew he dreaded that everything he'd done would be undone once he grew old and died. He sought immortality with the tears, yet feared that he would never find it. But Maelys did not know how to exploit that weakness, either.

So much for his fears; what about his hopes? Family was everything to Jal-Nish, though his wife had repudiated him many years ago, after a lyrinx's claws turned him into a monstrosity. His daughter and three older sons had died without issue and he had no living relatives apart from Nish, who had just rejected his father's offer and all he stood for. Though Jal-Nish felt desperately alone, he was too proud to ask for his only son's help again.

'Flames,' slurred Flydd. 'White, cold flames, burning but never consuming.'

He had been talking nonsense for ages, always about fire and darkness. He groaned and slumped back to sit on his heels, threads of vomit and blood-stained saliva hanging from his open mouth. Jal-Nish's head shot around, his fingers working instinctively on the shimmering surface of Reaper, only to let out a short, barking laugh. Flydd heaved up a black clot onto the dry moss; Jal-Nish, bouncing on the balls of his feet, resumed his vigil.

'Darkness aflame,' choked Flydd. 'Never the same; forever in pain; the flame to regain.' He spat out another clot and began to mumble incoherently.

And Maelys had helped to do this to him. Guilt-ridden, she tried to shut out his groans, for the sky palace would be here in a minute. Family was her only lever and Nish was all the God-Emperor had left – *or was he?* What if she could convince Jal-Nish otherwise?

Her heart began to thunder. Dare she try? Jal-Nish had been a scrutator, and possessed all their arts of interrogation and torture; he was practised at extracting secrets from even the most hardened opponents. He must be even more skilled now, for Gatherer controlled his wisp-watchers, loop-listeners, snoop-sniffers and all the other instruments, public and secret, with which he maintained control over the world. No one could resist Gatherer, with the possible exception of little Fyllis.

But Gatherer was on his sky palace, and that gave Maelys a slender chance. Could she pull it off, all alone? She quailed at the thought of trying, for deceit was foreign to her nature, but she had to, no matter what it cost her. She knew there would be a cost; she'd discovered that the first time she'd been forced to act against her principles.

Somewhere below the entrance to the cavern, rock crunched. Jal-Nish held up his hand and the grinding stopped as the winch cables were halted. He leaned out, peering down at the gigantic anchor embedded in the precipice below the cavern, which sounded as if it were tearing free.

'Slowly,' he said to Reaper. 'Take it slowly now.'

The grinding resumed; the sky palace inched closer. Flydd was raving about wraiths and darkness, and a woman dressed in red, but his eyes were empty. She began to fear that his old self was lost inside his renewed body and he was sinking into insanity, but she couldn't worry about that now. It was all up to her and she had to do two impossible things: first, find a way to save her family from Jal-Nish, and second, discover a means of escape.

The glimmerings of a plan came to her, so reckless that it just might work, though if she were caught he would put her to such agonies that the chroniclers would still be telling the tale in a thousand years. She looked away, struggling to curb her panic. How could a shy, bookish country girl even think to deceive the God-Emperor and his Profane Tears?

She had to find a way. Maelys glanced through the swaying curtains of moss and lichen that partly closed off the entrance. Jal-Nish was still looking out. She made up her mind; she would not give up on her family while she lived. She would do whatever it took, and pay the price later.

Taking a deep breath, conscious that she might not have many left, she called, 'Jal-Nish?' She could not bring herself to use the title *God-Emperor*.

He turned and put his head through the moss curtain, frowning at her. Maelys's knees went weak at the thought of what she was about to do. It couldn't possibly succeed; he would see through her instantly.

'Yes?' he said. The platinum half-mask covered the ruined left and central parts of his face, including his nose and chin, but left his right eye, brow and cheek exposed. 'What do you want, girl?'

Maelys couldn't bear to look at him, or Nish, who had previously rejected her so humiliatingly; or least of all, Colm, whom she felt sure was in love with her. She cared for him too, and admired him even more, since Colm, honourable man that he was, had previously declined to press his suit at such a difficult time for her. After this, he never would. What she was about to do would cost her all her friends, and mean the death of any hopes she held for Colm and herself.

'I'm pregnant!' she said hoarsely. 'By Nish.'

TWO

Colm choked. Nish jerked upright. The dead moss rustled where Flydd knelt, bloody strings swinging from his lips. Even the gentle giant, Zham, looked shocked.

Maelys couldn't afford to look any of them in the face. This meant life or death; nothing else mattered. She kept staring at Jal-Nish, and his one eye lit up for an instant, enough to give him away. Oh yes, he wanted what she could bear him – he wanted it more than anything in his empire. But then his face hardened.

'Cryl-Nish said, only half an hour ago, that he's not had congress with any woman since escaping from Mazurhize. Are you calling my son a liar?'

'No,' Maelys said faintly.

His cheek went purple. 'If he's not lying, you must be.'

'I'm not lying,' she gasped. This was much harder than she'd thought; she couldn't do it.

Jal-Nish turned to Nish. Say nothing, Nish, Maelys prayed. Leave it to me.

'Well, Cryl-Nish?' said his father.

'I have not had relations with her. As far as I know, Maelys is a virgin.' Nish's jaw clenched and his eyes flicked towards Colm.

No, Maelys prayed. Please don't say it, Nish. You'll ruin

everything. If you ever cared about me at all, please keep quiet.

He said thickly, 'Though *he* may have taken her on the way here – they were close enough when they arrived.'

Out of the corner of her eye Maelys saw Colm's look of outrage. 'I may be just a humble woodcutter to you, Deliverer, but I've behaved as a gentleman with Maelys, as I have with all women. While you, *surr*, are nothing but scum, no matter who your father is.'

Jal-Nish's fingers stroked Reaper, hooked through its silvery surface and Colm doubled over, gasping for air.

'Despite his manifest failings,' he grated, 'Cryl-Nish is my only son, and the chosen one. You will treat him with the respect due to his station.'

Colm collapsed, clawing at the dead moss covering the floor. Jal-Nish looked away indifferently and spoke to Maelys. 'Virginity is easily tested, girl. Think carefully before you say any more, for every untrue word earns you a deeper excruciation.'

Maelys *had* thought very carefully, but even so, she was starting to doubt whether she could pull it off. The story was already spinning out of her control. Besides, she had always been a modest girl, and in her family people did not talk about such matters, especially not to strangers; but there was no going back now.

'You may have me tested,' she said, flushing at the thought of it, even at speaking of such an intimate test, 'and you will discover that I am a virgin still. *Colm* does not lie. *He* is a gentleman.'

'Then you're a lying slut,' spat Jal-Nish. 'You've proven it out of your own mouth.'

The sky palace loomed into view, its white stone sails shining in a fleeting ray of sunlight. He stopped it with a backwards gesture.

'I'm neither a liar nor a slut.' Maelys felt her cheeks going even redder. 'I *am* pregnant, to Nish.'

'Why do you insist on this vicious falsehood?' Jal-Nish's

flesh-formed hand gripped a rock at the entrance, crushing it to dust. 'Faugh! I've had enough of this.' He turned to step out onto the plank and Maelys could not think how to stop him.

'There is – a way,' Flydd said hoarsely from the floor. 'We both know – it can be done, Jal-Nish.'

Jal-Nish spun on his boot heel on the swaying plank, strode back to Maelys and lifted her by the front of her shirt, staring into her eyes. She forced herself to meet his one eye, and again she saw that fleeting spark of hope in it.

'Well, girl?' he said, letting her down again. 'I have to know. And you must understand that, once I have Gatherer in my hands again, I can sort truth from falsehood in an instant.'

Yet you want this grandchild so desperately you can't bear to wait until the sky palace arrives. It was his weakness and her opportunity, though only if she could capitalise on it once she'd told her story, and Maelys still hadn't thought of a way to do that.

'Your son is a passionate man,' she said, 'a lusty man who had been deprived for ten years.'

'I know my son,' he said thickly. 'I was like that myself, before the tears raised me above such animal appetites. Get on with it.'

The cavern was perfectly still; there was no sound apart from the swishing of the moss curtain in the wind and the creaking of the monstrous mooring cables as the sky palace moved in the updraughts.

'I nursed Nish after he was wounded leading the Defiance in their victory over your army,' said Maelys. So far, so good, but she hadn't begun the real lie yet. Her eyes met Nish's, and it looked as though he was trying to say something, but she couldn't tell what.

'It was no victory at all,' sneered Jal-Nish. 'I was directing my troops via Gatherer. I let him win.'

No difficulty reading Nish's face now. He was a man

stripped naked to the world, his anguish showing in the shards of his cheekbones, the fingers like fishhooks; the raw, running eyes.

Maelys felt acid rising up into her throat, burning her. Jal-Nish was an even bigger monster than she'd thought. 'You deliberately sent thousands of men to their deaths, and left the rest of your own army dying in agony in that slaughter heap? Why?'

Jal-Nish chuckled. 'It amused me to let the so-called Defiance think they could win, for it will make their ultimate defeat all the more crushing. How did you do it, girl?'

Maelys could barely breathe. She couldn't speak for a moment, but she had to master herself. The soldiers were long dead; she had to take care of the living.

'Nish . . .' It was so difficult to say it; she felt a scarlet blush spreading up her neck and across her cheeks. 'Your – your son is such a lusty man that, even while recovering from that terrible arrow wound, he was . . . subject to an, er, nocturnal, um, flux.'

'Nocturnal *flux*?' Jal-Nish cried. 'Speak in a plain tongue, girl, and be swift about it, or Reaper will sear it out of your living mouth.'

'Even in the most terrible fever, and half dead, Nish became so aroused each night that he spilled his seed upon the sheets.' Her cheeks were so inflamed that they stung. 'I had to have him, any way I could, but Nish would not have me at any price.'

'I'm not surprised. My son is entitled to princesses; he could see nothing in such a plain little minx as you.'

Maelys was used to insults, she'd had a lifetime of them from her mother and aunts, yet she winced. 'And so,' she went on haltingly, 'on the second night of nursing him, while Nish groaned in his lusty delirium, I gathered up his seed and inserted it within myself, and now I'm pregnant by him. And still a virgin; it can only be his child.'

There was a shattering silence. Maelys lowered her

head, trying to see Nish out of the corner of her eye, but he had turned away. Not Colm, though. He was staring at her in appalled, contemptuous disgust. He was not a forgiving man: in his eyes their time together, and their friendship, had been a lie and a stain on his own honour. No matter what happened next, he would never forgive her.

'The chances of becoming pregnant –' began Jal-Nish.

'My clan are *very* fertile,' she said truthfully. 'And it was the right time of the month.'

'Well, Son?' said Jal-Nish. 'What do you have to say?'

Nish wore a faint smile. He was not displeased to be described as a lusty man. Boor, she thought. Oaf! Yet he met her eye and, surprisingly, she saw no censure there – indeed, a trace of admiration that she'd been game to take his father on. Despite his flaws, Nish possessed qualities that Colm would never have.

'I am, as we discussed earlier, a man of strong appetites,' Nish said. 'What Maelys says could be true. I lay in a fever for days, so how would I know what she got up to?'

Jal-Nish turned back to her. 'Why?' he said simply.

She'd scraped over the first hurdle but Maelys couldn't relax yet. Now was time for the plain truth. 'Ever since I was a little girl, and first heard the tale of Nish's heroism and nobility in the lyrinx wars, I've looked up to him. I admired . . . *admire* him above all men.'

'So you had to have him, any sordid way you could, to further your absurd fantasy.' His lip curled.

'I did not,' she said with dignity, 'for I knew Nish was far above me and out of reach. I come from a good family, yet I'm a simple country girl and the ways and doings of the mighty are beyond me.'

'Indeed they are!' said Jal-Nish. 'I would not have chosen *you* for my son; not for anything. Then why?'

'My mother and aunts knew how I admired Nish and required me to commit this dreadful wickedness, for it was the only way to save our clan – Clan Nifferlin.'

'Clan Nifferlin,' Jal-Nish said thoughtfully. 'An old clan,

13

once troublesome, but no more. All resistance failed with the death of the last male – your father, Rudigo – a week ago.'

That shook her, though her beloved father had been on the run since she was twelve, and had been captured long ago. She'd been expecting his death for a year, but even so, tears welled in her eyes.

'Father is dead? Please, did he suffer at the end?'

'Oh, I made him suffer,' said Jal-Nish with vengeful relish. 'Once I discovered your role in Cryl-Nish's escape, I kept Rudigo alive so he could suffer all the more.'

Maelys lowered her head. She couldn't speak; could not bear to think of her father in torment because of what her mother and aunts had forced her to do.

'Your aunts put you up to this,' Jal-Nish said, 'and somehow you, *a simple country girl*, succeeded against all the odds. You *have* saved your family, for the moment at least, for until proven otherwise your clan is bound to mine with indissoluble ties of blood. There's more to you than meets the eye, girl. Perhaps you aren't such a bad choice after all – *if you're telling the truth*. But I'll soon discover that, and if you have been truthful, you will have everything you've ever dreamed of.' He studied her, then Nish, then Maelys again. 'And if you've lied – well, I'll leave that to your *fertile* imagination.'

Maelys couldn't relax, for she'd merely won her family a tiny reprieve. It could be as little as an hour, once he took her onto the sky palace and tested her with Gatherer, or as much as a few weeks if she held out, and Jal-Nish had to wait until she had her next monthly courses. But the moment she did, Maelys would be revealed as a liar and a cheat, and both she and her family would be doomed. Claiming that she'd miscarried would not save her. Only Nish's child could.

Unless she could get away before he tested her. That was the second impossibility, though having achieved the first, however fleetingly, she felt bolder now.

14

Jal-Nish beckoned the sky palace forwards, impatient to get moving, but there came a terrific crack from below the cave. Gigantic lumps of rock flew in all directions and the mooring cable tore free and hurtled upwards, smashing the gangplank to metal splinters.

Jal-Nish teetered on the rim of the entrance as the cable flailed across the sky like a writhing worm, the massive anchor clanking on its end. The sky palace tilted and the tension of the remaining cables jerked it up out of sight. He cursed, then began shouting orders to his helmsman, via Reaper.

Maelys met Colm's eyes. He gave her a look of deepest contempt and turned away, and she knew she'd lost a friend forever. It hurt, but she put it to one side. Clan first – *always* clan first.

'Xervish,' she said softly. 'Try the crystal again. This is the only chance we'll get.'

He was on his feet now, holding the diamond-clear, thumbnail-sized crystal out on his shaking palm and staring at the fire burning within it – the power it had absorbed from the cursed flame below the obelisk standing in the centre of the marshy plateau. Flame reflected in his brown eyes. 'Can't,' Flydd said dully. 'Nothing left.'

'You've got to find it again. You've got to remember.'

'Art is gone. Body – renewed, but Art – didn't survive. Lost them. Hollowed out; empty; useless.'

Maelys had never heard such bitterness from Flydd before; and without his Arts, how could they hope to escape through the shadow realm to safety? It was a dangerous place where they needed all the protection they could get, and he had long ago woven such protections into his crystals, especially the fifth, the only one left. But no matter how dangerous the shadow realm might be, they had to go through it, for Jal-Nish had covered every other escape route.

'Xervish,' said Nish uneasily, 'please try again. Open the hidden door and get us out of here.'

15

'Arts – lost!' Flydd said through his teeth. 'She – must have taken them.'

'Who? Maelys?' Nish's eyes probed her.

'No!' Flydd gasped, retching again. 'Woman – in red.'

'What woman in red?' said Nish quietly, with an anxious look at his father's back.

'Was in my mind – during renewal. Thought she *was* me.'

'That doesn't make sense, Xervish.'

Flydd looked up blankly. 'Don't know. Memory in pieces.'

'It'll come back. You recognised us, so you've still got some memories. *Use them!*'

'Can't.' Flydd began to retch, spitting bloody muck onto the floor.

'The crystal is charged,' said Maelys, staring at it, though without Flydd's Art it was as useless as a lump of coal. 'Jal-Nish said it has power to open any barrier. Tell us how, Xervish. Hurry!' If renewal had gone wrong, internally, Flydd might be dying. All the more reason for her to act quickly.

Jal-Nish stepped inside. He'd overheard. '*For one who can use it*, I said. None of you can, no matter how you try. But try, by all means.' He smiled maliciously, then turned away and plunged his hand into Reaper again. The sky palace reappeared, listing steeply to starboard in the fierce updraught, and objects began to slide off its decks. Maelys felt her slim hope fading. With Reaper he would soon set the sky palace to rights. What could the God-Emperor not do with the tears?

However the sky palace listed further and Jal-Nish cursed. 'Pathway!'

With a metallic *zing*, a copper-coloured plank fizzed into existence between the cavern and the sky palace. Withdrawing his hand from Reaper, he began to stride up the plank. Coloured pressure patterns swirled across its coppery surface with every step, and it shortened behind him so that he was always walking upon its quivering outer end. Without turning, he thrust his arm backwards and a brown wall formed at the cavern entrance, then slowly solidified like baked clay until the light was blocked out. They were trapped.

'A lucky accident that the anchor tore out,' said Zham. 'Can we make something of it?'

'No accident,' slurred Flydd. 'Monkshart – Vivimord – determined – bring down – blasphemous God-Emperor.'

'And he wants Nish,' Maelys reminded them. 'You'd be better off with your father, Nish. Vivimord is insane.'

'But while Father has Reaper,' said Nish, 'Vivimord can't touch him. Which means –'

'Jal-Nish – playing with us,' said Flydd.

'He loves his little games,' Nish said bitterly. 'And more than anything Father loves to allow his victims to hope, so he can have the pleasure of crushing it. He wants us to dream that there's a way out –'

'Which means there's none,' said Flydd. 'He's set us up.'

Absolute silence fell, for no sound penetrated the seal at the entrance. The cavern was dark, save for the faint light from Flydd's crystal.

'He's not a god; just a pretender,' said Maelys. 'He didn't expect Vivimord to come through the hidden door at the back of the cave; nor did he know what choice Nish was going to make, or what I was going to say. And he can't know what we're going to do next. We've still got a chance. Teach us to use the crystal.'

'Secret Art – years to master. No novice can use – crystal – no matter how much – power it contains.'

His voice was cold; nothing remained of the charming, friendly Flydd she'd met just days ago. Why was he so bitter? Renewal had been a terrible ordeal for him, but he was alive and had a healthy and vigorous body. Couldn't he be thankful for that?

Nish snatched the fiery crystal out of Flydd's hand and thrust it into Maelys's. 'You've got a small gift for the Art. Try it – Father could be back any minute.'

'He could be waiting outside right now, laughing his head off,' said Colm grimly. 'We should have jumped off the cliff when we had the chance.'

'My family needs me,' Maelys hissed.

'And it's abundantly clear that you'll stoop to any depths for them.'

His words were another slap in the face. She wanted to do the same to him; felt an urge to hurt him, but Maelys turned away and clenched her slender fingers around the crystal, trying to think her way into its heart. Its light came pinkly through her flesh, flaring and fading; a pulse was beating in one of the veins of her wrist. Think! There's got to be a way.

She couldn't think of one; Maelys didn't know anything about her little gift, which had been suppressed too long, and now was stunted. Training in the Arts needed to begin in youth and, at nineteen, she was too old to ever achieve mastery.

Could there be a simpler way? She touched the crystal to the columns carved into the rear wall, left and right, high and low, and to the flat section in between, where the secret door had opened. Nothing happened. Maelys imagined Jal-Nish's mocking laughter.

She rubbed the crystal against her forehead and touched it to the taphloid hanging on its chain around her neck, again to no effect. Nish was frowning at her. Did he think their peril was her fault? In a way, it was, but surely it was better than the alternative? If she'd refused her aunts' demand in the first place, he would still be in his father's prison, going mad, and she and her family would be hiding in the mountains, slowly starving to death.

'You try it.' She passed the crystal to him. 'You're the one with the clearsight.'

'My gift is puny,' he reminded her. 'Totally insignificant.'

'But linked – to God-Emperor,' said Flydd. 'Gift came from – touch of tears, Nish.'

'I'll never forget it.' Nish was clutching the crystal in

both hands, one clasped around the other. 'During the war, Father thrust my hands right into the tears in an effort to bend me to his will. Fighting his compulsion almost broke me.'

'But you got free – single-handedly saved what was left of – mighty army,' said Flydd, sounding more coherent now. 'Fighting him strengthened you – Nish. Strength you can draw on now.'

'It's a wonder you still have your hands,' rumbled Zham. 'The touch of Reaper crisped Vivimord's belly like a roast pig, and he's a great mancer.'

'Father protected me, I suppose,' said Nish.

'Power of – tears has grown mightily since – beware!' said Flydd. 'Anything coming to you?'

'Not a thing.'

Maelys's eyes met Zham's. He was standing between the columns, holding his enormous sword. He gave her an encouraging smile, and it warmed her. She still had one friend left. Colm was grimly practising strokes with his notched blade; was he mentally using it on her?

'Nish,' she said, 'what if you used your clearsight to see what's happened to Xervish's Art?'

'I hadn't thought of that.' There was a long silence while Nish strained until a muscle began to jump in his jaw. 'I can't see anything.'

Panic was creeping over Maelys, suffocating her, but she couldn't give in to it. Whenever she wavered, the thought of Fyllis in the hands of Jal-Nish's torturers stiffened her spine for one last try.

'What about using *me*?' she said.

'I don't know what you mean,' said Nish.

'I'm not sure I do, either, but something strange happened to Flydd during renewal last night. After he'd used the fourth crystal, he had to draw on me. He took my hand and I could feel the heat running up my arm to my heart . . . the strength being drawn out of me . . .'

'How does that help?'

'What if he didn't just take from me? What if he *gave* as well?'

Nish frowned, the flickering crystal lighting the furrows across his forehead. 'Xervish? Could Maelys be the woman in red you were raving about?'

'She isn't wearing red.'

'Perhaps, in the fever, she seemed to be.'

Flydd shook his head vigorously, then winced. 'The woman in red looked nothing like Maelys. She wasn't beautiful; her face was stern and arrogant; and she was bigger, taller, and older.'

Maelys stared at Flydd. He thought *she* was beautiful? No one had ever said that before.

'Did you give *anything* to Maelys?' Nish persisted.

'Can't remember what happened during renewal,' Flydd said hoarsely. 'Few mancers ever do.'

'Is it the kind of thing you might have done?'

'Not unless I was desperate. What mancer would willingly give away the least fraction of his Art, knowing he might never get it back?'

'But you *were* desperate, Xervish,' Maelys said softly, glancing over her shoulder at the barrier. Jal-Nish could return at any second. 'Nish, use your clearsight on me, *quickly.*'

He put his hands around her skull, above her ears, and Maelys shivered at his touch. Nish didn't press hard, nor hold his hands there long, and when he drew away there was an odd look in his eyes.

'Xervish, I think you did pass something to Maelys, and yet . . .'

'My Art?' Flydd said hoarsely. 'My precious Art?'

Maelys hadn't realised that it meant so much to him, though when she thought about it, to have been a great mancer for so long, and then to lose it in a moment, must be like losing a limb. No, worse, for a man with no legs can walk with crutches, but losing one's Art would be like going back to the helplessness of infancy.

'There's something not right, though.' Nish swallowed.

'I've lost my Art!' Flydd cried. 'The one thing that has sustained me all my life. I'm naked without it.'

'That's not what I meant.' Nish was staring alternately at Flydd, then Maelys. 'My clearsight tells me that there's *more* of you now, Xervish.'

'That's absurd. If I've passed my gift to her, there should be *less* of me.'

'Can you remember doing that?'

'I can't remember *anything* save the woman coming into me. She had strange eyes – a reddish purple . . . now what does that remind me of?'

'Can you take your talent back from me?' said Maelys.

'Not without the Art . . . though there may be a way to use it where it lies,' said Flydd. 'Look deeper, quick.'

Nish put his hands on Maelys again, and shook his head. 'I can't tell. My clearsight is too feeble.'

'If only there were a way to strengthen it,' said Maelys, musing on what had been said. And how could there be *more* of Flydd when he'd lost his Art? That didn't make sense.

'If we could eat rock, we could chew our way to freedom!' sneered Colm.

'There is a way,' said Nish, ignoring him, 'though I'm not sure I've got the courage to try it.'

'I wouldn't,' said Flydd. 'Your father won't save you this time, Nish.'

Maelys didn't know what they were talking about. 'I'll try anything if it helps to save my family.'

'Not this way,' said Nish. 'I won't let you.'

Flydd's eyes were on Maelys. 'I do believe she would, Nish. She's braver than any of us.'

'Just tell me what to do,' snapped Maelys.

Thump. Something struck the barrier from the outside and it cracked like an ancient bowl. Nish was staring at it, his fists clenched rigidly at his sides and his jaw muscles standing out. He turned to her, and something shone in his eyes. Admiration? Surely not from Nish? Now he let out a long breath, but the fine hairs stirred on the back of Maelys's neck – what was he going to do?

He eased himself into the deep shadows to the left of the opening, crouched and pulled up great handfuls of dead moss until he was covered in it.

'Nish?' said Maelys.

'There's only one hope left,' he said quietly. 'It's do or die this time and I don't care which.'

'What are you going to do?'

'Stay back; distract Father so he thinks I've escaped. As soon as he breaks through, scream my name and leave the rest to me.'

'To the wall,' hissed Zham, sweeping them together in his long arms and thrusting them backwards as the clay seal began to crack and fall out. 'Pretend Nish has gone through the hidden door. When Jal-Nish comes in, we all attack him at once.'

Fragments crashed to the floor and misty light flooded in. Maelys reached out towards the wall and yelled, 'Nish?' as shrilly as she could.

'What the –?' cried Jal-Nish, then leapt to the floor of the cave.

Maelys spun around, trying to maintain the pretence that Nish had disappeared. Jal-Nish came forwards, staring at the closed door. 'How did he get away?'

'Get him!' roared Zham, hurling himself at Jal-Nish.

Nish propelled himself to his feet. Jal-Nish spun around, sure he was under attack, but Nish wasn't going for him. He dived and thrust his left hand deep into Reaper.

And shrieked.

THREE

'You should not have done that, Son,' said Jal-Nish with icy calm. 'I'm not going to protect you this time.'

Nish was writhing on the floor, frantically trying to jerk his hand free, but it was held fast and his wrist and forearm were blistering and growing redder by the second. Maelys caught a whiff of burning flesh and was glad Nish hadn't told her what he was going to do. If she'd done that to herself . . .

As everyone rushed Jal-Nish, he caressed the upper surface of Reaper. Zham was hurled sideways against the hidden door; a *crack-crack* sounded like ribs breaking. Colm went flying across the cavern, thudding into the left-hand wall with his shoulder and side. Maelys dived for Jal-Nish's ankles, trying to heave him off his feet, but was driven face-first into the moss.

Flydd must have thrown something, for Jal-Nish doubled over and fell to his knees, spit spraying through the mouth slit of his mask. Nish's shrieks broke off; he brought his free hand up and crashed it into his father's chin, sending the half mask clanging off the stone sill and over the precipice. Maelys caught a glimpse of the scarred, noseless, suppurating horror of Jal-Nish's face, destroyed by a lyrinx's claws thirteen years ago. Despite all the power the tears gave him, he had never been able to repair the injuries.

Jal-Nish's one eye glazed, his hand fell away from Reaper and he collapsed, unconscious. The quicksilver surface of the Profane Tear turned a dull, roiling red and a hideous clanging erupted from it. The rest of the crazed barrier exploded out of the entrance, tearing the curtains of moss and lichen away, and Maelys heard an answering clanging from bow and stern of the sky palace, a few hundred paces away.

Soldiers ran along the deck, the white armour of the Imperial Guard shimmering, their adamantine blades raised high. The ultimate crime had been committed: the God-Emperor's sacred person had been attacked and they burned to avenge the insult. They converged on the copper plank-path that linked the sky palace to the cavern.

'Kick the plank away,' said Flydd.

Maelys ran and took hold of it with both hands but it was so heavy she could not budge it. Only minutes to live, she thought, but a whole eternity for the dying. Nish's hand was still caught and his lower arm was smoking; his mouth opened and closed as if he were silently shrieking his lungs out.

Maelys couldn't bear to see his agony. She scrambled towards him on hands and knees. 'Nish, Nish?'

She had reached for his sleeve when Flydd shouldered her out of the way. 'Don't touch him, lest you end up the same way.'

'But . . . Nish . . . why did he do it . . .?'

Flydd scooped dry moss from the floor, wrapped it around Nish's wrist and heaved. The moss began to smoulder, then burst into flame. Flydd cursed but didn't let go. With a wrench, he tore Nish's hand free of Reaper.

Maelys nearly threw up, for his hand was a smoking ruin and smelt of burnt meat. She darted to the sill, tore up handfuls of wet moss and covered his hand in it. Steam boiled out; he gave another silent scream. She dragged him to the entrance and thrust his hand out under the cascading water.

Flydd ripped the sleeve off his shirt and pulled it over Nish's hand. Maelys had to help Flydd tie the knots, for renewal had cost him his coordination as well as his Art.

'I can do nothing for the pain, Nish,' said Flydd. 'Did you succeed?'

Nish tried to speak, but his face twisted in another silent rictus. When it finally passed he tried again. 'No choice . . . only way . . . bolster clearsight. Think it worked. Take . . . wrists.'

Flydd took his blistered wrist, Maelys the sound one, and Nish strained. 'I see it,' he slurred. 'See . . . way.'

'How?' said Flydd urgently. 'Zham? Colm? Hold the soldiers off.'

Colm was on his feet, swaying as he attempted to lift Zham. The giant's forehead was bloody and he was holding his side. He leaned against the rear wall and wiped blood out of his eyes with the back of his hand. Drawing his monstrous blade, he advanced unsteadily across the cavern. 'I'll hold them off as long as I can, surr.'

Tears sprang to Maelys's eyes, for Zham was utterly reliable, blindly loyal. She dashed them away. 'Nish? How am I supposed to give Xervish back his Art?'

'Don't . . . think – can. He's got to . . . *take* back. But without Art . . .'

In other words, it was impossible. 'Then how do *I* use it?' She shook his arm in her agitation.

On the floor, Jal-Nish kicked feebly, then slurred, 'They're coming for us – I warned you they were coming, Son. Why wouldn't you listen?'

'What's he on about?' said Colm.

'Father's paranoid,' said Nish. 'He thinks we're being watched by creatures from the void.'

'Maybe we are,' said Flydd. 'That's where the lyrinx came from, and they weren't the first.'

'Father sees enemies everywhere,' sneered Nish. 'The mighty God-Emperor lives in terror of being overthrown.'

Mocking laughter issued from the roiling surface of Reaper.

'How do I use the Art?' Maelys repeated.

Nish's eyes swam in circles. The pain was killing him. 'You . . . can't.'

She wanted to scream. 'Then you've maimed yourself for nothing.'

Nish shook his head. 'Together,' he whispered. 'You've . . . got to do . . . it together.'

'I can't perform any kind of mind-merge without my Art,' said Flydd.

'I don't know what a mind-merge is,' said Maelys. 'Father stunted my talent when I was little, to save me from the scriers. That's why he gave me my taphloid.'

'Yes!' cried Flydd. 'Take it off, quick!'

With her free hand Maelys lifted it over her head, feeling the wrench that she suffered every time she was forced to remove it. She felt naked without it, exposed to the world, for her unshielded talent created an aura which a skilled scrier would detect instantly.

Flydd snatched the taphloid from her hand, holding it by the chain.

'I can feel your great gift shining out in all directions, Maelys,' said Flydd, 'beating on me like hot sun on bare skin. You must focus it on me alone – though not as I am *now*. Look for the old, decrepit but true me; the one you met before I took renewal. Try to find that man, no matter how deep he's buried. *I* can't open the way, but he may be able to, *if* he still exists.'

Another painful, mocking laugh issued from Reaper. Maelys restrained an urge to kick it out the entrance.

'Take my wrist,' said Nish urgently. 'They're coming fast.'

She tried to do what Flydd had asked, but couldn't see him at all, for something obscured everything in her inner eye – a heavy, churning mass of black, burning from the inside out but never consumed, *Reaper*. This close, its power was singeing the fine hair on her arms. Reaper longed to consume her, and it was as corrupt as the man who had created it from the implosion of the Snizort node all those years ago. Those compressed forces had distilled everything good and noble out of it, and now it debauched everything it touched. It longed to corrupt her, to burn her to ashes . . .

'Maelys?' An open hand slapped her hard across the cheek.

She opened her eyes, tore her mind away from Reaper's pull. Flydd was glaring at her.

'You . . . struck me.' She touched her fingers to her stinging cheek.

'What's the matter with you?'

'Reaper!' She shuddered. 'It's too strong; too near. I can't resist it; I can't see anything but Reaper.'

'Try harder. You've got to look beyond it; there's no other way.'

There was shouting outside, then the clash of sword on sword. Zham swayed in the entrance as he fought the first of the crack Imperial Guard. He had the advantage of height and position, but clearly his broken ribs were troubling him and he couldn't hold the enemy off for long.

'Wait,' Maelys said. 'I was wearing my taphloid when I saw Jal-Nish using Gatherer in the Pit of Possibilities –'

Flydd slapped his hand across her mouth so hard that her lips stung. They both turned towards Jal-Nish, who was twitching again.

'It's coming for us,' Jal-Nish said. 'Oh, fire and flame, *it's coming!*'

She averted her eyes from his ghastly face.

'I wish you hadn't mentioned that,' said Flydd in a low voice. 'Reaper may allow Jal-Nish to register what we say, even when he's unconscious, and I don't want him to know what you saw in the Pit.'

It reminded her of the gloomy futures Nish had seen in the Pit of Possibilities. None of them had contained her;

was she destined to die young, soon, *today*? It shook her. If her fate was preordained, what was the point of fighting, or indeed, *anything*? No! she thought with a rush of anger. I refuse to believe it. I will fight on; and I *will* prevail.

Metal clanged on metal. Colm was standing to Zham's right, thrusting his blade at a soldier on the plank, just outside. Zham skewered the man behind him through the neck joint of his armour and twisted his blade out in a gush of bright blood. The soldier toppled off the wind-shaken plank, but another stood behind him, and many more behind him. The plank was bowed down under their weight.

Flydd slipped the taphloid into her hand. 'Try it!'

Maelys put it around her neck and felt the pressure of Reaper ease. She closed her eyes and tried to blank everything out save her memory of the old Flydd. It was hard, for there was so much to intrude – the thump of sword on armour, the grunts and screams of the fighting soldiers, and the howling updraught, which always picked up as the day drew on. Nish, beside her, was panting like a woman in labour from the escalating agony of his burned hand. Most distracting of all, she kept catching whiffs of the rotting flesh of Jal-Nish's terrible face.

Fyllis, splayed on the wall of Jal-Nish's torture chamber. That image helped her to focus on what had to be done – find the real Flydd. She felt the strength of his hand around her wrist and imagined it to be the old man's feebler grip.

It was working. Now she remembered him as she'd first seen him, just days ago: drinking and laughing with Nish on the rickety bench outside his amber-wood hut. She'd envied them their easy camaraderie and their long friendship, for she'd felt alone and abandoned since Nifferlin Manor had been torn down.

Flydd had led her out into the stink-snapper-infested marshes and questioned her about the most intimate and embarrassing details of her travels with Nish. Later, she remembered Flydd's fury as she had pressured him to take renewal. If she'd had an inkling of what it would do to him, she would never have opened her mouth.

Colm gasped and stumbled backwards, holding his left shoulder. Blood was seeping through his fingers. 'Just a scratch,' he said through gritted teeth, though the gash was as long as his little finger.

Zham swung his blade back and forth, sweeping another of the Imperial Guard off the plank, the man's helmeted head flying right and his body toppling to the left. Colm gripped his sword in bloody fingers and returned to his position. They were safe for another minute.

She conjured up that first memory again: Flydd, barely tipsy at all, laughing with a sozzled Nish. It felt like a lifetime ago. She tried to see into Flydd, to understand what drove him, good and bad. How had he held to his purpose despite being trapped at the top of Mistmurk Mountain for nine years, knowing that his plan to free Nish from prison had come to naught?

Flydd had never given up; moreover, he had maintained his sense of humour and that ferocious will to fight on, no matter the cost. He reminded her of her father, Rudigo, who had been forced to flee from Jal-Nish's vicious lieutenant, Seneschal Vomix, when she was little. Rudigo, whose tortured body now lay in the anonymous burial grounds behind Mazurhize. That was her fault too, for as a child she'd unwittingly insulted Vomix and it had drawn attention to her family's gifts.

Suddenly she *saw* Flydd – the real Flydd – just for a second, and again felt that burning sensation surrounding her heart and flowing down her arm to where his fingers clenched like an iron manacle. Nish stiffened and tried to pull away from her other hand, but she maintained the contact even though her head was spinning and her knees had gone weak. Must – hold – on. Must hold –

She was lying on the floor with Nish bending over her. Maelys felt cold now, to her very core; frozen and empty.

The taphloid was lying beside her and she reached out for the comfort of it.

'I've got back a trace of my Art,' said Flydd. 'I can see the way!'

He turned towards the rear wall, the fifth crystal shining through his fingers, and reached out between the columns. A dazzling flash lit up the cavern; the crystal burst and fiery shards flew out in a fan, though all were extinguished when they hit the hidden door, as if it had drawn the power from them.

One glowing fragment flew straight up, bounced off the roof and curved down in an arc towards Maelys, landing on her stomach. Had Flydd taken back all his Art, or was part of it still trapped in her? She didn't *feel* any different. The shard was useless, but she slipped it into the empty crystal compartment of her taphloid and waited for the door to open.

It did not.

More malicious laughter issued from Reaper as Jal-Nish groaned and came to his knees, unmasked and grotesque. 'You think you can best *me* that easily?' he said in a slurred voice. 'Even unconscious, I was more than *your* match, Xervish.'

With a bellow of rage, Nish leapt at his father. The uppercut started at floor level and ended with a sickening crack on the point of Jal-Nish's scarred jaw, lifting him off his feet, for Nish had hit him with all the pent-up fury of his ten years of imprisonment. Jal-Nish landed on his back in the moss, eyes open, but so deeply unconscious that Reaper's surface went still. The clanging started again. The Imperial Guards on the copper plank let out a collective roar. A sword rang on Zham's greatsword.

'Xervish?' said Nish, his battered knuckles bleeding onto the moss and his bandaged hand dripping yellow fluid. *'This can't all have been for nothing!'*

'It's over, Nish old friend,' Flydd said gently. 'That crystal was special; I spent years priming it to crack into the

30

shadow realm, and protect us while we were there, and without it we've lost. As I said on one other memorable occasion, we must face our end with dignity.'

Maelys had read that tale when she was little. Flydd was referring to the time during the lyrinx war when he and his allies had been taken by the corrupt Council of Scrutators in their attack on Fiz Gorgo. After a show trial on a great canvas amphitheatre erected many spans above the roof of the stronghold, all its people had been set to be executed there.

'I didn't hear you say it,' whispered Nish. 'I was trapped below in the burning tower.'

She'd read his part of the tale many times. In one of the greatest feats of heroism in all the Histories, Nish had cunningly attacked the scrutators and their hundreds of crack guards, rescued the prisoners and, with their aid, had turned ruinous defeat into an unimaginable victory, which had turned the tide of the hopeless lyrinx war and, two years later, had led to that astonishing, yet noble, triumph over the alien enemy. Maelys, reliving the tale, realised that she could forgive Nish almost everything because of the hero he had once been, and might be again.

Looking at him now, she could see that he was in agony, but he endured it in silence; he could show no weakness to an enemy who would ruthlessly exploit it.

'And you saved us all,' said Flydd, deep in a recovered memory.

'To die at my hands –' slurred Jal-Nish from the floor.

How had he roused so quickly? Maelys tasted despair this time; he could never be beaten.

Flydd forced a clump of moss into Jal-Nish's mouth with the toe of his boot. Jal-Nish fell silent, though his fingers kept moving. Reaper's surface rippled and Zham staggered backwards, falling against Colm and driving him to his knees.

Flydd stamped on Jal-Nish's fingers, but too late. With a single bound, a giant of a warrior sprang from the plank onto the sill of the cavern. He was almost as big as Zham,

31

brandishing a cutlass in one hand and a rapier in the other, and cutting and stabbing faster than the eye could follow. Zham came upright but his injuries had weakened him and some of the rapier blows were getting through. He was soon speckled with blood in a dozen places.

The cutlass flashed out to the left. Zham parried, but the warrior lunged and stabbed his rapier half a hand-span into Zham's mighty thigh. His leg wobbled and he nearly went down.

'Zham?' cried Maelys, seeing blood pouring down his leg. Something whirred in front of her; she did not see what it was.

With furious blows, Zham drove the warrior backwards onto the plank. Behind him a line of soldiers waited their turn, and many more were at the railings of the sky palace. The greatest hero in the world could not defeat them all. Maelys felt sick, for the end was inevitable now.

'Fly, little lady,' said Zham, turning to smile at her even as he defended furiously. 'I'm done for, but you can still get away.'

'No, Zham! The door is closed. It's over. Lay down your weapon.'

'Fly! I won't give up until you pass through.'

'Please, Zham.'

'Ever since I took up arms,' he grunted, 'I've known it would end this way. It's all I'm good for, little lady.'

He drove the warrior backwards a few steps, then reached down to grasp the plank and gave it a mighty heave. It twisted slightly; the huge warrior threw out his arms for balance and, as the twisting motion propagated along the plank, those men behind him did the same. One fell silently to the left; another cried out as he went off to the right. Zham twisted again. Could he pull the plank free? She allowed herself to hope, for Zham's strength was as huge as his heart.

Again that whirring, and this time Maelys looked down. The shell of her taphloid was changing; faces and dials she'd never seen before were appearing and disappearing there, as they'd not done in many years, and the hand on one dial was pointing towards the rear of the cavern. The fragment of crystal must have powered it for the first time in months, but it did not blank out her gift, as it had always done before she'd passed through the Mistmurk at the base of the Pit of Possibilities.

Hopeless, fatalistic thoughts rose up; again she crushed them and focussed on what she had to do. The taphloid must be enhancing her gift, for suddenly she could see Jal-Nish's jagged red and black aura again, and Flydd's pale green one flickering, and a tiny glimmer coming from Nish as well.

She turned, following the direction the little hand was pointing, and the hidden door between the columns was outlined in yellow radiance. A brighter oval in the middle marked a keyhole the size of her closed fist, and in a daze she thrust the taphloid at the hole.

An enormous groan made her look over her shoulder. Zham had lifted the end of the metal plank and the soldiers still on it. How could he do that with broken ribs? Grunting with the strain, he forced it to chest height and twisted it left, right, left. A dozen Imperial Guards fell to their deaths, some silently, others screaming in terror, but the giant warrior rode the twisting board as if his feet were glued to it, swaying from side to side and balancing himself with swings of his rapier and cutlass.

Maelys could see how it was going to end, for Zham had exhausted his strength, yet failed to dislodge his enemy. The warrior sprang, bounced on the swaying plank, lunged and thrust his rapier down. It went through Zham's unprotected chest and came out a couple of hand-spans from his lower back, sparkling like freshly polished metal with rubies dripping from its tip.

'Zham!' she wailed.

The end of the plank slipped through his fingers and struck the sill of the cave. The warrior tried to heave his weapon out but Zham's hands locked around his enemy's on the rapier's hilt, and held him. Putting his huge boot against the warrior's groin, Zham sent him flying into the three guards behind, knocking them down. The warrior went over the side, and they did too.

Maelys ran to Zham. 'Flee!' he said weakly, and fell to the floor, the impact pushing the rapier most of the way back through him. Blood was flooding from the hole in his chest; he was going to die.

The few surviving guards broke into a run, and others were scrambling over the side of the sky palace now that the way was clear. Soon they would pour into the cavern like a dam bursting.

'Thank you, faithful Zham,' she wept, kissing his brow. There was nothing more she could do for him. Family first; always family first. Her eyes swimming with tears, she turned away from the friend who had given his all and asked nothing in return, went to the rear door and thrust the taphloid into the keyhole. The door began to scrape open.

Jal-Nish twitched, rolled over and groped blindly for Reaper.

'Get in!' she screeched, leaping through into the darkness.

Flydd picked up his rucksack, which Zham had packed for him after renewal, slung it over his back, and followed, then Nish; Colm was still by the entrance, his sword out.

'It's over, Colm,' Flydd said gruffly. 'Come, if you're coming.'

Colm jerked the rapier out of Zham's chest with one hand, swiping at the leading soldier through the entrance with the other. The man ducked, then came on. Colm ran across the cavern, through the door, and Maelys put her fist into the glowing keyhole on the other side, then whipped it out again as the slab slammed shut, leaving them in darkness.

Four

As the stone door closed, Nish sagged with relief, for it had placed a physical barrier, however temporary, between him and his father. He couldn't see a thing, and there was no way to tell which way the cavern led from here, save by feel. 'Light!' he said hoarsely, for his throat was so dry it itched.

'Can't even make light,' muttered Flydd. 'I'm reduced to mere, talentless humanity.'

'It's all I've ever been,' said Colm.

'Then you can't possibly know any different.'

'Stop moaning, you old fool!' snapped Colm. 'Make the best of it.'

'You sound better, Xervish,' said Maelys hastily. 'As cranky as ever, in fact.'

Flydd managed a feeble chuckle. 'I'd imagined that being restored to a vigorous middle age would be like getting a new life, but it feels as if my old bones are loosely clothed with someone else's muscles. Every movement requires an effort of will; it's like learning to walk again.' He paused. 'I don't know how you did it, Maelys, but thank you.'

She said something, softly, but Nish missed it; he could not concentrate for the pain of his charred left hand. He

35

sucked at the wet sleeve covering the coconut-sized moss bandage. The moisture felt good on his cracked lips but the movement caused the agony of his burns, temporarily forgotten in the mad scramble to escape, to flare anew.

He bit down on a cry; giving way to pain could only make things worse. He had to be stronger than he'd ever been, for it was his only hope of escaping the monster on the other side of the door. But it was hard, very hard. The pain was worse than any of the many injuries he'd taken during the war.

This will be my first test, he thought. No matter how much it hurts, I won't make a sound. And if I'm strong enough for that, I'll take it as a sign that I can defeat Father.

Nish groped in the darkness with his good hand, touched something warm and yielding, Maelys's bosom, and jerked his hand away. At her sharp intake of breath he muttered, 'Sorry! Can't see a thing.'

She probably thought he'd done it deliberately, but he had bigger worries, not least the extraordinary story she'd told his father. Could Maelys really be pregnant with his child? He didn't think so, but if she was, even if she'd done it in such a sordid way, it would change both their lives. They would be bound together for all time, by blood. He had to admire the scheming little vixen. Maelys was braver than he was, and she never gave up.

He could sense her small, tense presence half a span away, and hear her quick breathing. She sounded as if she were cracking up and he couldn't blame her. She'd saved them but she could do no more, nor could Flydd, and Nish didn't trust Colm. It was up to him, now. He had spent months tormented by self-doubt and, to his shame, wallowing in self-pity, but he had to put all that behind him. After repudiating his father's offer to become his lieutenant, there was no going back, for they were enemies and would remain so until one of them died. It was time for Nish to take charge of his life.

36

Flydd and Maelys were talking about what she'd seen in the Pit of Possibilities, which reminded Nish of his own visions there, the first time. He could almost convince himself to discount his last vision – the one where he, the Deliverer, was acclaimed as God-Emperor – no matter how much he yearned for it, for Vivimord had as good as admitted sending it to him. But take it away and the other futures all ended the same way: in the failure of his quest, the triumph of the God-Emperor, and Nish's exile, madness, or death.

Despair pinched at his liver, a stabbing pain, but he endured that too. Never give way, not once; not even for a second. I reject all those possibilities and the pit itself, he raged inwardly. There will be no madness; no exile; no death. I will make my own future!

I won't become the Deliverer either, for that would mean submitting to Vivimord's plans for me, and he's just as corrupt as my father. But I *will* overthrow Father and restore peace and justice to Santhenar – though not as the God-Emperor. There will be no more God-Emperors. 'Whatever it takes, and however long, I'm going to do it!'

'What's that?' said Flydd.

Nish hadn't realised that he'd spoken aloud. 'We've got to get away from the door. Where does this cave go?'

'I don't remember.'

'Why not?' Nish snapped as the pain flared again. 'You had nine years.'

'And you took ten years to get here,' Flydd said mildly.

'How far is it to the shadow realm?'

'Not far; assuming I can find the power to enter it. Lead on.'

'I –' The pain nearly overcame him; Nish squeezed his eyes shut until the spasm passed. 'Feel around, everyone; find where the passage goes.'

'Right here,' said Colm from his left. 'It slopes down gently.'

'Go down, and we'll follow.'

'Whatever you say, *Deliverer*,' Colm said, the soles of his boots sliding on stone.

Nish didn't have the strength to be irritated. He went behind Maelys, wishing he had Zham's strong arm to lean on, and already missing his quiet, reliable solidity. But Zham was gone, as so many of his friends and allies had been lost. Nish needed to grieve for him but couldn't afford to; not here. Jal-Nish would already be recovering; his troops would be helping him back to the sky palace, where he would use Gatherer to search out all the secrets of Mistmurk Mountain, and hunt Nish down.

He choked but managed to swallow his despair. Just take it minute by minute, he told himself. Even agony can be endured for one minute, and if you can do that, you can suffer it for another. And so he continued.

They went down a long straight passage, clambered over a shallow crevasse which Colm discovered by falling into it and gashing his shin, then along a narrow, snaking tunnel with a gentle downslope and a strong smell of animal urine. Flydd kept stumbling, falling over and cursing his ill-fitting new body.

'Xervish,' said Maelys in a tiny voice. Ten or fifteen uneventful minutes had passed, during which Nish's unease grew ever stronger.

'What?' panted Flydd.

'When you began renewal, you talked about *forcing the barrier* and *holding open the shadow realm* for the hours it would take to get through it to safety. You said you needed at least three crystals to do that, but all we have is one tiny shard. How can we possibly get through without the crystals?'

He began to breathe heavily, as if remembering something he would sooner have forgotten. 'I don't know.'

'I thought the stone door –'

'It's just a normal door into the caverns that run through Mistmurk Mountain. The shadow realm is yet to come – if we can get into it at all.'

'What is the shadow realm?' said Nish. 'Is it like the maze we passed through when we escaped from Monkshart at Tifferfyte?'

Flydd stopped to catch his breath. 'Completely different. That maze was a dangerous place, but an empty one. It could drive you mad, and most people would become lost and die there, but it held no other threat. The shadow realm is like a nether world to the Three Worlds, bound to yet separate from them. It's the pit into which necromancers like Vivimord delve to further their depraved Arts, a perilous place full of dark and mischievous spirits.'

'Then why are we going there?'

'Because there's no other choice. Bad as it is, we've got a better chance passing through the shadow realm than we have staying here. We're not strong enough to fight Jal-Nish. We've got to disappear, though sooner or later he'll find us with the tears, wherever we hide. Therefore we've got to have a weapon, one he's afraid of, and the antithesis is the only possibility I know of. Besides, I spent years preparing my crystal to protect us while we pass through the shadow realm.'

'But it's broken.'

'The spells remain in the shard Maelys caught. Let's get moving.'

'So we won't be there long?' said Maelys anxiously.

'Just a few hours, hopefully . . .'

That sounded ominous. 'And then what?' said Nish.

'We return to the real world a long way from here; and from Jal-Nish.'

'And after that?'

'The instant I have regained my Art and my fitness, we go south to the Tower of a Thousand Steps. To approach the Numinator, I'll need all my wits about me.' He added under his breath, 'And then some.'

They continued down a steeper slope which was slippery with aromatic droppings. 'What's that smell?' said Nish. It was sickly sweet and spicy, like cane syrup mixed with pepper and cloves.

'Giant swamp creepers,' Maelys said from ahead. He could hear the revulsion in her voice. 'When I went down to the cursed flame earlier, there were thousands of them, all oozing and squirming over each other. Yuk!'

'Tasty, though,' said Colm. 'If we're trapped down here, at least we'll eat well.'

Nish, remembering the splendid steaks they'd dined on during their first night on the plateau, salivated. The swamp creepers were like gigantic black slugs the size of a muscular man's thigh, and almost all meat.

'I remember now!' cried Flydd. 'That's where we've got to go. The cursed flame is the one source of power available to me.'

'And Father will have it under guard,' said Nish.

'He may not know about the flame yet. Ah, this place has a familiar feel. I think I know where we are.'

'Lead the way, then – *what's that?*' said Nish, as thunder rolled down the passage.

'The God-Emperor's mancers must be attacking the hidden door,' said Flydd. 'Come on.'

They skidded down the slick surface, scrambled through a pit full of droppings which had an appalling stench and a faint luminosity, then climbed a broken slope equally coated with muck. By the time they reached the top they were smeared with it. Handicapped as he was, Nish fell many times, and each time his burned hand struck the rock it sent sickening waves of pain through him. He almost cried out, but managed to stifle it. I will not give in, he kept telling himself. I can beat Father; I must. He was thankful for the darkness, which concealed the tears streaming down his cheeks.

'Nish, are you all right?' said Maelys. Her hand touched his arm. 'Oh Nish,' she said quietly. 'I'm sorry – about everything.'

Her concern almost undid his resolve, but he could not reply. It was taking all his strength to endure the pain. He managed a grunt and after a moment she moved on.

After some twenty minutes of scrambling, during which they heard the thunder twice more, Flydd whispered, 'It can't be far now. Once we get to the bottom of this long slope, we should be below the flame – *back*!'

They crept backwards. 'What is it, surr?' said Nish.

'I caught the faintest reflection, a long way down, as if someone had put his head around the corner, then ducked back.'

'I didn't see anything,' said Colm.

'Good eyes are the one benefit I've got from renewal so far,' said Flydd.

'Apart from life!'

Flydd ignored the sarcasm. 'My renewed guts feel as though they're eating themselves, and my leg muscles slide up and down on my bones with every step. We'd better go back to that cross passage we saw a few minutes ago. I think there's another way into the flame chamber.'

'I got to it from beneath the obelisk in the marshes,' said Maelys timidly.

Did she think they were disgusted with her? Colm had certainly made his contempt plain. Nish no longer knew what he felt about Maelys, though she was as brave and resourceful as any woman he'd ever known, even Irisis – *No!* He could not, *would not* allow himself to make the comparison.

After feeling their way through absolute darkness for a good while, Flydd grunted, 'I smell moist air – cool air.'

'I smell nothing but the decaying turds of a million swamp creepers,' muttered Colm.

'Above the cavern of the cursed flame,' Maelys said, 'the air was warm, but below it a cool breeze was blowing up from the depths.'

'So we're below the cavern. Good,' said Flydd. 'Perhaps this way is not guarded.'

Nish thought that unlikely, but refrained from saying so. Despair is your greatest failing, he told himself. Don't open the door to it; not even a crack. While we're alive, there's hope. Things aren't as bad here as they were at Fiz Gorgo, and you pulled off a miraculous victory there. You can do it again. He closed his mind to the thought that miraculous victories had occurred a number of times in the Histories, but seldom had even the greatest of heroes done it twice.

'I can smell sweaty men,' said Maelys, now walking shoulder to shoulder with Nish.

'Just what you've been panting for,' said Colm.

'Shut up!' she hissed. 'Just shut up, Colm. I don't know what I ever saw in you.'

'Likewise!'

Nish couldn't stay silent any longer. 'Leave her alone or you'll have me to deal with.'

'Is that a promise, *oath-breaker*?'

Nish felt himself flushing. 'She saved us all, you fool!'

'And she'd do –'

'Enough!' hissed Flydd. 'What's the matter with you three?'

Now Nish could smell the soldiers' rancid sweat. The way *was* guarded, and as they crawled back into the reeking dark, he felt despair's door creaking open. Just a crack, but it was always there. With an effort of will he closed it again. 'Is there no other way to obtain the power we need?'

'There are only two entrances, and I dare say the other one is guarded as well.'

FIVE

Maelys sagged against the wall, feeling worse than ever. Colm's naked contempt was almost unendurable, and she could not understand why he was so hostile. She'd made no promises to him; they had never been more than travelling companions. With an effort, she put him out of mind. She'd had barely any sleep last night and not much the night before; every muscle in her body was aching and she was tired beyond rational thought.

Flydd's and Nish's muttering was like a harsh lullaby, and her eyelids drooped. She would snatch a few minutes' sleep while they worked out what to do. Maelys felt herself drifting, all her cares retreating . . .

The suppressed nightmare jerked her awake, reviving those paralysed minutes she'd spent on the slab with the cursed flame licking at her, and Phrune looming over her, preparing to take her skin and spill her blood into the flame, so as to revive his dreadful master.

The scene played over and over, until she was shuddering with the horror of it: the blade, the blood; Phrune's mutilated, leering face and Vivimord's groans issuing from beneath the slab; the heat of the cursed flame and the bouquet of precious amber-wood. The high, shadowed ceiling covered in the mucus crusts of swamp creepers, webbed by the corded nets of some unknown scuttling beast, all the way across that pyramidal opening –

Maelys's eyes flew open. 'Xervish!'

'Yes?' he said dully.

'There may be another way into the chamber of the cursed flame.'

She heard his sharp intake of breath. 'Where?'

'When I was on the slab and the flame flared, I saw a hole high above. It may be an old chimney, and if anyone has some rope, you might be able to get down it.'

'I've got rope,' said Colm. 'Can you find the top of the chimney, Flydd?'

'I think I know where to look.'

He led them up a broken slope, over a blade-like hump and around a twisting bend which felt as though water had once flowed down it. There were no droppings here, though Maelys could still smell them. Flydd stopped so suddenly that she ran into him and Nish into her.

'Hush!' Flydd said softly.

'What is it, Gorderz?' A slurred voice issued through a fissure in the rock to Maelys's left.

'Thought I heard footsteps, Snegg,' said another voice, sounding rather strained. 'Hold up.'

'This place makes my mind reel. Where are we?'

'No idea. What's happened to the others?'

'I thought they were with you,' said Snegg.

Gorderz cursed. 'The master won't be pleased.'

The intruders were only spans away through the rock; they would hear the slightest sound. Maelys steadied herself against the wall. Nish's shoulder touched her and she could feel him shuddering as he fought the pain. If he let out a squeak, they were lost.

The soldiers did not speak again, though Maelys was afraid they were still there, waiting for someone to move. Nish's breathing grew ever more laboured but she wasn't game to try and comfort him.

Finally the first man spoke again, much further away.

'Wait another minute,' said Flydd quietly. 'They're lost and afraid; if we go the other way we should be safe.'

There's no safety anywhere inside Mistmurk Mountain, Maelys thought.

They went on, feeling their way around a hairpin corner and along a passage so low that even Maelys had to negotiate it bent double. She could hear Colm's muffled curses as his backbone struck the knobbly roof.

'There's a crack ahead of me,' said Flydd when they emerged at the other end where there was room to stand upright, 'and it smells faintly of smoke. I think we can dare a little light here. Maelys, if you would open your taphloid.'

She did so, gingerly. Flame swirled within the shard, revealing a vertical, soot-stained crack a couple of spans high, though less than two hand-spans wide. 'The crystal is brighter here.'

'No wonder,' said Flydd. 'We're directly above the cursed flame. Close the lid to just a sliver of light. That's better. Go through, Maelys, and step with care.'

She squeezed sideways through the crack, at the risk of her remaining coat buttons, and felt around with her foot. 'I'm on a narrow rock shelf running around the inside of the chimney,' she whispered. Its walls were smoke stained and criss-crossed with crusted mucus tracks, some of which were fresh, judging by the shine. 'The chimney hole is practically blocked. Come inside; don't step in the centre or you'll fall through.'

Below, the chimney was a clotted mess of slime and droppings caught in corded cobwebs. Maelys felt her skin creeping. She didn't want to meet whatever made such thick webs, especially not in the dark.

The others worked their way through, and she moved around the ledge to give them space. Colm, who was tallest, blocked the crack with his body and Maelys opened the lid of the taphloid all the way. The chimney flared out around and above them but narrowed below the shelf.

Colm thrust his sword into its sheath, leaned the rapier that had killed Zham against the corner, then pulled a hank of fine rope from his pack and tugged on it, testing its strength.

'Down there?' said Flydd.

'That's where the smoky smell is coming from . . .' Swamp creepers gave Maelys the shudders, and though she wasn't afraid of ordinary spiders, the creature that had made those cord webs could be as big as she was. 'If you and Nish go down, I'll watch the way out with Colm.'

'Nish can't use his left hand.' Flydd frowned at the crusted mess blocking the chimney. 'Give that a poke with your blade, Colm. It doesn't look very wide.'

'Chimneys rarely are,' said Colm. 'That's why they use little kids as chimney sweeps.' He was looking coldly at Maelys, as if she were a stranger.

Not me, she thought. Haven't I done enough?

Colm ran the tip of his sword around the four sides of the chimney hole, then carefully lifted out the web and its clinging droppings, flicking them into a corner and wiping his hands on his pants. A warm spicy smell wafted up, of swamp-creeper slime, ordure and smoke. The exposed hole was no wider than her shoulders.

'It seems to narrow further down,' said Flydd, with the faintest of smiles. 'You're the only one who'll fit, Maelys.'

'You're pleased it's not you.' She felt petulant saying it, but she'd sooner fight a stink-snapper in the swamp than go down there.

'I certainly am, but if I had to go down, I would, and so will you.'

Not for the first time, Maelys cursed herself for being so little; she cursed her companions too, and her whole life. She'd been brought up to marry well and manage her manor and estate, and there had been a clear division between men's work and women's. Men did the hard, backbreaking labour, and most of the really dirty work. Climbing down this chimney was *definitely* men's work.

She heard a squelching slurp from the depths that had to be one giant swamp creeper crawling over another. 'You're not that big, Xervish,' she said desperately. 'I'm sure you'd fit – at a pinch.'

'Nope,' said Flydd. 'The renewed me has broad shoulders.'

'And I've got a big bottom,' she said recklessly. 'Huge, in fact.'

'Indeed you have.' Flydd gave her an appraising grin. 'Turn around; I'd better make sure. Don't want you getting stuck halfway.'

She did so, flushing, yet praying for once that it would be too big.

'It's large all right,' said Nish, grinning despite his pain.

Even Colm, who had been grim-faced ever since her lie about being pregnant, gave a faint twitch of the lips. Men!

Flydd measured her hips with his outstretched hands, then the chimney hole. 'Your bottom, while certainly of a traditional size, isn't large enough to get you out of trouble. Take your coat off and down you go.'

She might have refused, but Maelys felt she had to prove herself.

'I'll go down!' she said savagely. 'But you're going to pay for this.'

'I'll add it to the list,' said Flydd. 'I've a whole lifetime of villainy to atone for.'

She didn't budge. 'What am I'm supposed to do?'

'Ah!' He frowned. 'This is where it gets tricky. Your shard still retains the spells I wove into the fifth crystal years ago, and it should be able to open the shadow realm if you can recharge it. Take it to the cursed flame –'

'But when I touched the flame last time, it paralysed me.'

He felt in his pockets. 'Hold the shard in this.' He handed her a coil of fine wire.

She quickly formed a loop in one end and put the coil in her pocket, again reliving how close she'd come to being skinned alive by Phrune. Her stomach muscles tightened. He was dead, thankfully.

Colm fashioned a rope harness around her middle, avoiding her eyes and being careful not to touch her, as if she were tainted. He checked the knots and tied the other end of the rope around himself.

'We'll lower you until you're directly above the slab,' said Flydd. 'You won't need to set foot on the floor. Give three jerks on the rope once you're in place, then two and two more when you want to be hauled up again.'

'What if there are guards?'

'Give the second signal before they see you. We'll pull you up and try again later.'

Going down and up once would be bad enough. She couldn't bear to do it twice.

'There's one more problem,' said Flydd, 'though I don't see what we can do about it.'

'What's that?' she said gloomily.

'I don't know how much power your shard can absorb from the flame. It may not be much at all.'

'How will I know when it's got all it can take?'

'It'll burst.'

'So how do I know when to stop?' she cried.

'I haven't regained that memory.'

'Wonderful!' Maelys said sourly. 'Are there any other ways this can go disastrously wrong?'

'I'll give you a list when I think of them. If you fail, just come up. Have you got a knife? You'll need one if you get tangled up in a web, or . . .'

'Yes.' The huge blade Zham had given her up in the mires was still strapped to her lower leg, under her trousers. She unsheathed it.

'Go now.'

She took a deep breath, then went to her hands and knees and lowered her head into the hole, conscious that her bottom was facing them.

'Make sure the rope is tight, Colm. If I'm going down

headfirst, I'd hate it to slip over my hips.'

'As if that's going to happen,' Nish smirked.

She wanted to smack him. Colm pulled the harness so tightly around her small waist that it hurt. Maelys closed her taphloid and the chimney was plunged into darkness. She went down head first, arms outstretched below her, and as her feet scraped over the edge she felt him take up the slack. Colm might hold her in deepest contempt, but she was safe while he was holding the rope.

About half a span down she encountered a thick web clotted with droppings, though fortunately it was so old and dusty that it was no longer sticky. Zham's knife cut through the strands like a razor. She stretched out her free hand, and froze, for her fingertips were touching something round, cool and slippery.

It was a giant swamp creeper – the most disgusting thing she could possibly have encountered in the darkness – and she had to feel her way around it. She dared not open the taphloid for light in case the precious crystal fell out.

The chimney was wider here, not narrower. Even Colm could have come down it, she thought resentfully, and swamp creepers didn't bother him at all. On their first day on the plateau he'd killed one and carried it back to the camp over his shoulder.

Maelys tried to stop but her slippery fingers couldn't get a grip on the wall, and Colm kept lowering her on the rope. She dropped sharply; her right cheek glided across the swamp creeper's skin, coating her in sickly smelling, slimy gunk.

She tried to push herself back up but the swamp creeper moved under her weight and she fell headfirst into the gap between it and another. The chimney was blocked with a great mass of them, one upon the next. She kept sliding down between the loathsome, squirming creatures

Her forehead was coated in slime; it clogged her eyes, and with every breath sticky bubbles formed at her nostrils;

her mouth was blocked with a clot of ooze the size of a lyrinx's bogey. She spat it out explosively, shuddering with disgust, then twisted sideways and managed to get another breath, but her weight kept pushing her down and there was nothing she could do but go with it.

She slipped further; now all but her legs were surrounded by giant swamp creatures, all stirring and creeping over each other on their mucus tracks, making disgusting slurpings and squelchings which, this close, were deafeningly loud.

Maelys squirmed, trying to clear a space so she could get a decent breath, for she could feel herself starting to panic. She slipped all the way down into another great cluster of swamp creepers, enclosing her from head to knee. Her shirt had slipped up and a small creeper oozed its way across her bare belly. Another crawled over her mouth and nose. She desperately, frantically tried to batter it out of the way but her blows just skidded off.

Panic burst over her; she couldn't control it. Maelys thrashed wildly, shaking her head from side to side until she was dizzy, and a little space opened up in front of her nose. She spat out another mouthful of ooze, which reminded her unpleasantly of the barbed slurchie Colm had removed from her belly in the rainforest. Maelys sucked in a breath of smelly air and screamed her lungs out.

Colm couldn't have heard, for he kept lowering her. She continued to flail and scream until her throat hurt and she was so exhausted that she couldn't move her arms or legs. She slumped in the middle of the cluster, ever so slowly sliding down between the swamp creepers, too exhausted to do any more. The panic was gone. She no longer had the energy for it. She had given up.

Until that reminded her of Tulitine, the old seer who had helped raise the Defiance in Nish's name, months ago. Though Tulitine must have been nearly eighty, she had a lover not a third her age and a zest for life unmatched in anyone Maelys had ever met. Tulitine had helped and protected her, though she'd been disappointed in Maelys when she'd fled the Defiance camp after Phrune had identified her.

Maelys's courage had failed her then, but she was stronger now. She could not, would not give up. She was going to fight Jal-Nish until there was no breath left in her body – but fight cleverly.

If there was anyone in the cavern below, she must have given herself away. Or maybe not. She'd slid through a couple of spans of swamp creepers, which completely blocked the chimney here. If they formed as thick a cluster below her, her screams might not have penetrated it.

Surely there couldn't be far to go? Maelys wiped her eyes on the back of her hand, but it didn't help; every part of her was thickly enslimed. The swamp creepers didn't feel quite so bad now; their skin was no more slippery than hers. And they were harmless, she reminded herself; entirely vegetarian. She slid another arm's length, then stopped, for they were so tightly packed here that her weight wouldn't carry her any further.

Maelys realised that she was breathing heavily, the panic rising again at the idea of being trapped in this slimy darkness. What if she cut her way through? The thought was revolting; besides, she would have to work head-down in a puddle of swamp-creeper blood and body fluids, and might drown before she got through.

She couldn't do it, and sheathed the knife, but could she force a path through them? Maelys twisted left, then right, but a space didn't open up. Harmless the creepers might be, yet she might easily suffocate before Colm realised that something was wrong.

She pushed harder but couldn't exert enough force to move them. Got to have something to push against, she thought. She wriggled and jerked but couldn't get the tiniest breath. The panic was swelling, almost overwhelming her. Her lungs were heaving; she only had air enough for another few moments.

She couldn't stand this; she had to get out. Maelys tried to punch the closest swamp creeper out of the way, but her fist sank into it as if it were a fat man's belly, forcing a gust of cool air out of an opening below its head, *prrrp*. It had a humid smell of chewed-up vegetation somewhat like a cow's belch, but it was breathable, life-sustaining air.

Wriggling her legs and sliding her weary arms this way and that, she managed to slip one foot to the side of the chimney, then another. The stone, though slick, was rough enough for her to get a grip. She pushed against it, forced with her arms until she broke the suction between the swamp creepers, and a cluster fell away. She shot through the obstruction like a cork popped from a bottle, into an open space, and dropped a good span before the rope caught her. Maelys hung there, slowly revolving, gasping at the cold, spicy air.

She went lower as Colm continued to pay out the rope, and her down-stretched palms skidded across another clot of swamp creepers. They didn't feel any better than the ones above, but the sooner she began, the sooner it would be over. Maelys formed an arrowhead with her hands, wedged the swamp creepers apart, and began to wriggle through like a human tadpole.

This passage was just as unpleasant as the previous one, but she continued, keeping her head bent towards her armpit so as to protect her nose with her angled arm. It worked, mostly; after several more panting minutes her hands popped free and in place of the sickly swamp creeper odour she caught a faint, gassy warmth that she remembered from her previous visit. She was out of the chimney and suspended above the huge, coffin-shaped slab up through which the cursed flame issued.

Maelys scraped muck out of her eyes and wiped it off on her saturated shirt. Clots of muck splattered on the stone far below. After blinking furiously, she managed to ungum her eyelids and made out the flicker of the cursed flame at least eight spans down. It was no longer blue; the flame looked purple-black now. She couldn't see anyone in the cavern, though most of its expanse lay in shadow. Besides, if Jal-Nish's scriers had found a way in, they might have set up a wisp-watcher anywhere.

She couldn't afford to worry about that. If she were discovered, she would give the signal and pray that Colm could heave her up in time. Maelys closed her mind to everything except what she had to do.

In a couple of minutes she was settling on the slab, which was partly covered in the splattered remains of a fallen swamp creeper. Near the flame hole the stone was stained with blood: hers, Phrune's and Vivimord's. She shivered at the memories. How long ago had Phrune attacked her? Six hours? Eight? Ten? She felt quite desperately tired. There was no time to waste. If any soldiers came in, she would be clearly visible.

Don't think about what happened earlier. Just recharge the crystal and get going. She gave the rope three sharp tugs. Maelys popped out the shard, which was glowing fiercely now, passed it through the loop of wire and pulled it tight. What if the force of the flame could travel up the wire? She pulled her sleeve down so no part of her skin would be in contact with it, then gingerly reached out to the flame.

Nothing happened, save that the dancing colours in the shard brightened. It's all right, she thought, her arm shaking. I can do this. And last time it hadn't taken long to charge the whole crystal. She'd held her shard in the flame for the count of thirty. It must be nearly that long now – long enough. She daren't take the risk –

Bang!

The shard burst into a thousand flying fragments; one stung the back of her hand. She picked it out and sucked at the tiny drop of blood welling there. Their last source of power was lost. All was lost. Why, why hadn't she been more careful?

SIX

Maelys was about to give Colm the signal to haul her up when she noticed a coating of little crystals, like spilled sugar, around the star-shaped hole through which the cursed flame issued.

Crystals were everywhere, of course – rocks were full of them – but even in the days before the nodes were destroyed, crystals capable of storing power for use in the Secret Art had been rare and precious. They were far rarer now, and finding one was as difficult as searching through the myriad grains of sand on a beach for one lost jewel.

And yet . . . the cursed flame had charged Flydd's fifth crystal quickly, so even an ordinary crystal might absorb *some* power after being bathed in the cursed flame for hundreds, even thousands of years.

She studied the sugary crust of yellow sulphur surrounding the star hole, but these crystals had no glow. Besides, they could not be bathed by the flame or the sulphur would have burned – every apprentice healer knew that. To find crystals bathed by the flame she would need to search beneath the slab.

Dare she? Flydd had said to come straight up if she failed, but she had to make up for bursting the shard. She had let him down and her failure would only confirm the contempt Colm felt for her. Unfastening the harness from her waist, she slid over the edge of the slab, avoiding the congealed puddle of Phrune's blood, and crawled into the space beneath the slab. Here the floor was scattered with flakes of Vivimord's skin, for Phrune had dragged his master underneath so Maelys's blood, purified by the cursed flame, could heal him.

She brushed the skin aside with her sleeve and crawled up to the flame, which hissed from a crystal-encrusted crack in the floor. These crystals were different, being long, thin, and blue-green, but all intergrown. She prised carefully with the point of Zham's knife but the brittle crystals broke every time.

Rolling onto her back, she studied the underside of the slab. There were more such crystals inside the star hole, but she couldn't reach them without putting her hand into the cursed flame. However the underside of the slab, around the hole, was covered in squat pink crystals condensed from the flame; she could see their facets twinkling.

Squelch!

What was that? Maelys eased her head out from under the slab, thinking that she'd been seen. Why, why had she untied the harness? She was about to spring up for it when her eye caught a faint movement from the chimney above – flame reflecting off the mucosal sheen of a moving swamp creeper.

Feeling like a fool, she resumed her search. Most of the pink crystals were the size of grains of rice but there were occasional larger ones, as big as kernels of corn, a few of which had faint colours swirling within them.

It didn't mean that they contained useable power, but Maelys couldn't go back up the rope empty-handed. She scanned the underside, not for the biggest crystal, but the one with the brightest colours.

It was only as long as her little fingernail, though the colours were intense. She touched the tip of Zham's knife to the rock above the crystal and it fell into her hand. The moment she put it in the taphloid, it came to life, suppressing her aura the way the taphloid had been designed to. So the crystal did contain *some* power.

Squueelllllch!

She eased out, looked up at the chimney, but didn't see any movement this time. Better get going; Flydd would be anxious about the time. Maelys put her hands on the top of the slab and tried to spring up, but her feet went from under her and she landed flat on her back. She'd slipped in Phrune's congealed blood, and that reminded her of something she should have remembered the moment she'd landed on the slab.

She rolled away, her hackles rising. Previously, Vivimord had dragged Phrune's body underneath, then stood on the slab, cut his own chest and let his blood flow into the cursed flame in a despairing attempt to revive his acolyte. But it had failed, and Phrune's body had still lain under the slab when Vivimord staggered off to confront Jal-Nish.

There was no sign of the body now – someone had been here before her. Jal-Nish's troops might have dragged Phrune out, but they would hardly have carried his disgusting body away. Only one man would have done that – Vivimord.

Was he here still? She couldn't see anything in the deep shadows. Heaving herself onto the slab, she reached for the harness.

Squelch!

The sound had come from her right. He was waiting for someone to come to the flame, the only source of power here that Jal-Nish did not control. Vivimord and Phrune had despised each other, yet they were linked by terrible needs which only the other could satisfy, and until the day of her death she would not forget Vivimord's parting words.

You'll pay for this, Maelys Nifferlin! I know Black Arts that can make a corpse scream in agony, that can torment even

a bodiless spirit and cause lifeless bones to chatter in terror.
You'll pay and pay, and keep on paying a hundred years after
your agonising death.

Had he been talking about the spectral beings inhabiting the shadow realm? More than ever she did not want to go there. Her sore fingers fumbled with the knots of the harness as she looked over her shoulder. Vivimord could be anywhere, and there was no point calling for help, for the soldiers they'd encountered earlier must have been his men, not Jal-Nish's. Besides, Flydd, Colm and Nish would hear nothing through the clots of swamp creepers blocking the chimney.

Having checked that her harness knots were secure, she reached up and gave two sharp tugs on the rope, but it stayed slack. She signalled again; it was not answered. That dreadful squelching sounded once more, she looked around frantically, then out of the darkness it came.

In the dimly flickering flame she couldn't tell what it was at first. It was man-shaped, though it did not move like a man. It had a slow, stiff-legged, shuffling lurch, and every movement was accompanied by squelching sounds, as if something liquid was sloshing back and forth.

Maelys caught a glimpse of a round, waxen head punctured by blank eyes; the mouth was a bloated circular orifice with something long and dangling jammed in it. It looked like a man who had choked on the head of a squid, with its tentacles hanging halfway down his chest, flapping from side to side as he moved.

The cursed flame flared, the creature stepped out of the shadows and she nearly wet herself. It was Phrune's ghastly corpse, its intestines hanging out of its mouth. He had died that way after Maelys, in a desperate attempt to save herself, had thrust her taphloid through his lips and its contact had inverted his aura violently. But no one could have survived what he'd been through. His corpse must have been reanimated by Vivimord's Black Arts.

'Colm?' she squeaked.

Why wasn't he pulling her up? Had they been discovered; taken; *killed*? She tried to climb the rope but it was so slippery she couldn't get a grip. She gave it a furious heave and another span or two slid down – she hadn't pulled hard enough the first time; hadn't drawn down all the slack line trapped between the swamp creepers. Colm hadn't got her signal.

She pulled the rope down until it went taut, then heaved hard, twice, and twice more. Dead Phrune had covered half the distance between them already and the sight of him filled her with a sickening, paralysing horror. *Come on!*

She gave the signal again and finally the rope began to move up, though several spans of slack were pooled on the slab and Phrune was only five spans away. She unsheathed Zham's huge knife, the size of a short sword in her hands, and held it out.

The corpse gave a squelching choke – laughter? – and more white loops of intestine flopped out. She waved the blade back and forth, but how could she harm a man who was already dead?

The slack was being taken up more quickly now; perhaps Colm had realised that something was wrong. The corpse reached the edge of the slab and reached out for the last coil of rope. Maelys kicked it out of the way and slashed at the waxen-pale forearm. The tip of the knife parted grey flesh but he did not bleed.

The corpse slipped in its own congealed blood and fell against the side of the slab. Plump fingers gripped the edge; the gluey eyes fixed on her and he began to climb. As Maelys backed down to the other end, the rope tightened around her waist and began to lift.

Phrune was on the slab, straightening slowly, but as soon as her feet lifted off she began to swing towards him. She would thump into him, couldn't stop herself, and all he had to do was hang on.

'Pull, damn you!' she screeched, for Colm wasn't lifting her nearly fast enough.

She bent forwards, holding Zham's blade in both hands like a spear, and pointed it directly at Phrune's eyes. If she could cut them he might not be able to see . . . though he could still grab her blindly.

She was swinging at him from his right. He shifted to face her, which meant that he could see. His arms rose; he was going to duck the knife and grab her, and she was moving too slowly to avoid him.

She whipped the knife back, doubled up her legs and as dead Phrune came within reach she shot out both feet like springs and struck him on the jaw.

His head jerked backwards; his arms flailed and he nearly overbalanced, but his left hand struck her ankle and latched on. She kicked furiously but he would not let go. She swung around him on the rope, then struck at his wrist with her other foot and tore free, kicking Phrune again and again, hitting him in the back of the neck and the shoulders, knocking him to his knees, until the swinging rope carried her away.

Colm jerked her higher; she was now head-high above the slab as Phrune regained his footing and came at her. Another jerk and she was above his head. He reached up and his putrid fingers grazed her ankle, but could not get a grip this time; she slashed with the knife, only managing to trim his long nails before another heave lifted her out of reach. Colm had done it. She was safe. Maelys sagged on the rope, barely able to see for the tears of relief.

She hung there, limp and exhausted as Colm pulled her up another half span. Phrune's arm jerked upright, his plump fingers pointed at her waist, and she felt a tickling at her middle, as if invisible fingers were working there – the knots were untying themselves! She tried to hold them together but the harness was already undone. The rope burned through her fingers and she fell heavily to the slab at the corpse's feet.

Phrune lunged for her. For an instant Maelys was too stunned to move, then desperation fired her limbs and, as his oozing intestines trailed across her chest, she hurled herself onto the floor and scrambled around the other side of the slab. The rope had stopped moving up; Colm had noticed the weight go off it and must be waiting for her to tie on again.

If she could distract Phrune, she might just scramble up, grab the rope and hang on while Colm lifted her out of reach. She'd have to be quick, though. Unfortunately, the corpse wasn't moving; Phrune was just waiting beneath the rope. Her gaze flicked around the large chamber. The cursed flame illuminated it for a few spans, beyond which the shadows became progressively deeper.

Spying a scattering of precious amber-wood pieces on the floor from her previous visit, Maelys scooped up half a dozen and tossed them into the cursed flame. It flared up, illuminating the chamber for a good twenty spans. The corpse lurched away from the flame but the moment it died down Phrune resumed his position, guarding the rope.

The taphloid had done him terrible damage before – might it still hold some power over his remains? It was worth the risk. Turning away, she took it off and concealed it in her left hand, the chain wrapped around it for security. Maelys crept in, waving Zham's knife in her right hand. The corpse slowly rotated to face her. She slashed at his knees but he didn't move; whatever intelligence had reanimated him, he knew she couldn't harm him with a blade.

Let's see how you like the sting of my taphloid, she thought savagely, then darted in and slammed it against Phrune's pale calf, which was chest-high to her.

The corpse didn't react save to tilt its head to stare blindly at her. Of course – being dead, it had no aura, so the taphloid could not harm it. Nothing could, save hacking it into immobile pieces, and she could not risk getting that close.

Wait! When the flame flared, Phrune had lurched out of the way. Could he fear the fire, or was he repelled by the precious, sacred, *lucky* amber-wood that had saved her last time.

She sheathed the knife, pocketed the taphloid, and gathered all the amber-wood she could find, tossing it into the flame, which roared higher than Phrune's head. The corpse moved backwards, trying to shield its eyes with its hands. It was her only chance.

She vaulted onto the narrow end of the coffin-shaped slab, took two running steps and leapt high for the rope. Phrune hadn't moved.

Maelys wrapped a loop of rope around her wrist and drew her legs up out of reach, hanging on grimly as she waited for Colm to feel her weight and start pulling her up. He did so, jerkily, but to Maelys's horror the rope began to slip across her palms. It was coated in swamp creeper slime, and though she squeezed until her hands began to cramp, she wasn't strong enough to hold on. She was slipping, faster and faster, until she slid off the end and landed on the slab, right over the flame.

It only stung this time, though she could feel the paralysis from the cursed flame creeping upon her, slowly this time; perhaps it was still partly affected by amber-wood. The corpse came her way. Maelys threw herself off the far side, intending to bolt into the gloom, but her legs had gone numb from the knees down and all she could manage was an awkward stumble. She hadn't gone far when two long arms wrapped around her and held her tight.

'We have the bait,' crowed Vivimord. 'Now to set the trap!'

SEVEN

Nish moved in the darkness, bumped his burned hand against the side of the chimney and bit down on a gasp. As the moss bandage dried the pain was growing ever stronger, and he didn't think he could take much more of it. Even worse, there was no feeling in his last three fingers; might he lose them, or even his whole hand? He was beginning to think so.

Colm was on his left, the taut rope looped around his right hand so he would sense the smallest tug. Flydd was on the other side, murmuring a rhyme, trying to recover his lost Art.

He broke off. 'How's your hand?'

'It's troubling me a bit, but I'll be all right,' Nish lied. 'During my time in father's prison I learned to be stoic.'

After a while Flydd said quietly, 'That bad, eh? If I could find a trace of my Art, I'd work a healing charm.'

Talking about it made the pain harder to endure. 'Thanks,' Nish said curtly. 'How are you getting on?'

'A few memories are coming back, though my flesh still doesn't fit my bones.'

'It takes days to adjust to a new pair of boots,' said Colm. 'You can't expect to feel at home in a new body in a hurry.'

'One of the reasons why I'd always refused to take renewal.'

'Still,' said Nish, 'many people would kill to be young again – well, middle-aged, anyhow.'

'Some people will kill for a few coppers,' Flydd sighed. 'I have to admit that, despite my protestations, a part of me did want renewal, after nine years in a failing body. I knew it would either kill me, thus solving all my problems, or make a new man of me. In a way, I'm glad I was forced into it – but don't tell Maelys I said that,' he added hastily.

'What about the third possibility?' said Nish.

'That I'd survive but be damaged? I ignored it, and the irony is bitter. I could have endured *any* physical agony more easily than I can accept the loss of my talent. Mancery has been my life and soul, my Art and Science, my work and play, but most of all it has been the crutch which has held me up through every one of life's crises since I first began training in the Art as a small boy. I don't think I can cope without it.'

'It may come back,' said Colm.

'I wouldn't bet on it.'

After a long pause, Nish said hesitantly, for few mancers liked to be questioned and Flydd was no exception, 'Xervish, a while ago you seemed to remember something puzzling about your renewal. And you mentioned a woman dressed in red.'

'Xervish?' Nish repeated after a minute or two had gone by and Flydd had not answered.

'I had a strange, strange dream,' said Flydd. 'It was after using the third crystal – or was it the fourth? The fire flared up oddly –'

'Fires flare all the time,' said Colm.

'Not peat fires, when they're nearly out. Though mine was no ordinary fire.'

'What do you mean?' Nish said uneasily. Whenever he thought he knew what Flydd was talking about, he introduced some new oddity.

'Vapours seep up through fissures in the rock from bituminous layers deep below Mistmurk Mountain. The same vapours feed the cursed flame and the greater abyssal flame that is its uncanny source –'

'*What* greater flame?' said Nish. 'I haven't heard of any other kinds of flame.'

'I built the fireplace in my hut over a fissure, years ago,' Flydd continued as though Nish had not spoken, 'thinking that, once I grew too infirm to cut and carry peat, I would still have warmth and a blaze to cook on. And the well of dreams when I needed it . . .'

'Well of dreams?' frowned Colm.

'The seeping vapours induce prophetic visions in those who have the gift of the seer, which thankfully I do not, and by breathing their vapours, oracles can connect with the ethereal realm where the shape and timbre of the future is encoded.'

'Like the Pit of Possibilities?' Nish said uneasily, remembering the dark futures it had predicted, especially for Maelys, and among them the solitary bright possibility for himself. He had always craved the respect that high office brought and, despite seeing how power had corrupted his father, a little part of Nish still yearned for it.

'No!' Flydd said firmly. 'Not like it at all.'

That made little sense. 'Then surely, with the vapours, you would have had strange dreams every night?'

'On warm nights, when there was no need for a fire, I lit the vapours before retiring; I am no oracle and prefer my own dreams. But during renewal, when Maelys was asleep, the fire flared as though vapour had gushed forth, then died down and I heard a hissing beneath me. The mystical vapours had found a new path up through the rock and it was then that I had the dream – if it was a dream . . .'

No one spoke, and Flydd went on. 'I didn't feel myself at all; I felt like someone else. Her!'

'But . . . you haven't become a woman, *inside*, have you?' Nish wasn't sure he could deal with that.

'You know I haven't,' said Flydd, 'though it can happen. The woman dressed in red was standing by the greater, *abyssal* flame, and though I could see her, I was also looking out of *her* eyes.'

'Do you mean that you were in her mind?'

'It felt that way, though she could have been in mine.'

'What was she doing?'

'Trying to do something with the abyssal flame, but it wasn't working.'

'Perhaps she was an amateur,' said Colm. 'Out of her depth.'

Flydd chuckled at the unintended pun. 'Not at all. She's a master of the Art; or once was.'

'Where is the abyssal flame?' said Nish.

'Deep down. She had a stern, handsome face, from what I saw of it,' mused Flydd, all dreamy and distant. 'And she was dressed in robes that have not been worn since ancient times. I'm sure I've never seen her before, yet I feel I know her.' Clothing rustled against rock as he stood up. 'Maelys should have given the signal by now.'

Nish came back to the present with a start. 'She's been ages. Something must have gone wrong.'

He felt tense all over; his muscles were as taut as cables. Waiting here was like thumbing his nose at fortune; every minute Jal-Nish would be tightening his cordon around the mountain, and sending his scouts creeping further into its hidden passages, cutting off every way of escape save the one Flydd could not get into – the shadow realm.

'We'll give her a bit longer,' said Flydd.

'What is the shadow realm, Xervish?' said Nish. 'I'd never heard of it before you mentioned it the other day.'

'It's a nether world, a way station for spirits detached from the body after death to rest until they finally fade into nothingness. I've heard that it was benign once – though scary – but something that did not belong was trapped there in ancient times, and has corrupted it.'

'*What* something?' said Colm.

'I don't know. It's now the home of dark shades called revenants, and darker nightmares: it's the ethereal realm where necromancers delve to further their unpleasant Arts. In the later stages of the war, Chief Scrutator Ghorr, a mancer who had mastered more of the Dark Arts than anyone, set out to find the shadow realm, for he thought it might prove useful in the war, or, if the worst happened, provide a final refuge for a select few.'

'Your depraved council, no doubt,' said Colm frigidly. 'If they hadn't prolonged the war, I would never have lost my home, my family and my inheritance.'

Flydd ignored the bitterness. 'Ghorr decided it was too dangerous to use, so he sealed all known ways into the shadow realm.'

'Forever?' said Nish.

'Well, nothing is forever. What one brilliant mancer can lock, another will eventually unlock.'

'When was this?' asked Colm.

'About fifteen years ago, but destruction of the nodes broke the power that had been used to seal the entrances – that's how I can hope to get in.'

Flydd was being careful with his words. The scrutators had always been close-mouthed; they guarded their secrets with other people's lives.

'I felt a tug on the rope!' hissed Colm. 'Two and two. It's the signal.'

Nish could hear it rasping on rock and its coils settling on the ledge beside him, then Colm cursed.

'What's the matter?' said Flydd.

'Her weight's gone off it,' said Colm hoarsely. 'She's fallen!'

Light suddenly flared at Flydd's fingertips, bright enough to hurt Nish's eyes. 'You've got your Art back!' he hissed.

'Any fool can make a bit of light,' Flydd said in an imperious voice, rather higher than his usual tones, then stared at his fingers.

'Are you all right? Your voice –'

'It's nothing,' Flydd said harshly, in his normal voice. 'We've got bigger things to worry about than my state of mind.' He studied the coils of rope. 'Maelys wouldn't have been more than a span above the slab. She won't be hurt. She'll try again.'

'How could she fall with her harness on?' Nish swallowed hard. And she might be pregnant, with *his* child. Why had he let Flydd send her down? 'She must have been attacked.'

'She took the harness off,' said Flydd. 'Maelys has trouble following the simplest orders.'

Colm let down a couple of coils and they waited again.

'About your Art –' said Nish.

'A tiny bit has come back – no more than a gifted five-year-old might display,' Flydd said without expression.

'But you just said –'

'I don't want to talk about it!'

Flydd allowed the light to dwindle to the feeblest of glow-worm gleams. Colm sat rigidly upright, hands clenched into a knuckled knot over the rope. Despite his harsh words, he did seem to care about her. Flydd began muttering again, though Nish couldn't make out the words. He rubbed his knotted jaw. What was the matter with Flydd? That voice had definitely not been his – it could have been a woman's voice. What if the woman in red was trying to take him over?

Colm's hands jerked, then again and again. 'She's back!' He came to his feet, feeling the rope, but frowned. 'She's trying to climb it. Why doesn't she tie on?'

Flydd was staring down into the black hole. 'She's been discovered.'

The rope went slack. 'She's gone this time,' Colm said dully, and reached for his sword. 'They've got her.'

'Not necessarily,' said Flydd.

'We've got to go down,' said Nish.

'There's no more defenceless man than one climbing down a rope,' said Flydd.

'Maelys has been a good friend to me – a better one than I have to her – and I will *never* abandon her.'

'Nor I.' Colm's knuckles had gone white. 'Despite . . . everything.'

Flydd sighed. 'And sometimes I forget that I am no longer a scrutator, but just an ordinary man. Of course I won't abandon Maelys; I should never have sent her down in the first place. I merely wished to teach her a lesson.'

'But . . . none of us could have gotten through,' said Nish.

'I lied; chimneys don't narrow downwards; they get wider. Even Colm could squeeze through with a bit of effort and a liberal coating of swamp creeper goo.'

'She's braver than all of us put together,' Colm said, flushing in mortification.

'Indeed she is,' said Flydd, 'for we're men of action who've spent a lifetime learning our brutal trade. It's all new to Maelys, and very hard, yet does she ever refuse a challenge? Come on.'

'Where are we going?' said Nish.

'Down and in the back way: the first guarded way we came to. Leave the rope.'

'We may need it,' said Colm.

He tossed the rapier to Nish, who caught it awkwardly. It felt good to have a weapon again.

'If we haul the rope up, they'll know we're coming,' said Flydd. 'If we leave it, they'll have one more way to watch.'

'Father has enough men to watch a hundred ways,' said Nish.

'Years ago I protected these caves against him; his men won't find their way through easily.' The finger-light died.

'How come you didn't tell us that before?' said Colm, aggrieved.

'I've only just remembered that I'd done it.'

It explained why the men they'd encountered earlier had been lost and confused, though Nish didn't take much comfort from it. His father could have broken Flydd's enchantment by now.

'So how come Vivimord got in when you were taking renewal?' said Colm.

'When I set the enchantment,' Flydd replied, 'I didn't know he was my enemy. No single enchantment can protect against every mancer. This way.'

Nish couldn't imagine how Flydd knew where to go, for he couldn't see a thing, nor remember the myriad twists and turns they'd taken since escaping from Jal-Nish.

'Quiet,' whispered Flydd after some minutes. 'We're close.'

'How are we going to do it?' said Nish.

'With extreme violence. And no chance offered.'

No one became a member of the God-Emperor's Imperial Guard without losing most of their humanity, and they would ruthlessly exploit any hesitation. Even so, and despite all the killing he'd done during the war, Nish could not take another man's life without a qualm.

He hardened his heart. It was their lives or his; their lives or Maelys's; their lives or else the God-Emperor would prevail, and if the tears gave him the secret of immortality his brutal reign would last until the end of time. Nish could not endure that thought; Jal-Nish had to be overthrown.

They turned another corner and saw the faintest illumination reflecting off the stone wall from around the next bend.

'Wait here.' Flydd went forward silently.

Nish felt an urge to practise a few strokes with the rapier, a weapon he had not used in many years, but restrained himself. Flydd would not appreciate its point coming his way in the dark.

Shortly he was beside them again. 'There are three guards, sitting ten or twelve paces past the corner, just before the entrance to the flame cavern. They've got their backs to us, watching the other passage. At the corner, I'll make light and we'll rush them while they're dazzled. We've got to take them down without warning. If one gets away . . .'

'We know,' said Nish, holding the rapier point down so as to avoid accidents. He was longing for bloody action now. It would help to take his mind off the pain.

They agreed on battle signals and headed for the corner. Flydd peered around it, then moved noiselessly out. Nish followed half a span to his right, for the passage was broad here. A little way ahead, he made out a flicker coming from an opening to their left – the entrance to the cursed flame chamber. This side of it, three large silhouettes waited in the dark.

Flydd touched their wrists again, the signal that he was ready. Nish tensed; on the count of five a brilliant light burst forth from Flydd's upstretched fingers and they charged.

The man on the right was scrambling to his feet when the rapier took him in the back of the neck; he collapsed without a sound. On the other side, Colm had taken the head off his man with a single savage blow. Blood sprayed onto the tunnel roof and all over them.

Unfortunately Flydd stumbled and fell hard, and the third soldier took off into the dark so quickly that Nish had no hope of catching him. Before he could move, Colm swung his sword over his shoulder and sent it flying viciously through the air. It struck the fleeing soldier in the back and brought him down.

Colm went after him without a word and finished the job, returning with jaw set and eyes hard.

'That was a . . . mighty throw,' Nish said, uneasily, for it showed a side of Colm he hadn't seen before. Nish had killed with military efficiency, while Colm's blows revealed a violent rage, barely kept in check.

'I've suffered plenty at their hands,' Colm grated. 'In the past, your father's men showed me no mercy, and I'll give them none.'

'You never forget an injury, do you?'

'Why should I?' said Colm with a hard stare. 'All I ask for is what is mine by right.'

Nish withdrew his rapier, wiped it on the soldier he'd killed and helped Flydd up. The light from his fingers was just a glimmer and he was waxen pale.

'Bloody renewal!' Flydd muttered. 'Legs gave out as soon as I tried to run.' He studied the bodies. 'They're not wearing uniforms. I wonder why?'

Nish could not have cared less. His pulse was racing, and every heartbeat sent a fresh spasm of agony through his burned hand, but he had to endure it. He had to find Maelys – *if she was still alive.*

He wiped the worst of the still-warm blood off his face, went around the headless man, whose neck stump was dribbling blood, and headed into the flame cavern. Left, right, left he went, the light of the cursed flame growing; now the long stone slab Maelys had described was no more than twenty spans away, with the rope and harness suspended above, but there was no sign of her.

'Keep watch on the entrances,' Flydd said quietly. 'I'll look for her.'

Nish moved into the shadows, rapier out. He wanted to use it on someone, and if they'd hurt Maelys, he would.

Colm, keeping well clear of the cursed flame, went across to guard the unseen far entrance, though it seemed a useless gesture. Neither of them would be a match for his father's highly trained Imperial Guard, face to face.

The pain grew ever worse until it was impossible to think about anything else. In a sweaty daze, Nish watched Flydd moving towards the slab, eyes sweeping right and left.

He picked up something from the floor. 'Shards of my crystal: she overcharged it and it burst. The flame must be more powerful than I'd thought. And it's shrunk back? Is that because of Vivimord?' Flydd bent low. 'Congealed blood; hours old, so it can't be hers. It must have come from Phrune or Vivimord.'

Colm eyed the cursed flame warily. Nish couldn't blame him; he felt its power too.

Flydd inspected the slab, and the floor around it, from which he picked up Maelys's taphloid by the chain, wrapped it in a rag and pocketed it. 'This is bad. Why did she undo the rope? Because the crystal burst, and she could not return to confess such a failure?'

'Why not?' said Colm from the darkness.

'Her family blame her for the ruin of the clan. In their eyes she can do nothing right, and she's always been expected to make up for the failings of others, but when she tries, it always goes wrong – like the story she told back in the cavern.'

'It didn't sound like a story to me,' Colm said coldly.

'She acted to save her family in the only way she knew how. I'm sure you would have done the same.'

'Not that way.' Colm could not contain his disgust.

'You judge her harshly.'

'The line has to be drawn; she crossed it.'

'Let's all bow to Saint Colm,' Nish sneered, for his pain was getting the better of him.

'Pay your own debts before you criticise me,' spat Colm.

'We've got enough enemies without you two at each other's throats,' said Flydd. 'Clearly, Maelys was driven to make her failure good, to save us.' He hauled his reluctant flesh onto the slab. 'These footmarks are too big for Maelys. She encountered someone here, but not one of Jal-Nish's big men. Not with plump, stubby feet like these.'

'And not Vivimord either,' said Nish, coming closer. 'He's got long feet.'

'Come up.' Flydd reached down to give Nish a hand, and he scrambled up. 'Hold your burnt hand just above the cursed flame. It might help.'

'Is that how Vivimord was healed?'

Flydd jumped down and began to pace around the slab. 'Not exactly; Phrune shed his own blood into the flame, thence onto Vivimord who lay beneath, and the purified sacrifice healed him.'

72

'I don't suppose . . .?' Nish began.

'I wouldn't recommend it,' said Flydd. 'It's the *cursed* flame, remember, and if any two men were already cursed, it was those two.'

'I'm equally cursed,' Nish said bitterly. He held his hand above the flame, biting his lip as the pain flared to new levels of excruciation. 'I don't see how it can do any harm.'

Flydd walked into the darkness, head down, studying the floor. 'Phrune's sacrifice might have perverted the flame. It will take a long time to cleanse it.'

Nonetheless, with the possibility of healing right in front of him, the pain suddenly became unbearable and, desperate for relief, Nish stabbed his wrist on the point of the rapier and allowed his blood to fall onto the slab beside the star hole. It began to run into the flame, which flared red and green. He half-scrambled, half-fell off and crawled underneath, tearing the moss bandage from his charred and repulsive hand.

Blood began to drip through onto his wrist. It was hot and made his unburned skin creep as if thousands of stinging ants were running over it. He rubbed the blood across his burned hand and fingers, where he could see bone showing through charred flesh. It smelled awful – cooked.

'Aah!' he cried out as the pain doubled and redoubled; he just had presence of mind enough to keep rubbing the blood in.

'No, Nish!'

Flydd came back at a stumbling run and tried to drag him out. Nish kept him at bay with his feet. If his hand could be healed, even partially, it was worth the risk.

'It's not a sacrifice if it's your own blood!' Flydd added.

Drip, drip, drip. Nish felt sure it was doing some good; the pain was easing and the flesh didn't seem quite so charred.

'No, *no*!' cried Flydd, trying to climb onto the slab.

A trail of large dark drops fell, but they were icy and burned glacially as Nish smeared them across the back of his hand and down his little and ring fingers, where the cold took away the pain completely.

'It's working!' He held his hand up. Where he'd rubbed the cold blood in, new skin was rising up from charred flesh before his eyes; smooth skin, slightly darker than his own. 'Another few drops like those and I'll have my hand back, nearly as good as ever.'

'Get out, Nish. There'll be no more.' Flydd's voice was granite hard.

'What's the fool done now?' said Colm from the other side.

Nish caught the last drop, rubbed it in and crawled out. 'But it's healing me . . .'

'Those last drops were Vivimord's blood, mingling with your own, you fool. And you don't want –' His eyes dropped to Nish's hand, where new skin was still forming. 'You don't want any part of him in you; especially not his blood. Hold your hand out, quick!'

Nish obeyed. 'What are you going to do?'

Flydd grabbed Colm's sword and swung it high. Nish was slow to react; he couldn't believe that Flydd was going to do it until the blade started to fall, then snatched his hand out of the way just in time.

'What do you think you're doing?' he cried, backing away as the blade struck the floor. He was shaking.

'Better no hand than one tainted by Vivimord's black blood. Hold it out.'

'No!' Nish gasped. What had he done to himself?

Flydd looked as though he was going to come after Nish and amputate his hand by force, but finally he sighed, 'It's your funeral,' and handed the blade back to Colm, who wore a curiously satisfied smile. He wasn't displeased at what had happened, but Colm had never liked him, and the feeling was mutual.

'What's the matter?' said Nish. 'How could it be that bad?'

'How the devil would I know?' said Flydd. 'Though I

dare say we'll find out soon enough. Better see if I can recover anything from this fiasco.'

He crawled under the slab, soon humping out again with a small crystal cupped in his hand. The faintest colours moved inside it. 'She found a powered crystal, but then she encountered her nemesis, and it wasn't Jal-Nish. So that's why the soldiers weren't wearing uniforms.'

'Vivimord,' said Nish, feeling faint. 'That stinking, murderous maniac.'

'And without her taphloid she'd be defenceless.'

'Can you find him?'

'I don't think that will be too difficult,' said Flydd. 'It's not her he wants, Nish. It's you – and you've just linked yourself to him for the term of your *natural* life. If not beyond it.'

Taking a small phial made of white crystal from an inner pocket, he carefully filled it at the cursed flame and stoppered it tightly. Through the walls of the crystal the flames licked back and forth, red and black.

'What's that for?' said Nish.

'I don't know yet, but it's what the woman in red wanted me to do.'

And is she still in your mind, Nish fretted, possessing you and controlling your every thought and deed?

EIGHT

Vivimord had tidied himself up since Maelys last saw him. His healed, baby-smooth olive skin had been freshly oiled, including his long hairless skull, and the bloodstains washed away. The dark hollows surrounding his deep eyes were less prominent, while the black, egg-shaped swelling on his right cheek, where Maelys had struck him with her taphloid, had shrunk to the size of a plover's egg.

He bound Maelys, gagged and blindfolded her, threw her knife away then carried her through the dark, walking with a slow, measured tread. They went down many flights of steps, along a passage with an uneven floor and through a stone door whose hinges hissed as it opened and closed. The swamp-creeper slime became ever more itchy as it dried but she couldn't scratch herself.

On the other side the passage was smooth and clean; she couldn't hear Vivimord's footfalls, though shortly she made out a repulsive squelching which indicated that Phrune was close behind. She could smell him now: a revolting mixture of rancid oil, dead flesh and burst intestines, overpowering Vivimord's own faint odour of crisped skin and the balm he'd used to dress his wounds. Or did Phrune still provide that service, even in death? And if he did, what other services did he continue to provide for his master?

Maelys shied away from that thought, for it was too appalling. She had to concentrate on getting free and fulfilling her responsibilities; she could not allow Vivimord to use her as bait for Nish. If she could get a hand free, she might draw the taphloid from her pocket, and then, look out!

She swung her knee up, so as to feel the comforting weight of the taphloid in the pocket of her pants, but it wasn't there. It must have fallen out during her struggles. She was unarmed; helpless; lost without it.

More doors opened and closed, the last with a brittle crack as though stone had become frozen to stone over the depths of time. Warm, dusty air billowed out, and a faint smoky odour, though it wasn't the chamber of the cursed flame this time. They had gone down many flights and up none, so she must be far below it now.

Vivimord's footsteps echoed hollowly, indicating that this was a much larger chamber, deep within the mountain. As they went in she heard a faint whistling, which grew louder. Maelys counted fifty-four paces before he laid her down on a warm floor and removed the blindfold.

Some twenty paces away, a much larger, green-black flame whistled up from a structure of carved greenstone – a pedestal or circular altar big enough for a temple – and its light illuminated the whole chamber. She caught her breath, for she could have been in the audience room of a palace from the Histories, one suited to an emperor. Why was it hidden in an insignificant plateau deep within an empty rainforest?

The chamber was painted with murals that, even in their barbaric brutality, were beautiful, though this was not the vicious brutality of the God-Emperor's realm. Even Maelys could tell that. It was the glorious barbarism of a people who had fought for survival for so long, against impossible odds, that they knew nothing else.

The flame flared higher, emerald tongues within the black. Dead Phrune squelched to a stop behind her, his regurgitated entrails dangling and dripping. Maelys rolled away across the floor; Phrune came after her and stopped her with his fat foot.

Vivimord stared at the characters inscribed around the altar. '*All endeavours fail*,' he read haltingly. '*Time undoes all things*. And rightly so. The Charon were great, but fatally flawed, and now they have gone to extinction.'

Maelys knew enough of the Histories to understand what he was talking about. A few Charon, the Hundred, had escaped out of the terrible void between the worlds thousands of years ago and taken Aachan, another of the Three Worlds, for their own. At that time, Aachan was inhabited by the great and powerful Aachim, but the Hundred, led by the greatest Charon of all, Rulke, had seized their world and kept them in thrall for thousands of years. The Charon were extremely long-lived but, in some cosmic irony no one had ever understood, most had been sterile on Aachan, and over the aeons the Hundred had slowly dwindled.

Three Charon had subsequently come to Santhenar: Rulke, Yalkara and Kandor. Kandor had been killed in ages past. Rulke had eventually been incarcerated in the Nightland, a special prison remote from the laws that governed the real world, but had escaped and brought the *Tale of the Mirror* to its dreadful climax some two hundred and twenty years ago. He had been slain and the handful of surviving but sterile Charon, led by Yalkara, had gone back to the void, and to extinction.

'Why did they build this place *here*?' she said, speaking her thoughts aloud.

'For the abyssal flame, I expect,' said Vivimord. 'It's far more powerful than the cursed flame, and more difficult to use, but I'll find a way.'

Phrune made a hideous gurgling noise. Maelys's hackles rose.

'Why, Phrune,' said Vivimord teasingly, 'are you trying to tell me something?'

Again the disgusting noise.

Vivimord smiled thinly. 'You want to kill her – no, to *skin* her for me? You'll have to wait, my *dear* Phrune. Maelys is bait; you know that. Come, we must set the trap.'

He dragged Maelys by her bound wrists into a smaller room which lay in darkness. 'This was once a great lady's bedchamber and will do nicely for the purpose I have in mind. But if you fail me, Maelys, a surprise awaits you below.'

Phrune gave another squelch; Maelys sensed dismay in him, or anger.

'Surely I don't have to remind you that you're *dead*, Phrune?' said Vivimord. 'You have no feelings now – if you ever did. You may think that tormenting her will give you the same sadistic pleasure as before, but it's not going to happen. You'll never feel anything again.'

Squelch-squelch, quick and agitated.

'Don't be like that,' Vivimord said with mock sorrow. 'We can't allow our base lusts to get in the way of the greater plan, can we? I too want Maelys to pay for what she did to us – I shudder for retribution – but we must keep to our purpose if we're to get out of here *alive*, and turn Nish into the Deliverer. My Defiance are only leagues away, but first we have to reach them.'

Light sprayed from the tip of the whippy wooden rod he was holding, illuminating a blood-red bedchamber. Its walls were lined with red marble, the ceiling was shaped like a tent, though draped with several of the cord-thick webs that had so unnerved her previously, and the centre of the chamber was occupied by a large bed with eight posts and a three-spans-high canopy whose velvet curtains, though somewhat ragged and dusty, had lost none of their ancient magnificence.

'Turn down the bed, Phrune,' said Vivimord. Phrune slopped forward, but Vivimord added, 'on second thoughts,

I'll do it myself – lengths of intestine on the sheets would not be conducive to romance.'

'Romance?' she said hoarsely.

Squelch-slurp, went Phrune.

'Nor mere animal lust,' said Vivimord. 'Back, Phrune.'

Phrune retreated and Vivimord deftly flicked dust off the covers and turned down the bed.

'Better test the equipment; it's many years since I was last here.'

He touched the first of a line of polished platinum stubs on the head of the bed. Nothing happened. He pressed it harder and flames sprang up from engraved glass lanterns mounted on brackets around the four walls. Vivimord stroked his fingers clockwise around the stub; the flames dimmed. He touched another stub; a glow appeared in a pair of brass censers hanging to either side of a dusty chandelier. Trails of drifting fragrant smoke made Maelys's nose tingle. Suddenly the colours in the room seemed brighter and richer, but she itched worse than ever.

As Vivimord touched the third platinum stub, a faint, mesmerising music began from pipes and drums, like the sound of players drifting up from a distant ballroom to be heard in snatches by a listener on a high balcony. He listened for a minute, head to one side and toe tapping, as if briefly he had been transported to another age, then pressed the stub again and the music faded.

A fourth stub was separate from the others but Vivimord had his hand positioned casually, as if to conceal it from her, and when he took his hand away the stub was no longer visible. She was wondering why when he strolled to the foot of the bed and stood looking down at her, rubbing his chin.

'I wonder – what creature is it that you dislike above all others?'

Instinctively, she looked up at the tented ceiling, but the dimmed lanterns no longer illuminated it. Maelys shivered.

'Swamp creepers disgust you, don't they? I detected your screams when you were coming down the chimney. You can't bear the sight of them, or the smell. And to have them crawling over you, trailing their slime across your face . . .'

Maelys clenched her jaw and swallowed. Let him think that; it might give her a chance.

'They give you the horrors, and if you were trapped in the middle of a mound of them you might go insane, but they're not what you fear most, are they? I can read you, little Maelys. You're the bravest girl I've met in years, but you have a weakness.'

She didn't reply.

'Spiders?' said Vivimord. 'You don't like scuttling creatures with lots of legs.'

'I'm not afraid of spiders; I used to catch them in little pots and put them out of Nifferlin Manor all the time.' That wasn't quite true; she'd been terrified of the huge, warty toad-spiders that she'd sometimes encountered in the old ruins behind Nifferlin. Maelys was reminded of the thick, cord-like webs that had been everywhere in the chamber of the cursed flame. She'd never seen the creatures that had made the webs, but they must be worse than toad-spiders.

'But you didn't kill them, did you?' Vivimord said. 'You're soft-hearted, and that's a weakness.'

'They were no danger to me.'

'It still shows weakness. Do you know what an octopede is?'

She shook her head. To her left, dead Phrune let out a slippery, coughing bark; jeering laughter, perhaps. Vivimord was wrong, whatever he was talking about: Maelys feared no creature on Santhenar the way she feared her own kind, and especially Vivimord and Phrune. Animals could be violent and vicious, but they weren't malicious and they did not torment other creatures for their own sick pleasure.

'This is no laughing matter, Phrune,' said Vivimord. 'This is retribution, not revenge. Retribution is measured justice and, carried out dispassionately, it elevates us; revenge is a base emotion that eats us away from the inside and, in the end, destroys us.' He studied his former acolyte. 'You can't understand, can you? The senses were everything to you, alas. That's what brought you undone and robbed me of your service when I needed it most.'

Vivimord raised his right arm towards the ceiling. Maelys heard a faint *zzzzzttt*, then something long and corpse-white tumbled through the air, trailing a short length of corded web, and thumped down onto the bed.

Maelys gasped and clutched at her chest, for the creature had an elongated body nearly two spans long, rather flabby and warty, a long straight spine or sting at the rear, and short, plump legs extending sideways. A pair of fish-hook-like claws jagged at the covers, then it shot over the side of the bed into the darkness underneath.

She shuddered violently and felt like throwing up. She could not have said why it filled her with such terror – Maelys was sure she'd never seen anything like it, even as a child – but it did and she couldn't conceal it. What if an octopede had come upon her in the chimney? They had definitely been there.

Vivimord gave a thin, satisfied smile. 'I thought as much. Get on the bed.' Then he frowned. 'No, not in that disgusting state. Go through that door; you will find a bathing chamber. Clean yourself up and come back.' He gestured and her bonds fell away.

She hobbled on numb feet for the door he was pointing to: she had to get away. The squelching noises sounded behind her, but Vivimord said sharply, 'Stop, Phrune. You're dead; you no longer feel *any* lusts.'

Phrune made a mewling gurgle. Jerking the door open, she hurled herself through and banged it, feeling in the darkness for a catch or bolt, but there was none. However her fingers touched a glassy plate which began to glow faintly, as though the power that had once illuminated it was almost gone.

She was in a small triangular room lined with polished pink stone. It must once have looked magnificent, but all was badly stained by brown seepage, and efflorescences of white and yellow crystals grew from the joins between the tiles. It could not have been used in centuries. Centrally, a tulip-shaped tub made from clear crystal rose from a stalk of the same material. Water with a yellow tinge flowed over the sides and down into recesses at the base; yellow concretions like button mushrooms had formed there and the room had a musty, dusty smell.

Maelys dared not disobey Vivimord; besides, the itching was almost unbearable. She didn't undress, though: she took off her boots and socks, climbed three crystal steps and was sliding into the tulip tub when the door opened a fraction.

Vivimord's voice said, 'Don't try anything. My guardian is watching you.' The panel brightened fractionally.

Maelys's eyes were drawn upwards to the dimly illuminated ceiling. A corded web stretched across it to a corner which lay in shadow, apart from a pair of large, garnet-coloured eyes, close together, and the tip of one hook-shaped claw.

Muffling a cry, she crouched until the cool water was at neck level and scrubbed furiously at her clothes and skin, trying to rid herself of every remnant of dried slime. After a hasty glance at the octopede, which hadn't moved, she ducked her head and washed her face, surfaced like a porpoise, checked on the watcher, then ducked again and raked her fingers through her hair. She wasn't game to lose sight of the octopede for more than a few seconds. For such a flabby creature, the other one had been terrifyingly fast.

How did Vivimord plan to catch Nish? It looked as though he was planning a seduction, though Vivimord knew that Nish had rejected Maelys months ago, and that he was still obsessed with Irisis, whose perfectly preserved body was held in Jal-Nish's Palace of Morrelune. Nish would do almost anything to have her back, and what if Vivimord, whose Black Arts had reanimated Phrune's corpse, knew of a way to restore the dead to life? It was horrible; sick; depraved; so what did that make Nish?

She reminded herself that, though Nish had been sorely tempted more than once, he had done nothing about it, *yet*. Vivimord was the immediate problem, but Maelys didn't have the faintest idea of how to deal with him; he was too ruthless and clever. So why was he playing out this seduction scene? Just to torment her? Hardly. Every minute that passed meant a greater chance of discovery by Jal-Nish, so why not simply seize Nish when he appeared? Could Vivimord be afraid of Flydd?

Then why show her the octopede? To ensure that she did what she was told – and betray Nish? And she probably would. Vivimord had found her weakness. She couldn't bear to be at the mercy of such a creature, its disgusting, warty limbs on her, its hook-claws dragging her to its fanged mouth. She would agree to anything to get away from it.

NINE

Nish had no idea how Flydd was tracking Vivimord and Maelys through the tunnels of Mistmurk Mountain, unless it was by smell. Several times he got down on hands and knees to sniff at the floor, where Nish noted an occasional greasy smear, and once a faint odour of rotten flesh, though it didn't tell him anything. Where they were going or what Flydd planned to do when he got there was a mystery, though Vivimord with his powers restored was almost as formidable an opponent as the God-Emperor. What could Flydd do, with just enough Art to create light? Nish noticed he kept playing with the crystal he'd taken from beneath the slab, rolling it back and forth between his fingers or pressing it against his forehead, but if he was trying to draw upon its power, it was not working.

Nish trudged along at the rear, enduring the fierce pain from his partly healed hand; the healing process felt like clusters of spines growing through inflamed flesh. His thumb, first two fingers and half the back of his hand were covered in new skin, and so was his palm, though the remaining two fingers were deeply burnt and he might still lose them.

'I think this is it,' Flydd whispered, loosening his knife in its sheath but not drawing it. They had turned into a straight hall lined with polished stone, smooth and cold to Nish's fingertips. 'We'll go in darkness now.'

'What's down there?' said Colm.

'Quiet.' Flydd was staring fixedly along the hall.

Nish couldn't hear a thing, though when he rested his head against the wall for a moment, the stone had the subtlest vibration.

'A great chamber lies at the end of this corridor,' said Flydd, 'and it's a place of power, though not one I know how to use. The abyssal flame, the mother of all cursed flames, burns continuously here, fed by a source deep in the roots of the mountain; it's the reason Vivimord brought Maelys here. With the mountain surrounded, he can't get out without tapping a mighty source of power to – *what's that?*'

'I didn't hear anything,' said Nish.

'Nor I,' said Colm.

'Perhaps I imagined it,' said Flydd. 'My new mind jumps all over the place; I can't always be sure whether I'm living in the moment or remembering the past – or *her* past. Come on; Nish, stay close. Vivimord wants you, remember.'

Everyone wants me, Nish thought, and Maelys too. I'm beginning to understand what she has gone through these past months.

'What does he hope to do with this mighty source of power?' said Colm. 'Open the shadow realm?'

'*That* was a secret known only to two scrutators,' said Flydd. 'The vile and vicious Chief Scrutator Ghorr, may he lie rotting in the most infested pit of all, and myself. Ghorr would have told no one before he died; he loved the power of his solitary secrets too much. I feel sure that not even Jal-Nish or Vivimord know how to enter it – directly, I mean.'

'How else can it be entered?'

'It's rumoured that there was once a Charon portal here. That's one of the reasons I chose this place.'

Or the woman in red put it into your mind, not for our betterment, Nish thought, though he didn't dare say it.

'What do you mean, a *portal*?' said Colm.

'A gate which allows one to travel instantly from one place to another.'

'Then open the damn thing and take us somewhere civilised, as far away from the shadow realm as possible.'

'I don't know *how* to open it, yet,' Flydd said. 'And even in my prime I wouldn't have had the strength to open a portal sealed for centuries. However, its previous existence would have left a weakness in the fabric of space here, which, even without my special crystal, I hope to exploit to slip into the shadow realm. And then out somewhere safe, as quickly as possible.'

'But Vivimord –'

'He's a great mancer, and having recently been restored at the cursed flame, he'll be able to wield its power better than any living man. He may be able to reopen the portal and carry Nish and Maelys beyond our reach; that cannot be allowed to happen. If she does carry the first grandchild of the God-Emperor, Vivimord would have a hold over him that would be impossible to break, and an alliance between those two monsters must be prevented at all costs.'

At the end of the corridor Flydd leaned on one of a tall pair of doors until it opened a crack, and peered through. Nish made out a distant whistling.

'This is the chamber of the abyssal flame,' whispered Flydd. 'Prepare for battle, but don't strike until I give the order.'

Nish and Colm drew their weapons. Flydd kept his knife in its sheath; the faintest glow limned the fingers of his right hand. As they entered, the whistling became shrill, painful; a monstrous green-black flame flared spans high from an altar in the centre of the room. They stopped, staring at it. Colm was breathing heavily.

They were in a vast, magnificent chamber with polished stone walls and splendidly barbaric murals. Flydd continued and the flame drew down to a flicker, the whistle dying to a gassy hiss. All fell into shadow save for the greenstone altar through which the flame issued. Its circular top was a thick, ornamented disc, several spans across, with the flame hole in the centre and a pair of curved projections running out from opposite sides to form the tips of a stubby two-armed spiral whose grooves continued into the centre of the disc.

'That's odd,' Flydd said quietly.

'What is?' Colm was moving his blade slowly from left to right.

'I've been here many times over the past nine years, trying to find traces of the portal, and the flame hasn't changed by so much as a flicker. Someone's made it change.'

'Vivimord must be using it,' said Nish, suddenly feeling cold, though the room was warm. The unhealed parts of his hand throbbed mercilessly, while where the new skin and flesh had grown he felt those prickling clusters of needles. What if Flydd was right and the blood did link him to Vivimord?

'I'm afraid he is. It's time for desperate measures.' Flydd raised his hand, grunting with the strain, and yellow light burst forth from his crystal, reflecting dazzlingly off a thousand polished surfaces.

The barbaric splendour of the chamber imprinted itself on Nish's inner eye, then the abyssal flame was drawn below the aperture from which it issued and the yellow light radiating from Flydd's crystal was driven back into it. He groaned, clenched his fist around the crystal and shook it furiously. Momentarily the blood was visible flowing in his fingers, but the crystal went out and the chamber grew dark.

'Can you hear that?' hissed Flydd.

Nish made out distant heavy footsteps, as of a squad of soldiers running up a long stair, though they had an echoing, unreal quality. Flydd grunted and his fingers flushed pink for a second, then the light went out and he could not force another glimmer from the crystal.

'It's Father's army coming up from the rainforest. They've found a way into the base of the mountain.'

'Are they close?' said Colm.

'I can't tell,' said Flydd. 'Wait! No, I don't think so. Those sounds are being *sent* here, to panic us. Back to the door!'

As he moved away, Nish caught a faint whiff of smoke – no, incense, with a sweet, spicy odour. His head spun; he shook it and it cleared, but the needle pricks in his hand grew so painful that he couldn't think straight.

'What about Maelys –?' began Colm, somewhere to Nish's right.

'We can't help her if we're caught.' Flydd's voice seemed to come from a distance. 'This way.'

Nish headed back towards the doors through which they had entered, holding his rapier low, but soon began to doubt that he was going in the right direction.

'Xervish, where are you?'

'Here!' Flydd hissed.

His voice came from even further away; to Nish's left now, he thought. How could he have made such a mistake? He turned in the direction he thought Flydd's voice was coming from, hurried forwards then, *whack*.

He hit the floor and the rapier clattered away. Nish rolled to one side, thinking he'd been attacked, but his groping right hand came down on carved stone which had a circular shape. He stood up, feeling his way around it. He'd run headfirst into the altar.

What was he doing in the middle of the room? He rubbed his forehead and caught a stronger whiff of incense, though it didn't make his head spin this time; it seemed to clear it. His hand prickled again, and now it felt as though someone had taken hold of it and was leading him to safety. He jerked back and felt around but there was nothing in front of him.

'Xervish?'

He did not reply, though a pale shape wisped by off to Nish's right. Stumbling backwards, he trod on the hilt of the rapier and grabbed it, never more glad to have a weapon in his hand.

'Colm?'

He didn't reply either. Nish shivered; he felt even colder now, and really afraid. 'Xervish!'

It was as if he'd shouted into an amphitheatre full of mud, which absorbed every sound. How had Vivimord separated them so easily?

His new skin tingled and he rubbed at it absently. He had to find the door; Flydd and Colm must be waiting there. Nish put his back to the altar and, trailing the rapier's tip on the floor, walked directly away from the altar. When he came to the wall he would follow it along to the double doors.

The smell of incense grew stronger with every step. He was halfway across the chamber, as near as he could judge, when someone whispered his name. He stopped, squinting into the dark until his eyes ached, but could not see a thing.

He couldn't hear anything either, save his breathing. Those pounding footsteps had stopped when he'd hit his head, which surely proved that they had been sent to panic him.

'Nish?' It was louder this time – a woman's voice – though it also came from a long way away. It might have been Maelys; he could not be sure. Clearsight, I've never needed you more – show me the way. But his clearsight, though it had been enhanced by the kiss of Reaper, told him nothing.

He bumped into a column supporting the roof, felt his way around it and kept going, swinging the rapier back and forth like a blind man's cane. Shortly it scraped on something hard. He reached out but it swung silently away from him – it was just a normal-sized door, not either of the pair of huge double doors they'd come through a few minutes ago. From beyond he made out a faint music of pipes and drums, notes that stirred the senses and set them on fire.

He shook the feelings off – they had to be an enchantment sent by Vivimord or Jal-Nish to ensnare him, and he wasn't going to be taken in. Suddenly his burned hand throbbed like a warning of greater pain to come; the effects of the cursed flame were wearing off.

He tried to ignore the pain and the head-spinning incense; he had to think clearly now. Left or right? There was no way to tell. He caught another whiff of incense; it was stronger, richer and more perfumed this time, and again his head spun. Nish rubbed his face with his free hand, struggling to think straight, then turned left, but heard the voice again, coming through the door. A throaty woman's voice – a nerve-achingly familiar one.

'Nish?'

It couldn't be, for Irisis was ten years dead and he wasn't going down that path again. Only madness lay that way, and he'd nearly succumbed before, when Jal-Nish had offered him what he most wanted in all the world. Nish had managed to resist the temptation and was all the stronger for it.

Nonetheless, he pushed the door open; he had to satisfy himself that it wasn't her; that it was a trick. The stirring music grew stronger, an overpowering waft of incense seared his nasal passages, and he saw that he was in the boudoir of some potentate of olden times. It was pleasantly warm but dimly lit; all he could see was a magnificent bed, dark, costly curtains and bed coverings, turned down on one side, and the flames guttering in their wall brackets.

And the buxom young woman on the bed. It wasn't Irisis, but a smaller version of her, for the shoulder-length golden hair was exactly the colour Irisis's hair had been. He couldn't see the woman's face, just the curve of a cheek, one bare, soft shoulder and the outline of her figure beneath the covers.

Nish swallowed, the incense swirling through him like a drug that muddied the mind and enfeebled the will, the music driving his pulse and quickening his desire. The last time he'd lain with a woman – with Irisis – had been ten and a half years ago.

A vague unease stirred, though he couldn't remember why. Something didn't seem right but he could no longer tell; his mind felt like mush. He tried to fight the urge to go to the bed, but it proved too strong – he was led there by that ghostly compulsion, again tugging his burned hand. Nish no longer cared about anything else; both Vivimord and his father had vanished from his mind. He could only think of the woman on the bed and his flaming desire for her.

TEN

Maelys lay in the bed, unable to focus on a single thought. The drugged incense and mesmerising music had eaten away her will and she wasn't strong enough to break free. Neither the fate of her family, nor of Flydd, Nish and Colm, mattered. She was no longer afraid of Vivimord; she felt a sense of lazy, drifting peace.

As she'd emerged from her bath, fully clothed, a touch of Vivimord's fingers had left her dazed and compliant. With hand gestures he'd transformed her garments to a diaphanous bed gown, painted her nails and lips, and converted her shaggy black hair to golden-blonde locks that caressed her bare shoulders. He artfully arranged her in the bed and she could do nothing about it. Had he sent her underneath to face the octopede she would not have been able to disobey, for he was far more powerful than when she had first met him.

Now Vivimord entered and made a mirror in the air in front of her, to show her what she'd become, and her appearance so shocked her that the enchantment he'd laid on her cracked and she felt the blood flooding to her face.

Her upbringing had been modest, and had become puritanical after her father had fled from Jal-Nish. She had never worn lip paint, nor clothes that were the least revealing, but now she might as well have been wearing air.

'You've turned me into a slut!' Jerking the covers up to her chin, she scrubbed at her lips with the back of one hand, smearing crimson lip paint across her face. Her voice was deeper, more throaty and sensual, and she didn't like that either. 'Why are you doing this to me?'

'I've transformed you into a temptress, to trap Nish,' he said, removing the smears with a snap of his fingers. 'No easy feat, given the base materials I had to start with.'

She ignored the insult; Maelys was used to them by now. Vivimord's plan didn't make sense; why did he need *her* to trap Nish? 'Why me? You once thought I was completely unsuitable for Nish.'

'I've changed my mind about you,' he said cryptically. 'Besides, the need is urgent now, and I have no one else.'

She had to get out of here. She wasn't going to do his depraved bidding. Maelys tried to get out the other side of the bed without revealing any more of herself, no easy thing in the gossamer gown.

Vivimord dragged her back by the ankle. 'Either you obey my commands,' he said icily, 'or you will suffer retribution for what you've done to Phrune and me.'

'What do you mean?' she whispered.

'Once Phrune has taken your skin, I'll feed your shrieking remains to the octopede.'

He touched her on the forehead, restoring the charm, and she fell back on the pillows, unable to resist as he arranged her limbs as before and pushed up her breasts until they were bursting out the bodice of the gown. He brushed his hand over her eyes and Maelys felt herself drifting off to sleep. She tried to resist it but his lips brushed her ear as he spoke in a language she did not know; sleep claimed her.

Time passed and she woke, so listless that she could barely move, drifting, dreaming, the music reinforcing Vivimord's enchantment with every beat, the incense dulling her wits with every breath. She was unable to think two connected thoughts; her mind kept wandering into waking dreams no matter how hard she tried to concentrate.

She managed to turn her head and noticed the three platinum stubs on the bed head. Hadn't there been a fourth? She had a feeling that Vivimord had hidden it from her. She tried to reach up but her arm had no strength.

Later, the door opened and Nish appeared there, looking around dazedly. He seemed taller, younger and more handsome than before, though she knew that was also Vivimord's enchantment.

She wasn't drowsy now and suddenly Maelys understood what was going on. Vivimord wanted her to get pregnant by Nish and would use his Arts to make sure she did; then Vivimord, by keeping the child, would be able to control both Nish and his father.

Yet in her dazed state, it felt right. If she could only sink back and accept Nish, it would make her lie to Jal-Nish into truth, one he could never disprove, and once she was pregnant her family would be safe for as long as he lived. Why not? She could not stop Vivimord, so what was the point of resisting? It would save her from Phrune too, and the octopede.

Nish was staring at her so hard that it burned, though Maelys knew he was seeing the Irisis look-alike Vivimord had made of her. She refused to meet his eyes or encourage him in any way. Give him nothing of yourself, she thought laboriously. Expect nothing from him and you won't get hurt. Lie with him; save your family, and your life. Get it over with. It won't be so bad.

Unfortunately, Maelys had always been a romantic and this was the very opposite of how she had imagined her first time with a man would be. But Nish looked very handsome now, and his robes befitted a prince. Perhaps he did care, a little.

He pushed the door closed and began to walk towards her. His eyes were glazed, the pupils dilated, and his breathing was fast and shallow. He was also being controlled by Vivimord; he did not want her at all. The realisation made another crack in the enchantment, though when she thought of little Fyllis in the hands of Jal-Nish's torturers, Maelys knew that lying with Nish was a small price to pay.

She took a deep breath, rolled onto her back, feeling her breasts straining against the gauzy fabric, and smiled until it hurt. She could not help remembering the time she'd tried to do her duty and seduce him, and the ghastly humiliation as he'd repudiated her. Maelys dreaded it happening again.

Nish began stripping off his princely robes – which had to be an illusion – as he approached. He climbed onto the bed, his eyes dark pools of longing for the woman she was made up to be.

Maelys had no experience in the arts of the bedchamber, so she lay back on the pillows, closed her eyes and left it up to him. Her nerves were singing from the incense, and Vivimord's enchantment must have been working again, for the moment Nish began to caress her, his touch awoke feelings that she had never felt before, though she had read about them in the Great Tales. She did not resist; she could not. She did not want Nish to stop.

This isn't you. A tiny voice hammered on the closed doors of her mind, trying to get through. *And it isn't Nish either. Vivimord is moving both of you like puppets. Stop it,* now.

But Nish's caresses felt so good, the nothings he was murmuring in her ear so right. She wanted them to go on forever.

Anything Vivimord wants is wrong. Fight him for all you're worth!

She did not. Nish drew the covers aside, looking down at her like a prince at his princess, but as Maelys felt the cold air on her skin she was reminded of her mortifying state of undress and it undermined the enchantment a little more.

As Nish leaned over her, the prince illusion slipped; she

saw that his eyes were dull and there was blood on his right cheek, and matted in his hair. Blood under his fingernails, too. Where had it all come from? His clothes were soaked in it. He'd been in a fight; he must have killed a man. She felt sick. Vivimord hadn't bothered to clean Nish up for her; her feelings did not matter.

His left hand, the burnt one, was swollen like a five-fingered balloon; it was a mixture of smooth new skin – how had that come about? – and blistered, weeping flesh. His dirty fingers touched her, and she felt so disgusted that it tore the enchantment apart. This was wrong, wrong, *wrong* and bound to end disastrously, as any alliance of the two most corrupt men in the world inevitably must. She had to stop it.

Her darting eye fell on the platinum stubs and she remembered the fourth, to the right of them. Vivimord had hidden it from her; might it offer some means of escape?

'Nish, no!' She pushed him away so hard that he slid off the edge of the bed and fell heavily to the floor, whacking his injured hand. He let out a shriek and drew his knees up against his chest, rocking from side to side.

She regretted it instantly, and was on her hands and knees, peering down at him, when he cried, 'Maelys?' in a choked voice. Pain had cracked the mesmeric spell on him and his eyes hardened; he must be remembering her previous mortifying attempt at seduction.

'Nish, run! It's a trap.'

The door slammed back against the wall and Vivimord stood there, his eyes ablaze and the blotched lump on his cheek a livid purple.

'Quick, Nish!' she screamed.

He got up, shaking his head dazedly, but Vivimord blocked the door. He smiled, pushed it shut and moved towards them.

'Get back on the bed, Deliverer. You have a duty to perform, for the good of your people and the stability of the realm.'

Nish looked up at Maelys, then at him, and shook his head.

'You *will* mate with her, Deliverer.'

Nish rubbed the back of his burned hand; he was shaking his head furiously. Vivimord reached out to touch him on the forehead but Nish backed away.

'You're breaking his enchantment, Nish,' Maelys yelled. 'Keep fighting him.'

Vivimord drew his fingertips down Nish's chest; his eyelids fluttered, then he got up and turned towards the bed like a zombie. Maelys watched him come, stumbling and pale, but when he was just a few steps away he looked up and met her eyes, and there was such dumb, helpless despair in them that her skin crawled. Nish could not endure this any more than she could.

It was a thousand times worse than before. Under no circumstances could Maelys lie with Nish while Vivimord was standing here, pulling his strings. She couldn't help Nish but she could stop this from happening, and frustrate Vivimord.

As he stalked towards her, she threw herself backwards against the bed head. Where was the fourth platinum stub – the hidden one? Dare she try it?

'Nish, onto the bed, quick!'

He didn't move; he was completely in Vivimord's power. She slid her hand across the bed head, past the three stubs, feeling with the heel of her palm for the fourth. She sensed just the faintest indentation, and pressed it.

Vivimord grinned wolfishly and she knew she'd just failed a critical test.

ELEVEN

'Nish? Colm?' said Flydd, squinting into the darkness. The thundering feet were now so loud that they drowned out his thoughts. It sounded like a small army running up steps, though he didn't think they could be close; the climb from the base of the mountain would take hours. However he was having difficulty distinguishing between reality and Vivimord's Arts of Bemusement and Illusion. He knew Vivimord was close by, though. Flydd could smell him.

He shook his head but the fuzziness didn't improve, though he well remembered the crystal clarity of his old mind, before renewal. What if he never regained it? However even that loss was insignificant compared to the nagging ache that was the disappearance of his Art. Curse Maelys for pressuring him into taking renewal; and curse himself for succumbing to the temptation he'd resisted for so long. He'd sooner be dead than try to live with the few pathetic fragments of the Art remaining to him; and even those could be the temporary gift of the woman in red.

What do you want from me? he raged silently.

'Flydd?' said Colm in a cracked tone, from some distance to his left.

He was afraid, and well he might be. Flydd was too.

Once he would have enjoyed the challenge of pitting his wits against another master, but there was no pleasure in being an ordinary man hunted by a master.

'What are you doing way over there?' Flydd hissed.

'I thought you were going this way.' Colm's voice approached. 'Cursed place – it tangles the mind.'

'Mine too,' muttered Flydd. 'Though it's not the place that tangles it – it's Vivimord. Where's Nish?'

'I thought he was with you.'

Flydd swore under his breath. 'Nish!' he said, not too loudly.

Nish didn't reply.

'What's happening?' said Colm, with forced calm. 'Is Vivimord trying to pick us off one by one?'

Flydd pressed his hand against his chest, for he had a burning pain there. What a laugh it would be if his renewed heart was giving out already. 'He doesn't give a damn about us, and he doesn't pick fights needlessly. All he wants is Nish.'

'Nish!' Colm bellowed. 'Where are you?'

'Shh!' Colm's voice hadn't echoed in the vast chamber, which was odd; but everything about this place was odd.

'How can he not hear us?'

'I'd say Vivimord has got him, but we'd better make sure.'

They circumnavigated the chamber three times but found no sign of him, and no openings save the double doors by which they had entered.

'Vivimord was so quick!' Flydd wanted to bang his head against the wall. 'He plucked Nish out from between us in seconds and I haven't got the faintest idea where to look for him.'

'You know Mistmurk Mountain inside and out. You must be able to find him; and Maelys.'

'Vivimord was ever a master of illusion, and now he's been rejuvenated at the cursed flame. You saw the fire dripping from his fingers when he fought Jal-Nish in the cave – Vivimord's powers have been redoubled, and I've lost mine.'

'We've got to look for them, Flydd.'

'I wouldn't know where to start. This place is a labyrinth.'

'They can't be far away.'

'Vivimord could be anywhere, even in this room, but hidden. I can't break such powerful Arts; can you?'

'Only with a blade to the heart!' Colm said savagely.

'Phrune is dead; he can't hurt anyone now. But if you get the chance to take Vivimord down, don't hesitate, for he's as big a monster as the God-Emperor. Let's go back to the altar. That's where Nish disappeared, and we may be able to pick up the traces. There's power at the flame, too; power aplenty, if only I could remember how to use it.'

As they headed back, Flydd's confusion began to fade and suddenly, when they were just a few steps from the altar, the abyssal flame leapt up spans high, emerald-green shot with black, illuminating the barbarically beautiful chamber. Its shrill whistling was painful to the ears.

'The running feet have stopped,' said Flydd, his heart sinking. 'Vivimord's got what he wanted. Though to get through Jal-Nish's cordon he'll have to activate the closed portal, so surely he must come back to this flame? Can I set a trap for him?'

Colm was pacing, ever more agitated. 'We've got to go after them, Flydd.'

'If we do, we'll probably be leaving them further behind. No, this place is the key, I'm sure of it. I'm staying here.'

'Flydd –?'

'Shut up! I've got to think it through.'

He sat on the base of the altar and put his head in his hands. In his prime he would have come up with a plan in an instant, but now his mind was like fog. 'Keep watch by the door, Colm.'

Why was he so unsure of himself? He'd been a commanding figure for more than forty years and, as a scrutator on the council, he'd been one of the most powerful people in the world.

Because authority had to be earned, and it could only be maintained by using it. He was out of practice. The world had changed; the old ways were gone forever. Jal-Nish had remoulded the world in his image and Flydd no longer understood it.

Above his head the flame flared and shadows drifted through his mind, like an image seen out of the corner of an eye – billowing red curtains with someone concealed behind them. The woman in red was peering through a framed hexagonal glass, *at him*. Her finger pointed at him, Maelys's taphloid grew hot and he felt a stabbing pressure behind his temples. It wasn't exactly pain; more like something pushing through a barrier. It disappeared and he tried to focus on the woman behind the curtains, but her image was gone.

Flydd realised he'd been holding his breath, but didn't let it out. Something had changed; she'd done something to him. He felt more clear-headed now; or was it more *awakened*? Did that mean she was ready to put her plan into action?

'Is something the matter?' said Colm, who had his back to the flame and was watching the doors.

'I had a vision that reminded me of my renewal dream, though why would I see *her* now?'

Could her appearance be due to the power of the flame, or did she want him to do something here? If she did, it was unlikely to be for his benefit. Flydd gnawed his lip; he wasn't used to being kept in the dark and couldn't bear to be manipulated. He didn't want anything to do with this perilous flame either, yet it might offer the only way out of here.

Drawing the taphloid from his pocket, he held it up towards the flame to see what would happen when their innate powers met. The flame's note changed to a deeper, more muted whistle. Colm drew a sharp breath; the green flame dropped fractionally and a series of little silvery bubbles rose up within it, black shadows and emerald fire drifting across their surfaces, before popping halfway to the ceiling with streams of trailing green specks. Flydd thought he saw her image in one bubble, hands out to him as if she were trying to tell him something.

Why was the flame affected by the taphloid? She can't have known he'd have it. No, but she would have expected him to be carrying his charged crystal, and Maelys had put the crystal she'd found below the cursed flame into the taphloid. Could the two flames be linked?

Flydd rocked back and forth, wondering about the bubbles, then thrust the taphloid at the flame. This time only one bubble appeared, but it was the size of a melon and spinning rapidly. Within it he saw the red curtains again, only they weren't curtains but the robes of a dark-haired woman, standing on a pinnacle in a wild wind. A huge moon hung above her and she was gazing into a scrying cup. Flydd's point of view shifted dizzyingly until he was looking down into it as if through her eyes, though this time she did not know he was there.

She was staring into a black, empty landscape, a place like nowhere he had ever seen before. Everything was black – no, it wasn't a landscape but a vast structure, for a smooth black floor extended further than he could see. Now he heard her, inside his head, her voice tight with strain.

I must find a way in. I can't hold the place together much longer. But what if it finds out?

The black shapes shifted, dissolving into one another; the bubble burst and her image was gone. Flydd staggered, for his heart was thundering and his knees felt weak.

'I heard her,' said Colm, shivering. 'That was the woman in red, wasn't it?'

'It was.'

'What was she doing?'

Flydd wasn't going to mention the image he'd seen

through her eyes; it was too worrying. 'I don't know, but she must have mastered the flame, to be so intimately connected to it now.'

'Why did she come to you during renewal?'

'How would I know?' Flydd snapped. He paced around the altar, cursing the craters in his memory. Dare he take the chance on her? Dare he refuse her?

Colm was looking ever more alarmed. He's regretting not taking the easy way out the other night, and jumping off the precipice, Flydd thought. Perhaps he should have.

'What's she trying to hold together?'

Flydd shrugged.

'Could it have anything to do with the shadow realm?' Colm wondered aloud. 'And where did you hear of the shadow realm, anyway?'

'From Rassitifer, an itinerant sorcerer, but a good one, and a friend for many years; I trusted him. He found a way inside, and that's where he suffered the wound that killed him. It left no mark, no scar, but he wasted away from within.'

'What did he die of?'

Flydd squirmed. 'Not even the council's healers had seen anything like it – he'd been eaten away inside; his vital organs were no more than soot, crawling with . . .'

'Maggots?'

'Whatever it was, it wasn't any kind of life I'd seen before. Meddle with the shadow realm at your peril.'

'And you planned to take us through it?' Colm's voice rose. He was as brave as any man when dealing with the known, but how could he cope with this?

'Only because there was no other way out. Besides, I was a greater mancer than Rassitifer; I thought it was worth the risk, and I'd prepared that crystal to protect us on the way through.'

'But you haven't got the crystal,' cried Colm. 'And you've lost your Art, so how the bloody hell are you going to protect us if you do find a way in?'

'I – I'll have to find a way,' Flydd said weakly. Just how was he supposed to forge a protection when he couldn't remember where the dangers in the shadow realm lay, nor the spells and protections he'd planned to use there?

'Well, you'll be going on your own. I'd sooner an honest death on an enemy's blade than what's going to happen to you.' Colm was circling around the altar, well clear of the flame, his head turned away as if he couldn't bear to look at it, which was another oddity in a day full of oddities.

'You'll probably get your wish. Go and check the doors.'

Colm went across, opened them carefully and slipped out into the dark. Flydd paced. There was something special about the flame, and it had to do with the woman in red, *and what she'd done to him during renewal.*

Why had she been in his head at that time, as if she'd been trying a mind-merge with him? Why would anyone with such powerful Arts want to rifle through the mind of an old fogy like him?

Because she wanted him to do something she could not do herself, which suggested that she couldn't use her own powers, or was afraid to. Did she want to attack her enemy without leaving anything that could be traced back to her? Not me, Flydd thought. *I will not be used!*

Colm crept back, head lowered, again shielding his eyes from the flame. 'I heard no one outside.'

'It's as I'd thought – Vivimord sent those footsteps to distract us.' Flydd took in Colm's fearful expression, his averted gaze, and remembered that he had also avoided the cursed flame. 'If I didn't know better, I'd think you were scared of fire.'

'Little fires I can manage,' said Colm in a bare whisper. 'I've trained myself to cook on them; I had to. But big ones . . . and especially any kind of uncanny fire –' A shudder racked him.

'What happened?' Flydd said more kindly. There wasn't time for counselling, but he couldn't have Colm cracking up on him either.

'I was a little kid the first time,' Colm said haltingly. 'It was during the war. The lyrinx war,' he added unnecessarily, for it had lasted a hundred and fifty years and raged across the known world, and there had been no war since it ended. 'We lived in the mountains of Bannador, on the great Island of Meldorin. Across the Sea of Thurkad. That's where the war began, in the mountains.'

Flydd knew it far better than Colm could have, but remained silent.

'We were burned out of our manor by the lyrinx, or the human scum who served them. I was too young to understand, though I can never forget our home ablaze with uncanny fire and the old servants screaming and running across the yard, burning, burning . . .

'Mum and Dad couldn't fight the lyrinx. The whole of Bannador was ablaze; there was war and blood and fire everywhere. The enemy were determined to burn us out. Even Thurkad fell, a few years later – the greatest city in the world.'

And the oldest, Flydd thought. The priceless treasures of more than three thousand years had been lost that day. He often reflected on how long it had survived, and how quickly it had been destroyed.

'It happened again as we fled in a wagon to the coast.' Colm's eyes were black pools of horror. 'We were attacked from the air, and the wagon and horses were burned with uncanny fire; we lost everything we had left.'

'I'm sorry,' said Flydd. There was nothing more to be said, for such human tragedies had happened a hundred thousand times during the war, on both sides.

'We ended up in a refugee camp on the other side of the Sea of Thurkad, near Nilkerrand. At least, it was *called* a refugee camp.' Colm's voice dripped bitterness now, the bitterness he could not hold back whenever he talked about his life, and some day it was going to consume him. 'In reality it was a city of slave labour, walled in with a palisade and patrolled by armed guards, where even the littlest children worked day and night, every day of the year, making equipment for the war.'

The cursed war, though long over, continued to intrude into all their lives. And Chief Scrutator Ghorr's corrupt council had given up trying to win it, for the war had allowed them to maintain their grip on power and wring it ever tighter. Had Colm known that, his hands would have been around Flydd's throat in an instant, though it had not been Flydd's doing.

'We spent years in that camp,' Colm went on. 'Terrible years where I saw my parents dying before my eyes. They couldn't take any more; if they hadn't had me and my sisters to protect they'd have wasted away and died. But it all came to nothing in the end, of course,' he said savagely.

'That's where I met Nish,' Colm went on after an interval. 'He dropped out of the sky, half-dead, clinging to the wreckage of an air-floater.'

'The very first air-floater,' said Flydd. 'As it happens, I sent him out on it, though I didn't expect it would carry him halfway across the continent of Lauralin.'

'We took him in at the risk of all our lives, and in return Nish promised to help me regain my lost heritage. Though he never did.' The fury was gone. Colm sounded defeated, as though nothing mattered any more.

'He might yet do so,' said Flydd. 'Once this is over.'

'Ha!' Colm snorted. 'Not long after he came, the camp was attacked with uncanny fire. I remember flames leaping above the roof and a horde of lyrinx swooping down on us. People ran in all directions but the gates were closed, and nearly everyone died. We escaped but I lost Mum and Dad and my two sisters. I searched for weeks; months; *years*; but I never found them. Do you wonder that uncanny fire arouses such terror in me?'

'I'm really sorry, Colm.'

They crouched with their backs to the altar, with the overhang above them and the flame roaring in their ears, and after a minute or two Colm stopped shuddering.

'We've got to succeed,' said Flydd, trying to convince himself. 'If Nish is lost, we're the sole resistance.'

'Save for the Defiance,' said Colm.

'If Vivimord did win, he'd be worse than the God-Emperor, who is, at least, an accomplished ruler. Under Vivimord, the world would fall into civil war, and that would be the worst outcome of all, for even a dictator like Jal-Nish is better than anarchy. The fate of Santhenar is up to me, and if the only way out of here is to walk the shadow realm, I've got to do it – *alone if necessary.*'

'I'm not going there,' Colm repeated.

Please let there be another way, Flydd thought, for several more memories had come back, of things Rassitifer had told him about the shadow realm. How could he hope to get through without the protection of the spells he'd put into the lost crystal? 'I'm sure the abyssal flame is the key,' he mused, 'if I can only discover how to use it.'

Colm half-rose, staring towards the double doors, which were faintly illuminated by the flame. 'The left-hand door just moved.'

They crawled behind the altar. 'If it was Vivimord, I'd know it, so it must be Jal-Nish's advance guard. Prepare to defend yourself.' Flydd drew his knife, knowing it would be useless against soldiers armed with swords. The flame had to be the answer, but how was he to use it?

Colm seemed unnaturally calm now. 'I've been expecting to die for so long, it's almost like an old friend at the door.'

'When Death puts his blade to your throat you'll find the will to fight. Let's see if I do something with her flame, to scare them off. Follow my lead.'

'I have been,' Colm muttered, 'and look where it's got me.'

The door was pushed wide and in the darkness beyond it Flydd made out green iridescent reflections – the abyssal flame reflecting off the armour of the God-Emperor's Imperial Militia, his second-best troops.

If the woman in red had wanted him to use the flame all along, she'd have to show him how. He stood up, keeping cover behind the altar, and raised the taphloid, hoping it would reveal another glimpse of her. The abyssal flame flickered and wavered away without showing him anything. His chest tightened.

'There's three of them,' said Colm. 'Two with scimitars, the third with a war axe. They're mighty big.'

'Size isn't everything.'

The original Flydd, though a small, gaunt man, had slain many a warrior in combat through his skill with a sword, not to mention his low cunning and a dash of mancery in emergencies. Unfortunately his renewed body still didn't fit and he was afraid it would let him down again. But how else was he to fight?

Use the flame, fool!

Her voice was even hoarser and more strained, as if it had taken a mighty effort to speak to him. How am I to use the flame, Flydd thought, but received no answer.

The leading soldier shouted, 'There they are; behind that altar,' and they moved in.

Exposing the metal side of the taphloid, he thrust it as close to the flame as he could bear its prickly, tingling heat. A huge bubble formed and swirled up on a current of air, turning slowly, and this time he saw clearly what was imprinted on it. Everyone must have, since the bubble was transparent.

The woman in red was standing by a fire, holding a crystal chalice in her left hand, and raised it high as if saluting an unseen observer. Green flame flickered in the bowl. She lowered the chalice, drained it in a long swallow and tossed it over her shoulder to smash in the fireplace. Looking up suddenly as if she'd seen him, she pointed at Flydd with her right index finger.

He felt a burning pain in the centre of his forehead – a pain he remembered from renewal – as if the sun's rays had been focussed there. Was she attacking him, or *waking something?* She slumped backwards into a chair, in evident distress, and the bubble popped.

His heart skipped several beats, then began to race. The pain became a wedge driven into his skull, sharper than before. He staggered and clutched at his head, but the pain disappeared and his knife hand began to tingle.

Use the flame, she had said, and its touch had also tingled. Knife to flame? He reached out with the tip of the knife, and as soon as it entered the flame the knife shook in his hand and began to make a faint humming sound.

Sword clashed on sword. Flydd looked around dazedly, knowing he'd lost precious seconds. Colm had his back to the altar and was fighting for his life against a soldier half a head taller and twice his weight. Another man was coming at him from the left, swinging the war axe, while the third was advancing on Flydd, carving the air with a span-long scimitar. They weren't planning to take prisoners.

Colm had been driven to one knee and his assailant was raising his scimitar for a blow that would split him from skull to buttocks like a side of beef. Flydd lunged at the soldier, swinging the singing knife in a wicked slash, in the faint hope that he would falter.

The note of the blade rose as it moved and a fiery lance of light extended from it, carving a streak across the soldier's iridescent chest plate. Flydd's fingers stung. He could barely hold the knife, which was vibrating wildly, singing piercingly. His heart began to hammer like a set of native drums and his chest burned from front to back.

The soldier screamed; steam wisped from the thin line which the light had carved right through his armour, followed by curtains of pulsing blood. His legs buckled and he fell.

The other two soldiers were frozen in place, staring at the dead man. Flydd's hand was throbbing now; he swung the shrieking blade in a wobbly arc towards the soldier nearest to him. The light lance passed across the man's throat, just above his armour, as he turned to run.

He kept turning but his head did not. Colm gagged, for the soldier's eyes remained locked on his, while his body was facing the other way, the sheared-off head perched neatly on his stub of neck. He kept moving and head and body separated; the eyes went dull in the flame-light and the head toppled off, bouncing twice before coming to rest near Flydd's foot. He nudged it out of the way, then had to let go of the shuddering blade, whose light was carving smoking arcs across the murals and the ceiling.

It clattered to the floor and the light went out. The beheaded soldier managed two more steps, blood fountaining from his neck, before slamming into the floor. The soldier with the war axe was pounding for the doors.

'Stop him!' Flydd gasped, barely able to stand up because his muscles were spasming violently. He slumped onto the base of the altar, legs kicking.

Colm swung his sword around his head and hurled it viciously at the fleeing man, but he had already crashed through the double doors and run. 'Missed!'

'He's gone to warn the God-Emperor of this deadly new power,' Flydd said ruefully, as Colm limped after his blade. 'Curse him!' He inspected his swollen fingers, which were covered in little white blisters.

'How did you do that?' said Colm as he came back.

'*I* didn't.'

TWELVE

M aelys was propelled towards the far wall so furiously
that the air whistled around her ears. She threw up
her hands in a hopeless attempt to protect herself, but
passed straight through the wall and felt no more than cold
rippling along her body. She slid down a glassy slope, the
gown riding up above her, passed through a circular hole
and kept falling.

Splat! She landed hard on something familiarly soft
and slimy-oozy that had to be a mass of swamp creepers,
and slid between them up to her hips. Yuk! They felt even
worse on her bare skin. She flailed and kicked her way
out until she lay precariously on top, in danger of slipping
back in with the slightest movement.

As her eyes adjusted, Maelys discovered that she was in
a deep circular stone pit, at least as wide as the bedchamber she'd been ejected from. Two small pale eyes gleamed
five or six spans above her, suspended in the angle between
the domed roof and the wall. The swamp creepers began
to squirm all around her and she drew her legs up towards
her stomach, feeling sick.

'Sweet, sweet revenge!' Phrune gurgled from on high.

His nauseating face was looking down at her through the circular hole, and he'd swallowed his intestines, allowing him to speak.

'This is legitimate retribution,' Vivimord reminded him. 'I was testing you, Maelys, to see if you were suitable for Nish after all. I really thought you were, for you're a remarkably clever girl; you've thwarted both me and Jal-Nish, time and again. Had you done what was required of you in the bedchamber you would have been pregnant by now, and I would have honoured you above all other women. But when you broke my enchantment it proved you could *never* be trusted, and now you're going to die in a way that will be a lesson to everyone in my realm.'

'You have no realm,' she spat, 'you murderous lunatic!'

'Ah, but I will have one, and you will become my first public exhibit, *and lesson.*'

She could not bear his gloating triumph, nor Phrune's sick bloodlust. Maelys looked away but could see no means of escape, for the curved walls of the pit offered no handholds. Several corded webs hung high above, well out of reach, and from their faint shimmer they must have been freshly made. If she touched one, she would be stuck fast; *prey.* That left only one other way out, though it sickened her to have to beg for her life.

'Please, give me another chance. I'll have Nish's baby . . . or anything.'

'I don't give *anybody* a second chance,' said Vivimord, 'and certainly not you. You're a threat to the Deliverer, Maelys Nifferlin, and any one of a thousand pliable girls will eagerly take your place.'

'Are you going to leave me here to die?' she said hoarsely. Somehow she doubted it.

'*A lesson to all*, I said. A public exhibit. Do you see the two pale eyes under the roof?'

Maelys swallowed, but it didn't help, for her throat was parchment dry. Besides, she *knew*, before he said another word, but she listened with a dreadful anticipation.

'It's a vigorous young octopede,' Vivimord said with relish, 'freshly mated and ready to breed. They live on the blood of swamp creepers, milking them like a herd of cattle, but to reproduce, octopedes need warm-blooded creatures – or, rather, *hosts*.'

She let out an involuntary cry.

'After it feels you all over, and paralyses you with its sting, and does other unspeakable things that you'll discover soon enough, it will spear you in the belly with its ovipositor and lay its eggs in you. After the way you've stalked Nish these past months you may find that a trifle ironic. Once you've been *inovulated*, I'll take you with me, paralysed but conscious, and make a live exhibit of you in my court so all the Defiance can see the little octopede grubs hatch – *and feed*.'

Maelys felt paralysed already. She reached up towards him, to beg for her life, but no sound came forth. She knew it was hopeless.

'I'll leave you to your fate, Maelys. Jal-Nish's army is close now and I've got to keep him away until I can round up your friends. I'm going to make examples of them too, all save Nish. He's the key to all our futures.'

Vivimord withdrew, though dead Phrune remained at the hole for a few seconds, staring down at her with those empty eyes before, with a twitch of the head that extruded a white length of entrails, he was gone.

Maelys studied her nemesis. The octopede was far bigger than her, and had an elongated, squishy body like a long balloon squeezed in two places. Its white, sagging skin was covered in warty pustules that oozed a creamy substance. It resembled the skin of a particularly unpleasant toad, and no doubt the ooze was poisonous. The plump, stubby legs ended in little clinging hooks while the lance-like tail flicking back and forth must be the ovipositor with which it would deposit its eggs inside her.

She rubbed her slippery arms, which were covered in goose pimples, and slid backwards across the swamp creepers. To think she'd been afraid of them. The enemy of my enemy is my friend; was there any way she could use them?

The octopede's oval eyes slanted across the front of its sloping head. A pair of hook-shaped claws were upraised, the pincers opening and closing rhythmically. It began to creep to the centre of its web, watching her all the while. The urge to give way to her deep, numbing fear and scream was almost overwhelming, but she had to resist it. Panic would be fatal.

The beast began to lower itself on a glistening cord extruded from a ring of spiky spinnerets at its posterior. It was curled into a semicircle with its ovipositor pointing at her and its hook-claws opening and closing, *clacker-clack*.

Her throat grew tight as she remembered how fast it had moved in the bedchamber. It could drop on her, catch her in its claws or spear her with the ovipositor, but how was she to fight it? She would be hard-pressed to avoid it; she couldn't even stand up on the slippery swamp creepers.

She scanned the walls in case she'd missed some means of escape, but they were solid stone. The only way out was past the octopede, unless . . . unless there was a hole down below. Could she burrow down through the swamp creepers? The thought was revolting, but she checked on the octopede, now swaying on its web, and knew she had no choice.

She began to take deep breaths as it lowered itself on its web cord. The swamp creeper gunk felt disgusting but she reminded herself that they were on her side – they would be shielding her from the common foe.

The octopede uncoiled and dropped sharply on its line, its plump limbs extending towards her, and the clacking of its hook-claws became more staccato. *Go, now!* Maelys upended herself and dived headfirst into the squirming mass of swamp creepers, clawing them out of the way as she tried to pull herself lower.

It was easy for the first half span, for she slid between

them under her own weight, but below that the swamp creepers were ever more tightly packed and every hand-span she moved down took a greater effort. As she clawed at the huge slugs, she imagined the octopede hanging above her exposed legs, ready to sting.

She pulled them down but a huge swamp creeper jammed under her knees, leaving her right foot and part of her leg exposed. She heaved again, her panic rising.

A shocking pain speared through the back of her calf. The octopede had got her with a hook-claw and Maelys could feel her flesh being torn. She would have screamed but could not spare the breath.

She wrenched free and dragged herself lower in the squirming mass. Her calf was a shrieking agony; it felt as though it had been ripped open. Maelys gasped and lost the last of her air, but if she came up for more the octopede would be on her instantly. She groped down as far as she could reach in case there was a hole below her, but felt nothing save more creepers; creepers everywhere.

Her lungs heaved; she would have to go up. Wait – when she'd been struggling down the chimney, when she'd tried to punch a swamp creeper out of the way, she had gained a breath from its air bladder.

Maelys put her mouth to the clotted opening of the nearest swamp creeper – yuk! – and forced her fist into its middle. Smelly cow's breath gushed out and she sucked it down until her lungs were full. The panic faded, though only a little.

She burrowed deeper then did it again, and again, until she must have been a span and a half below the surface and the weight of swamp creepers above her was so great that she could barely inflate her lungs. If she went any lower she would be crushed to death. She probed and her fingers touched hard stone – the base of the great well.

It was solid. She rested a moment, trying to ignore the agony in her calf, then wriggled on, squeezing air out of the nearest swamp creeper whenever she needed a breath. She criss-crossed the floor but found no opening; there was no way out from the bottom. Up half a span where the pressure was blessedly less, she began to move in rising circles around the sides but discovered no exit there either, even when she'd risen to within a single swamp creeper of the surface and could breathe unaided again. What was she to do? Tulitine, she thought, I need your help more than ever.

Maelys had a feeling that the old woman would be proud of her now, and it made a difference, since her other friends had turned out to be less than steadfast. Colm was disgusted and contemptuous, Flydd had seemed to be re-evaluating her, and as for Nish – the incident in the boudoir could only have reinforced his disdain.

After enduring years of carping criticism from her mother and aunts, Maelys longed for the approval of people she admired, and none more than Tulitine, who was old and had neither the mancery of Flydd nor the skill at arms of Colm, yet possessed an inner strength greater than either of them. If Tulitine could fight even Vivimord, in her own small ways, Maelys could overcome this obstacle, and the next.

She eased towards the surface, trying to emulate the random squirming of the swamp creepers, and felt that she was doing a good job of concealing herself until the creeper above her head let out a squeaking note of pain. She looked up to see it hooked out of the way and tossed against the far wall; the monstrous octopede was hanging directly above, eye to eye with her.

Maelys's mouth opened in an involuntary scream but she managed to keep silent; if she once gave in to her fear it would spiral out of control and that would be the end. She couldn't get out of the octopede's way quickly enough; if she tried it would attack from behind, and once it caught her with those little foot-hooks she would never get free. Stealthily, maintaining eye contact all the time, she slid her right hand underneath a swamp creeper and cocked her arm.

The octopede's eight plump legs suddenly stood out like inflated balloons; it was going to strike. Maelys hurled the swamp creeper up at it with all the strength she had, so hard that it wrenched her shoulder.

As the octopede flashed down, the swamp creeper struck it on the head, knocking it sideways into the wall. Ignoring the throb in her shoulder, Maelys scooped up another swamp creeper and, as the octopede swung back, spinning in a circle, she aimed for its web cord.

The swamp creeper bounced off but the tough web did not break; the octopede began to spin the other way as it swung across the pit. Its two hook-claws were extended, ready to attack the moment it came within range.

Maelys wriggled into a vertical position, trying to get a firmer footing on the mass of swamp creepers lower down so the ones around her legs would hold her upright and give her more leverage. A huge swamp creeper was squirming to her left, the biggest she'd seen so far. Did she have the strength to throw it? Her shoulder was shrieking and suddenly she felt very weak, but she had to fight that too. One last try.

She held the swamp creeper on the flat of her palm, hanging over each end like a monstrous slug; and being so slimy they were hard to throw straight. She hurled it at the octopede's middle; it flew straight for once, and knocked it right off its cord.

It landed on its back on the swamp creepers and began to rattle its claws furiously, struggling to turn over on the slimy surface. The swinging web cord passed by and Maelys knew it was her lifeline out of here, if she could climb it.

It was just within reach, but she was so coated with mucus she wouldn't be able to get a grip. She rubbed her hands against the gritty stone wall until the slime was gone and, as the cord swung back, stretched as high as she could reach, caught hold with her right hand, and stuck fast. Web cord was sticky to anything but an octopede.

It was still trying to turn over, and would soon succeed,

for it had impaled a swamp creeper on its ovipositor and was using it for leverage, skidding on its back across the surface. If it came close enough, it could attack with either ovipositor or hook-claws.

She didn't try to pull free; that wasn't going to work. With her left hand, she scraped muck off her arm, slid her hand in under the stuck fingers, prised and prayed.

After a few seconds, it reacted with the gum on the web cord, breaking it into strands that she could peel away. Maelys forced her inner hand up all the way and the stuck hand popped off. She glanced over her shoulder; the octopede was still thrashing, sliding this way and that, coming ever closer.

Could she climb the cord? Maelys didn't think so; she had never been athletic. She reached up with her slippery hand, touched the cord higher up and it stuck, though not tightly; she could just pull free. She enslimed her right hand and tried to spring up, so as to grab on higher.

She didn't budge; suction from the surrounding swamp creepers held her legs in place. Her right hand caught the web cord above the left, slipped, then caught again. She held on grimly, pulled the other hand free, rubbed more slime on it and took a grip higher up, then did the same with the first hand.

It was like trying to pull her feet out of deep, sticky mud. She pointed her toes, thrashed her lower legs and finally the suction broke. Maelys drew her legs up above the swamp creepers, knowing she was far from safe.

She was exhausted; her wrenched shoulder was throbbing and blood ran down her torn calf to drip off her heel. The octopede spun around, its hook-claws waving in the air. A host of finger-like protrusions above its mouth were stirring, as if they had picked up the smell of her blood.

In a single movement, it turned over. The ovipositor pulled free of the impaled swamp creeper and arched over the octopede's back, dripping pink fluid onto its warty skin. Tiny hooks on the ends of its stubby legs latched onto the swamp creepers and it began to undulate across them like a caterpillar, heading directly for her blood.

Maelys hauled herself up another few ells, feeling her strength going. She'd never had strong arms and they had little left to give. Up again, she told herself. Just one more heave and you'll be out of reach.

She took hold higher up, without thinking to replenish the muck on her hand, and stuck fast. Now she was really in trouble. Tearing the lower hand free, she rubbed it across her slimy stomach and started to prise away the stuck hand. She had to be exquisitely careful; if she lost her grip she would be impaled on the ovipositor, which was sticking up below her, catching her blood as it fell.

She managed to free herself and climb another handspan, but the blade-sharp ovipositor was not far below her bare feet and the octopede was arching up its rear section in an attempt to reach her. She jerked her feet up, only to realise that the cord was dangling below them. If the octopede caught hold she would be trapped.

Kicking the hanging end sideways, Maelys hung from one hand for interminable seconds while she tried to hook the dangling cord with her arm. After three attempts, with the octopede stabbing ever closer to her feet, she managed to drape the cord over her shoulder. She rubbed the slime away, stuck the cord there and clung on with both hands, panting. She was safe for the moment, but there was so far to climb.

Maelys had to keep going. The ovipositor speared up at her, just missing her left foot; the octopede was now clinging to the swamp creepers with its front legs and arching its rear section off the ground, giving it another third of a span of reach. She dragged herself up further, sobbing in desperation. Her throat was burning and her arm muscles were starting to cramp.

The octopede swayed upwards, stabbing again and again; the tip of its ovipositor slid up between her toes, almost to her knee, and the skin began to sting. She jerked her legs higher, holding her knees against her belly as it kept stabbing below her bottom. If she weakened, even for a second, she was finished.

She had to get up out of reach while she still could. Maelys found the strength to pull herself up another few hand-spans, but could go no further. Her muscles were trembling and wouldn't hold her long, but in a flash of inspiration she wiped the slime off her right hand, stuck it to the cord and it held her. She hung there, panting, allowing her muscles to relax for the first time.

The octopede could not reach her now, but it wasn't finished yet. It tilted its ovipositor back over its head and circled around on the swamp creepers, its foot-hooks alternately piercing their leathery skin then pulling free. What was it up to?

She hastily gunked up her left hand and was working the stuck one free when she noticed the spinnerets at the octopede's rear pointing towards her. Maelys's stomach lurched; she dragged herself up another few hand-spans and stuck on, looking down fearfully.

A wave passed along its rear section; the flabby sac contracted and a liquid jet shot up at her, solidifying into sticky web in the air. Maelys jerked herself sideways and the jet shot past a finger's width from her knees, arching across the pit to fall near the far wall.

The octopede's foot-hooks released; it moved slightly, hooked on again, pointing its spinnerets squarely at her this time, and fired. She swayed aside as the jet shot past her ankle, but Maelys couldn't play this game any longer. Next time it would get her. She had to climb the cord no matter how much it hurt.

And it hurt more than anything she'd ever done. Her arm muscles were shuddering with the strain before she had gone a quarter of the way. The octopede fired again but did not reach her this time, and undulated across the swamp creepers to the side wall. There it began to climb, clinging to tiny cracks in the stone with its foot-hooks.

It was halfway up the wall already, while after all this time Maelys was only halfway up the cord and going ever slower. She now realised, with the despair of utter certainty, that she wasn't going to make it. She would still be a couple of spans below the hole in the roof when the octopede reached the web above her.

Though every muscle in her body was screaming with exhaustion, she kept going; she wasn't going to succumb to it, and she couldn't let Vivimord win either. She was going to fight them to her last gasp. She was *never* going to give in, no matter what.

Maelys still had three spans to go but the octopede was near the top of the wall. Two-and-a-half spans: it began to creep across the roof, upside down, its warty body dangling. Two spans; she was gasping, grunting, her mouth as dry as paper. The octopede reached its web and headed across to the cord she was suspended from.

She stopped and stuck on. What was left? Only to let go, plunge headfirst into the mass of swamp creepers and hope that she broke her neck. But she probably wouldn't, and even a broken neck need not be fatal. The octopede's eggs would still incubate inside her paralysed body, and besides, Maelys clung to life more desperately than ever. Life was hope; life meant she still had a chance. Think!

The octopede reached her cord, clung there for a moment, its pale, slanted eyes on her, and a pair of curved brown fangs above its mouth slowly extended like a cat unsheathing its claws. That must be how it paralysed its victims.

Maelys went down half a span and allowed the cord's stickiness to hold her again. If attacked, she would let go and fall; she had no other options. Or did she? Could she use swamp creeper mucus against the octopede?

It was worth a try, though she didn't think it would work; the beast had eight little foot-hooks to cling on with. It had walked across the bed of swamp creepers, after all, by hooking into their leathery skins.

Scooping a handful of ooze off her thigh, Maelys cupped her hand around the cord and slid down two spans, coating it liberally. She slid down a further span, allowing friction to wipe the remaining muck away until the web's stickiness was just enough to hold her, but she could still pull free when she needed to.

What would the octopede do? Had it ever played such a game with one of its victims before? She doubted it; the caverns of Mistmurk Mountain had been uninhabited for centuries. Maelys didn't think it could be an intelligent creature, but there was always a possibility that it understood what she had done, and if so it could avoid her trap by lowering itself on another line beside hers.

She felt exhausted; light-headed from hunger. Maelys couldn't remember the last time she had eaten. Even thinking was hard now. The octopede began to come down, watching her all the while. She wasn't acting like its other prey, and it was wary of her. Could she make it *more* wary?

Unpeeling one hand, Maelys brandished it at the creature, then bared her teeth and hissed. It stopped on the cord, its head swaying from side to side, its ovipositor erecting and the glistening fangs sliding in and out, then began to move down slowly. She needed it to come at her in a rush so it would have all its feet on the slippery line at once. What if she pretended to attack it?

She pulled herself up by her arms and let out a shriek of defiance, though it came out as thin and fake, and the octopede didn't seem to be taken in. It swayed upwards but its legs stiffened; it was going for her.

Maelys took a tight grip with both hands; she did not know what it would do or how it would attack. Her gut cramped; one more pain in a long line of them. If there was a part of her body that wasn't aching, she couldn't think of it.

It came down the cord more quickly than she had expected. Maelys choked back a cry and tried to scramble down, but the slime on her palms had worn off and she was stuck to the web.

'Aahhh!' This time her scream was pure terror. She wrenched until the skin of her palms stung, but her hands would not come free.

Tiny drops of venom appeared at the hollow tips of the octopede's fangs. Her hands were loosening, though not quickly enough for her to jump. What if she doubled up and tried to kick it off the cord? No, it was too fast; besides, bare feet were no use against claws and fangs.

The octopede shot onto the mucus-coated section and its foot-hooks slipped, for they hooked *around* the cord, not into it. It slid down under its own weight, dragging the rest of its body onto the slippery section. The foot-hooks clamped on furiously but could not gain any purchase; it was sliding directly towards her.

Once it slid below the slippery section it would catch hold, and then it would be in a position to strike. The front pair of hooks locked onto clean cord, stopping its head end instantly, but the shock tore the upper six foot-hooks away from the slippery cord and the octopede fell outwards, its ovipositor carving a semicircle through the air then spearing at her.

She threw herself sideways on the cord but, as the creature swung upside down, its weight tore the two front hooks away and it fell. Maelys's hands were still partly stuck; she could do no more than tuck her head under her arm and hang on.

One snapping claw struck her hard on the shoulder and it tried to hook in, but the octopede had already fallen past. The heavy beast plummeted down and slapped onto the swamp creepers, sending a squirming ripple out, as if from a stone thrown into a pond.

It didn't move; perhaps it was dazed or hurt, and Maelys saw her chance. She had to take it, for she'd never get another. She took careful aim at its head section, just behind its eyes, peeled away the last of the gum holding her to the cord, and dropped.

She had no idea what was going to happen. If she

missed, she might break her ankles; she would certainly be at its mercy. The octopede had not realised the danger, for it was randomly moving its legs as she plummeted down, and she hit it at full speed.

The warty skin of the barrel-sized head section resisted the impact for a moment, then burst and she plunged through, splattering stinking yellow and green innards everywhere. The ovipositor shot up at her but, as her knees buckled, it passed over her shoulder and a stream of little white grubs was forced out.

Maelys threw herself to one side, scrambling out of the disgusting mess and plunging knee-deep into swamp creepers. She jerked her legs out and scrubbed furiously at the stinging yellow and green muck all over her feet and legs.

At a movement behind her, she glanced over her shoulder. The octopede's pale eyes had gone dull; was it dying? She couldn't be sure, couldn't take the risk, either, for its lower sections were still moving. It was still dangerous.

The left hook-claw snapped at her. She backed away, scraped up swamp creeper ooze and rubbed her legs with it until the stinging died down to a dull throb.

There was still green muck on her left foot, and some unidentifiable sausage-like organ had stuck between her toes. She flicked it away, revolted, wiped her fingers then scrambled backwards as the ovipositor, swinging through the air, fired a stream of grubs at her.

Only then did she notice that the swamp creepers were stirring, sliding over one another to feed on the splattered innards, and the little grubs, which they passed over and swallowed. They weren't entirely vegetarian after all.

The octopede began dragging itself backwards by its foot-hooks, towards the wall. If it reached it, it might still prevent her from getting out; might even do the gruesome business with its grubs. No! she thought. I've got to kill it. And then she had a brilliant idea. Picking up a swamp creeper, she tossed it into the ragged cavity she'd burst through the head section.

The swamp creeper began to feed on the octopede's insides, so she threw another in, then another, until the beast was so weighted down it could no longer move. Shortly they began burrowing down its insides into the undamaged segments, and before long all the little grubs had been eaten. She'd won the first battle.

But, she had to get out before Vivimord came back for her, and she had to have a weapon. She wasn't going to let him off, either. If she got the chance, he was going to die.

She wasn't game to go near the ovipositor, but the left fang was dangling from its venom bulb, half torn off by the force of her impact. Coating her hands liberally with protective muck, she wrenched the bulb and fang off, plugged the tip of the fang with a globule of ooze, then wrapped all in a strip torn from the bottom of her gown and tied it around her neck.

It was an awfully long climb up to the hole, and she was quite desperately exhausted and sore, but she knew she was going to make it. Nothing was going to stop her this time. *Nothing!*

She caught hold of the web and began to pull herself up.

THIRTEEN

Flydd rubbed his stinging hand as he tried to come to terms with what had just happened. From what he remembered of the Secret Arts, he couldn't explain it.

'Was that *her* again?' said Colm.

'It looks that way.'

'Is she *here*?' Colm kept his eyes averted from the hissing flame.

'I don't know, though I know when I'm being used. We've got to get out.'

'You said the flame was our only hope.'

'But I don't think it's meant to be used *here*.'

'How else can we use it?'

'I don't know. I don't understand anything! Guard the door. I'll see if I can find another way out.'

Colm took up position by the door, his bloody sword upraised. 'They're coming! It sounds like his whole army.'

'And this time the sounds are real, which means that Vivimord can't keep Jal-Nish out any longer.' Flydd walked around the altar, staring into the flame. 'How did that power come to my knife? What's she trying to tell me? How to get away?'

'Xervish!' Colm said urgently.

He was near to cracking. Flydd could see it in his eyes

as they reflected the flames. 'I haven't found the way
out.'

'Get a move on. They're nearly here.'

Flydd ignored him. He had to focus all his wits on finding the way – *her* way. He could hear the pounding boots
now, hundreds of them, and felt a shiver of fear. 'Bar the
doors.'

'With what?'

'How the bloody hell would I know? Use your initiative.'

Colm thrust the dead soldiers' swords through the U-
shaped door handles and studied the result. 'That won't
hold them back a minute.'

Flydd left it to him. I'm not even asking the right questions, he thought, trying to conjure up his mental image
of the woman holding the chalice. Who could she be? She
must have been a mighty sorcerer once.

The army thundered up the passage towards the doors.
He had mere seconds to find the way. If he wasn't meant to
use the flame here, how was he supposed to take it where
it was needed? Ah!

He brought his knife to the flame until the blade began
to sing anew, then used the beam from its tip to cut a small
rectangular block from the altar, no longer than the palm of
his hand. Holding the block carefully, he eased the singing
blade into it, almost to the bottom, then carefully turned
it in a circle and broke out the cylinder of rock. Cutting its
top off, he wetted the sides with his tongue – *sizzle* – and
slid it in. It fitted perfectly, making a stopper for the empty
bottle.

Taking it out again, he reached out and gingerly held the
bottle to the fire, upside down, until it was full of green-
black abyssal flame. Could such a small amount of flame
be enough to open the way? It would have to do; there
wasn't time to make another bottle. He stoppered it, tied
the stopper on with a piece of string and pocketed the bottle alongside the phial containing the cursed flame. If only
he knew how to use them.

The swords rattled as someone pushed on the doors. 'Xervish?' Colm hissed. 'Are you all right?'

Flydd was pressing his fist to the centre of his chest again. The burning pain was stronger than before, and anxiety seemed to make it worse. He felt quite ill with it. 'Yes,' he lied. 'Come here.'

Colm ran back to the altar, reaching it as an armoured shoulder hit the doors hard. The swords held, though Flydd knew they would not survive many more blows. His knife was dead again. He recharged it in the flame.

'Make another bubble,' said Colm. 'She might show you the way this time.'

Crash! The doors burst open, the swords snapping under the force of the impact, and two soldiers pushed in. Flydd saw dozens more behind them, the flame reflecting off their upraised blades.

Flydd thought he knew what to do, but he was afraid. What if the flame paralysed him, as the cursed flame had Maelys? Yet it was the woman in red's flame; might that protect him? No time for hesitation now; he had to follow his intuition – *or hers*.

He stripped the cloth off the taphloid, sprang up and, holding it by the chain, thrust his hand into the flame. Colm choked and turned away. The flame burned, though not with the heat of a normal fire. Flydd held his hand there for as long as he could endure the prickly heat, and a few seconds more, whipping it out as a monstrous bubble emerged from the hole in the altar, temporarily blocking the flame, which gushed out on all sides in tongues of green and black. Why the bubbles, he wondered. Were they the easiest way she could communicate with him, from wherever she was?

The bubble rose, slowly revolving, though this time, to Flydd's dismay, he couldn't see anything in it. He'd been expecting the woman to solve his problems, but how could she? She must be far away, for every communication took a greater effort and seemed to hurt her more.

'How am I supposed to get out?' he muttered.

Down. The voice in his head sounded really strained now.

'What do you mean?' he said, low and urgent. 'Am I supposed to *go* down, or out? Speak to me!'

She did not answer. He felt that her strength was failing. Was she trapped as well?

'If this chamber was built as a way for her to recharge her power,' Flydd added, 'why doesn't she use it?'

'She can't get to it,' guessed Colm.

'Take them!' ordered an officer with a plume of ochre feathers rising from the top of his helm. The soldiers advanced. 'Battle mancers, neutralise Flydd.'

A pair of robed mancers pointed their rods at Flydd. He ducked behind the altar. Did her instruction mean to go down, or to *send* something down? The flame, perhaps? Following his intuition, he thrust his hand into the flame again and roared, 'Down!'

To his surprise, the bubble dropped sharply, pushing the flame out to all sides like the petals of a buttercup. A green wisp made his hand tingle until the vent blocked and the flames went out.

The room grew dark, apart from the glimmering hemisphere of the bubble. The whistling note of the abyssal flame was cut off and the room became as silent as stone. The soldiers froze; even the mancers went still, arms outstretched. Flydd didn't understand what he had done, nor why the God-Emperor's battle mancers, who were hardened to every kind of atrocity imaginable, seemed to be afraid.

'Cut them down!' said the plume-helmed officer.

The floor seemed to move in a circle beneath Flydd's feet. 'Down and down and down again!' he said softly, concentrating on the bubble, though he did not see how it could work. He no longer had the Art for it.

Suddenly, silently, the bubble was sucked down through the vent and the whole floor circled the other way. The only light came from a pencil beam, with the same glimmer as the bubble, shooting vertically from the vent and making a small green circle on the ceiling, many spans above.

'Lantern bearers, unshutter your lanterns,' shouted the officer.

Dozens of metal shutters rasped open, but no light came forth.

'Lantern bearers, re-light your lanterns.'

After a pause, a man yelped. 'They're lit, sir,' he said in a hoarse whisper. 'I burned my fingers on the flame but it's not giving out any light.'

'Nor mine,' said another.

The officer's voice grew hard. 'Mancers, make light.'

One mancer bellowed like a trapped buffalo and a fizzing sound issued forth, but the blackness remained impenetrable. The other's rod shone white at the tip before fading again.

'Troops, move around the walls.' The officer's voice rose. 'Stand shoulder to shoulder until you encircle the room completely, then move in to the altar. Allow no one to get past. Take Cryl-Nish Hlar and the black-haired girl, if you can find them. Kill the others.'

'What are we going to do, Xervish?' Colm said, beside him.

Flydd could feel the woman straining to tell him something, and he could sense her pain, but nothing came through. Pushing the bubble down had been the right thing to do, but it hadn't saved him; it hadn't shown him anything either; or had it? Maybe he hadn't gone far enough. His eye followed the pencil beam up to the ceiling, where a spiral engraved on the stone appeared to be the twin of the one on the top of the pedestal. And it, he recalled, looked as though it was meant to turn. Could it open some secret passage or path, and if so, how was it operated?

He ran through those methods of opening he could recall, though most relied on knowing particular words of command, on solving fiendishly difficult puzzles or on mechanical devices of great cleverness and subtlety. But he could not be expected to know such words of command, nor solve such puzzles in an instant. Besides, this was her flame, and as far as he knew she had dwelt here alone. The answer would surely be simple, and encoded in the one word, *down*.

'Down!' he said softly.

Colm began to duck below the altar.

Flydd gripped him by the shoulder. 'Not you; stand firm. *Down!*' he said to the bubble, using his most commanding tone and, with a rumble that shook the floor, it continued on its downward path.

The shaking intensified until Flydd had to hold onto the altar with his free hand, but it began to separate into two sections at the spiral engraved on the stone. Now he could feel the floor cracking, no, *separating* from the altar and moving outwards, carrying them with it. Vapour hissed up. The ceiling also seemed to be spiralling apart though there was not enough light to see it clearly.

The altar section twisted itself down through the ever-widening hole. Flydd staggered and nearly fell in as the other section went too. Was he supposed to follow? He could not see what lay below, nor any way to get down, but going to the source of the flame seemed like a bad idea. Then, as he teetered on the edge, he heard rock being torn open in the depths. Had he set off some trap or curse?

It definitely did not help; it hadn't revealed any way out. The floor opened just behind them, in a ring centred on the altar hole but a few spans out, leaving them on a narrow doughnut of floor. Flydd was eyeing this new opening when, with a roar and a rush, a column of vapour shot up, and ignited. The abyssal flame was back, a hundred times greater, a vast ring of green-black fire surrounding them.

Colm shuddered, his eyes took on an insane blankness and he barely choked down a shriek. He was cracking and

Flydd could hardly blame him: the flame was his worst nightmare.

'Hold on, Colm,' he said softly.

The soldiers were equally wide-eyed, but they were tough, disciplined men who obeyed orders without question. They began moving around the wall to encircle the flame, and more were streaming in through the doors.

'What's going on –?' It sounded as if a band had been clamped around Colm's vocal cords. He screwed his eyes shut, took a deep breath and opened them again, staring at his feet. 'We're between the pit and the flame, and *there's no way out!*'

Flydd was beginning to think the same thing but, before anything else, he had to calm Colm. If he broke down it would make their situation impossible. 'Get ready to fight.'

He held his knife as close to the raging flames as he could bear, but this time it made no sound.

'What's the matter now?' Colm shrieked, running around in circles.

'The perversity of the Art,' Flydd muttered. 'Things seldom work the same way twice, especially when you really need them. Stay calm; I'll get us out yet,' he lied, for he had no plan at all.

What if the abyssal flame were linked to the cursed flame, as he'd speculated earlier? He knew the cursed flame had some connection to the obelisk at the centre of the plateau, which was an ancient Charon memorial as well as a warning that all things must fail. Could it also be a signpost pointing straight down to the vast power of the abyssal flame which the woman in red could no longer reach?

It made sense. What if she'd come to him during renewal because she'd read his intention to go through the shadow realm, and realised that he could help her? She must intend him to use the power of the flame to open a portal into the shadow realm, from the obelisk. He closed his mind to the step after that – what she would do once he'd given her what she wanted. If this was the only way out, he was going to take it, no matter the consequences.

'Show me the way,' he said softly, eyeing the creeping soldiers.

She did not reply; he would have to work it out, but how was he to activate a link between the flames? By mixing them? Flydd opened his phial and bottle, and allowed wisps of their flames to merge in the air. The flames went blue and began to revolve in a tight spiral that reminded him of a galaxy he'd seen while studying the stars in his prentice-ship, near sixty years ago. The spiral spun in on itself, ever faster, only to collapse into nothingness. He hastily stoppered his bottles as the rock groaned below him.

The circular altar hole closed over, shot open again and a set of stone steps twisted up from the depths like an auger to form a tight, rail-less stair moving towards the opening in the ceiling.

'That's it.' With each turn of the steps Flydd felt the strength drain out of him, as if he were heaving it up with his own muscles. He slumped to his knees. 'That's her escape route.'

But were they supposed to go up, or down? The ceiling opening was dark; whatever lay in the depths was equally indeterminate.

'Jump through the flame!' shouted the plume-helmed officer. 'Take them!'

The leading soldiers hesitated on the other side of the ring of fire. It was not a difficult leap, had it not been for the uncanny flame, but no doubt they'd heard of Flydd's singing blade and no one wanted to be first to feel it.

'Take them, you stinking dogs,' the officer bellowed.

A group of soldiers moved forwards, slowly and uneasily. Colm was panting raggedly and did not know where to look, for the maddening flames were all around.

'Do what you like, Flydd. I'm going up.'

Head down, covering his eyes, he stumbled onto the

rotating stair, whose blade-sharp apex was already six coils above them and slowly rising.

Oddly, though, the rising treads did not carry him up with them, and he began to lurch up the steps. Fresh blood stained his shoulder where he'd been cut during the fight that had killed Zham; the wound had broken open again.

Flydd put his knife to the flame and felt the remaining strength being drawn from his own bones, though the knife remained mute. He backed towards the stair. Three soldiers ran towards him, attempting to leap the annulus of flame together; if they got through he was a dead man. He held up the useless blade and made a humming sound in his throat.

The officer laughed mockingly. 'The blade isn't working and he's got no Art. He's helpless.'

The running soldiers hit the flame but were hurled back, statue-stiff. Another man checked them. 'They're dead, surr. Stone dead!'

Flydd took no heart from it; it wouldn't take the battle mancers long to find a way across. His body felt worse than before: exhausted and ill-fitting. As he dragged himself up the steps, three more soldiers crept forwards, raised the statue-like corpses to the vertical and toppled them across, attempting to form a body bridge. Two fell into the depths but the third body spanned the gap. The living soldiers were flung backwards, as stiff as their fellows, however another three soldiers threw the bodies across the gap. This time two spanned it, and only one of the living fell.

A soldier tried to walk the body bridge but fell onto the dead men and lay there, legs dangling off to the left, arms hanging to the right. Unlike the others, he was still alive and twitching, but unable to move. Not far away, a dozen soldiers waited their turn, fearful yet eager to get the reward for Flydd's head.

He continued up to the tenth turn of the stairs, where he looked down into the slowly widening annulus of fire. Something green and black swelled and pulsed in the depths. The stair was still rising, though he could not see what was supporting it. Previously, the abyssal flame had begun at the top of the altar, but its base was creeping ever lower into the subterranean abysses, feeding on itself. What would happen when it got to the bottom? You don't want to find out.

He was halfway to the ceiling, some twenty turns of the staircase above the floor, when he stumbled, missed the step and nearly went over. The first of the soldiers had crossed the bridge and was on the stair, climbing more quickly than he could. He searched the flame for another of those glimmering bubbles that had been so helpful before, but could not see any.

Previously he had created them with the taphloid. As he reached out to the flame with it, it swung against his wrist and its touch was like boiling lye; a little circle of skin blistered before his eyes. The soldiers were coming up rapidly now, their swords out. He had the advantage of height, though it did not nullify the greater reach of their weapons.

Flubber-flub. It came sweeping in through the open doors, banked and curved towards the flame – an entirely new creature-construct of Jal-Nish's, something he'd never heard of before. It was like a flying wing – no, more like one of the stingrays Flydd had seen gliding through the shallow water of the bay where he'd played as a child, so many years ago. It was slate green with a broad, arrow-shaped head, the mouth opening on its underside; its delta-shaped wings stretched out a good span and a half to either side, and it had a whip-like tail plus an erectile sting which lay along its backbone.

Another followed it, and a third, flying with sinuous undulations of their leathery wings, though such heavy creatures must also be using the Art to keep themselves aloft. They didn't look particularly dangerous, yet if one perched at the top of the stairs he would not be able to pass.

136

Was this the way out, or had he missed something? He swung the taphloid through the flame. *Bubbles, come!* It was a cry of desperation, but he'd also commanded the flame as though it was his right to do so – no, *her* right – and a series of small bubbles rose up towards him.

'Mancers, destroy them!' shouted the plumed officer.

A small, cloaked figure in the doorway pointed at the bubbles with his right hand and they popped one by one before Flydd could read anything in them. At first, Flydd thought the mancer was Jal-Nish, but it was not wearing a mask, and it was far shorter – a dwarf of a man, in fact. He reeled.

'*No!* It can't be.'

'Who is it?' said Colm, who was just a few steps above now, watching the wing-rays warily. He was still breathing heavily, though the panic had receded. The wing-rays were circling the top of the stairs, blocking the way. Flesh-formed creatures as they were, they seemed immune to the flames.

'I know that little man.' Flydd clung to the treads above him as his knees buckled. 'He was a great friend once; an unshakeable ally; a masterly mancer and one of the bravest men I've ever met.'

The soldiers were still climbing towards them, but the dwarf stopped them with a hand gesture and Flydd made out a brassy glint in his fist.

'Come down, Xervish.'

The dwarf came forwards with that characteristic rolling gait, like a sailor walking the deck of a heaving ship. He was a handsome man with a leonine mane of hair that was as thick and full as when Flydd had last seen him ten years ago, though there were grey streaks in it now. He looked distinguished, from the neck up.

His voice put the matter beyond doubt, for it was rich, throaty and cheerful. He was Klarm, once known as the dwarf scrutator, and he had gone over to the enemy. It was one of the most bitter blows Flydd had ever suffered.

'I thought I knew you, Klarm,' said Flydd. It took all his strength to keep his voice steady. 'Clearly, I never did.'

'I haven't changed,' said Klarm. 'There was no point in being a powerless renegade, snapping uselessly at the God-Emperor's ankles. The war was won ten years ago –'

'The war was lost the day Jal-Nish came back from the dead in his air-dreadnought, and you know it.'

'Whatever you say, Xervish, but he controls the world, and all the Arts now –'

'Not this one!'

Klarm stared at the column of flame, now roaring ever higher and buffeting the wing-rays aside, and Flydd thought he saw a momentary unease in his old friend's eyes, before Klarm went on.

'– and there's nothing to be gained by fighting him. It behoves those of us who have mastered the Arts to use them for the world's betterment. Surely you can see that?'

'I see only a former friend who sold out for the basest of motives,' Flydd said thickly.

He did not want to believe his eyes, for if Klarm had gone over to the enemy, could *anyone* be trusted? This was unbearable. It was one thing to lose dear friends to the war, cut down in their prime; that was one of life's inevitable tragedies. But for a former friend to willingly serve their most bitter enemy shook Flydd's faith in human nature, not to mention his own judgment.

'You judge me,' said Klarm, 'yet you know nothing about my life these past years.'

'You're right. I do judge you, and I find you wanting, but I'll finish that debate when I have you at my mercy, *traitor.*'

The dwarf raised his right hand and Flydd saw that brassy glint again. Klarm rarely used rod or staff, wand or crystal; his favoured device was a little brassy object he called a knoblaggie. No one else employed such a device and Flydd had never fathomed how it worked, which might turn out to be a fatal weakness.

'It gives me ten times the power of before, Xervish,' said Klarm. 'And you've lost most of your Art. You can't resist me. Come down.'

Flydd noticed another silvery bubble rising on the side of the ring of flame furthest from Klarm. It was so small that he might not notice it, though the dwarf was amazingly competent in everything he did, and his keen eyes missed little. Flydd had to distract him; had to keep him talking.

'What mighty position has he given you, *old friend?*' he shouted down, looking away from the bubble, not much bigger than a grape, that was slowly coiling upwards in the flame. 'Did you take over as his chief lieutenant when Vivimord left him? I know how you crave power.'

It was a lie intended to provoke; Klarm had been the best of men to serve with, for he had never been ambitious for himself. His greatest pride had been to do whatever job he had been tasked with to the best of his abilities.

'You know me better than that, Xervish.' Klarm scanned the flames but the bubble was concealed in a fiery green knot. 'A position was offered but I did not take it; I'm a mancer, not a governor.'

And a very good mancer, better than Flydd himself, in some respects. How much more had Klarm learned from Jal-Nish and the tears while Flydd had been trapped on Mistmurk Mountain? Just for a second, he envied him.

The bubble was stationary now, well out of reach, and he could not draw on it from so far away. He had to keep Klarm talking.

'If only he could have trusted you,' said Flydd, 'he might have made you second only to himself, for you're a man of rare qualities. But the God-Emperor fears rivals, and he knows that a man who has turned his coat once will do so again, *when the price is right.*'

'I did not turn my coat.' Klarm showed that Flydd had nettled him only by a slight stiffening of the spine, a small man trying to appear taller. No one else would have picked it, but Flydd had known Klarm for a very long time. 'I only accepted his offer after he controlled the world and all resistance had ended.'

The bubble was moving up again. 'And the remaining traitors, your former *friends*,' Flydd sneered, 'rounded up. You must be pleased to know that the job is done. How many pieces of gold will he pay you for my head?'

'I've never served for love of gold; you know that too. I wish there could have been another way, Xervish, for I love my friends even when they've done wrong. But I love duty more and, having sworn to the God-Emperor I cannot do otherwise than honour my oath. You would have done the same, had our positions been reversed.'

Klarm spoke truly; in the long decades of the war, Flydd had often been forced to choose, and every time he'd come down on the side of duty rather than friendship. A great leader could do no less, and when there had been no choice but to sacrifice a friend to the greater good, he'd done it. It had always left a bad taste in his mouth afterwards, but the war had to be won. Losing it had been unthinkable, for that would have meant the end of humanity on Santhenar.

'Which capture gave you the greatest pleasure, Klarm?' said Flydd, bursting with frustration at the slow rise of the bubble. If he continued to taunt the dwarf, he might reveal something about the fate of their friends. 'Who got away that day, apart from you?'

In his mind's eye Flydd relived those last frantic moments after Klarm had engineered their escape and they'd bolted across the town square to steal Jal-Nish's undefended air-dreadnought. Flydd had got there first, along with Yggur, Fyn-Mah and General Troist. Flangers, that noble, troubled warrior, came next, with Klarm gasping at his side, his little legs going three strides to Flangers's one.

But Nish, well behind them, had been struck down, and Irisis, who never forgot a friend, turned back to help him, knowing she was dooming herself.

'You remember what happened as well as I do,' said

Klarm, 'and you're trying to find out if there were any other survivors. I'm telling you nothing.'

Curious, Flydd thought. He doesn't parrot the God-Emperor's lie, *every one of your old allies is dead.* Was Klarm afraid to lie to Flydd in case he picked it? Could someone else have survived? He felt his eyes pricking at the thought; oh, to not have to fight the God-Emperor all alone.

Klarm's eyes narrowed; he was no longer looking at Flydd, but just below him. The bubble, which had grown a little, was clearly visible now. Klarm threw out his arm, the knoblaggie glinting in his fist, but Flydd was quicker. Lunging, he snatched the bubble out of the air, and felt the most terrifying pain he had ever experienced.

FOURTEEN

Maelys swung across onto the roof of the swamp-creeper pit, fell into thick dust and lay there, unable to move. Climbing the octopede's web cord for the second time had been like hauling herself up a thousand-span-high cliff. Every bone ached, every muscle burned; her torn calf was shrieking and she was shaking uncontrollably. She rolled over onto her back, eyes shut, reliving the nightmare. It had been even worse than Phrune's attempt to skin her alive at the cursed flame.

But it made no difference to the smouldering knot of determination inside her. *No one* got away with abusing her the way Vivimord had. He must be stopped, and there was only one way to do that. For someone as gentle and soft-hearted as Maelys, it was a life-changing revelation. Vivimord had to die.

She'd gone a little way down this path months ago, when Seneschal Vomix had pursued her through the labyrinth below Tifferfyte. At one stage she'd had him at her mercy, but she could not bring herself to cut down a helpless man, monster though he was. Look what had come from that failure.

This time, if she got the chance, she would kill Vivimord, *and* Phrune, no matter the consequences. She had no idea how to make Phrune die permanently, but she was going to find out. And she'd better get going; Vivimord could come back at any moment. Jal-Nish was hunting her too, to take her back so she could incubate his little grub of a grandchild – or so he thought. And he'd better not discover otherwise.

She rolled over, and it hurt, but no amount of pain was going to stop her. Maelys came to her hands and knees and began to crawl up the glassy slope. Time passed in a daze; she could not have said whether the journey to the boudoir wall had taken ten minutes or ten hours. She could think of nothing save what she was going to do when she got to the top.

When she touched the wall she'd been thrown through, it shivered like the surface of a pool and her hand slipped in. She eased forwards until her eyes crossed the cool barrier. The bedchamber was empty.

Maelys crawled in. Apart from the rumpled covers and scattered flakes of dried swamp-creeper slime, like the stuff she was covered in now, there was no sign that anyone had been here. She could not see the octopede either – perhaps it was the one she'd killed below. Her feet still burned from contact with its innards.

Desperately thirsty, she dragged herself into the bathing chamber, clambered up into the tulip tub and lay in the water with her mouth open. Her injured calf throbbed, but she did not move. She could not.

Eventually the cold roused her; Maelys scrubbed the last of the octopede entrails off her inflamed skin and felt better. She slid to the floor, only then realising that she was in her old clothes; Vivimord's temporary enchantment had exhausted itself. She could not find her boots though.

She tore a strip of cloth off her shirt, bandaged her calf, went out into the bedchamber and headed for the door, barefoot, but it was no longer visible; the walls were completely blank. She wanted to scream, yet only cold logic was going to get her out.

Nish's rapier lay near where the door had been. The weapon was far too long for her, and unwieldy, but at least it was light. How to find the way out? The door must be hidden by illusion, and Maelys knew that illusions cost power for as long as they were maintained. Therefore, since he knew her to be trapped, why waste his strength on unnecessary detail? And if this illusion was designed to deceive the eye, could she break it by using another sense? Touch, say?

Closing her eyes, Maelys ran the tip of the rapier across the wall where the door should be. It made a loud scraping sound, but she had to take that risk. After covering many spans of wall, the tip slipped into an invisible crack. She felt it with her fingers. It ran vertically; it had to be the edge of the door.

By sliding the rapier tip up and down in the crack she found the latch, and when she pushed hard on it, it slid in silently and the door came ajar. At once she heard the hiss of the abyssal flame, and raised voices coming from a distance. Extinguishing the wall lights, she cracked the door open. The altar was gone, the flame chamber now brightly lit by a vast doughnut-shaped ring of green-black fire soaring up towards the ceiling, though her doorway lay in the shadow of a nearby column.

A pleasant, fruity voice spoke. Maelys went very still, for the room was full of Imperial Militia, plus several battle mancers and one of the God-Emperor's black-robed scriers. An all-seeing wisp-watcher was mounted on his back, its blind eye turning this way and that. Maelys felt a rush of fear, for the sight brought back those terrible times from her childhood, hiding in the ruins of Nifferlin Manor while the searchers tramped back and forth, dragging away cousins, uncles and aunts, never to be seen again, and drawing ever closer to her family's miserable hiding place.

She shook her head, put childhood behind her and eased back through the door, for the soldiers encircled the flame and were pressing steadily in. The men facing her across the circle might see her if she moved.

144

'Come down, Xervish. There's no escape from here.'

The voice belonged to a tiny robed mancer, a handsome dwarf with swept-back hair. Flydd was trapped halfway to the ceiling on a coiling set of steps arising from the centre of the fiery ring, and Colm was further up. Maelys couldn't see Nish or Vivimord.

A plumed officer shouted orders and the circle of soldiers closed on the flame. Maelys pulled the door shut. There were too many of them; there was nothing she could do.

She bit down on a momentary despair; she had to be even stronger. From outside there came a boom, a fizzing whip-crack, a series of roars and the sound of pounding feet. Had she been discovered? She stood to one side of the door, holding the rapier out.

No one came through; after a couple of minutes the sounds died away and she forced herself to open the door. The flame chamber was empty, though the fiery annulus roared higher and brighter and louder than before, and it was growing every minute. The floor shook with its fury and an ominous crackling came from the depths.

The annulus had been bridged by the rigid bodies of many soldiers, but as it slowly widened they were falling into the deep. She put her head around the column. The chamber was so brightly lit that she could see into the furthest corners. Dead men lay scattered across the floor, including two lying in a red heap at the base of the stairs – Flydd and Colm?

Her throat went dry. They could not have been killed so quickly, so easily – could they? Maelys had to restrain herself from running across.

A furtive movement caught her eye, high above, and she was glad she had not moved, for it was Vivimord, right at the top of the stair. As he heaved someone off onto a platform through a small gap in the flame, the illusion he'd used to conceal himself must have slipped momentarily. And the man he was dragging, slumped over and barely able to walk, was Nish.

Maelys could not forget the awful despair she'd seen in Nish's eyes as Vivimord had compelled him to come to the bed earlier. It had moved her, for she had seen into Nish's soul, into the torment of a man struggling to overcome his own demons and do what he believed was right, yet forced to a base act by a stronger foe. He must still be under the compulsion.

She wasn't game to go out the double doors; Jal-Nish was bound to have left guards, or a scrier with a wisp-watcher. Vivimord disappeared into a tunnel high above and Maelys, quaking, knew she had to follow him now or lose him and Nish. She crept out into the flame light, feeling as though a target was painted on her back.

First she had to cross the corpse bridge, and she'd better be quick. Only three statue-stiff soldiers remained and, as she approached, the annulus widened, sending the shortest of the three tumbling headfirst into the crack. The body next to him wasn't much taller; it must soon follow.

She checked again, but could not see anyone alive. She crept towards the bridge, repelled by the idea of walking across men's bodies. It seemed so callous, but there was no other way across. She stared at the crumpled remains at the foot of the steps. Could they be Flydd and Colm? There was so much blood she couldn't tell.

The dead soldier on the right only rested on his helm and boot heels and she dared not put any weight on him; with the annulus creeping ever outwards, they would both end up in the abyss. The body on the left was much taller; his head and shoulders rested on solid stone, though the green flame licked up on either side, and occasional tongues of fire wisped up between his legs. It looked more dangerous than the cursed flame and she was really afraid of it.

Taking a deep breath, she stepped onto his shins. Had the flame killed the poor fellow?

It was hot above the flame; not as hot as normal fire, but still uncomfortable. She stepped carefully across onto his marble-hard belly, swayed and nearly threw her arms out into the flame. The annulus widened another ell and the soldier's helm made a scraping sound as it slipped on the floor. Now he was only supported by the back of his head and his boot heels. Maelys froze, afraid to move in case it toppled him, but even more afraid of remaining where she was.

She was gauging how much of his helm remained on solid stone when his eyes opened. Maelys's knees went so weak that she nearly toppled off. He wasn't dead, just petrified; maybe none of the soldiers making up the bridge had been dead.

He was a handsome young man, no older than her nineteen years, and he was staring up at her with pleading eyes. His full lips parted and he whispered, 'Help me.'

Maelys felt a pang in her heart. For all his size he was no more than a boy, but even had he been her best friend, he was twice her weight and she could not save him. He was going to die.

'I'm sorry,' she said, avoiding his eye. 'There's nothing I can do.'

As she took another sliding step onto his chest, Maelys heard his helm slip. She swayed wildly, left then right, and her right hand went into the flame. The prickly warmth of it ran up her arm, and it fell leadenly to her side. The paralysis, or petrification, began to creep down her right side and up her neck. She could feel herself stiffening and knew she would not be able to stay upright much longer. She tried to move, but couldn't.

The paralysis crept across her chest and belly, which grew hard; she felt sick, faint and weak. The octopede's curving fang grew burning hot as she became icy cold wherever she'd felt the creeping paralysis, then suddenly it was gone.

It had to be the fang: perhaps the octopede had spent so long in the abyssal flame chamber that it was immune to its effects. The young soldier's helm scraped again; he couldn't last long. Her next step should have been onto his face, for she was afraid to stretch too far in case she pushed him in, but she couldn't bear to walk on those pleading eyes.

'Please help me,' he whispered, but she stepped over him onto the floor and kept going, and did not look back even when his helm slipped the rest of the way and he fell to his death with a gasping, boyish wail.

The steps had been reduced to a ragged skeleton of stone that might collapse at any moment. What Art could have eaten them away? They'd been solid when she'd looked out the door not long before.

She had to force herself to inspect the two blood-drenched corpses, and then to pull the locked bodies apart. Her heart was racing as she exposed their faces, but she did not recognise either of them. Did that mean Flydd and Colm had escaped, or had they been taken away? She looked up but there was no way to tell, and if the soldiers had taken them, there was nothing she could do about it. That made her decision simpler; she would go up, after Vivimord.

Further up, a pair of soldiers were jammed into the tread of a step that was just a skeleton of stone. There was blood everywhere, still oozing from the base of the step and from one severed, dangling arm, though their bodies were incomplete. The rest had fallen through. Eyes averted, Maelys climbed around them, clinging to the ribbons of stone which were all that remained of the stair. The floor began to shake in circular motions that made her feel seasick, and the skeleton stair wobbled with every quake, shedding flakes of rock like confetti.

She scrambled up and up, knowing that there was virtually nothing holding the stairs together; its stony skeleton could fall apart at any moment. She forced herself on, afraid she was walking into a trap but having nowhere else to go.

The flame roared in a great ring around her. It was licking across the ceiling now, and charred lengths of octopede web plus flakes of swamp-creeper crust began raining down. What was up there? She couldn't tell; everything shimmered with heat haze.

She reached the top and saw an upcurving ledge through the flame. Dark entrances ran off it, to left and right. She would have to jump through the flame onto the ledge and hope she survived paralysis, for the stair was about to collapse and she could not go down. Maelys eyed the roaring flame, worked her legs up and down a couple of times in practice, and sprang.

A blast of heat, then instantaneous and total paralysis struck her. She landed stiffly on the ledge, hitting her knee and the side of her head. She felt nothing through the numbness, though it was going to hurt once it wore off. She lay there, growing even colder, and afraid she would never move again.

The fang began to burn and the paralysis faded, though not as quickly as before, nor as completely. The power of the fang must be exhausted and she'd better not touch the flame a third time.

She got up, aching all over, sniffed her away around until she picked up the faint odour of Vivimord, then hobbled after him into the darkness, holding the rapier out in front of her.

The mere thought of him made her heart race and her fury rise in a hot wave. Just let him try and take her now. Just let him try.

FIFTEEN

Flydd, who was lying on his back on the steps with Colm staring down at him, realised that he'd screamed. Every bone ached, his teeth felt loose and the hand that had grasped the bubble was strangulation-purple. The bubble had burst, though before that he'd been looking out through eyes not his own, at something happening far away. The body he'd been clothed in had, unmistakeably, been that of a woman, and the transition had really hurt. But what had she been looking at? He couldn't make sense of it.

He shuddered at an echo of the pain and his knife hand tingled; the blade was alive again. He cut an experimental arc in the air between himself and the soldiers coming up the stairs. The knife screamed – no subtle weapon this – and carved the leading soldier's head and shoulders off his torso as though it had been no more than a joint of meat at the dinner table. The man to his left lost the top half of his head. The soldier below them fell down several steps, trying to scrub the blinding blood out of his eyes, and the rest retreated to the floor.

Flydd, shocked, turned it towards the robed mancers and the cold-eyed scrier behind them, who was studying him via a wisp-watcher mounted on his back. Jal-Nish selected his scriers from the most depraved men in his realm, and Flydd had no compunction about cutting him down.

The mancers ducked for cover and the scrier slipped behind a column, out of reach. Klarm alone had not moved; it was as if he was testing Flydd. Flydd couldn't kill his former friend in cold blood but he waved the shrieking blade at the wall above Klarm's head: a warning.

He somersaulted backwards through the double doors, then thrust his head and hand around the left-hand one, the knoblaggie out, and its blast tore chunks from the stairs below the butchered soldiers. With a shrilling swish, Flydd gave him a haircut. Smoke rose from Klarm's hair and he ducked out of sight.

Flydd cut down a pair of soldiers crossing the body bridge and they fell into the flames. Another two died at the base of the steps. 'Up, Colm,' he gasped. 'All the way.'

A wing-ray shot at them out of nowhere, eyes green with reflected flame, wing tips rippling. He carved it in two and it fell into a squad of soldiers, bringing half of them down. The others dragged the pieces off the crushed and thrashing men.

Colm plodded up, out of sight. Flydd followed painfully, for his bones seemed to be slipping and sliding inside his leg muscles again, and his bruised feet hit each step with a thud.

He couldn't work out what he'd seen through the eyes of the woman in red. She'd been crouched behind a brass-mounted lens the size of a small cartwheel, swinging it this way and that, and staring frantically through it, but at what? He'd seen only billowing mist shot with shifting, wraith-like shadows – ice-white and soot-black. Did the lens look into another place – or another *dimension*? Her heart had been thundering. What was she so afraid of?

He vaguely remembered seeing those peculiar shadows before, back in the cavern with Jal-Nish. Or had it been earlier, during renewal? He could not recall. Flydd's unease deepened. She was manipulating him to do something she could not do herself, or was afraid to, and he could see no way out of it.

The stair appeared to terminate a span up through the circular opening in the ceiling, where Flydd made out entrances to left and right. Another knoblaggie blast shattered the step below him, slamming chunks of broken rock into his left leg.

He scrambled up around the curve of the steps until he was sheltered from Klarm's line of fire. Flydd felled two more soldiers walking across the body bridge, though it would not delay the others long. Jal-Nish could call upon thousands of men, and would not care how many lives he wasted.

Klarm kept blasting with his knoblaggie, but the range was long now, and Flydd was not hit directly, though by the time he crawled up the last steps into the ceiling opening he had been peppered by stinging fragments of stone and the lower half of his body was a mass of bruises.

He leapt off the stair, through a gap in the flames, onto a sloping ledge with passages running to right and left. Below, at least a hundred troops had lined up to cross the body bridge, while Klarm, the two mancers and the scrier were in conference behind them. Flydd crept up to the right-hand opening, keeping low, but ran into a solid wall. The way was sealed, and so was the passageway to the left. He could cut through, but the enemy would only follow. He had to stop them.

Flydd put his back to the wall, still puzzling about what he'd seen through the woman's eyes, and whether she'd meant him to see it. He didn't think so, and that was chilling, for it implied that something was out of her control.

He was watching the soldiers when he felt her presence within him again. Flydd could feel the tension in her, and sense a fear that all her plans were going to come to nothing, for some shadowy nemesis was drawing ever closer to her.

He *almost* saw it, then, in her mind's eye – a wraith-creature (he could think of no other name for it) formed of white shadow and black fire, creeping, darting and continually changing its form to blend with its surroundings. He certainly *felt* it – a rage that had been burning for an eternity, and a determination to recover . . . what?

Flydd shook his head and the extraordinary feelings faded like a dream. He was back in her mind and she, fuelled with a resolve born of desperation, was trying to find the courage to take a momentous step. *Dare I defend myself with the most awful power of all? I must!*

She was at the obelisk in some past time, for it stood upright and the glyphs carved into it were fresh and clear. At its base, a round opening was lit from below by the cursed flame roaring up the chimney from the flame chamber. The woman in red was looking fearfully over her shoulder, clutching a handful of flame; she touched it to her forehead, pain speared through his and he saw her portal spell clearly for the first time.

Springing up, cat-like, she snatched a long spike off a table and held it out in her extended arm, pointing towards the base of the flame. The tip of the spike turned red and began to sing in the way his knife had; a beam carved down through the opening and shortly the flame changed to abyssal green. She caught some in her hand but did not use it, just pointed the spike down, growing ever more tense. The flame gushed higher but a shudder racked her. *I dare not.* She closed her hand, extinguishing the flame, and her image slowly faded from his mind.

He couldn't tell what she dared not do, but in that fleeting moment Flydd had *seen* her Art and thought he understood it. He could feel power within him now, the power of *her* Art, and he used it to complete his renewal at last. She was using him but he would worry about that later. His loose bones settled into their enclosing muscles, his saggy sinews snapped tight, and for the first time he felt at home in his renewed body. He slid out into the open.

'What are you doing?' cried Colm.

Flydd didn't answer; there wasn't time, for half a dozen troops were on the stairs, holding out shiny shields to reflect any knife-beam back at him, and the rest were waiting their turn. Leaning over the edge of the ledge, he focussed her Art, though not to shear flesh this time. The knife had to be forced to cut rock, metal, and anything else in its path. He sent the power of the shrieking blade slanting down through the annulus to sever whatever was anchoring the stair below and, with luck, collapse it into the abyss. Drawing every bit of power the woman had woken in him, he sent it into the knife.

Its scream made Klarm and the mancers clap their hands over their ears; the last wing-ray, gliding in circles below the ceiling, dived headfirst into the floor and did not move. Klarm blasted up at Flydd, knocking pieces out of the ledge.

Flydd swung the knife and bisected the dark-robed scrier, who died with a squeal that lasted until the air in his lungs was gone. Flydd felt no pity for him; scriers were vicious and merciless, and it was fitting that he die as he had lived.

The stair shook in wild circles, hurling the soldiers many spans to the floor, or into the abyss; he heard bones break. He cut down through the annulus again, expecting the stair to collapse, but it stilled, creaked, fell silent. Only then did he realise that it was fading, parts of it disappearing as if painted with an invisibility brush.

Klarm sent up another blast, narrowly missing him. He wasn't holding back now. Flydd ducked out of sight. Klarm prodded at the lower invisible sections with his knoblaggie, then ordered another half-dozen soldiers to climb the stairs, and the rest out through the double doors. The six soldiers started up, anxiously, and Flydd couldn't blame them. He allowed the first to climb halfway before slanting a knife beam in behind the reflective shield and cutting him down. The second and third fell to their deaths when

154

the steps they were standing on vanished, leaving a mere skeleton of stone around the edges. Klarm ordered the surviving three down.

With a grim smile, Flydd turned back to Colm, who was standing at the entrance to the blocked tunnel. 'Our first victory.'

'They'll soon cut us off.'

Without warning, the cool green flames beside them darkened to a deep green-black, and grew hotter, though not nearly as hot as normal fire. Something had changed.

'What is it?' said Colm, panting like a dog on a hot day.

'I should have been more careful. I think I've cut open the reservoir that feeds the flame.'

A minute ago the abyssal flames had been bouncing harmlessly off the ceiling, but now the stone began to droop. The ring of fire thickened into a circular column, sending tongues of flame licking out towards them. White fumes crept along the ceiling.

'The flame's out of control,' Flydd said, 'and it's not going to stop. Run!'

He carved a hole through the wall blocking the right-hand entrance, and leapt into the tunnel behind it. Colm followed and they raced up a steep slope into the darkness.

'Where are we going?' panted Colm.

'To the obelisk, as quick as we can.'

A few minutes later a passage ran off to the right, but the sound of marching feet echoed from it.

Flydd swore. 'Klarm's soldiers have found another way up. They're trying to cut us off.' He pressed on hastily, but soon the rising tunnel curved back and they heard the flame again. They turned the corner and saw that it had dissolved up through the floor not far ahead, flinging globules of rock at them, and eating ever upwards.

'They *have* cut us off,' said Colm. 'There's no way out.'

Flydd checked the knife in his blistered hand. Rainbow colours swirled across it, as if the metal had been overheated, and the blade was bent. Its steel could not

155

withstand the uncanny stresses imposed on it and if he used it again it was likely to fail, but he dared not take the risk of swapping it for Colm's scimitar. It might not sing at all; the blade might even shatter.

Ahead the roof was sagging, the flame dissolving a circular shaft up towards the surface of the plateau.

'I've never seen anything like it,' Flydd said. 'The flame seems to be unbinding the very forces that hold solid rock together.'

Tramp-tramp. 'They're close!' said Colm. 'And I'm not going to be taken alive.'

He seemed to have gained some control over his fire phobia and could glance at the column of flame without cringing. There was a defiant gleam in his eyes and an aggressive angle to his chin that Flydd remembered from the first time he'd met Colm.

Shield.

It hadn't been a voice in his head this time, just the image of a transparent cone standing on its base. 'There is one way out,' said Flydd. 'Straight up.'

SIXTEEN

Colm's eyes widened. 'Look what it's doing to the rock. It's unnatural.'

Liquified rock formed puddles on the floor of the tunnel and began to dribble towards them, sweeping up the debris in its path. A piece of dry grass, blown into the tunnel in ages past, was carried along on top, yet did not even smoke. The liquid rock wasn't hot, and that was downright uncanny.

Flydd squirmed at the thought of what the flame would do to them, but there was no other way. He studied the circular opening. 'The abyssal flame isn't nearly as hot as normal fire, and once it eats through into the cavern above, a tunnel slopes up steeply towards the surface, as I remember it. If we can get into it first . . .'

'You're insane.'

'She wouldn't have sent me this way unless there was a way out.'

'*You don't know this is the way!*' Colm hissed. 'She might be trying to trap you.'

'No, she needs me to do something for her, and I'm sure I've got to go up.' Flydd edged towards the flame with the tip of the blade out. The flame was only warm on his skin, but the knife grew so hot that he could barely hold it. As the tip grew red-hot, bordering on white, the blade bent into a half twist at the hilt.

Jerking his hand away before the blade failed completely, Flydd stumbled backwards and reached as high above his head as he could, praying that he'd understood what she'd shown him. 'Duck down! Make yourself small.'

Colm crouched, pulling his arms and legs close together. Flydd angled the blade down and out, then rotated, careful to keep the tip pointing out beyond any part of himself or Colm. The blade hummed as it carved a circle around them, and as he completed it a grey cone sprang into being, just like the one she'd shown him, enclosing them on all sides. The warmth of the flame was cut off, though its dazzling light was barely diminished.

Flydd stopped channelling power through the knife and took a step forwards. The cone moved with him. 'Come on.'

'Where?' A muscle twitched along the line of Colm's jaw.

Flydd couldn't blame him. The cone would protect them from many dangers, but could it survive where he had to take it? 'There's a way to get past the flame,' he equivocated. He could not tell Colm the truth.

Colm looked askance at the flame. His larynx bobbed up and down, and his eyes dilated until Flydd could see twin flames reflected there. 'You're mad.'

'Very probably,' Flydd said dryly. If he couldn't separate himself from the woman in red, he probably would go mad.

A spear shot above their heads, passed in one side of the cone then out the other.

'That wasn't supposed to get through,' he muttered.

Flydd made the cone again, using all the Art she'd shown him. It hurt in the centre of his chest this time; *she* might have been capable of channelling such power without harm, but he could not. The cone went a speckled blue and grey, like a wild duck's egg and, feeling as though he was carrying an enormous weight, he stepped towards the crackling flame.

Colm didn't budge; the moving cone struck his elbow, *zzzt*. He let out a yelp and clutched his arm.

'Don't touch the cone,' Flydd said over his shoulder.

'You might have mentioned that beforehand.' Colm cupped his elbow. 'I don't see any way past the flame.'

If he knew what Flydd had in mind, Colm would fight him all the way. Flydd pressed forwards, his renewed heart pounding painfully. This was going to take all the Art he had, and there was no way to test it first. If it wasn't enough, or if he got it wrong . . .

'What the blazes are you doing?' cried Colm, for Flydd was heading directly towards the curving wall of flame.

He smiled mirthlessly.

'Flydd!' Colm grabbed him by the shoulder and tried to heave him around. He'd worked it out. 'You'll burn us alive.'

Flydd shook him off. 'It's the only way out, and the cone will protect us.' I hope.

The blow to the side of the head rocked him; he staggered and nearly fell, and Colm, eyes wide and mouth gaping, leapt at him, mad with panic. Flydd didn't have the strength to fight him; he reached up with the twisted blade and drew the point of the cone down until it touched Colm's head. The younger man crumpled as if he'd been hit with an axe.

Flydd pressed on. It took an effort to move, for he was carrying Colm's dead weight on the base of the cone. He heaved it across to the flame, then hesitated. If he was wrong, it would be a most unpleasant way to die. But there was no alternative. He pushed over the edge into the flame.

The cone tilted sideways, and dropped. Flydd's heart spasmed; he was sure they were going to plummet all the way down to the abyssal source. The cone kept dropping, but he fought it, drawing power – her power – until his galloping heart seemed about to explode. The cone rocked left, right, turned upside down, dropping him on top of Colm, then righted itself and began to bob up and down within the flame.

The burden was even heavier now; Flydd could barely stand up for the weight, and it was so bright in the flame that he had to cover his eyes. The firelight was beating against his skin, drying it to a crisp; even with eyes covered, his mind's eye was full of green.

It was uncomfortably warm now, and getting warmer, for the cone, like a greenhouse, was allowing heat in but not letting any out. If he couldn't find the way to the surface soon, they would be baked.

A spear shot by, though this time it bounced off the skin of the cone. Another spear struck it harder, making it slowly rotate. The dissolving rock above them was falling in heavy drops that slid off the steep sides of the cone, though the racket was so loud he couldn't think for it. Flame gusts buffeted them; it was taking all his strength to keep the cone within the flame and slowly rising into the roof cavity.

He could smell smouldering hair – his or Colm's. Even if his head had been on fire, he didn't have the energy to slap it out. Rock collapsed in a deluge; the cone twisted and rolled, throwing him onto Colm again, then shot up and burst out into an empty tunnel.

Flydd directed it away from the flame, but couldn't hold it; it toppled onto its side, rolled around in a curve, and he could finally let go. The cone vanished; his ears were assailed by the roar of the flame. Cinders flew in all directions and the air had the blistered, metallic reek of a foundry.

'Come on,' Flydd croaked.

Colm lay on the floor unmoving. Flydd's cheeks were burning. He rubbed his hands and the skin rustled like dry paper.

Taking Colm under the arms, he dragged him away

from the flame, around a corner and into blessedly cool, moist darkness. The roar and crackle were muted here; he could think again. He laid his burning face against wet rock, rubbed his hands over it and pressed them to the back of his neck.

Colm groaned and kicked a foot.

'Get up,' said Flydd. 'This place is a labyrinth, but Jal-Nish's scriers will soon track us down. We've got to get to the obelisk first, or we've failed.'

He lifted Colm to his feet. Colm clung to his shoulder and they lurched into the darkness, moving by feel, since light would be an instant give-away. Around two more corners and the roar of the flame was just a slow reverberation of the air, though Flydd could feel it shaking his bones, which, in the envelope of his renewed self, felt much more sensitive than before.

Colm was recovering now; his fingers no longer clawed into Flydd's shoulder and his footfalls were more even. 'If you ever do anything like that again,' he said in a low, emotionless voice, 'you're a dead man.'

He wasn't joking. Below the surface, Colm churned like lava in the crater of a volcano, and one day he was going to explode.

'I can hear the abyssal flame again,' said Colm about half an hour later, as they felt their way up a sloping ramp of broken stone seeping with smelly water.

In the distance Flydd made out a faint, booming crackle. 'So can I.'

'That can't be good.'

'It's extremely bad.' What if it burned all the way up to the plateau, and the uncanny flame met the cold sludge of the marshes?

Flydd slumped against the side wall, pleased that Colm had regained his equilibrium, at least. 'I feel nearly as bad as I did before renewal.'

'I feel the way you *looked* before renewal.'

'You poor devil!' Flydd chuckled. 'I think we can venture a little light here.' Pearly glows formed at each of his fingertips, like shining peas. 'We can't be far from the surface now. I can smell the swamp.'

'It's a change from smelling you.' Colm scooped a handful of muddy water and rubbed it over his face, where it mixed with the dirt, smoke, flaking skin and old blood.

'And you stink like you just crawled out of someone's coffin,' said Flydd with a dry snort. When Colm wasn't wallowing in life's injustices he could be good company.

'Yeah, yours!' Colm grinned, teeth flashing white in his filthy face. 'And damn glad I am to be out of it.' He inspected the rubble slope above them, which ended in a hole too small to crawl through. 'It won't be easy to get up there without causing a rockslide. How far does it go, do you think?'

Flydd shrugged. 'Could be spans.'

'Then the rubble will take hours to shift. Which we don't have.'

'We may not even have minutes.'

'Use the knife, Cut a way out.'

'It's dead and I can't recharge it without the flame – if at all.'

'Blast a hole with one of your spells, then.'

'I don't remember the Art for that. I'm worn out, Colm. Aftersickness has drained me dry.' Flydd leaned against the side wall and allowed the light to fade to tiny fingertip glimmers.

'I need that,' said Colm.

Flydd brightened his fingers again. 'What for?'

'Where mancery fails us, we'll have to make do with muscle.' Colm went up to the blockage and began to tear at the rubble, pulling rocks out and tossing them down the slope past Flydd.

'Careful,' said Flydd. 'The troops will hear you.'

'Don't see as it makes any difference. If we can't get through damn quick, we're done for.'

He wrenched at a cabbage-sized rock in the centre of the rubble but it wouldn't budge.

'It's like the keystone of an arch,' said Flydd. 'Wriggle it from side to side, carefully, or you'll bring the lot down on us.'

'We're going to die sooner or later,' Colm said indifferently.

'Let's make it a lot later.'

Colm jerked and heaved, and suddenly it gave, and the rubble above with it. Flydd, who was several spans further down, scrambled up onto a little rock ledge. Colm didn't have time; he turned away and took the blows on his back. Wheelbarrow-loads of broken rock drove him to his knees, then further up a blockage gave with a roar and a deluge of smelly mud poured down on him.

Flydd reached down as Colm was washed past and hauled him out of the flood. He was a cake of stinking ooze matted with rotting reeds, but he looked cheerful for once.

'If they didn't know where we were before, they do now,' Flydd said dryly.

'We'll be out on the plateau in a minute.'

Flydd's stomach was churning again. Once they got to the obelisk he must use the woman's Arts to open the shadow realm, and what would happen then? Was he no more than a diversion, to be sacrificed so she could escape her enemy?

The sound of the flame was growing louder again. It was now a roaring and a cracking, a booming and a blasting and a shattering, as if it was tearing solid rock to pieces. A spear of pain seared through his chest. He didn't think he was having a heart attack, though it might have been less painful if he was.

He crawled up the mud-clotted rubble to another blockage. 'Give me a hand with this,' he panted, trying to prise out a rock without toppling it on himself.

Clash-clang. 'Can't!' Colm grunted from well below.

Flydd glanced down. The younger man was stabbing at something, and Flydd caught an occasional flash that might have been eyes or teeth, though he couldn't tell if it were man or beast. 'Don't let it get past. We're nearly there.'

Colm came to his feet, then lunged. There was an inhuman snarl and he fell backwards onto the slope, but bounced to his feet and lunged again.

Flydd wrenched at the stone, slid it to one side and was struck by another deluge, water this time. When it shrank to a malodorous trickle he saw a faint grey light above.

'We're here, Colm. *Colm?*'

'I'm all right,' he said breathlessly. 'Just.'

He clambered up beside Flydd, who smelt blood on him. 'It nearly got me, whatever it was,' Colm added, 'but I got it first.'

'Good man.' They scrambled out into the marshes, the sodden ground squelching and sinking underfoot. 'Keep a sharp eye out for stink-snappers,' said Flydd in a low voice. 'We haven't come all this way to be eaten by a carnivorous plant.'

'Give me an honest, savage beast anytime. Can you see anyone? Brrr!'

Mistmurk Mountain rose from tropical rainforest, but its flat top stood over a thousand spans high and it was always cold here. Ground mist lay in a thin blanket over the pools and mires that covered all but the stony outer rim of the cloverleaf-shaped plateau, though when Flydd stood up his head poked above the undulating surface of the mist. It was a cloudy night with just the hint of stars.

'No, but they're out there. Jal-Nish will have another army along the rim.' Flydd knew he wouldn't see them from here. They'd be hiding, waiting.

He scanned the sky and saw nothing. Once we're spotted, he thought, it will take them a good while to get here. In that time, he had to find what he was looking for, and make it work.

He turned around, searching for landmarks. The marshlands were relatively featureless but after nine years on the plateau Flydd knew every pool, reed and moss-covered rock – like that black outcrop to his left, shaped like a pointy, half-peeled lemon, where most of the moss had been grazed off by swamp creepers.

'This way.' He began to trudge along the winding strip of firm ground between the pools and mires. 'It's not far to the obelisk.'

The ground quivered, rippling the ponds to either side. Steam hissed up from the mire ahead; it had a sulphurous stench.

'I think the flame is getting hotter,' said Flydd.

The pond beyond was bubbling; a swamp creeper floated upside down on its surface and the air smelled like boiled meat.

'I don't suppose . . .' began Colm.

Flydd was salivating too. 'We haven't got time,' he said regretfully. 'Besides, that water doesn't smell too good.'

'Since it's probably my last meal, I'll risk it.' Colm skewered the swamp creeper with his sword, hacked it into chunks and sank his teeth into one. 'Delicious. Want some?'

'The way my renewed stomach feels, I won't risk it.' Flydd swallowed mouthfuls of saliva, feeling as though he hadn't eaten in a week.

On the right, an expanse of black mud was slowly rising. Only hours ago it had been a large pool, but the last of the water was draining away, leaving fish and legged eels flapping in the muck. Get moving, or you'll suffer the same fate, Flydd told himself, and struggled on.

'There it is,' said Colm, belching cheerfully.

'Quiet!'

The tilted stone obelisk was four or five spans long and partly covered in moss and trailing feathers of lichen that largely obscured the ancient Charon symbols engraved into the stone. The growths had been charred off its upper section by an earlier blast from the sky palace, tilting the stone and uncovering the opening through which Maelys had first gained entry to the cursed flame chamber. The obelisk was warm and Flydd could feel the tingle of power now; the woman in red must have opened him to it.

'*Now* I understand. The obelisk forms the solid pole of a portal. In ages past, she brought the cursed flame here, using the conjunction between solid stone and ethereal flame to make her portal.'

'I wondered why you filled that phial at the cursed flame.'

'I had a different purpose in mind, but if I have to use it here, I will.'

The ground shook and a stone's throw to their left a geyser erupted in the marsh, followed by an explosion of boiling mud. That's where the abyssal flame was going to come up, and it was dangerously close. Flydd threw himself behind the obelisk. Colm was struck in the chest by a huge clod of hot mud and reeds and was knocked off his feet. He cried out, clawing away the boiling, clinging muck.

Flydd dragged him into shelter. 'Stay down. This is only the beginning.'

Colm cooled his scalded chest in a puddle as steam belched up from dozens of fissures, obscuring everything. They crouched under the tilted obelisk as the explosions continued; it was like being next to a mud volcano. Boiling mud was blasted up and out in every direction; chunks the size of oxen rained down, splattering on the obelisk and sliding off its edges to form steaming piles on either side of them.

'It's the end of the world,' said Colm, his eyes huge.

'Not yet, but I'm doing my best,' Flydd said sardonically.

The explosions, and the deluge, grew ever louder, the rain of mud more intense. Colm said something but Flydd didn't catch it; the noise was deafening. The ground was shuddering wildly now.

'I said, what if the obelisk falls on us?' Colm shouted in his ear.

Flydd had been thinking the same thing. 'It'll end all our worries. If we go out we'll be buried in hot mud. It'll stop in a minute.' As soon as all the mud above the abyssal flame boiled away, and then what? He felt a little shiver of anticipation. The abyssal flame was too powerful, too uncanny. It wouldn't go out tamely. It was preparing the way for something monumental.

The mud eruptions cut off, though the ground was still shaking. He peered around the edge of the obelisk. The mist and steam had been blasted away and there was just enough starlight to make out a crater wall some fifty paces off, though he wasn't high enough to see inside it.

Then, with a whistle that grew to a roar, the abyssal flame burst through its last barrier and shot upwards, a ruler-edged rod of green and black fire climbing a hundred spans into the sky. A shockwave blasted outwards, tearing up reeds and overtopping pools. The mud wall collapsed abruptly, deluging Flydd to the knees, and it was still scalding. He pulled himself out and retreated further under the obelisk.

When the debris settled, he scrambled up to the tip of the obelisk, and in the light of the flame he could see all the way to the edges of the plateau. A line of shadows rose up along the rim. In every direction, as far as he could see, the God-Emperor's Imperial Militia were climbing to their feet, their armour winking in the glare.

'They must be three thousand strong,' said Colm, joining him at the top.

'At least,' said Flydd.

'And there's no way out.'

'Bar our portal to the shadow realm.'

In a sudden silence, the sky palace materialised high above them, its white stone sails shining in the light. Flappeters were wheeling around it, riding the updraughts; flocks of bladder-bats appeared from apertures in the sky palace; a wing-ray began to curve down towards them.

'No way,' said Colm. 'None at all.'

SEVENTEEN

Maelys felt as though she'd been following Vivimord for a lifetime, as he drove a dazed, uncomprehending Nish before him. She had tracked them up the perilous stair and through the dark corridors above it, finding her way by smell. There was no sign of dead Phrune but she could smell his unguents on Vivimord's ruined skin. Phrune must have gone back to the pit for her, and discovered her escape; he would be hunting her now.

She turned around, holding the rapier out like a silver spear, but saw no living thing, nor any walking corpses, thankfully, though as she went on she could feel his dead eyes on her.

She hadn't learned any more about Flydd or Colm's fate, though it did not seem possible that they could have escaped the soldiers and Vivimord. So that meant it was all up to her, again. Every success was topped by another disaster, but she had to fight on. She could not allow herself any self-doubt or hopelessness, else she would not be able to continue. Nonetheless, those feelings were always just below the surface.

She kept them at bay by renewing her vow. She was going to destroy Vivimord and Phrune, and rescue Nish. And then . . .?

She simply did not know. Her old life and old dreams had been so thoroughly destroyed that Maelys could not imagine any future beyond the struggle against the God-Emperor, not even if, by some miracle, they won.

As she walked, she was trying to think of a way to rescue Nish, but no plan came to mind. Without her taphloid she could not attack Vivimord from behind, for he would detect her aura before she came close enough to strike.

Maelys was edging around a corner when she saw the flame again, rushing up an eerily shimmering shaft. Vivimord could hardly have gone that way; he must have turned back, but how close was he? She squinted against the brightness. There he was, just ten paces away! She ducked back. His head was bowed and he was dragging Nish, whose eyes were closed, his arms sagging. Vivimord must have renewed the enchantment on him.

She scuttled back the way she had come until she saw a cranny in the tunnel wall; Maelys squeezed into it and waited for them to go by, praying that Vivimord would pass on the other side of the tunnel, far enough away that he would not detect her aura. The cranny was unnervingly webbed with cords and had a faint odour of octopede, but it was too late to look for another hiding place. She crouched in the base of the cranny with the rapier pointing up over her head, just in case.

Vivimord stopped a few paces past her, sniffing the air. Maelys had never wanted her lost taphloid more, both for its concealment of her aura, and as a weapon she knew he feared. The rapier would be little protection against him.

'Where the devil has he gotten to?' he muttered.

Vivimord sounded agitated and she wondered why, since he had what he wanted. He hurried on, stopping frequently to sniff the floor and examine it for tracks, the dark radiance of the cursed flame dripping from his hooked fingers. She followed, keeping no more than thirty paces behind. Being so close posed a grave risk if he turned back, but she was afraid to let him get further ahead in case she lost him.

Several times she saw brighter glimmers as he used his Art to find the path, before finally he said, 'Ah!' and turned up a steep slope, no wider than his shoulders, hauling Nish behind him.

Maelys followed, her heart thumping. At the top she waited until she heard him moving down the next tunnel before going after him. She was so tired that every step was a struggle, and was plodding along, squinting at the swinging puddle of black light coming from his fingertips, when Vivimord suddenly crouched and light stabbed out from his fingers.

She thought he'd discovered her, until it illuminated something large and black flapping out of the darkness ahead of him. The wing-ray let out a brittle cry and shot over his head, dripping blood, to disappear in the darkness between Vivimord and her. Maelys didn't hear it hit the floor, which meant that it was still alive and would attack her next. And even if she killed it, Vivimord would discover her when he came to investigate the ruckus.

She ducked down, holding the rapier out to protect her face, praying that the wing-ray would pass over her head and keep going. She saw nothing, heard nothing, then a thumping blow drove her backwards a good span. It had driven itself onto the point of the rapier and every furious flap was forcing it further along the shaft towards her. Maelys couldn't hold it and wasn't game to pull the rapier out in case the beast came at her. Feeling its cold breath on her hand, she let go and threw herself out of the way.

'What the blazes was that?' she heard Vivimord cry, and his black light began to grow again.

She crawled back to a curve in the tunnel, defenceless now. He would recognise the rapier, deduce that it was hers and hunt her down, but she dared not retreat further for fear of dead Phrune. She knew he was coming after her.

Light crept from Vivimord's hand, streaking low along the tunnel floor, and she realised that he was also afraid. The mountain was full of troops and scriers now, and not even Vivimord's illusions could hide him from the direct gaze of Gatherer. A narrow beam touched on the body of the wing-ray, whose fleshy wings were undulating like waves on the sea. He studied it from several paces away while she held her breath and felt the backs of her hands prickling. His acrid sweat was unpleasantly strong. The floor of the tunnel moved underfoot and the muted roar of the flame grew louder. Vivimord hastily turned away.

He hadn't seen the rapier. He must have thought that his blast had brought the wing-ray down. She was about to move when he spun around, arm upraised. Had he seen her; heard her; *sensed her aura?*

Vivimord was absolutely still. Black flames dripped from his fingers again, and if he came after her, he could blast her down as easily as he had the ray. Her palms oozed sweat; projections on the floor were cutting into her knees, and her stomach was so empty that it hurt. Then the light was drawn back towards his hand, and died to the faintest glimmer as he turned away. It took a long time before she could find the courage to follow.

It was completely dark now but she could tell where the ray was by its wing flutters. She approached gingerly, unable to tell whether it was badly injured, perhaps dying, or about to wriggle free. She was reaching down to feel for the rapier hilt when she remembered that barbed stinger in the middle of the creature's back. She couldn't risk it; the rapier would have to be abandoned.

She went sideways until she touched the far wall of the passage, keeping as far from the wing-ray as possible, and continued. After following Vivimord for some minutes she heard him squelching through mud, then scrambling up a rubbly slope, dislodging small rocks as he went. Water trickled down and momentarily the smell of the marsh blew his reek away.

Nish must have fallen, for she recognised his pained cry.

'Get up there, Deliverer,' Vivimord grated, 'and be quick about it. Flydd can't hide from Gatherer up top, and neither can I.'

So he had been following Flydd. Relief flooded her; she wasn't completely alone. Maelys crept to the mud at the base of the slope and waited for them to move away, for she could not move silently over the rubble. She started up, then stopped. What if Vivimord had sensed her and was waiting at the top?

Something clacked behind her, like an iron-shod boot on stone. The God-Emperor's troops must have picked up the trail. She had to take the risk. Peering up the slope, she made out a darkly ragged opening against the night sky, curtained with the straggling roots of marsh plants – it was the plateau at last. And five minutes from now she could be dead; or Vivimord could have won; or, more likely, the God-Emperor would have taken the lot of them.

She had just reached the top when the ground lurched upwards, collapsing the steep bank of an empty pond next to the opening; a river of muddy slurry poured down the hole and the rubble began to move under her feet. Maelys snatched at the roots as she fell, twisted them around her wrists, and they held.

As she pulled herself up, the marsh burst open some distance ahead and slightly to her right, and boiling mud lumps began to splatter down all around. She scrambled across to an intact section of the overhanging bank, covering her head with her arms. If it collapsed she would be buried alive, which had a slight edge over being cooked in boiling mud.

Despite several more lurches and shudders, the bank held, but as the mud eruption paused, she heard that boot clack again, and a deep male voice.

'It's started. Get up there.'

Lanterns were approaching the base of the rubble slide.

She would be discovered in seconds. She had to risk the eruption.

Maelys dragged herself up the bank and was creeping through the marshes with clots of hot mud raining down all around her, when there came a shattering boom from not far ahead, and a wild gust of hot wind knocked her flat on her back. The greeny black abyssal flame roared up, casting brilliant light and deep shadows across the top of the plateau.

And there, hanging in the sky high above, was the God-Emperor's sky palace. The trap had been sprung and there was only one way out of it – Flydd's spell into the shadow realm. If he'd discovered how to make it work. If he was still alive.

'If you don't open the portal now,' Colm cried, 'it'll be too late.'

Flydd, who was standing on the tip of the tilted obelisk gnawing his upper lip, didn't answer. He could hear soldiers pounding up steps directly below the obelisk, making for the cavity at its base, and others would be storming up the rubble slide he and Colm had just climbed. At the same time, Jal-Nish's Imperial Militia were moving steadily in from the edges of the plateau, tightening the noose, while flappeters, bladder-bats and wing-rays guarded the skies. Now the sky palace hung high above them, all the more ominous because it was absolutely silent.

'Jal-Nish has blocked every avenue of escape save the one I no longer want to take: the portal to the shadow realm. But I have no choice – as a novice at the perilous art of portal making, aiming it anywhere in the real world would almost certainly be fatal.'

Flydd held the phial containing the cursed flame against his forehead, hoping that it would wake his lost Art so he would not have to rely on the woman's ominous mancery, but nothing came to him. Before renewal he'd known how to open the shadow realm; he had rehearsed Rassitifer's spell many times in case he'd needed to use it in an emergency, but that memory had not returned.

It left no alternative but to follow her perilous procedure. Dare he?

'Flydd!' choked Colm. 'Do something.'

Flydd twisted the bung out of the phial and touched a fingertip to the wisp of cursed flame coming from the top. His finger began to go rigid, but a little charm – one of hers – came into his mind to prevent the paralysis. He worked it and gingerly touched his finger to his forehead. Heat twisted in, like a corkscrew; faded.

He tried to draw power from the flame the way he had seen her doing it, but nothing came to him. 'Why isn't it working?'

'Maybe *he's* blocking you.' Colm glanced up at the sky palace, shivered, then slid down to the base of the obelisk and scrubbed mud off his blade with a handful of reeds.

'Could Jal-Nish be blocking *her* Art? How could he understand what he's never seen before?'

'Perhaps the tears allow him to understand all powers.'

'If he'd understood the flame, he would have ordered his scriers to use it against me down below.'

'Unless he's playing with you,' said Colm. 'He does love to torment his victims.'

'Jal-Nish never puts personal pleasures ahead of his own safety. I'm a threat to him, so he'll secure me first, or kill me. Perhaps I need more power. She used a mere wisp of the cursed flame, but it's her Art and she could be subtle. I don't have time for subtlety.'

'There may be a reason for it,' said Colm. 'The portal spell may be dangerous.'

'No doubt it is, though hardly more than *him.*'

Flydd glanced up at the sky palace. It was measurably lower than before, and the abyssal flame, roaring ever higher, might have been seen a hundred leagues away. The next few minutes would determine what kind of a symbol it became in the Histories – a beacon of hope, or a mark of despair.

174

He drew out the bung but this time touched the rim of the phial to his forehead. The shock was like a heated auger boring into his skull, but when it passed, the portal spell had not worked. If only he still had the fifth crystal, the most powerful of all. He'd primed it years ago and it would almost have opened the path into the shadow realm by itself, had he not lost the power to set the spell off. If he'd had it, he could have thumbed his nose at her and whatever she wanted from him.

Wishing was futile. He had to have more power, far more than was held in this tiny phial. Dare he draw upon the power of the abyssal flame itself? The power now being wasted, flaming into the heavens, must be enough to open the shadow realm a thousand times. Assuming he could draw upon it without killing himself; and let the whole damn world go to ruin if he failed!

Vivimord was creeping across the marshes, dragging Nish through the mud behind him, and Maelys followed as closely as she dared. She would not be heard in the roar of the flame, but she would be clearly visible in its lurid light if Vivimord glanced back.

He topped a small rise, then crouched in a hollow, out of sight. What was he up to? She crawled after him, wishing she still had the rapier and fantasising shockingly about sticking it in one side of him and out the other. She hadn't gone far when an unpleasantly familiar sound swept towards her, *flutter-flap*. It was a flappeter, the most fearsome of all Jal-Nish's flesh-formed creations. Maelys went still and kept her head low, glad of the camouflaging mud that covered her from head to toe.

The flappeter cruised over her and kept going. Maelys slowly lifted her head. She could see the obelisk clearly now, and a man's outline at the top: Flydd! Her eyes pricked with tears of relief. He was alive!

His arms were upraised as if he were attempting mancery. She stood up carefully, fists clenched, for the flappeter could pluck him off before he realised it was there. She was about to shout a warning when he swung his arm backwards; green fire stabbed at the creature, which swerved wildly, almost crashed into the swamp, then began to climb away, smoke rising from its lower feather-rotor.

It had taken a lot out of Flydd, though. He was bent double, choking or throwing up, and the peril had not gone away. A flock of bladder-bats descended, and lights were advancing from every direction – the Imperial Militia were coming. As she watched, Vivimord disappeared behind the column of flame.

She had to warn Flydd about Vivimord, though Maelys couldn't see how to do so without alerting him to her presence. She crept on, keeping low, and was edging past the fury roaring up from a circle burned through the marsh when she smelt the ghastly odour of perfumed oil and rotting entrails, and was caught from behind in two oily hands.

'Slybbily meee,' slurred dead Phrune, licking pieces of intestine off his green lips.

EIGHTEEN

Flydd wiped his mouth as he watched the flappeter climb away, knowing he hadn't done it much damage. It would soon be back, if the bladder-bats or wing-rays didn't get him first.

'Get on with it,' Colm said from the ground.

Flydd spat over the side. 'My mouth tastes like something a stink-snapper has been digesting for a week.'

Colm chuckled. 'That's another death to look forward to, if Jal-Nish doesn't get us first.'

Flydd managed a smile. 'I'll try the portal spell again, though I'm sure I did it perfectly last time . . .' Unless he was missing something. He had attempted it three times now, and felt blocked each time. He simply could not draw on the monstrous power of the abyssal flame. There had to be another way.

The woman in red had used the flame during his renewal hallucination; he now remembered what she'd done, but still he could not get it to work. She was using him to do something she could not do herself, and yet he had no choice. He didn't think she was on the God-Emperor's side, or Vivimord's.

He was going through his memories of her, trying to see if he'd missed anything, when he noticed something she had avoided thinking about earlier; something she hadn't wanted him to discover. Whatever she was hiding, it had to do with the power she'd considered using a while back, then rejected because it was too dangerous. Dare *he* try? It could hardly be more dangerous than allowing Jal-Nish to win.

He explored the memory she'd tried to hide. Whatever this new power was, it lay buried deep below Mistmurk Mountain, at the base of a narrow, ring-shaped shaft bored through a thousand spans of rock down to the source of the vapour which fed the abyssal flame. The source was concealed by that flame, and hidden below the centre of the hearth from which it emanated.

Flydd whipped out the bung of the stone bottle in which he'd captured some of the abyssal flame; it flickered greenly black over the lip. He hesitated for a moment, doubting himself, then swiftly upturned the bottle against his forehead for a second and thrust the bung back in.

Bone-grinding, scalding pain tore into his head; sickening waves followed it, slowly fading. He closed his eyes, and it was as though a door had slid open at the base of the mountain, and a hatch swung back at the centre of the abyssal flame's hearth, to reveal what lay beneath.

It wasn't the source of the abyssal flame at all, nor of the vapours that fed it. It was a small rectangular box made from clear crystal – cut from a single diamond, perhaps – and within it he saw the faintest movement. There was something white inside; small and white and restless. Flydd did not see how it could hold the power he so desperately needed; power to overcome whatever was blocking him and blast open the entrance of the shadow realm, but there had to be a good reason why it had been hidden so carefully.

Dare he? He'd die if he didn't. And it probably wouldn't work anyway.

He traced out the way of power – the way to use the abyssal flame and open that box, *her way*. At the moment he had that thought, the flame brightened and roared higher. Flydd shuddered at what he was about to do, but he was going to do it anyway.

Using the abyssal flame as a focus, he reached down, down, down to the very core from which it came, to the hearth through which the vapours that fed it issued. Using the power of the abyssal flame against itself, he spun it into a spiral, ever tighter, until it formed an irresistible emerald spear. He took that spear and hurled it down through the hearth, cleaving it in two.

The halves of the hearth fell to either side and the spear continued down, directed with unerring aim, until it struck the top of the little diamond box, met resistance, and overpowered it. The lid shattered, the webbed and layered protections inside it tore, and a small white flame was released. It was such a tiny flicker that Flydd felt sure he was the butt of a monstrous joke. How could that be the power he was looking for?

Noooooo! screamed the woman in red into his mind, so desperately that he felt her throat tear and tasted blood in the back of his mouth. *Not the chthonic flame, you fool.*

Too late! He had committed a mancer's most cardinal sin. He'd used power without knowing what he was doing, and there was no way to fix it now – the chthonic flame, whatever *that* was, was out of its box, and every one of its protections had been broken.

He had to keep going now, and quickly. The next step was to form the structure that would become the portal's entrance. It would shelter them from the raw power needed to open the woman's long-closed portal and direct it to the shadow realm. Could he do it? Making portals was one of the greatest Arts of all, one that few master mancers from the Histories had ever done successfully. And even with *her* knowledge, Flydd began to doubt himself.

What shape should the entrance take? In mancery, such things mattered, and if he gave it the same shape as the woman had used when she'd made her portal long ago, resonances of time and place would make this one easier to create. Flydd closed his eyes, opened himself to her memories and saw spirals everywhere: on the obelisk, down at the altar, and even in her memories. That had to be it. Taking power from the abyssal flame for the last time, he focussed it, used her portal spell, and its entrance slowly whirled into physical form around the base of the obelisk.

It looked like pale red glass, and had a central dome from out of which spiralled four narrow arms, so elongated that each wrapped around the dome several times. Why four arms? The spirals down below had all been two-armed. He touched the glassy wall but felt nothing; it was just an image, yet to take on physical form.

The roaring abyssal flame suddenly broke into a series of flares, as though its conduit were trying to cough something up. As if that had been a signal, the Imperial Militia must have broken into a run, because the steadily moving lanterns drawing in from the edges of the plateau began to jiggle. The troops were converging on him and getting into position to attack. The flock of bladder-bats let out a massed squeal and dived.

The green flame coughed twice more and died down, plunging the plateau into darkness. In the sudden silence Flydd could hear his ears ringing. Pain gnawed the centre of his chest; acid rose up his throat. Had the flame gone out completely? If it had, he'd made a catastrophic blunder.

'What's going on?' said Colm, shivering. 'What have you done, Flydd?'

'I don't know.'

The abyssal flame suddenly belched higher than before, rushing up past the sky palace and buffeting that monstrous structure like washing on a clothes line. The flame went transparent, almost invisible in the darkness; the pain in his chest was like teeth chewing on his lungs, then the flame turned a brilliant, icy white. That tiny chthonic flame, fuelled by the vapours seeping from deep below the mountain, had grown into a conflagration. Flydd was paralysed by the horror of what he'd created, and he had an awful feeling that they were all going to pay for his folly.

'No,' he whispered. 'No, no!'

'I don't see how you could have made things any worse,' said Colm, standing with his arms crossed protectively over his chest, looking up.

This flame was freezing; Flydd could feel it from a distance. Ice began forming around the edges of the vent and growing upwards in jagged arrays of crystals. He felt just as cold inside, but there was no going back now.

'Things can always get worse.' He headed towards the vent. 'Very much worse.'

'Flydd?' cried Colm. 'We're almost within range of the soldiers' spears.'

'I need fire.'

He didn't want to go near it; he definitely didn't want to carry it back. The chthonic fire must have been hidden for a reason and he recalled the woman's fear of it. And if she was afraid, he should be more so, but the abyssal flame was gone and he had no choice.

He churned through the mud, which had baked hard in some places, was deep and liquid in others, yet near the edge of the flame was already freezing solid. The ice around the edges of the vent had a peculiar pale green tint. Could it be used to contain chthonic fire?

Flydd reached out and gingerly touched his bent knife to a tendril of chthonic flame. The knife went white and made alarming cracking sounds, but held. He carved an oval flask from the peculiar green ice and held it out on the point of the knife until it was full of fire; the knife became so cold that its hilt stuck to his fingers. He thrust the stoppered flask inside his coat with the others, where he could feel the cold burning. Flydd swiftly cut a second flask, pyramidal this time, filled it and stowed it as well. He'd done as much as he could.

The next step was to solidify the portal entrance with them both inside. Once that was done they would be safe – from everything outside it, at least. Flydd made his way back to the obelisk and climbed one step up its slope. Opening one of the chthonic fire flasks, he drew power from it as he'd seen her do, fingertip to forehead. Agony! Mist formed around the obelisk and drifted through the red glass spiral, for its walls were still intangible. How was he to complete it? He didn't know. He couldn't think straight for the pain boring into his skull.

Colm scrambled up the obelisk. 'They're nearly here.'

Flydd could see the jiggling lanterns from the corner of his eye.

Colm sprang up to the tip, swinging his sword in a vertical arc. Flydd jumped. A bladder-bat squealed as the blade went through one wing and into a bladder filled with the floater gas that kept it aloft. The gas hissed out; the creature's other wing scraped down the side of the obelisk, then it splashed into the mud, dead.

'Thanks,' said Flydd. 'You'll have to keep them off.'

'At last there's honest work for me to do.'

The implication being that mancery was dishonest work. After today, Flydd couldn't blame him for thinking it.

Phrune's fingers tightened on Maelys's wrist. She swung around, striking at the corpse with her fists, useless though that was – it was animated by Vivimord's necromantic Arts and the only way to stop it was to chop it into little pieces, but she was unarmed.

The abyssal flame sputtered, then changed from green to a brilliant, frozen white. Maelys didn't have time to wonder about the ominous transformation; the light illuminated dead Phrune more starkly than sunlight, and he was clad in rags through which his skin had the bleached grey of a fish's belly. His reek was overpowering now, and something white and slippery dangled from his left hand: a long loop of intestine with a slip-knot at the end.

Phrune let out a slimy chuckle and began to pull her to him. He was twice her weight and far stronger; if he got his arms around her that would be the end. Maelys tried to wrench free but, though his palms had that familiar oiliness, his fingers and thumb had locked around her wrist.

She had only one advantage; he was slow and lumbering, and she was quick with life. Maelys yanked up a clump of reeds with her free hand and smacked Phrune across the eyes with it. He blinked away the mud, focussed his empty eyes on her and gave a slow pull on her arm.

She jammed her feet against a ridge of baked mud and strained backwards with all her weight, but wasn't heavy enough to heave him off balance. Phrune kept pulling, his lacerated mouth open in a deathly grin. She threw herself forwards and dived between his legs before he could react.

She hadn't broken his hold on her wrist, though, and it was wrenched so badly that she thought the bones were going to break. She steadied her wrist with her free hand, jerked Phrune's arm between his legs and heaved with all her might. His feet left the ground and she threw her shoulder against him, toppling him onto his face.

He still wouldn't let go, but Maelys fell with him, driving her knees into his back and pushing him through a thin hard crust into liquid mud, hitting him with her weight again and again until at last his fingers gave enough for her to pull her throbbing wrist free. She jumped up and down on the back of his head, forcing it into the mud as hard as it would go.

Nothing could stop Phrune, though, and when she saw his hands clawing at the reeds and his knees drawing up, she leapt onto the firmer ground next to the white flame, which had been baked hard by the abyssal flame's heat and was now freezing even harder.

Oh for a stout stick or a heavy rock, but no trees grew on the plateau and the only rock was solid bedrock. Her one hope was the flame itself. She backed towards the brink, the cold freezing her muddy clothes, leaving a good pace between herself and the edge so she wouldn't slip in.

Would Phrune recognise the danger? That depended on whether he had any intelligence left or was just a corpse animated by his master's Arts.

He rose slowly to his feet, dripping mud, and came at her. Maelys moved along the rim so he would have to approach from the side, which would give her the best chance of knocking him in. He could do the same to her, of course, unless Phrune had something worse in mind.

He moved sideways so as to come at her head-on, which suggested that there was some intelligence at work within him. She backed around the rim, desperately trying to think of a way to finish him. He had endless patience, but she had little time. Vivimord was probably attacking Flydd right now.

The ground was uneven here, consisting of the hollows of pools drained when the flame had burst up through them – some baked hard, others with just a firm crust over deep, soft ooze – and the head-high banks between the pools. She climbed the bank behind her, slid down the other side, crossed the next dry pool and clambered up the bank after that, onto its edge. Maelys was backing across it when she felt the ground crumbling under her feet. The other side had been undermined and had fallen away, leaving a thin crust of moss and earth with nothing supporting it.

She moved to the brink of the flame shaft, then jumped off the undermined bank to the hard base of the pond, and waited. Shortly Phrune clawed his way to the top, saw her below, and stopped. She moved backwards but he remained where he was. Did he suspect a trick?

She took another step backwards, trying to stare at him fearfully, which wasn't hard. Alive or dead, Phrune was terrifying. Another step.

He moved at last and his right foot came down on the undermined section, which crumbled beneath him. Phrune toppled, fell to the floor of the pond, but to her dismay landed solidly on his stubby feet. She ran at him, put her hands against his chest and shoved as hard as she could.

He fell backwards towards the flame but, as he was going over, one flailing hand caught her shirt and pulled her with him, and Maelys was already off-balance. She dropped to her knees and jammed them into the ground, praying that the fabric would give, but her shirt tore down to a seam and it held.

He teetered on the brink, trying to pull himself towards her, but Maelys could feel her knees slipping under his greater weight. He swayed forwards, backwards, forwards again and with the recklessness of desperation she propelled herself up, drove her head into his belly as hard as she could, then threw herself backwards.

His insides made a disgusting sloshing noise and began to slide out of his mouth, but his fingers relaxed on her shirt and he toppled into the freezing white flame. She watched him fall, squinting against the glare, until he was out of sight, surely burning to ash and gone forever.

Maelys's heart was clattering and she could barely stand up, but she had to get to the obelisk. Colm was halfway up it, swinging at a flock of bladder-bats, while the obelisk was surrounded by long glassy red spirals. Flydd's shadow realm spell must be working after all.

She was heading for it when the flame gave a series of belches and a transparent figure rose out of it. No, a series of identical figures, five of them, each the image of dead Phrune. They swung around until they formed a line, their ruined mouths opened in the same moment, and they broke into silent laughter.

NINETEEN

Flydd was exhausted, as though all the power he'd used so far had been drawn from his own bones. He felt quite hollowed out, yet still the spiral had not solidified to protect them. Why not? *Was* Jal-Nish blocking him until he could get all his forces into place?

Colm, who was balanced on the tip of the obelisk, drenched in frozen blood and frosted fragments of bladder-bat, could barely hold his sword arm up. The creatures kept coming, and above them six flappeters flew in tight circles, waiting their chance. The advancing army was only a few hundred paces away, struggling through the trackless swamp. Another few minutes and they would be here.

'If you want a fight, Jal-Nish, you'll get one!' Flydd roared at the sky. 'You were never my equal in the old days and you're not now.'

'Don't provoke him,' Colm croaked. 'It's a hollow boast, anyway, since you all ran away from him ten years ago.'

'Do your own job and don't tell me how to do mine.'

Colm propped himself up on his sword, momentarily, then struck wearily at another bladder-bat.

'I need more power,' said Flydd. 'More and more and more, and curse the consequences.'

He staggered back to the freezing flame and thrust his

blade into it, praying that the metal could take the strain. The blade shrilled like hot iron thrust into a quenching trough, and as he returned he could feel its power dissolving the barrier that had been blocking him all this time. The spiral arms, now full of trapped fog, were starting to solidify. The one closest to the chthonic flame was almost set, though the other arms and the centre were still open.

Flydd climbed partway up the obelisk, whose upper two-thirds angled out the top of the dome. 'Colm! Get inside.'

'The flappeters are coming. I've got to hold them off.'

'You can't fight flappeters with a sword, and once the spiral sets, you'll be stuck outside.'

And so would Nish and Maelys, if they were still alive, but it was fruitless agonising about that. If he and Colm got away, at least they would have saved something from the fiasco, and given the God-Emperor a small kick in the teeth.

Colm slid down the obelisk and jumped in. Flydd traced a spiral in the air with the bent blade, and the arms began to set. The portal spell was finally working.

The sky palace dropped sharply and the advancing army broke into a run. Flydd laughed aloud. 'You're too late, God-Emperor!'

Now to open the way into the shadow realm. He called on more power, until the white knife wailed. The chthonic flame doubled in height, and redoubled, soaring a thousand spans into the heavens.

The spirals were setting like red crystal, the outside world thinning. A jag of light stabbed down from the sky palace, striking the eastern arm, but was reflected harmlessly away.

'The God-Emperor trembles,' Flydd gloated. 'He's terrified of the chthonic flame, an unknown power to him; and afraid of what I might do with it.' He raised his fists to the sky, white knife in hand. 'Be very afraid, God-Emperor!'

'Shut up!' cried Colm. 'You're begging fate to strike us down.'

'He fears the strong, Colm, but he *despises* the weak.'

Through the dome the chthonic flame glowed white, searing its way upwards as if to ice-weld the world of San-thenar to the endless void. Huge flakes of snow began to fall.

'Flydd?' choked Colm, shuddering. 'What have you done? It's out of control.'

'It'll have to burn itself out. I can't stop it.'

'Open the damned portal before the flame freezes us solid.'

'I thought you didn't want to go to the shadow realm?'

'I don't!'

'And neither do I,' Flydd muttered. 'But I'd sooner die there than give Jal-Nish the satisfaction.' The portal was coming. He could feel it, just out of reach, but he was still blocked from opening it.

Thump-crash. Below him, three soldiers pulled themselves up from the cavity at the base of the obelisk and began to dig their way out from under the dome. Others were trying to smash into the arms. They would fail but, if enough of them kept at it, and Jal-Nish maintained his strikes, they must eventually break through.

The Imperial Militia began to close the ring around them. Another booming cry rumbled down from the air palace.

'*ATTACK!*'

Flydd tried again, expecting to be blocked, but *fssssshh-htttt*. A shadowy opening began to form, though not in the centre of the spiral, where it should be. It was at the end of the arm to his right, though he could not see it clearly. He shivered and rubbed his eyes, his unease rising.

'What is it now?' said Colm.

'The portal should have formed at the obelisk. Why has it formed over there?'

Colm shrugged. 'What does it matter, as long as it works?'

'I don't suppose it does,' said Flydd. 'Come on.'

The outside was lit by a series of bright flashes coming down from the sky palace, and a tap-tapping sounded, as of a hammer on crystal. Afraid that the spiral was going to shatter under Jal-Nish's attack, he bolted up the curving arm, which was thick with fog. The bottom of the arm was below ground here, so he was running on mud and earth.

The arms curved around the obelisk twice, but it wasn't until he passed the terminus of another arm that he realised he'd gone up the wrong arm of the spiral.

He pressed his nose to the wall. At the end of the next arm, a clot of vapour was swirling in to a dark centre; it had to be the portal. He felt an overwhelming rush of relief, until something moved on the far side of it, human-shaped. Could it be the woman in red? It didn't move like her.

'Is that Jal-Nish?' said Colm.

'Don't think so,' Flydd grunted, now regretting his shouted challenge. If Jal-Nish stood between him and the portal, he'd failed. He couldn't fight the God-Emperor.

The mist thickened until Flydd couldn't see anything. But surely Jal-Nish wouldn't risk himself; he would have sent a powerful mancer to block the way.

As he ran back to the centre, each of Jal-Nish's blasts was like hammer blows that shook the spiral, and it was growing hot from all that expended power.

'It can't take much more, Colm. And neither can I.'

'I thought you said the spiral would lock everything out.'

'Any normal attack. Not an army with all the power of Reaper behind it.'

He reached the centre, where the portal should have formed, and entered the next arm, the correct one. Dozens of soldiers had pushed between the spiral arms and were attacking the sides; others had climbed on top and were trying to smash it in with hammers and war axes. They grimaced and brandished their weapons at him. He tried to ignore them, but more troops were running up all the time, along with robed battle mancers and grim, grey-skinned scriers with wisp-watchers on their backs. They would be sending everything they saw to Gatherer, and Jal-Nish would see it more clearly than if he were here.

Klarm appeared, pointing the brassy knoblaggie at him. Treacherous Klarm, and if he couldn't be trusted, no one could. Win or lose, you're all alone, Flydd.

Yellow light stabbed from the knoblaggie, to bounce harmlessly off the wall. Flydd put it out of mind and jogged on. Each spiral arm wrapped around the centre twice, so he had to make another two circles before he reached the end.

Running through the sticky mire was exhausting; he could barely lift his feet. He dropped back to a walk, following the right-hand wall so he would know how far he'd gone, and trying not to look at the hundreds of brutal faces lined up along the outside. He felt like a rat in a maze, with his nemesis awaiting him at the other end.

The fog was so thick here that he practically had to swim through it, swinging his arms and legs against its uncanny, clinging resistance. Flydd couldn't tell if Colm were still behind him; with the constant blows on the spiral he couldn't even hear his own thoughts. He passed a scarred face he recognised from the previous turn, then Klarm, who had his hands out as if pleading with him. Flydd turned his face away.

It was taking so long! A couple of minutes later he went past the same faces again, and then again, as though he were on a treadmill to nowhere. Jal-Nish's arts must have stretched the spiral arm out, or twisted it into an endless loop. Suddenly afraid, he broke into a run, squelching through the boggy mud, and finally broke into fresh, untrodden ooze. Whatever had been restraining him before had let him go, but why?

He was nearing the end of the arm, dread growing with every step. It was darker here, for the end was completely surrounded by troops, each man trying to be first to smash a way in and claim the prize. Even the strongest mancery could be overcome by brute force, if enough of it could be brought to bear. It was Jal-Nish's strength, and Flydd's weakness.

He went on, step by slow step, holding his knife out. Seeing a moving shadow ahead, he went for it, and the white tip of his blade was just an ell from the man's belly when he recognised him.

'Nish? What the blazes are you doing here?'

Nish managed a slurred grunt. His eyes were dull, his arms hung limp; he looked as though he'd been drugged, or spell-dazed. The mist swirled and only then did Flydd make out the baby-smooth arm around Nish's neck, and the long face marred by that black excrescence on his cheek. It hadn't been Jal-Nish blocking him, but Vivimord! Vivimord had stopped him from opening the portal until he could get into position to take it.

'Open it, Flydd,' he said quietly.

'So you can escape with Nish.' Flydd tasted the bitterness of abject failure. Why hadn't he realised who his real enemy was? 'I'll destroy us all before I give in to you.'

'No one goes through the agony of renewal only to throw it all away. I've beaten you, Flydd. Open the portal.'

How Flydd wanted to wipe the twisted smile off his face. 'You don't know me at all,' he spat.

He dared not attack Vivimord directly, for that would put Nish at risk. What if he blasted the portal wide open? It might create an opportunity to attack. The chance was slim but he had to take it.

Drawing the power of the chthonic flame from the white blade, he visualised the entrance to the shadow realm the way Rassitifer had taught him, and hurled power into the misty vortex behind Vivimord. It faded from black to pearl. Vivimord moved towards it, dragging Nish with him. He wasn't struggling; Nish hardly knew he was there.

Mist began to whirl into the vortex; the portal was creeping open, the shadow realm just a leap away. 'Colm?' Flydd said softly.

'Here,' came from directly behind him.

'Be ready for anything.'

Though Flydd had little experience of portals, he knew that no two were alike, and that it was impossible to predict what would happen when this one opened. Might it suck them through, or would there still be some barrier to be forced before they could enter the shadow realm?

'And after we go through,' he added, 'hang onto me.'

'Why?' said Colm.

'Because aftersickness will be so bad I might not be able to stand up.' Opening a portal required a stronger Art than he'd ever used before.

The portal opened with a roar and freezing air blasted out, churning the mist. Flydd, blown off balance, slipped and fell. Vivimord let go of Nish and somehow – Flydd had no idea how – tore the portal from his control.

Klarm's face appeared through the wall; he pressed his knoblaggie against it and strained with all his strength, but fruitlessly. He stared at the knoblaggie in dismay, then tried again. Nothing. Flydd's heart stopped for a good five seconds, for he knew what it meant. The chthonic flame was overwhelming all other powers and, if the tears failed, even for a second, it could be catastrophic.

The soldiers resumed their attack with greater fury. Flydd tried desperately to regain the portal but he'd done too much, too soon, with a body that still didn't feel like his, and he had nothing left.

And Vivimord was too strong; he'd been healed at the cursed flame and its power flowed in his veins; those black flames still dripped from his fingertips. He was stealing the portal, directing it to some unknown destination, and Flydd knew he'd never get it back.

In one last desperate effort he snatched Colm's sword and leapt at his enemy, but Vivimord turned aside, casually tossed a loop of mist over Flydd and pulled it tight around his neck.

Nish was given a hard shove in the back and disappeared

into the portal. He was gone; lost. With a tweak of Vivimord's fingers, the mist noose pulled ever tighter. Flydd dropped the sword and tried to force his fingers under the noose but there was nothing to grip; it was as intangible as the mist it had been made from, yet it was cutting into his neck and crushing his windpipe. It was the simplest of spells, one that a journeyman sorcerer could break, but in his powerless state Flydd could do nothing to save himself.

'Colm, help,' he gasped, falling to his knees, but Colm had a silvery mist-noose around his own throat.

With ironic salutes to Flydd, to Klarm and to the sky palace high above, Vivimord backed towards the portal. He'd won. But then, as he was about to step into it, the mist stirred on the other side of the vortex, at the tip of the spiral arm, and a battered, mud-covered apparition staggered out.

'Maelys?' Flydd subvocalised.

Vivimord looked up sharply, as if he'd sensed something, though Flydd still had the taphloid in his pocket and it must have partly shielded her aura.

Maelys had eyes for only one man. Her young features twisted, she sprang, raised a octopede fang high and stabbed it into the middle of Vivimord's back. He staggered and fell to one knee but she followed him down, pressing the fang in and twisting it as far as it would go.

'Die, you cur!' she gasped.

He swung at her but she squeezed a sac attached to the fang; yellow venom oozed out from around the wound in his back and he squealed like a pig in a slaughterhouse. One swinging fist struck her in the face, and as she went down, the long fang tore free.

Maelys collapsed, holding her jaw, which hung at an odd angle. Vivimord staggered two steps into the portal, his knees wobbling uncontrollably, and tried to close it behind him. The mist-nooses turned back to mist; Flydd could breathe again. He drew on the power of the chthonic flame – it really hurt this time – and tried to stop the portal from closing. If he could hold it for another minute the venom might bring Vivimord down. The zealot's left leg had buckled and his face was distorted in agony, but he fought back and the mist tightened around Flydd's throat again. He had to ignore it; had to hold the portal with his last breath. He strained but instead felt the most extraordinary sensation, as if the spiral were being pulled apart.

And it was. The four arms shifted slightly, then separated into a pair of two-armed spirals. He was in one, Vivimord and Nish in the other, and there was no way to get to them. Vivimord's spiral spun until it became a blur, and vanished.

'They're gone!' Flydd croaked, watching the mist noose drift away and dissolve back into the air. 'We've lost Nish now. By the time Vivimord is finished with him, there'll be nothing left.'

The hammering on the spiral, which had stopped during the struggle, resumed in greater fury.

'They're breaking through,' said Colm, rubbing his throat.

The red crystal wall was cracked in several places and could not last much longer. Flydd dragged a flask of chthonic fire from his pocket, unstoppered it and forced the remaining portal open a crack.

Not yet. I'm not ready.

There wasn't time to worry about voices in his head; the woman in red had been using him all this time. No more! He forced the portal wide open.

Noooooo! she screamed again; again too late.

A vast surge of force burned through him, as if he'd linked the tiny flame wisping up from the flask to the column of chthonic fire blasting into the sky. *I'm back!* Flydd thought. I'm a real mancer again. He took a step into the portal but, remembering how quickly Rassitifer had taken that fatal injury in the shadow realm, Flydd froze.

'Wass 'at?' mumbled Maelys, holding her jaw. Colm was staring up at the sky, open-mouthed.

Flydd made out a massed scream of terror, so loud that it penetrated the solid walls of the spiral, and looked out to see the soldiers, mancers, scriers, and even Klarm, running for their lives.

What had he done? A moving reflection flashed across the spiral and the dreadful realisation struck him. The sky palace, suddenly robbed of the power which held its enormous weight suspended in mid-air, was falling directly towards them, for the chthonic flame had overwhelmed the power of the tears which held it up.

'Get out of the way, Flydd!' shrieked Colm, heaving Maelys to her feet and trying to push into the portal.

The army was doomed, and Klarm as well, for the sky palace was going to smash the centre of the plateau to smithereens and blast everything off it in a hurricane of shattered rock. Not even the spiral could resist that kind of impact. Nothing could.

But still Flydd hesitated. Without his own Art, he would be practically defenceless in the shadow realm. He could not use the Arts he'd been given by the woman, for they relied on the flame, and once he passed through the portal it would be beyond his reach.

'Flydd!' Colm screeched.

Was a quick death here worse than a lingering one in the shadow realm? He had only seconds to choose. Suddenly, with a scream of agony, she was in his mind, a part of him as she had been once before.

Thrice-cursed fool. You'll owe me a lifetime of service for this.

Flydd felt hot threads weaving back and forth across the centre of his head, as if those parts of his mind separated since renewal were finally being rejoined, and he felt more of his Art return.

Go, you fool. I'm with you now.

The sky palace was hurtling down, directly at them. He wasn't sure he had enough Art to survive the shadow realm, but she was within him still; *she* might. Holding the two flasks of chthonic fire out, he drew power and opened the portal the way he had learned from her.

As Flydd stumbled through, he looked up. Moments before impact, a wing-ray lifted off from the deck of the sky palace, a small figure riding on its back. Jal-Nish was abandoning his army, his servants and even his mancers, and running for his life.

The portal opened all the way and Colm leapt through with Maelys. Flydd lurched after her, and the last he saw of Mistmurk Mountain was the sky palace thundering towards the flame, driving it back down the monstrous shaft, then slamming into the plateau so hard that it rifted it from one side to the other. The scene was obscured in a pall of mud, steam, dust and the pulverised bodies of the God-Emperor's entire Imperial Militia, three thousand men.

Colm and Maelys were tumbling head over heels ahead of him, carried towards the shadow realm's grim, thorn-wreathed entrance, through which Flydd could see shades swooping and revenants leering in anticipation. They looked even stronger than he'd imagined. He swallowed and tried to draw away; he wasn't ready. Neither his memories nor his Art were coming back quickly enough.

He felt her sigh of relief – *At last!* – as she went with him – but then her horror as she realised where he was going.

Not there! *What are you doing to me?*

Pain sheared through his skull; the portal was torn from his control again. No, he thought. Not this time. Whatever the woman in red wanted, he did not. He fought back but she beat him off, wrenching the portal out of his grip.

Way behind him he could just make out its distorted opening, wreathed in blasted chthonic fire. He drew on it and the portal was his again. It snapped shut and he felt her separate from him agonisingly, as if a healing wound had been torn open.

Noooooo! she screamed for the third time. *Not yet! Not there!*

Lightning flashed all around and the entrance to the shadow realm disappeared, replaced by utter blackness. Flydd felt more pain, worse than before, but this time it was her pain until her presence completely separated from him and he felt her spinning away, her control slipping. She was falling out of the portal, lost, gone.

He rolled over and over in the air. 'Colm? Maelys?'

No answer. He flashed by a woman's face, *her* face. She was clawing at a transparent wall from the other side, and he sensed her terrible anguish.

You've failed me, you fool.

'And you used me!' he snapped.

I saved you, she raged. *Do you think I went through all this so you could leave* me *behind?*

'What was I supposed to have done differently? Where are you, anyway?'

He was carried past and did not hear her reply, if she made one, and she faded from sight. He continued to fall through darkness for a long time, until, without warning, he went sliding across a smooth, cool surface and came to a halt not far from Colm. Maelys lay a few paces further on. A small pool of light bathed them, but beyond it he could see nothing.

'Are we in the shadow realm?' whispered Colm.

Flydd rolled onto his back. The floor was black and as hard and smooth as glass, and he knew where they were though he had never been here before. It was the place he'd seen in her scrying cup down at the abyssal flame.

Maelys sat up, holding her dislocated jaw with both hands. She frowned ferociously, then jerked hard and forced her jaw back into place, biting back tears of agony.

'Where are we?' said Colm, getting up. 'This doesn't look like the shadow realm. Not the way you described it.'

'I'm dreadfully afraid,' Flydd said haltingly, 'that we've ended up in a far worse place.'

'Where?' mumbled Maelys.

'The Nightland.'

'But,' said Colm, 'isn't that –?'

'It's the place where the greatest of all the Charon, Rulke, was imprisoned for a thousand years, and not even his genius, nor his mancery, could get him out.'

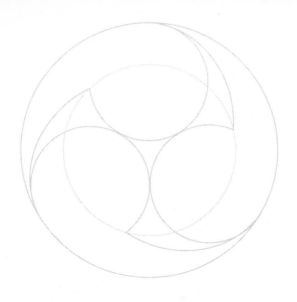

PART TWO

THE TOWER OF A
THOUSAND STEPS

TWENTY

Save for the roaring green flames, and later the hissing, spitting white ones, Nish knew little about Vivimord dragging him up the stairs and halls of Mistmurk Mountain and out onto the plateau. Once there, Nish saw the zealot glaring at him, and the needle pricks in the back of his hand stung venomously; he tried to run but his numb feet would not move; he fell but felt nothing as he hit the ground . . .

Later he remembered, though distantly, as if through a spinning hole, Maelys stabbing a curved fang into Vivimord's back and him squealing like a pig. Nish would have cheered, had he been able to speak.

His memories of the time after that were equally fragmentary, for Nish was too dazed by Vivimord's ensnaring spells. He vaguely recalled whirling through a black, empty space, then being pushed out into darkness and smelling the humid odour of rainforest. A river poured over rapids nearby, and people were talking. The portal was still open nearby; he could hear air rushing through it all the while.

Later he caught a glimpse of Vivimord, stripped to the waist, scrubbing frenziedly at the wound in his back. Nish's burned hand flared with pain, he gasped and an elderly woman bent over him and spooned something bitter into his mouth. Her face looked familiar, though he could not remember where he'd seen her before. She began dressing the burn on his hand . . .

Two peasants with dirt under their fingernails hauled him to the portal and he was carried to a stony hilltop where the wind blew wild and hot, though it was the middle of the night. The old woman was dressing his hand again, frowning at what she saw and muttering phrases over it. Despite her efforts it throbbed all the time, save where he'd rubbed Vivimord's blood into it. Those patches were cold, prickly and unbearably itchy, but his other hand was strapped to his chest and he could not scratch.

His wits felt dull; he was unable to follow any train of thought for more than a minute. The one thing Nish remembered clearly was that mortifying encounter with Maelys in the bedchamber. He'd thought she wanted him, and he had certainly desired her, until she broke Vivimord's enchantment and escaped. Clearly she, a slip of a girl, was a lot stronger than he was.

'Maelys,' he said, not realising that he was thinking aloud, 'how could I have been so wrong about you?'

'It's too late for her!' the zealot hissed in his ear. 'She *struck* me, Deliverer; she's doomed to the most agonising death-in-life I can come up with.'

Vivimord's teeth were bared, the blemish on his cheek looked purpler than ever, and he had a hand pressed to the fang wound. He winced, then slid his hand under his shirt and across his belly, where the skin crackled. Every day he seemed to be suffering more, and less able to endure it.

His eyes met Nish's. 'The octopede venom makes it so much harder to bear, and I have no one to salve my ruined skin. Curse her for robbing me of Phrune as well; curse Maelys for everything.'

Nish didn't care how much Vivimord suffered – the more the better – but he thought it wise to hide his feelings. 'I'm sure the old healer can soothe –'

'No *woman* can ease my pain!' He pressed the fang wound again, gasped, 'Blood!' and turned away.

Nish forgot him instantly, for he was still thinking about Maelys. After escaping Vivimord's enchantment she must have killed an octopede, whatever that was, torn out its fang and tracked Vivimord all the way up to the obelisk – to save him, Nish? Was there nothing she could not do? She put his own resolve, his own courage, in the shade.

I can't fight him, Nish thought despairingly. I haven't got the strength any more. He'd lost the moral courage that had previously sustained him, some time during the decade of his imprisonment, and no matter how much he fought, no matter how many times he struggled to the surface, hopelessness always pulled him under again. Like a sot trying to give up the drink, his resolve would last for a day, a week, even a month, but sooner or later his self-doubt became insurmountable and the temptation to give up, irresistible.

Several days after his abduction he was carried from the gate onto a patch of tough blue grass between two standing stones; a third slab was precariously angled across them. They were high in a mountain range Nish did not recognise and the air was mild and dry. The peasants set him in the shade and the old woman began to change his dressings, muttering a useless healer's charm over his hand and *tcching* under her breath. Nish let out a groan of misery, for he'd grown so used to her that he hardly noticed she was there.

'What is it, Deliverer?' she said quietly.

She hadn't spoken to him before but now he recognised her voice. She was the old healer who had helped to rally the Defiance to him, months ago. Nish could not remember her name.

'I can't do it. I've tried to fight Father and Vivimord, but I fail every time. Even that victory I had over Father's army months ago was a lie. *He let me win*, just to undermine me even further. I can't fight on; I've got nothing left.'

Her eyes were clouded yet he felt that she saw him clearly. She looked over her shoulder, laid her seamed hand upon his brow and said quietly, 'You must fight him, for the world needs you and only you can save it. Gather your strength, and I'll help you when I can.'

Nish couldn't speak; the offer was as extraordinary as it was unexpected, and absurd. The healer was a spry old thing but she couldn't be far off eighty. She could not take on the mighty, any more than he could.

'I have a lover younger than you,' she said with an impish smile. 'Don't tell me what I can or cannot do; don't even think it.'

He remembered the smile. 'You were the seer who touched me that day after we escaped from the labyrinth below Tifferfyte. You helped to form the Defiance.'

'Indeed I did; my name is Tulitine, and without me there would have been no Defiance, for I read you and certified that you were indeed the son of the God-Emperor. And I convinced the people to rally to you.'

'In Monkshart's name,' he said bitterly. 'You were either his servant or his dupe.'

'Always in *your* name, never in his. I had my doubts about Monkshart then, and subsequent events have confirmed them, but at the time there was no choice. No one else could have pulled the Defiance together in time.'

'And now he's in charge again.'

'Only until you're ready to take control, Nish. The moment you can find the strength within you, I'll help you to bring him down.' She looked over her shoulder again and lowered her voice. 'And it may not be long.'

Nish snorted. 'That time will never come. I'm a hollow man.'

'With an iron core. It's a little rusty at the moment, a trifle bent, yet once you learn to stiffen it, as you had to during the war, it will support you even in the worst of times. Remember your past, Nish.'

'That only makes it worse.'

'Not the heroic past you use to beat yourself with, but the time before that, when you were a craven youth, a greedy, unpleasant young man who had to learn to reach for the heights rather than wallow in the mire. Think about that youth, and remember how he turned himself into a man, and a hero. And only then, remind yourself of your destiny, *and go after it.*'

She was right. Too often Nish had compared his present tormented self to the commanding hero he'd been at the end of the war, and could only see how far he'd fallen. Yet when he thought about the youth he'd been before the hero – an unhappy prentice artificer in a distant manufactory, brutally flogged for his crimes – it was clear that he'd risen a long way. And if he'd done it once, surely he could rise again, if not by himself as he'd always tried to do in the past, refusing all aid, then with the help of those allies he had left.

He looked up at her wrinkled old face. 'You're right to chide me, Lady Tulitine –'

'I am no lady,' she said with a throaty chuckle, 'but go on.'

'I will do it!' Nish took her hand and pulled himself upright on his litter. She did not let go and, with her hand gripping his, Vivimord's hold slipped fractionally and he felt a surge of courage.

'Never again!' he exclaimed. She raised a white eyebrow. 'Never again will I succumb to the despair that is my enemy's closest ally,' Nish said fiercely. 'I will pretend to be compliant until I'm ready to strike, but all the time I will be working to undermine Vivimord and bring him down. And when he's gone, I *will* become the Deliverer, if that's the only way to topple Father from his throne, but I'll only do it on my terms. Yet should I succeed, I will not take his place. I dare not.'

She looked deep into his eyes, her own cloudy eyes reading him and gauging his resolve. 'Yes, you can do it, Nish, and you must, for the world is in terrible danger, and neither Vivimord nor your father has the power to save it. You might not succeed; the odds are against you and the fates give you just one slender chance, but you have to take it. Sleep now; gather your strength, but give no hint of your resolve. When he comes, pretend that you're fully under his enchantment until I say otherwise.'

'Where is he taking me?'

'I won't know until we get there.'

'What's happened to Flydd and Colm? And Maelys?'

'They are in dire peril and I don't know if they'll survive. You can't depend on them, Nish. It's all up to you now.'

And she went out.

Nish was taken though the portal twice more, its entry and exit always in hot lands where the sun stood vertically at midday. They had to be in the far north of Lauralin, or whatever lands lay beyond it. He was in no hurry to reach their final destination, for whenever his prickling hand told him that Vivimord was approaching, Nish found his resolve shrinking to nothing. Only when the zealot had gone, and Tulitine was close by, could Nish find the strength to oppose him; to go on.

Finally the portal opened on a sloping hill at the edge of a sweeping curve of rainforest, and Vivimord stepped through, grimacing and rubbing his chest. The peasants carried Nish out and Tulitine followed. Forested mountains lay all around, while down the slope a pocket handkerchief of cleared land was covered in thick, blue-green grass. A pretty town, its cottages and meeting hall made of rough-sawn timber, nestled in the curve of a stream. It was raining gently, but the rain was blood-warm; patches of mist drifted on the mountain slopes and the air was so thick with humidity that it was stifling.

Vivimord's face was creased with pain lines which grew deeper every day. How much longer could he endure it, Nish wondered, without Phrune to salve his terrible injuries.

The zealot touched Nish on the forehead. 'Rise, Deliverer. You're safe from your father at last.'

But not from you! 'Where are we?' Nish said haltingly, pretending to be groggy from the enchantment.

'One of the few places on Santhenar where your father cannot reach. Or at least, where he has not taken the trouble to do so. The hidden land of Gendrigore.'

'Gen-drig-or-ay,' Nish repeated. 'Never heard of it.'

'It lies at the northernmost tip of Lauralin, bracketed between the cities of Taranta and Fankster. Gendrigore is a peninsula but it might as well be an island, since the only way to reach it is via the track across the mighty mountain chain called The Spine, which separates Gendrigore from Crandor and the rest of Lauralin. This land cannot be approached by sea; it is entirely surrounded by cliffs, and the currents that race past them are impossible to navigate. It is equally difficult to come at by flappeter or air floater on account of the treacherous updraughts, the deadly storms, the exploding volcanoes and the impenetrable, clinging mists.'

'It sounds like the end of the world,' said Nish.

'It's a poor land, far from civilisation; Gendrigore has no cities to speak of, and few resources save wood and grass, neither of which can be carried out over The Spine.'

'Father will still have spies and watchers here.'

'A few, but it's as good a place as any to plot the return of the Deliverer.' He gave Nish a piercing glance.

The healed skin on the back of Nish's hand prickled, but the enchantment must have been weaker today, for he felt a wild urge to strike the zealot in the face. Nish restrained himself; he must give nothing away until Tulitine said the word. He trusted her, and until then he would be compliance itself.

'Indeed,' he said. 'I know my duty to the world. Father must be overthrown and I'm going to do it.'

'Excellent! But you let me down in the mountain,' said Vivimord, rubbing his chest and screwing up his face.

'Why would you not mate with Maelys and give me what I wanted? Surely you did not find her *that* unpleasing?'

Nish, resenting the implication about her, said stiffly, 'It was Maelys who fled, not I.'

'Yet I sensed reluctance in you . . . and when I sent young women to satisfy you months ago, you rejected them all. The Deliverer must be seen to consort with women, Cryl-Nish. Nothing else will do, *in public*. Yet, ah, if your private tastes lie in another direction –'

'They don't!' snapped Nish. 'I was grieving the loss of my beloved Irisis.'

'After ten years?' Vivimord exclaimed. 'That is beyond the call –'

'Time stood still while I was in Father's prison. I could not truly grieve until I had my freedom, but I'm done with that now. I've accepted what I cannot change; it is time to live again.'

'Splendid! I'm sure the young women of Gendrigore would fight to besport themselves with the Deliverer. May I send them to your bed?'

Lust flared and, despite everything, Nish could not resist it. Besides, he reasoned, somewhat conveniently, Tulitine had told him to be compliant until she gave the word. 'You may,' Nish said curtly, 'as long as they in no way resemble Irisis.'

The days went by, Nish occupying himself with long walks through the surrounding forest and along the nearby sea cliffs, savouring the quiet and solitude. He had regained his strength and health now, save for his burned hand, which was stiff and still painful. He did not think he would ever have full use of it, and whenever Vivimord approached, the skin prickled and he felt that familiar dullness behind his temples which told him that the zealot was reinforcing his enchantment.

Vivimord was, however, having unexpected difficulty in recruiting a new Defiance. The people of Gendrigore had welcomed Nish and Tulitine, but they were suspicious of the brooding zealot and few would listen to his rhetoric, which elsewhere Nish had seen sway multitudes, or his subtle threats. They were a peaceful folk who had little interest in the outside world. They had heard of the Deliverer, of course, but the God-Emperor did not interfere in their lives and they saw no compelling reason to march against him.

Vivimord's manner grew ever more agitated; there were black circles around his eyes and he was constantly touching the wound on his back, and the crisped skin of his chest and belly, as if the pain could never be assuaged.

One night Nish was shocked out of sleep by a furious bellowing. 'Let me go! Let me go at once, or I'm going straight to the Deliverer.'

It was still dark, though it could not be long until dawn. He rolled onto his back, frowning. Vivimord's voice had lacked its usual arrogance; he sounded like a man caught out and trying to bluster his way through.

'We caught him blood-handed, Mayor,' said a male voice Nish did not know. 'It were poor Tildy the milk lass this time – throat cut, just like the other two. Swine was on his knees beside her body, catchin' her blood as it were apumpin' out, and arubbin' it over his face and chest. Shoulda' took his head clean off his shoulders. I shoulda' done that.'

Nish sat up, feeling sick, and began to dress. A youth had been killed on their second night here, and a young woman the night after that, and both had their throats cut. Still under the enchantment, he hadn't thought much about the murders, but the accusation made sense. Previously, Vivimord had only been able to obtain relief from the agony of his ruined skin, seared by the touch of the tears when he'd saved Jal-Nish at the battle of Gumby Marth all those years ago, by covering it in tissue leather made from the flawless skin of a youth or a girl.

Phrune's blood sacrifice at the cursed flame had restored

Vivimord and given him the smooth skin of a child, but only hours later Maelys had attacked him with her taphloid, striking him on the cheek and burning that egg-sized excrescence there. In his agony he'd fallen directly onto Reaper, which had blistered his chest and belly like crackling on a roast pig.

Blood must be the only relief left to him; fresh blood. And since Phrune was no longer around to give up his own, Vivimord had been stalking the innocent and defenceless.

Nish thrust the flap of his tent aside and strode out barefoot onto the wet grass. Two men held pitch-covered torches high, the wood flaring and spitting sparks in all directions. Another two, burly woodsmen, were dragging Vivimord behind them, tied hand and foot to a long pole. Its lower end cut through the sodden grass, leaving a waver-ing trail of mud in its wake. The zealot's face was stained with red; so was his shirt, and the excrescence on his cheek was thick with smeared blood, as if he'd anointed himself there. Townsfolk and farmers ran towards them from all directions, carrying torches.

'Deliverer!' Vivimord spoke in his most commanding tone, and there was much of the Art in it too. 'There's been a dreadful mistake. Order them to set me free; the very future of the Defiance depends on it.'

Nish's hand prickled and his forebrain went as dull as if he'd been drinking all night. He could feel Vivimord's Art beating at him, and the familiar shrinking inside. He didn't have the strength to fight him; and besides, he now real-ised, the accusation had to be a terrible mistake.

He was about to say so when Tulitine laid her hand on his left arm. 'Don't listen to his lies, Nish. This is the moment you have been preparing for all this time; the hour when *you* must take command.' Her damp grey hair strag-gled about her shoulders, and she looked haggard, though her gaze was as resolute as ever.

Barquine, the mayor, came running up with his gilded rod of office. He studied the prisoner, smacking the rod into the palm of a meaty hand. He was a cheerful, stocky, moustachioed man who had made Nish welcome from the beginning, but he did not look cheerful now.

The pressure in Nish's mind eased and he knew that Tulitine was right. Now was the hour, and if he could just resist Vivimord's enchantments, the zealot was finished. I can resist him, Nish told himself. I must *and I will*.

'Deliverer,' Vivimord said commandingly, 'order these simple fools to let me go. They've got the wrong man.'

He must have employed more Art this time, for again Nish began to disbelieve the charges, and even Barquine seemed to be wavering. The torchbearers formed a circle around the prisoner on his pole, and the townsfolk a larger circle around that, frowning and muttering among themselves.

'What is this?' Barquine held his rod of office across his chest like a shield, and his knuckles were white. 'Why have you trussed up the Deliverer's most trusted advisor?'

'We found –' began the taller of the woodsmen.

'You cannot touch me!' hissed Vivimord. 'I am the Deliverer's man and he is a guest in your country; therefore the laws of Gendrigore do not apply to me. Order them to release me, Cryl-Nish.'

It was hard to resist his entreaty; Nish felt like a sapling bending before the gale of Vivimord's Art, and if he tried to fight it he would be torn apart. But Nish met Tulitine's eye and remembered what she'd said about the core of steel within him; rusty on the outside but still strong at the centre. He imagined it running up his backbone, stiffening it, and spoke deliberately, precisely.

'The laws apply to you if I say they do.' Nish folded his arms across his chest and prayed for the strength to defy his enemy.

Vivimord reeled on his pole; the bloody excrescence on his cheek swelled. 'Deliverer!' he said warningly.

Tulitine touched Nish's right shoulder; the pressure eased. 'And I say they do!' Nish burst out while he still had

211

the strength to speak. 'Mayor Barquine, I place Vivimord's fate in Gendrigore's hands.'

Barquine inclined his head in acknowledgement. 'What are the facts of the matter?' he asked the men holding the pole.

'Since the second slayin', four nights ago, we took it upon ourselves to keep watch,' said the shorter of the original two torchbearers, a burly man clad in nothing but knee-length canvas pants. He had the muscles of a blacksmith or a bull wrestler, and his chest was covered in black hair with small charred and frizzed patches burnt through it.

Definitely a blacksmith, Nish thought.

'We heard a cry, down behind the old dairy,' the smith went on, 'and caught the devil at it. He had poor Tildy down, her throat cut from ear to ear, and as the innocent blood pumped from her he was arubbin' it over his face and belly, and acryin' out like a man doin' the business with a woman, if you take my meaning.'

'That's a lie!' Vivimord roared. He must have realised that he was losing command of them, for he attempted to draw himself upright on the slanted pole and said, with most of his old authority intact, 'It was *I* who found that man at it, on my morning constitutional.' He pointed a bloodstained finger at the smith. 'He took the girl by force, then killed her to avoid being found out. It is he who must be put to trial, not I.'

This time there was such Art in his voice that Nish was swayed, and so were all the townsfolk. He could see their faces hardening, their eyes swinging from Vivimord to the burly blacksmith. Nish *knew* that most of Vivimord's power came from his Art of rhetoric, but could not bring himself to disbelieve.

He was about to order Vivimord released when Tulitine said quietly, 'Vivimord is covered in blood, yet the blacksmith hasn't a trace on him. How could he cut the girl's throat without getting blood all over him?'

'He did it from behind,' said Vivimord. 'After he'd had his lustful way with her.'

'There would still be blood on his knife hand.'

'Not if he were skilled at killing. Not if he were quick.'

'You know a lot about the business of killing.' Tulitine's voice was so low that everyone had to strain to hear, but it was all the more effective for that.

'I fought at the God-Emperor's right hand during the war against the lyrinx.'

There was a sharp intake of breath from the crowd.

'And perhaps you serve him still,' Tulitine said silkily. 'Blacksmith, take us down to the body.'

The smith let go of the pole, which was taken by another man, and led them silently across the sodden grass to the stream which partly encircled the town, and thence along it to a roofless stable set among tall trees, its wooden slab walls sagging with age and rot. Within a set of cow bails, on the manure-covered earth, lay the sad remains of Tildy the milking girl. Beside her body was an overturned stool; a dangling rope was still tied to the bails, where the beast she had been milking at the time of her death had broken away.

'Keep back.' Tulitine bent to inspect the body, the patterns of blood, and the footmarks on the ground. 'The girl has not been taken, by force or otherwise. Her killer came up behind her and cut her throat while she was milking. And you're the only man with blood on him, Vivimord.'

'The killer must have washed himself in the stream,' said Vivimord, straining to use his Art, but it no longer seemed to be working.

'There are no marks down the bank. No one has washed themselves here today.'

'Further along, then. He could have bathed anywhere.'

'There hasn't been time; the body is still warm. And the cry was heard, when?' Tulitine wasn't looking at the blacksmith, but at the taller man holding the pole.

'Not half an hour ago,' he replied. He was dark featured

213

and prematurely balding. 'And we found the knife he used to kill poor little Tildy.' He held out a wavy-bladed weapon made from black metal. It was smeared with damp blood.

'The knife is his,' said a voice from the crowd. 'Vivimord always wore it on his right hip as he strutted about our town like an arrogant rooster, knocking honest, hard-working people out of his path.'

'Someone stole it last night,' Vivimord said weakly. The power of his voice was diminishing with every new piece of evidence, as if he was losing confidence in his Art. Tulitine now stood tall, her old eyes blazing, fighting him all the way.

'There are bloody fingermarks on the hilt,' said the balding man. 'And look at his hands – they're huge. I'll bet you can match the finger marks to him.'

Two men forcibly folded the fingers of Vivimord's right hand around the hilt, and everyone crowded around. His fingers fitted the blood marks perfectly.

'It proves nothing,' said Vivimord. 'Lots of men in the town have big hands.'

'Not like yours!' said the balding man. 'We've got worker's hands. Your fingers are creepy, like a long-legged spider.'

'And there's blood under his nails,' said Tulitine. 'The girl's blood.'

'I bent over her,' said Vivimord, 'trying to save her life.'

'Any man who saw as much death in the war as you did would have known that Tildy's wound was fatal. Draw up his shirt, lads.'

'Get away from me!' Vivimord's eyes were darting this way and that. 'I can't bear to be touched.'

'Yet you held your victims down while you cut their innocent throats from behind. Do it.'

The balding man drew Vivimord's shirt up, all the way; it made a tearing sound. The townsfolk surged forwards again. His chest and stomach were thickly coated with dried blood, and where the bloodstained shirt had been torn away from his skin, it was revealed to be hideously thickened and scarred, with crisscrossing cracks that wept clear yellow fluid.

'Well, Nish – er, Deliverer,' said Barquine. 'The evidence is clear against Vivimord, and he is your man. What are you going to do about his crime?'

TWENTY-ONE

'He's not my man,' said Nish. 'He brought me here, under duress.'

'Yet you're known as the leader of his Defiance.'

'Deliverer!' Vivimord extended his bound arms as far as they would go and ratcheted up his Art. 'This accusation is a vicious lie. An enemy has set me up for this crime, to prevent you from ever casting the blasphemous God-Emperor down. You know you cannot succeed without me.'

Nish felt his confidence faltering, for it could be true. Jal-Nish might have set this up – was there any place on Santhenar his power did not reach? And what if Nish did need Vivimord to help overthrow his father? For the good of the suffering people of the world, he could ignore this one crime, couldn't he? After all, Tildy was dead; it didn't matter to her.

'I – I don't know. I must think for a moment.'

'Then think swiftly,' snapped Barquine. 'And not of your bonds with this man, whatever they may be, nor your goal to overthrow your father. Think only of justice for poor Tildy, who did no one any harm.'

Nish nodded stiffly and walked into the forest. Dawn was breaking. He knew what had to be done, deep down, but what if he were wrong?

'You've dealt out death aplenty in battle, Nish, and I dare say slept soundly afterwards. Why do you shy at delivering justice?'

Tulitine's voice came from the deep gloom between two gnarled trees which leaned towards each other to form an inverted V.

Nish jumped. 'I *will not* become my father.'

'I never heard that what Jal-Nish meted out was justice.'

'You know what I mean.'

'I don't believe I do.'

'Father has tempted me unbearably, over and again. You cannot know how he whispers in my mind, offering me the things I want most in all the world.'

'I know exactly what you want, Nish. You long for wealth and authority, the love of beautiful women, and most of all, respect. You want people to look up to you for all you've achieved, but you're terrified of failure, and of their contempt.'

His stomach clenched. 'How do you know me so well? Are you a sorcerer who can extract the secrets of the innermost mind?'

'You said it all in your fever, months ago. And I can read your every thought on your face, and in what you say and do. Or don't do – like dealing with Vivimord now you have the chance.'

Nish ignored that. Before he could accept her help he had to confess his deepest desire and his greatest failing – the one which, were it offered to him again, he did not think he could refuse. That's where he'd gone wrong last time. He'd kept it secret and it had grown until it almost overpowered him.

'Father holds Irisis's perfectly preserved body in a glass coffin in his palace of Morrelune, and he told me that, if I came back to him, he would restore her to me.'

Tulitine stiffened in the gloom, then reached out and put a hand on his shoulder. 'Can the Profane Tears give

217

him the power to reach into the shadow realm, and even below that?' she said thickly. 'It cannot be – no one can come back from death. *No one!*'

She was shaken, which gave Nish pause for thought. Flydd had also said that it was impossible to raise the dead, but what if Jal-Nish *could* restore Irisis to him? His heart soared at the thought, even as he recoiled in self-disgust for being seduced by it.

'Necromanty is the greatest abomination of all, and yet you're swayed by what it can give you,' Tulitine said icily. 'Be very, very careful, Nish. I'd thought better of you. If you can consider such depravity, you're closer to becoming your father than I'd realised.'

'That is why I shrink from dispensing justice to Vivimord,' he said quietly. 'Because I fear what will come of it.'

'How should justice be dispensed, Nish?'

Nish hesitated, for he knew she was going to disagree with him, and why, but it had to be said. 'In Vivimord's case, deep in the forest and well away from watching eyes. A swift slash across the throat, the way he killed the girl, then a pyre to burn the body to ashes, and the ashes scattered to the winds.'

'You are very wrong if you think justice can be done in secret. Justice must be public, and impartial, else it looks like revenge and only inspires more killing.'

'If it's done publicly, Father will hear of it; he has spies everywhere, even here. He will make Gendrigore suffer a thousand times over for the justice meted out to Vivimord.'

'But he and Vivimord are enemies.' Tulitine came out from behind the trees.

'Yet Vivimord once saved Father's life, at great cost to himself, and Father does not forget such things.'

'If you deal with Vivimord in secret, Gendrigore will believe that you let a depraved murderer go out of weakness. That could fatally undermine the Deliverer.'

'Are you trying to talk me out of it?'

'I merely point out the consequences. It's up to you to make the choice, and you must do it at once.'

'I dare not kill him as he deserves, Tulitine. You know how power tempts me. I dare not take one single step on the corrupt path. I *will not* become my father.' Nish put all thoughts of Irisis firmly behind him. 'Yet neither can Vivimord be allowed to go unpunished.'

He trudged back to the scene of the murder, oppressed by the thought that, whatever his choice, ill would come of it. He walked up to the mayor, looked him in the eye and said in a carrying voice, 'Vivimord's crime was against Gendrigore, not me. He will be tried according to the laws of Gendrigore.'

Vivimord protested his innocence all the way back to the town green, and exerted his Art ever more powerfully, until Nish felt dazed from it, and ordered that the men dragging the pole have their ears blocked, and everyone else keep out of earshot. He stayed well behind, and once away from the zealot's influence Nish had no doubt that Vivimord was guilty.

'What form will the trial take?' he asked Barquine on the way.

'In matters such as this the accused is tried by ordeal,' said Barquine. 'If he survives, he is acquitted and will be expelled from Gendrigore.'

'And if he does not survive?'

'Then clearly he was guilty.'

Swift, summary justice, and Vivimord was such a monster that Nish could not disagree. And yet . . .

'You look troubled,' said the mayor. 'Do you doubt our justice?'

'Not at all,' Nish said hastily. 'The law is the law, and I know, from experience, Vivimord's character. Few will regret his passing, if he is convicted. But I should warn you that he was once the right-hand man of the God-Emperor –'

'What is that to us?'

'And Vivimord saved Jal-Nish's life. If he is harmed, the God-Emperor could well seek retribution.'

'I see.' The mayor paced off across the grass, mud squelching up between his bare toes.

Nish watched him go, feeling anxious for these kindly people. They had treated him well, yet, isolated here by cliff and mountain and impenetrable forest, they could not imagine the depravity of those who fought to control and dominate the outside world. Jal-Nish might well hate Vivimord for his betrayal; might well seek to kill him to end the threat to his own reign; yet if Gendrigore put Vivimord to death, it would be made to pay. Nish wished he'd carried out his original intention, but it was too late now.

Barquine was gone a long time. Perhaps he was consulting the town elders. The sun had risen before he came striding back, anxious but determined.

'The laws of Gendrigore stand,' he said abruptly. 'The Spine has protected us for twice a thousand years and we do not fear your God-Emperor. Bring the prisoner to the sea cliffs for trial.'

Vivimord was dragged off, bound to his pole, cursing them in a low voice. Again Nish felt the power of the zealot's mancery, and feared he might yet sway the peasants to let him escape.

'I would stop his mouth,' Nish said quietly to Barquine. 'Vivimord's chief sorcery is in his voice, and few people can resist for long.'

'I can feel it working on me.' Barquine gave the order and Vivimord's mouth was filled with rags so he could not utter a sound, then two gags were bound tightly over them. 'They will have to be removed for the ordeal, Nish. The trial must be fair. The accused must be allowed to speak.'

He strode off. The men dragged Vivimord towards a path through the forest, in the direction of the sea cliffs. The townsfolk followed.

Tulitine came up beside Nish. 'Would you take my arm, Nish? I'm feeling my age this morning.'

Nish did so. 'What is a trial by ordeal?'

'It's an old form of justice, long abandoned in more *civilised* lands,' she said as they headed after everyone else. 'Some say that proving a man guilty or innocent by ordeal is just like tossing a coin, but I think otherwise. Destiny also sits at the judgment table and, given a choice between the ordeal and trial by the corrupt jurors of the God-Emperor, I know which I'd choose.'

After walking for half a league or so, they emerged from the forest onto a sloping strip of land covered in scrubby, thick-leaved bushes and small trees, then onto a band of grass and herbs; beyond that was the bare rock of the cliff edge. The sun was just visible over the forest behind them. At least a hundred people had already assembled on the rock and more were coming along the cliffs, and emerging from other paths through the forest. There were storms out to sea and lightning flashed along the horizon.

Nish smelt salt and rotting seaweed, and heard the crash of waves breaking on the cliffs far below, and the echoing boom as the swell rolled into sea caves. The sky was overcast and looked like rain, but then, it always looked like rain in Gendrigore.

A number of tall tripods were mounted along the cliff edge, made from tree trunks. Each had a wooden arm extending out over the edge, from which was suspended, on a plaited rope, a large wooden basket with a bamboo floor and an umbrella-shaped bamboo roof. Each rope ran up, over a rolling block at the end of the arm, and down to a hand winch fixed to one of the legs of the tripod.

'They're fishing baskets,' said Tulitine. 'The fisherwomen are wound down in their baskets until they're a few spans above the water. They lower their lines and crab pots into the water, and wait.'

'Doesn't sound like much of a life,' Nish murmured.

'Life is what you make of it. They can talk to each other, watch the ever-changing seas and the colours of the sky, lie back and think, sleep. What more could anyone want?'

'It's very exposed.'

'The rain is warm here; and the breezes mild.'

'What if the rope breaks, or a gale dashes them against the cliff?'

'Then they'll die, as we all must some day,' she said sharply. 'Life is dangerous, Nish, whether you're a cliff fisherwoman of Gendrigore or a lapsed hero on the run from an all-powerful father and his own crippling self-doubt.'

He avoided her eye. 'How does the trial by ordeal work?'

'I expect we'll find out soon enough.'

The trial proved simple and dignified. When everyone had assembled, the mayor simply said, 'Let the trial of Vivimord, also known as Monkshart, begin.'

Two sturdy, black-haired young women swung the arm of the nearest tripod in; a third, who could have been their mother, wound the winch and lowered the hanging basket to the ground. A bamboo door was unfastened and swung open. The three women joined a fourth, who was small, old and wiry – the grandmother, perhaps. They untied Vivimord from the pole, keeping his wrists and ankles bound, and his mouth stopped.

'The trial is carried out by those most injured by the crime,' said Tulitine. 'In this case, the women of Tildy's family.'

They hauled Vivimord to the basket, his feet dragging, and pushed him inside. He did not deign to struggle, though his dark eyes shot apocalyptic fury at them. Never had Vivimord been treated with such contempt, and he could not bear it.

The women said no word as they followed him inside, lashed his wrists to the side of the basket and fixed a thin rope around his waist. The other end was tied to the floor. The youngest woman, and the oldest, remained inside and closed the door. The other two began to raise the basket with the winch.

It took many turns of the winch handle to lift it but they did not falter for a moment.

'It is a matter of pride that they do not give way to human weakness during the trial,' said Tulitine. 'No pain, no weariness may delay the ordeal, for that would be an ill omen.'

'For someone who didn't know what was going on a while ago, you're very well informed,' sniffed Nish.

'I spend more time watching and listening, and less talking.'

Her acid tongue reminded him of Flydd, and again he wondered what had happened to him and Maelys, but that was fruitless.

Once the basket was several spans above the ground, the winders locked the winch and heaved on ropes to swing the tripod arm, and the basket, out over the cliff. It began to swing back and forth in the wind. They tied the arm in place and began to lower the basket towards the sea. The work was easier now but they kept up the same steady pace at the winch.

It took a good half hour before the basket was lowered to the point where the ordeal would take place, some fifty spans below them and a few spans above a huge, swirling whirlpool, one of a line of three formed between clusters of toothed rocks by a racing current. This whirlpool was ten spans across, and two or three deep, and its perimeter was flecked with creamy foam.

The women in the basket raised their right hands. The women at the winch locked it, then signalled to the mayor with their closed fists. Barquine gestured to the assembled townsfolk along the cliffs, drew his head back and walked to the brink. After studying the basket, the whirlpool, the sea and the sky, he held out his right hand, palm downwards.

Nish edged closer to the brink. He did not like cliffs, but he wasn't going to take his eyes off Vivimord for an instant. The two women cut the ropes around the prisoner's ankles, and his wrists, and opened the door. The older woman held Vivimord's knife pressed against his back while the younger cut the gags. They were taking no chances with him.

Vivimord spat out the rags and his roar of fury echoed up the cliff. He lunged at the older woman like a striking snake, trying to hurl her out the door. She must have expected it for she slashed him twice – once across the excrescence on his cheek, and again in a zigzag pattern down his scarred chest. Black burst from the excrescence like an exploding buboe; blood poured down his chest. She pressed the knife to his throat, her free arm hooked though the side of the basket, while the younger woman held him back with the rope.

'The symbolic cuts,' said the mayor. 'A cheek for a throat, if you like, yet he lives so that justice can be done.'

'Jal-Nish owes his life to me,' Vivimord bellowed, using no rhetoric this time, just naked, quivering rage. The back of Nish's hand throbbed. 'He once swore an oath that he would never see me harmed, and he will send an army to avenge this insult. Jal-Nish will see Gendrigore wiped from the face of Santhenar, and its people sold into everlasting slavery.'

Vivimord threw out his arms as if to cast a mighty spell, but the younger woman sprang, kicked him in the back with both feet and sent him flying out. He plunged down towards the whirlpool, trailing the rope, and hit the water with a tremendous splash.

'If he is carried down and drowned,' said Tulitine, 'he is proven guilty. The rope is there so the body can be checked for signs of life. Should the whirlpool cast him out, he is judged innocent and the townsfolk will haul him up again.'

Vivimord bobbed up and floated for a second, spread-eagled on the spinning water like a four-legged spider, with the rope trailing up from the middle of his back. He slowly rotated towards the centre of the whirlpool, reached it and was sucked under in an instant.

One of the women in the basket let out more rope, until

it lay in loops on the whirling surface. Several loops were drawn under. Nish realised that he was holding his breath. No one spoke, anywhere along the cliffs. The wind had died away and the humidity suddenly became oppressive. How deliciously cool it would be in the water.

There came a concussive thud, then a pink dome of water formed at the centre of the whirlpool and expanded upwards until the whirlpool's motion had been cancelled and the sea surface went flat. The dome kept expanding, rising, and Nish made out a figure rising with it, propelled upwards at fantastic speed. Vivimord burst up from the water dome as if flung by a mighty hand, slowly rotating in the air and trailing blood from the stumps of his legs, which had been sheared off below the knees. His mouth was wide open and he was screaming, though no sound could be heard.

He described a spiral through the air like a seal thrown by a leviathan of the sea, the broken rope trailing behind him and his blood making a ragged curtain of red.

A vast creature thrust its streamlined black head up through the collapsing water dome. Nish could not tell if it were shark or whale, or something else entirely, but as Vivimord spun down it caught him by the thighs, shook him back and forth as a terrier shakes a rat and hurled him upwards, almost to the height of the fisherwomen's basket.

Vivimord came tumbling down again, screaming shrilly, and the sea creature snapped at him again. For a moment Nish thought its jaws were going to close over Vivimord's head, which would surely be proof of his guilt if any more were needed, but he gave a convulsive jerk, turned right side up, the vast maw slammed shut and bit him off above the knees.

The leviathan seemed to nod in the direction of the watchers on the cliff, then submerged silently. Vivimord, now making a dreadful cracked screech, spun in another loop, blood spraying from his stumps. His agony-etched eyes fixed on Nish, and the mayor, and Tulitine, and he cried, 'Revenge eternal, until the very pit of the abyss cracks open,' then smacked into the water.

Nish's restored hand burned as fiercely as if it had been thrust back into Reaper. At every point where Vivimord's blood had touched the water a cloud of red fog formed, and the clouds spread and grew until they merged and he disappeared beneath them, save for his upthrust fist. Nish's left fist clenched so tightly that he could not open it. He shuddered, then the fog billowed up to conceal all. When it dispersed a minute or two later there was no sign of the zealot.

Someone sighed; the woman holding the wavy-bladed knife dropped it into the water, then everyone on the cliff line cried out in unison, 'The Maelstrom of Justice and Retribution has spoken. Vivimord was guilty and has paid the price.'

Flecks of red foam revolved on the surface of the water. The women at the winch slowly wound the basket up again, and everyone headed back to the town green for Tildy's funeral rite, and the wake to follow.

Tulitine remained at the top of the cliff, staring down into the green water and frowning. Nish, burning fist clenched in his pocket, went back to her. 'What's the matter? Don't you feel that justice was done?'

'Few would argue that Vivimord has suffered a just punishment . . .'

'But?' said Nish.

'There is no body.'

'There seldom is when people drown at sea.'

'With mancers as powerful as Vivimord, one must always check the body – and then burn it to ash and scatter it to the winds, as you said earlier.'

His unease grew. 'After all that, you still don't think he's dead?'

'The body can't be recovered, so there's no proof that he is. Even more disturbing, the whirlpool, which has existed for hundreds of years, is gone.'

Nish hadn't noticed that, but she was right. The whirl-pools further up and down the coast were spinning exactly as they had always done, but of the Maelstrom of Justice and Retribution there was not a trace.

'Then we'd better get ready for war,' he said grimly.

TWENTY-TWO

Maelys lay on her side on the cold floor, surrounded by flakes of dried mud, trying to erase that image of the sky palace smashing into the plateau. She could not bear to think of all its crew, and all those soldiers, wiped out in an instant. Though they were servants of the God-Emperor, they were also human beings with families. Having lost her own clan, she could feel for their tragedies.

And after all she'd done to reach the portal in time, she had failed to save Nish or to take Vivimord down, or end dead Phrune. She had a feeling that the five spectres liberated when he'd been consumed by the chthonic fire would be worse than he had been, alive or dead. Why five? Was that a product of the Black Arts Vivimord had used to animate his corpse?

Nish was lost, no one knew where, and all her differences with him had dissolved once she'd seen the torment in his eyes in the bedchamber, the pain of being controlled by another. Nish had been so deeply in the zealot's thrall that she could not see how he would ever escape from it. And if Nish was the only man who could bring down his father, what hope was there?

Only one – it was more urgent than ever that they find

the antithesis to the tears, and that meant reaching the Numinator.

She rubbed her aching face. Having spent her childhood helping the clan healer, Maelys had known how to fix a dislocated jaw, but it would be painful for a long time.

She sat up and the pool of grey light illuminating her shifted slightly. She could still see Flydd, but only Colm's boots were visible now. Around them, nothing could be seen save the black, glassy-smooth floor extending in every direction until the darkness of the Nightland obscured it.

'I thought you were supposed to be crippled with after-sickness, Flydd,' said Colm. His voice sounded odd here, as if he were further away than he looked.

'I expected to be,' said Flydd. 'Don't know why I'm not.'

'Xervish?' Maelys said, feeling a trifle breathless. 'I'm really worried about Nish.'

'So am I,' said Flydd, 'but there's no way of finding him.'

'He looked like a zombie,' said Colm. 'Vivimord must have broken his mind.'

He did not sound upset about it, which strengthened Maelys's growing dislike of him. 'He's a lot stronger than you think!' she snapped.

'That he is,' said Flydd. 'I've stood beside Nish in many a struggle and I've had no more reliable ally .'

Colm scowled and changed the subject. 'What happened to the chthonic fire when the sky palace crashed?'

'I'd say it was sealed into the depths under a plug of molten rock,' said Flydd. 'Trapped forever.'

'I saw a woman on the way here,' said Maelys thoughtfully. 'She was clawing at the clear wall, trying to get in. Was that your woman in red?'

'It was.'

'She looked terrible.'

'She's afraid.'

'What of?'

'I don't know. The portal was meant to bring her here,

evidently, but I didn't know that. When I directed it to the shadow realm she took it from me and brought it here instead, but couldn't get to the portal in time.'

'Why did she want to come here?'

'When I was briefly in *her* mind, I saw something I wasn't meant to see: some kind of phantom hunting her, a creeping thing of white shadow and black fire, constantly changing its form. I've never heard of anything like it.'

'I hope it can't get in here,' said Maelys, rubbing her cold arms.

'I hope so too,' said Flydd, 'though I've got a good bit of my Art back now, and I'm starting to think I might regain the rest, in time.'

'Xervish,' Maelys said uneasily, '*Rulke* isn't still here, is he? I'm sure I've read –'

'No, he'd long dead. He was freed from the Nightland by Tensor the Aachim some two hundred and twenty years ago. Tensor had waited more than a thousand years to take his revenge. He was a brilliant man but an even bigger fool; he killed Rulke and that folly has been shaping the world ever since. Had Rulke survived, the lyrinx would never have gained a foothold on Santhenar; there would have been no war, no scrutators, and no God-Emperor.'

'And I would never have lost my heritage,' said Colm.

'You would not have inherited Gothryme in the first place.'

Colm sat up and glared into the darkness.

What's the matter with him now, Maelys wondered. 'Where is the Nightland, anyway? And how do we get out?'

'I don't know, to either question,' said Flydd wearily. 'It was created by the Council of Santhenar – the greatest mancers of the ancient world – as a prison to trap Rulke, the most powerful mancer of all time, and hold him until they could find a way to put an end to him. The Council were learned men and women who had devoted their long lives to the Art, and they had far more power than I do. It's said that they made this place from a fold in the wall of the Forbidding, an intangible barrier which closed Santhenar off from the perils of the void.'

'Why did they want to trap him?'

'Many reasons: some noble, others base. The Charon were few – only three of them are known to have come to Santhenar – but mighty, and they lived for thousands of years. Just a hundred of them, The Hundred, took the Aachim's world from them, and the conquest would never have succeeded without Rulke. He was a threat to Santhenar too.'

'What happened to the Nightland after he was freed?' said Maelys, rubbing her jaw, which ached every time she opened her mouth. Her rudely bandaged calf was even more painful. 'Did the Council leave it in place?'

'As I recall the Histories – and I haven't got all my memories back yet – the Nightland collapsed after he went free.' Flydd frowned. 'No, that must have happened later on, for the *Tale of the Mirror* says that Rulke returned here, briefly. As scrutator I was required to know the Histories by heart, especially the banned ones like the *Tale of the Mirror.*'

'Who banned that tale?' said Colm. 'It's a matter of personal interest to me.'

'Why is that?' asked Maelys, picking dried mud out of her hair and flicking it away.

'I don't see it's any of *your* business,' he said coldly.

It was like a slap across the face. Why did he feel so betrayed? She had never given him any reason to think she cared for him other than as a friend, but clearly he'd hoped otherwise. Damn him – it was lucky he'd revealed his true harsh and moralistic colours early.

'I'd like to know what your personal interest is, Colm,' said Flydd.

'Llian of Chanthed wrote the *Tale of the Mirror,*' said Colm, 'and he married Karan, a distant cousin of mine. After they, er, *died*, my branch of the family inherited the estate.'

'Llian was a great teller, wasn't he?' said Maelys. 'I remember Father talking about him when I was little.'

'He made himself out to be,' Flydd said darkly, 'though he's now known as Llian the Liar.'

'Not by everyone!' snapped Colm. 'My family never believed that story, nor the one about Karan Kin-Slayer.'

'I don't see why you're taking it so personally,' said Flydd. 'They've been dead two centuries. You've got to forgive and forget.'

'I *never* forgive an injury,' grated Colm, giving Maelys another cold glance.

'Then you'll always be shackled by your own bitterness,' said Flydd. 'But since you've asked, the tale was banned because the Numinator ordered that it be banned – presumably because Llian the Liar made parts of it up, or changed them to suit himself – and the scrutators obeyed the Numinator's orders without question – *or else.*'

He grimaced and rubbed his chest, where a deep torture scar, from the time he'd dared to enquire about the Numinator, had reappeared after renewal.

'I suppose the Council maintained the Nightland in case they recaptured Rulke,' Maelys speculated.

'Not all this time,' said Flydd.

'Why not?' said Colm.

'Because he's long dead, and so are the mancers who created it. It doesn't make sense that the Nightland still exists.'

'Maybe it will just go on forever,' said Maelys, resting her throbbing jaw on her arms and closing her eyes.

'Nothing lasts forever,' said Flydd. 'Everything fails and dies, in the end. It took mighty Arts to create the Nightland, and more power to keep it in existence for all the centuries that it was Rulke's prison, so why is it still here?' He got up and paced around in a circle, hands clasped behind his back. The puddle of grey light followed him, leaving her and Colm in the dark. 'Why didn't it collapse to a singularity two centuries ago, when the Forbidding was broken?'

Maelys couldn't have cared less. She wanted to sleep for a month.

'Something must be maintaining it,' said Colm.

'That would take monstrous power,' said Flydd, 'and not even the God-Emperor has power to waste.'

Maelys heard Colm walk away with quick, anxious steps that did not echo. She sighed; after the pursuits, terrors, torments and betrayals of the past days, she found the Nightland peculiarly soothing. It was chilly but she was used to that, for Nifferlin Manor had been high in the mountains. Cold was better than heat.

She took a quick sideways glance at Flydd. His jaw was clenched but he did not speak, for which she was grateful. She craved quiet and solitude until her shredded nerves could repair themselves. Before she left home, the forests of her family estate had provided a much needed refuge from the constant bickering of her mother and aunts. Perhaps the Nightland could provide a similar solace.

Maelys lay on her back and rolled from side to side, allowing the cold to ease her overheated muscles, feeling her pulse slowly returning to normal. They were safe from Jal-Nish, and Vivimord. Nothing from the real world could touch them here. Flydd would find a way out, and there was nothing she could do to help. She pillowed her head on her arms and closed her eyes . . .

Flydd was still breathing heavily as he tried to recover his equilibrium. Nine years he'd spent trapped at the top of the plateau where one day, even one year, had been as uneventful as the next – until Nish had appeared just a few days ago. Flydd's world had been turned upside down; the time since then had been one crisis after another and he was finding it hard to cope.

A mancer's mind was least affected by renewal, for the brain could not be remade from scratch like the rest of the body. That was his problem. He had a strong, middle-aged body that he was slowly growing into, but he still had the mind of an old man.

And there remained blanks in his memory, particularly

to do with the woman in red. Why *had* she come to him? He felt sure it had not been an accident. Could she have picked him out long ago, even planted the idea that had brought him to Mistmurk Mountain, to do something that she could not, and bring her here? And he'd failed her at the critical moment, so what would she do now?

Colm came pacing back. Maelys was asleep, a little mud-covered ball. He scowled.

'Why are you so hard on her?' Flydd asked quietly. 'Without her courage and determination we could not have escaped.'

'I salute her courage and determination,' Colm said, tight-mouthed, 'but I cannot forgive her methods, or her morals. I once thought – well, I know better now, after what she did with Nish . . .' His face twisted in disgust. 'She's the most calculating woman I've ever met, and she's bound herself forever to the God-Emperor. I hope she's satisfied.'

Whatever Maelys wanted, and whatever she did in pursuit of it, was no business of Flydd's. But even so . . .

'Colm, you're a bloody fool.'

'What are you talking about?' Colm snarled.

'Maelys isn't pregnant. She made up that lie to save her family.'

Colm drew in a sharp breath. 'I don't believe you.'

'I was a scrutator, on the Council,' Flydd said simply. 'One of our unsung Arts was telling truth from falsehood, and I was better at it than most. Maelys is an honest, truthful person and she hated making up such a sordid lie, but she's a loyal daughter and sister, and there's nothing she won't do to save her family.'

'Jal-Nish was a scrutator too. *He* believed her.'

'He wasn't a full scrutator long, and only briefly; he never had *our* training. Besides, he's desperate for a grandchild. He wanted to believe Maelys and, after all she's done to defy and thwart him, he's developing a grudging admiration for her. He realises she's a worthy partner for the son of the God-Emperor, and a suitable mother for his grandchild.'

'So *she's* safe, then,' said Colm sullenly.

'She would be if she *were* pregnant, but once Jal-Nish discovers she's not, he'll crush her, no matter what her other qualities, for deceiving him. Once we return to the real world she'll be in peril of her life.'

'Maybe we should leave her here until the job is done.'

Flydd stared at him. 'Maelys isn't a bag of treasure to be hidden.' He reached over and shook her by the shoulder. 'Wake up. We can't stay here.'

'Like it here,' she said sleepily. 'Nice and quiet; cool. No flame.'

'We've got to find the way out before it's too late.'

'Tomorrow.'

'We've got to look now. My portal will have weakened the barrier around the Nightland, but it will soon repair itself, and the longer we take, the harder it will be to get back to the real world . . .'

Assuming we can. Flydd wasn't entirely sure that there *was* a way out. Taking the four containers from his coat, he lined them up on the floor – first the white crystal phial containing the trapped cursed flame, followed by the abyssal flame in its square stone bottle, and lastly the oval and pyramidal green-ice flasks containing the freezing chthonic flame. The green ice condensed from the chthonic flame showed no signs of melting. Inside the flasks, the white fire swirled, glacier slow, and glacier cold.

Maelys sat up, combing the hair off her face with her fingers. 'What are they for?'

'I don't know yet.'

'What did you mean by, *too late?*'

'The Nightland was the most secure prison ever built and a mancer of my talents, considerable though they once were, should never have been able to make a portal to it. I would not have, had the woman in red not forced my portal away from the shadow realm, to here.'

'But she didn't get in, *did she?*' Maelys peered into the dark.

'No, she didn't get in,' said Flydd.

'Then she can't harm us,' said Colm. 'Can't you get us out the way you got in?'

'The Nightland was designed so *no one* could get out. There may be no way to open it from inside.' Flydd got up abruptly. 'Let's go for a walk.'

Maelys followed Flydd and Colm across the black floor for ten or fifteen minutes, but they might as well have been standing still for all the difference she saw. The Nightland was utterly featureless: it had no walls; no roof; no landscapes, structures or furnishings.

She stopped, looking around anxiously. 'I don't think we should go any further. What if we can't find the way back?'

Flydd kept going. 'The barrier that walls the real world off from the Nightland touches all points of it equally, so it should not matter where we are.'

'What's *that?*' said Colm, moving carefully to the left. Flydd let out a sigh and followed.

Maelys hurried after them. About thirty paces away, a transparent device of wheels and levers, wires and glassy plates, hung in the air. Flydd prodded it with his fingertips and they went straight through.

'The Histories tell that Rulke built all manner of devices here, trying to find a way out, and to make war on his enemies once he did. Virtual devices, formed from the fabric of the Nightland, like blueprints in three dimensions. That's how he designed his construct.'

'What's a construct?' asked Maelys.

'A metal conveyance that could create its own portals and jump from one part of Santhenar to another.'

'The Aachim built constructs on Aachan,' said Colm. 'Thousands of them came to Santhenar through a portal when Aachan was being destroyed by volcanoes.'

'But they did not invent them; they merely copied Rulke's, and imperfectly.'

They continued, seeing other suspended devices every now and again. Some were large and complex, and seemed almost real, while others appeared mere afterthoughts which hung in the air as thin as smoke.

'I could use a drink,' said Colm. 'My throat tastes like dried mud.'

Splash. Maelys, now a few paces ahead, had walked straight into a waist-deep pool. The chilly water stung her injured calf; it was black, motionless, and seemed thicker than normal water, for it barely rippled as she moved. She climbed out hastily. Black droplets wobbled through the air, taking ages to fall, and skidded across the floor in globules like spilled quicksilver.

'How could I have missed that?' she said, irritably flicking drops away.

'It wasn't there,' said Flydd.

She stared at him, hands on hips. 'What are you talking about?'

'The Nightland was designed to keep its prisoner alive for as long as he lived, so it had to provide water, food and air, if nothing else. Colm wanted water, therefore it appeared.'

Colm scooped a handful of the dark liquid and held it up. It quivered on his palm and he looked at it askance. 'I'm not drinking that.'

'It's a trifle black, I admit,' smiled Flydd, 'but what would you expect in the Nightland?'

'I'm afraid to expect anything,' muttered Colm.

Flydd dropped to his knees by the pool, gathered a double handful and drank noisily. 'It has a slight taint, but I'm sure it's not harmful.'

'I'm not!' Colm tasted the water, very tentatively, then shrugged. 'But if there's no way out, what does it matter?' He drank deeply, and washed his face and hands. 'I'm starving,' he announced loudly. 'I'd like a grilled rump of young buffalo, with mustard and pepper, a mug of dark ale and a plateful of those nut and honey pastries Mother used to make when I was little.' He looked around expectantly.

Flydd chuckled. 'It doesn't work like that. We're in a prison, after all. Whatever it provides for us will be nourishing, but I doubt it'll be tasty.'

Maelys went back to the pool. The globules were hard to swallow and made her burp, sending a host of tiny droplets soaring out of her mouth and away. 'Pardon me,' she said politely, then giggled and turned her head, firing more droplets in a soaring arc. She crouched under the water and scrubbed the worst of the mud off.

They continued, and shortly came to a low oval table, as black as everything else in the Nightland, on which sat three loaves of bread, plus platters, knives and a large black mound with a strong, yeasty smell.

'I'm not eating that,' said Colm, staring at the mound. 'It looks like a flappeter's dropping.'

Flydd, unperturbed, sat on the floor and extended his legs under the table. Maelys's mouth flooded with saliva. She sat opposite, drew one of the loaves towards her and began to cut neat slices from it, as if serving guests at Nifferlin Manor. She passed three slices to Flydd.

'Thank you,' he said gravely, inclining his head to her.

She pushed a platter of slices towards Colm, who ignored them, then took a single slice for herself and bit into it. 'It's not as good as we had at home, before . . .' Maelys stopped chewing as the memories flooded her, and had to wipe her eyes. 'It hasn't got much flavour.'

'Try the black stuff,' said Flydd, watching her, like an emperor his food taster.

She felt like retorting, 'Try it yourself!' but dug the knife into the mound. It had a soft consistency, like butter, so she spread it on a corner of her slice and tasted it.

'Yuk!' she said, swallowing without chewing. 'It's horrible.'

'But nourishing,' said Flydd. 'Pass it over.'

'So I'm your official taster now, am I?' said Maelys.

'Someone's got to do it.' He spread the black paste thickly on his slice, took an experimental bite, gagged and swallowed hastily. 'Delicious!'

'Liar! It's absolutely disgusting.'

'I've eaten worse.'

After they'd finished, Flydd lay on his back beside the table. 'Before I attempt the portal again I've got to rest, but my mind is too full for sleep. Has anyone got a tale to divert me?'

'You both know my story,' said Maelys. 'But we don't know Colm's –'

He glowered at her. 'Why don't you mind your own –?'

'An excellent idea,' Flydd interposed smoothly. 'Tell us your story, Colm. Down at the abyssal flame you gave me just the bare bones.'

'The tale is so bitter I can scarcely bear to begin it,' said Colm.

'Half a million families were dispossessed during the war with the lyrinx and they all have bitter tales.'

'My family dwelt at Gothryme for more than a thousand years,' Colm said, tight-mouthed, 'and we were robbed of it.'

'Maelys's family held Nifferlin for just as long, and her entire clan is dead or scattered. Why is your tragedy worse than hers?'

'She can go back, but Gothryme Manor and all its land, poor though it is, has been given to others.'

'Maelys can't return while the God-Emperor lives. You're holding out on us, Colm.' Flydd didn't look curious, merely expectant, as if he already knew what Colm was going to say. 'Gothryme,' he repeated.

The name was vaguely familiar to Maelys, in the way that hundreds of places she'd heard about were.

'You know all about it!' Colm said fiercely. 'The scrutators knew everything. They had the *Tale of the Mirror* banned.'

239

'That was long before my time,' said Flydd. 'Later the tale was rewritten to correct certain grievous inaccuracies inserted by the Teller. I'm told that Llian the Liar was a most unreliable narrator –'

'He was the greatest Teller of all!'

Flydd shrugged. 'What's it to you, anyhow?'

'Gothryme belonged to Karan Fyrn, and she was the heroine of the *Tale of the Mirror*, as it was originally written. My ancestor Macolm, nine generations ago, was her distant cousin and never expected to inherit anything. It should all have gone to Karan and Llian's children . . .'

'Until she murdered them, and Llian too,' Flydd said softly. 'Then killed herself. Karan Kin-Slayer she's been called ever since. She was no heroine; that was another of Llian's lies. She broke the Forbidding, or caused it to be broken, which brought the lyrinx to Santhenar and began the greatest of all wars. No wonder her name, and Llian's, are among the most reviled in all the Histories. Your family gained no honour from inheriting Gothryme.'

'It's still tainted to this day,' said Colm softly, 'and so is my family name, but Gothryme is my heritage.'

'You won't get it back while the God-Emperor remains in power.'

'It's not my *only* heritage, and I'll gladly accept your aid in recovering the rest.'

Flydd frowned. 'You're asking for *my* aid?'

'I've done all you asked of me, and I'd thought I'd earned a little consideration in return. Evidently not.'

Flydd sighed. 'Long ago I vowed to help overthrow the God-Emperor, Colm. Surely you realise that must come before any personal matters, no matter how pressing? But do go on.' He sounded as though he was humouring Colm.

'Karan was left a treasure by Faelamor, the leader of the Faellem people, just before she led them back to her own world of Tallallame.'

'Ah, yes,' said Flydd, his eyes lighting momentarily.

240

'Faelamor's fabled trove. I've wondered why it was left to Karan.'

'Faelamor had done her a great wrong and wished to atone for it.'

'Well, that's what the *original* tale said,' Flydd conceded.

Two angry red spots appeared on Colm's cheeks. 'Faelamor left the remaining treasures of her people to Karan, and that trove lies under a perpetual concealment in a cave in Elludore. An ebony bracelet handed down the generations will dispel the illusion and reveal the treasure.'

'I'd like to see it,' said Flydd with rather more interest than before.

'Where's Elludore?' asked Maelys.

'It's on the eastern side of the Island of Meldorin,' said Flydd. 'Elludore is a rugged, forested land north of Thurkad, between the mountains and the sea. Do you have the bracelet, Colm?'

'Mother gave it to my sister, Ketila. She was three years older than me, but my family were lost in a lyrinx attack not long after I met Nish. I told you that.'

'Then the bracelet is lost or destroyed,' said Flydd.

'I imagine so, but surely with your powers you can dispel illusions?'

'You're asking me to abandon the struggle against the God-Emperor to help you find a few trinkets?' Again Maelys got the impression that Flydd was toying with Colm.

'You have to hide until you're fit to take him on,' said Colm. 'You can hide in Elludore as well as anywhere.'

'You've got a nerve!' said Maelys. 'We're supposed to be finding the Numinator, not fighting your battles for you.'

Flydd raised a hand to her. 'Go on, Colm.'

'You can dispel illusions, can't you?' Colm looked pathetically eager now.

'*Many* illusions, if my powers come back fully, though a perpetual illusion created by the greatest illusionist of all is another matter entirely. But Colm, Faelamor's treasure trove is mentioned in the Histories, and therefore thousands of people must have known about it over the past two centuries. Even its location in Elludore – in the ridge-and-valley land called Dunnet – must have been identified long ago.'

'No one else knew the location of the cave, or even which valley it lay in,' said Colm. 'There are millions of caves in Dunnet.'

'Or Karan Kin-Slayer would have taken it,' said Flydd, 'before she went mad and slaughtered her family.'

'It was always said, in our clan, that she spurned the gift of her enemy.'

'A rumour she may have put about herself, to conceal the treasure from marauders.'

'I'm sure it's still there,' Colm said heatedly, 'Will you help me?'

'Do *you* know the location of the cave?'

'The secret was told to me when I was a boy.'

'And you still remember where to find one small valley among thousands in a trackless wilderness?' Flydd said with a trace of scorn. 'Elludore must be two hundred leagues from Bannador. Have you ever been there?'

'Once, when I was little. I'm sure I can find it, and I'll know the place when I do. It has one particular . . .' he shivered, '*landmark* that can be found nowhere else – if it still exists after all this time.'

'Are you going to tell me what it is?' said Flydd, clearly intrigued.

Maelys was too, but Colm had that familiar tightness about the mouth and jaw, and the fixed look in his eye, that said he wasn't going to say. It was the first thing that had struck her about him – how closed off he was. His past was a nagging thorn that he might never get over, even if he recovered the treasure trove.

'I've got to have it, Flydd,' Colm said, 'with your help or without it. Our line has been tainted since Karan's time, and I've lost my family and my estate. This is the only thing I've got left.'

'I don't even know if the portal spell will work here,' said Flydd.

'But if you can make it work, why not head for Elludore? It's the perfect place to hide while you regain your Art.'

Flydd was breathing heavily. 'Perhaps I will. Faelamor's fabled trove – what mancer wouldn't want to set eyes on that?'

Maelys thought there was an odd, greedy tone to his voice. Surely not.

'Assuming we can get there,' Flydd continued. 'Portals can only be opened in a few special places.'

'But surely Faelamor's cave *is* a special place?' said Colm.

'Not necessarily for portals. Elludore, Elludore,' said Flydd, uneasily. 'That reminds me of something unpleasant.' He walked around the table several times. 'No matter; whatever it was, it happened long ago. I can't think about this now, Colm. Losing Nish has thrown me and I don't see how we can defeat Jal-Nish without him.'

'We were going to find the Numinator,' Maelys pointed out. 'That's why you took renewal in the first place, Xervish.'

'Ah, yes.' Flydd didn't look pleased to be reminded. 'And the Numinator must be approached carefully. It may have been weakened by Jal-Nish's rise, but it will not be powerless.'

'How do you know it still exists?' Colm burst out. 'This quest seems like a waste of time to me.'

'My deepest scars – the ones that survived renewal – still throb at intervals, the way they used to when I was tortured. The Numinator is still alive, all right, and it guards its privacy jealously.'

'It may have fallen under Jal-Nish's control by now.'

'I don't think so. At the end of the war, just after he reappeared so shockingly, I mentioned the Numinator to Jal-Nish in passing, and he didn't know what I was talking about. Not being on the inner Council, he had never been told that most secret of all secrets. And the Numinator would have had plenty of time to hide itself, after the nodes were destroyed.

'So how do I get to it?' he mused. 'And survive?'

TWENTY-THREE

'What if you offered the Numinator something it wanted badly?' said Maelys.

Calling the Numinator *it* felt strange, yet there were many intelligent, non-human creatures in the void, and it had appeared not long after the Forbidding, which protected Santhenar from the void, had been broken.

'I've already thought of that.' Flydd pressed his hand against the bottled flames in his inside pocket. 'These are a magnificent gift for any mancer, even one of the greatest: a source of power unaffected by the destruction of the nodes. What secrets may be uncovered by a diligent study of these uncanny fires? Dare I give them to the Numinator, though? Will the gift gain us a boon in return, or be used against us? The gratitude of mancers is unreliable at the best of times.'

'Don't I know it,' Colm said pointedly. 'You can agonise for the rest of your miserable life, Flydd, or you can just get on with it.'

'The future of Santhenar is at stake!' Flydd flashed. 'I'll decide what to do in my own time.'

'Can you tell us *anything* about the Numinator?' Maelys asked hastily. 'Where did it come from? What does it do; what does it want?'

'The Council never knew, though the Numinator's great age argues either for someone with blood from one of the longer-lived human species – that is, Aachim, Faellem or Charon – or a mancer who has taken renewal, and more than once; or a non-human creature that entered the world at the time the Forbidding was broken.

'If Chief Scrutator Ghorr knew its origins, he told no one and the secret died with him. All we knew was that the Numinator created the Council of Scrutators nearly a hundred and fifty years ago out of the Council of Santhenar, which had existed in one form or another for thousands of years. The Numinator shaped our Council to its own purposes, of which only one was winning the war.'

'What were its other purposes?' asked Colm.

'It wanted to *control* Santhenar, though not to exercise power over it – the Numinator was never interested in power for its own sake. It required the Council to collect information on every single person in the world: their ancestry, looks, family traits, habits, talents and gifts, and compile it in registers.'

'What for?' said Maelys curiously. Nothing she heard about the Numinator made sense.

'No one knows,' said Flydd. 'A copy of each register was placed in Ghorr's strongroom in the scrutators' hidden bastion, Nennifer, and from there it vanished. However I did learn, by means I won't go into, that the Numinator dwelt in the frozen south at the Tower of a Thousand Steps.'

'Where is that, anyway?' said Colm.

'It lies on the forbidden Island of Noom, in the middle of the Kara Agel or Frozen Sea, an Antarctic wasteland so bleak that only ice bears and seals, walruses and snow leopards can survive there. A few trappers and prospectors cross in and out in the brief and bitter Antarctic summer, but no one winters near the Kara Agel.'

'Save the Numinator.'

'And perhaps ice runs in its veins instead of blood.' Flydd shivered and pressed a hand to his chest again. 'I most passionately don't want to go there. Though my torture was half a century ago, I can still feel the scourges flaying the flesh from my body for daring to speculate about the Numinator.'

'It may have given up by now,' said Colm.

'It has held to its plan for at least a hundred and fifty years.'

'It could be dead.'

'I don't think so,' said Flydd. He looked at Maelys. 'The thought of Noom arouses terrors that you cannot imagine, yet I must go there sooner or later. The Numinator knows the Histories better than anyone on Santhenar, even Jal-Nish. If there is an antithesis to the tears, that's where we'll find out about it. But not now; I've got to sleep. The way may be clearer in the morning.' He looked around. 'Ah!'

Maelys followed his gaze and saw, about twenty paces away, a simple straw mattress, like Flydd's former bed in his amber-wood hut on Mistmurk Mountain, covered in a single blanket. A good distance to the left, a black replica of Colm's bedroll lay on the floor, while further off stood a wooden bed identical to the one Maelys had slept in when she'd been a little girl. It even had the same patchwork quilt her mother had made. Tears formed, but she didn't brush them away.

'Good night,' she said, and headed towards the bed, her only hope of comfort in an alien world.

It was smaller than she remembered, but Maelys didn't try to imagine it differently in the hope that it would change to fit. She crawled under the covers, pulled them up around her ears, gave a little sigh and fell instantly asleep.

Maelys did not dream, so far as she was aware, but woke feeling restless, having no idea how long she'd slept. Flydd was flat on his back with his legs spread and mouth open, snoring. Colm lay on his side in his bedroll, knees drawn up to his chest and an arm wrapped around them – a revealing posture. Was he unconsciously trying to protect himself, or to keep the world at bay because he could rely on nobody but himself?

Colm wasn't her problem. Sliding out of bed, she walked away from the dim illumination that surrounded them. The floor was cold under her bare feet but, being still warm from bed, she found it soothing and stimulating. At a point where Maelys could just see the twin glimmers on Flydd and Colm, she began to pace in a great circle around them. She needed to walk but dared not lose sight of them, else she might never find her way back.

On her second circle, Maelys thought she heard a faint call. She looked back to the lights but they were not moving.

Hello.

This time it was clearer, a rich male voice, though it sounded far away. An attractive voice, she thought. Trustworthy. She searched the blackness for a sign of the man who had spoken, but the Nightland remained as impenetrable as ever. She didn't answer.

Who are you?

Or was the voice in her head? She couldn't tell. Maelys kept silent, for it occurred to her that the Nightland must still exist for a reason. It might be used as a prison for all manner of desperate scoundrels; why else would someone expend all that power to maintain it? She took a few steps into the darkness, in the direction from which the voice seemed to be coming.

What's your name?

He didn't sound like a villain. His voice sounded young, gentle and, well, *nice.* Maelys wasn't foolhardy, though, and such impressions would not have carried her another step towards him except that he also sounded lost, and terribly lonely. She knew those feelings; she'd suffered them since childhood, and she felt for him.

She checked on Flydd and Colm again. She must have gone further than she'd thought, for they were just small points of light in an infinite blackness.

'What's yours?' she said softly.

I'm Emberr, he said, in a rich burr.

'Emberr!' Maelys tried to roll her r's the way he had. She liked the name – it sounded safe, yet strong. 'Where are you?' She went slowly forwards, still wary, taking no risks.

This way. A point of light appeared in the distance. *Please come.*

She stopped. She wanted to see him, but dared go no further. 'I'll get lost.'

He gave a cheerful chuckle. *You can't get lost with me as your guide.*

'Are you a *prisoner?*' Her voice quavered.

No, but I am trapped here.

Maelys believed him; she just *knew* he was telling the truth. She continued, step by step, and when she finally came to her senses and looked back, Flydd's and Colm's lights had disappeared.

That shook her; she turned in a full circle but there was nothing to be seen save Emberr's beckoning glimmer. Was he telling the truth? She believed so. Could she trust him to guide her back? She hesitated, coolly analysing her feelings for the least uncertainty, the tiniest unease. Feeling none, she went on.

Maelys walked through the dark for a long time, and every so often the small glow illuminating her touched other virtual contrivances hanging in the air to left or right. She gave them no more than a passing glance. Their design and purpose was unfathomable.

As she went on, the light grew steadily, and shortly she made out a pretty little cottage with lights streaming through windows all around, surrounded by a low fence. Flower gardens luxuriated on either side of the path to the front door, while behind she made out a vegetable garden, fruit trees and a small forest fading into the night. It would have been beautiful, had all not been in shades of Night-land black.

She stood at the front gate, afraid to go further. It was made of old, weathered wood; she ran her hand along it and splinters dug into her skin. It felt so real, so homely, yet Maelys was not such a fool as to think it might not be a trick. The stuff which made up the Nightland could be formed into any shape that could be imagined, if one had the Art for it.

'What is your name?'

His voice was much louder now; she could hear it properly, rather than just inside her head. He might have been standing on the other side of the door.

'Maelys.' She spoke in the barest whisper.

'Such a pretty name. Come closer, Maelys, so I can see you clearly.'

She didn't move. 'How did you know I was here?'

'I smelled your perfume from a league away.'

'I'm not wearing any.'

'You smell like the most beautiful perfume in the world.'

What a romantic thing to say. Maelys imagined that she smelled of sweat, mud, swamp creeper and perhaps even a trace of Phrune, but she was touched nonetheless. No man had ever said anything romantic to her before. Yet as soon as he saw her, all ragged and grubby and dressed in boy's clothes, Emberr would realise how wrong he'd been.

'Come inside,' he said.

Maelys was well brought up and wary; she was not that smitten. 'Come out where I can see you.'

The door opened. She swallowed; licked her dry lips; for a moment she was blinded by a flood of warm yellow light, the one thing in this place that wasn't black.

He stood in the doorway, a silhouette against the light, then the door swung shut behind him and he came slowly down the steps. He wore only a kilt fastened about his waist with a fabric belt. He was tall, which she liked, but not too tall, which she also appreciated. He had broad shoulders and a strong chest, a narrow waist and long legs. His hair

250

was dark, curly and worn long, which she was not used to in a man, though she conceded that it looked right on Emberr. He was handsome and strong, yet she had been right about him: he had a kind face.

The moment he saw her, his eyes widened and he stopped in mid-step, staring.

'Is something the matter?' said Maelys.

'You're . . . not what I expected.'

'Oh!' she said dully, thinking him disappointed. He'd expected a tall, elegant princess, as was his due, not a small, grubby girl who was inclined to be buxom.

He looked her up and down, drinking her in and marvelling at her. 'It's not what you're thinking. Not at all. You're beautiful, Maelys.'

It wasn't flattery; he meant every word. She bit her lip; this was too much. Was she in some weird Nightland dream? If she was, she didn't want to wake from it. But then, she thought, how many girls does he know? If I'm the only one he's met, it's no wonder . . .

'What are you doing here, Emberr?'

'I was born in the Nightland, so I can never leave.'

'Never!' she cried involuntarily. Poor man. She leaned forwards, staring at him just as avidly, and gained the impression that he was reconsidering a previously made plan.

'Unless someone takes my place.'

She took a hasty step backwards, thinking that it was a trap after all, but he was staring into the distance, sadly, pensively. 'How do you know?' she said.

'My mother told me, a very long time ago, that I could only be freed from the Nightland if a woman took my place. I was too young to understand what she meant, and mother never came back to explain.'

'Is that why you lured me here?' Maelys said coolly, getting ready to run, though she had no idea which direction to take to find Flydd and Colm. What a fool she'd been – she should have realised it was a trap.

251

'I didn't *lure* you,' Emberr said sadly. 'I merely called you, and you came. I used no magic at all.'

Yes you did, she thought. The most irresistible magic of all. But she said, 'I'm not as big a fool as I look.'

He slumped on the bottom step and put his head in his hands. 'I knew this would go wrong. I don't know anything about people.' He looked up at her. 'Maelys, I would never ask you to take my place, nor try and trick you into doing so. I was born here, and I can survive in the Nightland if I must, but it would destroy you.'

'But . . .' said Maelys.

'I'm not unhappy here, for I know nothing else, but I'm terribly lonely. Yet if I have to live my remaining years here, I can endure it.'

She believed him, and it was so sad that her eyes stung. It was such a waste. She pushed the gate open and went a step along the path, before stopping. 'There must be a way to get you out.'

He looked up at her. 'Only the way I mentioned – by an exchange with a young woman. The rules which govern the Nightland were embedded within it when it was created, and nothing can change them. You'd better go – your friends are calling you.'

Maelys couldn't hear anything. She stared at his broad chest, feasting herself on him. He was everything her romantic soul dreamed of – the perfect mate – save that he was trapped here forever.

'There must be something I can do.' She could not think of a thing.

'There's nothing. Please don't mention me to your friends.'

'Why not?'

'My mother has a terrible enemy, one who will not hesitate to harm me if it ever finds out where I am. No one must ever know about me.'

It was the last thing she had expected him to say, and she could not doubt his sincerity. It drew her closer to him.

She wanted to tell him of her own enemies, her own desperate flight, but did not want to add to his troubles.

'All right,' she said reluctantly, and turned to go.

'Wait!' He reached out to her. 'Will you swear it?'

'I swear that I will tell no one about you.'

'Thank you. And there is one other thing,' he said softly.

'Of course,' she said without thinking.

'Would you kiss me, Maelys? I have never kissed a woman.'

Danger signals went off in her head. Was this what he'd been aiming for all along? If she kissed him, would it trigger a spell that would trap her forever and allow him to go free? But why would he need a spell? He could leap up and catch her in a few bounds.

'Nor I a man,' she said, and went towards him, knowing she was a reckless fool, but she wanted this more than anything and for once she was going to give way to her feelings.

He stood up as she drew near, staring at her with an intensity that sent shivers up her spine. He held out his arms and she went into them. He ran a finger along the line of her jaw where it was swollen, and she flinched.

Emberr frowned and carefully turned her head to one side and back, touching the bruise with a fingertip. 'Someone *struck* you?'

'A very evil man; but I attacked him first; and I got him, too.'

'Even so.'

Emberr laid the flat of his palm on the bruise and the pain faded away completely. He did not question her, but bent his head and kissed her on the mouth, and she yielded to his arms, still half-expecting it to be some hideous trap but quite unable to resist.

He did not kiss her passionately; it was just a delicate, lingering brush of the lips, yet it was more sensual than any touch she could have imagined. She pressed herself

253

against him, clinging to him, only dimly realising the hardness growing between them. Emberr arched away at once and she tried to push herself against him, seeking the comfort of human touch, but he let go and stepped back, looking down at her with those soft brown eyes.

'Thank you,' Emberr said. 'I will never forget you, Maelys, but you must go at once. I'm protected here but you are not.'

'But . . .' She rubbed her tingling lips, wanting more.

'Go quickly!' he said hoarsely. 'That way!' He pointed over her shoulder.

She saw moving lights in the distance. She looked back at him, wanting him more than she had ever wanted anyone, but with a wave of his hand the cottage, the gardens and the forests vanished, and so did Emberr.

Who was he, and why was he trapped here? There were no answers. Maelys stumbled back towards the lights, more alone than she had ever been, and terribly afraid that she would never see him again.

TWENTY-FOUR

'That was foolish,' Flydd said as she met them, though he did not seem angry. 'Whatever possessed you to wander away?'

'Sorry,' Maelys said distractedly, trying to control her face so as to not make him suspicious. 'I woke feeling restless. I needed to walk.'

He was smiling and seemed so much more relaxed than before. 'No harm done. The sleep has done me good – I think I know a way out of here. Let's see if we can find one of Rulke's virtual devices – the right one.'

'Which one?'

'The model for his construct. He couldn't use it to make a portal and escape because he didn't have the power.'

'Why not?'

'He could make *things* from the matter of the Nightland, but they would always remain part of it, for Rulke could draw on no power that did not come from here. But I can.'

Flydd held up the pyramid-shaped ice flask. Chthonic flame swirled lazily inside it.

'It took a gigantic column of white fire to break into the Nightland,' Colm pointed out, 'and even then you barely managed it. How do you expect to get us out with that piddling flame?'

'I was opposed by Jal-Nish and Vivimord, if you recall,' Flydd said mildly, 'and I'd never done it before. But if we can find Rulke's virtual construct, the most subtle engine for making portals that has ever been devised, the tiniest amount of power should suffice. The chthonic flame trapped here ought to be enough for several such portals, and that's just as well, if we're going to Elludore first.'

'But you said . . .' began Colm, confused.

'I've decided I'm not yet ready to face the Numinator. A trip to Elludore would give me the chance to grow into my renewed body and get it fit for the task. By then the rest of my memories may have come back, too, and hopefully my Arts.'

They searched for what felt like a day and a night, though Maelys found it impossible to keep track of time here – it did not seem to run the way it did in the real world. Flydd inspected all the virtual devices they'd encountered previously, and every other one they came to, but none proved to be what he was looking for.

Maelys, footsore and too weary to stand up, sat on the cold floor, unable to think of anything but Emberr, Emberr, Emberr. In his arms she had felt complete for the first time in her life, and all she wanted was to be there again.

'What's the matter with you?' said Flydd, staring down at her. 'You're mooning about like a love struck calf.'

Colm laughed cynically.

'Nothing,' she lied. 'Just tired.'

Flydd walked away, rubbing the stubble on his jaw, then stopped abruptly. 'Wait!' he cried. 'I remember now.'

'Remember what?' asked Maelys, afraid of what he might be thinking.

'An important detail. Rulke escaped from the Nightland after Tensor exploited a flaw in it, trying to lure him out so as to kill him. But Rulke was too strong. He got away, returned briefly to the Nightland, and Karan Kin-Slayer and Llian the Liar ended up here as well.'

'I'd prefer that you called them Karan and Llian,' Colm said stiffly. 'We know what murdering scum the scrutators were, and to my mind, they were the liars when they rewrote Llian's tale. Most of them, anyway,' he added hastily as Flydd clenched his fist.

'Whatever keeps you happy,' Flydd said coldly. 'The tale states that the Nightland was collapsing, and there's no reason to doubt Llian the – him in *this* matter, at least. Over time the Nightland had leaked power into the void, and at the end there wasn't power enough left to sustain it . . .' He frowned.

'What's the matter now?' said Colm.

'I repeat my earlier question. Why is the Nightland still here, two hundred and twenty years later, seemingly as vast and whole as ever?'

'Perhaps it's a new one, just recently made.'

'Not with all Rulke's relics in it. This is the original Nightland, sustained for all this time at an incalculable cost of power. Why?'

To protect Emberr, who was trapped here, Maelys thought, but dared not say so. If she mentioned his name, Flydd would go after him and try to use him in some way. She felt terrible, keeping such a vital secret from Flydd, but Emberr was already in danger and Flydd would only make it worse. She could not put Emberr at risk; she'd given him her word.

Flydd's glance rested on her. He knows I'm keeping something back, she thought. I'll never keep the truth from him.

He turned away, muttering, 'I'm worried now. Every minute we spend here increases the risk of discovery.'

'Who by?' said Colm.

'The one who owns the Nightland.'

They tramped back and forth for many more hours, without finding any sign of Rulke's virtual construct. Maelys followed their footsteps, eyes closed, stumbling with weariness. Her previous sleep could not have been more than an hour, for she was quite overcome by drowsiness.

'Aha!' Flydd was squinting off to her right. 'I think we should go this way.'

'Why?' said Colm. 'It looks the same in every direction.'

'Intuition tells me that this is the right way.'

'Intuition? You?' Colm's voice dripped scorn.

'It surprises me too,' said Flydd, 'but I'm going to follow it.'

After ten or fifteen minutes they came to a broad, curving crevasse filled with smoke-like vapour and spanned by a cracked arch of some hundred rising steps, and as many descending into the mist-shrouded distance of the other side. They climbed the bridge one at a time, in case their weight proved too much for it, and entered another section of the Nightland where the floor smoked like ice, and luminous vapours swirled up and around them with every movement. Pools of water black as ink lay in holes so deep that they seemed to have no bottom.

After negotiating a path between hundreds of such pools they came to the remnants of a once magnificent palace, now broken and distorted as if it had been compressed into a mote, then expanded again. And this part of the Nightland had colour: sombre reds, browns and yellows which were like a rainbow compared to the unrelieved black of everywhere else.

'What happened here?' said Maelys.

'This must be the part of the Nightland that collapsed,' said Flydd. 'Rulke's part. Someone tried to restore it, though not very successfully.'

'How could one section collapse and the other not?'

'I have no idea.'

They went inside, through great halls all twisted as though they'd been wrung out like washing, and imposing audience chambers that were equally deformed. One was the size of a dog kennel on the inside, though its outside walls joined seamlessly with the normal-sized rooms surrounding it. They entered the most magnificent library Maelys had ever seen but the books were all crumpled and ruined; they had expanded to full size but the shelves had not.

'Rulke must have had a colossal ego,' Colm observed, 'to have created all this when there was no one else to see it.'

'He was a great man who had been used to the best of everything,' said Flydd. 'He liked to build things, and he had infinite patience. I might have done the same, had I been sentenced to a thousand years here.'

'You spent nine years on Mistmurk Mountain,' Maelys pointed out, 'and you were satisfied with a little wooden hut.'

Eventually they came to a glorious, though to Maelys's mind intimidating, bedroom that was hardly deformed at all. The floor was tiled with red marble, the walls draped in rich velvets and silks, while the bed was a head-high platform supported on six posts of carved ebony, with a canopy so high that it could barely be seen.

'I couldn't sleep there,' she said, 'no matter how tired I was.'

'I doubt he used this room for *sleeping*,' said Flydd with a sly grin.

'I don't know what you mean,' frowned Maelys.

'I heard the Charon were lusty devils, men and women,' said Colm.

'He could create anything he wanted for his pleasure,' said Flydd. 'Or *anyone*.'

I wouldn't want to lie with Emberr *here*. Maelys, realising what a shocking, wicked thought she'd just had, flushed so red that her cheeks burned.

'Now we've embarrassed innocent little Maelys,' Flydd chuckled. He ruffled her messy hair and walked through into the next room. 'Hello! What's this?'

It was roughly the size of a large covered wagon, though it hung in the air as if weightless. It had a skin of blue-black metal, shaped in alien curves and ominous bulges that no blacksmith of Santhenar could have duplicated. Oddly shaped levers and knobs protruded from the top.

Flydd exhaled loudly. 'It's Rulke's original model for his construct – the very first construct of all, and still the most potent. With such a perfect plan as this, and unlimited power, another could be made. This belongs in the Great Library – if it still exists.'

Maelys pressed her burning cheek against the cold doorway. 'Shouldn't you destroy it? After the last war –'

'I doubt that I can influence it in any way.' Flydd swept his arm against the side of the construct and it curved straight through. 'Besides, after the nodes failed, Lauralin was littered with dead constructs, and I never heard that Jal-Nish had succeeded in activating one, for all the power of his tears. Did you, Colm?'

Colm shook his head. 'The God-Emperor has air-dreadnoughts, and he had his sky palace, but his only other flying devices are flesh-formed.'

There was a faint noise in the distance, like a piece of ice shattering on a hard floor. Flydd spun around, tiptoed to the door and looked out.

'I keep forgetting that any kind of depraved being could be held in such a secure prison as this.'

'And any kind of evil prison warder,' said Colm.

Maelys could only think of Emberr, trapped here for as long as he should live. If only there was a way to get him out.

'Let's see if the construct can be made to work,' said Flydd.

He withdrew the pyramidal ice flask from his coat, wincing as frost formed around his fingers. That had not happened in the real world. The chthonic flame was moving sluggishly. He walked around the virtual construct, studying it from all angles. Maelys followed him at a distance, not because she had any interest in the device – she'd experienced far too much of the Art lately – but because the floor here was so cold that it hurt her bare feet if she stood still.

He began to trace the shape of the construct with his

fingers, as high as he could reach, circumnavigating it again as if trying to imprint it on his memory. Maelys reached out to touch it, but felt nothing at all. It was just patterns of light and shadow.

Flydd walked into it, and from outside she could see his dim outline holding the ice flask up like a lantern. Colm yawned, strolled away and stood leaning on the wall with his eyes closed.

Maelys suppressed a yawn of her own and followed Flydd in. Her skin tingled as she passed through the skin of the virtual construct; everything was a formless blur for a few seconds, then the farthest layers faded and she saw a pair of high-backed seats, plus a confusion of levers, knobs and glassy plates, all illuminated by dark red light.

'That's odd,' said Flydd, who was to her right.

Maelys turned towards him but was assailed by such an attack of vertigo that she staggered. Everything swam sickeningly across her field of vision for a moment before settling down again.

'What is?' she managed to gasp.

'I don't know. It's different to the constructs I travelled in during the war, and it's going to take time to understand how it works. Go and get some sleep, Maelys. There's a bed in the next room.'

'I couldn't sleep there.' The thought of lying in Rulke's bed gave her the shivers.

'You're out on your feet. Get moving; I can't rely on you the way you are.'

She went out reluctantly, past Colm who did not acknowledge her, and into Rulke's bedchamber, where she stood beside the huge bed. Flydd was right; she had to rest and there was nowhere else. Her toes felt like frozen knobs.

Climbing the bedpost reminded her of climbing the web cord to escape the octopede; her sore muscles screamed at the abuse. Maelys flopped onto the bed and pulled the velvet quilt over her, trying not to think about the lustful acts

Rulke must have committed here during his long incarceration, but the only way she could get him out of her mind was to focus on Emberr instead.

It didn't help – it made her feel all hot and panicky. Maelys stuffed a fold of the quilt into her mouth to stifle a groan, and it was a long time before she fell into a restless sleep.

'Ah, there you are,' said Flydd when she reappeared. 'Feeling better now?' She didn't look it. Her hair was tangled, her eyes had dark circles around them and her face was flushed.

'Slightly.'

'You should be. You've been asleep for almost two days.'

'Two days!'

'This place has an odd effect on some people. And you look as though you've been sharing Rulke's lusty dreams,' he said cheerily.

Maelys avoided his eye. Such a modest girl, he thought.

'Have you had any luck with the portal?' she asked.

'On the plateau you said that making a portal to the real world was perilous,' Colm observed.

'Indeed, but I'm no longer a novice at it, and I've learned a lot from Rulke's virtual construct,' said Flydd. 'I think I can get us to Elludore with it, safely, and possibly make another portal after that . . . I hope so, for it's a good seven hundred leagues to the Island of Noom, the way the secret paths run, and that's the best part of a year of walking, in rough, trackless country.'

'Assuming the God-Emperor doesn't catch you first,' said Colm, who was still propping up the doorway. 'Which he will.'

'It would be devilishly difficult to avoid the notice of his spies and watchers on such a long journey,' Flydd agreed. 'Besides, we don't have time. Jal-Nish's defeat will only drive him harder to hunt us down . . .'

'What's the matter?' said Maelys, for Flydd was staring at the construct. 'Is something about it bothering you?'

'Perceptive, too,' Flydd said to himself. 'It should have been dead, but it isn't.'

'What do you mean, *not dead?*' Colm shot upright.

'It's been used, and there are still traces of power within it, yet the Histories say Rulke *never* made a portal out of the Nightland, because he couldn't. Tensor freed him the first time, and when Rulke returned, through a portal he'd made from the real world, he left it ajar so he could escape again. He didn't use this construct because he didn't need to.'

'Perhaps he returned again,' said Colm.

'It's possible,' said Flydd, 'though by then he would have had his *real* construct, so much more powerful and subtle than a virtual one could ever be. And a couple of years later he was dead, as was Tensor. By the end of the *Tale of the Mirror*, almost all of the great mancers were dead or gone forever, so who came to the Nightland and used this virtual construct after that, *and why?'*

'They could have come before the end of that tale,' said Maelys.

'No, else all traces of the construct's use would have been wiped clean when the Forbidding was destroyed. This place was made from the Forbidding, remember, and its destruction should have destroyed everything in it, including the virtual construct. Why didn't it?'

'Because someone protected it.'

'And I keep asking, why go to such immense trouble to protect an empty prison?'

Perhaps it wasn't empty back then, Maelys thought. What if there was someone in it who could never leave? But that would make Emberr hundreds of years old, so who was he, and how did he end up here?

'To keep other prisoners here,' said Colm. 'One of them must have used it.'

'This construct can only be empowered by a force

brought in from outside,' said Flydd, 'but prisoners would have been stripped of all possessions before they were sent here – no prisoner could have used it. If someone entered from outside to check on the prisoners, they would have come via their own portal, so why would anyone need to use this one? And if there were prisoners here, why would their warders leave the virtual construct empowered, which would give them a chance to escape?'

'Does it really matter after all this time?' said Colm irritably. 'You're always chasing thoughts around in circles, Flydd. Get the damn thing working. I want to feel good solid earth under my feet again.'

'I know how to make it work. And since it's still live, that won't take long.'

'Will you take me to Elludore? Please?'

'Perhaps I will. I can get back my Arts there as well as anywhere. And I too would like to see Faelamor's legendary trove.' His eyes glinted in a most un-Flydd-like way, then he stepped inside. 'Come through. Colm, tell me everything you know about Elludore. It's not a land I know, and I've got to find a safe place for the portal to open, and see the destination clearly, or we'll never get there.'

TWENTY-FIVE

It felt as though Maelys was sliding down an endless tunnel lined with silk. Half an hour must have gone by before, without warning, she dropped nearly a span into long, dry grass. Her knees folded, she hit the ground softly and opened her eyes. Feathery seed heads caressed her bare arms and tickled her nose; she hastily suppressed a sneeze, not knowing whether it was safe to make a sound. It was late afternoon, clear but cool, and the sun was falling behind snow-clad mountains. It would soon be dark, and cold.

She was on the upper slope of a steep hill, one of a cluster of five whose crests were grass-covered, though forest on their lower slopes extended out to the horizon in all directions. To her left a brick fireplace large enough to roast an ox was topped with a chimney five or six spans high. Beyond it a broken stone wall ran straight for twenty or thirty paces, with smaller walls extending off it; squared stone littered the grass as far as she could see. It looked like the ruins of a manor or country house, or perhaps a monastery.

A tear formed in her eye at the thought of beloved Nifferlin Manor, torn down to the foundations by the God-Emperor's troops. She dashed it away.

The grass rustled to her left. 'Colm?' she said quietly. 'Xervish?'

No answer; perhaps they hadn't come through yet. They'd left the Nightland together but the portal had thrown her into that lightless tunnel and she'd lost them.

What if they hadn't come through at all? She suppressed a twinge of panic. She had no coin, no weapon, no boots; just the clothes on her back and the taphloid around her neck, which Flydd had returned before they left the Nightland. And Elludore, if this *was* Elludore, was an unknown land far from anywhere she knew. It could be a lawless land where an unaccompanied woman would be in peril.

'Xervish?' she called, more loudly. Her injured calf throbbed.

The afternoon was absolutely still. She limped across the crest and peered down the other side of the hill, seeing nothing to alarm her, though any kind of predator could be hidden in the long grass. What if Flydd and Colm had ended up somewhere else? Her chest grew tight at the thought, the familiar anxiety of abandonment rising up to choke her. She forced it down again and tried to think.

It would be freezing up here tonight but she wasn't game to light a fire, for it would be visible for leagues; besides, she had neither food nor water, and there would be no water up here. Yet if she went down to the forest Flydd and Colm wouldn't know where to look for her.

The grass rustled again, just behind her, and she looked down to see a large black and red snake winding its way between the stems, just a flashing strike away from her bare feet. Terror froze her to the spot, and Maelys nearly wet herself when the snake stopped and raised its head to stare at her.

She didn't know what to do; snakes had been rare in the cold uplands of Nifferlin, and though she'd seen them on her travels since, there had always been someone with her. She'd never had to deal with one all by herself. What was she supposed to do? She wasn't game to run, sure that it could strike more swiftly than she could leap, and what if there were others close by? She wouldn't see them if she were running.

She didn't move, apart from an uncontrollable curling of her toes into the powdery dirt. The snake's head turned this way and that, its eyes staring into hers. Don't worry about me, she thought desperately. I'm no threat. I've never killed a snake in my life.

A hundred thumping heartbeats she stood there, watching the snake as it watched her, before it lowered its head, wriggled elegantly through the grass and was gone.

Maelys picked her way back to the stone chimney, inspecting the ground ahead and to either side before each step; she had never felt more vulnerable. The chimney looked solid enough, and there would be a better view from the top. Reluctant to climb the outside, which would leave her exposed to view, she stepped into the fireplace and looked up. At least there would be no swamp creepers in this one.

It was still sooty, and rather narrow at the top, but any of the boys at Nifferlin Manor would have been able to scramble up it, so surely she could. The sun was falling rapidly towards the snowy mountains and it would soon be dark. She scrambled up; the last third of the climb proved a tight squeeze and she tore her pants squeezing through. I don't have to worry about falling down again, Maelys thought ruefully.

Some leagues to the east the land sloped steeply down to a broad plain covered in forest save for a few small patches of cleared land. The plain ran north and south further than she could see. Beyond must be the long narrow Sea of Thurkad, though she couldn't make it out through the haze.

Behind her, in the west, the land rose ever higher, though it lay in the shadow of the setting sun and she could see no signs of human habitation there. Manors or farmhouses occupied two of the other nearby hills, though none of their chimneys were smoking, which surely meant that they were abandoned. South of her, however, perhaps a league away, a village was clustered around a larger building; a communal barn or inn. No, not a barn; she could definitely see smoke rising from its chimneys. It must be an inn, and a substantial one.

Maelys could see no sign of Colm or Flydd further down her hill, nor were there any tracks in the grass. Should she wait, or head down to the village, barefoot? Either alternative was fraught – she knew all too well how unfriendly country folk could be, especially to people who spoke differently, and had no money.

The sun dropped below the mountains, the temperature fell sharply and the choice was made for her – it would take half the night to reach the village in the dark, but with nightfall all kinds of predators would be on the prowl.

She climbed down, rubbed her chilly fingers together and went looking for firewood. There was none up here; nor could she find a sharp stick with which to defend herself. She had to have shelter though, so gathering what broken stone she could lift, she built a curving wall in front of the fireplace.

It was only hip-high when the last light faded, but better than nothing. She felt more secure crouching in the fireplace behind her shelter, until the night noises began. Something swooped past the chimney, and in her imagination it was a savage skeet, or some beast flesh-formed by the God-Emperor's Arts. A cat-call, not far away, was answered by a howl somewhere to her left, and Maelys almost cried out. Curse Colm and Flydd; why hadn't they come through? At least they were armed. Any large predator could leap the wall and trap her inside.

The next cry was closer; Maelys imagined she could see two yellow eyes moving towards her in the darkness. Scrambling to her feet, she felt for the handholds in the chimney and hauled herself up as fast as she could go.

Her left foot was dangling in the centre of the fireplace

when something struck her wall, knocking a stone off the top layer, and let out a screeching howl. Maelys yelped, jerked her foot up, then felt for a handhold and headed higher.

The creature, whatever it was, scrabbled over the wall and began to claw at the chimney. Afraid that it could climb, she pulled herself up to the narrow point, but this time she stuck there, and no matter how she strained Maelys could not force her way up any further.

That night was one of the longest she could ever remember. The beast remained there for at least an hour, and she could smell it. It was rank as an old fox, though far bigger, and its breath reeked as though it dined on carrion.

It jumped out over the wall and she dared to hope that it had given up, but it began to howl until it was answered by other howls, not far away. They weren't wolves, but something just as savage. It ran around the chimney at least a hundred times before rushing the fireplace again. This time a whole pack followed it, all screeching and snarling at each other, then clawing themselves a span up the chimney on the backs of the pack, to snap at her feet. Maelys twisted around, managed to wriggle her hips up through the constriction and clung to the top of the chimney, looking down. Dozens of pairs of eyes reflected the starlight.

Frost began to settle on the stone. Maelys eased her legs and body down the chimney where the stone was still warm from the sun, though the rising stench from the pack of beasts was nauseating. She supported herself on her arms but dared not sleep in case she fell down among them.

The night dragged on, every second an eternity, and it wasn't until the sun rose that the creatures slunk away. They looked like jackals, only with bigger shoulders, huge, bone-crushing jaws and dragging haunches.

Pulling herself up to watch them go, Maelys was clinging on, feeling ill from lack of sleep, when she saw a pair of horses climbing the hill. She slid into the chimney and peeped over the top. The two riders stopped halfway up, pointing to tracks in the grass and then to the pack of hunting beasts, now creeping on their bellies into a patch of longer grass. The riders looked up in her direction, one pointed, and they rode towards her.

There was no way to escape them. They would see her tracks in the grass, and the rude wall that, clearly, had only been built yesterday, so what was the point of hiding?

Never give up; something might distract them at the last minute. Withdrawing below the level of the chimney, she made sure she had a solid foothold and kept still.

The horses' hooves made barely a sound on the powdery ground. As they approached she heard a mutter of conversation, and a man laughed. They knew she was here and she could do nothing to defend herself. Her imagination was running through a series of probable fates when there came a rapping sound on the side of the fireplace and Flydd's voice said, 'Maelys, you can come down now.'

She almost fell down the chimney in relief. She climbed down to the hearth, scrambled over the wall and stopped, staring. She didn't recognise either of them.

'Our faces are too well known.' Flydd's voice came from the older of the two men, who was grey-haired, bearded and yellow-skinned. 'A strong illusion was needed so Jal-Nish's watchers and spies would not recognise us.'

Colm was weather-beaten, tanned and bald apart from an arc of hair behind his ears. They were wearing clean clothes, looked freshly bathed, and Flydd had even had a haircut.

He studied her, head to one side, smiling. Maelys flushed; she felt sure he was laughing at her filthy, bedraggled appearance. Her arms and clothes were smeared with soot; her face must be as well, and her pants were torn on both hips where she'd forced herself up through the narrow point of the chimney.

'I – I thought you were my friend,' she wailed. 'I – can't – take – any – more,' and she burst into tears.

'I ache all over,' Maelys groaned as she slid off Flydd's horse into the mud outside the inn at a village called Plogg, a good six leagues from where she had prematurely fallen out of the portal. She hit the ground and her knees buckled, for she'd been riding in front of him all day on a lumpy and poorly made saddle. Her backside was one massive bruise, the insides of her thighs were rubbed raw and her new boots pinched. But worst of all, she was dressed as a boy again and her bound breasts were even more painful than her bottom.

Flydd steadied her. 'I don't feel so good myself. Using the virtual construct was more painful than I expected.'

'You are all right, though?'

'I will be in a day or two. And you haven't helped, have you?' he said to his horse, patting it on the flank. 'My new body has thighs as soft as a maiden's.'

'What would you know about maidens' thighs?' she snapped.

'I've ridden that saddle many a time,' he chuckled, 'and it's a damn sight more comfortable than this one. Why, I remember –'

'*Thank you*,' she said coldly.

Colm was looking around in satisfaction. 'The inn at Plogg is exactly as it was when I came here as a boy – three storeys of mossy white stone, a host of chimneys like cut-off witches' hats, and a front door decorated with a pair of eels standing on their tails.'

'Lampreys, to be precise.' Flydd indicated the hanging sign above the door, *The Laughing Lampreys*.

'What's a lamprey?' said Maelys.

'It's like a parasitic eel. It attaches to a fish with its sucker mouth and feeds on it.'

'What about people?' Maelys said uncomfortably.

'I've met just as many parasites among humans.' He chuckled.

'That's not what I meant.'

'I know what you meant. Lampreys don't attach to land

animals, as far as I've heard. Come on – I'm wet and hungry. Now, don't say anything about our quest.'

Colm led their horses down the street to a stable. 'Ah, I'm weary,' said Flydd, clinging to the doorknocker for a moment. 'Let's get in out of the rain,'

'Are you sure you're all right?'

'It's just aftersickness. I haven't suffered it in years, and it hits me very hard in this new body. After making two portals in a row, it's amazing that I can still stand up.'

'Will it get worse?'

'I hope not.' He turned to Maelys, who had hesitated in the muddy road, feeling shy. 'Something the matter?'

'I've never been in an inn before.'

'You astonish me. I've stayed in thousands and they're all the same – dirty linen, bedbugs and food I wouldn't feed to my dog. In some inns, the food *is* dog.'

'I thought the scrutators had the best of everything.'

'They *could* have the best of everything, if they chose to, and many did. Personally, I've never found that a good way to rule. To know what the common people think, you've got to live amongst them.' He reflected, then added, 'Well, some of the time. There are limits.'

'I hope the food isn't dog here,' said Maelys. 'I'm starving. I don't feel as though I've eaten proper food in weeks.'

'You haven't; we were in the Nightland for the best part of a month, Santhenar time.'

'What?' She stared at him. 'You're making it up.'

'I'm not. I asked the date when we bought the horses.'

'It only felt like a few days to me.'

'Time runs faster there, evidently.'

Not for poor, lonely Emberr, she thought.

He rapped with the knocker, and shortly the door was opened by a short, bald man, so pale that it looked as though he'd never been outside. He had transparent eyebrows and unnervingly pink eyes. 'You'll be wanting a bed at this time of day,' he said in a flat voice.

'Three beds, taverner.' Flydd pushed through into a

foyer lined with coat pegs, most of which were occupied by dripping cloaks or heavy coats. Maelys followed, standing behind him and feeling uncomfortable. 'There's three of us.'

'You want a bed *each*?' exclaimed the innkeeper. 'Can't be done. You'll have to share.'

'We'll have two rooms, at the very least, with no one else in them. Just us and your fattest bedbugs.' Flydd laughed.

The innkeeper looked hurt. 'Mistress puts oil of turpentine in the wash. No bedbugs here.'

'Excellent, taverner. We'll have your freshest, cleanest sheets as well.'

'They were only changed a month ago.'

Flydd clinked two coins in his pocket, meaningfully.

'If you want to pay for fresh sheets,' said the innkeeper, beaming, 'that's different. Don't get many through here as do.'

'I don't suppose you get many visitors at all, in these empty lands,' said Flydd.

'More than you might suppose, lately. Some nights we turn people away to the stables, but a large party left this morning, hurrying west. Come in.'

Flydd stopped him with a hand on his shoulder. 'What's west of here?'

'Just rocks and trees, but these folks were the sort you don't ask questions about, if you take my meaning.'

'Bandits?' Flydd said, almost too casually. 'We'll want to keep well away from them.'

'Not bandits,' said the innkeeper out of the corner of his mouth. 'God-Emperor's men; soldiers *and scriers*. Come through – you're letting a draught in.' He bustled away.

'Just wipe my boots first,' said Flydd, closing the door behind the taverner.

He took Maelys's arm. 'Why do you suppose a party of the God-Emperor's people are hurrying west?' he said softly.

Her heart lurched. She looked up into his fierce eyes;

273

he wasn't so different from the old Flydd after all. 'They can't know we're here. They just can't!'

'Jal-Nish soon will. I've underestimated him badly; I should have known better. He leaves nothing to chance, and his humiliation at Mistmurk Mountain will only have stiffened his resolve. I deliberately chose our destination at the last possible moment to make the portal difficult to track; I dare say that's why you went astray.'

'Then why are they here already?'

'They've had a month, remember? From the instant we fled the plateau, Jal-Nish's spies and record-keepers would have been set to work, tracing our every connection so as to work out all the places we might have gone, and sending people to every one of those places to intercept us the moment we appeared. He would soon have discovered that Colm's family came from Gothryme, and that he was heir to the manor. Jal-Nish, or one of his tellers, would have remembered the connection to the *Tale of the Mirror* and the treasure left to Karan Kin-Slayer in a cave in Elludore. A treasure that could give me the power I so desperately need,' he said in a low voice. 'Only Colm knows where the cave is, but Jal-Nish's scriers –'

'What's the matter?' said Maelys.

'I thought I heard something.' He put his ear against the inner door, then the outer, listened and shook his head. 'Wipe your feet. We'll talk later.'

Maelys heard footsteps coming up the outside steps. 'That must be Colm now.'

She opened the door. It wasn't Colm, but a tall and extremely buxom woman in her middle thirties, with flaming red hair and a lush, scarlet mouth curved into an enigmatic smile. She stopped on the step below Maelys, but still looked down into her eyes.

'What have we here?' she said. 'A little door boy?' She reached into her coat as if to tip Maelys, who coloured and stepped backwards.

'I'm a g-guest here.'

'Really?' said the woman. She looked up, saw Flydd, and her dark eyes widened momentarily.

He nodded absently to her, his mind on other matters, but she brushed past Maelys and extended her hand to him, smiling. 'Bellulah Vix, but *you* can call me Bel. What's your name? You don't look as though you're from these parts.'

'I'm Lorkentyne Pumice,' lied Flydd in an accent so neutral that it would have been impossible to tell where he came from. He took her hand and his eyes went blank momentarily, then shook it, wincing at the strength of her grip. 'Just taking the air for a day or two. And you?' he added politely.

'Buy me a cup of mead and I'll tell you everything.'

'I'm afraid I've other business to attend to, Bel.' Flydd looked as though he regretted having to say it.

'Nonsense, Lorky,' said Bel, as though the decision had been made and there was nothing more to say. 'You'll do your other business all the better for spending a relaxing hour with me.'

Flydd looked taken aback; surely no one had ever spoken to him in such a confident and familiar way before. 'Another time,' he said with a greater degree of reluctance.

'Right now.' She linked her arm through his and turned him around. Flydd looked back almost pleadingly, as if to say, 'Get me out of this,' as Bel led him inside, flipping a coin over her shoulder to Maelys.

'My bags are outside, lad. Treat them as delicately as you would a lady.'

She laughed heartily and the door banged behind them. Maelys stared at it. Bel's profile, as she turned to go through the door, had been vaguely familiar. Where could she have seen her before?

TWENTY-SIX

Maelys, who had caught the copper coin without thinking, limped down the steps and carried in Bel's bags,
which were extremely heavy. She could not have said why
she did it, save that the woman had a natural authority
which, because of Maelys's upbringing, she found difficult
to defy. But how could Flydd be taken in by her? Was he
really that low from aftersickness?

A blast of aromatic heat struck her as she entered the
taproom, which appeared to occupy most of the ground
floor of the inn, though it was lit only by a pair of lanterns
above the counter and a smoking open fire on the other
wall. The floorboards were strewn with dried ferns and
pungent thyme, several long trestle tables ran down the
centre of the taproom, and there were smaller tables in the
shadows to either side.

Two of the trestles were occupied by groups of men and
women sitting around steaming jugs of mulled drink; a
gaggle of small children played hide and seek between the
legs of the trestles. The tables near the fire were also full,
though the ones along the rear wall were empty.

Flydd and Bel stood at the counter, Flydd ordering
drinks from a thin barmaid. Bel slipped off her grey cloak
to reveal a clinging crimson gown, quite unsuitable for

this weather, which displayed the most voluptuous figure Maelys had ever seen. The older woman was positively bursting out of her stays – or would have been if she were wearing any. A common tart, Maelys thought sourly.

Bel folded the cloak and laid it over Flydd's arm as Maelys staggered up with her bags. Flydd said something to her and they both laughed. Maelys scowled, thinking they were laughing at her, but Bel turned and smiled, saying, 'Thank you, lad,' in such a warm and welcoming way that Maelys was disarmed. Still a tart, but a good-natured one.

Bel's gaze slipped to Maelys's chest momentarily before she turned back to Flydd, and Maelys felt a spasm of panic. She knew! It was much harder to fool a woman about such matters.

'I'll have your best room, taverner,' Bel said in a carrying voice.

'Sorry lady, we're full tonight.' The albino looked at Flydd. 'Unless the gentleman . . .'

'We're not sharing,' said Flydd. 'But we'll be gone at first light.'

'You can have a room tomorrow,' the taverner said to Bel. 'You'll have to sleep in the stables tonight.'

'Damned if I will,' said Bel. 'What do they need two rooms for? They can have one and I'll take the other.'

'We need both,' said Flydd, though less firmly than before. He glanced at her bust, swallowed and looked away.

'All right. You and the fellow with the horses can have one; I'll share the other with the lad. I'm sure my virtue will be in no danger from such a little chap.' Bel gave a throaty chuckle.

'His virtue might be in danger from you, though,' said a red-faced fat man, sitting by the fire and tapping a long-stemmed pipe on the hob.

The whole room laughed, and Bel as loudly as any of them. She ordered drinks for everyone and bestowed a knowing smile on the taproom. 'I'm fixed up for the night, as it happens. Bring our drinks to the table by the back door, bar lass. *Lad*, take my bags up to our room.' She tossed Maelys another coin.

Maelys caught it, quivering in fury. What was the matter with Flydd? His eyes slid across Bel's splendid bosoms again, which were practically exploding out of her gown, then back, lingeringly. A leg of ham could be concealed in her cleavage and you'd never know, Maelys thought spitefully. Coarse, vulgar strumpet – how could Flydd be taken with someone like her?

Because he'd been a lusty man, even into his sixties, until the scrutator's torturers had cut his manhood from him. Maelys had seen enough during his renewal to know that Flydd had got it back and, after so many years, perhaps his male urges were irresistible. Having grown up in a female household, men had always been a mystery to Maelys, but the aunts had never stopped talking about their base, wicked and unquenchable lusts.

She looked helplessly at the taverner. 'Up the stairs to the top and go right, all the way to the end,' he said. 'Would you like a hand?'

'I can manage, thanks.' She hauled Bel's bags up the steep and creaking stairs.

The room at the end was small, cold, and half of it was taken up by a rustic cabinet bed with sliding wooden sides. It was common for travellers of the same sex to share a bed, but Maelys had slept alone since she was little and couldn't bear to lie with a stranger, especially one as loud and coarse as Bel; there was no choice but to sleep on the floor. It was a miserable prospect, for the boards were bare and a chilly draught blasted under the door.

On the way downstairs, she saw Colm at the counter, scowling into a large tankard. His face was drawn; he looked as though he'd suffered a bitter blow. 'Where the blazes did *she* come from?' he muttered, as though Bel was Maelys's fault.

'How would I know?' she hissed, perching on a stool

beside him. 'She just latched on to Flydd. She won't take no for an answer.'

'Why didn't you stop him?' he muttered. 'She's a land lamprey if ever I saw one.' Bel leaned towards Flydd, her bust swaying as though desperate to escape its moorings, and Colm said stiffly, 'Oh, I see. Want a drink?'

Maelys had occasionally tasted the mild small ale brewed for the labourers at Nifferlin, but had only touched proper drink once before, when Phrune had given her the drugged liqueur in Tifferfyte.

'Yes, I do. A big one.'

Flydd and Bel were leaning across the table towards each other and the air between them was sizzling. Maelys felt infected by it too, though the other patrons were talking and drinking as though nothing unusual had happened. Perhaps Bel regularly plied her trade here.

Colm looked at her sideways. 'A big drink? Are you sure?'

She nodded vigorously. The barmaid tapped a large mug from a barrel and set it on the counter in front of her. The beer was a deep brown, with a myriad of bubbles bursting through a deep capping of foam.

Maelys took a long draught without tasting it, gasped and banged the mug down on the counter. Nifferlin small ale had a sweet, nutty flavour, but this drink was so bitter that it puckered up her mouth.

'How can anyone drink that stuff?' she said, wiping her mouth on her grubby sleeve and streaking chimney soot across her face.

Colm managed the ghost of a smile. 'If you drank enough you'd come to like it.'

'Why would I want to?' She checked on Flydd and Bel. She was holding his broad hand across the table, staring down at it as if reading his palm. 'We've got to do something, Colm.'

He stared into his drink as though to read his own future there. 'No, we don't.'

She lowered her voice. 'We're supposed to be incognito and he's making a spectacle of himself. Everyone will remember us.'

'If you don't like the company he keeps, go to bed.'

'I've got to bring him to his senses. It's the responsible thing to do . . .' But Maelys had kept Emberr secret from Flydd, so who was she to lecture anyone about responsibility? No, it had to be done.

She turned away. Colm grabbed at her arm but she ducked under it and marched over to the table. What alias had he used? She couldn't remember, and she couldn't call him Xervish.

'Surr,' Maelys said, 'are you sure this is wise?' It sounded lame, but she couldn't be more specific. There were spies everywhere in the God-Emperor's realm, even in remote backwaters like Plogg.

'Go away, boy!' Flydd growled without looking up.

Bel smiled and dropped her eyes to Maelys's chest as if she could see straight through her boy's clothes to what lay hidden beneath. 'Your master is weary and saddle-sore, lad. He needs the kind of respite only I can give.'

Maelys wasn't giving in that easily. 'Er, *master*,' she said to Flydd, 'you don't know her.'

'He soon will,' grinned Bel. 'Every luscious bit of me.'

Even Flydd looked taken aback at that. He took a long pull at his mug, swallowed and allowed Bel his hand again. Maelys surreptitiously tried to see how much beer was left. Surely he couldn't be drunk on half a mug?

'He's drunk on my charms, aren't you, Lorky?' Bel said teasingly. 'I'm all you've ever dreamed of, and much, much more. In all your life you've not had the kind of night I can give you.' She began to suck his fingers.

Maelys looked away, disgusted, but Flydd was four times her own age, and if he chose to fall into the arms of the first scarlet woman he met, she couldn't stop him.

'We've got to leave early in the morning, surr,' she said quietly.

'He'll be up at dawn, I promise you,' Bel said with a throaty chuckle. 'Run along, lad.'

Maelys blushed, for her meaning was perfectly clear. She stormed back to the counter, where Colm was draining his tankard. 'I'm going to bed!'

'Don't be silly; our supper will be here in a minute. Come over here. We need to talk.'

Colm led her to a table in the angle between the counter and the wall, furthest from the fire or anyone else, and set their drinks down. Maelys noticed that he took the chair against the wall, where he could see the whole room and no one could approach him from behind.

'Did you ask the way,' she said in a low voice. 'To your valley?'

'Yes, but . . .'

A cook's boy came from the kitchen, carrying their dinners on a tray – thin slices of hot grilled meat on slabs of bread, and on the side a jumble of steaming vegetables, none of which were familiar to Maelys. She waited until the boy had gone before speaking.

'A party of travellers went west this morning – the God-Emperor's men. The taverner mentioned them.'

'I heard it in the stables,' said Colm. His big fists clenched on the table. 'Jal-Nish must know we're coming, and what we're looking for.'

So that's what the matter was. Maelys felt for Colm; nothing ever went right for him. 'We'll have to call it off.'

Agitated, he hacked meat and bread, speared it on the point of his knife and wolfed it down, staring at his plate all the while. Maelys was cutting her meat into neat portions when she remembered that she was supposed to be a rude, grubby lad, not a well-mannered girl. She picked up a large piece with her fingers, swallowed it without chewing, had another swig of beer and even managed a small belch.

'Don't overdo it,' scowled Colm. 'You've already attracted enough attention.'

How dare he treat her like a child! She lowered her head and attended to her dinner in silence. The meat was tough but tasty, the bread gritty, and the vegetables had a bitter taste, but she ate every morsel. She was so hungry she could have gnawed splinters off the table leg.

Colm threw down his knife, his meal barely touched. 'I can't call it off!' he hissed. 'I'm going on by myself if I have to.'

Bel's eyes were on her. Maelys leaned forwards, saying quietly, 'What's the point, Colm? Without Flydd you'll never see through the illusion.'

'This is the only thing left to me,' he said slowly, tapping his fists on the table with every word. 'I've lost everything else – my family, my estate, everything I've ever worked for, and –'

For a terrible moment she thought he was going to say, '– and *you*,' but he bit the words off.

'I can't give up Faelamor's treasure, no matter the cost.'

'I don't think Flydd would want you to go alone,' said Maelys.

'I'll be gone before the tart's finished with him. And you can't stop me.' He glared at her.

'I wouldn't *try* to stop you. The things I've done to try and save my family . . .' Her ears began to burn. Why had she reminded him?

'*Indeed!*' He nodded stiffly. 'Good night. I'm leaving at dawn.'

She felt a lump in her throat. Despite their differences, he'd been good to her once. 'I'll get up to say goodbye.'

'All right.' He set off upstairs.

Bel was leaning right across the table, nibbling at Flydd's palm. Maelys was revolted; in her family, no one would have dreamed of acting lasciviously in a tavern. Noticing Bel's eyes on her again, she went up to her room.

But it wasn't her room now; Bel would be sharing it. Maelys turned the lantern low and lay diagonally across the bed, fully clothed, as if to stake her claim on it, but sleep would not come. She shoved the draught excluder against the crack under the door and threw herself on the bed again.

It wasn't long before they came up the stairs. Flydd was laughing and snorting at the same time, Bel making a low, throaty chuckle. They stopped on the landing below and Maelys heard their lips smacking together, the disgusting slurping noises going on for ages, like two swamp creepers mating. She pulled a pillow over her head and tried to block them out.

They came up the last flight and Maelys groaned aloud, only now realising what Bel wanted the room for. How could she, Maelys, have been so dull-witted as to not realise? She would have to go to the stables. She sat up, rubbing her eyes, but Bel – Maelys could tell it was her – began to pound on the door next to Maelys's room.

Footsteps stumbled to the door and it was wrenched open. 'Oh, for pity's sake!' Colm cried. He stamped across the floor, then back to the door and Maelys heard him thumping down the stairs. Flydd and Bel fell into the room, laughing like drains, and the door banged.

The snorting and lip-smacking, and then the symphony of the bed, continued for hours. Maelys was grinding her teeth down to stubs when the tumult cut off as their bed collapsed.

TWENTY-SEVEN

Maelys shot up in bed, wide awake, her heart pounding; she had just recalled where she'd seen Bel's profile before. Front-on her features were unfamiliar, yet from the side the curves of her nose and chin were oddly reminiscent of the woman in red, as Maelys had glimpsed her on the way to the Nightland. Could she be Bel, transformed by spell or illusion, and if so, what did she want from Flydd?

What if the woman in red was one of Jal-Nish's mancers? Yes, that had to be it. She must have been manipulating Flydd all along, in another of the God-Emperor's twisted schemes to raise their hopes so he could have the satisfaction of dashing them irretrievably.

She eased off the bed, trying not to make a sound. She had to tell Flydd without alerting Bel, though in his current state he wouldn't be easy to convince. How could he have been taken in so easily? Because the woman in red had been in his mind since renewal. Bel must have bewitched him at the door – at that moment when his eyes had gone blank – while he was weak with aftersickness.

Surely dawn could not be far off, though Maelys could see nothing through the dirty sheets of mica that served for window panes. Unfastening the window, she slid the sash up and put her head out. It was still dark.

The inn was still, and so was the night; there wasn't a breath of wind. No night bird's cry broke the chilly air, no rat scurried across the rafters; not even a cockroach was stirring.

Thup-thup.

Her stomach muscles knotted, for the sound was unmistakable – it was a flappeter, not far away. Bel must have summoned it; no doubt she'd already rendered Flydd helpless. And Colm was gone. He'd been so furious that he couldn't have slept – he would have headed directly for Dunnet, where his hidden valley lay, and must be at least a league away by now. Maelys was all alone, and no one here would dare support her against the God-Emperor.

Thup-thup, louder this time. The flappeter must be planning to land on the roof. She was out of time. Jamming her new boots into her pack, she eased open the door. It stuck on the draught snake and she picked it up thoughtfully. The sand-filled sausage was heavy; she might knock Bel down with it if she could take her unawares.

There was not even a snore from Flydd's room now. Maelys lifted the latch, careful not to let it clack. The door hinges let out a faint creak and she froze, but when there was no sound from the bed she slipped inside.

She crept across, feeling her way, and made out Flydd's nasal breathing. One knee encountered the foot of the bed.

'Xervish?' she whispered, forgetting that they were travelling incognito.

With a little sigh, someone rolled over and Maelys caught a waft of expensive perfume, not the kind that a rustic tart would be able to afford. But if Bel was one of Jal-Nish's most accomplished mancers she could have whatever her heart desired.

Swinging the draught snake back, Maelys aimed where she expected Bel's head to be, and felt it strike flesh – probably her shoulder. Bel cursed, snapped upright and tried to tear the draught snake out of her hands.

With an almighty crash, the flappeter landed on the steep roof above their heads. Maelys could hear it scrabbling there, and torn-up shingles sliding down the roof and crashing onto the road at the front of the inn.

'What?' groaned Flydd, sitting up with pearls of light swelling at his fingertips. He was naked, bleary-eyed and there were scratches across his arms and chest.

'It's a flappeter, you stupid dunce!' Maelys cried. 'Bel must be one of Jal-Nish's mancers. She's betrayed you.'

Flydd stared at Bel, bewitched, uncomprehending, helpless.

She scrambled out of bed, threw her gown over her head in one elegant movement and jumped into her shoes, which fastened themselves. 'Out the back way.'

'Don't go with her, Xervish,' Maelys cried. 'She'll take you straight to the enemy.'

Bel was on her in an instant, lifting Maelys by the shirt front and shaking her. 'Get out of the way, you stupid little fool.' She tossed Maelys at the wall.

She slid to the floor, groaning. There was a thumping and crashing on the roof, as if soldiers were trying to smash a way in. Flydd hauled his clothes on. Maelys clambered to her feet, the draught snake hanging from her hand, not knowing whether to whack again or run for her life. All over the inn, people were shouting and screaming.

'Soldiers coming through the roof,' a man shouted.

'And outside the doors,' yelled another.

Someone fell down the lower stairs and began to groan.

'There's no way out,' said Flydd listlessly.

'Through the window,' said Bel. 'Onto the roof.'

'Xervish?' cried Maelys. 'Don't listen to her. There's a flappeter up there.'

Bel's backhanded blow crashed into the side of Maelys's head and knocked her down. Spots floated across her vision and, before she could move, Bel picked her up, upside down, threw her across her ample shoulder and was at the window. She thrust it up and scrambled onto the sill, the aged wood creaking under her weight as she caught the top of the window and supported herself there for a moment, one-handed. Maelys, folded over her shoulder, had her face pushed into Bel's stomach, which was firmer than it had appeared.

To Maelys's astonishment, for Bel didn't look as though she'd taken a day's exercise in her life, she began to climb the front of the inn, her toes finding footholds between the stones, her soft hands lifting her weight, and Maelys's, easily. Maelys, terrified that she'd slide off Bel's shoulder, clung to her flimsy gown.

The flappeter was still *thup-thupping*, supporting itself on its feather-rotors. Maelys didn't want to go anywhere near it, but she couldn't escape without falling. She pressed her knees against Bel's back and locked her arms around her waist.

Bel chuckled. 'Won't do you any good, *boy*. If you fall, my gown will tear off and I'll be dangling here in the altogether for the whole world to see.' It didn't sound as though either prospect bothered her.

Flydd emerged from the window and looked up the sheer face of the building. Maelys made out the whites of his eyes. 'I can't climb that!' he said.

'Wait, I'll come back for you.' Bel climbed another span or two and said to Maelys, 'Grab the edge of the roof and pull yourself up.'

'I can't!' Maelys hissed. 'I'll fall.'

'One less problem for me to worry about.'

Maelys reached out with one hand, her fingertips scraping across the rough stone, and felt an indentation between two blocks. Taking hold as best she could, she tried to slide off Bel's shoulder, but slipped and her fingers were torn free. Bel threw her weight against Maelys, squashing her against the wall and forcing the air from her lungs. Maelys found a better grip and attempted to climb, but her fingers weren't strong enough to support her.

Bel put a hand between her legs and heaved her effortlessly onto the roof. She sprawled on the splintered shingles with her feet in the guttering, getting her breath back as Bel turned to go down for Flydd. Could she possibly be on *their* side? Maelys looked up at the flappeter and knew otherwise. She'd put them right into the enemy's hands.

The flappeter was a huge, elongated shadow hovering above the ridgepole. The gutter was half-full of shingles and she could just make out a hole smashed through the roof. She couldn't see the rider, which was a mercy – he must have gone down the hole. She flattened herself on the roof, for the flappeter was more dangerous than any rider.

Little Maelys! What a pleasure it is to see you again.

Maelys nearly fell backwards off the roof. 'R-Rurr-shyve? I thought you were dead?' Months ago she had killed Rurr-shyve's rider and managed to gain a tenuous control over the flappeter, but subsequently it had fallen into a river near Tifferfyte and she'd believed it had drowned.

It takes an awful lot to kill a flappeter. The Imperial Militia lifted me from the river with an air-floater and sent me back to the flesh-formers of Farentyl, to be restored. Improved. *You can't touch me this time.*

It rotated on the ridgepole, its hooked feet clasping and unclasping, sending more heavy shingles sliding down the roof at her. Rurr-shyve was a good five spans long, half of which was the heavy tail which it could swing hard enough to smash down small trees. It could hover on its feather-rotors or walk awkwardly on its pairs of thin legs, and its long head had two pairs of horns.

It emitted a honking hoot, no doubt calling the soldiers. Maelys scrambled backwards along the wooden gutter, not game to take her eyes off the beast. There was no hope of escape now.

Flydd was heaved over the edge onto the roof a few spans away. Rurr-shyve made a purring sound in its throat and darted its long neck at him. He yelped.

Two soldiers ran out the front door of the inn and looked

up. Maelys, peering over the guttering, could see them clearly, for someone had thrown bales of straw into the street and set them alight, sending a blaze spans high into the air. More soldiers were running up the stairs.

'Xervish, you've got to do something,' she whispered.

'Don't have strength to take on – flappeter.' His voice was slurred; he was still ensorcelled.

She shook him but it made no difference, and now it sounded as though the soldiers were scrambling back up through the roof; they couldn't be allowed to get through. Maelys scrabbled up towards the hole on hands and knees. Rurr-shyve's long neck swung towards her but it couldn't reach without lifting in the air. Its feather-rotors began to beat more rapidly.

The movement sent shingles sliding down at her, and they were heavy enough to break her fingers. She stopped one with the heel of her hand and tossed it up through the hole in the roof. There came a satisfying cry of pain, so she hurled more shingles, as fast as she could catch them. After the fourth a man cried, 'Aaargh!' and she heard him go crashing down.

A second soldier cursed but Maelys didn't think he'd fallen, and Rurr-shyve was coming for her.

'Xervish, help!'

Bel was crouched further along the gutter; Maelys couldn't see what she was doing but she'd made no move to stop Maelys throwing her shingles, so why had Bel brought them up here? Because there was no end to Jal-Nish's convoluted and malicious cunning.

Flydd stood up, thrusting his hands at Rurr-shyve, but gave a grunting cough, fell on his face and began to slide towards the edge. She went backwards on her belly, and hit the wooden gutter hard. It held; she wedged her feet in and broke his fall; threw her arm across his back to steady him, but felt sticky wetness there. He'd been shot, probably with a crossbow bolt. It did not feel like a grievous wound, though he was losing a lot of blood.

A soldier's head popped up through the hole, holding a blazing torch. 'I see them,' he roared. 'We've got them.'

A second man followed, clad in leathers – Rurr-shyve's rider. Firelight glinted off the control amulet mounted on a chain that ran across his forehead. Rurr-shyve hovered at the edge of the roof, preventing her from climbing down, and with Flydd incapacitated there was no hope anyway. It was taking all her strength to hold him.

Bel suddenly stood up, thrust her arms high and cried three words in an unfamiliar tongue. A sudden breeze plastered the gown against her opulent figure. A gasp escaped her; her left knee wobbled; her arms shook as if she were holding up a huge weight but she forced them higher, grinding out more words.

With a shrill cry, Rurr-shyve sideslipped away, but Bel slammed into the roof, face first. She began to slide down but hooked her fingers over the edge of a shingle and held on. Maelys stared at her. That Bel had just used all the power at her command was evident, but if she were one of Jal-Nish's mancers, why go to all this trouble?

A pair of closely-spaced carmine sparks shot across the sky, accompanied by an unnervingly shrill and ululating whistle that came ever closer. It passed high overhead, and vanished.

BOOM-BOOM.

The sound, deeper than thunder, shook the roof, dislodging more shingles. One thumped Flydd in the back and he moaned. The whistle rose in pitch, coming from the other direction; the pair of sparks curved around towards them.

Abruptly the whistle was replaced by a sobbing moan; a yearning cry; then a trumpeting roar as something monstrous raced their way.

'No!' Bel said faintly, struggling to her feet. 'I didn't call a *male.*'

'What . . .?' said Flydd.

'I can't control a male; I'll try to seize the other.'

'Can't do it,' said Flydd. 'Not without amulet.'

'On your bellies!' hissed Bel, flattening herself on the roof.

Maelys pushed Flydd's face against the roof as a second flappeter, twice the size of Rurr-shyve, thundered above them. Bel cried three more foreign words – evidently orders. The larger flappeter skidded in a tight circle, hovered and rotated its long head to stare at her. There were tinges of red in its globular compound eyes, though that might have been reflections of the burning straw. Its neck extended towards Bel; its maw opened and, with a steamy hiss, a yellow cloud boiled towards her.

She sprang sideways right over Maelys's head, landing with a thump that shook the rafters. Bel had avoided the cloud but a yellow tendril wisped out and touched Flydd on the left hand. He yelped and his hand jerked convulsively; the skin was already swelling. Maelys wiped his hand with her sleeve and felt the vapours stinging her forearm.

Bel, weak-kneed and wobbly, repeated her orders, harshly. The flappeter stared at her, eye to eye, and made as if to breathe at her again. She drew herself up, pointing directly at it, and the male shuddered, lowered its head submissively, rotated in the air and squirted something rank along the ridgepole.

Extending several pairs of legs, it hooked into the nearest soldier's chest and lifted him, squealing and spurting blood, high into the air. It turned towards Rurr-shyve's rider, who frantically pressed his hand against the now-wriggling amulet on his forehead, shouting, 'Rurr-shyve, Rurr-shyve!'

A hook-ended leg scraped down the rider's forehead, snapping the chain. With a cry of pain he dived for the amulet, which was sliding down the roof, but missed. Another pair of legs caught him by the shoulder and belly, dragging him up besides the soldier, then they were sent flying over the edge and fell to the road in front of the tavern.

Rurr-shyve shrilled in sympathetic pain. The amulet slid into the gutter beside Maelys. She reached for it but drew back as its eight metal legs snapped out and the curled leaves of its segmented body opened to display its mechanical innards. But it was the key to Rurr-shyve, and the only way out of here. It began to scuttle along the gutter, trying to get to Rurr-shyve. If it did the flappeter would be free, and uncontrollable.

Could she control Rurr-shyve again? She had to try. Maelys snatched the amulet off the side of the gutter and closed her fist around it. It struggled furiously, the tiny metal claws tearing at her until she slid her fingers between several of its legs and squeezed hard, whereupon it went still.

Bel, now ashen in the light of the blazing straw, spoke another phrase. The male flappeter let out that trumpeting roar again, flew down to the road and, to Maelys's horror, began to eat the head of Rurr-shyve's rider. Rurr-shyve bellowed in agony and shot across the ridgepole, only to stop suddenly and settle there. It began to sniff the ridgepole.

'What's that about?' said Maelys.

No one replied.

The amulet began to struggle again. Maelys pressed it against her chest, between her breasts where Rurr-shyve's original amulet had once hung. The amulet went still, then slowly folded its legs.

Rurr-shyve turned slowly, staring at her. *So, little Maelys thinks she can best me again? She'd better be stronger this time.*

'I will be,' said Maelys savagely.

Rurr-shyve was still sniffing; suddenly its tail shot up.

'Now!' whispered Bel.

'What?' said Maelys.

'Get on its back.'

'What about Xervish?'

'Just go!'

Maelys didn't hesitate, for more soldiers were gathering outside, and maybe Bel was on their side after all. With hindsight, how could the woman in red have been one of Jal-Nish's mancers? If she had been, why would she have helped them to escape the plateau?

Maelys crawled up the slope, put one foot into the left stirrup and pulled herself into Rurr-shyve's front saddle. Bel staggered across the steeply sloping roof, picked Flydd up and heaved him up onto the rear saddle. Rurr-shyve lurched sideways and Flydd nearly fell off. Maelys reached back to steady him. Bel slid a pale, plump leg over Rurr-shyve and slid in behind Flydd.

Maelys expected the flappeter to throw them off, for such creatures bitterly resented being ridden, even by their bonded rider, but the sniffing beast ignored them. Below, the male had eaten the head and chest of the rider and was crunching into the fallen soldier. The other soldiers had retreated, evidently afraid to attack one of the God-Emperor's precious flappeters, and a robed scrier was calling into a loop listener. The male looked up, saw Rurr-shyve with tail upraised, and lifted into the air. Rurr-shyve lowered its tail and fled.

The male emitted another urgent, yearning cry, raised its own tail and rotored after them, and only then did Maelys realise, with a thrill of horror, what was going on. Rurr-shyve must be a female.

'We've got to get off! Right now!'

A soft hand slapped over her mouth. 'Don't move, don't speak!' Bel whispered over the *thup-thupping* of the feather-rotors. 'Interfere with the mating dance and we all die.'

'Why did you call a flappeter?' hissed Maelys, turning around. 'Couldn't you think of a better –'

'Best beast I could reach –' Bel sagged sideways.

Not you too! Maelys couldn't do anything for her; Rurr-shyve was rolling from side to side in the air and swinging her tail up and down; an invitation?

'To conjure such a beast from – so far – almost beyond *my* capacity.'

'*Who are you?*' Maelys hissed, but could barely hear

herself over the trumpeting of the male. It must have been three times the weight of Rurr-shyve and, whether it mated with her in the air or on the ground, they could not survive it.

Bel said exhaustedly, 'Fading fast. Look after Xervish.'

She slumped against Flydd's back, breathing noisily, but forced herself upright again and appeared to be pressing her right hand to the wound on his back. Maelys felt heat wash through her and sensed something stir in Flydd, as if he was finally being released from her bewitchment.

'Direction?' slurred Bel.

Flydd managed to raise his head. 'West-north-west, about four leagues; a deep, narrow valley surrounded by knife-sharp ridges. Entrance a slot between buttresses of rock. But there are many valleys; without Colm . . .'

'Amulet!'

Maelys handed it to her and, with limp gestures, Bel directed Rurr-shyve in that direction, flying just above the treetops. The flappeter resisted, turning her head to left and right, whilst raising and lowering her tail invitingly. It had gone bright yellow, and the horns on her head were glowing; the pair thrusting out sideways were a pale orange and the pair projecting forwards the dull red of warm coals. Sticky saliva dribbled from her mouth and was blown back along her flanks; acrid puffs of a stinkbug stench from her breathing tubes burned Maelys's nose.

The male let out another bellow. It was not far behind; the brilliant yellow of Rurr-shyve's tail reflected off its largest pair of eyes, while both its pairs of horns were a fiery red. Its dark body could barely be seen but the erect tail, which terminated in a fan of oval discs almost as extravagant as the tail of a peacock, shimmered with waves of colour.

Rurr-shyve slowed and turned its long neck to look back; the male dived towards a little clearing in the forest, then came zooming up right in front of Rurr-shyve, whose feather-rotors reversed and beat frantically as it came to

294

a stop in mid-air. The male hovered, waving its iridescent tail suggestively. Rurr-shyve went forwards a few spans, then backwards, then forwards again, but as the male darted towards her she slipped to the side and raced away, her own tail flat. The male, its flanks coated in windblown trails, turned to follow, and so the pursuit went on.

Bel seemed very weak now. She was clinging to her saddle horn with one hand while she tried to direct the flappeter west-north-west with the other. She managed to drive it in that direction for a league or two before Rurr-shyve, whose cries were becoming ever louder and her tail-raisings more lasciviously inviting, suddenly dived towards a treetop.

Maelys choked. 'They're going to mate!' It had been bad enough next to Flydd and Bel last night, but these flesh-formed monstrosities – yuk! 'Bel? *Bel?*'

TWENTY-EIGHT

Maelys could see right through Bel – she was barely there. What was the matter?

She solidified fractionally as Rurr-shyve settled on a sturdy branch in the crown of a spreading tree, then bent its knees and raised its yellow tail. Pores along its flanks dilated, gushing a greenish vapour which drifted into their faces. Maelys caught a whiff; it had hardly any smell, but she felt more intoxicated than she had after drinking that beer last night. The male was boring down towards them, bellowing with lust, its paired horns throbbing red. The rainbows of colour pulsing across its tail discs lit up the tree's canopy.

The thought of being caught between a pair of mating flappeters made her feel ill. She tried to heave Flydd out of the saddle onto a nearby branch, though she had no idea how she was going to get him down to the ground. She wasn't sure she could get herself down.

'On, Rurr-shyve,' said Bel ineffectually. 'Hurry.'

Rurr-shyve didn't take any notice, for Bel was no longer in control. Maelys took back the amulet and tried to speak into Rurr-shyve's mind the way she had done months ago, but couldn't reach her. In the intoxication of the mating ritual the flappeters must be oblivious to anything else – rather like Flydd and Bel last night, Maelys thought sourly.

'Help me with Flydd.' She tried to haul his weight out of the saddle.

Bel made a distressed sound in her throat, but managed to partly solidify herself and dragged Flydd across a small gap onto the wildly shaking branch. She wavered there and nearly went over the side, until Maelys steadied her.

'This way,' Bel said limply, backing down the steeply sloping branch, holding Flydd.

Maelys didn't understand how she could stand upright without falling off; clearly Bel was a brilliant mancer, th   ps lacking in judgment.

Rurr   ather-rotors came to a stop and drooped. In the light   er lurid tail, Flydd's face was the colour of mud. Maelys held him as best she could, her feet slipping on the damp bark, as the male flappeter hovered above Rurr-shyve. The brilliant colours racing across its tail fans could have been seen back at Plogg. The male gave a steamy hiss, settled on top of Rurr-shyve, and it began.

Their mating made a racket that must have been audible a league away; such roaring, bellowing, grunting and bleating Maelys had never heard before. Their pores issued more intoxicating vapours until the crown was shrouded in a green-tinged mist; vile-smelling gunge dripped from their gaping mouths, and their tails thrashed so wildly that a windstorm of shredded leaves drifted down. The whole tree was shaking as Maelys scrambled from branch to branch, occasional flashes from the male's tail lighting up the forest floor.

'Hold him steady.' Bel's voice was barely audible above the racket. 'I'll do the rest.'

Maelys had no choice but to trust her, though she could not imagine what Bel wanted, or what she was planning to do to them. But if Bel collapsed, or faded away, Maelys had no hope of getting Flydd to safety before the troops arrived.

Slipping on the wet bark, they slid down into a fork just wide enough to hold all three of them. Bel was no more than a shadow slumped against the trunk, breathing shallowly.

'Are you all right?' said Maelys.

'Too weak – can't hold myself here . . .'

Why not? Maelys didn't have a clue what was the matter with Bel. Above, the bellowing appeared to be coming to a climax. A rainbow ray briefly penetrated the clouds of shredded bark and leaves, revealing thin grey strands dangling towards them and oozing down the trunk. Maelys shuddered.

'On!' With a gasp of pain, Bel resolidified, took Flydd over her shoulder and scrambled down, one-handed. Maelys followed, feeling for every foothold, for she could no longer see anything.

The tree shook. 'Aah!' Bel cried weakly.

There was a rustle and a thump. Flydd groaned. Maelys reached the ground and groped around in the dark. Flydd lay on his face in a thick bed of dry leaves, but Bel had vanished.

Maelys felt his back. Bel's healing spell had scarred over the wound, though the area was inflamed and she could feel something hard underneath – a crossbow bolt. The moment they reached somewhere safe it would have to come out. She hauled him to his feet.

'Can you walk?'

'Have to, won't I?' he said limply, sagging on her shoulder. 'Where's – Bel?'

'Drawn back where she came from, I suppose. Where do we go from here?'

'Don't know.'

'We've got to get away, fast. That scrier called for help and it won't be long in coming.'

And wherever Bel had conjured the gigantic male from, it was a staggering feat of mancery that would not have gone unnoticed. Their position was hopeless, for Flydd was too heavy to carry.

'This way,' said a voice from the darkness. 'Hurry.'

Maelys's knees sagged with relief, for it was Colm, and few men were more at home in forests than he was. Realising that she still held the amulet in her free hand, she weighed up whether to keep it or not. No, Rurr-shyve would undoubtedly come after it and to escape they needed all the help they could get. She tossed it into a bank of leaves. Yet even if they got away, could they trust their good fortune? Jal-Nish might simply be waiting for Colm to lead him to the trove.

'Xervish?' Maelys said that afternoon, looking over her shoulder to check that Colm wasn't in earshot. He was twenty paces back, down on hands and knees, drinking from the rivulet they'd just crossed.

Flydd grunted. Every movement caused him pain and his cheeks had a rosy, feverish glow. He seemed mortally embarrassed that he'd been taken in by Bel and would not meet her eyes. She didn't want to talk about last night, either, but she had to.

'About Bel . . .' she said tentatively. 'How could you –?'

'I don't want to discuss it. I must have been out of my mind to let one of Jal-Nish's mancers get so close to me.'

She realised suddenly that, because Flydd had been under the enchantment, he didn't know what Bel had done to effect their escape. 'I don't think she was –'

'No more! Don't ever mention her name again.'

He looked so fierce that she moved away hastily.

'Surr,' she said quietly.

'Go away,' he gritted.

She went.

'What's Bel up to?' Flydd muttered. 'Or rather, what has Jal-Nish put her up to? Was everything that happened at Mistmurk Mountain part of his plan, too, even the woman in red? And if it was, what is he trying to get me to do that he dares not do himself?'

'This is it,' Colm said the following morning, as they trudged out of the trees onto a bank of pale gravel and saw two towering buttresses of white limestone ahead, like a wall with a slot cut through it, with the river tumbling over a shallow sill between them. 'We're definitely in Dunnet now, and I'm sure this is the right valley.'

Bel's healing charm must have continued doing its work, for Flydd had perked up during the night, though he winced with every step and she often noticed him feeling the arrow wound. 'The test will come when we enter the valley,' he said, 'though it looks like cave country.'

'The test will be getting out again,' Maelys muttered.

The only way in was along a narrow, water-washed ledge on the right-hand side of the stream. It ran up and down, then curved around the base of the buttress. On the left-hand side, the racing river tore at the broken rock.

'A few well-placed troops could keep an army out,' Colm said with satisfaction as they headed in.

'If we had them,' said Flydd. 'Ah, I remember now. An army tried to attack this valley once, though they didn't attempt to force the entrance. They came over the razor-topped ridge.' He shivered in the cold wind blowing down the river, and fell silent.

To left and right, the valley walls consisted of layers of cliffs, one above another, separated by steep tree-clad slopes. The valley floor was gloomy, for no sun reached it at this time of the year. Maelys could see dozens of caves, several close to the river at the base of the lowest cliff, but most in the higher cliff layers.

Over the next few hours they searched every cave they came to, but Flydd detected no illusions, perpetual or otherwise.

'It could take weeks just to search this one valley,' Maelys said wearily, 'and what if it's the wrong one? There could be a hundred valleys just like it.'

Colm wasn't daunted. 'I've waited most of my life for this day. I'll search ten thousand caves if I have to.'

Day after day they climbed up and down to check the caves, camping in them at night and hiding their tiny cooking fires with screens of woven reeds, but there was no sign of the enemy. Jal-Nish has to be holding his troops back, Maelys thought. There's no way his scriers wouldn't have found our trail by now.

They continued, working their way ever upstream, and now in the deep, narrow valley the forest closed in on them. The trees were even taller here, the air over the water cold and misty, and the valley had a dank, silent air.

'I don't like this place,' said Maelys, standing by the dark stream and pulling her coat around her. 'It feels as though we're being watched. There could be an army hidden up above and we'd never know.'

'There is, but it can't harm us,' said Colm enigmatically. 'Let's try that one.' He pointed up the flank of the valley.

Flydd grunted and led them up the slope, but Maelys's unease grew with every scrambling step.

He topped a small rise and stopped abruptly. 'This is the place, all right.'

Maelys came up beside him, cold inside and out; Colm stopped on his other side. Just ahead was a vast tangle of white, brown and yellow objects – many long and thin, others round as balls. She took a couple of steps forwards and her teeth began to chatter; she could not stop them. 'But they're bones – *human* bones! Hundreds of them.'

'Tens of thousands of bones,' said Flydd.

Colm went pale, turned away abruptly and sat down, head in hands. 'It didn't seem so bad when it was just an old tale.'

Flydd walked to the base of the pile, where he prodded some rib bones with his foot. She could not read his expression.

'Xervish?' said Maelys. 'What happened?'

'Two centuries and more ago, near the end of the Time of the Mirror, Yggur and Mendark, two of the very greatest mancers in all the Histories, led an army here secretly to take back a device held by Faelamor. They employed every concealment known to their separate Arts, and also brought a team of master illusionists to hide the army and confuse her.'

'But something went wrong?'

'The plan failed, utterly. Faelamor discovered them long before they got here. She broke the concealment and created a counter illusion that was too much for the illusionists. Most died, the rest went insane, and she lured the army to its doom. She marched it over a cliff – that cliff,' he pointed up the sheer limestone face of the upper cliff '– in the impenetrable fog.'

Maelys could see that day in her mind's eye and felt sick with the horror of it. 'Why did a whole army have to die? If she was the greatest illusionist of all, why didn't she hide whatever they were looking for until they gave up?'

'I expect she wanted to teach them a lesson – that all their might, and indeed the towering Arts of Yggur and Mendark, were as nought compared to her mastery. Two thousand men fell to their deaths that hour, and neither Yggur nor Mendark ever recovered from the defeat.'

Maelys closed her eyes, but she could imagine it all too clearly. The terror of the fall, the agony of their smashed bones, the ghastly waiting of any injured survivors to die.

'This valley hasn't forgotten either,' said Colm soberly. 'Not a single plant grows within the boneyard.'

'Plants will, one day,' said Flydd. 'Nothing lasts forever.'

'Save perpetual illusions,' said Colm.

'Perhaps. Faelamor's cave would not have been far from where the army fell. To the right, I'd say.'

For a few minutes, they followed a trail worn by cloven-hoofed animals, up and down, around a series of fallen boulders, then along the base of the cliff. To their right the ground fell away steeply towards the river; ahead it became a sloping apron before a black opening in the white rock.

'That's the cave,' said Colm hoarsely. 'It's got to be.' His eyes were streaming and he did not bother to hide it.

Maelys did not follow at once, for again she had the unnerving feeling that they were being watched. She slid behind a tree, looking up the valley and down, as far as she could see. Nothing moved in her field of view, but with all the cover here, Jal-Nish could have an army hidden close by. Would he make his move now that the cave had been found, or wait until the illusion had been dispelled?

She followed Flydd up to the cave and stopped just inside until her eyes adjusted. The cave was well protected from wind and weather, while a natural groove in its ceiling, somewhat soot-blackened, would have helped to funnel out smoke from a cooking fire. The floor was scattered with charcoal from camp fires of long ago and the dry dung of a variety of small animals. She saw nothing else.

'This place doesn't look grand enough for the leader of all the Faellem,' said Maelys. 'It looks like any other cave.'

'The Faellem lived in harmony with nature,' Flydd said absently. 'They did not care excessively for possessions, or built things. As long as they were comfortable, the cave's simplicity would have appealed to them.'

Colm paced back and forth, his back bowed and his shoulders slumped. 'I don't think there's anything left.'

'Faelamor was a master illusionist,' Flydd reminded him. 'The greatest that ever lived.'

'Then break her illusion, if it still exists.'

Flydd didn't move. 'It's not that easy.'

'You haven't tried! I've been brought here under false pretences.'

'Oh, don't be so pathetic! You nagged me to come here, if you recall, though I told you more than once that I might not be able to break her illusion.'

'I'm sorry. Please try.'

'Colm, I can't yet tell if there *is* an illusion. I've got to have something to start with, and it all takes time.'

'Then why did you come?' Colm said, very controlled. 'Why allow me to hope?'

'Because you begged me.' Flydd turned back to his study of the floor, and again Maelys noticed a faint gleam in his eyes.

'Then it's over,' Colm said dully. 'I've nothing left to hope for.'

No one said anything. Nothing Maelys could say would give him any comfort.

'I think you're looking for this.' The woman's voice came from behind them.

TWENTY-NINE

Maelys spun around. A woman not much taller than herself stood at the entrance to the cave, her hair tumbling halfway down her back. She was silhouetted against the light, so her features could not be seen, and at first Maelys assumed it must be Faelamor herself, back from the dead, for the woman held out a small ebony bracelet.

'Colm?' she said in a dry little voice. *'Colm?'*

Not Faelamor. Colm swallowed noisily, tried to speak but nothing emerged save a hoarse croak. He tried again. 'Ketila?'

'Yes. It's me.' She just stood there, staring at him as if at the rising sun.

'I thought you were dead,' Colm whispered. 'Though I never gave up hope. Is little Fransi . . .?'

Ketila's throat quivered. 'Eaten by a lyrinx,' she said slowly, deliberately, as if she hadn't spoken in a long time.

He staggered and caught blindly at Maelys's shoulder. 'Oh, oh! But . . . it would have been quick. She would not have suffered . . .'

'Fransi suffered.' There was a whole world of torment in her words. 'Oh yes.'

'Why wasn't I there? If only I'd been there –'

'It would have eaten you too.'

'At least my worries would be over.' Then, softly, 'What about Mother and Father?' He was pleading with Ketila; please, please say that they're alive.

'They died soon after we lost you, escaping from the slave camp. They attacked the lyrinx that had taken Fransi, with their bare hands. They had no chance.'

Though Colm must have expected it, he shrank down on himself, each death a blow hammering him deeper into the dirt. He swayed, his nails digging in and out of Maelys's shoulder. She could not bear to imagine what that night must have been like.

'No chance.' His arm fell to his side. 'All the heart had gone out of them long ago. They would have been glad to die.' He went forwards, slowly.

Ketila moved backwards and the light from outside fell on her face. She was not yet thirty and might once have been pretty, but was now thin and drawn. Her skin was weathered from sun and wind, grief had etched deep lines around her mouth, and her eyes had an unnervingly blank stare.

'What are you doing here, Kettie?'

'Don't call me that,' she said sharply, fighting back tears.

'Sorry, Ketila.'

'I can't bear to be reminded of the good old days.'

'In that terrible camp?' he exclaimed.

'I was happy there. We were all together; we had each other.'

'I never thought of it like that,' he said quietly.

'I searched everywhere for you that night,' said Ketila. 'And for weeks and months afterwards, but no one had seen a twelve-year-old boy answering your description.'

'Nor a fifteen-year-old girl like you,' said Colm. 'Nor Fransi; nor Mother and Father. I never gave up looking, but I had lost hope.'

'I knew you'd find your way to Dunnet eventually, if you were still alive.'

'How long have you been here?'

'Eight years.'

'All by yourself?'

'Since I lost everyone, I prefer to be alone . . . In the war, I learned that no one but your family can be trusted. I went through a lot in the years it took me to find this place.'

Maelys could only imagine it – a young woman, travelling alone for years through the lawless chaos of those dark times.

'Oh, Ketila,' said Colm, and took her in his arms.

Ketila kindled a small smokeless fire between the boulders down the slope, out of sight of the bone field, and they ate smoked fish from her stores, and drank sweet-sour tea made from a local herb. Afterwards Flydd walked away towards the bones, but Maelys remained by the fire. She had never seen Colm so alive, not even during those brief weeks together on the way to the plateau. He kept jumping up and sitting down again, pacing between the rocks, staring hungrily at his sister and looking away again, and all the while beaming as though he could not believe his good fortune.

Ketila maintained her reserve. Mostly she stared into the fire, lost in her thoughts like a lifelong hermit. Occasionally she looked up at Colm and, momentarily, there was a glow in her eyes.

Maelys sat well to the side, keeping watch. She didn't want to intrude; besides, the enemy could come down the cliffs, or up the river, at any moment and she wasn't going to be taken by surprise again.

'I felt so guilty,' said Ketila. 'I still do.'

'Why?' said Colm. 'You never did anything wrong.'

'I'm the oldest. I should have been looking after you and Fransi.'

'You couldn't look after me – I was always in trouble and I never did what I was told. And I forced Mother and Father to take Nish in. If only I hadn't.' He bowed his head.

'What difference would that have made?' she said in the brisk fashion of an older sister. It was the first trace of animation Maelys had seen in her since dinner.

'If I hadn't, Nish would have been taken into custody at once, and maybe the lyrinx –'

'They didn't come for him, Colm; they didn't know he was there. It was the war – just the stupid war – and without Nish we might never have won it.' Her eyes shone for a moment. 'I was quite taken with him once, you know.'

Maelys sat up. Ketila had known Nish back when he was Maelys's age – would he fit the legend, or fall terribly short? Had Nish done something to make her mistrust humanity so?

'Really?' said Colm in astonishment.

'I was just fifteen. Remember how Mother forced me to wear those horrible black wooden teeth, and painted spots and warts all over me?'

'It was the only way to keep you safe. A pretty girl in that lawless place . . .'

'Then Nish dropped into the camp from a balloon he'd flown halfway across the world. He was already a hero; he'd killed a nylatl; he'd fought lyrinx, and beaten them.' Her eyes were shining now. 'He told such stories in those few nights he slept in our hovel; I'll never forget a word of them. And Nish was a gentleman, too. He was so kind to me, though I was just a kid he would never see again. The thought of him sustained me in my darkest hours.' Ketila sighed.

Maelys studied her from under her lashes. They weren't so different after all, for Maelys had nurtured a silly romantic dream about Nish ever since reading his tale when she was nine. And I wasn't wrong about him after all, she thought. Ketila's story proves that Nish was once as noble as the stories say. Poor Nish, tormented beyond endurance by his father until he believes himself a failure. Poor Nish, who promised the world he would overthrow his father, and then went back on his promise. How can he ever redeem himself?

'I never wanted him, romantically,' said Ketila, as though she'd read Maelys's face and wanted to distinguish them from each other. 'It was just hero-worship. And after I was left on my own . . . I don't want any man, *ever*,' she concluded fiercely.

Flydd came wandering back and sat down, wincing and rubbing the scar on his back. The crossbow bolt had to come out, but now was not the time. No one spoke. Maelys could feel her stomach muscles knotting; they were wasting precious time. She glanced at Flydd, who had leaned back against a rock with his eyes closed, fingers drumming on his knee.

'We've got to get moving!' she burst out. 'They could be in the valley already.'

'Who?' said Ketila.

'The God-Emperor's army,' said Flydd. 'Colm?'

Colm stiffened, then emptied the dregs of his tea onto the ground. 'What did you find after you dispelled the illusion, Ketila?' he said quietly, struggling to keep the eagerness out of his voice.

'I didn't dispel it.'

'Why not?'

Ketila still looked wary, and Maelys didn't suppose that would change in a hurry, after spending half a lifetime on her own.

'It's your heritage, not mine,' said Ketila.

'We could share it.'

'I never wanted it, Colm; all I wanted was home and family. A little cottage would have been enough for me if I could have shared it with the people I loved. But you were different. You could never be happy with what you had – you were always reaching out for more; always expecting what could never be yours.'

She rose, sliding the ebony bracelet up and down her arm, and headed to the cave. They followed. At the entrance, she held the bracelet up.

'It's made of precious ebony from the world of Tallallame,' said Flydd from below, 'which had special powers even in that magical land. But objects carried between the Three Worlds change in unusual ways –'

'Change in what ways?' said Colm.

'No one would have known save Faelamor herself, for it's different every time. Would you go in, Ketila?'

She did so, and Maelys noticed, from behind, how little there was of her. Though she had ample stores of dried fish and other foodstuffs, and the valley was abundant with game, Ketila ate no more than was necessary to sustain herself.

As she advanced with the bracelet, a myriad of shadows sprang up from the floor to form a confusion of tangled, moving shapes. But they were not quite shadows: they had the outlines of people with subtly aura-tinged edges. The hairs on the back of Maelys's neck rose.

'Come back a step,' said Flydd, holding his right hand out. His lips moved, though Maelys didn't hear anything.

As Ketila stepped back, most of the shadows sank into the floor again, though one remained, the barest outline of a small female figure bending over a fire set on the floor. Ketila's arm shook; the figure faded to a wisp and disappeared. Other figures, male and female, rose and moved about the cave, though seldom were they visible for more than a few steps.

'The first woman would be Faelamor,' said Flydd. 'And the others, no doubt, her people; the Faellem were a small folk. Faelamor dwelt here for months, perhaps years, though *she* would not have left much of herself behind – only when she used her Art, and that sparingly. Move your arm to the left, Ketila.'

As she complied, several larger, bulkier shadows rose and moved about, though only one could be seen clearly, a big man swinging a pick into the earth floor, then bending over to look at what he had uncovered. Behind Maelys, Colm groaned.

'Shh!' said Flydd. 'Ah, I think I understand. Faelamor brought her most precious possessions here long ago, and hid them, protected by her perpetual illusion. She may have returned many times, taking some items or adding others, and each time renewing the illusion.'

'And the other shadows?' said Colm. *'That man?'*

'Villains and fortune hunters who came after her death, attracted by the tale and the lure of what lay hidden here. Hundreds could have entered the cave, though only those with sufficient Art to touch the illusion will have left their shadows behind. Don't panic, Colm. *He* took nothing away.'

Ketila moved around the cavern under Flydd's direction; the shadow figures rose and fell. They saw Faelamor's outline many times, plus other small slender folk who could have been her people. A taller woman came, then more men digging under the direction of a robed figure whose face was not visible from any angle. A small, curvaceous woman came and went, plus other shadows so faint that not even their sex could be determined. Finally, what could only have been a pair of Jal-Nish's scriers turned up, armed with wisp-watchers, though they did not seem to find anything either.

Colm was growing ever more agitated. 'The enemy may be encircling the valley even now, Flydd. Why isn't the bracelet dispelling the illusion and showing us the trove?'

'I don't know; we'll have to use trial and error.'

Flydd had Ketila walk around the walls of the cavern, then spiral slowly in to the place where the miscreants had been digging, an insignificant hollow in the floor. She touched the ebony bracelet to the hollow and through the dirt Maelys saw a brighter, richer shadow: a long, wide, shallow box, full of scrolls, parchments, cups and bowls made from precious metals, plus items of jewellery and a small wooden ball. Colm sighed and fell to his knees beside the hollow.

'Dig carefully,' Flydd said. 'Even the box is precious.'

Colm began to dig with a pointed stick, while Ketila watched him in silence. Soon the corner of a wooden box was revealed, its pale timbers stained with the colour of the earth in which it had been buried for centuries. He scraped the earth off the top, and all around it, then levered carefully. The box rose out of the earth and the last of the dirt crumbled away. He lifted it in trembling fingers, slid the cracked lid off and rocked back with a cry of despair.

'It's gone!'

The box was full of earth, ash and charcoal. He shook it out and crumbled it on the floor, raking through the little pile with his fingers, over and over and over, desperately sifting it ever finer, but of the scrolls and precious items they'd seen in the shadow play, nothing remained save a few crumbling fragments of charred parchment and an empty leather pouch.

'We've been robbed, Ketila.' Colm's fingers clawed at the dirt.

'No, Colm. Just you,' she said quietly.

'I would have shared everything with you. I told you that.'

'Our tainted heritage destroyed Mother and Father. They had given up long before the lyrinx took Fransi, and they were glad to die with her, even though it left *me* all alone. I don't want any part of our heritage. All I want is my brother back.'

'Poor, penniless and miserable,' he choked. 'A stinking, unwashed peasant who can never hope for more.'

'All your life you've festered about your inheritance,' she said sharply, and if you'd got it when you were young, you might have been happy, but it's too late now. Even if you do recover it, you'll be consumed by bitterness. I never expected anything, but now I've got you back my life is complete.'

'Is there anything else?' said Colm. 'Try the bracelet again.'

'There's nothing,' Flydd said quickly. 'You've got it all.'

'A lousy broken box!'

Outside, there was the sound of a stick breaking. Maelys, who was closest to the door, looked out. 'Just a dead branch falling off a tree, but . . .'

'The enemy won't be far away,' said Colm in a dead voice. 'We should have run while we had the chance, but it's too late now. You're right, Ketila – this hopeless dream has consumed my life, and now it's probably betrayed us.' He stalked to the doorway, put his hands around his mouth and bellowed, 'I renounce my heritage, every last stinking crumb of it!' He turned to Ketila, his once handsome mouth twisted. 'There; it's done. Come on.'

She caught his arm. 'I know every ell of this valley, and the two valleys on either side. We can still escape them.'

As she pulled her tall brother out the door, the bracelet oscillated down her arm and Maelys noticed a tiny shimmer on the floor in the darkest part of the cave. She started towards it. Outside, Ketila's and Colm's footsteps dwindled down the slope.

'Xervish?' Maelys said. 'Did you see that?'

'Shh! I did. Be careful.'

She squatted down, and where she'd seen the shimmer, the top of something round just protruded above the dirt. She was about to prise it out when Flydd threw himself at her, knocking her out of the way.

'Don't touch it.' He stood over the round object, legs spread, breathing heavily.

'What is it?' she whispered.

'I–don't–know.'

He bent over, rather red in the face, and began to excavate the object from the hard-packed earth with one of the splintery strips of wood from the box. It looked like a dirty, rudely carved wooden knob or ball, about the size of an orange. 'Grab that leather pouch we saw earlier.'

313

She fetched it for him, and when the ball was fully exposed on a little pinnacle of dirt he scooped it up in the leather pouch, pulled the drawstring and slipped the pouch into his pocket.

'I'll give Colm a yell.' She went to the entrance.

He caught her arm and dragged her back roughly, hissing in her ear, 'Don't say a word about it.'

Maelys pulled free and stared at him, shocked. 'It's valuable, isn't it?'

'I think it's a *mimemule*, and if it is, it's more valuable than everything that was stolen.'

'What's a mimemule?'

He shook his head. He wasn't going to tell her.

'But – it's Colm's,' she said.

'He renounced his heritage,' said Flydd, breathing hard. 'That makes it treasure trove, and finders keepers.'

'You didn't find it; I did.'

'But you didn't take it, Maelys.'

'You said not to touch it.'

'And you didn't, so now it's mine.'

Maelys searched his grim face, trying to understand. That unnerving gleam she'd seen once or twice previously was back in his eyes, and she remembered him telling Colm, hastily, that there was nothing else here. Had he done so deliberately? Had he set all this up, even come here intending to take the treasure if he could? Surely not, unless she didn't know him at all. 'You can't do this to Colm. It'll destroy him.'

'Oh, yes I can. Why do you think I came here?'

'I *thought* you came to help Colm.'

'I came in search of a weapon against the great enemy, and this might help me to find one. Colm can't use it anyway – it's steeped in the Art of another world and he's quite talentless.'

'But he could sell it and buy Gothryme back.'

'This can't be sold,' Flydd said hoarsely. 'Not ever. It's mine now, and you're not to say a word about it. Hush!'

He put his foot over the hole in the floor and took her arm again.

Heavy footsteps approached the cave and Colm appeared. 'Will you come on! Ketila knows a safe way out.' He looked from Flydd to Maelys, frowning. 'What's the matter?'

'Just a minor disagreement about how to proceed,' Flydd said, crushing her wrist warningly, 'but we've sorted it out now. *Haven't we, Maelys?*'

Flydd wasn't a greedy man – at least, the old Flydd hadn't been – and surely he had a good reason for keeping the mimemule. Such an enigmatic old device, made long ago by one of the greatest of all masters in the Art, might be deadly in the wrong hands. It would certainly be useless to Colm, who did not have any trace of a gift, and she understood that such a perilous device should never be sold for mere money, so why did she have the feeling that Flydd was, essentially, stealing it?

Furious at the position he'd put her in, she nodded stiffly. After Colm went out, she said, 'I feel as though I've aided and abetted a common thief.'

His head snapped up. 'If that's what you think, little Maelys,' he said coldly, 'you'd better watch your back. You never know what a *common* thief might do next.'

She followed him out, her faith in humanity shaken. Ketila was several spans up a crevice in the cliff and Colm was starting up after her.

'Where are we going?' said Colm.

'The Island of Noom.' Flydd's tone was like a death knell.

'Isn't that –' began Ketila.

'It lies in the frozen southern wastes,' said Flydd, 'but if I can find the right place to make a portal we won't have to walk *all* the way.'

'What are you looking for?'

'A lookout on a ridgetop, with a clear view in all directions, and no trees or upstanding rocks between us and the horizon. Do you know such a place?'

'Yes,' said Ketila, 'though it won't be easy to get to.'

'There's no choice. I've never been to Noom, so to make a portal there I need the perfect starting point.'

They climbed the crevice, turned left along the slope, then into a crack running up the higher cliff. Maelys's feelings of dread were growing ever stronger, for in the back of her mind she could feel the rhythmic beating of Rurrshyve's feather-rotors. Surely that meant the flappeter was close, and because they had once been linked in the contract between flappeter and rider, it might be using that link to find her.

'They're nearly here,' she said in a choked gasp. Nothing made sense any more. Flydd had stolen Colm's heritage and she was supposed to go along with it. Right and wrong no longer seemed to have a clear meaning.

At the top of the crack Ketila scuttled along a narrow path near the edge of the cliff, weaving between tussocks of razor grass which stabbed at Maelys's knees through her pants. To her left was a sheer drop of some fifty spans onto broken rock, and every time she looked down her heart lurched and she imagined those poor soldiers in the fog, lured to their deaths. It was so horrible she couldn't bear to think about it, but the memory of the bones kept it in her mind.

And Faelamor had killed them: the same Faelamor who had owned the mimemule Flydd had stolen from Colm. Had she used it to create that illusion? If she had, it must be tainted by all those deaths. What sort of a person would kill two thousand men just to teach their masters a lesson?

Ahead, the cliff ran out in an overhang like a thick lower lip, after which it curved around to the right in a tangle of razor grass and thorny shrubbery at the base of the higher cliff.

'Up there!' Ketila headed towards a barely visible cleft.

Maelys plodded after her. Flydd crouched low and went to the edge of the overhang. 'I can see the whole valley from here.'

'Be careful,' said Ketila over her shoulder. 'You can be seen, too.'

Flydd flattened himself further. 'A column of troops has just turned the corner below Faelamor's cave – I can see them against the white rocks. We've got to go faster.'

They scrambled up the cleft and onto the sharp white spine of the limestone ridge. To the right, the land dropped steeply into the adjacent valley, but they weren't going there. The meandering ridge crest was broken by a series of steep pinnacles and Ketila was making for the tallest of these, a square-sided pyramid which stood a good fifty spans higher than any other. If its top was the only place suitable for making a portal to Noom, they had to reach it, though Maelys felt desperately afraid. The sides were precipitous and it would be a dangerous climb, even if they had all the time in the world. They had to get to the top before the enemy came within range, for on the climb they would be exposed and helpless.

They went up the south face, the steepest of the four but the easiest, for a winding crevasse ran into the limestone, just wide enough for them to inch up. Ketila went first, since she'd climbed it before. Colm followed, then Flydd, slow because of his back wound, and Maelys last.

A *thup-thup* came out of nowhere and the male flappeter shot overhead, carrying a rider and two archers this time; it banked so they could bring their bows to bear. An arrow chipped stone from the rock behind Maelys, and another tore Colm's hat off. He caught it in mid-air and kept going.

Maelys's eyes followed the flappeter, which had swept by and out over the centre of the valley, where it began to circle. Its rider was leaning forwards, speaking into a glistening loop – a speck-speaker – telling the army exactly where they were.

She could see them now. Hundreds of soldiers were scrambling up clefts everywhere it was possible to force a path. Fit, strong and well equipped, they would climb three spans to her one. She looked up, trying to gauge the distance to the top. It seemed an impossibly long way.

'How far to the lookout?' panted Flydd.

'Ten minutes for me,' said Ketila, 'but I don't see how we can get there.'

'Why not?'

She pointed north along the cliff line. A head ducked back out of view. More soldiers were coming along the crest of the ridge, straight for them.

Ketila climbed faster, with Colm at her heels, but they were rapidly widening the gap to Flydd, the only one who could save them. Maelys clawed her way up the crevasse, breaking her fingernails and tearing skin off her palms. The flappeter was coming again, its bowman leaning over the side and pointing a club-headed arrow at Flydd.

Ketila had squeezed her thin body further into the cleft and was looking down, her face quite blank, save when she looked at her brother.

Maelys reached Flydd, who was labouring badly.

'How long will it take to make the portal, Xervish?'

It had taken ages to use the virtual construct in the Nightland and she couldn't imagine it would be any quicker here. And at the top of the crag they would be completely exposed. There didn't seem to be any way out this time.

Flydd shook his head; he didn't have the breath to answer.

The troops were swarming along the ridge and up the cliffs; the huge flappeter rotored in for another attack. Even if they reached the top of the crag, if the portal took more than a minute to make, it would be too late.

Ketila was only a few spans from the crest, hurling rocks at the flappeter's eyes, and at the two archers on its back. They hadn't fired at her yet, for the flappeter was bouncing wildly in the wind, but if they got a clear shot she would die.

It sideslipped away, but in the same breath Rurr-shyve came at them out of nowhere with a new rider and two archers. Maelys cursed her folly in throwing away the amulet. If she'd kept it, she might have had a hope of influencing Rurr-shyve: either turning it away, or into the path of the male.

Colm was clinging to the side of the cleft, hanging on against the blast of Rurr-shyve's feather-rotors. She couldn't come closer without her feather-rotors hitting the rock; it was the only thing saving him.

Maelys climbed above Flydd and reached down her hand. His grip was weak now; he seemed to be fading, yet there were still three spans to go. A white flash caught her eye, far away to the left, the sun reflecting off an approaching air-floater, and it was like being punched in the stomach. Every time they had a minor victory, Jal-Nish and his troops regrouped and fought back stronger than before. They had destroyed an army at Mistmurk Mountain but he simply raised another one. He could rouse the whole world against them.

Flydd settled on a little platform beside her. His face was pallid and sweaty, his cheeks slack, and he had a tremor in his right arm.

'How are you doing?' she said quietly, concerned for him despite what he'd done in the cave.

'I've had better days.'

'Can you make it to the top?'

'Haiiii!' shrilled Ketila, and began hurling rocks furiously.

She must have had plenty of practice during her lonely years in the valley, for she was a very good shot. A fist-sized rock smacked into the giant flappeter's watermelon-sized right eye, caving it in. It lurched away, trumpeting in pain, with its leather-clad rider pressing his hands over his own right eye and screaming in sympathetic agony.

The link between flappeter and rider must have failed momentarily, for it sideslipped directly for Rurr-shyve. She shot down into the valley, wailing shrilly. Having mated with the giant male, she was bonded to it as well.

In quick succession, Ketila hurled rocks at the two archers on the male flappeter as they struggled to get a clear shot. The leading archer was struck so hard on the hand that it tore the bow from his fingers. He swayed wildly in the saddle and managed to catch his bow by the string, but before he could recover, Ketila, her face twisted in a snarl, hit him in the back of the head with another rock. He slid out of the saddle, swung upside down from one foot by the stirrup, then fell.

But Rurr-shyve came zooming up from the other side, appearing out of nowhere, and the rear archer fired at her. The arrow skimmed her neck, caught in her knotted hair and slammed her backwards into the crevice so hard that her teeth snapped together. Ketila's eyes rolled up in her head and she toppled forwards.

THIRTY

A t the moment the red fog disappeared from above the whirlpool and revealed that Vivimord was gone, Nish knew in his heart that he had made the wrong choice and that Gendrigore's peaceful existence would soon be over. He went heavily back to the tents and sorted through Vivimord's gear. There wasn't much – just clothes, which he burned, since not even the meanest peasant of Gendrigore would have worn them – some potions and ointments which he threw out, a book written in a script he could not decipher, which he put away for later, and a sabre with a basketwork handle, which he kept, because metal weapons were hard to come by in Gendrigore, and of poor quality.

The sabre was beautifully made, of the same black metal as Vivimord's wavy blade, and Nish knew he would soon have need of it. It was a trifle long for him, but he would have to get used to that, for no smith in Gendrigore had the skill to cut down such a blade without ruining it.

The Maelstrom of Justice and Retribution did not reform, and the townsfolk expressed some unease about it in the inn that evening, though after a vigorous and well-lubricated debate they gave the next whirlpool the same name and got on with their affairs.

In the morning, the sea leviathan that had attacked

Vivimord was discovered, floating upside down and blackly bloated, at the point where the former whirlpool had been. This was seen as a bad omen, but by the following afternoon a hundred sharks and ten thousand eels had reduced it to a skeleton which sank out of sight and, to Gendrigore, the matter was finally closed.

'We're not afraid of the God-Emperor,' said Barquine, the mayor, several nights later. He and Nish had taken to sitting on the deck of the open-air inn with their feet on the rail, watching the mist roll in over the forest, as it did every afternoon that it wasn't actually raining. Such afternoons were rare at any time, for it was always raining in Gendrigore.

Nish took a hearty pull at his beer. Though it had come up from cellars excavated ten spans into the rock below the inn, it was tepid. It was good beer, though, strong and dark with a powerful flavour of roasted malt and a bitter aftertaste from some local herb used in place of hops, which were unobtainable here.

'I swear this is the finest beer I've tasted in more than ten years.' He raised his glass to Barquine.

'Considering that you spent most of that time in your father's dungeon, and the rest on the run, that isn't much of a compliment,' said the mayor. 'But I'll take it as given, and so will my brew-girl, when I tell her.'

'Brew-girl?' frowned Nish. 'Brewing beer is a man's job in Gendrigore, isn't it?'

'Not since Alli took over, and if she hears you say so there'll be a warty toad in the bottom of your next mug. I taught her everything I know about brewing, and she surpassed me within the year.'

'She can brew my beer until the polar ice melts and floods the whole world,' said Nish with a sweeping gesture that slopped beer down the mayor's shirt. He hastily returned his tankard to the rail.

Barquine casually wiped his shirt, as though it was an everyday occurrence. 'You're a travelled man, Nish,' he said, chewing on a sprig of lime leaves to cover the smell of his drink before he went home. 'Are there really polar lands where nothing lives and nothing grows, and even the sea is covered in ice?'

'So I'm told. I haven't been that far south, myself, but my old friend Xervish Flydd, once a scrutator, flew over such lands in a thapter, a flying machine, during the war. And I once crossed high over the Great Mountains, the highest peaks in the world, where there was nothing but snow and rivers of ice as deep as the sea cliffs of Gendrigore are tall.'

'That would be a marvel indeed. I've seen snow once or twice; it falls every winter at the top of The Spine that keeps the marauders of Lauralin out of our land, though it seldom lasts long.'

'Mayor . . .' began Nish after he'd finished his beer and, for once, had not started on another. Today it was doing nothing to ease his troubles, for he knew the time had come to act.

'Barquine, please,' he said.

'Barquine, I'm worried about my father. You don't know what he's like.'

'I've a fair idea, Nish, for we hear the tales, even here. There's no need to worry about us. Many tyrants and scoundrels have tried to conquer our land, and all armies, save three, foundered on the way up over The Spine, the only way into Gendrigore. The path is so high and rugged that no army can climb it and still fight when it gets to Blisterbone Pass. Of those three who reached Blisterbone, two armies did not survive the descent.'

'Isn't there a second pass? I'm sure I heard someone talking about it.'

'There's Liver-Leech Pass, but it's even higher and more dangerous. If an army can't cross the lower pass they won't attempt the higher one. And even if some survivors do cross Blisterbone, and climb all the way down the path on our side, they'll be starving and riddled with fevers that hardly touch us. Your father is a mighty foe, I grant you, but The Spine will break him too.'

Barquine had been saying much the same for days, and Nish did not think he would ever face up to the peril. No one in Gendrigore was concerned about the God-Emperor, and there was no one he could talk to about his fears, for Tulitine had gone into the forest with her lusty farmhand after Vivimord's death, and had not returned.

Nish had also tried to convince the townsfolk to get ready for war, and they had listened politely, since he was the son of the God-Emperor and a former hero, but when he called them to arms they went home to their beds and thought no more about the matter. The God-Emperor lived half a world away and it was impossible to imagine him interfering in their humble lives. Nish trekked to the nearby towns and villages, and received the same response everywhere.

What more could he do? How could he help a land which would not help itself? Yet he had to do something; he could not stand by.

He offered the young people military training, thinking that they would flock to him for the chance to learn about the martial arts, for when Nish had been young, a hero of the wars would have attracted thousands of youths.

But they did not care to learn the art of war in Gendrigore. A few dozen young men and women appeared that first evening, though they were more interested in seeing him in action than in learning themselves, and after a couple of hours, most had drifted off, never to return. Those who did stay followed his orders, more or less, but they chafed under his discipline and saw little sense in the sword, spear and shield exercises he made them repeat a thousand times until they had them right.

Nish was walking back to his tent in the moonlight after another fruitless training session when Tulitine appeared from the forest, not far from where Tildy had been killed.

He turned to meet her, but she bypassed the town, walking so quickly that he had to trot; he caught her at last after she crossed the sloping green on the way to the path which led down to the sea cliffs.

It was another sweltering night, and he was dripping with sweat. She must have heard him running after her, but did not turn around. Could she be entirely without fear? 'Tulitine?'

'Yes, Nish?' she said, maintaining an unbroken stride.

He felt like a child running after an indifferent adult. Falling in beside her, he wiped his sweaty face. 'Where have you been?'

'Surely you weren't worried about me?'

'A little. And . . . I missed you.'

'Really?' she said with a hint of amusement. 'Are you lonely in Gendrigore? I've always found the people of this land to be excellent company – especially the ones who creep into your tent in the middle of the night.'

He ignored that. 'Have you been here before?'

'I've been *everywhere* before.'

He would ask her about that sometime. 'They are good company. I particularly like the mayor . . .'

'And sporting in bed with the young women,' she said teasingly.

'Them too,' he muttered. Since Vivimord's death he had seldom spent the night alone, but it was embarrassing having an old woman refer to such matters. Even more embarrassing that she so openly enjoyed the favours of men a third her age, but he did not want to dwell on that. 'It's just – they don't take things seriously.'

She stopped momentarily as they passed into the strip of forest between the town green and the sea cliffs, sniffing the air, before striding on. The humidity was even more oppressive here, and the mosquitoes unrelenting. He waved his arms back and forth but it made no difference. The moment he stopped, they settled in speckled swarms on his face and hands and the back of his neck.

325

'They are serious about everything that matters,' she corrected. 'Their fishing; their farming and herding and gathering; their families, their town and their country.'

'You know what I mean. I've tried to warn them about Father, but they won't listen.'

'Why should they?'

'Because he could destroy this place with a wave of his hand.'

'But they know otherwise. In its entire history, Gendrigore has never been successfully attacked.'

'The past is an uncertain guide to the future, Tulitine.'

'Indeed, but the Range of Ruin – the only part of The Spine that can be crossed – has no paths, and even if you get to Blisterbone Pass, the way down runs along cliffs so steep that a mountain goat would have trouble negotiating them. The rain up there is torrential, the jungle so thick a walker must hack her way through it, and infested with every kind of biting, stinging, creeping and crawling creature imaginable. The ground-clinging mists mean that you cannot tell whether your next step will go down on crumbling rock or over the edge of a precipice, and the fevers can turn your lungs to mud or your bowels to water within a day.'

'If anyone can find a way, Father will. He'll happily lose two armies if it ensures the third gets through.'

They walked out of the strip of forest into the band of small trees paralleling the cliffs. The timber tripods of the cliff fishers stood up like black tent frames in the moonlight.

Tulitine went to the edge and sat on the bare stone with her legs dangling over. Nish sat a little further back, enjoying the cool breeze on his face and the relative absence of mosquitoes and gnats. No wonder she spent so much time here. The booming of the waves against the lower cliffs had a metronomic regularity that he always found soothing.

Down to his left, a trio of dolphins burst through the

swell, one after another, standing on their tails and waving their heads in the air, and Nish could sense their delight in their sport. The first dolphin shot into the newly named Maelstrom of Justice and Retribution, rode the currents around for several revolutions and then leapt out the other side, chittering to its fellows.

Nish laughed for the sheer pleasure of seeing their joy. Tulitine was leaning forwards, chin resting on her knee, listening to their calls. They circled the whirlpool a few more times, then dived under the swell together. After they had gone, and Nish was gazing idly at the moonlight reflecting off the foam, he saw a light below him, moving in the wind. He felt the sweat break out on him anew – surely it couldn't be Vivimord, back from the dead?

'Tulitine,' he whispered. 'A light.'

She chuckled, then lay down on her back on the warm rock, looking up at the stars. 'It's the fisherwomen.'

'At this time of night?'

'A good fisher fishes when the fish are feeding. It's a lovely night for it. If you look closely you can see a school swimming just below the surface.'

Nish couldn't see any fish, but streaks of silver shimmered up and down as the wet lines moved through the waves. Some minutes later he noticed a larger flash as a fat tunny was hauled up hand over hand, flapping on the end of the line. 'She's got one.'

The old woman didn't answer. He could hear her steady breathing, though he didn't think she had gone to sleep. 'Tulitine?'

'Yes?' she said quietly.

'When we were talking earlier, I got the impression that you were advancing Barquine's arguments rather than your own.'

'I might have been.'

'And I'm wondering if you're not a little worried, too.'

'Not for myself.'

Getting anything out of her was like pulling teeth, but

Nish persisted. 'Yet you're afraid for Gendrigore. You don't believe it's as safe as they think.'

'As you said, the past is not an infallible guide to the future.'

'So you believe that Father can conquer Gendrigore.'

Tulitine sighed. 'This is not a wealthy land – or rather, the wealth of Gendrigore lies in its forests and the creatures that inhabit them, but there is no way to tap that wealth from outside. Gendrigore is not rich in jewels or ores, rare spices or costly fabrics. It's rugged and rocky; its patches of fertile farmland are small, steep and difficult to farm. It has little that can be traded outside its boundaries, and so there is no pressing reason to plunder, or invade.'

'Are you saying that previous attackers weren't serious?'

'Must I spell everything out for you? I'd have thought, as the son of the God-Emperor, that you would understand.'

'You must!' Nish snapped, nettled. He didn't like being compared to his father in any way, nor did he appreciate the implication that, as the son of such a monster, he should also be a master of the cunning arts.

'Gendrigore's previous attackers were small armies driven solely by greed, and any prisoners they took would have told them how poor this country was. After discovering that they had little to gain here compared to what they had already lost, they did not persist.'

'Father isn't driven by greed,' said Nish. 'Gendrigore has nothing he wants, apart from me. But if he's learned of Vivimord's death, he will punish Gendrigore for the insult done to the man who saved his life. He cannot do otherwise, and once he begins the attack he dare not fail, for that would show weakness. He was defeated on Mistmurk Mountain; if it happens again it could encourage rebellions all over the place and fatally undermine him, so Father will crush Gendrigore out of existence to teach the rest of the world a lesson.'

'He must,' said Tulitine.

'Do you think he's on the way?'

'I have been reading the wind, and listening to the cries of the birds and the squeaks of the bats, and the calls of the dolphins.'

What was she trying to tell him? That she was a Wind Talker and a Bird Caller? Or was she merely in tune with the natural world?

'What do they tell you, Tulitine?'

'The bats squeak about a great army on the march from Pashnak and Huccadory, cities east of here in Northern Crandor. The dolphins talk of a fleet of ships leaving the safe harbour of Turtle Haven, heading west towards Gendrigore.'

He sprang up so hastily that he slipped on the wet rock near the cliff edge, and his arms windmilled for a few seconds before he regained his balance. He moved well back. 'Why didn't you tell me this before?' he said hoarsely, shocked at his carelessness.

'I knew how you would react,' she said dryly, 'and I didn't want you to fall over the cliff before I was sure what the signs meant.'

'But you're sure now.'

'The cry of that dolphin confirmed it. A battle fleet is sailing east, though that doesn't mean your father intends to attack Gendrigore.'

Nish knew in his bones that Jal-Nish was coming. 'Barquine said Gendrigore can't be attacked by sea. Is that right?'

'I believe so. The few inlets along Gendrigore's coast are cliff-bound, and the currents that race between the reefs surrounding this little peninsula are vicious. Only a foolhardy captain would approach such a shore.'

'Jal-Nish cares nothing for the lives of his men,' Nish mused, 'but he won't risk the humiliation of losing a fleet. It will be carrying more land troops, and all manner of engines of war. How long do we have, Tulitine?'

'They will reach Taranta in days, and disembark there. The land armies? Perhaps another week and a half.'

'The troops from the fleet won't head for The Spine until the armies arrive. Father only attacks when he has overwhelming strength. How long would it take his army to march from Taranta to the top of The Spine?'

'You'd have to ask Barquine, though I expect it would take another week.'

'And how long for Gendrigore's army, *which it doesn't have*, to get into position to defend Blisterbone Pass?'

'A couple of weeks, from here.'

'How big are Father's armies?'

'The birds and the bats didn't say. They're not very good at counting.' She smiled.

Panic tied Nish's intestines into a painful knot. Jal-Nish would hardly come with an army of less than ten thousand men, plus battle mancers, flesh-formed beasts and all manner of terrible engines of war. How could Gendrigore oppose such a force, even with its advantages of mountain and cliff and wild, wild weather? It wasn't a populous land, and its few towns and many villages were far apart. It would take weeks to round up a core of raw recruits, assuming he could convince them to come at all, and if a militia of a thousand men could be raised, he would be astonished.

'A thousand untrained, ill-disciplined and badly armed youths,' said Nish, 'against a professional force of battle-hardened men ten times that number – it doesn't bear thinking about.'

'It's not quite that bad, Nish. No army could cross Liver-Leech Pass, though the survivors of a broken army might scale The Spine to Blisterbone, if the weather allows it. But there a few hundred men, if they stood fast, could hold the pass against an army in the wet season, which is now.'

'What about the dry season?'

'Gendrigore doesn't have a dry season. There's only the wet season, and then the *really wet* season, and in the really wet season not even a forest rat could cross The Spine, for there are no bridges, no fords, and every gully is a torrent of wild water and rolling boulders that will grind every-thing in it to paste.'

'How long is it until the *really wet* season?'

'A few weeks, if it comes on time, and it lasts for five months. so if you can hold Blisterbone until it begins, Gen-drigore will be safe for half a year. A lot can happen in that time.'

'If The Spine becomes impassable, how do we get down again once the really wet season comes?'

'In great haste,' chuckled Tulitine. 'It takes a week or two to build up.'

'Leaving a small window for the enemy to follow us.'

'Not in the really wet season. Your father would call his generals back, be sure of it.'

The Spine sounded like a nightmare but Nish couldn't see any choice. His new-found resolve was burning in him, and if he had to fight his father all the way he was going to start here, right now.

'I'll try to defend the pass, if I can raise a force. I dare say Gendrigore will have armour, weapons, and so forth?'

'Nearly everyone hunts from time to time; they have bows and know how to use them. And I imagine there'll be a rusty sword or two lying around,' she said lightly, 'though most would have been reforged into more useful tools long ago, since iron is rare here, and expensive. But as for armour – who could wear it in this climate? You'd collapse with heat stroke.'

Nish rubbed his stinging neck, dislodging a thousand gnats bloated with his blood. He'd moved too far away from the edge. 'There won't be time to make many swords, even if I can get the steel; good swords take ages to make from scratch and they won't be a match for the equipment Father's soldiers have. Our smiths can make spearheads, at least, though amateurs with spears against trained swords-men . . . No, to defend the pass I've got to have a force armed with bows, spears and swords; a few hundred, at least, and they'll have to be trained.'

He thought through all that had to be done before they could leave for the pass, then sank his head in his hands. The conclusion was inescapable. 'It can't be done. If it takes a week to round up a small militia – I can't possibly call them an *army* – and another fortnight to get them into place, there won't be any time for training.'

Tulitine laid her old hand on his arm. 'It looks bleak, I agree. You can't possibly fight him in battle and win, so you must find another way.'

'What other way? Father thinks of everything. He will have identified his army's every weakness by now, and found ways to strengthen them.'

'Then forget about trying to identify his weaknesses. Work out his army's strengths and try to find ways to turn them against him.'

'I've no idea how,' Nish said acidly. 'Perhaps you'd care to point out a way for me.'

'I'm a healer, not a warrior. I don't fight wars.'

'I wish I didn't.'

THIRTY-ONE

'Ketila, Nooooo!' Colm threw his arms up to catch her but she was already falling out past him.

Maelys managed to get a couple of fingers to her billowing shirt but the weathered fabric tore apart. She watched Ketila all the way down to the rocks at the base of the cleft, then wished she hadn't.

'Ketila!' Colm screamed.

In all her life, Maelys had not heard such anguish. He threw his arms up, clawing at the sky; his mouth was a raw hole, his eyes black pits of despair. Then he started down the crevasse, springing from rock to rock with reckless desperation.

'She's gone, Colm,' said Flydd, swaying into his path.

'Get–out–of–my–way!'

Flydd put his arm out, blocking the way down. 'You can't do anything for her. I'm really sorry.'

'Ketila could still be alive and I'm not leaving her to die alone, Flydd. I'm all she's got.'

He tried to force Flydd out of the way. Flydd raised his hand, touched Colm in the middle of the forehead and his eyes went blank.

'You can't do this to me,' he said in a dead voice.

'Go up!' It was a command this time, with all the Art Flydd could summon behind it.

Colm gave a terrible moan, deep in his throat, but he went. Maelys followed, barely able to look at him, or Flydd. She did not glance down again, for Ketila must have died instantly. Even so, she would not have stopped Colm.

'Why did I throw away the amulet?' she whispered. 'With it I might have kept Rurr-shyve back. I might have prevented this. If only I had . . .'

Colm turned stiffly, his white-hot stare on her. *You allowed her to die*, he seemed to be saying. *It's your fault.* Maelys's eyes locked with his and she could not tear away.

'Go up!' said Flydd.

Colm went, and Maelys followed, every nerve screaming fool, fool!

Flydd dragged himself up the crevasse on will alone, until finally they reached the top. It was a dome some five spans wide, with a chilly wind rushing across it. The male flappeter was spiralling down, still trumpeting in agony. Rurr-shyve's rider was circling the pinnacle and the archer who had fired the fatal shot held a clenched fist high in triumph. The leading soldiers coming along the ridge to the north went to their knees and aimed their bows.

'Surely they can't hit us from there?' said Maelys, ducking just in case.

'If they put enough arrows into the air, one or two are bound to find their mark. Get down, Colm.'

Colm stood on the brink of the crag facing the archers, as if daring them to shoot him. A flight of arrows soared up at them. Maelys flinched. The archers following them up the cliffs were almost within range.

'Keep low,' said Flydd. 'Stand by me and be ready.' He lowered his voice. 'The instant the portal opens – if it does – take hold of Colm and make sure he comes through.' He knelt down and took a small grey globule from his pocket. It had a rubbery appearance.

'What's that?' said Maelys.

334

'An envelope formed from the wall of the Nightland.'

'And it's for?'

'I inflated it around the virtual construct before I came through the portal, then allowed the envelope to shrink to its original size. Everything inside it should have shrunk proportionally.'

'What if it squashed the virtual construct into a blob, like parts of the Nightland had been squashed?'

'The construct isn't solid, so it can't be squashed . . . at least, I hope not.' Flydd did not sound as certain as he had previously. Holding it out on his palm, he began to mouth the words of the mancery that would restore it to full size.

Maelys kept watch on their attackers. For the moment, the male flappeter didn't offer any threat, though Rurr-shyve was climbing rapidly into the window of clear air to the north-east, the one place unaffected by the archers' attack.

A rain of arrows flashed silver as they climbed into late beams of sunlight, then fell around the left side of the crag. None hit, though one shattered not far from Maelys, driving splinters into her left knee.

Hurry, Flydd. She didn't say it. He knew.

The archers fired again. Rurr-shyve had climbed above the level of the crag and was hovering, waiting for the arrows to fall. Down below, the male flappeter was climbing slowly. Its rider had regained control.

Arrows rattled on the sides and top of the crag. One speared through the back of Colm's right boot heel, another flashed past Flydd's outstretched hand. He dropped the globule but caught it again, still mouthing the spell. His eyes were screwed up as he attempted to visualise their destination.

The Island of Noom – the Tower of a Thousand Steps. After all she'd heard about the Numinator, it was impossible to think they would be safer there. And yet, surely anything had to be better than Jal-Nish?

Flydd completed his spell, but the little envelope of the Nightland failed to expand. The archers on the ridge fired a third time and this volley was tighter, focussed on the top of the crag. The male flappeter was climbing rapidly now, heading straight for them, toothy maw gaping, its collapsed compound eye fluttering in the wind.

'It's racing Rurr-shyve,' she said absently, watching it hurtle towards them, fluid leaking from its eye.

'Why won't it work?' muttered Flydd. 'Can some other Art be interfering with it?' Laying the envelope carefully in a hollow where it would not be blown away, he went down on his belly and peered over the edge.

Maelys went with him. 'What are you looking for?'

'Mancers, or scriers, though I can't see any. Those men are just soldiers, yet something is interfering with my Art.' He began to take objects out of his pockets: a tiny knife, a wooden comb with half its teeth missing, a collection of coloured pebbles. 'Hold these for me.'

He put them in her hands, then drew out the dirty leather pouch containing the mimemule he'd taken from the cavern, but the instant she took the pouch, there came a *pfft* behind them.

The envelope of the Nightland split open like a flower and the construct expanded up out of it, two spans high and floating in the air, whole and complete. Before Flydd could speak the Words of Opening, a funnel-shaped portal snapped into being directly in front of it and freezing air howled out, coating the curving rim of the funnel with frost. Icicles grew before their eyes, iron hard and sharp as spikes. The funnel kept lengthening on the inside, though all she could see at the other end was fog. It cleared suddenly and beyond the small circle that formed the exit of the funnel, Maelys saw a frozen wilderness of grey ice.

'Go through!' cried Flydd over the roar of the wind.

Maelys hesitated, but Rurr-shyve was falling towards them; the male flappeter was hurtling in to their left and a tight knot of arrows arching towards them from the right. She ran, caught Colm's arm and, before he could resist her, dragged him against the wind into the funnel. The wind slammed into her, but she pushed harder, harder, forcing herself into the mouth of the funnel, where a countervailing force caught her and Colm and sucked them through. Blue lights flashed in her eyes; she felt a gut-wrenching inner twist that brought the taste of Ketila's smoked fish up into the back of her throat, then she and Colm were hurled out the other end into a grey land that did not look as though it had ever seen the sun.

Flydd came tumbling after her. 'Get out of the way!' he screamed, clawing across the ice to his right.

Maelys looked back as the male flappeter hurtled through the virtual construct, scattering its myriad intangible components, its feather-rotors reversing as it tried desperately to brake in the air. Its rotor beats punched a hot fist of compressed air through the portal, sending Maelys tumbling across the ice.

The male could not brake in time; it loomed ever closer, a monstrous winged shadow; its head entered the mouth of the portal, where the gate-force caught it and dragged it in, but it was too big to fit.

Its feather-rotors were sheared off to a blood-gushing stalk, its four pairs of legs ripped out and smashed into spindly segments. Its immensely long body was sucked through in a storm of bloody feathers and fragments of leathery skin and scale, thrashing wildly, its maw snapping and its tail swinging from side to side.

It shot out the other end of the portal, bellowing in agony, shattering lumps of ice and flinging shards in all directions. The remains of the leather-clad rider, crushed to a paste along its spine, slid off and plopped redly to the ice. The flappeter's tail smacked into a boss of ice too big to break and its front half was swung the other way, right at Maelys. She tried to run ahead of it but her feet slipped and she went down. The flappeter's neck and shoulder came driving towards her, its good eye and ruined one rolling in different directions, its huge mouth open. Thick blood was still spraying from its rotor stalk.

The good eye focussed on her just before it struck and the span-long maw twisted around to snap at her. Maelys didn't have time to reach for her knife; she just swung at it with the object in her hand – the leather pouch with the mimemule inside.

The pouch grew so heavy that she could hardly move it, and momentarily she felt herself to be a warrior swinging a mighty war hammer. It crunched straight through the eye and the tough carapace surrounding it, into the flappeter's forebrain, splattering grey and white matter in all directions.

Its ruined head thudded to the ice. The four pairs of leg stumps waggled back and forth and the tail continued to twitch blindly, then it went still. Maelys slumped beside it, covered in congealing muck and shaking all over. She didn't have the faintest idea what had happened, though she felt as though she *had* swung a warrior's war hammer, and the muscles of her right shoulder were so strained she could barely move it.

The portal was gone. Colm was standing a few paces further off, staring at the dead creature, though she did not think he was seeing it. His eyes were expressionless pits, at least until Flydd got up and limped over. As he crossed into Colm's field of vision, his eyes registered such hate as she had never seen before. Flydd's dazing spell had worn off.

'Take me back to Ketila,' Colm ground out.

'I can't,' said Flydd. 'When the flappeter went through the virtual construct, the mancery at its core tore it apart. Without it I can't reopen the portal.'

Colm stalked across, drew his knife and put it to Flydd's throat. 'My sister lies dying at the bottom of the crag. Take–me–back.'

'She fell fifty spans onto rock,' said Flydd. 'She would have died instantly.'

'Take–me–back.'

'Do your worst,' said Flydd limply. 'I couldn't open the

portal again if the Profane Tears lay unguarded on the other side.'

Colm's knife hand jerked, and a thin line of blood appeared on Flydd's throat, but he did not move nor acknowledge it in any way. After a couple of frozen minutes, Colm hurled his knife into the ice, stumbled away and fell to his knees, weeping in broken, choking sobs.

Flydd, rather wobbly at the knees, helped Maelys up, saying softly, 'How did you do that?'

She rubbed her sore shoulder. 'I have no idea. I imagined I was attacking the flappeter with a war hammer and, momentarily, I was.'

He frowned, checked that Colm wasn't looking – he wasn't – and held out his hand. Maelys gathered a handful of the gritty, crystalline snow, scrubbed bloody muck and scales off the leather pouch and handed it to him. Flydd slipped it into his pocket without looking at it, but Maelys couldn't stop thinking about the mimemule. It had brought the virtual construct to life and, in an instant, created a portal that had previously taken Flydd an hour and a half to make. Not to mention the war hammer. Did it make whatever one imagined, or really wanted? No, there had to be more to it than that.

'It might have been better to let him go down to Ketila,' she said quietly. 'He's a broken man, Xervish. He's lost everything.'

'He knows where we're going,' said Flydd, 'and what we're looking for. The Numinator is a secret the God-Emperor may not be aware of and I could not allow Colm to reveal it, *under any circumstances.*'

She shivered at the meaning behind his words; the ruthless scrutator inside him was not entirely dead. She'd liked and admired Flydd from the moment she met him, and knew that he felt the same way about her. Now she wondered what he might do to her if she ever stood in his way.

Her teeth chattered; it was desperately cold here. The blood and brains of the flappeter had frozen already; her toes were aching in her boots and icicles were forming on Flydd's short beard. Colm began pacing back and forth, stamping his feet in a vain attempt to keep warm. The sun hung a hand's breadth above the northern horizon but there was no warmth in its rays, and it was as dark as an overcast winter's day after sunset.

'My directions weren't too wide of the mark, in the circumstances,' said Flydd. 'We're on the inner edge of the Kara Agel, the Frozen Sea, and if I'm not mistaken that's the Island of Noom just over there.'

Maelys looked in the direction he was facing and did not like what she saw. The Frozen Sea was a mass of ice, smooth in places, heaved up into broken slabs in others, with a dusting of snow which the wind had blown into dune-like drifts, rippled like sand. Elsewhere the snow had been scoured away to reveal bare grey ice. The Frozen Sea extended further than she could see in all directions, save to the south, the direction in which Flydd was pointing, where a low, rocky shore could be seen perhaps a third of a league away. Snow-covered hills ran off into the distance, yet she could not see a single tree, nor any signs of life.

'What a miserable place. Why would anyone choose to live here?' She rubbed her arms, shuddering with the cold; every breath hurt her nose and throat and lungs. Their clothes were utterly unsuitable for this climate, and they had no food with them. Wherever they were camping tonight, she hoped it was not far away.

'To hide from the world?' said Flydd. 'Or to work on a great project unhindered? I cannot say, but here the Numinator has dwelt for more than a hundred years.'

'The Tower of a Thousand Steps had better be nearby or we'll freeze to death before we find it. How long until nightfall?'

'Not long. The days are only a few hours long at this time of year, and the nights are eternal. Let's get to shore. We might find something to eat there.'

'Can't we eat the flappeter?'

'I wouldn't recommend it, since it's a creature flesh-formed by the God-Emperor himself, and he's fond of his little jokes.'

She was rubbing her freezing arms when it occurred to her that the word mimemule was suggestive. Did it mimic thoughts, or turn them into reality? 'Xervish,' she said quietly. 'If the mimemule –'

'Not now!'

'What I meant was, we've got to have warm clothing. Furs!'

'I see. Good idea.' He pulled out the leather pouch, touched his fingers to it, feeling the shape of the ball inside and subvocalising, *Fur-lined pants and coat and boots and hood for us all, now.*

Her garments transformed instantly, as did Flydd's, then Colm's. Colm stopped abruptly, looking down at his feet, then plodded on.

'How does that work?' said Maelys.

'Later.' Flydd surreptitiously closed his hand over the pouch and it vanished. Withdrawing the containers of trapped fire from his pockets, he vanished them as well, then looked sharply across at Colm. He need not have bothered. Colm was oblivious.

THIRTY-TWO

They slept in a snow cave dug into a hard-packed drift between rocks. It was miserable, even in their furs, and they had no fire, for Maelys hadn't seen a tree or bush, or indeed anything living bar a crust of lichen growing on the exposed rocks. But not even the polar cold was as frigid and unrelenting as the bitterness and rage emanating from Colm. He blamed her for Ketila's death as much as he blamed himself; no, more, for she had thrown away the amulet that might just have kept Rurr-shyve out of firing range. But more than either of them he blamed Flydd for not allowing him to go down to her and ease her last moments, then die with her and put an end to his agony.

'Don't mention my fire bottles here,' said Flydd in the morning. 'They don't exist.'

Since he could not conjure food with the mimemule without alerting Colm, they left as soon as the sun slid sideways over the horizon. Flydd set off confidently inland, as if he knew where he was going, or following some lead he did not care to share with them, and within the hour they were climbing a hill whose dark, nodular stone protruded through a thin cover of snow.

'That looks like an arch at the top,' said Maelys, and it was, a massive arch of grey, hard stone, different from the rock it was founded upon. Its pillars were spans across at the base, square in outline, and carved with curving symbols or glyphs incised finger-deep into the stone. They reminded Maelys of the ones carved into the obelisk at the top of Mistmurk Mountain.

'Curious,' said Flydd as they climbed a steep track up to the arch, slipping on black ice. 'It looks like Charon work. Could the Numinator be . . . no, of course not – they're extinct.'

He was walking bent over. The crossbow bolt was troubling him but she could not cut it out here, either. Colm plodded along behind, head down. When they walked, he followed some twenty paces behind. The moment they stopped, he did too, always keeping his distance.

Beyond the arch, nothing could be seen but grey – grey cloud, grey sky, and a grey range covered in grey ice. The wind was stronger here and she had to keep her head lowered, for whenever she looked directly into it her eyes watered and the tears froze on her cheeks. Colm was standing down the slope, his hair and beard covered in frost. He had not spoken all day, and showed no interest in his surroundings.

'The Tower of a Thousand Steps,' said Flydd quietly, though there was a hard edge to his voice.

He had been tortured on the Numinator's orders, Maelys recalled. Had he come for revenge? Is that why Flydd had agreed to lead them here?

'Where?' She could see nothing save the ice-hung crags of knotted schist to either side.

'Look through the arch.'

'I am.'

'Look down.'

She wasn't tall enough to see over the hump, so she stepped forward until she stood right in front of the arch, and squinted down into the shallow valley on the other side. Maelys cried out in wonder. 'A tower made of glass!'

Through a low-hanging mist she could just make out

what appeared to be a frozen lake – at least, partly frozen, for there was a curving rim of clear water in the middle, surrounding a small island. Jagged ridges ran up to a hill at its centre, from which the tower rose sharply to form a spire hundred of spans high. Between the two ridges closest to them, low down and not much higher than the level of the lake, a small opening in the hill appeared to lead into the base of the tower.

Flydd came up beside her. 'Not glass, but ice.'

Maelys shivered. 'How can anyone live in such a bleak place?'

'It would take a particular kind of person. Though I dare say the tower is a lot warmer on the inside.'

'But it's ice!'

'So is an igloo, yet people live comfortably in them all winter. Come.'

He stopped by the arch, though, momentarily looking anxious.

'Xervish?' said Maelys.

'Even the faintest of my scars throb at the memories,' he said softly. 'The pain permeates every cell and nerve. Not even renewal could erase the memory of what the Numinator did to me, and one day I'll make it suffer an equal torment.'

'Xervish?' she repeated, alarmed. Renewal had definitely changed him; these days she seldom saw the tough but kindly old man she'd been so taken with on the plateau.

With an effort, he unclenched his jaw. 'Don't worry. I won't allow personal difficulties to distract me from what we came here to do. Let's go through.'

She caught his arm. 'Wouldn't it be better to go around? I don't like the feel of the arch.'

'I'm not going to slink in like a jackal,' he said, striding through.

Maelys held her breath, just in case the arch was enchanted to keep people out, but nothing happened. She followed him down the slope, struggling to stay on her feet on the icy path. Flydd's head darted around at every sound, every shift in the wind eddying across the knotted rock. Despite his brave words, he was frightened. He must be afraid that the Numinator would torture him again.

It was darker on the valley floor; mist hung around them, cold and dank, obscuring the tower and the way ahead. Maelys pulled her furs more tightly about her but could not keep the chill out. No wind stirred the air, and they plodded towards the frozen edge of the lake, their boots breaking through humps of crusted snow to the ice beneath.

At the edge, Flydd stopped. The ice on the lake looked as solid as stone here, though an irregular ring of clear water encircled the island. No, the ring of water, and its boundary with the ice, was in constant motion. Fresh ice was rapidly extending out from some edges, while at others it was melting just as quickly. Little bulges and embayments were constantly being created and destroyed as ice and clear water swept around the island, ice sometimes touching the inner shore momentarily before collapsing into treacherous water again.

'How are we supposed to get across?' said Maelys. 'There's no boat, no bridge . . .'

'It's a puzzle,' said Flydd. 'The patterns of water and ice are meant to keep intruders out, and we'll have to solve it to get across.'

Maelys was no good at puzzles, so she studied the tower and waited for him to find a way. Its sides were decorated with arching, pointed crests and horns of ice. The place looked bleak and forbidding.

'All right,' said Flydd at length.

He led them out in a meandering line on the hard ice, which was almost black, all the way to the shifting grey boundary that marked the freezing and thawing inner barrier, like a moat around the island and the Tower of a Thousand Steps. There he stopped, frowning.

'Flydd?' said Maelys, looking up at the top of the tower anxiously.

345

'Not now!'

He was still standing there half an hour later, his head sweeping this way and that, following the shifting patterns, and his lips moving all the while. Despite the wonderful fur-lined boots, Maelys's feet were getting ever colder. She couldn't feel her toes any more, though she could sense something at the top of the tower – a cold, hard presence that surely must have seen them ages ago. Why had she convinced Flydd to come here? She was completely out of her depth. She turned to look at Colm, still twenty paces back. He was staring at the cracked ice beneath his feet, as motionless as ever.

'I have it!' said Flydd. 'Come on, and keep right at my heels. You too, Colm.'

Colm looked up at him blankly, then shuffled forwards.

'Ready?' said Flydd. 'One, two, three, then run with me, all right?'

'Yes,' said Maelys, gulping.

'One, two, three.'

He ran out towards the edge and off the hard black ice onto the thin grey stuff, which rocked beneath him. Maelys leapt after him, her numb feet hitting the ground as stiffly as wooden legs. She could see right through the ice she was standing on, and what was that gliding through the water below it?

Flydd caught her by the arm and yanked hard. 'Run, you bloody little fool! Run as though your life depends on it; for surely it does.'

She ran after him. Just ahead, the berg they were on thinned to nothing, and beyond that was a patch of open water, about a span across. If she fell into it she would die, even if they got her out, for the cold would stop her heart. Flydd sprang high, rocking the berg beneath them. Maelys followed, landing a little shorter and skidding on slick ice. She just caught herself before she slid off the thawing side into the water, let out a squeal at her narrow escape, and pounded on.

Flydd was thumping up a shallow rise, but at the top he propped and turned sharply to the left. Maelys almost went over, for the rise ended in a crevasse where the berg was splitting in two, and this gap was spans across, too far to jump. She scrambled down and raced after him, jumped another gap, then another and another.

Flydd was constantly twisting and turning, and sometimes doubling back on himself, never running in the same direction for more than a few paces. It was like a competition as well as a race, for as fast as he ran, the bergs were forming in front of him and thawing behind. Ice a third of a span thick simply dissolved away in seconds, and ice of similar thickness formed in an instant on otherwise clear water.

'One false step,' he panted, 'one miscalculation, and we're gone.' His cheeks were red and his eyes were glowing. He was exhilarated by the contest.

He went skidding sideways, then raced around a boss of ice like the dome of a citadel, emerged on the other side and tried desperately to stop, but slid down a glassy slope towards an uncrossable gap. He could not stop; the ice was so slick that he might have skated on it. He was going to end up in the water, and so was she.

At the last second Flydd propped on a chunk of nodular ice, managed to turn towards a slightly narrower gap, though one that was still far too wide to leap, and sprang for all his might. He soared high in the air and Maelys's heart was in her mouth – he was going to land in the water.

At the last instant the water froze beneath him, just as he must have predicted; he struck the little berg with both feet, rocking it in the water, stumbled, then sprang for the berg on the other side of the gap.

'Haaaiiiii!' he roared in triumph, raising his fist to the sky, then ran on without looking back.

Maelys followed him across, her heart pounding and her knees weak. She was sweating in her furs already. The race went on for another few minutes, and Flydd nearly went into the water many times. Maelys had more narrow escapes than she cared to think about before she finally lurched off the last recrystallised berg onto solid ground and fell to her knees. Shortly Colm came after them, lathered in freezing sweat, and stopped twenty paces away.

'That was brilliant, Flydd,' she said, panting. 'Or is the Numinator's power fading?'

'It isn't,' said Flydd.

'Oh! You mean it let us in?'

'Do you really think the Numinator became so powerful, and survived so long, without knowing when there were trespassers in its domain?'

Above them loomed the monstrous ice tower, topped with blade-like laths of ice towering into the brittle heavens. The low sun, picking its way through gaps in a lead-grey overcast, threw glittering reflections off every crystal face. Shielding her eyes, she peered between her fingers. The Tower of a Thousand Steps was magnificent; awe-inspiring; terrible, and surely its master must echo it.

'How can any one person *need* such a vast dwelling?' she whispered.

'The Numinator has very great needs,' Flydd intoned. 'Terrible, desperate needs.'

Maelys swallowed hard.

Colm broke his long silence. 'You should not have come here. You will not get out alive.'

She stared at him. 'Don't you mean, *we* will not get out alive?'

'What do I care whether I live or die?'

Maelys wanted to shake him. There wasn't a trace left of the Colm she'd once admired. I've lost plenty too, she thought, but you don't see me whining about it all the time. Maelys bit her tongue. Had she just seen little Fyllis fall to her death, and been able to do nothing about it, and blamed her companions, she might have felt the same.

'We've got to go on, no matter what,' she said. 'There's no other way.'

348

'Hush!' Flydd had his head up like a dog sniffing the air. A shudder shook his muscular frame, then he turned towards the arched opening in the blue ice on which the tower was founded. 'That will be our way in.'

A path of crushed ice curved down towards the opening. The razor-crested ice ridges hemmed it in on either side, rising ever higher as the path fell.

Flydd threw his shoulders back, raised his chin and strode down the path, hiding his anxiety. Maelys waited for Colm to follow, but he was staring into space again, so she headed after Flydd, almost running to keep up. It wasn't until they'd gone a few hundred paces that she realised she was treading in his footsteps, keeping directly behind him as if he could shield her from view.

'The Numinator's eyes are everywhere,' he said without breaking stride.

She stopped, hand pressed against her thudding heart, then continued. The entrance was a tall open rectangle at least three times her height. Within, every surface glowed with the blue of thick ice, though Maelys could make out nothing but straight-sided shapes fading into darkness.

She took a step, stopped, then another, until she stood directly underneath the lintel of the doorway, and looked up sharply. Nothing moved within her field of view. The opening was made of flat ice so smooth that it might have been freshly planed, but inside, where it was sheltered from the wind, frost needles as long as nails grew from every surface. The drifts of snow on the featureless floor were untracked.

'It's empty.' Colm's voice showed a trace of animation for the first time since his sister's death. 'The Numinator must be gone.'

'The Numinator is still here,' said Flydd, his eyes darting again. 'Were *he, she or it* gone, the tower would have collapsed into a formless rubble of ice.'

'The destruction of the nodes might have destroyed the Numinator,' said Maelys.

'That tragedy undoubtedly weakened it,' said Flydd, 'but would have angered it too. Beware! This tower is maintained by the Art and, whoever the Numinator is, its power is far greater than mine.'

'Then why did we come here?' said Maelys. 'How can we hope to prevail?'

They went in slowly, the crusted ice crunching underfoot, until the entrance could no longer be seen. The spaces were dimly lit by light transmitted through the ice and all had an eerie grandeur, a majestic simplicity, but there was something vaguely familiar about the place, too. Maelys was studying the glyphs etched deep into the ice along a wall when she realised what they were.

'Xervish, these characters are also like the ones we saw on the obelisk. Does that mean this place is . . . Charon?'

'The Charon are extinct, I told you; had they built it, here, the ice would have collapsed long ago.' Flydd's voice was a trifle hoarse.

'Like the Nightland was supposed to?'

He did not reply to that, but went on, 'The Numinator may not be human. And if not, that would explain something I've always wondered about.'

'What's that?' said Maelys.

'How it has lived so long. We know it's at least a hundred and seventy years old, for it was a cunning, experienced sorcerer when it took on the original Council of Santhenar, and it was powerful enough to defeat the combined mancery of the greatest mages of all. Only the Charon, Faellem and Aachim were naturally long-lived, but both Charon and Faellem are gone.'

'The Numinator must be Aachim, then,' said Maelys. 'There are still plenty of Aachim on Santhenar.'

'No Aachim would decorate their architecture with Charon characters.'

'Why not?' said Colm, who had come up behind them.

'Because a hundred Charon took the Aachim's world from them, and held them in thrall for thousands of years.

350

They hated their masters with a passion we could never understand, therefore the Numinator can't be Aachim, either.'

After walking through one featureless ice hall after another, they entered a large rectangular room, a good hundred spans long and wide, and at least ten spans high. Its walls were lined with shelves, stretching from floor to ceiling, that had been formed from clear ice, and upon them stood row upon row of large books, like merchants' ledgers, bound in red or brown leather.

'Ah!' said Flydd. It was a deeply felt sigh of understanding.

'What?' said Maelys.

He didn't answer, nor did he go to the shelves. Flydd stood inside the doorway, staring towards the far end of the room and wearing an enigmatic smile. Maelys waited for a minute or two, but when neither he nor Colm moved she went towards the nearest shelves; she had to satisfy her curiosity.

To her surprise, she could read the writing down the spines of the ledgers. The nearest one said, *Bloodline Register 13,809, Thurkad*. The ledgers on the shelves nearby bore different numbers, but all had the same place name, for Thurkad had once been the greatest city in the world.

'Bloodline register?' said Maelys aloud. 'What does that mean?'

Flydd did not reply, so she eased the register from the shelf and opened it. It was huge and very heavy – she could barely hold it. Inside, the page was ruled into columns, with names on the left – women's names and dates, notes on their monthly cycles, state of health, male names with descriptions as well as lists of abilities, talents and ancestral charts, details about sexual congress, and a variety of symbols. Occasional rows contained details related to pregnancies – weight changes, complications, miscarriages and births. The last column was headed *Gifts and Talents*, but she could not tell what the symbols meant.

Maelys knew what it was immediately, for Clan Nifferlin had kept such records for their prized breeding animals.

She snapped the register closed, feeling ill. 'It's a stud book, but for *people*. This is what the scrutators were doing for the Numinator. Why, Xervish?'

He was still staring into the distance. 'I don't think anyone ever found out – not even Chief Scrutator Ghorr, may he still lie rotting in the sump of the Uttermost Abyss.'

Maelys took down another book from a different place, and subsequently a third from the other side of the room. The places, names and dates were different, though the contents were the same everywhere. 'But . . .' She stared down the endless rows of the vast room until they blurred in the distance, trying to work out how many registers there were; how many names there had to be. It was beyond her ability to calculate. 'There must be *millions* of names here.'

'Every single person who has lived in over a century,' Flydd said soberly. 'It's the reason why the Numinator set up the Council of Scrutators in the first place.'

'That doesn't make sense,' said Colm. 'The scrutators ran the world.'

'And we were very good at it,' said Flydd. 'We ran it ruthlessly, but efficiently – for the Numinator.'

'Why didn't you all get together and overthrow it?'

'The Chief Scrutators never wanted to.'

'Why not?'

'Because the Numinator is different to every other villain you've ever heard of in the Histories. The Numinator was never a rival for the power of the scrutators; it didn't give a fig for power, conquest or wealth. As long as the scrutators did their job and sent the bloodline registers, the Numinator never interfered.'

'Surely some of the other scrutators must have objected to being told what to do?'

'Oh, they did,' said Flydd.

'What happened?'

352

'Do you remember my scars, before I took renewal?'

Maelys shivered at the memory.

'I was one of the lucky ones,' said Flydd. 'I lived.'

'But surely . . . the Numinator must have given the Council that power for a reason . . .?'

'The only reason we ever had was to complete the bloodline registers.'

'I don't understand,' said Maelys.

'That's all the Numinator *ever* asked of us.'

'For more than a hundred years?'

'That's right.'

'Why?'

Flydd shrugged. 'I didn't know, but we'll learn nothing more here.'

It was incomprehensible to Maelys that anyone could have pursued such a monumental project so single-mindedly, and for so long. How could anyone develop a plan that might take hundreds of years to complete? What could drive them to it? And had the Numinator succeeded, or failed?

They continued through the hall of registers to the far end, then out and down a broad flight of steps into a lower level. Some colour had come back to Colm's cheeks – the mystery had aroused his curiosity. Maelys prayed it would last, for the cold rage that was his other face was unbearable.

This chamber was much smaller – no larger than one of the public halls in Nifferlin Manor. It was divided into a number of cases made of ice, though here the ice was cloudy and it was hard to make out what was inside. The shapes were suggestive, though, and despite the cold the room bore a faint, unpleasant odour of decay.

'They look *human*,' said Maelys.

'It's a cemetery,' said Colm. 'The ground here must freeze as hard as iron, and when people die there would be no way to bury them –' The bitterness was back. He would never bury his sister, nor any of his lost family.

But the Numinator was more powerful than all the great mancers of Santhenar put together, Maelys thought. It could easily thaw a plot of ground to bury the dead. There had to be some other explanation, and it might lie inside the cases.

The nearest was a rectangular box, rather larger than a coffin, with walls a hand-span thick; she could see nothing through them. The lid was thinner, though. She put her hand on it and could feel the cold searing through her glove.

'Come away, Maelys,' said Flydd, who was standing in the middle of the room, head tilted to one side as if listening to something on the edge of hearing. 'Whatever is inside, it's the Numinator's private business.'

It seemed an extraordinary thing for him to say, after bringing them all this way. Maelys couldn't hear anything, and she wasn't going to stop now. 'If we can't look around, we should never have come here.'

'We should never have come here,' echoed Colm.

Maelys forced her gloved fingers into the gap between the lid and the case, and lifted. The lid was very heavy, and she could only raise it halfway. She gasped.

A young man lay within. He was naked and his skin was a blotchy purple, as if he had been out in the cold for hours, but there were blue-grey patches of decay here and there, and the smell of corruption was stronger. His yellow eyes were open and staring, though he was undoubtedly long dead, but there was no sign of what had killed him.

'What strange eyes.' They were oval, and more catlike than human, with pupils that were contracted to vertical slits. He had a long face with a bulging forehead and a raised crest running across the top of his shaven skull, though his chin was just a minuscule bump. Ice crystals clustered on his lips and at his nostrils; feathers of ice hung from his lower eyelids.

'Maelys, come away,' said Flydd, taking her elbow and dragging her aside.

'Xervish, what is this place?' She jerked free and stumbled to the next case. It contained a young woman's body. Her head was shaven and she too had the cat eyes and the crest over her head, though hers was not nearly as prominent as the young man's had been. And she had three pairs of breasts.

'Xervish?' she said. 'Who are they? *What* are they?'

The third case held another woman, apparently normal save that her fingers were twice the length of human fingers and could have wrapped right around the back of her hand. As with the others, there was not a mark on her to indicate how she had died.

'She must be Aachim,' said Colm, who had followed her. 'The Aachim have exceptionally long fingers.'

Flydd was beside Maelys now, staring in, then abruptly he thrust the lid down. 'Enough! Come.'

'Xervish?' she repeated.

'I – don't – know!' He caught her arm, jerking her away. 'Don't pry into what is none of your business or you'll end up in the next box.'

He hauled her down to the other end of the chamber, walking very fast. Maelys tried to pull free but he wouldn't let go; she stumbled along with him, feeling a mixture of fear and resentment.

And the bodies had all smelled, she realised, as if they had been going off, though that did not make sense either. In the cold rooms on the south side of Nifferlin Manor, haunches of meat had kept all winter, and there had been hardly any smell, yet Noom was far colder than Nifferlin. Bodies should have lain here in their ice cases preserved forever.

They did not need to open the boxes in the next chamber, for the ice was clearer here and she could see through the walls. Each box contained a young man or woman who had apparently died in the prime of life, but all had some oddity: one a flaring crest like a sail growing out of the top of his head, another a tail extending down to the back of her knees, while a third had knuckles the size of lemons, but no fingernails.

Maelys no longer wanted to know the truth about the Numinator. She tried not to look as Flydd led her along through chamber after chamber on this subterranean level, but could not prevent herself from staring at each new body, each fresh horror. And they *were* horrors here, for the dead men and women grew ever stranger until they were scarcely human at all.

THIRTY-THREE

Flydd flung her through the door into the next chamber, then froze, grey-faced and haggard. He looked like an old man again.

A bench of ice ran along either side of the room, and arranged along it were skeletons no more human than the bodies in the cases. One had cat feet and a tail with traces of orange fur still clinging to it, another had fingers half the length of its body. Maelys turned away, sickened, but in front of her were more skeletons in huge ice amphorae, and others suspended from the ceiling on wires, the bones held together with fine gold threads.

'It looks like a schoolroom,' said Maelys.

'Perhaps it was,' Flydd said sombrely.

The room after that smelled putrid. It contained smaller jars full of preserved, unborn creatures with huge heads, staring, lidless eyes and unpleasantly non-human features. Many of the jars were cracked, though, and several had leaked brown fluid which had frozen on the shelf around them. Down the far end, the jars were broken and their contents, spilled onto the bench, must have thawed, for all had gone an unpleasant grey-green colour before freezing again.

'Is the Numinator breeding *people*?' said Colm, his handsome mouth twisted in disgust.

'It looks that way,' said Flydd. 'Or at least, *was* breeding them.'

Maelys was thinking of the thousands of bloodline registers and the millions of names in them, every single person on Santhenar. 'Why would anyone breed people? Is the Numinator trying to create an army?'

'I doubt it,' said Flydd. 'As I said, the Numinator never showed any interest in conquest or power. As long as the scrutators kept sending the registers, it didn't interfere.'

'Unless people pried into its affairs.'

He rubbed his chest, eyes closed.

'Flydd?' Colm said in a low, warning tone.

'What?' Flydd snapped.

'Behind you.'

Maelys spun around. Standing in the open doorway, about twenty paces away, stood a figure as strange as any she had seen in the glass cases. It was a man, tall but thin to the point of emaciation, with a narrow head and dark, fixed eyes. Despite the cold he was clad in only a loincloth and sandals which looked as though they had been carved out of wood. His big hands hung by his side and the yellow fingernails were shaped into points. His broad, flat feet also had sharpened nails. She waited for Flydd to use his Art against the fellow, but Flydd did nothing.

'You will come with me,' the man said in a thick, bubbling voice.

'Who are you?' said Maelys, unable to suppress a shudder. 'Are you the Numinator?'

The man's meagre lips twisted into a humourless rictus. 'I am Whelm.' He pronounced it *Hwelm*. 'Come.'

A faint smell seemed to be seeping from his pores. Maelys could not place it. It wasn't exactly unpleasant, but it wasn't attractive either. 'Whelm?' A vague, unpleasant memory stirred, from one of the Great Tales. 'Weren't the Whelm–?'

'They were a race born to serve,' said Flydd. 'A race for whom the very idea of freedom was anathema. They were once Rulke's servants, but after he was imprisoned in the Nightland they eventually swore to the great mancer, Yggur. For many years they served him at his stronghold of Fiz Gorgo, but when Rulke escaped they rejected Yggur to take on their former name, Ghâshâd, and serve Rulke anew.'

'What happened when he was killed?' said Maelys, staring at the Whelm, who was staring at her.

'The Ghâshâd were broken, and because of their crimes they were forced to swear that they would take no master evermore. They became Whelm again, returned to the freezing southern forests and have not been heard of again unto this day. But you broke that vow,' Flydd said, looking up at the tall Whelm. 'You have taken another master.'

'Aye,' said the Whelm, gravely. 'We were masterless, desolate and desperate, until the Numinator came and saved us. The Numinator ordered us to serve, and who were we to disobey? To live is to serve. Come.' He flexed his fingers.

Maelys studied the yellow pointed nails, then the gaunt face of the Whelm, and decided that she was going to do exactly as he had said. 'Are you taking us to the Numinator?'

Again that humourless twitch of the mouth. 'You are trespassers. You do not have the right to ask questions.'

He extended a skeletal right arm down a corridor to his left. Maelys hadn't noticed it before. 'What are you going to do with us?'

'You will do useful work until the master is ready to deal with you.'

Again Maelys hesitated, expecting Flydd to resist, or at least give her some lead, but he was already walking towards the corridor. Why was he so acquiescent?

The Whelm's wooden sandals clapped on the ice floor as he walked, or rather stalked, with an odd, jerking motion, but he would say no more. They went ahead, following his pointing arm, down to a small room lit by a single lantern. There they were set to work at bloodline registers for the town of Banthey, on Banthey Isle in the tropical north. Through thick ice panes in the walls to left and right, Maelys saw other people engaged in seemingly identical tasks, but there was no way to contact them, and each had their own Whelm guard.

They had to compile lists of names from the registers, but only those few who had a five-digit number beside them. It was tedious work, and often there would only be one such number in the entire register, but a Whelm stood behind each of them and, whenever a page was turned too quickly, or someone missed a five-digit number or noted one down incorrectly, the sharpened nails dug into their neck.

'If they know when we're making a mistake,' said Colm, rubbing his stinging, nail-scored neck at the end of a painful and miserably cold day, one of many that had all been the same since the Whelm caught them, 'why don't they do the damn job themselves? It'd be a lot quicker.'

'I don't think that's the point,' said Flydd.

'Then what is the point?' said Colm.

'We're finally going to find out.'

Another male Whelm had appeared in the doorway. 'You will come now,' he said in a voice like bubbles rising through a vat of mud. Maelys thought it was the Whelm they had first encountered, but couldn't be sure. Whelm features were of a kind.

'Where are you taking us?' she said.

He didn't reply, but led them down a long hall, then out into a broad open space whose ceiling was so high that Maelys could not make it out. Maelys looked back and the building they had been held in was revealed as a slab-sided, flat-roofed bastion, perhaps ten floors high, completely enclosed by the gigantic Tower of a Thousand Steps. Ahead some hundred paces was the inner wall of the tower, curving all the way around the bastion, and rising up in a sheet of ice which slanted back over their heads as though they were inside an enormous cone standing on its base.

The Whelm led them through a small door at the base of the inner wall, and onto a broad staircase of diamond-clear ice that ran up inside the wall of the tower in a series of flights to form a pentagon shape. Here he ushered them past and she identified his smell – fish oil mixed with onions.

'Is this the Tower of a Thousand Steps?' said Maelys.

He pointed up, and up they went. The Whelm's sandals clapped against the treads; he was slow but tireless. They climbed until even Maelys's travel-hardened legs were aching. She began to count, but lost her way at four hundred and sixty, and after that there was no point.

The ice walls of the tower were like vast, sloping panes which might once have been transparent, but were now so fretted by time and wind that they were like sand-blasted glass. They allowed light in, but revealed nothing of the surrounding land.

After a seemingly endless climb they came out onto the uppermost floor of the tower. The roof soared above them like a five-sided glass steeple, the ice a russet colour that let in even less light. Flames flickered in a dish the size of a circular bath, and the misty air above it swirled up lazily, the mist changing from red through all the colours of the spectrum to violet at the top of the spire, then falling in slow whorls and eddies down the steeple walls to the floor and rolling in to the centre again.

As Maelys's eyes adjusted she saw a simple bed and dresser against one wall, and a table against another, to her left. The table was piled high with bloodline registers and she didn't realise that someone was sitting behind it until they moved.

She jumped. It was a woman with shoulder-length hair the colour of spun gold. Maelys stared. She'd expected to encounter a cold-eyed mancer, or even some fierce, intelligent creature from another world. It had not occurred to her that the Numinator, who had ruled over the most powerful mancers in all the world, might be female.

The woman stood up and came out from behind the table, and Maelys was in no doubt that here was the Numinator at last, for her presence was like a freezing wind, a blow in the face, a shard of ice through the heart. She wasn't tall, or physically imposing – Colm towered over her – and was dressed in a simple, dark gown which concealed rather than revealed her slender figure. Her face was neither young nor old, but extremely forbidding. There were crinkles at the corners of her eyes, and lines curving down from each side of her mouth. Flydd stiffened beside Maelys. Even he was intimidated.

The Numinator held herself poker-rigid. She had once been a striking woman, but Maelys did not think she had ever been a likeable one. She radiated an aura of vast self-control and intense dislike. Maelys also knew, without knowing how, that the Numinator was nothing like any other power in the world. Indeed, the very fact that she had cut herself off from the world showed how indifferent she was to the things that powerful men like Jal-Nish and Vivimord pursued so desperately.

'Why have you trespassed on the forbidden Isle of Noom?' The Numinator's voice was overly precise and formal. Everything about her seemed controlled – almost frozen in time.

Maelys glanced at Flydd. He was staring at her as if he expected *her* to speak first.

'Go on, Maelys,' he said. 'Coming here was your idea.'

Maelys clenched her jaw but bit her tongue painfully. Tasting blood, she swallowed. Why had Flydd put her forward? Was it his promised revenge because she'd pressured him to take renewal? She no longer understood him, if she ever had. No, it could not be that. He must be working to a plan and she had to go with it. What could she say that would sway the Numinator? Nothing, so she would simply tell the truth.

'The God-Emperor holds the last of my clan.' She met the Numinator's glacial eyes and tried to hold them. 'If I can't save them, no one can, and my story has been repeated many times since the God-Emperor came to power. He must be overthrown and –'

'You're overly bold for your age,' said the Numinator. 'How old are you, girl?'

'N-nineteen, Numinator.'

'I can't ever remember being so young,' the Numinator mused. 'I don't recall having a childhood.' The eyes focussed on Maelys again. She could not tell their colour – they might once have been grey, or green, or even blue, but they were leached of all colour here. 'I know of no way to touch the God-Emperor.'

'But you controlled the Council of Scrutators for more than a hundred years,' Flydd said quietly. 'Indeed, you *created* the Council.'

'The puppet master speaks,' said the Numinator, staring at him as if to peer right inside his head. 'There is something familiar about you.'

Flydd said nothing. The Numinator studied him, her head tilted, her back held rigid. 'Take off your coat and shirt!'

'What?' cried Flydd, not moving.

'Or my Whelm will do it for you,' she added quietly. 'They number seven hundred, and obey my every command. Nothing can shake their loyalty.'

'A previous master said the same,' said Flydd, 'if I remember the Histories.'

A wintry smile touched her stern mouth, momentarily taking decades off her age. 'You dare quote the Histories to *me*, who lived them?'

She gestured to the Whelm standing at the top of the stair, but before he could move Flydd whipped off his coat, dropped it on the floor and unfastened his shirt.

The Numinator glided forward a few steps, stopped and made a twirling motion with her fingers. Flydd turned around, slowly, until he faced her again. His cheeks were a trifle pink, though that might have been the cold.

Her eyes went out of focus for a moment, as if she were thinking hard, then the wintry smile fleeted back and she said, 'Xervish Flydd.'

Flydd gaped. 'How can you tell?'

'You were flogged to the bone for inquiring about me, many decades ago now, and such scars cannot lie. Even after taking renewal, Ex-Scrutator Flydd, the deepest scars remain, and they tell me your name as surely as a print from your finger. Why did you put the girl up to it? What happened to the courage you were once famed for?'

'I grew old, and it faded with the decay of my body. I was ready to die but Maelys Nifferlin pressed me to a renewal I would have done anything to avoid, and rightly so, for, renewed or not, I am not half the man I was, even on my death bed. She put *me* up to it, and she can explain herself.'

'And you protest too much. You can't play your scrutator's games with me, Flydd, for I read men like books. You may dress.' She turned back to Maelys, saying, 'Well, girl? It seems you are also more than you appear.'

'I'm not, but last year, in the Pit of Possibilities, I saw that the God-Emperor had a weakness,' said Maelys. 'If you can tell us where to find the antithesis to the tears –'

'Antithesis?' said the Numinator in an odd, angry tone.

'The spell or artefact or . . . or force that can destroy –'

'I know what antithesis means!' The Numinator crooked a finger at the watching Whelm, who shepherded them into the corner nearest the top of the Thousand Steps.

She began to pace, eyes closed, hands held up above her head as if carrying a coffin at a funeral. She turned in a circle, then in a second circle linked to it, making a figure eight, and a third and fourth – a cloverleaf. Every footstep was slow, sliding and deliberate, as though it represented a single, precisely calibrated thought. Watching her feet, which moved like a metronome below her gown, Maelys saw that the ice formed a slight depression there.

The Numinator had paced the same path so often that she had worn down the floor beneath her.

Finally she turned back to them, and her face was cast into a grimmer curve than before. 'I know of no antithesis to the tears.'

THIRTY-FOUR

Flydd made a faint noise in the back of his throat. Colm let out a harsh bark of laughter; it sounded half insane. The Whelm shuffled its wooden sandals.

Maelys felt a shriek building up and had to restrain herself from giving way to it. The journey had been wasted; everything they'd gone through since leaving the plateau had been for nothing.

'She might be lying,' said Colm.

The Whelm's right hand closed around Colm's throat from behind, the sharpened nails pricking through his skin and causing five beads of blood to bud there. The yellow nails of its left hand cut through Colm's coat and shirt to his belly. Colm went still, his eyes bulging. He definitely wanted to live now, and Maelys was pleased to see it, though she was afraid his change of heart might have come too late.

'Never speak ill of the master,' hissed the Whelm. His gaze turned to the Numinator. 'Shall I tear his throat out, master? Or offer you his living bowels on a platter?'

The Numinator looked faintly disgusted. 'Release him, Whelm. No one can harm me here. His words mean nothing; less than nothing. Take them down and put them back to work. The great project is behind schedule.'

'But . . ' said Maelys, thinking of the countless days they had spent going through the registers so far, and the endless work to go. 'How long?'

'Surely you didn't think you could just leave?' said the Numinator. 'You trespassed on my privacy, deliberately, and you have to pay for it.'

'What do we have to do?' Maelys said dully.

'When the God-Emperor destroyed all the nodes, he damaged me and undermined my power. My life's work, which was almost complete, has to be redone by the most monumental labour, and I can no longer do it alone.'

'What great work?' said Colm, but the claw-nails pricked into his throat again and he broke off. Five blood-beads oozed down his neck.

'Never question the master,' the Whelm grated.

'Enough, Gliss,' said the Numinator, and he returned to the top of the steps at once, though his eyes were staring fixedly at Colm's throat and he was trembling.

He wants to kill Colm, Maelys thought. The Whelm are fanatically loyal and they can't bear any threat to their master, nor any insult. The quickest way to eliminate the threat is to kill, so they'll kill any of us without compunction. The thought was chilling, for it made them far more difficult to deal with than the God-Emperor's soldiers. Nothing would sway the Whelm; not mercy, kindness, forgiveness, empathy.

'How long?' said Maelys despairingly; they'd come all this way, wasted all this time, for nothing. Her family was in terrible danger now, for Jal-Nish was unpredictable and might destroy them at any moment. She had to find the tears' antithesis; she just had to.

'Why, as long as you all shall live,' the Numinator said with another chilling smile.

The pain swelled into a shrieking knot, as if the Whelm had torn open Maelys's chest and clenched its sharpened nails into her heart.

'No!' she gasped. 'You can't. I've got to –'

'You're trapped, girl. You can't do anything. Take them down, Gliss, and put them back to work.' The Numinator returned to her table and began to study her ledgers as if they were no longer there.

'But if you're powerless –' began Maelys.

The Whelm's right hand thudded onto her shoulder.

'*Never* think that I am powerless, girl,' said the Numinator without looking up. 'I am diminished, certainly, but my Arts suffice to maintain my realm; and control everything and everyone in it.'

The Whelm's metal-hard fingers turned her towards the top of the Thousand Steps. Colm followed.

'I have a gift for you, Numinator,' said Flydd. 'Something you may never have seen before. A gift of power.'

The Numinator looked up sharply. 'There are few forms of power that I'm not aware of.'

Flydd drew the white crystal phial from his pocket and held it up. The red and black flame still flickered there, ominous in the dim light. 'I trapped this from the cursed flame that still burns beneath the ancient Charon obelisk on Mistmurk Mountain.'

The Numinator sat stiffly, staring at the phial. 'I have been there. I read the glyphs on the obelisk and understood their true meaning. I have seen the cursed flame too, but it does not have the power to help me now.'

Flydd stood there, swaying back and forth on the balls of his feet, then transferred the phial to his left hand and slipped the right into his pocket.

The Numinator smiled thinly. 'I won't leave it for you to work some minor havoc with. Gliss?'

Gliss came forwards and Flydd, with a show of reluctance, handed him the phial. When Gliss had returned to the top of the steps, Flydd said, 'But did you know that the cursed flame is fed from a deeper source – the abyssal flame.' He raised the stone bottle. 'One that is far greater and more perilous.'

'I have also seen the abyssal flame,' said the Numinator.

'The gift is no use to me.' She gestured to Gliss, who took the stone bottle as well. 'Take them down.'

'I will lead them below at once, master,' said the Whelm.

Flydd held up his left hand, and put his right hand in his pocket again. 'Ah, but have you seen this? It is the ultimate unknown power, so unlike any other force on Santhenar that I cannot understand where it came from.'

He withdrew a cloth-wrapped package and held up the oval ice flask containing the trapped, pure white, freezing chthonic flame.

'What is that?' the Numinator said sharply.

'It came from a crystal chest hidden below the source of the abyssal flame, at the very base of a shaft bored deep into the rock below Mistmurk Mountain.'

'That seems like a prodigious effort for such a little thing,' said the Numinator, though she seemed wary. 'I sense no great power in it.'

'As I said, the chthonic flame is a power like no other on Santhenar.'

'*Chthonic* flame?' She shot upright. 'And it was hidden? *By whom?*'

Maelys wondered if he was going to mention the woman in red, but Flydd merely shrugged.

'Bring it here.'

Flydd went forwards with the flask. The Whelm followed at his heels, hands stretched towards Flydd's throat, until the Numinator rapped, 'He cannot harm me, Gliss. Flydd, place it on the table.'

Gliss returned to his position, his jerky movements more exaggerated than before, and staring shard-like at Flydd all the while. If he got the chance he would eliminate the threat to his master, permanently.

Flydd placed the flask on her table and stepped back.

'What else do you know about the flame?' Her frosty eyes were fixed on him now, as if daring him to try and conceal anything from her.

369

'Nothing. I wasn't aware of its existence until just before we fled the mountain. I found it by the merest chance.'

She continued to stare at him for a minute or two, then gestured to Gliss. 'Put them back to work.'

Late that night, Gliss heaved open the ice door of their cell and crooked a finger at Maelys. 'Come.'

'Me?' Her voice went squeaky. 'What for?'

'No questions. *Come!*'

There was no point resisting. She couldn't escape the Numinator and her seven hundred Whelm, and even if, by some miracle, she did get out of the ice tower, without shelter she would freeze to death within a day.

'Where are you taking me?'

Gliss did not reply, but it became clear once he began hauling her up the Thousand Steps – he was taking her back to the Numinator and it could not be for any good reason.

The scrutators had flayed the flesh off Flydd's bones because he had dared inquire about the Numinator, and Maelys's crime was of a higher order. She was not strong enough to endure a flaying.

Her legs started to shake, and soon her knees were wobbling so violently that she could barely stand up. She fell down, but Gliss kept dragging her, unheeding, and her kneecap struck the edge of a tread so painfully that she cried out. The Whelm did not stop and she forced herself to her feet again.

The Numinator had Flydd's measure; he could do nothing here, and neither could Colm, so it was up to her *again*. That was the only advantage of being little and young: people underestimated her. Maybe the Numinator would too. If an opportunity came, she had to be ready to seize it.

They finally reached the Numinator's steeple-topped eyrie and she gestured at Gliss, dismissing him. He glowered at Maelys but left. He did not take her seriously as a threat. Good so far.

'Come here, girl.'

The Numinator was sitting bolt upright by the fire in a chair formed from ice and covered in the white pelt of a large hunting cat. Her feet were placed on the floor, perfectly aligned; her long-fingered hands rested on the arms of the chair. She reminded Maelys of Mistress Hatyn, the ferocious tutor in the schoolroom at Clan Nifferlin, in the days before the war ended. She had been equally organised and controlled; no one had ever got away with anything while Hatyn was in charge.

Maelys, realising that she was creeping like a mousy child, straightened her back, forcing herself to meet the Numinator's eye. The Numinator gave the faintest, derisive twitch of the lips, as if to say, *You think you can stand up to me?*

'How did you come here, girl?'

She did not want to answer that. 'My name isn't *girl*. It's Maelys. Maelys Nifferlin.'

'I know your name, and your clan. Every name on Santhenar is in my bloodline registers.'

'Stud books is what I would call them!'

'And you are a vulgar little trollop.'

The Numinator was trying to provoke her, which meant that she wanted something. Perhaps they could bargain. 'Who are you?' she said, because she couldn't think of anything else to say, and couldn't bear to be stared at in that unnerving silence.

'I am the Numinator and I hold your fate in my hands.'

Why state the obvious? The Numinator must have some weakness, some very great need, and Maelys had to find out what it was.

'How came you here?' the Numinator repeated. 'You did not walk all the way from the south; neither did you fly in an air-floater.'

Surely she knew about the portal? And if she did not, why not ask Flydd? Because Maelys was more likely to give something away?

'I didn't really understand it,' said Maelys.

'Liar! It was a portal, wasn't it?'

How could she deny it? The Numinator must be able to see everything from up here. 'Yes,' said Maelys, then it occurred to her that Flydd might have wanted it kept secret. Portals were extremely difficult to make.

The Numinator sat up even straighter. 'And Flydd created it? How, precisely?'

'I don't know anything about mancery . . .'

'But you know what he did. You saw him make it. Speak!'

The Numinator leaned forwards, fixing her frosty eyes on Maelys and rubbing a ring on the middle finger of her right hand, and Maelys felt so overpowered, so flustered, that she spoke without thinking.

'Only the second time.'

'The *second* time? Are you telling me that Flydd *twice* made a portal?'

It was impossible to resist her; Maelys simply did not have the will. The Numinator must have bewitched her in some way. 'Three times,' she whispered. 'Once when we escaped from Mistmurk Mountain, and then . . .' She dared not mention the Nightland, for that would lead to Emberr, 'and then to get to Plogg –'

The Numinator held up a slender, veined hand. 'Plogg is a village in Elludore, and that is a land I know well. Why did you go to Plogg?'

'It was close to a hidden valley . . .' Maelys trailed off, for the Numinator wore an enigmatic smile.

'I checked my registers last night. Your companion, Colm, was heir to a small, impoverished estate in Bannador called Gothryme, and feels he was robbed of it. His heritage – the entirety of it – is recorded in the Histories and even mentioned in the twenty-third Great Tale, the *Tale of the Mirror*. You were going to Dunnet, were you not, to find the treasure left in a cave there long ago, concealed by a perpetual illusion?'

372

'Yes,' Maelys said faintly. If the Numinator knew everything that had ever happened on Santhenar, how could
Maelys possibly take her on? But she had to. Never give
up, she told herself. Never, never, *never*.

'And did Colm find his heritage?' said the Numinator.

Maelys was on very dangerous ground. She dared not
mention the mimemule that Flydd had vanished, else the
Numinator would take it. The mimemule, whatever it was,
was her only hope of escape from Noom.

'The illusion had been broken. The treasure was gone.
There was just a wooden box full of dirt and an empty
pouch.'

It was the hardest lie she had ever told, even more difficult than lying to the God-Emperor about being pregnant
with Nish's child. She forced herself to meet the Numinator's gaze, but lightly.

The Numinator frowned. 'But Faelamor was the greatest illusionist of the age. How could any mancer break her
illusion?'

'I know nothing about such things.' Maelys was standing
as rigidly as the Numinator, her fingers curled like butcher's hooks. Relax, you'll give yourself away. Her fingers did
not want to relax.

The Numinator tapped her nails on the icy arm of her
chair. 'The treasure is irrelevant. But *three* portals, one after
another – how could any common mancer do that?'

Maelys remembered Flydd questioning where his ability, or his knowledge to make portals, had come from. Dare
she ask? It seemed overly bold, but she had to be, else she
must fail.

'What are you saying, Numinator?'

The Numinator was staring into the flames, rubbing
her right forefinger against her thumb. 'Making portals
is one of the greatest and most difficult of all the Secret
Arts – so difficult that, over the course of the Histories,
hundreds of years have often gone by without *any* suc-
cessful portals being made. To make a single portal is

exhausting, and cripplingly so for all but the greatest mancers . . .'

So how *could* Flydd do it, even with the aid of the woman in red?

'Xervish Flydd was never a truly great mancer,' the Numinator went on. 'His genius lay in other areas – leadership and strategy. I would have thought a portal beyond him, even at his peak. But *three* portals, one after another, and soon after taking renewal, beggars comprehension. Unless . . .' She looked up into Maelys's eyes. 'You pressured him. Were you there while he used the renewal spell?'

'He required me to watch.' Maelys did not want to be reminded of that horror again. 'He wanted me to know what I'd done to him.'

'Tell me about it. Omit not the least detail.'

Maelys did so, and when she'd finished, the Numinator sat back, frowning. 'Is that all?'

'Have you taken renewal?' said Maelys.

'*I* have no need of it,' the Numinator said loftily.

Therefore she wasn't old human – so who was she?

'Did anything unusual happen to him?'

'I wouldn't know. I'd never heard of renewal before . . .'

'You're withholding something,' said the Numinator. 'Keep nothing back – or else.'

'During renewal,' said Maelys, 'Flydd saw a woman dressed in red. He thought he *was* her, at one stage, or that she was him, but he later realised that was just a hallucination. He saw her afterwards, too, when he was hunted through Mistmurk Mountain. She taught him about portals. That's how we escaped.'

'A woman in red?' The Numinator looked at Maelys sharply. 'It still does not add up. One mancer can't simply *tell* another how to make a portal; there is a craft to it and it requires long practice. Tell me how the first portal was made, and where it was intended to go.'

Maelys felt that every word was a minor betrayal; she

wanted to defy the Numinator but her will to resist was being overpowered by some mighty spell or Art. She told the Numinator about Flydd's original plan to escape via the shadow realm, how it had been frustrated by the destruction of the fifth crystal, and all that followed.

'I do not know this shadow realm,' said the Numinator, frowning. 'At least, not by that name. How did he make the first portal?'

'I can't say,' said Maelys. 'We were separated for ages; I only reached him as it was opening. I think it had something to do with the chthonic flame.'

'And then the portal took you to the shadow realm? Tell me about it.'

Maelys didn't know what to say, and the Numinator seized on her hesitation. 'Don't even think about lying to me, Maelys Nifferlin.'

Maelys, thinking of the lie she'd already told, felt a flush moving up her cheeks. What if the Numinator could tell? She dared not risk another lie; Emberr's life was at stake. 'We did not go to the shadow realm. We . . . we ended up in the Nightland.'

The Numinator's right hand clenched so tightly on the arm of her ice chair that steam rose from it, then, with a little crack, it crumbled into chunks. The fire died down to the faintest flicker in its bowl, just enough to illuminate her right cheek. A shower of droplets fell from the point of the steeple, high above. One splashed on the top of Maelys's head and it burned like ice.

'There is no Nightland,' said the Numinator. 'It collapsed to nothing as its one prisoner, Rulke, escaped for the last time. How do you know it was not the shadow realm?'

'Flydd said it was the Nightland. There were all sorts of virtual devices in it, including Rulke's original pattern for his construct. That's how Flydd made his second portal – he powered the virtual construct with the chthonic flame you took from him.'

The Numinator drew in a sharp breath and held it for a

long time. Bringing the fire to life with a hand gesture, she pulled her chair close to it, then closer still, rubbing her hands together. Her fingers had gone blue; she hunched over the flame, trembling.

'It makes no sense,' she said at last. 'When Rulke escaped the second time, the Nightland was collapsing to a singularity, for the power that had held it together was exhausted. How can it still exist two hundred and twenty years later?'

'Flydd asked that very question,' said Maelys. 'He said it would take an immense amount of power to maintain such a huge place, and why would anyone go to all that effort, for nothing . . .' Thinking of Emberr, she felt her cheeks grow warm again and struggled valiantly to control herself. Not for nothing.

'A *huge* place?' said the Numinator. 'The Great Tale says that it was tiny by the time Rulke escaped, and shrinking towards nothingness.'

'Flydd thought it had rebounded,' Maelys ventured.

'No!' the Numinator exclaimed. 'Such things do not happen by themselves. If the Nightland still exists, it's because someone has made it so. The God-Emperor? Is it his ultimate prison?' she mused. 'Or the best hiding place of all – his perfect refuge in times of danger? No, I don't think so. I don't believe he even knows of its existence, *so why is it there?*'

Don't react, Maelys told herself, thinking of Emberr. He was in danger from his mother's enemy and she had to protect him.

The Numinator rose from her chair and glided towards Maelys; she was within reach before Maelys realised what was happening. She turned to run.

'Stop!'

Maelys froze, unable to defy the Numinator.

'You know something. Speak!'

Maelys shook her head and tried to back away. She wasn't game to speak, for she knew her voice would betray

her. Her feet wouldn't move, and she leaned so far backwards that she overbalanced and hit the ice.

The Numinator crouched beside her, her stern, sad face
just an ell away. 'Speak, girl! What else did you find in the
Nightland? *What is it for?*'

Maelys had to remain silent; she'd promised Emberr
that she would keep his secret. But she could not hold out
against the Numinator's overwhelming power. 'Emberr,'
she gasped, rolling her r's just as he had on that perfect
day when they had met.

The Numinator reared backwards onto her heels.
'But . . . that is a *man's* name. Speak, girl! Tell me
everything.'

'I met a young man called Emberr,' said Maelys. 'He was
tall and handsome . . .' The Numinator was frowning at her
again. 'What's the matter?'

'Why is he there? Who holds him prisoner?'

'He's not a prisoner,' said Maelys. 'He was born there.'

'Born there?' The Numinator was so shocked that momentarily she lost control, her mouth opening and closing like
a stranded fish.

'That's what he said. Because he was born in the Nightland, he can never escape – at least, unless a woman takes
his place. That's what his mother told him.'

'Ahh!' The Numinator's eyes glittered. 'And who was his
mother?'

'He didn't say,' said Maelys, really afraid now. The
Numinator knew something and it was not to Emberr's
advantage. 'He said that she left him there but could never
come back.'

A fire was burning in the Numinator's eyes now. 'When
was this?'

'Emberr didn't say. A long time ago.'

'What about his father?'

'He didn't mention him.'

'I wonder . . .' said the Numinator. 'No, it's not possible,
after all this time.' She raised her voice. 'Gliss?'

The Whelm's sandals clapped up the steps. 'Master?'

'Take her down again, then ensure I am not disturbed, *under any circumstances*. I have much to do and little time in which to do it.'

THIRTY-FIVE

Maelys was so worried about Emberr that it took her ages to get to sleep, but when she did, she began to dream about him at once. It was a powerful, sensual dream where he had taken her by the hand and was leading her up a winding path towards a pretty glade . . .

'Maelys. *Wake up!*'

It was Colm's voice. She clutched her furs about her, yearning to go back to the dream, but it was gone. 'Yes?' she said irritably. It was still pitch dark.

'Flydd has found a way out. Hurry!'

She felt for her fur-lined boots and dragged them on. In the cold, the leather had gone as stiff as wood. 'How?'

'Just come!' he hissed.

It didn't seem possible, but Maelys asked no more questions. Her mind was already full of them. Could the Numinator be the enemy of Emberr's mother? When she had heard about him, her eyes had blazed.

Maelys recalled a series of crackling shrieks in the night. At first she'd thought that someone was being tortured, but had come to realise that the sounds had been mechanical in origin – like monstrous slabs of ice being torn apart and put back together again. The Numinator was making something, up in her eyrie.

She picked up her pack and felt for the door. 'Where are you, Colm?'

'Here!' he said from behind her.

'How did you get in?'

'Flydd made a hole in the wall.'

She felt about and found a smoothly scalloped opening in the ice, leading into the next cell. 'Ow!' The ice had burned her, but with a stinging, freezing fire which had blistered her fingertips. Looking down at the hole in the wall she noted a faint white flicker there. Flydd had brought two flasks of chthonic fire to Noom, but had only given one to the Numinator. He must have used the other and the white fire was eating away the ice.

Maelys raised her stinging fingertips to her mouth, but thought better of it and wiped them on the wall instead. A lick of flame began to eat at that ice, too, though it soon went out.

'Maelys?' said Flydd urgently.

She scrambled through the hole, careful not to touch the sides, and into Flydd's cell. It was identical to hers though faintly illuminated by a patch of white flame spreading outwards from a hole in the far wall, into Colm's cell. Maelys looked askance at the fire. It did not feel right, or safe.

'I think she was telling the truth,' said Flydd. 'I don't believe she knows anything about the antithesis to the tears and there's no point us being here.' He was crouched in the darkness at the rear of the cell; Maelys could only see the curve of his back. 'I'm wondering if the Numinator has spent so long brooding on her obsession with the bloodline registers that she's gone insane.'

Maelys didn't think she was insane at all, but felt too bruised by her interrogation last night to say so.

'She won't harm us while we can do useful work,' Flydd went on, 'but she won't let us go either. We've got to escape, now, while she's distracted.' Another of those ice-tearing shrieks shivered down from above. 'I'd like to know what she's up to.'

'She questioned me again last night,' said Maelys. 'She used some kind of spell on me. I couldn't hold out . . .'

'Her Arts could make the very stones speak,' Flydd said curtly. 'What did you tell her?'

'She seemed really interested in your power to make portals, one after another. She found it, er, incredible.'

'As do I.'

'I also mentioned the woman in red. The Numinator knew I was holding something back and forced me to tell her about the Nightland. She was shocked; she couldn't believe that it still existed, and said some great mancer must be maintaining it.' Maelys, guiltily, didn't mention Emberr. She felt bad enough that she'd broken her promise and revealed his name to the Numinator.

Another crackling shriek echoed down.

'What is she doing?' mused Flydd, looking up. 'She's using mighty amounts of power up there – and my chthonic flame, I think.' He stood up. At the base of the wall, the ice twinkled with the white fire that was steadily eating through it.

'I don't like that stuff,' said Colm. 'It doesn't feel natural.'

'It's not,' said Flydd. 'And had we possessed any other weapon, I would have had nothing to do with chthonic fire, either. This way.'

'Where are we going?'

'To find those workers we saw the other day. We've got to have help. We can't escape on our own.'

'Can't you make another portal?' said Colm.

'Not without the virtual construct.'

'Where are the other prisoners held?'

'I don't know,' said Flydd, 'though I don't suppose they'll be very far away.'

'There will be guards,' said Maelys. 'Whelm.' She was really afraid of the Whelm, afraid of their obsessive loyalty; even more afraid of their inhumanity.

'Seven hundred of them, the Numinator said,' Flydd

mused. 'And Whelm see better in the dark than we do. They're relentless in pursuit, but slow and awkward in a fight.'

'Plus they're armed,' said Colm. 'We're not.' Their weapons had been taken before they had been put to work on the bloodline registers.

'Let's see what I can do about that.'

Flydd swiftly drew three elongated outlines on the wall with the lip of his pyramid-shaped flask. He stood back while the flickering white fire ate into the ice, then kicked through in the middle and the lengths of ice fell into Colm's cell. Flydd picked one up in a cloth-covered hand and wiped it. The flames faded and he was left with a rude club, as hard as stone. He handed it to Colm, wiped down the second, smaller club and gave it to Maelys, and took the last for himself.

'A crude weapon, but robust.'

'A knife would be better,' said Colm.

'One sideways blow and the blade would snap. Our cudgels will cave in a dozen Whelm skulls before they break.'

Maelys let out an involuntary cry. She did not like to be reminded about how brutal battle really was.

'If you take up a weapon you must be prepared to use it,' said Flydd, 'and face up to what you've done to another human being with it, good or evil.'

'I know,' she said faintly. 'It's just – I was gently brought up.'

'Not so gently that you didn't see animals butchered for food, or wild beasts killed when they threatened the herds or the children. The Whelm won't be gentle if they catch us, and treating them gently will reveal a weakness that they will exploit ruthlessly.'

Maelys swallowed, pulled down the sleeve of her coat to protect her hand and grasped the ice cudgel, following them into the next cell. Shortly they were out in the corridor. It was lighter here, for the rays of a half-moon came dimly through the right-hand wall.

'This way, I think,' said Flydd, turning left.

Colm followed close behind, then Maelys, taking little notice of their surroundings, which in this gloom looked ever the same. From high above she kept hearing the shrill crackle of tearing ice, and felt sure the Numinator was constructing a portal to the Nightland. If she was, it could only be because of Emberr; he was in danger from his mother's enemy, and who could that be but the Numinator? Was she planning to kill him? And if she was, it was all Maelys's fault.

She froze in the middle of the corridor, staring upwards. Flydd's last gate hadn't taken long at all, and maybe, powered with chthonic fire, the Numinator's portal would be just as quick.

She took a couple of steps back the other way, trying to hear, but the tower was silent now. What if the portal was finished; what if the Numinator was already going through it? *Emberr!* She'd only met him for a few minutes but felt she'd known him always. He'd spent his life all alone, yet his only concern had been for her. She couldn't bear to think of the Numinator harming him.

She would have to tell Flydd. Maelys could only imagine his fury when she revealed that she'd deceived him so terribly, but it must be done. She turned down the corridor, rounded the corner, and stopped. Halls ran in three directions and she could not tell which way Flydd and Colm had gone.

'Xervish?' she said softly, afraid of alerting the Whelm.

There was no reply. In the distance she heard the unmistakable clap of a wooden sandal against the floor, though she wasn't sure which hall it had come from. Maelys hesitated. She had one chance in three of finding Flydd now; less if the hall she took branched again. And she had at least one chance in three of blundering into a Whelm.

The odds were against her. It's a sign, she thought. I'm meant to go the other way. But she hesitated, more afraid of the Numinator than she had been of Jal-Nish. Ever since childhood, Maelys had been intimidated by powerful, dominating women.

Courage, Maelys. It was as if old Tulitine were speaking to her, and Maelys had never known her to be afraid of anyone. Drawing the taphloid from between her breasts, she squeezed it in her fist and cried silently, Tulitine, give me strength.

It helped a little. She had to take on the Numinator, for Emberr's sake, and she'd better hurry. Testing the weight of the club, she turned and headed towards the Thousand Steps, following the path Gliss had used last time. She reached the stair without encountering anyone and began to climb, not thinking about what she was going to do once she reached the top. She couldn't plan that far ahead.

Halfway up, as Maelys stopped for a breather, the sound of tearing ice echoed down the stairs. Was the Numinator nearly done? Ready to go through?

Clap, clap. It was a Whelm on the steps below her, and coming up rapidly. 'Master?' called a woman's voice, higher than Gliss's, and less gurgling. 'Master, there's someone on the Steps.'

The wooden sandals clapped once more, not so heavily, then Maelys heard a faint, swift padding. The Whelm was coming after her, barefoot. Maelys began to run but could not keep it up. A thousand steps was a mighty climb and she'd already done it twice in the past day. Her legs hurt, right into the bones.

She looked down but there wasn't enough light to see anything below her. She had to climb faster. The Whelm were slow, Flydd had said. We can outrun them. But they were also iron-hard and could keep going forever. She couldn't tell how far there was to go – perhaps four hundred steps. She'd never make it.

Maelys pressed on, step after exhausting step. The ice cudgel grew heavier every second, and its cold was burning through her sleeve. She didn't think she could hold it much longer. She swapped it into her other hand, used it as a cane for a moment, and continued.

As she reached the next landing, a triangle of glassy ice between two steep flights, Maelys caught sight of something moving below her, just a fleeting change to the pattern of dull light and pitch darkness. The Whelm was less than fifty steps below, and gaining. She wasn't *that* slow. Maelys's throat was raw from gasping the dry, frigid air, but she had to press on. She might be Emberr's only hope.

Soon she realised that there was no chance of beating the Whelm to the top. She would have to attack before the woman leapt on her from behind, but how? The Thousand Steps was composed of one steep flight after another, running up a five-sided stairwell, but there was no central column to hide behind; neither had she noticed any doorways through which to strike from darkness. The upper part of the Tower of a Thousand Steps seemed empty, as if it had been built for one purpose only: to raise the Numinator's eyrie as far as possible from the bleak landscape of the Isle of Noom, and the grim museum and necropolis in the basement of the inner tower.

It was lighter up here, and as she climbed the next flight the moon broke through again, shining brightly through a small patch of clear ice, right into her eyes. Momentarily Maelys couldn't see clearly and knew she would find no better place for an ambush. She went up a few more steps, crouched low, transferred the club to her right hand and tried to prepare her sore muscles for action.

She would only have one chance. If the Whelm got her nails into Maelys she would not get away, and even up two steps she would have little advantage in height. She would have to strike hard, fast and true, and pray that her first blow was a disabling one.

The Whelm's feet were slap-slapping against the ice; and she was panting. The tension in Maelys's stomach was painful now and, as if the Whelm had detected her anxiety, her footfalls slowed. Maelys peered over the step but couldn't see her. She must be waiting in the darkness lower down. Maelys let go of the club handle and rubbed her freezing fingers against her coat sleeve.

Gripping it again, she tried to calm her racing heart. The moon was drifting in and out of the clouds, the light flaring and fading. The Whelm had stopped panting; Maelys couldn't hear her at all.

She couldn't hear anything from above, either, which might mean that the Numinator had completed her portal and was on her way to the Nightland. To kill Emberr? Maelys wanted to shriek, just to break the tension.

Slap-slap. The Whelm was coming on. Maelys could see her now, rounding the lower angle, plodding up with that awkward gait. She stopped one flight below and in a shaft of moonlight Maelys saw that she was not much older than herself, though thin and bony like all the Whelm. Her short dark hair was cut straight across at the back of her head, and she had huge black eyes.

It made a difference. Maelys wasn't sure she could attack a young woman. She clung desperately to the ice club, feeling the sweat freezing on the palms of her hands and her heart racketing under her breastbone.

The Whelm moved up; she was almost to the point when the moonlight would shine in her eyes. One more step, Maelys thought. The Whelm was looking up and hadn't seen her, flattened in the pool of shadow on the step.

She took another step, but as Maelys sprang to her feet the light faded as the moon passed behind a cloud. The Whelm saw her and lunged.

Maelys, taken by surprise, swung the club, but she was off-balance and had moved too late. The Whelm caught her arm, tore the club out of her hand and sent it flying down the steps. Before Maelys knew what was happening her right arm had been twisted up behind her back, the Whelm's free arm came around her neck and she was caught in an unbreakable headlock.

In the depths below them a tocsin sounded, low and mournful.

'Master?' called the Whelm anxiously. 'It is I, Sitchah –'

'I said no interruptions!' the Numinator's voice came faintly from above.

'Master, the prisoners have escaped. I – I caught the girl on your steps. She was armed.'

After a brief pause, the Numinator, sounding rather strained, said, 'Bring her up.'

'Master?'

'At once, Whelm!'

Sitchah drew a deep breath, as if distressed, then said, 'At once, Master.' She smelled of fish oil and onions too, though not as strongly as Gliss and the other males.

Maelys was forced upwards, Sitchah holding her so tightly that Maelys's feet barely touched the treads. They reached the last flight before the top.

It was much lighter here, for a pulsing glow extended down from the Numinator's fire, and the steps were littered with shattered pieces of ice, fallen from above and frozen to the treads. Several threads of chthonic flame trickled down the riser of the top step, eating into it. Maelys's skin crawled.

Sitchah forced her up another step, then sprang sideways, stifling a gasp and looking down at her left foot. She had gashed it deeply on a shard of ice; blood was pouring from her sole to stain the step.

She hobbled up another step, then another, but it proved impossible to avoid the iron-hard, brittle shards, and soon every footstep left a bloody print. Maelys had to admire Sitchah's determination: no pain, no injury could prevent her from doing her duty to her master.

Or could it? Maelys allowed her weight to fall to the left, forcing the Whelm to move that way. Sitchah winced as her foot came down on another shard, then began to pick a path up further to the left, heading towards the faint white flicker of chthonic flame. Maelys kept leaning that way, hoping Sitchah hadn't noticed the flame, which wasn't very bright.

They were just five steps below the Numinator's eyrie now, Sitchah gasping with every step. The soles of her feet must have been gashed to the bone.

Three steps, and Maelys could see into the eyrie, which had been completely rebuilt. The upper third of the ice steeple was gone, as were the books and the table. Wind whistling across the open top of the steeple caused a sobbing reverberation of the air; it was as cold as outside and tiny ice crystals were drifting down, winking in the light of the fire, which now blazed in a broad metal dish in the centre of the eyrie. The fire was different, too. The chthonic flame had been emptied from its ice flask and, well-fed and unconstrained, burned two spans high.

It was surrounded by five miniature ice steeples, four spans high at the left-hand end and six at the right, supporting a sloping slab of ice, like a roof over the white flame. Maelys couldn't see the Numinator until she moved behind it. She wore grey-green pants, an ice-grey blouse, and a stiletto made from ice was strapped to her right thigh. The hollow core of the blade was a brilliant, poisonous yellow. Maelys's gut tightened. So the Numinator *did* intend to kill Emberr.

Her arms were upraised, her hands placed together in a steeple that mimicked the way her tower top had been, and her fingers glistened with chthonic fire, though it didn't appear to be burning her.

'Guard her until I get back,' she said without looking at Sitchah.

The Numinator drew her hands out and down, as though pulling a bubble over herself, all the way to her feet. Now glistening with white chthonic fire, she went backwards half a dozen steps, took a running dive through the flame, and vanished.

'Master!' cried Sitchah, pushing Maelys up the steps. Her shredded foot came down on the chthonic fire threaded across the top step, she shrieked in agony, and her grip relaxed momentarily.

Maelys tore free, thrust her down the steps and raced towards the ice steeples. There was no time to think. Emberr was in mortal danger and she had to help him, but she didn't know how the Numinator had made the portal to the Nightland, or even if it could be used again. But surely she would have left it open so she could return?

Maelys raced between the second and third steeples, under the sloping slab of ice, and felt a slight shock, and a tingling all over, as if she were no longer in the normal world. She was within the portal, but where was the opening to the Nightland? Should she dive through the flame as the Numinator had? Surely there had to be more to it than that?

The pyramidal ice flask was sitting on the floor, with the stopper beside it and a tiny drift of fire rising up from it. And the Numinator's hands had been shimmering with chthonic flame, as if she'd rubbed it over herself. Maelys wasn't sure she dared. The Numinator might have protected herself with all manner of spells before she used the fire.

A groan came from behind her, and her head whipped around. Sitchah was staggering up the last steps, lacerated across her chest and legs from where she'd fallen down the shard-covered steps, but nothing save death could prevent her from doing her duty.

There was no time to think; Maelys had to act now. Upending the ice flask, she poured its contents, about five drops, into the middle of her palm. It burned hot and cold at the same time, not just on her skin but beneath it, as if it had penetrated all the way to her bones.

She ran three steps to where the Numinator had stood, rubbing the chthonic fire over her fingers and hands until they burned and shimmered, then raised her arms, steepled her hands as the Numinator had, held them there for a moment and drew them down to the floor, all the way to her feet. To her surprise, it worked and a glittering bubble enveloped her. She went backwards to the point where the Numinator had stood, staring at the chthonic fire in the metal bowl.

If this failed, she would die. If Sitchah got there first, she might also die, for Sitchah had failed her master and it was Maelys's fault.

Taking a deep breath, she ran and dived through the chthonic fire. It seared all the way along her body, even to the soles of her feet in their boots, then the Tower of a Thousand Steps and the whole world vanished.

THIRTY-SIX

Nish was tearing out his thinning hair. He had talked himself hoarse trying to convince the mayors of Gendrigore to raise a militia, but they would not listen.

'A dozen armies have broken on The Spine,' Barquine kept saying, complacently quaffing his beer, 'and the God-Emperor's forces will meet the same fate.'

Nish could see the catastrophe approaching like a tsunami, but what more could he do? No outsider, not even the Deliverer, could raise an army in Gendrigore without the support of the mayors.

Tulitine maintained her watch from the cliffs, listening to the birds, bats and dolphins, and reporting on the progress of Jal-Nish's forces, though it was not until they had begun to gather in Taranta that she drew Barquine aside. He listened, looking ever more grave, then set down his beer unfinished and shouted for the fastest runners in the town.

Scribes set down his message on a dozen tally sticks, and each runner set out in a different direction to carry the call to arms to the rest of the province, though it would take days for them to reach the provincial boundaries and pass the message to the other two provinces.

Before any runners had returned, however, all Gendrigore knew of the threat, for red-sailed ships could be seen

out to sea, well clear of the menacing rocks and treacherous currents, watching the coast day and night.

'What are they doing?' said Hoshi, an apprentice potter.
He was one of the few young men from Nish's little militia who had shown any appetite for training and Nish was
grooming him for leadership. He took every opportunity
to teach Hoshi the art of war, though with limited success.
He simply went straight for his opponent and whacked as
hard as he could. A cheerfully unsubtle youth, he had no
head for either strategy or tactics.

They were perched at the cliff edge by the fishers' tripods, watching the enemy. Nish was peering through
Barquine's battered brass spyglass, the only one in all
Gendrigore. He rubbed his eye with his scarred hand,
winced, and slid the brass tubes further apart to focus
better.

'Spying on us. See them there, up in the basket at the
top of the mainmast?' He handed the spyglass to Hoshi.

He trained it on the figures at the top of the mast, and
swung it towards the stern. 'What's that at the back?'

'Where?' Nish shaded his eyes and squinted. Something
dull-black and leathery crouched there, though he could
not make out what it was. 'It's not a flappeter.' He held out
his hand and Hoshi put the spyglass in it.

Nish focussed, looked away then focussed again. 'I've
never seen anything like it. It looks like a bat, though no bat
grows a tenth that size. Could it be a gigantic bladder-bat?'

The creature suddenly pulled its wings, which were
very bat-like, right in and wrapped them about itself until
it resembled a black ball the size of a beer barrel, though
it did not look like a bladder-bat. 'They're lifting it onto
something . . . it's hard to make out in the shadow of the
sails . . . looks like a javelard.'

'What's a javelard?' said Hoshi, picking yellow potting
clay out from under his fingernails.

He turned to smile at Gi, a sturdy, dark-haired young
woman with a round, cheerful face. She had also trained

392

hard these past days and had the blisters to prove it. She strode up, swinging a long ivory-wood staff which the town blacksmith had shod with brass at either end. She was a better tactician than Hoshi, though her gentle disposition made her a lesser soldier. She held back when she should have gone for the jugular.

'A javelard is like a catapult for throwing heavy spears,' said Nish.

The javelard snapped and the black beast was propelled hundreds of spans into the air, looping up then down like a cannonball, and flying directly at them.

'Look out!' cried Gi.

Nish scrambled to his feet and threw himself backwards as the ball-beast approached at frightening speed. When it was just a few spans away its wings unfurled and swung back like an arrowhead. A jet of brown vapour exploded from its posterior, propelling it at them like a rocket.

It had a feline head with long, vampiric teeth, and it went straight for Nish. He tried to weave out of the way, stumbled, and it would have got him had not Gi, after a momentary hesitation, cracked it over the side of the head with her staff.

It made a high-pitched chittering sound, rotated in its own length, and red bulb-like eyes extended an ell out of its head. Both eyes were fixed on Nish, who had the unnerving feeling that it knew who he was, or was remembering his image, to be shown to the nearest wisp-watcher as soon as it returned to the ship. That could not be allowed. His father must not learn that Nish was hiding here – he would definitely make war on Gendrigore then.

'Kill it, quick!'

He had left Vivimord's sabre back in his tent. Nish snatched a knife from his hip sheath and slashed at the creature, which blasted again and shot up out of reach. Gi ran underneath and tried to whack it out of the air. It spat a green gob at her, just missing her face and making the grass sizzle where it landed.

Hoshi hurled his spear at it, but it slipped sideways; the spear shot past its shoulder, out over the cliff, and was lost. The creature rose higher, rocking on its spans-long batwings. Nish scanned the ground for something to throw at it.

There were no rocks – the cliff edge was solid stone. The creature gave him a knowing look, then its rear parts began to swell; once they went off, it would jet beyond reach. Gi was staring at the sizzling patch on the blackened grass, shuddering. She hadn't seen combat before, and had no idea what to do.

Nish had seen more than he cared to remember. Running three steps, he snatched the staff out of her hand and sent it spinning up towards the beast's leathery right wing, too large a target to miss. The brass cap punched straight through the soft leather of its wing membrane and the spinning staff shattered the gracile bones. The creature dropped sharply and couldn't recover. It spun down, just missing the cliff and the fisherwomen's basket directly below it, and smacked into the water beside the defunct whirlpool.

It floated there on its spread wings, struggling to move, until a dark shape came up underneath it and, without ever breaking the surface, pulled it down. The ship unfurled its red sails and turned away.

'Well done, Deliverer,' said Gi, retrieving her staff and wiping it on the grass. 'Sorry. I should have thought of that.'

'Nish,' he said absently. 'Call me Nish.' No one said 'Surr' in Gendrigore. His eyes followed the ship until it disappeared in the haze, and he could not help thinking that the beast had already reported his presence here.

The runners returned, along with local volunteers and promises of more, a total of fifteen hundred men from the three provinces of Gendrigore. From what Nish knew of The Spine, and the crude mud-maps he had seen, he was cautiously optimistic that fifteen hundred would be enough, even if not all of them could reach Blisterbone Pass. If he could get most there in time, and hold it for a week or two, the really wet season would isolate Gendrigore for half a year, and in that time, anything could happen.

The local militia, as yet barely three hundred strong, was poorly armed and virtually untrained, but he had run out of time. They were to rendezvous in the foothills leading up to The Spine with two other small militia sent from the southern and eastern provinces, Gendri and Rigore, in six days.

The weather was perfect for marching, overcast and relatively mild, but they made slow progress, for Nish's troops took neither the threat, the march nor his training seriously. Every village broached barrels of beer, mead or fruit wine in their honour, and the revelry went on until late in the night. It proved impossible to rouse them early each morning, and even old Tulitine, who set out not long after dawn, was waiting in the next camp before the limping, sore-headed militia reached it. His only consolation was that the numbers swelled daily and he would have his full complement of five hundred by the time they reached the rendezvous point, Wily's Clearing.

On the fifth afternoon of their march Nish had just given orders for the setting up of the camp when a young man burst from the forest above them, looking around wildly. His breath came in ragged gasps and he was so thickly coated in mud that he might have been dragged through a buffalo wallow.

He looked frantically back and forth, gasping and trying to speak, until someone pointed him in Nish's direction. Nish started to run to him but stopped and, holding himself upright like the experienced and unflappable captain he must appear to be, strode across.

'I'm Cryl-Nish Hlar, called Nish,' he said. 'Captain of the militia. Do you have a message for me, lad?'

'Name's Ekko. Been on watch – lookout – Blisterbone. Barquine –' Ekko folded over, so exhausted that he was slurring his words.

Gi crouched beside him, listening to the gibberish. 'He says, er . . . Barquine sent a carrier dove to his village, Nilvi, two weeks ago, ordering the watch, since Nilvi is closest of all to the pass.'

So Barquine had taken Nish's warnings seriously after all; at least, seriously enough to keep a lookout for the enemy. 'What did you see?' said Nish, as more people ran across, until they were surrounded by most of the militia.

'Watch-fire on Titan's Peak, three days ago,' gasped Ekko, 'then on Currency Crag. The alarm. War –' He bent double again and brought up a dribble of green vomit. 'War is coming to Gendrigore.'

Ekko shuddered and stood up; he was extremely thin, covered in bruises, and his skin was loose, as if he'd lost a lot of weight in a short time. His eyes were deeply sunken, his nostrils crusted, and every bit of skin was lumpy with insect bites.

Nish had been expecting such news, but the desperation in the young man's eyes shook him. 'We thought as much lad. We're prepared.'

Ekko looked around at the staring youths, then brought up more muck. 'The God-Emperor's troops are as number-less as the leaves of the forest. Where is our army?'

Chills radiated out from the middle of Nish's back. 'This is it; well, a third of it.'

Ekko looked at the motley woodcutters and peas-ants armed with home-made bows, spears, axes and a few rusty swords, then collapsed. 'All lost,' he whispered. 'All – lost.'

Tulitine bent over the lad, then shook her head and called for a stretcher. 'By the look of him, he was a well-built fellow when he left home. Now he'll be lucky to last the night.'

'What's happened to him?'

'He's run all the way from the lookout at Blisterbone, the best part of twenty leagues, and he can't have stopped for four days, up mountain and down, over some of the roughest country in the world. Hadn't you better get this rabble into shape?'

'I will,' Nish said grimly. 'There'll be no drinking or wenching tonight.'

'See you set a good example, then.'

The militia were quiet now; too quiet. 'They need something to do,' Nish said to Gi and Hoshi after Ekko had been carried to the healers tent. 'We'll have target practice with bows and spears, but first I'm going to round up all the grog and tip it in the river, and send the camp followers packing.'

'I wouldn't do that, Nish,' said Hoshi. 'Collect their grog, yes, and put a trusted guard on it, but if you throw it out . . .'

'They'll mutiny?' said Nish, a dangerous glint in his eye. 'During the war against the lyrinx, the penalty for mutiny was death.'

'They won't mutiny,' said Gi, carefully cutting half an ell from her black hair with a long knife. 'They'll just go home.'

'Desertion in the face of the enemy is as bad as mutiny, and the penalty –'

'Is death,' said Gi. 'That's your answer for every problem, Nish –'

'It's not my answer,' he snapped. 'It's the way war has to be, to defeat the enemy.'

'It's not *our* way,' said Hoshi. 'We don't glory in war the way you do – Gendrigore has always taken care of our enemies.'

Nish gritted his teeth and reminded himself that he was a guest in this land, and the self-appointed captain of an army they'd never wanted to form. 'Not even Gendrigore can take care of my father. The whole world answers to his command, and whatever he wants, he gets.'

'And he wants you most of all,' said Gi quietly. 'Perhaps you should give yourself up to your father, Nish, and we can all go home again.'

'I did not order Vivimord put to death; Gendrigore did.' Nish knew it was a weak thing to say as soon as the words left his mouth. If he hadn't come to Gendrigore, it wouldn't be threatened now. 'Gendrigore has shown itself to be rebellious and Father will be out to crush it whether he gets me or not.'

'What good will crushing us do him?' said Gi, puzzled.

'To exercise power over the lives and deaths of others is Father's greatest pleasure.'

'That doesn't make sense.'

'It's the way some powerful men are. Believe me, I've seen it too many times.'

'I do believe you, and it still doesn't make any sense. Besides, Vivimord is dead. Your father can't know what happened to him.'

'We never saw the body.'

'He was eaten.'

'With great wizards, you always have to see the body,' said Nish, repeating Tulitine's words. They made plenty of sense now. 'And the Maelstrom of Justice and Retribution disappeared, which seems a very bad omen to me.'

'You don't know Gendrigore, Nish,' she said softly. 'That's not how we read omens here.'

'How would you read them?'

'The whirlpool is gone, but there is another whirlpool. Life goes on. Justice has been done and your father cannot know what happened to his friend.'

'Of course he can. The whole of Gendrigore was talking about the execution weeks ago, and father has secret spies and watching devices everywhere on Lauralin; *even here.* He will know.'

'Now you're frightening me,' Gi said. 'I will gather up all the drink and guard it myself.' She turned away, young, afraid and out of her depth, but determined to do her best.

That's what Gendrigoreans were like and he loved them for it.

'Let's get the targets set up,' said Nish to Hoshi. 'We've still got an hour of daylight.'

Hoshi carved man-sized blazes into half a dozen trees on the edge of the clearing, then organised the men into lines to fire at them. The archers fired, and mostly hit their targets, which was to be expected, since many of them lived by hunting. The men and women using slings came forwards, took aim and swung.

'Only one hit out of eighteen,' said Hoshi, inspecting the targets. 'Still, early days yet, Nish.'

'They've got a full week to learn how to throw, so there's *nothing* to worry about.'

'Very good,' Hoshi said with a flash of white teeth. He'd missed the sarcasm. 'First rank of spearmen, come forwards.'

Thirty men, and a few women, ambled up. One was picking his teeth, another his nose, while a third was whistling so loudly that he could have been heard a hundred paces into the forest. Another group were chattering among themselves as if they were going to a party.

Nish felt like banging their heads on the targets. In the days of the war, the men under him had followed his orders without question, for everyone in Lauralin, from the smallest child up, had been used to the unrelenting discipline of the scrutators. How was he supposed to impose his authority on a people unused to discipline, when he had no authority in this land? There had to be a way to get through to them, but he couldn't think of one.

'Spearmen, throw your spears,' said Hoshi.

Only five spears hit their targets, and two spearheads shattered on impact. Nish frowned. 'I wouldn't have thought the trees were that hard. Just as well the others missed, eh?'

'Er, yes,' said Hoshi, giving him a puzzled glance. He did not know what was wrong.

The second row of spearmen advanced to the line. Nish was heading for the targets to check the spears when Hoshi roared, 'Stop, you fools!'

Nish dropped flat as a flight of spears whistled overhead, all but three spraying to either side of the targets. Another spearhead shattered. He remained on the ground until a red-faced and abashed Hoshi had routed the spearmen, then Nish directed them a furious glare and went to the targets. Hoshi came trotting after him, along with Forzel, a tall, handsome joker who was always immaculate. Everyone else wore homespun, but Forzel was clad in fine cottons and wore a silk kerchief around his neck.

'Who made this rubbish?' Nish said furiously, holding up one of the broken spears. The long, leaf-shaped blade had shattered halfway down. 'The steel isn't tempered properly.' The broken metal tip had a rough, crystalline inner surface. 'It's not steel at all . . . it looks like cast iron. You can't make spear heads out of cast iron.'

'It won't shatter on a man's flesh, Nish,' said Hoshi defensively. 'It'll kill him dead and all.'

'Unless he's wearing armour,' said Nish, grinding his teeth, 'and Father's men will wear chest plates at the pass, where it's cool. Hoshi, this won't do. The spearmen need a lot of practice, but at this rate they'll have broken all their spears before we set eyes on the enemy.'

'We could take the heads off and just throw the shafts,' Hoshi said brightly.

'The balance and weight will be wrong. When they have to throw the real thing, they'll throw short.'

'Then we'll make straw men for targets and hang them from the branches.'

'Good idea; at least the spearmen can get in some practice tomorrow afternoon.' He raised his voice. 'Slingers, aim and fire.'

This time none of them hit their targets. Forzel,' said Nish, 'keep them at it as long as there's light.'

He walked away, trying to calm himself, but the pain in

his gut was back, worse than ever.

'It'll be all right on the day,' Hoshi said encouragingly. 'What else could possibly go wrong?'

And that was the worst omen of all.

THIRTY-SEVEN

'Where the devil is Maelys?' said Flydd, looking around irritably.

'It's not like her to get lost,' said Colm from behind him.

'It's just like her to get lost, *actually*. Maelys was always going off on her own when she travelled with Nish, and for someone who pretends to be so meek and mild, she's got a reckless streak.'

Flydd turned, cursing her under his breath, though it was his fault. He'd pressed on too quickly, and she might easily have taken a wrong turn in this blackness.

Clap.

Colm nudged his arm. 'Whelm!' he whispered.

'And not far from the junction of the three corridors, I'd say.'

Flydd began to ease his way along the wall. They were on the side of the tower shaded from the moon now, and there was no light at all, but he had a feeling that there was more than one Whelm at the other end.

He put his ear to the wall and subvocalised a spell of enhancement, hoping it would work. You never knew in a place like this, pervaded by another mancer's Arts.

'There's an odd tang in the air,' said a thick-voiced Whelm, a male. 'I don't like it.'

'Our master is hard at work in her eyrie,' said a woman with a husky voice. 'Never question our master's work.'

'I do not,' the first Whelm said hastily. 'But the master looked shaken after she questioned the black-haired girl.'

'Because the Nightland still exists?' asked the woman.

'No – because there's someone hiding in it.'

'Did you hear that?' whispered Colm.

'I wondered why Maelys was behaving so oddly,' Flydd said quietly.

'She was distracted for ages after she got lost in the Nightland.'

'So she met someone there and kept it from me, the stupid little cow. I'll kill her!'

The Whelm female spoke again. 'There's an odd smell in the air. It's that old conjuror, Flydd.'

'Old conjuror indeed!' sniffed Flydd. 'If they come this way I'll conjure the very life out of them.'

'Run and check on the prisoners!' cried the thick-voiced male. 'I'll search these passages.'

Flydd cursed. 'They'll soon discover my holes in the walls.'

Before they could move, a tocsin pealed in the distance. 'We'll never get back to Maelys now,' said Flydd. 'This way.' He turned down the corridor, trailing his fingers along the wall.

Colm grabbed him by the shoulder. 'We can't leave her, Flydd.'

'I thought you despised her.'

'I do, but I'm not the kind of man to leave a companion behind.'

'Neither am I; but we can't fight seven hundred Whelm on our own.'

'Then what's the plan?' Colm hissed.

'We rouse the other prisoners and fight our way out. In that diversion, we may be able to find Maelys.' Flydd pulled free and pressed on.

He nearly fell down a set of steps, cursed and felt his

way below, trying to make no noise. 'Get a move on,' he muttered at the bottom. 'There'll be Whelm everywhere in a minute.'

'It goes four ways here. Which way?'

'Hmm,' said Flydd. 'I lay awake for most of the night, making a mental plan of the tower. The hall of the bloodline registers was on the left at the bottom, and the rooms with all the preserved bodies further on, then down. The level below that surely holds the prisoner's cells and, if there are guards, we'll have to overpower them as quietly as possible, then free the prisoners and run.'

'If they've been here for years, they'll be as cowed as slaves.'

'They're all we've got.'

Shortly they reached the hall of the bloodline registers and hurried through its darkness. The spines of the individual registers glowed green all around them. Despite his words, Flydd was fretting about Maelys as they pushed through the doors at the other end, then into the chambers with all the jars and coffins. The ice-clear lids shone a milky yellow, eerily illuminating the faces and bodies below.

What single-minded determination the Numinator must have, Flydd thought, to have followed her plan all this time, every idea and action directed to a single purpose. Not even the destruction of the nodes had stopped her. He could admire her for that, if nothing else.

He reminded himself of the scars she had given him, and the pain he would not forget even if he took renewal a dozen times. No, he had to put all extraneous thoughts out of mind and concentrate on breaking out of here. With his flask of chthonic flame, and the mimemule, that was still possible, but what then? Noom was unrelentingly harsh, and almost impossible to survive during the winter.

Clap-clap.

'They're on their way,' said Colm.

They ran through the dark for some minutes, Flydd

turning this way and that following his mental map, then down another set of stairs to the lowest level. The clatter of running Whelm grew ever louder.

Flydd reached a door and jerked at the latch but it did not budge. 'It's locked, and in a way I can't fathom.' He pressed his nose to the ice, which seemed extremely thick here.

'Use the flame,' said Colm. 'Burn a hole though it.'

'I'm having second thoughts about that.'

'It worked beautifully last time.'

'It worked a trifle too well, and that makes me uncomfortable.' Flydd looked up sharply. 'Did you hear a faint fizzing sound?'

'Yes,' said Colm. 'I don't know where it came from, though.'

'I don't like it. This place is a little too strange for me.'

'They'll be here any second.'

It sounded like a hundred Whelm, and taking no trouble to disguise their coming; the clatter of their wooden sandals was deafening and they were making a dull grinding sound, as if they were all moaning and gritting their teeth at the same time.

'Something must have gone wrong,' said Flydd. 'Something's happened to the Numinator, and they're afraid.'

'Afraid for her?'

'Of course. And equally afraid that they'll be bereft of their master yet again, and left alone in a hostile world. They'll fight to the death to prevent that happening.'

'Can't you blast the door off its hinges or something?' said Colm.

'Even if I could, we may need to shelter behind it to hold them off.'

Flydd pressed his forehead against the door, ignoring the biting cold. What was he to do? The more he thought about the chthonic flame and where it had come from, the more perilous it seemed. Who had put it in that crystal casket at the bottom of the shaft, and why had they hidden it so carefully? Questions he should have asked himself before breaching it, but it was too late for regrets now.

'There's nothing for me here,' he muttered. 'I've got to get away. The world is at stake and I must be just as focussed as the Numinator – but on bringing the God-Emperor down.'

Feeling in a pocket, he discovered a splinter of precious amber-wood, left there from one of his walks across the top of Mistmurk Mountain before renewal. Amber-wood had an enchanting fragrance, and it helped to conceal the user from watching eyes, especially those watching with the Secret Art. But it also brought good fortune and he had never needed it more.

Unstoppering the flask of chthonic flame, he dipped the splinter in and traced a circle on the wall, just wide enough to squeeze through, some twenty paces beyond the door. White fire licked up from his trace marks and he heard that fizzing sound again.

The fire soon ate through the ice. He pushed the circle in, climbed through the hole and, as soon as Colm had squeezed his lanky frame in, wiped away the cold fire. Coating the edges of the circle with meltwater, he fitted the circle of ice back in place.

'It'll freeze to solid wall within a minute,' Flydd said, rubbing his hands furiously to warm them.

'But they'll see the circle in the ice. They'll know we're in here.'

'In the dark, it may be some time before they notice it. I'll just jam the lock.' He went to the door, melted ice in his hand with white fire and poured the water into the lock, where it froze instantly. 'Come on.'

They were in an empty cell whose door was open, one of many along a corridor. Most of the other cells looked unused; walls, floors and ceilings were pure, clean ice.

'This had better be the place,' said Flydd anxiously. The racket of the Whelm's wooden sandals could be heard through the thick walls.

'*Anywhere* could be the place,' Colm said pessimistically. 'I don't think the Numinator is predictable.'

Colm barred the door of the corridor. They continued, opening doors to left and right, but it wasn't until halfway along that they found an occupied cell. Someone small and dark-haired lay asleep on a narrow bed formed from ice. Flydd illuminated the cell with finger light. It was a woman, in her mid-thirties.

'Hello,' he said quietly.

She shot up in bed, the thin furs falling away, and put her hand up to keep the light out of her eyes. Her skin was very pale, as though she had not seen the sun in years, and she looked vaguely familiar. But then, most people did, for Flydd had met so many people in his time as scrutator that it was rare for him to see an entirely new kind of face.

'Who are you?' he said.

'My name is Chissmoul, surr,' she said quietly, avoiding his eye.

Again that familiarity, but he could not remember why. Curse his fragmented memory.

'Where are the others?'

'Further along to the left. You – you're not a prisoner, are you?'

'No, we've escaped – this far anyway.' Flydd gave a mirthless laugh.

Giving him a puzzled glance, she slipped out of bed. She was solidly built and wore a woollen shirt, buttoned high, trousers of the same material and thick socks. She pulled on a pair of boots, and a woollen hat over her short hair. 'I'm ready, surr.'

'Don't you have a coat?'

'We never go outside, surr.'

His heart sank. She could not survive on Noom without furs; none of the prisoners could. 'Show us the way.'

Chissmoul set off down the corridor, then stopped and said shyly, not looking directly at Flydd, 'Do I know you, surr?'

'I don't know. Do you?'

'You look strange, but the way you speak . . . it reminds me of –'

'Spit it out, lass!' Flydd said peremptorily.

'The scrutator, Xervish Flydd.'

He stopped short. 'I am Flydd. I've taken renewal – reluctantly.' It seemed important he say that. He did not want anyone to think he'd done it of his own free will, and that was curious. In the olden days, he hadn't given a damn for other people's opinion of him. Must be getting soft, he thought.

'Chissmoul, Chissmoul,' he mused. 'You look familiar, but renewal took my memories and many of them have not come back.'

'I was a thapter pilot in the war.'

'Of course! You were the really shy one, yet you flew your thapter as though you were born to it, and with a reckless daring I'd never seen before.' In his mind's eye Flydd could see her laughing face now, after she'd just pulled off some desperate manoeuvre with ease, which none of the other thapter pilots could have done without crashing their machines.

'The war was terrible, yet those were the best days of my life. I've never felt so alive, flying across the sky, at one with my thapter. But I'll never fly again.'

'Those days are gone forever, along with many other wonderful things that were no longer possible once the nodes were destroyed.'

'I have my memories,' said Chissmoul softly, opening the door of another cell. 'You will remember this man, too. We came here together.'

The man who lay on the bed was almost as gaunt as a Whelm, and at first Flydd did not recognise him, for little of his former good looks remained. His sandy hair was thin and lank, his grey eyes as dull as the eyes of a fish on a slab. Only the jutting jaw was unchanged, though the bone had less flesh on it than Flydd remembered.

'Sergeant Flangers!' Flydd cried, unable to contain his joy, for Flangers had been a hero of the lyrinx wars, an honourable man and a loyal soldier. He had also been forced to betray his soldier's oath, and had not recovered from it, though that had been many years ago. 'Are you all right?'

Flangers stared at him, uncomprehending, until Chissmoul said gently, 'It's Scrutator Flydd, come back from the dead, *renewed* by the mancer's Art.'

'Not quite from the dead,' said Flydd. 'But very close.'

Chissmoul helped Flangers out of bed. 'I've been better,' said Flangers, standing up shakily. 'Old injuries still plague me, surr, and they'll be the death of me before too long.'

Flydd thought so too. He hadn't hoped for much down here, so he wasn't disappointed, though a dying soldier and a pilot without her craft were bound to be liabilities.

'But I'll do what I can for you, surr, for old times,' said Flangers. 'The menace of the God-Emperor is almost as bad as the one we fought ten years ago, and defeated.'

'Almost,' said Flydd, offering Flangers his arm.

Flangers gestured that he would walk alone, so they followed Chissmoul out. 'How did you come here, old comrade?' said Flydd.

'We ran for a long time, after Jal-Nish took over the world with his sorcerous tears. The remainder of our fellowship scattered, then met up again, those who had survived.'

'And many did not, I imagine.'

'General Troist was taken first, then killed while trying to escape. At least, that's what was said.'

Flydd stopped for a moment, bowing his head, then walked on. It was another blow. 'That is very bad news, though not unexpected. Troist was a good man, and steadfast to the very end. I wonder what became of his family?'

'I cannot say. Then the dwarf scrutator, Klarm, was taken. I never knew what happened to him –'

'We do!' Flydd said harshly. 'Klarm went over to the enemy. He is now a lieutenant of the God-Emperor.' If he survived the crash of the sky-palace, which I doubt.

'No!' cried Flangers. 'Klarm was the bravest man I ever met. I cannot believe it.'

'I saw him with my own eyes, just weeks ago. He attacked us.'

'How could he betray us?' Flangers persisted. 'Klarm wasn't that kind of a man.'

'Our fellowship was long broken, and we were all thought to be dead. In that situation, a man with a slippery conscience might tell himself that it wasn't a betrayal.'

'An honourable man can always tell the difference between right and wrong . . .' Flangers stopped suddenly, swaying on his feet, and Flydd knew what was the matter with him. He'd been put in precisely that situation by Perquisitor Fyn-Mah, forced by her direct order to fire on his superiors in an air-floater, and that conflict had eaten the heart out of him. 'But what would I know?' he said tiredly. 'I'm just a man of war.'

'What about Fyn-Mah?' said Flydd.

'Also dead. She was fleeing from the enemy when her horse was shot from under her. She broke her neck and died instantly.'

'Ah!' cried Flydd. He'd never been close to his prickly subordinate, but they'd worked together for a long time and he'd always admired her. 'Malien?'

'No one ever saw her again after she fled with Tiaan.'

'And Tiaan?' Flydd held little hope for her – she'd thwarted Jal-Nish and he would have made her pay.

'No idea, surr.'

They reached the end of the hall, where Chissmoul twisted the knob and thrust the door open. It was so dark inside that Flydd could make nothing out, until someone laughed in a way that raised his hackles.

'She's got you too!' a man spoke in an oddly triumphant tone of voice, one unfortunate taking pleasure in another's downfall. 'That completes the picture.'

'You know who I am, even though I've taken renewal?' said Flydd, the hair on the top of his head stirring.

The man stood up. Flydd made out the faintest double flash, as though he wore broad, shiny bracelets on his wrists. He was very tall.

'I would know you anywhere, Flydd, even after the renewal you swore never to take.'

Flydd wasn't going to make excuses to this rival of long ago. 'What kept you here? Surely you, of all people, could have broken free long ago? Your Arts, after all, are unique, and as I recall they relied less on the power of the nodes than anyone's. Not even the power of the tears could take all your power from you.'

'Not all, no. Unfortunately, the Numinator's servants took me by surprise and put these on me.' The bracelets flashed again. 'They are bonded to me like my own bones to my flesh. I cannot remove them, and while their enchantment persists I may not use the least part of my Arts.'

'That must be galling.' Flydd couldn't feel too much sympathy for him – they had been rivals far too long – though he did understand. In the last months of the war they'd managed to achieve an uneasy comradeship.

'I've endured the loss of my powers before, and I can endure it again.'

'So I believe. So who is the Numinator, anyway? If you recognised me so easily, surely you must know her true identity?'

'I've never met her,' said the man in the shadows. 'I've not even seen her from a distance.'

'How curious,' said Flydd. 'She showed herself to us freely. Well, no matter. Let's see if we can get you out of here, Yggur.'

THIRTY-EIGHT

Yggur chuckled and held out his arms, on which the bracelets gleamed silver. 'Why did you take renewal?'

'Another time,' Flydd snapped, studying the bracelets in dim finger light. Without understanding how they worked it would not be easy to break their hold.

'Sensitive, are we?'

Flydd studiously ignored the jibe. 'How did you end up here?'

'Jal-Nish hunted me a good way across Lauralin, with a band of fellow miserables that grew smaller every day. There was no hiding place from which he could not winkle us out with his all-seeing tears. The Numinator was my last hope; no one else had the power. As it turned out, she did not, either, and I now think we were lured here. The moment we arrived I was beset by a horde of Whelm – Whelm! *Me!* – and these bracelets fitted to me. She's got little power of her own, Xervish. The destruction of the nodes robbed her of most of it, and destroyed her work – I dare say you've seen the decaying evidence of it by now.'

'We saw it.'

'The bracelets take all the power I can draw upon, and channel it to her. It's all that's holding the Tower of a Thousand Steps together.'

There came a furious attack on the barred door at the other end of the hall. 'Is there any other way out of here?'

'I'd be the last person to know,' said Yggur. 'As the Numinator's most dangerous prisoner, and the Whelm's former master, way back in the *Time of the Mirror*, my movements here have been severely constrained. What about you, Flangers?'

'As a soldier and a *former* hero, I haven't been allowed to roam either.'

'The Whelm made me work all over the place,' said Chissmoul in that quiet little voice. 'Up in the tower and down in the pits, but I don't know of any way out save across the shifting ice on the moat.'

'Then let's waste no more time looking for one,' said Yggur. 'We'd better get through to the others –'

'What others?' said Colm, who had been very quiet since they'd lost Maelys.

'The Numinator has another hundred and fifty prisoners here, and her Whelm bring in a few more every week. They take anyone from the nearby lands who can read. The work of cross-checking her registers goes on sixteen hours a day.'

'What for?' said Flydd. The nagging question had gone unanswered for too long.

Yggur did not answer. At the other end of the hall, the attack on the ice door grew ever more furious.

'They're nearly through,' said Colm. 'Do something, Flydd, before they massacre us all.'

The cries of the Whelm could be heard clearly now, and they sounded desperate.

'What's the matter with them?' said Yggur. 'I've not seen a trace of fear in them in the seven years I've been here.'

'Only one thing can make Whelm afraid,' said Flydd, 'and better than anyone you know what that is.'

'A threat to their master,' said Yggur. 'But no one can threaten her here. She can see an enemy coming for fifty leagues.'

'Only if one comes via the material world! Chissmoul, where are the other prisoners?'

Yggur caught his arm. 'What did you mean by that, Flydd? How *did* you get here?'

'Later,' said Flydd, pleased to have Yggur at a disadvantage. Too often, in previous times, it had been the other way around. 'We'll have to fight our way out, and five against seven hundred isn't the kind of odds I relish. I'm going to release the rest of the prisoners and find a way to arm them.'

'This way –' Chissmoul broke off, staring at the ice wall, down which a thread of glistening white fire was making its way.

'What the blazes is *that*?' said Yggur.

'Chthonic flame,' said Flydd. 'I found it in the caverns within the plateau of Thuntunnimoe – Mistmurk Mountain.' But why was it trickling *down*? It could not have come from the fire he'd used to escape his own cell; not here.

'I know about Thuntunnimoe,' said Yggur. 'It has a Charon obelisk on top – a warning to keep away, among other things. And you took this *chthonic* fire from within?'

'Deep down. There wasn't any choice, not with the God-Emperor and Vivimord closing in on us, both desperate to get Nish back.'

'So Nish still holds out?' Yggur said admiringly. 'He's got a backbone of adamant, that young man!' He moved closer to the wall, studying the chthonic fire from just a hand-span away. 'It's eating away the ice. This is a perilous force you've liberated, Flydd. I do hope you know what you're doing.' Yggur's tone implied that he didn't.

'I said there wasn't any choice,' Flydd said darkly, irritated that Yggur still had the ability to rile him. 'We would have died, otherwise.

Yggur pressed his nose to the wall, watched the tiny trail trickle past, and frowned. 'You might still have made the wrong choice.'

'What are you talking about?'

'You do know the story of the girl who opened the forbidden box and unleashed pestilence upon the world?'

'Of course!' Flydd snapped.

'I suggest you reflect upon it.' He turned away. 'See how it burns through the ice, Chissmoul?'

She shivered. 'It's as though it's *feeding* on it.'

'We would do well to reflect upon that as well. Come on.'

He turned away, limping from an age-old injury, then set off, his long legs taking such lengthy strides that Flydd found himself trotting to keep up. That irritated him too, and he dropped back to a fast walk.

Yggur chuckled.

'What's so funny?' Flydd snapped.

'You, Flydd. You're a treat. I haven't felt so good in all my years of imprisonment.'

'To make you happy, I'd gleefully double them.'

'Weakest jibe yet. You've lost your touch, old friend – renewal has diminished you.'

Flydd scowled, for Yggur was right. With an effort, he put his feelings to one side. They would always be rivals, yet they had to work together. They reached a buttress of solid ice, a good span thick and rounded at the base, as if it was slowly flowing and spreading out under the weight of the inner tower. Beside it the wall was thinner, no more than a couple of hand-spans.

'Here, I think,' said Yggur. 'Would you agree, Chissmoul?'

She studied the wall, head to one side. 'Yes.'

Flydd withdrew his ice flask and twisted at the stopper.

'What's that?' Yggur said sharply.

'The chthonic flame I took from Thuntunnimoe. It's how we've been getting through walls and keeping ahead of the Whelm.'

Yggur held out his hand. Flydd grudgingly placed the flask in the middle of his palm. Yggur studied it warily, then carefully eased the stopper out. A tiny ice-white flame wisped up. Yggur slammed the stopper in and twisted it until it was tight.

'Put it away, you fool. Don't use it again – *ever.*'

Flydd felt furiously angry, but bit down on it, for that would only be aiding the enemy. 'I take your warning, but if it's necessary to use it for our survival, I'll use it.'

'I hope you *don't* live to regret it.'

'Hadn't you better tell him about the other one?' said Colm, who was looking more troubled every second.

'*What* other one?' Yggur cried, spinning on one foot. His bracelets twinkled in the white firelight as though they were inset with diamonds.

There was a monumental crash behind them. The Whelm were into the first hall. 'There isn't time to discuss it,' said Flydd. 'We've got to move.'

Flangers drew himself upright, took the ice cudgel Flydd had left on the floor, and hobbled back along the hall to stand guard. Chissmoul and Colm went with him.

'We'll discuss it right now,' said Yggur. '*What other one?*'

'I brought the Numinator three bottles. I had no hope of gaining her cooperation unless I could give her some power she'd never seen before.'

'And in the three bottles? Please tell me you haven't given her the chthonic flame, Flydd.'

'I gave her the cursed flame, the abyssal flame which feeds it and, from the greatest depth of all, the chthonic flame,' Flydd said limply.

'You stupid, useless fool! We've got to get it back.'

'It's too late. She must have used it already . . .'

Yggur followed his gaze to the wall, down which two more threads of twinkling fire were running, eating into the ice and spreading. What if it *was* feeding on the ice? Flydd thought.

'What has she used it for?' said Yggur.

Flydd gave no answer.

'I've got to have power,' muttered Yggur. 'I feel as help-less as a child. Since you've got such colossal forces to lavish on our enemy, do something with these.' He held out his wrists.

Flydd laid his hands on the bracelets, trying to sense his way into the spell-binder they contained. Feeling something shifting restlessly within them, he strained with all his might. The bracelets grew burning hot under his hands and he smelt burnt hair. They had singed the hairs on Yggur's arms, though he did not flinch.

Flydd, feeling the strength draining out of him, jerked his hands away. 'I don't know if it's helped, but I can do no more just now.'

Yggur rubbed his wrists. 'I've got a trace of my power back and . . . it feels as though the Numinator's hold over me has weakened. As though she's far away . . .'

Flydd and Colm exchanged glances.

'What have you done now?' cried Yggur.

'We think Maelys was concealing something from us, and –'

'Who the devil is Maelys?'

Flydd explained, briefly. 'The Numinator questioned Maelys alone last night, about the portals I've made. I think the Numinator has used the chthonic flame to make a portal, and has taken Maelys back to the Nightland –'

Yggur looked as though he were going to have a fit, but contained himself and said quietly, '*The* Nightland? Rulke's prison?'

'The same. It didn't collapse after he left it, as everyone thought. Or if it did, it has been carefully restored, and maintained ever since, though who could do such a thing?'

'Not I,' said Yggur. 'All the old human mancers on Santhenar, working together, could not have rebuilt the Nightland after the Forbidding was broken. They would not have had the power.'

'Then who?'

'The question is unanswerable, as is the more important question – why? And since the Numinator has already used chthonic fire, it may be too late. Once taken out of the flask it can never be put back. See how it's eating away at the ice? If it can't be extinguished, the roof of the inner tower will fall in on us.'

Flydd was digesting that when Yggur said sharply, 'You said *back* to the Nightland. Have you been there already?'

Flydd explained that as well, and how they had come here via Dunnet, though he did not mention the mimemule. 'The Nightland was as big a surprise –'

'They're coming!' whispered Flangers, backing down the hall with the cudgel over his shoulder, ready to swing.

'I've got to use the fire to get through this ice, Yggur,' said Flydd.

'I said no!' Yggur put his hands on the wall, pushed, and Flydd smelt singed hair again. 'For seven years she's drawn on my power to hold this place together. I could not stop her, but I've learned how to follow the paths she's taken with it, and how she's used my power. If she's truly gone, with what you've given me I might just . . .'

With gritted teeth, he strained until the bones in his arched back creaked. Lines appeared on the wall – the outlines of the blocks from which it had originally been constructed. 'Ice, *unbind!*'

Water began to dribble out from the edges of the block he had his hands on. He pushed hard and, after a brief moment when it seemed the block would not budge, it glided away smoothly on a film of meltwater and fell out with a loud crash.

From the other side of the wall, a woman cried out fearfully, then Flydd heard a clamour of voices. He scrambled through the hole and held up his hands. They quieted at once.

'I am Xervish Flydd. Some of you may know my name.' A low, excited buzz spread through the throng before him. The light was dim, and he could make out no more than a mass of thin figures. 'I came to Noom to get you out.' The lie was excusable, in the circumstances. 'The Numinator is not here at the moment . . . which gives us our best chance, but you must all do exactly as I say.'

Chissmoul ducked through the hole, then Flangers and Colm. Yggur was still on the other side.

'How can we get away?' said a scrawny man near the front. Flydd could make out no more than an enormous prow of a nose. 'There's five hundred leagues of snow and ice in every direction.'

A considerable exaggeration, but there was no time to argue. 'The same way I got here,' Flydd said. 'Through my vast command of the Secret Arts – Arts that the God-Emperor thinks *he* controls – ha!'

He held up the flask so everyone could see the swirling fire inside it. Yggur climbed through and stood up, wearing an ironic smile, though he made no move to interfere. Damn right! Flydd thought mulishly. He wears the bracelets, not me.

'The Whelm are after us,' he went on, 'but they're afraid. Their master is not here and they're leaderless.'

'Which means they'll be terrified and panicky,' said the man with the big nose. 'And merciless.'

'Trust me, and I'll get you out of here,' said Flydd weakly, knowing that he was losing them. It would never have happened in the olden days, when he had often swayed multitudes with his rhetoric.

'A hundred and fifty of us can't fight seven hundred armed Whelm,' said beaky nose. 'The Numinator treats us well enough, and it's better to live as her slaves than die at the hands of these brutal Whelm. Go away and fight your own battles.'

Yggur, who was leaning against the wall, stood up to his full height and raised his bracelets so they caught the light of the chthonic fire, which was oozing down these walls as well.

'You don't know Xervish Flydd, save as a name from the past, but you do know me, and you know that my power, tapped by the Numinator through these bracelets, is all that is holding up the Tower of a Thousand Steps. The Numinator has gone – and she may never return – but Flydd has given me some of my power back. We are leaving to continue the fight against the God-Emperor, so you have no choice. Once I leave, the tower will collapse whether the Numinator returns or not.'

'We won't let you leave,' said the beaky-nosed man. 'We're not dying just so you can get away. Take him, lads!'

A group of men at the front surged forwards and Flydd felt the icy teeth of panic on his liver – the situation was out of control and he could not think how to regain it.

Yggur didn't move, though he stood more stiffly erect and the bracelets gave off little flashes. 'You know better than that, Lazus,' he said, looking to the left. 'And you, Pordey. Don't you?'

Two of the leaders stopped, and all the others with them.

'He's bluffing,' said the beaky-nosed man. 'He's got no power. Take him.'

Yggur smiled grimly and extended a long arm towards him. 'My phantom hand, an invisible hand which is an extension of this one, is going to reach in through your chest and squeeze your heart until it bursts . . .'

'Go on, then,' the beaky-nosed man said, with a knowing smile.

Yggur reached a little further and stiffened his fingers as though forcing them through something hard. The beak-nosed man gasped and clutched at his chest. Flydd heard cracking sounds, like ribs breaking, then Yggur slowly clenched his fist. His arm did not shake.

The man's face went red, then white. His lips turned blue, he beat awkwardly at the air with his hands, then screamed as bright red blood was forced out his mouth, nostrils and eyeballs.

He collapsed to his knees, slumped forwards and fell on his face, dead before he hit the ground.

'Was that really necessary?' said Colm, looking sick. He opened the distance between himself and Yggur.

Yggur stared at the body as if contemplating giving its heart another squeeze. 'He would have hindered us every step of the way,' he said quietly, 'if we got out at all. Now the problem is solved.' He raised his voice. 'Does anyone else dispute my command?'

No one answered.

'Can you really do that?' said Flydd. He had seen more violent death than most men, but the display left him awed, and uneasy. No one had ever understood the roots of Yggur's strange power, nor his impossibly long life, for that matter.

'It's marvellous what the power of suggestion can do to an angry man with a weak heart,' said Yggur ambiguously.

'Then use your power to get us out of here.'

Yggur held up his braceleted wrists. 'The Tower of a Thousand Steps is not an easy place to escape from. Its power is linked to *hers.*'

'You'd better think of a way.'

'And you'd better do something about the hole in the wall before the Whelm come through.'

'Call the biggest of the prisoners over and help me heave the block back in.'

'No, I need it.'

'What on earth for?' said Flydd.

'Weapons!'

THIRTY-NINE

Flydd had done what he could to seal the hole with webs of ice as thick as bars, but it would not hinder the enemy long and, unfortunately, there was no other way out of the cells.

'They're coming!' Flangers said hoarsely. 'We'll have to fight them as they come through.' He hefted Flydd's cudgel and stood to one side of the hole.

'Surr,' said Chissmoul to Yggur, 'he's too weak to fight. They'll kill him in the first minute.'

'Flangers can't *not* fight, Chissmoul. He was a professional soldier; take that and he'll have nothing left.'

'If he dies, I'll have nothing left,' Chissmoul said, white-faced.

What could he say? Flydd eyed the ice walls, which were laced with chthonic fire now, spreading out from each oozing thread and slowly eating the surface ice away. Every so often a small chunk would fall and smash on the floor; within, the ice was honeycombed with water-filled holes.

'How long can the inner tower hold?' Colm said quietly.

'I don't think there's any way of telling.' Flydd wiped drops off his face. 'Perhaps not long at all.'

'The core of the wall is still solid,' said Yggur. 'It'll last a while yet.'

He was standing over the block of ice he'd pushed out, rubbing the bracelets. 'Now I've got some power, let's see what I can do with it. For the past seven years, the Numinator has drawn upon my power to shape and strengthen her ice tower, and those skills have flowed back to me. With a little effort, I should be able to form ice with as much skill as a sculptor carves marble.'

Yggur smoothed his hands across the great block, ignoring the biting cold, and seemed to be calculating its dimensions. 'Spears are the only weapon suited to untrained soldiers.' He spoke to the stone, softly. 'Split and split and split again – split eight times over.'

With a dull crack the block split in two, and each piece split again and again, eight times, until hundreds of long ice stakes went tumbling across the floor.

'Blade tips!' Yggur picked up one of the stakes and shaped its tip into a spearhead with his fingers. This proved a greater strain; he swayed on his feet.

Ice cracked away from the leading end of each stake to form a leaf-shaped point about a hand-span long, bladed on either side.

'Javelins, become as adamant,' said Yggur, now screwing up his face as if he'd swallowed a cup of fishhooks.

'What's the matter?' said Flydd.

'When one must use a power held in another's thrall, aftersickness is swift, and cruel.' The spears did not look as though they'd changed, apart from a slight creaking of their crystalline structures, but Yggur swayed on his feet.

Flydd steadied him. 'And will get crueller, as I know all too well.' He raised his voice. 'Take a spear each and prepare to defend yourselves.'

The prisoners came forwards, picking up their weapons gingerly, as if they had never handled one before and did not want to do so now. It was not a good sign; it meant they still saw themselves as helpless slaves rather than as prisoners determined to escape. There was going to be blood on the floor before they won free – assuming they did.

423

Flangers hefted his spear with a wince that he tried to disguise.

'For those of us who know how to use weapons,' said Yggur, 'I'll make something a little more ambitious.' Holding three spears together, he formed them into a long sword. 'Use it carefully, Sergeant Flangers. This isn't as brittle as regular ice, but it'll shatter if you strike the wrong way.'

Flangers made a space for himself and swished it through the air. 'It's a fine weapon. Perfectly balanced, though a trifle light. It won't cut far into an enemy.'

'Ice *is* light,' said Yggur. 'I can't do anything about that. But it'll cut deep enough, if you swing true.'

By the time he'd made blades for himself, Colm and Flydd, Yggur was staggering from aftersickness and holding his belly with his free hand.

'Stand back,' said Flydd as the Whelm began to smash at the ice webbing over the hole. 'I'll take charge of our defences. Flangers, you're my first lieutenant. Defend our left flank.'

The Whelm, a host of gaunt, staring shadows, were prising at the hole, bent on making them suffer for daring to defy their master.

'We can't defend this place,' Flydd said to Colm, who was standing by Yggur, sword in hand. 'We've got to get out before they surround us and break in from all sides.'

'There's a stair in the far corner,' said Yggur, nodding in that direction. 'We should make for it, and hope we can force our way out through the sealed door at the top.'

'Where does it lead?' said Colm.

'To the top of the inner tower. It contains the cells, the hall of the registers, the work rooms and the coffins. It's ten floors high, and lies entirely within the Tower of a Thousand Steps, though it's completely separate from it.'

'Why is that?' said Flydd.

'I don't know,' said Yggur. 'The outer tower is five times as high, but unused save for the Numinator's eyrie. Perhaps she did not want it tainted by what was done below.'

'We won't get out of here by going up,' said Colm. 'We should go down.'

'There's no choice. They've got this level surrounded.'

Colm lowered his voice. 'We'll never get a hundred and fifty terrified people up the stairs. And if we do, we'll still be trapped, only at the top.'

'Attack!' shouted the leader of the Whelm. They burst Flydd's ice defences and surged through the rectangular hole, far faster than he had expected. Within seconds a dozen were in the room, swinging long black, jag-edged blades.

'Stand!' shouted Flangers, defending with his ice-blade, though his illness made him slow. Too slow?

Perhaps it's for the best, Flydd thought. Flangers had atoned over and over for breaking his soldier's oath, yet it had not been enough for his unyielding personal code of honour. He was the best of men but the forced betrayal had eaten him away inside, just as the chthonic fire was consuming the tower's ice from within, until all that remained was the husk.

But the bonds of comradeship were too strong. Flangers had stood beside him many times during the war, and Flydd could do no less than back him now, even at the cost of his own life. Which proves I'm no longer a scrutator, he thought wryly. Few scrutators had ever risked their lives when there were others to die for them. Just me and Klarm, but he couldn't think about that. Klarm's betrayal was still too painful.

Flydd leapt forwards, as he had not been able to do for many years, and took pleasure in his renewed body, so much stronger and faster than the old one. I've finally *fitted*, he exulted. And won't it be ironic if I only have minutes to live?

A Whelm leapt at him, hacking with his jag-blade. Shorter and stockier than most, and less awkward, he was on Flydd before he could get the ice sword into position. Flydd swept it up as the Whelm slashed, but the ice sword, struck side on, shattered.

Cursing, Flydd scrambled backwards, looking frantically for the leftover pile of spears, but it was well out of reach. The Whelm lunged and Flydd threw the sword hilt at his face. It cracked into his forehead; the Whelm slipped on broken ice and Flydd kicked him in the belly.

He went down. Flydd fell on him as the Whelm's head struck the floor, trying to wrench the jag-blade out of his hands. It wouldn't come – the Whelm's grip was unbreakable.

Flydd heaved him bodily off the floor, but the Whelm would not let go. He was kicking at him, going for the belly with those sharp-nailed toes. Flydd, painfully aware that his back was undefended, put his boot heel on the Whelm's throat and pressed down until his windpipe gave.

Even in death the Whelm clung to his sword. Flydd prised the flat fingers off, hefted the sword, which was extremely heavy, then swung around. There were dozens of Whelm in the room, and more scrambling through the hole all the time. He had to block it and there was only one way to do that, whatever Yggur said.

Unstoppering the flask of chthonic fire, he passed it around the edges of the opening. White fire licked up and tongued down, forming a tracery across the hole. The Whelm hesitated on the other side, afraid to risk the uncanny fire.

Flangers had formed his spearmen into a square, its concave front bristling with spears, and the formation was difficult to attack, for the Whelm could not get close without running onto the points. However they had learned that a swift sideways hack would often snap the brittle spears, and were slowly advancing in a wedge.

Three or four Whelm lay dead on the floor, and another was twitching feebly, but at least a dozen of the prisoners had fallen and a large group had thrown down their spears and were backing into a corner with their hands up. Flydd had to do something or their terror would infect the rest and the cause would be lost.

426

'Colm!' he hissed. 'You're good with a sword, aren't you?'

'Relatively speaking. I was never a master.'

'I was *taught* by a master, but my renewed sword arm lacks the skill of the old one. We've got to counterattack and we need a third, one we can rely on.' Yggur had been a skilled swordsman but could barely stand up for aftersickness, while Flangers had his square to look after.

'I'll do it!' Chissmoul thrust out her spear as if taking down a Whelm twice her size.

'You!' Flydd couldn't hide his astonishment, for she was no bigger than Maelys.

'I was a good thapter pilot,' she said defensively.

He laughed. 'The best I ever saw, *and* the most reckless.'

She smiled faintly. 'All skills suited to a warrior. And Flangers taught me well, on the way here. I can't live without him, surr. If he dies, and I know he will, I must also die.'

It made her one of them. 'Get yourself a proper weapon and come with me. Take my left flank, one pace back.'

Chissmoul twisted the jag-blade out of the hands of a dying Whelm and took up position. Flydd knew he could rely on her. Colm was on his right, and he was skilled with a blade, but Flydd wasn't so sure about him. Colm had always been an unknown, a loner, and after Ketila's death Flydd had never been confident that Colm would not turn on him at the worst possible moment. And if he discovers I've taken the mimemule, Flydd thought, a trifle guiltily, I'm a dead man.

'We've got to attack the Whelm on their right flank,' he said, 'or they'll tear right through the square. Defend me – that's all I ask. Ready?'

The Whelm wedge was driving at the concave front of the prisoners' square, making a coordinated attack on their brittle spears. Within seconds the ice spears of the front row had been shattered and they were defenceless, buckling and about to break.

'Hold, hold!' roared Flangers from the other side. 'Second row, push through and attack.'

The prisoners could not cope and Flydd did not blame them. 'Stand firm!' he yelled. 'Just a few seconds more.'

The front row, faced with an unwavering line of jagged Whelm blades, threw down their shattered spears and, desperate to get away, tried to force their way back through the lines. The second and third lines of spearmen were torn open; spears pointed at the floor, the roof, anywhere save at the attacking Whelm, who fell upon the backs of the front line and cut them down in a few bloody seconds.

Flydd cursed bitterly. 'The fools! Why couldn't they have stood fast?'

The Whelm plunged deep into the prisoners' formation, cutting swiftly and ruthlessly as though the mayhem helped to ease their own pain. The next line of prisoners turned to flee, but only presented their undefended backs to the enemy.

'Come on,' Flydd hissed, 'or the lot of them will be dead. Useless fools!'

They simply weren't trained for battle. Flydd lunged after the Whelm, picked out the leader and thrust the jagsword at his back.

The blade felt unbalanced in his hands; it did not want to go where he swung it. It angled into the Whelm's back, low down, but twisted sideways. It made a nasty gash but the Whelm turned and came at Flydd, swinging his jagsword in arcs like a farmer using a scythe.

Flydd just managed to get his sword to the other's blade as it hacked towards his belly. The weapons met with a mighty clang and a flurry of sparks. The Whelm jerked backwards and Flydd's blade, caught on one of the jags, went with it.

Taken by surprise, he was dragged to the Whelm, skidding on his knees. With a cunning flick-twist, his opponent freed his own blade and hacked at Flydd's head.

He ducked just in time. The blade cut through his hair;

428

one jag caught in a knot and jerked his head sideways so hard that his neck bones went crack. Flydd tore free at the expense of a clump of hair and a piece of scalp, and drove his sword at the Whelm's unprotected groin.

The Whelm sprang backwards with such haste that Flydd knew he'd found a weakness.

'Cur that you are,' grated the Whelm, 'surely even your kind know the rules of combat?'

So the groin was off-limits to the Whelm. It was good to know. 'I only follow one rule,' Flydd panted. 'The winners make the rules, and the losers *die*.' He hacked left, then right, trying to draw the Whelm away. The fellow seemed to be weakening; blood was running down his right leg from the back wound.

Flydd stabbed at the groin again. This time the Whelm did not withdraw fast enough and the jag near the tip of the blade caught in his loincloth. Flydd pulled back and tore the rag away. The Whelm reeled, instinctively tried to cover himself, and it was an easy matter to skewer him through the chest.

To his left, Chissmoul was labouring with the heavy blade, which was far too long for her, only just managing to parry her opponent's blows. On the right, Colm was using his ice sword like a rapier, lunging forwards and pricking his opponent with the tip, then whipping it back to protect the brittle blade.

The Whelm were not master swordsmen; they lacked both dexterity and practice. However they were strong, Flydd thought gloomily, as well as tireless and determined to prevail for their master.

Chissmoul slipped on the bloody floor and fell to her knees, gasping. Two Whelm came at her, one from each side, and Flydd couldn't get to either of them in time. The taller of the Whelm dragged Chissmoul upright by the hair, baring her neck for the other, who swung back his jag-blade to hack her head from her shoulders.

Flydd cried out and made a frantic effort to get to her,

but knew he was going to fail. Chissmoul's eyes were staring; not at her attacker, but over his shoulder, meeting her death bravely. She closed her eyes.

The ice spear came out of nowhere, hurled with such force that it tore through the back of the shorter Whelm's neck, out his throat and struck the taller Whelm in the right shoulder. Blood sprayed in his face, momentarily blinding him, then Chissmoul reached up and, in a wrestling manoeuvre Flydd had never seen before, used the taller Whelm's height to throw him over her head into the other Whelm as he collapsed.

Flydd cut the taller Whelm down, absently, then turned around. The room was a slaughterhouse awash with blood, but the last of the Whelm had fallen. So had a couple of dozen of the prisoners, and the rest had jammed themselves into a corner, eyeing the Whelm beyond the fire-webbed hole, who were trying to use a blanket to put out the white fire blocking the hole.

'That was a mighty throw for a dying man,' Flydd said to Flangers, who had come from the other side of the room carrying a broken ice sword in one hand and three spears in the other. There was a spring in his step that hadn't been there before, and his formerly grey cheeks had a healthy glow. 'How did you know Chissmoul was in danger? Surely you can't keep the whole battlefield in your mind at once?'

'Every man, and every weapon,' said Flangers. 'When I was a sergeant, I had to – how else could I look after my men and defeat the enemy?'

'It's a skill few other sergeants have had.'

'It won't be enough next time. They'll break through there and there, and there.'

He pointed and Flydd made out shapes through the ice, hammering furiously. 'We can't defend this chamber, can we?'

Flangers shook his head. 'Not a hope. The prisoners are a rabble.'

'They were taken because of their book learning,' said Yggur, leaning on a broken spear. 'I doubt there's an experienced fighter among them.'

'And if we force them to fight,' said Flangers, 'they'll die. You can't make a warrior out of a clerk in less than a month – if at all.'

'Up there.' Yggur nodded towards the top of the stairs.

They clattered up the broad, curving stairs, which were walled off at the top with solid, spans-thick ice. 'When the Numinator built this,' said Flydd, 'she was making sure no one could ever get through. You'll have to unmake the blocks, Yggur, since I'm not *allowed* to use chthonic fire.'

'Sarcasm was never your strong suit, Flydd.' Yggur put his hands on the wall, but hastily peeled them off. The ice was so cold that skin stuck to it. 'I don't believe I can.'

'Why not?' Flydd said peevishly.

'The bracelets take power from me as quickly as I can draw it, to maintain the tower.'

'I gave you some power back.'

'But the tower is under threat from chthonic fire now, and it's taking more. I feel drained all the time, like a well pumped dry. Removing that block of ice, and making the ice weapons, took my last reserves.'

'You'd better join the clerks in the corner, if that's the best you can do,' Flydd said, turning away. 'There's no choice, then. I'll have to use the fire.'

He boiled ice with it until the chamber was full of mist, to conceal what he was up to, and set to work. The ice was so thick here that he had to use half of the white fire remaining in the flask, then they huddled at the top of the stairs, feeling the vibrations from the Whelm hammering at the walls and waiting for the fire to do its work.

'It's taking an awfully long time,' Flydd muttered. He wanted to pace, to relieve his anxiety, but there was no room.

Screams echoed up from below and the surface of the fog, which hung thickly in the lowest third of the chamber, began to churn.

'They're through!' said Yggur. 'Better move fast, Flydd.'

'Doing all I can,' Flydd grunted. He was using his Art to drive the flame through ice set as hard as metal, but it was slow, draining work.

'We've got to hold the Whelm off,' said Flangers to Colm and Chissmoul.

Before they could move, the prisoners stampeded up the stairs. Flangers roared at them to let him through, and brandished his sword in their faces, but could not move them. The prisoners below were pushing ever up, forcing all before them.

More kept moving up, until Flydd was squeezed against the fiery ice so tightly that he could scarcely draw breath. Behind him, prisoners were gasping, screaming, collapsing; the smaller and weaker among them would be crushed, but there was nothing anyone could do about it.

Flangers wriggled along the wall and shouted in Flydd's ear. 'What if we jump over the side, surr? We might be able to get them down again.'

'It's four spans, soldier. You'll break both legs when you hit the floor and the Whelm will finish you off. Clear a space for me. I can't work.'

Flangers shouted orders, but the crush grew ever tighter. Below, men and women were screaming; and then came the terrible sound of jag-blades tearing through unprotected flesh.

'It was a sorry day when you came here, Flydd,' said Yggur, supporting himself against the wall, head and shoulders above the crowd. 'The Whelm are terrified of any threat to their master, and this rebellion is the greatest threat they've ever faced. Do something quick, else they'll butcher all of the prisoners.'

Flydd felt sick. They hadn't asked for this, and there was little they could do to protect themselves. He clutched the green-ice flask in his right hand, feeling its chill eating into him, and tried to remember the way he'd drawn upon chthonic fire next to the obelisk on Mistmurk Mountain to open the first portal. Could he find that kind of power again and force it to work for him?

He thought himself into the heart of the flame, attempting to recover the mental state that had given him power previously, but instead the outer wall of the chamber appeared to thin and what he saw was not Noom's bleak landscape of rock and ice beyond the moat, but a roiling nothingness with mists and whirlpools of light scattered across it, separated from him by a transparent membrane. Could he be seeing into *the void*? It seemed impossible, but what other explanation was there?

Then he saw the woman in red again. Her ghostly form drifted towards him until she came up against the barrier that separated them. Her hands scratched at it, as if she were trying to get through, just as she had on his way to the Nightland. Flydd couldn't see her face, just the curves of cheek and jaw.

Someone screamed and pointed, and the crowd surged away from the spectral figure. Flydd clung desperately to the fire-eaten ice, afraid he'd be carried off the side of the stair. Behind him there were more screams and a series of unpleasant thuds as people fell to the floor below.

He shook his head, concentrated on driving the chthonic fire deeper into the ice, and the woman in red faded away.

'Every single thing you do makes it worse, Flydd,' said Yggur, forcing his way through the crowd, which parted before him like soil carved by a plough. 'Who was that?'

'I don't know,' Flydd said uneasily, 'though it's not the first time I've seen her. I first saw her during renewal, though I dare say that was a trauma-induced hallucination.'

'I wouldn't be so sure. You know of the great mancer, Mendark, I assume?'

'Of course. He was one of the greatest in all the Histories.'

'He took renewal as many as twelve times, by some accounts; far more than any other mancer ever managed.

He didn't believe that renewal hallucinations were hallucinations at all – he said they were aspects of reality.'

Flydd froze, searching the elusive memories of his own
renewal for something disturbing. 'That can't be so,' he
said slowly.

'Why not?'

'Because I hallucinated that she was a part of me – and
not just mentally.'

FORTY

'If there's an ell of flat land in Gendrigore, I'm yet to see it,' Nish grumbled as they scrambled up a steep and extremely wet slope through dense forest. 'How far is it to The Spine?'

They hadn't made up any time, and he was painfully aware that his father's mighty army would be climbing the range by now. If they reached Blisterbone first, as was increasingly likely, there would be nothing to stop them. Imagining what it would be like to defend against a vastly superior enemy with the advantage of height, he shuddered. It would be a massacre, and an entirely pointless one. They simply had to get to the top of The Spine first.

'We'll reach the foothills tomorrow mornin',' said Curr, their guide.

A dirty, wiry little man, bald of head, leathery of skin and blank of expression, he was constantly chewing string-tied wads of leaf which stained his lips, teeth, chin and fingers blue. Curr had turned up not long after Ekko, and announced that he'd been across The Spine a dozen times and had been sent to be their guide.

'Foothills!' cried Nish. 'I've seen mountains smaller than the hill we're climbing now, and it doesn't even have a name.'

'Very rugged country, The Spine,' said Curr. The string of his latest wad hung from his lower lip, and beads of blue saliva dribbled down his chin with every word. His shirt and thick orange chest hair were stained with it. 'Kept us safe for more'n a thousand years, it has.' And it'll turn back the God-Emperor's army too, you young whippersnapper, he seemed to be saying.

Nish averted his eyes. 'And the other two provincial militias will rendezvous with us at Wily's Clearing before the climb?'

'Don't know nothin' about arrangements. Just a guide, I am.'

'But there is a good spot for all our forces to come together there?' Nish asked anxiously.

'There's a clearing big enough for all the troops you'll have.' He hawked and spat blue phlegm into the grass.

The wet season had been unseasonably mild for the past week, with only a torrential downpour every second day, but as soon as they reached Wily's Clearing, a precipitous opening in the forest not much bigger than a horse blanket, it began to rain in earnest. Nish closed his eyes and pointed his face to the sky, savouring the cool drops on his sweat-drenched, insect-savaged skin.

'About time!' he said, rubbing it over his face and looking around. 'Where are the detachments from the east and south?'

'That'll be the men from Rigore province,' grunted Curr, pointing into the trees.

Nish made out a handful of troops sitting on a log, passing a wine skin about. The Rigore pennant, featuring a laughing dolphin bursting through a wave, hung from the branch of a tree. No guards had been set out, no defences prepared. Nish, as an old soldier, was disgusted.

'There don't seem to be very many. I was promised four or five hundred from Rigore province, and slightly more from Gendri.'

'Expect they're down at the river. There's a fine bathin' pool there, for those what like that sort of thing. Don't hold with bathin', myself.'

Nish exchanged glances with Gi, whose snub nose was turned up. Curr's assertion was redundant – he could be smelt a hundred paces away, against the wind.

'What about Gendri province?' said Nish.

Curr shrugged. 'Shoulda been here days ago. 'Course . . .'

'What?' said Nish.

'Mostly sod-turners over east. Wouldn't know one end of a spear from the other. Better off without them.' Curr walked off, hawking to left and right.

Gloom settled over Nish and he could not shake it off. His quest had been cursed from the beginning. 'Hoshi, make camp, then put up the targets and get everyone practising. Gi, come with me.'

He went across to the men on the log. They were a rough lot, almost as dirty as Curr, unshaven and dressed in mud-stained rags. The roughest of them all, a big, burly man with a green feather in his broad-brimmed hat, was swigging from the wine skin and belching loudly.

As Nish approached he lowered the skin, wiped his mouth and said, 'What do you want, shrimp?'

Nish felt an instant and urgent dislike of the fellow, so strong that it took an effort to conceal it, but he began politely, 'I'm Cryl-Nish Hlar, and I –'

'I know who you are, you white-faced runt. I said, what do you want?'

Nish restrained himself. 'I'm the commander of Gendrigore's combined militia.'

'Be dammed! I'm not serving under no poxy turd of a foreigner.'

'That has already been decided by your betters,' said Nish between his teeth. 'Where's your commander, soldier?'

The burly man lurched to his feet, swaying wildly, but

recovered. 'I'm the commander here, you slimy little poop. I'm Captain Boobelar and I'm not serving under you.'

Nish knew that he would have to break Boobelar; he also knew that now was not the time. Boobelar would have to be taken by surprise, and crushed, for he knew nothing else. Once it was done, Nish knew, the men of Rigore would bow to his authority, but they would forever hold a grudge against him for taking down one of their own, and if they caught him on a dark night he'd get a beating, if not worse. Just what he needed on the eve of battle.

'My apologies, Captain Boobelar,' said Nish, stiffly sketching a salute. 'I did not recognise you out of uniform.'

Boobelar did not know what to make of that. He nodded curtly but did not return the salute.

'Where are the rest of your men, Captain?' said Nish. 'I was promised five hundred from Rigore.'

'Rigore can't afford to waste five hundred on a wild goose chase. It's harvest time. I've brought eighty, and even that's too many.'

'Eighty is no good to me!' cried Nish.

'Then we'll go home again,' said Boobelar, taking another swig and tossing the skin over his shoulder at a soldier lying on his back at the other end of the log.

It struck him in the face and he started up with a shocked cry, 'Is it the enemy already?'

The other men laughed, and Boobelar loudest of all.

'Let's not be hasty,' said Nish, red-raw inside at having to mollify this brute. 'The enemy is already on the march from Taranta with a mighty army. They may already be climbing The Spine.'

'How do you know?' said Boobelar.

'The watch fires have been lit, and a runner has come from the lookout above the pass.'

Boobelar swallowed, his triangular larynx bobbing up and down.

'It's true then,' said a soldier with a red birthmark in the shape of a horseshoe on his right cheek.

Boobelar glanced at him. 'What if it is, Lucky? They'll break on The Spine, like every other army has, and we'll grow fat on the loot we plunder from their rotting bodies.'

The man called Lucky licked his lips. He had three teeth, one on the top and two on the bottom.

Nish desperately hoped that it was true, and that he could hold Blisterbone Pass with as few as a thousand men. He would have that number when the Gendri militia arrived. 'Is there any sign of the army from Gendri?'

Boobelar grinned, displaying a full set of fractured yellow teeth. 'The best news of all.'

'What?' Nish's spirits rose fractionally. 'More than five hundred? A thousand?' With a thousand more, he would feel relatively confident, if only they got to Blisterbone first.

'They're not coming,' snorted Boobelar. 'We won't have to share the loot with them.'

'Not coming?' Nish couldn't keep the dismay out of his voice. This campaign was a nightmare; no, a farce.

With a wolfish laugh, Boobelar reached backwards for another wine skin. Someone put one into his hand. He turned his back to Nish, farted, then lay on the log and expertly directed a stream of purple wine into his mouth.

Nish dropped his hand onto the hilt of Vivimord's sabre, but withdrew it. Boobelar's gestures were an insult and a challenge, and he wasn't going to fall into the trap. He would challenge Boobelar at a time of his own choosing. Until he crushed him, though, he would look weak in the eyes of his men. Assuming I *can* crush him, Nish thought. Boobelar was a head taller and half as heavy again, with muscles honed from years of labour. Nish was fit from months of walking, but he was not strong enough to take this man down in unarmed combat.

And if the troops from Gendri were not coming, could he afford to crush Boobelar and lose one more man? Indeed, was there any point going on with so few? Yes, even leaving Gendrigore's fate out of the equation, he had to go on.

If this was to be the first real battle of the war against his father, he had to fight it, *and he had to win*, even if he only had five hundred. He had to find a way.

He desperately needed advice, but the one person he could turn to was never around when he needed her. Tulitine hadn't been seen for days and no one knew where she had gone.

After dinner, Nish sat by the embers of his cooking fire where the smoke provided some relief from the incessant mosquitoes, mud flies and blue-eyed gnats, and from Curr's squalid reek. Nish was trying to get a picture of the track that wound over The Spine, but the guide was not being helpful.

'So how long is it to the pass now, Curr?'

Curr took out his blue-stained chaw, studied the soggy mess in the firelight, and put it back. 'For me, five days. Your useless lot might do it in seven, if they walk hard and nothin' goes wrong.'

'Is there any chance the supply wagons can come partway up the track? It would be a big help if they could, otherwise we'll be awfully burdened with supplies.'

Assuming the supply wagons ever got here. The bulk of their supplies were coming from Gendri, which was closest to The Spine, but since Gendri's troops had failed him, maybe the supplies weren't coming either. How long could he afford to wait? No more than another day, and if they hadn't turned up by then Nish didn't know what he was going to do.

Curr snorted, spraying blue saliva out in a poisonous cloud. 'Forget everythin' you know, captain.'

'What's that supposed to mean?' Nish snarled, for it had been a rotten day of a lousy week and he could not imagine tomorrow being any better.

'You keep calling it a *track*. Ain't no road, no track, no path. It's the worst country you ever saw for walkin'. One minute yer up to yer neck in snake-infested swamp, the

440

next yer inchin' sideways along a ledge with a hunderd-span drop below yer and rotten rock crumblin' underfoot. Ridge goes straight up for five hunderd spans, then down the other side, then up another ridge, and another, and another. By the time you get to Blisterbone, with all the ups and downs, yer've walked halfway to the moon. You couldn't lead a horse over The Spine, and yer talking about *wagons*!'

Curr got up, scratched his scrawny haunches and walked off.

Nish felt like getting so drunk he couldn't stand up. They would have to carry all their supplies on their backs, but they could only carry enough food to last them a fortnight up such precipitous paths. If all went well they would have just enough to get to the pass, fight a quick battle and come down again. If they had to wait, or defend, for days, they would run out of supplies, and once these were gone they would have to live off the land or starve. But living off the land was very time consuming; no army could do so and fight at the same time; not up there.

So they would have to fight, and win, within days of reaching Blisterbone.

Or fight and die, in which case the lack of supplies would not matter.

It began to rain in earnest in the night, and it grew ever heavier until he could not sleep for the drumming on the canvas of his tent. Just what we need on the first day of the climb, he thought, though he had been expecting it. Gendrigore was a wet place and this was the wet season, and nowhere was wetter than The Spine that cut it off from the world. He couldn't imagine what it would be like in the really wet season.

'Nish? Are you awake?'

It was Tulitine, outside the flap of the tent.

'Can't sleep in this,' he muttered.

'Just as well. There's a lot to talk about.'

'Come in.'

He sat up and lit his lantern. Tulitine came in, water running off her oilskins to join the streams of water winding their way across the sloping floor of the tent.

'Where have you been?' he asked.

'Here and there, listening to the wind in the trees and the croaking of the frogs.'

'Why does everyone in Gendrigore talk in riddles?' he muttered.

'Those who demand plain speaking aren't always equipped to deal with what they hear.'

'What's that supposed to mean?'

'The truth isn't always obvious, even if the facts are clear. Sometimes truth is a riddle nested inside a paradox, and until you can puzzle out that paradox and solve the riddle you won't know which way to act.'

'Are you saying that I shouldn't try to defend Gendrigore?'

'It may be right for Gendrigore, but wrong for you – or the other way around. It may be right for you both, but wrong for Santhenar.'

'What's Santhenar got to do with it?'

'I don't know . . . but some of the forces determined to overthrow the God-Emperor may be worse than he is.'

'Do you mean the Numinator?' Nish often wondered about Flydd and Colm, and Maelys. Had they found the Numinator by now? If they could enlist the Numinator's aid it might turn the tide their way, assuming they were still alive, of course.

'The riddles written in the wind are more enigmatic than usual.'

Nish sat, head bowed, as the rain pounded down. He had never felt less certain of his path and her words had not helped. 'Tulitine, I don't know what to do. Rigore has only sent eighty men, most of them drunks and troublemakers only here for the looting, and I don't think Gendri is sending anyone. Is there any point in going on with so few?'

She didn't reply, and he added, 'I don't suppose you've heard any whispers about Flydd, Maelys and Colm? I really need help. I'm lost.'

She sighed. 'None at all. All right, Nish, here's the plainest speaking you'll ever hear from me. The enemy is making better progress than anyone expected and you can't wait for the supply wagons. You must leave at first light and make a forced march all the hours of the day, and tomorrow and the day after. You've got to reach the top of Blisterbone Pass before Jal-Nish's army does. If they get across before you do, Gendrigore is lost and so are you, and Santhenar may be doomed.'

'What do you mean, *Santhenar may be doomed?*'

'I've read the omens, but I know no more. Good luck.' She offered him her thin hand.

'You're not coming?' he said, dismayed. Though his troops were only ten or fifteen years younger than him, they felt like a different generation. They hadn't grown up in a war where every waking thought was directed to the struggle for survival against a superior enemy. None of them knew anything about the real world beyond Gendrigore's borders, and he could not turn to them for advice.

She didn't say anything.

'Of course you're not,' he said. 'How could I have imagined otherwise? This is a road for the young and reckless.'

'And I'm too old. I couldn't climb The Spine with a heavy pack, and there would be nothing for me to do there anyway.'

'Do you mean . . .?'

'You know I do. For anyone badly injured up on The Spine, it will be a death sentence. Up there, bad wounds can turn septic in a day, and anyone who can't walk must be left behind. You can't carry the injured in that kind of country, Nish.'

His lantern went out, though Tulitine had not gone near it, and with a rustle of wet oilskins she was gone.

We can't wait for the supply wagons, he thought, and

they can't go any further, so what are we to do without them? I'll leave a man behind to tell the wagons to wait, if they arrive, until the force from Gendri gets here. If they come.

Who said things could not get any worse?

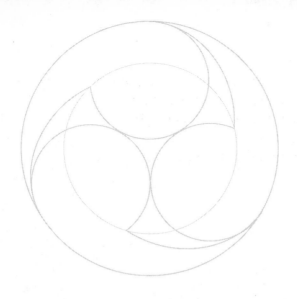

PART THREE

THE RANGE OF RUIN

FORTY-ONE

They set off at first light, Curr leading, Nish following as close behind as he could bear the stench, scrambling on blistered hands and bloody knees up a ridge through rainforest festooned with vines. The bedraggled army followed, grumbling at the early start. There was no track to follow, just an unmarked slope that went up and up forever.

The heavy rain intensified; it was now a downpour so fierce that Nish could barely see and couldn't hear. The whole mountainside was running with water and the ground a sponge into which his boots sank so deeply that mud flowed over their tops. Every step took an effort, especially for him. The Gendrigoreans were used to such conditions; he could never be.

He soon realised how skin-deep his fitness was, for the first hour was more exhausting than his climb to the top of Mistmurk Mountain, about a month ago; the next hour loomed like an even higher peak. He staggered on, head down, drenched to the skin and feeling faint from the dreadful, stifling humidity. Got to keep going, he kept telling himself. If he showed any weakness, his sad little army would turn back. He had to be as hard as iron and as tough as the best of them. They would expect no less of the son of the God-Emperor. The only way to lead men was from the front.

Three days went by and it was raining just as hard. It had not let up for a minute and Nish felt as though his continually wet feet were rotting. He wasn't game to take his stinking socks off in case the skin came with them.

'This must be how the world ends,' he said to Hoshi, who had come back from the leaders. Despite all Nish's efforts, a third of his men had passed him today. He stepped carefully onto what looked like solid ground and sank thigh-deep into clinging mud.

Hoshi heaved him out, as he had done a dozen times already. He was still smiling, though not as broadly, nor as often. Even the hardiest of the Gendrigoreans were struggling in the impossible conditions.

'Not much further to go today, according to Curr,' said Hoshi. 'We'll camp on the top of the ridge. A great overhang of rock there will shelter us all, and we might even get a fire going. Can you make it that far, Nish?'

'I'll make it, however far it is,' Nish gasped, praying it was only another hundred paces. His iron determination had not yet failed him, but determination was not enough when the soles of your feet were covered in burst, weeping blisters and your muscles kept locking up with cramp.

He staggered up and ever up, reaching the campsite less than an hour later. It was on a saddle-shaped ridgetop with steep slopes to either side, the sodden ground covered in shattered trees and broken rock. Further along, the ridge reared up in an axe-shaped precipice of seamed brown stone whose top was concealed by the low-hanging clouds.

'I thought there was shelter?' said Nish. 'An overhang or something.'

'Musta fell down,' said Curr. 'Rock in The Spine is rotten – too much rain. Whole mountain fell down once – shook the ground all the way to Rigore.'

The precipice looming above them looked none too

secure either, but Nish was too exhausted to care. 'We'll camp here. At least there's plenty of firewood.'

'If you can get it to burn you're a better man than I am,' said Curr, spitting a blue deluge onto a nearby log.

Nish wasn't going to fall into that trap. 'I'll leave that to those who know how.' He raised his voice. 'Let's get the targets strung up while the tents are being pitched.'

There was a collective groan from those nearby, though they complied readily enough. There had been no time for target practice since they'd begun the climb and, as each passing day brought them closer to the enemy, few now doubted that they were going to see action.

Nish pitched his tent on the smoothest patch of ground he could find, made his way around the precipice to one of the less public waterfalls cascading down the side of the ridge and stood under it, fully dressed, until the worst of the mud was washed out of his hair and clothes. Everything he owned was saturated; for the past three nights he had slept in his muddy gear and woke feeling like a pig in a wallow, though at least the mud had kept the insects away.

He stripped off, dropped his clothes onto a rock and scrubbed himself clean, then washed his slimy socks and mud-caked boots. As he'd suspected, the skin was peeling off his waterlogged feet in sheets.

'Bad idea, bathin' up here. Never know what might come after you when you're all pink and naked.'

Nish spun around. Boobelar was standing between the rocks twenty paces away, wine skin in hand, all his cracked teeth showing.

'As long as it's not the enemy,' Nish said, pretending a calm he could not feel.

'You don't know who your enemy is up here.'

'I've got a pretty fair idea.' Nish's chances weren't good. There was no one in sight and he'd left Vivimord's sabre back in his tent; if he took this brute on bare-handed there was only one possible outcome.

449

Boobelar moved towards him, hand on the hilt of his blade, drawing the moment out. Nish eyed the shattered rocks littering the ground. Some had sharp edges; if he was lucky he might get in a telling blow.

Boobelar grinned and took another couple of steps. Nish felt like a fool; he should never have let his guard down; should never have come around here all alone. Even if Boobelar didn't intend to kill him, he certainly planned to inflict such punishment that Nish would be forever damaged in the militia's eyes. Since they had little innate respect for authority, his position as captain did not elevate him, and once they lost respect for Nish the man he would never be able to lead them.

He went backwards until he was under the edge of the waterfall. His clothes were just to the left but he could not afford to go for them – half dressed he would be even more helpless. Nor could he shout for help – no cry would be heard over the waterfalls – and if he ran he'd shred his feet on the rocks and Boobelar would take him from behind.

His only hope was to attack Boobelar bare-handed, and beat him, but that wasn't going to happen, unless . . . could he use his clearsight to tell what Boobelar was going to do next? It was such an unreliable gift that Nish seldom tried to use it any more, but it had been enhanced a trifle that day he'd put his hand into Reaper in the cavern on the edge of Mistmurk Mountain . . .

He picked up a fist-sized piece of rock shaped like a hand axe and stepped forwards onto a relatively smooth patch of ground between the rocks, the best arena he could find. Boobelar drew his sword and came on.

Knowing his cause was hopeless, Nish sought deep and despairingly for his clearsight, and for once, found it. What did Boobelar have in mind? How would he strike, and which way? Nish tried to see into his mind, but nothing came.

The soldier was not a subtle man, but he was a cunning one. Would he feint, or pretend to slip and lure Nish forwards? He gave the clearsight all he had, suddenly saw himself through Boobelar's red and yellow eyes, and recoiled, for he'd seen right into the festering mess that was Boobelar's drink-addled mind.

'Ugh!' he gasped, cutting off the clearsight, so sickened that the stone slipped from his hand.

Before he'd recovered, Boobelar, leering like a maniac, was upon him, and Nish felt sure he was going to die. Boobelar knocked him backwards with a fist like a small club, right through the waterfall, and Nish slammed into the rock face. Water thundered on his head, temporarily blinding him, the dropped sword clanged on stone, then he was caught in a headlock, dragged forwards and thrown belly down over the curve of a boulder. His chin hit the lower side and his head spun.

Nish was scratching at the rock, dazedly trying to get up, when he heard Boobelar coming up behind him, roaring with laughter. What was he going to do? Surely he wasn't planning –

Whack! The blow drove him so hard against the rock that he felt its little projections breaking the skin across his belly, groin and thighs. His whole backside was shrieking. Boobelar had struck him with the flat of the sword and all the strength of his arm behind it.

'Deliver yourself from this, Deliverer!' The soldier's wild laughter rang in his ears.

Nish tried to get up. *Whack, whack!*

He felt as though the flesh of his backside was splattering off and his bones were being crushed by the assault. Did Boobelar intend to beat him to death with the sword? It wouldn't take long at this rate, and Nish couldn't do a thing about it.

'Hoy, what the blazes is going on?'

It was Gi's voice, though she couldn't help him. Gentle Gi wouldn't last a second against Boobelar. 'Keep away,' Nish gasped.

'Get away from him!' Gi shouted. 'Come on, lads!'

Boobelar gave Nish a final shattering whack and disappeared over the steep edge of the ridge. Unable to move, Nish lay over the rock, arse-up, letting the mortifying tears fall where they may. This was the end of his command and his quest. There could be no coming back from such a humiliation.

Gi came running up with Forzel and Clech, a huge, gentle fisherman with a perpetual squint from staring out to sea.

'Are you all right, Nish?' she cried. 'Clech, get after Boobelar.'

Clech's boots pounded away. Gi took Nish's shoulder but he slid bonelessly off the rock onto the ground. He couldn't move; couldn't speak; and definitely could not meet Forzel's eyes, for he was a perennial joker and Nish could only imagine what he'd make of this scene.

Gi ran back for balms and bandages. A grimly silent Forzel helped Nish up, and when his many cuts and abrasions had been treated, dressed him and assisted him back. Nish crawled into his tent, too sore and sick to eat. By nightfall Boobelar's men would have spread the story through the camp, and Nish would be a laughing stock, his reputation ruined. The militia would never follow him now.

He huddled in his wet bedroll, knowing he should go out and address them at once, to try and save himself, but unable to face the ordeal. It would not have surprised him if they all deserted in the night.

When he rose the following morning, after what felt like the most painful and miserable night of his life, the militia was still there. His backside was a swollen mess of purple bruises that were spreading up his back and down his thighs, and he could barely stand up. But he had to; the mortifying moment could not be put off any longer and, whatever came from it, he would face it with the few shreds of dignity he had left.

Hoshi was just outside. Nish beckoned him over. 'Would you –?' His voice went hoarse. 'Would you call everyone together? I have to tell them what happened and give them the opportunity –'

'No!' said Hoshi, more firmly than he had spoken to Nish before.

It was starting already. 'I'm your captain!' gritted Nish. 'It's an order –'

'You don't know Gendrigore, Nish. We don't make heroes of men like Boobelar, who kill for a living. Our heroes are ordinary folk who have fought against the odds, even if they've failed.'

'I don't know what you're talking about,' said Nish.

'We don't think the less of you because a swine like Boobelar beat you black and blue. We admire you all the more because you had the courage to take him on unarmed, when you knew you couldn't win.'

Nish found this difficult to understand, for he had grown up in the old school, where everyone knew their place and it had been ruthlessly enforced. 'But how can I maintain discipline when –'

'We don't obey you because you give us orders, Nish. We follow you because you care about us, and for our beautiful Gendrigore. We follow you because we believe in you.'

'But –'

'We have looked out for our captain,' said Hoshi. 'The matter will never be mentioned again.'

'But –'

Hoshi held up his hand and Nish broke off, humbled and overcome. The matter was not mentioned again, on that day's march or afterwards, and Nish did not see a single smirk or secret smile on the faces of his militia.

In the early afternoon he was having a leak behind a tree when Boobelar's company hobbled past, every man of them sporting black eyes and battered faces. Nish's own troops had swollen hands and bleeding knuckles, even gentle Gi. He could have wept for their simple, stubborn loyalty, and their refusal to allow him any shame for what he had been through. He loved them, every single one.

But it could not erase his humiliation; it burned him night and day, lessening him in his own eyes. After making such an elementary blunder and leaving himself exposed to his enemy, how could he rely on his own judgment in the battles to come, when lives would be lost at every miscalculation or failed strategy? How could he believe in himself when at every critical choice he would see his naked body splayed over a rock, having his arse whaled by an addled thug?

Maybe the militia would follow him as confidently as ever, but Nish felt eaten up from the inside. He was no longer sure he had the self-belief to lead them in the battle of their lives.

That day was a nightmare; for the first hour Nish could barely stagger. But he forced himself to, enduring the pain and making every step into another blow against Boobelar. How he was going to pay.

Nish would not accept the frequent offers of a helping hand; he could not, for in his mind that would only reveal another weakness. He had to do it alone, no matter how it hurt. And the next hour hurt even more.

Each succeeding day felt worse than the one before, yet Nish drove himself harder, for they did not seem to be getting anywhere. When he finally clawed his way to the top of each ridge he could only see more ridges, looming ever higher until they blurred into the rain, and there was never any way to get to the next ridge without climbing down a precipitous slope and up the other side. Every day his terror grew that they would get to Blisterbone and find it held against them by thousands of jeering Imperial Militia.

The business between him and Boobelar wasn't finished, either. It could not be until he crushed the man, or Boobelar killed him. He could see it in the captain's eyes every time they met. Boobelar said not a word, and neither did his troops, but the sore continued to fester.

'I'm sure we've climbed this ridge before,' Nish panted

on the afternoon of the sixth day. 'It looks really familiar.'

'In that case, you'd see our tracks,' said Curr.

'The rain would have washed them away.'

'Land all looks the same up here,' said Curr. 'It even fools me sometimes.'

'We must be getting close now,' Nish said on the seventh day of the climb. He had stopped with Gi, Hoshi and Curr for a few minute's rest. They slumped to the ground but Nish stayed on his feet; if he once sat down, he did not think he would ever get up again.

It was still raining as heavily as before, but it was milder at this altitude, and occasionally, when they emerged from forest onto an open ridge and the wind was blowing hard, he felt pleasantly cool.

'Couple of days to Blisterbone,' Curr grunted.

'You said it would only us take seven days.'

'It would have if you'd put your backs into it.' Curr spat onto the ground between Nish's feet.

He became ruder and more disrespectful by the hour, and in the olden days Nish would have had him flogged for insolence, but without Curr he would never find the pass. Besides, he had too many other problems to worry about – like their rapidly dwindling food supplies.

The militia had consumed far more than he had expected, and so had he, for the forced march in these conditions had been utterly exhausting and everyone had lost weight. Had they eaten any less, they would have been burning the flesh of their own bodies and growing weaker every day. As it was, he'd already left twenty-two people behind suffering various fevers and ailments, and another twelve with broken limbs and sprains. They would be helped down on the way back – if the militia came back – and if it did not, most of them would die. He had to keep up the strength and morale of the able-bodied; they had to reach Blisterbone Pass first, and then they would have to fight for their lives, so Nish ordered the cooks to keep doling out the food. If they ran short on the way home, at least they'd be walking more downhill than up. Well, slightly more downhill.

Nish's other problem, which grew more pressing as they approached their destination, was his ignorance of the enemy's progress. There was no point labouring up to Blisterbone if the enemy already held the pass.

'You'd better go ahead and find out where they are,' he said to Curr.

'Won't do you no good,' said Curr.

'Why not?'

'They'll have a hundred scouts out, and fifty scout hunters. You'll just be telling them we're on the way.'

'Father has spies and watchers everywhere. He must know we're coming.'

'But not where we are. If you send up a scout, it'll just be telling his men that you're close.'

'If they've taken the pass and are on their way down, I've got to know where they are so I can make a battle plan.'

Curr sighed ostentatiously and hawked another gob at the fire. 'Look, Nish, yer a decent fellow, for a white-skin and a foreigner, but you can't fight the way you're used to, up here.'

'I've got to make plans.'

'Battle plans are no good on The Spine, son – the land is too rough, the jungle too thick. This ain't like a clear battlefield, where you can see everyone. You can't see yer own men, and you never know where the enemy is. They can attack from any direction, and you won't know it until their spears take your throat out. Send out a detachment, you lose sight of them and there's no way to give them new orders. When the fightin' starts, it's every man for himself until they're dead, or you are.'

'So the biggest army always wins,' Nish said bitterly.

'The one that uses the land best wins.'

'How can I do that when I can't see the enemy's formations?'

'You don't fight in formation. You fight them in secret, with pits and traps and snares. Poison the water, roll boulders down on their camps, attack at night with spears and arrows, then scatter and hide. Never show yerself if you can avoid it, for someone stronger and faster will always catch you. Never fight hand-to-hand unless yer've no choice. Fire, run, hide, then fire again.' He got up and walked off.

'That's not a very noble form of warfare,' Hoshi said quietly.

'There *is* no noble form of warfare,' said Nish. 'War is maimed men left to die in agony, towns full of women and children put to the sword, lands razed, stock butchered, forests burned . . .' He put his head in his hands.

'What's the matter?' asked Gi.

'Curr is right. It's the only way, though I don't like shooting men in cold blood either.'

After a long pause, Gi said, 'I heard you were a javelard operator during the war, firing from the top of one of those metal caterpillars.'

Most javelards had been mounted on the top of clankers, which were eight, ten or even twelve-legged armoured mechanical monsters driven by a force, now gone, called the field. Unfortunately, or perhaps fortunately, clankers had failed when the nodes were destroyed, taking the fields which empowered the Art with them.

'I've used javelards,' said Nish. 'In open battle.'

'Did you always warn the enemy before you shot him?'

'You don't warn your enemy in war. You just shoot.'

'In the back?'

'Sometimes,' Nish said uneasily, not wanting to be reminded of those times.

'Even if he doesn't know you're there?'

'You kill or be killed until the battle is won, or lost.'

'If the God-Emperor's troops see one of us within range,' Gi said quietly, 'will they shout a warning, or just shoot?'

'They'll shoot, of course. They'll slaughter the lot of us and sweep down into Gendrigore, and hiding in the forests

457

won't serve your people this time. The God-Emperor's armies will starve them out, Gendrigore will fall, your people will be carried off into slavery and that will be the end of resistance on Santhenar. Gendrigore will become a symbol – that there is no country, no matter how small, that Father won't take the trouble to crush, to ensure his realm is unchallenged.'

'Gendrigore did not challenge him.'

'The moment Gendrigore put Vivimord to trial, it spat in the God-Emperor's face, and he could not ignore it. That was my fault.'

'Gendrigore brought Vivimord to justice and executed him, not you,' said Gi.

'Your people thought they were executing a murderer, and that would be the end of it, but I knew differently. I put the responsibility in their hands, not because I thought it was the right thing to do, but because I could not bear to act like my father. That cowardly choice is going to cost Gendrigore dearly.

'I see the answer now. There's only one way to win this battle, if our tiny militia *can* win it, and that is to fight Curr's way. I will do whatever it takes to turn Father's army back, and pay the price, even if it costs me my soul. I will never give in until the war is won – or lost beyond recovery.'

'Finally you're talking like the Deliverer,' said Hoshi.

FORTY-TWO

Yggur looked at Flydd quizzically. 'What if the woman in red didn't just influence you during renewal? What if she actually entered you?'

'I haven't got time for such nonsense,' Flydd snapped. 'The prisoners are being slaughtered as we speak.'

'You can't avoid the question forever. I saw it in your eyes the moment you appeared here.'

'Saw *what*?'

'You were changed, Flydd. Changed more than any mancer should be after ten years, even one who has gone through the trauma of renewal.'

'How the hell would you know? You've never been renewed.'

'I knew you well, once, and over the uncounted centuries since my birth I've known a dozen mancers who survived renewal. You're not the same man you were when we last met.'

Flydd turned away, desperately trying not to think about what Yggur was saying. He didn't want to consider the ugly possibility; couldn't bear to face it.

Yggur caught him by the arm. 'Ask yourself this, Flydd. Where did your ability to make portals come from, and how did it come so easily to you in a world stripped of most of its Arts?'

'*She* taught me how to make the portal,' Flydd gritted.

'You know as well as I do that one mancer can't just *tell* another how to work a spell. You have to *know* it from the inside out.'

'All right! She got in my mind at a moment of weakness; she must have put everything there that I needed.'

'It still came too easily, Flydd, and you know it. If I'd made a portal to the Nightland I'd have been crippled by aftersickness for days, yet by all accounts you hardly suffered at all. You made another portal out only a couple of days later –'

'A month had gone by when we returned to Santhenar,' Flydd snapped.

'The only passing time that counts is the time of the place where you spend it – the Nightland. Two days between portals, and no aftersickness – it should not have been possible. And then you made a *third* portal from Dunnet. You ought to be dead, yet you look better than I do. Why Flydd?'

'Not now, damn you!' Flydd could feel the pressure boiling up in him. He wanted to strike out at Yggur. He didn't want to consider that the woman in red had changed him, might even have left part of herself inside him, to control him at some future time. Instead, he directed his fury, and his deep-seated fear of what she had done to him, into the chthonic fire webbing its way across the wall of ice, to blast a way through it.

A boom shook the steps. Rotten, fire-eaten ice crumbled out of the lower walls in several places and more Whelm scrambled in. Half the prisoners fell down on the stairs in a wave that proceeded from top to bottom.

When the steam and flying ice had cleared, Flydd saw a neat tube blasted through the ice wall in front of him, expanding outwards on the far side.

'We're through!' he roared. 'Come on.'

He crawled in. Three Whelm guards lay on the far side, crushed under the ice. One was still kicking.

'And this,' said Yggur, 'if you need further evidence.'

'What are you talking about?'

'The old Flydd could not have done what you just did, using nothing more than cold fire. The woman in red has changed you, Flydd, and good is not going to come of it.'

Flydd didn't answer; it was too disturbing. He saw a square staircase to the left, various rooms and corridors ahead and to the right. 'Chissmoul, do we go up?'

She nodded. 'We must. They'll have taken the lower stair by now.'

'Where does this one lead?'

'All the way to the top of the inner tower.'

'Is there any way out from there?'

'Yes, but we'd have to fight hundreds of Whelm to get to it.'

'Can we defend the top?'

She hesitated before answering. 'I expect so . . . for a while.'

'Then that's what we'll have to do. Come on.'

He ran for the steps and began to scramble up them. They were very steep, and also speckled with chthonic fire. 'Is the whole damned place fire-eaten?' he cried as his boot plunged through the tenth step into icy water. Jagged ice tore at his calf as he pulled free.

'Not yet, but the fire seems to be feeding on ice,' said Yggur. 'And unless we can put it out, it's not going to stop until it's consumed the entire tower.'

Flydd felt a chill of fear. 'And what then?'

'The moat water will stop it spreading any further, fortunately. The Numinator won't be pleased, though.'

'That's the least of my worries right now.'

Flydd stopped on the first landing, for Yggur was already lagging behind, and Flangers was labouring. Colm and Chissmoul continued up out of sight. Behind Flangers, the leading prisoners were pushing up, stumbling and fearful.

461

They were torn between an uncanny death at the mancers' hands or a brutal one from the Whelms' jag-blades, and little to choose either way.

The floor rocked sideways, sliding Flydd and Yggur across the landing and throwing most of the prisoners off their feet.

'What was *that*?' asked Flangers. He was as brave as any man in the face of physical danger, but was not equipped to deal with the uncanny.

'Felt like a foundation stone crumbling,' said Yggur.

'Is the inner tower going to fall?'

'Not for a while,' said Yggur. 'Her bracelets are taking every speck of power I have, to maintain her realm, and this ice is stronger than brick or stone. Small breaches will heal themselves, for any liquid water that forms will put that patch of fire out and then freeze, welding the ice together again. Where it is rottenest, that part of the wall will collapse, but the rest of the tower should stay together – for a time.'

'Just long enough for us to get to the roof,' Colm said gloomily. 'And then the inner tower will fall down.'

When they reached the top, Flydd echoed his despair. The roof of the inner tower was flat and some fifty paces across, surrounded by a chest-high wall of ice as clear as window glass. Three suspended aerial walkways, equally spaced around the perimeter wall, ran across to a narrow platform encircling the inside wall of the Tower of a Thousand Steps, which curved around and soared above them like the inside of a gigantic cone. On the far side of their roof, another stair ran down inside the inner tower.

'We can't defend the roof either,' said Colm. 'Not with five ways for them to attack us.'

'Flangers?' said Flydd. 'What do we do?'

'Block the two stair wells,' said Flangers. 'Flydd, you'll have to do that. You too, Yggur. You've got to find the power somewhere, surr,' Flangers added hastily, for mancers were notoriously short-tempered and quick to take offence. 'I'll see if we can deal with the walkways.'

Flydd and Yggur headed for the second staircase, since the one they'd climbed was choked with scrambling, desperate prisoners. 'You do it,' said Yggur. 'I've worked out how to hold back a little power for myself, but I'm saving it for an emergency.'

Flydd raised an eyebrow. 'And this isn't?'

'This is just a skirmish. The real battle is yet to come.'

Flydd drew power from a patch of white fire and concentrated on the roof of the stairwell, several spans down. It was much harder to break the ice this time, for it was more solid here and he felt hollowed out from overusing his Art, but after much straining the blocks above the bend of the stair separated and fell in.

'I don't think it's blocked completely –' Flydd slumped to his knees, his head whirling and his stomach churning with aftersickness. *She* was back in his mind's eye and she wanted something.

'What's the matter?' said Yggur, splitting a block over and over, making more spears.

'I saw the woman in red again.'

'What was she doing?' Yggur rapped.

'Trying to get through to me,' Flydd said faintly, 'but she's faded away.'

'Good riddance!' Yggur inspected the ice rubble below. 'One or two Whelm might still scramble through there, but they won't find it easy to fight on that shifting slope.'

'Nor will our untrained prisoners with their brittle spears.'

Yggur took an armload of ice spears up, then went down to the fallen blocks to make more. Flydd headed across to Flangers, Chissmoul and Colm, who were at the end of one of the aerial walkways. These consisted of a series of ice planks frozen onto cables of clear, woven ice. There was no sign of the enemy.

'This ice must be spell-toughened,' said Flangers, hacking at a cable. 'Not even a Whelm jag-blade will make an impression on it.'

'It is,' said Yggur, laying down another armload of spears, 'and the tower draws upon my power from time to time, to bolster the cables anew.'

'What if you were to hold it back?' said Chissmoul who, having been a thapter pilot, understood the ways that power could be drawn, and blocked.

'I'm not sure that I can; the bracelets are still in charge.'

'Here come the Whelm!' someone yelled.

Flydd peered over the edge. Far across, on the cone-shaped inside wall of the Tower of a Thousand Steps, lines of Whelm were clambering up a set of rungs to the platform that encircled the inside of the Tower of a Thousand Steps. Once the Whelm reached the platform they could run around it to the walkways, and attack across all three at once.

Without warning the roof of the inner tower swayed left and right, then jerked downwards half a span, sending slow waves across the suspended walkways and pulling their curves tighter.

'Another course of the tower has crumbled,' said Yggur.

'It had better not fall any further,' said Flydd.

Yggur, now shaking with aftersickness, added another armload to his pile of ice spears. 'Arm yourselves,' he said hoarsely to the wide-eyed prisoners, and they obeyed at once.

Yells and screams broke out behind them. The last of the prisoners were coming up, closely followed by a pack of Whelm. A band of prisoners tried to fend them off with ice spears, but the Whelm smashed the spears with sideways sweeps of their jag-blades.

Flangers, leading a squad of spearmen, drove them down. Flydd ran to their aid, knocking the useless defenders out of the way with his shoulder and leaping down onto the top step. He'd worked out how to use the jag-sword now. The elegant swordsmanship he'd learned from a master decades ago was useless here; neither could he cut and thrust as he would normally do in battle, for the jags caught on clothing and flesh, and it was difficult to pull free.

The best way to use a jag-sword was as an edged bludgeon. When swung hard enough it would shear through flesh and bone, and one blow was normally enough to disable an opponent, or kill him.

A pair of Whelm lunged up the steps, and Flydd felt a spasm of fear. Though he had the advantage of height and speed, it was difficult to get a good swing going in the narrow stairwell. He hacked straight down at the Whelm on the left, who ducked but left his sword upraised. Flydd's blade struck it with a clang and another flurry of sparks, and the jags caught. The Whelm held Flydd's sword; he couldn't free it in time, and the second Whelm leapt up two steps, raising his weapon for the blow that would cleave Flydd in two from skull to navel.

It was a clever strategy, clearly much practised, and he had no choice but to abandon his sword. He threw himself backwards but his heel caught on the edge of the top step and he landed on his back on the roof, winded.

The leading Whelm leapt up beside him and raised the jag-blade high to skewer Flydd to the floor. He couldn't get out of the way; couldn't move.

'Stay down!' Yggur roared, and pointed his left hand at the tightly stretched ice cables at the far end of the nearest walkway.

The Whelm stopped, staring, jag-sword upraised. Flydd heard a shrill hiss as the woven ice fibres unravelled at high speed, then the cables snapped and hurtled towards the inner tower, their wiry ends lashing about furiously. The ice planks of the walkway were sent flying in all directions, embedding themselves deeply in every surface and smashing down two prisoners who had been slow to react.

Yggur dropped to the floor; an iron-hard cable end sang over his head, and Flydd's, slammed into the Whelm's right cheek, tearing his face off, then continued on its unstoppable way.

The Whelm fell backwards down the steps but his jag-blade hit the roof, point first, between Flydd's thighs, then toppled and thumped him in the groin, chest and mouth so hard that tears sprang to his eyes.

The other Whelm was on his feet. Flydd spat out blood, sat up and hefted the jag-sword. Swinging it sideways so hard that he wrenched his back, he sent it spinning at the Whelm, who could not move quickly enough to avoid it. It struck him in the belly and knocked him down half a dozen steps.

Flydd got up weakly, holding his groin, the pain coming in waves so intense that he wanted to throw up. He could not look at the faceless Whelm, who was crawling blindly up the steps, still trying to do his duty. Thankfully, Flangers put the fellow out of his misery.

'You'll have to block the stairs, Flydd,' said Yggur in a faded voice. 'I can do no more.' He was on his hands and knees with his forehead touching the floor.

'I don't have much left either.' Flydd studied the lay-out of the stairs, identifying its weak points as a matter of habit. 'I'll have to go down. I can't do it from here.'

'They'll have a clear view of you.'

Flydd shrugged. 'See if you can do something about the other two walkways.'

With the destruction of the first walkway, the inner tower had taken on a list, and walking across the sloping, slippery ice was difficult and dangerous. Flydd slid down the sloping stairs, trying to make sense of what he'd heard earlier. Had the Numinator opened a portal to the Nightland? And who had Maelys met there? The questions were unanswerable, but they raised a more urgent one. What would the Numinator do when she returned and saw the destruction? Would she call her Whelm off? The main tower looked solid but the inner one was badly damaged and, without being strengthened with the Art, must fail. Its collapse would bury the hall of the bloodline registers and all those unpleasantly suggestive bodies, skeletons and malformed creatures in jars, ruining her lifetime's work.

He hobbled down the steps until he was directly below the weakest point he'd identified in the stair roof. The Whelm who had fallen lay dead with a broken neck, and others were scattered below him, stuck with ice spears. Flydd clutched at his groin, trying to ease the pain, then reached within himself to draw power one more time. It was harder than ever now; he couldn't concentrate, and he could hear the leathery feet of more Whelm padding up the stairs.

Now! He drew power hard, directing it into the ice above him which, being almost untouched by chthonic fire, was as hard as adamant. His power made no impression on it. He tried again, but again saw the woman in red, dimly as though through a transparent barrier. Her arms were out-stretched pleadingly, but what did she want? For him to let her through?

As if he was going to add to their troubles by calling her. Every muscle ached from overuse of power, and every bone. He had taken far more from himself than any mancer should have, and he was going to pay for it.

He tried to dismiss her from his mind, but the look in her eyes kept breaking his concentration, and then he realised that her face was vaguely familiar, though from a long time ago.

He'd once had a brilliant memory for faces, though that had gone with renewal. He could not think why he knew her of old. Too late; the Whelm had rounded the curve of the stair directly below and seen him.

From the ranks below the leaders a stream of spears arched up at him, shining in the dim light. He thrust his arm up, directed all the power he had left at the weak point in the stair roof, then scrambled backwards as the ice fell in gigantic blocks, smashing the treads to rubble.

Most of the spears were brought down by the falling ice, but one shot over his shoulder and slammed into the steps above him. He scrabbled up on hands and knees, desperate to get out of the way. He didn't think he'd completely blocked these stairs, but it would buy them time.

Yggur had brought down the second walkway. The third was only connected to the inner tower by one cable, but seven Whelm were pulling themselves across it, clinging upside down by their hands and feet. Terror was etched deep into their faces but they were determined to do their duty.

Yggur lay flat on his back, barely able to move. He'd taken more from himself than he could spare. Colm and Chissmoul were hacking furiously at the remaining cable with jag-swords, one on either side, but their blows were having no effect on it.

Two more Whelm clambered onto the cable, hanging upside down like gangly sloths, .

'Surr!' cried Flangers, who was staring down the first staircase. 'They've found a way up!

'And more will follow,' said Flydd. Which should he attend to?

He left them to Flangers and Chissmoul, staggered across to the cable end and touched the stopper of his fire flask to it.

Crack! The cable snapped with such force that the Whelm clinging to it were catapulted in all directions. Flydd didn't see what became of them, though not even Whelm could survive such a fall.

The tower tilted left, rocked to the right and plunged down at least five spans before it steadied, tilted at an angle of twenty degrees. The rubble blocking the first stairs disappeared as though it had slid down a plughole, carrying the Whelm with it.

'If the inner tower keeps this up, we'll be in the basement by breakfast time,' Colm said wryly.

Flydd went over to Yggur and helped him up. 'When I drew power then, I saw the woman in red again; and I know her face from somewhere – from long ago.'

'I didn't recognise the image I saw earlier.'

'It wasn't a good likeness. She changes her face from time to time.'

'Well, don't use chthonic fire again,' Yggur said limply.

'I'll try not to.' Flydd walked away. The immediate threat of the Whelm had eased but they would soon find another way to attack. They were relentless.

He found the prisoners against the outer wall by the second stair. A few still held ice spears and other weapons, though most were blank-faced and apathetic. They were no use to him, yet he could not abandon them.

Flangers lay slumped against the wall further around, a red stain flowering below his right shoulder. Chissmoul knelt in front of him, attending to the wound.

'That looks bad,' Flydd said, crouching over him.

'I've taken worse,' said Flangers. 'It was a clean spear and it hasn't hit anything vital. It's damn painful, though.'

'I can imagine,' said Flydd. Flangers wouldn't be swinging his sword anytime soon. The odds were lengthening.

He leaned on the wall, taking advantage of the brief respite to run through his options. 'I don't know what to do,' he said to Colm, who was hanging over the outer wall and appeared to be throwing up. 'We can't fight seven hundred. If the Numinator comes back soon, I'm tempted to surrender and pray that she's merciful.'

Colm wiped his mouth on his bloody sleeve and straightened up. 'She won't be.' He bore a gash on his forehead and a bloodstained bandage was wrapped around his left wrist.

'I suppose not. I –'

The tower tilted so far to the left that the prisoners came sliding across the roof towards Flydd. It swayed back to the vertical and slumped another four or five spans in one stomach-lurching rush, before steadying briefly, then slipping down a little further.

Colm began to throw up again. Flydd looked over the wall. The inner tower had dropped about fifteen spans since they'd reached the roof, and was now only half its former height. The ring-shaped area between it and the surrounding Tower of a Thousand Steps was filled with water, floating pieces of ice, bloodline registers, and bodies.

Ice coffins containing those less-than-human corpses, plus jars and amphorae of all sizes with their gruesome contents, were floating amongst pages from the registers. The lower levels of the inner tower must be completely flooded, and every subsidence forced coffins and frozen corpses out into the water. At least the Whelm could not get in from below, unless they swam. Unfortunately, it left Flydd with no way to escape.

The tower sank another span, sending fountains of brown water up on all sides and filling the air with unpleasantly smelling mist. The fountaining water froze in the air and fell back with a million little splashes.

More Whelm were scrambling up the rungs; the platform encircling the inside of the Tower of a Thousand Steps was crowded with them. From the exaggerated jerkiness of their gait, and the wailing and banging of closed fists on their bare chests, they were in torment.

'The master must be dead, else she would have protected her tower!' cried a gangly male, standing on the brink of the platform and rending his clothes in his anguish. 'She'll never return now.'

Another Whelm appeared behind him, a gaunt fellow wearing a black loincloth and a crown of iron barbs. Holding a staff of black iron in his left hand, he banged it on the floor of the platform so hard that chunks of ice crumbled away. He stared across the ring of foul water and his glittering eyes met Flydd's.

'There's no sign of her, and even her eyrie is failing,' the Whelm cried. 'Once more we are masterless, miserable Whelm.'

'What are we to do?' cried the other.

'Bring down the Tower of a Thousand Steps on their heads. Bring it all down!'

FORTY-THREE

'Can she be dead?' said Flangers.

'I doubt it very much,' said Flydd. 'Whelm are an overly emotional race. They'll soon discover their error, I'm sure.'

'Who's that?' said Colm, eyeing the gaunt Whelm wearing the crown of iron barbs.

'A Whelm sorcerer,' said Chissmoul. 'His name is Zofloc; he's the closest they have to a leader.' She shivered. 'He has no eyelids, and eyes like worms impaled on fish hooks, and he never takes them off you.'

Flangers rubbed the neat bandage Chissmoul had made over his shoulder wound. 'Other Whelm have no interest in us; not even in the women prisoners. Even the lowest Whelm see us as beneath them, but Zofloc is different.'

'It was as if he was trying to look right through my skin,' said Chissmoul.

Flangers scowled and gripped the hilt of his jag-blade. 'Where can his power come from?'

'From *me*,' growled Yggur. 'Via the Numinator's bracelets. Get down!'

Flydd ducked behind the wall. A flight of arrows, fired from the platform to their left, skidded across the roof, and screams from the thronged prisoners told that several missiles had found a mark. They scrambled to shelter behind the wall, though Flydd noted chthonic fire creeping across it too. This tower can't last another hour, he thought despairingly. I can do no more to defend it and when it fails we'll be dumped in the icy water, where the Whelm will pick us off with arrows at their leisure. Our only hope lies in the Numinator coming back and saving us, and what a feeble hope that is.

And the irony is, the God-Emperor will never know what happened to his sole remaining enemies. We'll just vanish. The Numinator won't say, if she has survived, and nothing could induce the Whelm to spill their master's secrets.

More Whelm were climbing the rungs, carrying equipment on their backs up to the platform where Zofloc waited, staring unblinkingly at the inner tower, arms folded across his scarred chest.

'What are they doing?' said Chissmoul.

'They've got lengths of twisted metal pipe,' said Colm. 'Copper pipe and glass vessels, and – a huge copper cauldron.'

More pipework was set down on the platform, then a frame assembled from wood, and three Whelm began to fit a contraption together under the supervision of the lidless-eyed sorcerer. The cauldron, which was a good span across, was set on a tripod standing on a hearth assembled from bricks, and filled with ice. A circular copper hood was fitted to the top and clamped tight; coils of pipe were connected to it, spiralling up before passing through an enormous block of ice, and down into a large glass flask.

'It's a still,' said Chissmoul. 'Dad had one at home when I was little, and he showed me how it worked. He used to make spirits from fruit and vegetables and grain – well, anything he could get his hands on, really. He was a bit of a drinker, poor old Dad.'

'What happened to him?' said Flangers.

'He made a bad batch and it killed him.' She sighed. 'We had great fun, Dad and I – when he wasn't drinking.'

'What could they distil out of ice?' said Colm.

'If you put ice in a still,' said Yggur, 'all you get out the other end is water . . .'

'Unless the ice is laced with chthonic fire,' Flydd said dully.

Chunks of black, bituminous material were stacked on the hearth beneath the cauldron. The sorcerer Whelm kindled them by thrusting the end of his staff into the pile. Flames licked up around the cauldron, and soon white fire began dripping into the flask. It looked far brighter than the chthonic flame in Flydd's flask had been, and it had a luminous glow.

Shortly the hood of the cauldron was raised and the water tipped over the edge into the swirling brown flood far below. The cauldron was refilled with fire-laced ice and the process repeated, over and over.

'What can Zofloc want with so much chthonic fire?' said Flydd a good while later. The sorcerer already had far more of it than Flydd had brought to Noom in his little flask.

'He's planning something apocalyptic,' said Yggur, who was sitting up now and looked a little better. 'You've got to stop them, Flydd.'

'I can't,' said Flydd. 'I've got nothing left.'

'Dig deeper. This is the end of the world.'

It wasn't like Yggur to indulge in hyperbole. Flydd felt a chill creep over him, but he could not think of a thing to do. He settled against the wall, shivering, and with every passing minute felt worse. Aftersickness, long delayed, was hitting him hard.

Minutes passed. Every so often a flight of arrows would come at them from a new direction and everyone would scramble around the wall, leaving one or two more bleeding prisoners behind. None of the arrows were aimed at Flydd's little group, however.

'Zofloc is saving us for a special fate,' Yggur said cynically.

The sorcerer Whelm looked like a man who ruled through fear and took pleasure in others' pain, Flydd thought.

473

The distillation continued until the flask was so thick with white fire that its luminous glow lit up the underside of the Tower of a Thousand Steps high above them. Zofloc gave orders and the Whelm began to decant the concentrated chthonic fire into smaller vessels.

'Flangers,' said Flydd, 'you've got good eyes. What's he doing now?'

'They're not as good as they used to be,' said Flangers. Chissmoul helped him up and he stared down at the Whelm. 'Sorry. I can't tell.'

'It looks like they're sealing fire into little rods or darts,' said Chissmoul. 'And fitting them to the tips of arrows.'

Flydd had forgotten that, as a pilot, she'd also had fine eyesight.

'What would chthonic flame do if it were fired into human flesh?' said Yggur quietly.

Flydd's scalp crawled. 'I wouldn't want to find out.'

The sorcerer took one of the dart-tipped arrows. Someone handed him a bow. He fitted the arrow to the bow and swung it around. Yggur ducked hastily, until he realised that the arrow had been aimed down at the water.

'What the blazes is he doing?' said Flangers.

The sorcerer released the arrow, which struck one of the floating, not quite human bodies. The body jerked; its legs and arms thrashed, then it rolled onto its back and began to splash clumsily towards the inner tower. Bubbles dribbled from its open mouth and its eyes shone with the colour of white fire. Zofloc took aim at another floater.

'He's turning the dead into animated corpses, like Phrune,' said Colm.

'How do you stop a corpse?' said Flydd.

'With another corpse,' said Yggur.

'Have you ever animated a corpse before?'

'Of course not!' Yggur cried. 'I abjure the necromantic arts, in all their forms.'

'We'd best not try, then, else Zofloc might seize control of them as well.'

'Block the stairways.'

'I haven't got the strength.'

'Get the prisoners onto it.'

Flydd dragged himself across to the prisoners and ordered them to defend the two stairways. They did not move.

'Look over the side,' he said. 'See the dead in the water. They're not human, are they? But they're coming for you.'

The prisoners set to, furiously heaving the shattered ice blocks into piles to block the stairways at the last turn. Before they had finished, the tower shuddered and settled another five or six spans, jerking down in stages. Brown water spurted up the steps like the sea through a blowhole, sending the workers tumbling over one another and coating everyone in noisome muck that reeked of death long postponed and well overdue. An ice amphora was blasted up to shatter against the perimeter wall. Its contents, the preserved body of an unborn child with a bony crest across the top of its head and a stubby tail, fell to the roof. Chissmoul stared at it, shuddering, then edged it down the steps with the toe of her boot.

One of the prisoners, who was hauling blocks well down the stair, let out a screech and ran on the spot, his bare feet slipping on ice. He made it up a couple of steps, but a dark shape lunged, sank its teeth into his calf and dragged him down into the darkness. Rending and crunching sounds ensued. The remainder of the workers fled up the steps, leaving the stair unblocked, and nothing could induce them to go down again.

Shortly the first of the animated corpses appeared. She would have been a pretty young woman had her skin not been a sickly green. She was followed by a large, shaggy fellow with claws for nails and body hair as thick as felt, though it was falling out in patches across his barrel chest like the coat of a dog with the mange.

Flangers struggled to his feet. He was even paler and had a shake in his good arm.

475

'You can't fight a corpse, Sergeant,' said Flydd.

'Fighting is all I'm good for.'

'The dead don't feel pain or injury; you can't harm them.'

On the other side of the roof, the prisoners began to scream, then stampeded across. More shaggy figures were clambering out of the second stair.

'What about fire?' said Colm. '*Real* fire, I mean.'

'We haven't got anything to burn.'

'Sorcerous fire then.'

'I couldn't light a splinter at the moment.'

Flydd tried not to listen to the screams as the animated dead attacked the prisoners. There was nothing anyone could do. He held Flangers back.

'Stay with us, soldier, and that's an order.'

'It's my duty to protect the weak and the innocent, surr.'

'It's your duty to be here when I need you. The fate of the world may depend on Yggur and me getting out of here, and that depends on you.'

Flangers remained where he was, though he did not look pleased about it.

The prisoners had worked out a way of attacking the corpses: a dozen men and women would take hold of each one and hold it down until its head could be cut off and hurled over the side. It was crude and moderately effective – the headless bodies blundered about in circles, attacking whatever they touched, whether human, ice or other corpses. But more dead were coming up all the time and soon they would outnumber the prisoners. Flydd could feel the tension gnawing at him, the familiar burning pain in the middle of his chest. He didn't have the strength for it, but if he couldn't save them now, no one could.

'There's only one way left,' he said to Yggur. 'Assuming I can make it work.'

Flydd withdrew the mimemule from an inner pocket, stripped his concealing illusion from it, and laid it on his palm while he tried to prepare himself. This was really going to hurt.

'Is that what I think it is?' said Yggur, perking up visibly.

'I have no idea what you think it is,' Flydd said evasively. 'Quiet. I've got to think.'

'I think it's a *mimemule*.' Yggur hauled himself to his feet. 'And to the best of my knowledge there was only ever one mimemule on Santhenar.'

'Not now, Yggur,' Flydd said warningly, for Colm was walking their way and the last thing Flydd wanted was for him to discover the truth. Too late – he'd seen it.

'What's a mimemule?' said Colm, gazing at the grubby, battered ball of wood.

'A mimicking device,' said Yggur, 'and therefore forbidden to the Faellem, but Faelamor –'

Colm's head shot around. 'Faelamor?' He sniffed the air.

'She brought it from Tallallame,' said Yggur, ignoring Flydd's frantic efforts to shut him up. 'It was one of her greatest treasures, for it could be used to mimic almost anything, even devices of great power. Where did you get it, Flydd?'

'I've had it for ages,' lied Flydd. 'Hush, this is a difficult Art to master –'

Colm snatched the mimemule from Flydd's hand, put it under his own nose and sniffed deeply. 'You bastard!' he roared, his eyes starting out of his head. 'You stinking, thieving mongrel. I know that smell – it must have been buried in Faelamor's cave. This is part of my heritage, and you stole it from me.'

Flydd flushed. 'You renounced your heritage, if you recall, and stormed out of the cave.'

'You hid the mimemule, you filthy liar, then took advantage of me. And you . . . you . . .' Colm was almost incoherent with rage. 'You provoked me to renounce my heritage! You must have been plotting to take it from me all the time, even back in the Nightland.'

Yggur was staring down at Flydd from his lofty height, looking faintly disgusted.

'I did not; not at all.' Flydd snatched the mimemule back and held Colm at bay with his jag-sword. 'You stormed out of the cave, if you recall, and it was only then that Maelys found –' Why, why had he mentioned her name? He'd made things worse, far worse, and there was no way to get out of it now.

'You mean *she* was in on it too?' Colm shrieked, so loudly that the animated dead turned their heads towards him, and so did Zofloc the sorcerer on the distant platform. 'I knew there was something sick about you, the moment I met you. And as for Maelys, the little bitch –'

Yggur, who had been watching Flydd's discomfort with a certain amusement, put up his hand and said quietly, 'That'll do, Colm. You're undermining the prisoners' faith in us, and it can only make things worse. Besides, since you did renounce your heritage, the treasure belongs to the first person to find it.'

'He knew I didn't mean it,' Colm said savagely.

'Then why say it? How is anyone to know what you intend? Too late to cry about it now; it's done. What's your plan, Flydd?'

'The mimemule created the portal that brought us here –'

'Really?' breathed Yggur. 'How did you do that?'

'I'd brought Rulke's virtual construct with us. The model on which his real construct was based.'

'Clever! How did you know it was in the Nightland?'

'I must have read about it in the Histories. Or the *Tale of the Mirror*.'

'That bit wasn't in the final tale. It was deliberately left out at my request, just in case.'

Flydd felt another chill, but just shrugged. 'Who knows where I might have read it in the archives of the scrutators?' And yet, he was sure he never had read it, *so how could he know*? 'I tried to get us out of Dunnet with the virtual construct but I couldn't get it to work –'

'Dunnet!' Yggur looked shaky again. 'You've been to Dunnet. Were . . .'

For once Flydd felt for him, for that valley had been the scene of his most devastating defeat and he was still scarred by it. 'The bones of your men lie where they fell.'

Yggur slumped against the ice wall, breathing heavily. 'I'll never forget that day, as long as I live. A whole army dead, for nothing.'

After a decent pause, Flydd went on. 'Anyway, Maelys accidentally touched the virtual construct with the mimemule bag and the portal opened instantly.'

Yggur stood up again and, with an effort, regained control of himself. 'So the mimemule mimicked the virtual construct. How interesting. Why didn't you make another portal hours ago?'

'I didn't have the strength. And I was afraid that the Numinator had opened another, up at the top of her tower. Two portals so close together could be deadly.'

'Indeed. But the portal could still be there, and you've got even less strength now.'

'Enough of your confounded questioning! I'm desperate now. Though I haven't got much white fire left. If I can make a new portal, it may not remain open long.'

'Not long enough for all the prisoners to get through?'

'Probably not, so what do I do? I'm damned if I go without them and doubly damned if I can only save half of them. And then there's Maelys.'

'Your partner in crime,' said Yggur. Colm clenched his fists.

The prisoners stampeded across the roof again, with forty or fifty animated dead close behind.

'Better use the mimemule,' said Yggur. 'Quick!'

Flydd upended the fire flask onto the mimemule, clenched his fist about it, thought about how the last portal had come into being, and prayed. The funnel of the portal opened with a boom that shook rotten ice down from above and dropped the inner tower another few spans into the rising brown water. It had reached the top of the stairs now, and if the tower slipped another span, water would flood over the wall.

A hot wind boiled out of the portal, condensing to steam which formed little whirling needles of ice in the frigid air of Noom. 'It's worked,' said Flydd, staggering with after-sickness. 'Go through, everyone!'

No one moved. 'There's someone at the other end,' said Chissmoul.

'What? There can't be.' Flydd peered down the funnel, which was a good hundred paces long, but his eyes were still watering too much to see.

'There is. It's a woman.'

Flydd cursed. 'This portal must have intersected with the Numinator's one, and she's coming back from the Nightland.'

'It doesn't look like the Numinator,' Chissmoul said uncertainly. 'It's much taller and bigger all around.'

Flydd rubbed his streaming eyes but only saw a red blur.

Yggur laughed. 'It's your woman in red, Flydd. You get to meet her in the flesh at last –'

'What's the matter?' Flydd felt a deep unease.

Yggur took a couple of steps forwards, staring down the tunnel, his jaw slack. 'I know her,' he said wonderingly. 'But . . . that's not possible.'

'How could *you* know her?' said Flydd.

'Because that woman was in the *Tale of the Mirror*, which I lived through. I thought she was dead. I thought the lot of them were dead.'

'What are you talking about?' said Flydd. He could see her coming now. She resembled the woman in red, though only slightly.

'They went back to the void to die, but at least one of them did not die,' said Yggur. 'Your woman in red is Yalkara.'

'Yalkara?' Flydd said dazedly. 'The Charon?'

'After Rulke, she was the greatest of all the Charon, and one of the few survivors of The Hundred who came out of the void all those thousands of years ago and seized the world of Aachan for themselves. That's why her face was familiar – you would have seen engravings of her image in the Histories. How did she survive; and what is she doing here?'

A very good question, Flydd thought, and here's a better one. Why did I hallucinate about her during my renewal, and why have I seen her shadowing me since?

And what can the second most powerful of the Charon possibly want from me?

FORTY-FOUR

Water surged up the stairs as the inner tower slipped down another few ells. Fragments of rotten, honeycombed ice showered down from on high. Those animated corpses who still had heads stirred; from the platform where Zofloc had built the copper still a lone archer fired arrow after arrow. The surviving prisoners, reduced to half their original number, surged out of the line of sight, a terrified, mindless herd.

Flydd only had eyes for the figure walking slowly down the portal tunnel. He could see her clearly now – a tall, statuesque woman of no particular age, wearing dark magenta robes that would have looked terrible on anyone else, though the colour suited her olive skin perfectly. They trailed out behind her, rippling in the blast. No one would have called her beautiful, for her long face was too strong featured for that. Her hair, the colour of fine white silk, was worn shoulder-length and barely moved as she walked.

'Yalkara?' he croaked as she approached the mouth of the tunnel, for his mouth had gone dry.

'That I am,' she said in a deep, raspy voice.

'I am Xervish Flydd –'

'I have known you.' As she stepped out of the tunnel

onto the roof of the inner tower, steam rose around her boots. The staring prisoners moaned and backed away. The Whelm archer stopped firing, his bow hanging loosely from its string. Even the sorcerer Whelm, Zofloc, laid down the chunk of chthonic fire-riven ice he had been hefting into the still to stare at her.

'Aiieeee!' a Whelm cried, distantly.

Flydd stared at Yalkara, trying to work out what she had meant.

Yggur chuckled. 'She used you, Flydd, and you never knew.'

Flydd flushed as he took Yggur's meaning. '*You* were Bel?' When she turned her head he could see the resemblance, just, though Bel had been plump and soft. There was nothing soft in Yalkara; she was as hard as the Whelm's black metal jag-swords.

'At the time,' said Yalkara, 'I was so weak the only guise I could manage was the one you lusted after so desperately. Where is the other portal?'

Flydd looked up. The underside of the Tower of a Thousand Steps, fifty spans above, was faintly webbed with white fire now, and he could see another platform there. 'Right at the very top of the tower, I assume.'

'Show me the way.'

'Why did you use me?' Flydd grated. It irked him that she'd used him as the woman in red, and as Bel. Maelys had tried to talk to him about Bel on the way to Dunnet, he recalled, but he'd refused to listen, refused to believe that she wasn't one of Jal-Nish's mancers, using him for some cunning purpose the God-Emperor didn't dare do himself. It irked him even more that he didn't have the faintest idea what was going on. He'd known everything, once, and he didn't like being kept in the dark.

'Because I needed to,' said Yalkara, turning away. 'Yggur.'

Yggur inclined his head to her.

'You appear to have developed a backbone since our

last encounter,' she went on. 'You were anguishing over some woman, as I recall.'

Yggur flushed, ever so faintly, and Flydd took a grim pleasure in seeing it.

'I thought she mattered to me,' said Yggur. 'I must have been wrong, since I can no longer remember her name.'

Yalkara smiled knowingly. 'You will never forget her name. Take me to the other portal.'

'Answer my questions, first,' said Flydd. *'Why me?'*

She grimaced. 'I don't have time for this.'

'Make time. You came to me when I took renewal. *Why me?'*

'Oh, very well! You were the only mancer of any consequence I could touch. I dared not go near your God-Emperor, or his acolytes, and nothing would have induced me to approach Vivimord. I could not risk becoming entangled in such a depraved mind in my helpless state.'

'Where were you?'

'Trapped in the void, which touches all places equally. Besides, Thuntunnimoe, which you call Mistmurk Mountain, was mine once, and I have a special bond with it. It is one of the few places on Santhenar to which I am still linked.'

'So you entered my mind during renewal, seeking to influence me.'

'I sought to *take control* of you at the moment you were weakest. I tried to meld my mind and yours but it did not go well – there's always a risk of that with renewal – and the trauma caused you to forget your Art. My intervention made things worse. You would have been easier to control if I had kept away until renewal was complete.'

'Why did you need to control me?' cried Flydd. 'What do I have that you could possibly need?'

'You were planning to use the shadow realm to escape, and that place is not so far removed from the Nightland. I schooled you in the Art so, instead of the shadow realm, you might open the way to the Nightland for me. I invested everything in you. I led you to Thuntunnimoe in the first place; I put the idea into your mind that it was a perfect refuge for you; I came to you in your vapour-induced sleep and taught you about the cursed flame. At every critical stage of your escape I was beside you, making sure you had the Arts you needed to survive, but you proved difficult to control and kept thwarting me.

'Then, at the critical moment, and despite all my earlier suggestions, when you opened the portal you forced it towards the shadow realm after all. I had to tear it out of your grasp and point it to the Nightland by myself. It nearly killed me; the pain was so awful I could not reach the portal in time, and you went without me. After ten years of striving, I had failed.'

The anguish was visible on her face, but she did not seem the weaker for it. On the contrary, Flydd thought.

'I kept seeing you,' he said. 'Just flashes of red shadow and a fluttering of robes. I was sure you were hunting me.'

'I was, but there is no way into the Nightland from the void.'

'So that's why you came to Flydd as Bel,' said Colm, mouth twisted.

'As you escaped the Nightland, I managed to latch onto your portal, trying to get in. Unfortunately it only allowed travel one way, so I rode it to Santhenar, near Plogg, and disguised myself as Bellulah.'

'You used me!' Throughout his life, Flydd had used countless people to get what he wanted, yet he smouldered at the thought of her using him. He wasn't blind to the irony, but it still irked him.

'I paid your price,' said Yalkara. 'Bel gave you a night you'll remember all your life, and you can't deny it.'

Again that knowing chuckle from Yggur.

'Why didn't you take the flasks of white fire when you had the chance?' said Flydd.

'I dared not touch it. If chthonic fire had been the

answer, I would have gone back to the Nightland two centuries ago, instead of going to the void –'

A dozen animated dead were advancing towards them. Yalkara held out her hand, palm upwards; the fire-filled darts slid from their bodies and they slumped to the roof, lifeless again. On the platform, Zofloc raised his bow, its dart tip glowing. She snapped her cocked wrist at him and the dart burst, spurting distilled fire everywhere. He beat furiously at his skin as she turned back to Flydd.

'But . . .' he said.

'Chthonic fire is *mine*. I brought it here from Aachan in ages past, and long before that, I took it from the exploded core of a comet in the deepest part of the void. Chthonic fire is a potent force whose essence easily slips between the dimensions of space and time; that's why it enables portals so powerfully – and animates the dead. But it's a perilous material to handle, especially for us Charon. Would that I'd known that when I first found it.'

Yggur bestowed a knowing glance on Flydd; *I warned you.*

'That's why I hid it deep below Thuntunnimoe,' Yalkara continued, 'and surrounded it with all manner of protections so no one would ever find it. No one on Santhenar knew it was there – I knew it would never be safe otherwise, nor would the Three Worlds be safe from it. But I made a terrible mistake. By trying to possess *your* mind, and giving you the Arts you needed to create a portal, I left open a tiny chink in my own psyche. Then, when you were struggling to escape from the God-Emperor, and you could find no other way to open the portal, desperation showed you that chink in my mind. You saw where I had hidden the chthonic fire and broke open the forbidden casket.

'You should not have brought it here.' She looked up at the Tower of a Thousand Steps, its structure threaded with white fire. 'As you will shortly discover.'

'But *you* could have used it safely at the obelisk,' said Flydd. 'There's no ice on Mistmurk Mountain.'

'Chthonic fire is inimical to us, and I no longer have the power to use it safely. Nothing endures forever, not even us Charon; my once great Arts are failing. I showed you how to make the portal because I no longer had the power to do so myself.'

Fool, fool! Flydd remembered how smug he'd felt, that he'd learned how to make it so easily.

'Then why didn't you force me to make a portal at Plogg, when I was under your enchantment?'

'It couldn't be made there – your incoming portal had twisted the fabric of reality too strongly. The nearest suitable place was the pinnacle you used at Dunnet. I had to keep you alive to get there, and you must admit I did my best. Not even the God-Emperor could have done what I did that night, though it nearly killed me.'

'But you didn't seize the portal I made on the pinnacle.'

'I couldn't reach it in time either. I was too weak. I had to gather my strength to take your next portal.'

'How did you know I would make another?'

'You weren't going to *walk* back from Noom. But you didn't make the next portal – the Numinator did – and she was gone before I could take it from her.' Her lips compressed to a white line. 'But now I must, for she's after the same thing as I am.'

'And that is?' said Flydd.

'I've answered all the questions you have a right to ask. The Nightland is my business.'

'So it was *you* who recreated it after it collapsed, and held it in place all this time.'

'I did – to the vast diminution of my powers, and I maintain the Nightland still, though not even *I* can hold it much longer. That's why I had to use you. I was desperate – too desperate.'

'What are you holding it for?' said Yggur.

Yalkara did not reply. Withdrawing a brass-framed lens from her robes, she peered through it, straight up. Colours danced there. 'Ah!' she said. 'I see how this works.'

She stepped backwards into the portal, spun the lens on its engraved handle, and a spasm twisted her strong face. Flydd gasped as the portal was torn from his grasp, then she traced a spiral into the middle of the lens with a finger-tip and the far end of the portal swung vertically. Yalkara shot upwards through the length of the portal, towards the top of the tower and out of sight.

'Aiiieeee!' cried a host of Whelm, straining forwards like a pack of wild dogs.

The dead on the roof began to grope blindly for the darts Yalkara had ejected from their bodies. High above, a bright light flared; a dull boom echoed down. Every white tracery of fire on the ice flared, before fading again. The inner tower dropped sharply and a wave of stinking water surged over the sides.

'It's going under this time,' cried Colm.

'Let's get going!' said Yggur.

'But the portal only goes up.'

The dead were moving purposefully towards them, even the headless ones, and in the deep water surrounding the inner tower hundreds more began stroking in their direction.

'Up beats under,' said Yggur. He raised his voice. 'Into the portal, everyone.'

Flydd was waiting for the prisoners to go first, but no one moved. 'Flydd, Colm, Chissmoul, Flangers, don't wait,' snapped Yggur.

Flydd pushed into the funnel-shaped portal entrance, followed by a jostling throng, and was hurled upwards into the Tower of a Thousand Steps with a stomach-lurching jerk. He expected to be ejected in the Numinator's eyrie, but the portal ended a couple of spans above the upper platform. Evidently the portal wasn't meant to carry this many people and, once they'd entered it, it had contracted to half its previous length.

'The portal's shrinking!' he yelled, jumping down onto the ring-shaped platform that ran all the way around the inside of the tower. An oval hall bored through the ice ran off to his right. 'Jump, or you'll end up back where we came from.'

On the rooftop of the inner tower, fifty spans below, the prisoners were forcing their way into the portal-tunnel and being carried up, but there were still about twenty outside and they weren't going to make it. More dead were churning through the stinking water and clawing over the wall, which was now awash, then pulling the prisoners under as if they were to blame for the horrors the Numinator had visited upon them.

Flydd strained to hold his end of the portal in place until the rest of the prisoners could scramble out, but it continued to contract downwards. Its mouth was level with the platform now; if it contracted further, anyone leaving it would fall fifty spans into the water. Another ten prisoners scrambled out, then a clot of five, punching and shoving each other in their desperation to escape, and finally another five or six, one after another.

'Yggur?' Flydd yelled. He couldn't see him in the portal, or on the flooded roof of the inner tower, and he couldn't hold the mouth in place any longer. 'Drag them out,' he gasped.

Colm began to heave people out of the portal and hurl them to the left. Chissmoul was doing the same, as best she could, but the portal suddenly contracted until the exit stood half a span below them.

'Floria!' shrieked a stocky young man, standing at the edge of the platform. 'Jump.'

A yellow-haired woman reached up to him with both arms. 'I'll never make it, Gaz,' she wailed. 'It's too far.'

'I'll catch you. Jump.'

Floria did her best, and her upstretched hands clasped onto Gaz's, but he was leaning out so far he couldn't hold her. Her weight pulled him over and they plunged down, wrapping their arms around each other, and into the water beside the tower. Three of the dead converged on the point where they had disappeared, and dived. None of them came up.

The tunnel shrank again. Now it was a span and a half below them. Yggur appeared, labouring up its slope, for the failing portal was no longer carrying people all the way. He reached the mouth, picked up a terrified woman and hurled her bodily upwards onto the platform. He did the same with a youth and an old man wearing spectacles as thick as marbles, then turned to the few people below him, but they were sliding down towards the water where the inner tower roof had been. It was completely gone now, breaking apart underwater to form bobbing brown icebergs. The last of the dog-paddling prisoners from the roof were pulled under.

Yggur tossed up one last prisoner, a slip of a girl cling- ing leech-like to his left ankle, then perched on the rim and sprang upwards like a gymnast. He would have made it save that his weight forced the portal's exit down. He hit the edge of the floor with his upper chest, bounced off, fell but managed to catch on with one hand.

Flangers grabbed his wrist and tried to hold him, but Yggur couldn't get a grip on the ice and his fingers were slowly slipping free, and Flangers was being pulled out- wards as well.

Chissmoul ran and caught hold of Flangers with both hands but couldn't hold him either, and finally in despera- tion she stood on Yggur's hand with both feet. It held him just long enough for Colm to catch his other hand, take his weight, and together they heaved him up.

'Thanks,' Yggur said, shaking his squashed fingers and scowling at Chissmoul. 'For such a little thing, you cer- tainly weigh a lot.'

Demure little Chissmoul put her hands in the middle of his chest, and alarm shivered across Yggur's face, for he was standing on the brink. Flydd chuckled.

'Thank you, Chissmoul,' Yggur said, more gracefully. 'I though my end had come.'

She walked backwards and he followed her to safety. 'But you've lived more than a thousand years, surr. How could *you* die?'

'I don't age as other men do, but I can be killed as easily as anyone.' He looked down at the prisoners who had fallen out of the portal and were thrashing in the water. 'Poor devils.'

'It could have been us,' said Colm.

'But it wasn't,' said Flydd, eyeing the Whelm, who were scrambling into an opening in the wall behind Zofloc's still. 'We've been spared so we can die a different but equally horrible death.'

'Where do we go now?'

'They must be heading for the Thousand Steps.'

'They're trying to cut us off from reaching the Numinator's eyrie,' said Yggur. 'How do we reach the Thousand Steps?'

'They can't be hard to find,' said Flydd. 'The tower isn't very wide up here. Follow me.'

He darted into the oval hall and ran down to another hall, then glanced left and right. To the right he saw steps. 'Ah! This way.'

He hurried to the Thousand Steps and began to climb. 'Should be called the Tower of a Million Steps,' he muttered, feeling his age before he'd gone two flights.

Below, he could hear the racket made by the Whelms' wooden sandals, hundreds of pairs of them, coming up in dreadful haste. Flydd felt sure they would catch the stragglers before the top, but didn't dare put on an extra burst of speed. That would leave nothing for the end, and the end was not far away.

He was labouring now, gasping with every step, and many of the prisoners had passed him already. Colm went by, his long legs moving tirelessly. He did not glance at Flydd as he passed, and Flydd knew that nothing had been forgiven.

On he struggled, ever upwards. Only Flangers was

below him now, with Chissmoul supporting him, but they weren't going to make it. The Whelm were only two flights below, and as Flydd turned, a brutally scarred male aimed a short spear at Flangers's back.

Flydd wrenched off a piece of fire-riven ice and hurled it down at the Whelm. It burst in his face and he fell backwards, crashing into the two Whelm below him and carrying them down as well. Zofloc, directly below them, ducked aside and allowed them to fall. He held something glassy in his left hand, swirling with luminosity – the flask containing the distilled fire.

A chill crept down Flydd's back. If those few wisps of chthonic flame he'd brought here could do all this damage, what ruin might a whole flask of concentrated chthonic flame wreak?

They staggered up the last few flights together. The prisoners, under Yggur's direction, were building a wall of ice blocks across the top of the stair into the Numinator's eyrie.

Flydd was so weary he had to crawl over the wall. There was no sign of Yalkara. 'Where's the portal to the Nightland?'

'Yalkara must have hidden it after she went through. Get us out of here, Flydd. Anywhere.'

Flydd slumped beside the fire bowl. 'At the moment I couldn't make a portal from one pocket to the other.'

'Then we'll have to fight on until you're better; or it doesn't matter any more.'

'Or the Numinator comes back through her portal to finish us off.'

FORTY-FIVE

Maelys slid blindly across the black floor of the Nightland and came to a stop against a fluted column
whose upper end soared beyond sight. She was stinging
all over from the chthonic flame, even inside her furs and
boots, and her eyes were watering so badly that she could
barely see. She wiped them on the inside of her coat, noted
the tiny white flickers die there, and looked around.

The Nightland was the same impenetrable gloom as
before, however she had the impression that her arrival
had made a loud cracking noise, which surely the Numinator must have heard, so where was she? Maelys crawled
around the buttress and made out a glimmer in the distance. Could that be her?

The light seemed to be growing and spreading, and
Maelys felt a spasm of panic, for her column was too
obvious a hiding place. Which way to go? Away from the
approaching light was too predictable so she turned right.

Maelys's innards were knotted again, but at least the
effect of the flame had faded to a peculiarly sensual tingling
all over; it felt as though all her senses had been height-
ened. The floor had such a creamy silkiness that every
movement was like having the soles of her feet stroked.
Her ears were hot inside and she could hear sounds she'd

never heard before: a faint breathy sigh, as though the Nightland was breathing, and a distant thumping like a slowly beating heart.

No – that was the Numinator's metronomically regular footsteps and she was heading this way. Maelys could see her clearly now, for she was shimmering all over with chthonic fire, and she held the ice stiletto in her right hand. Its poison-yellow churning core looked deadly.

You fool, Maelys told herself. You should not have followed her. The Numinator was fanatical about her privacy and would not tolerate any intrusion on it. But if Maelys had not come here, she would never see Emberr again; if she had not come, Emberr would have been killed.

Where to hide? Maelys noticed that her hands were still covered with a faint tracery of chthonic fire – not nearly as bright as the fire lapping the Numinator, but enough to give her away in the Nightland.

Pulling her sleeves down, and her hood low over her face, she crawled away, worrying she might even be leaving a fiery trail. She looked back. Tiny worms of light glimmered at the base of the column, and the Numinator could hardly miss them if she looked that way, but Maelys couldn't see any on the floor.

She had just set off again, head down, when she felt a slow surge of air, as from a large door being slammed, and made out a hiss, as of a sharply indrawn breath. The Numinator was looking around in alarm.

Maelys lay flat on the floor, watching her from the corner of her eye. Was the Numinator afraid that prisoners were held here, or beasts from the void? It was an uncomfortable thought, but even if there were, Maelys had to get to Emberr and warn him. She'd broken her word and betrayed his trust, and she had to make up for it.

The Numinator shook her head and continued, following a series of zigzagging curves sweeping out to left and right. If she kept to that pattern, the next time she headed right she would see Maelys.

As soon as she turned away on the other arm of the zig-zag, Maelys changed course and scuttled into the deepest darkness she could find. Since she had no idea where she was, it made no difference which way she went.

The Numinator turned sharply and headed directly for her, the poisoned stiletto jerking up and stabbing down with every stride. She must have seen her. Maelys was unarmed, for she had lost her club on the Thousand Steps; she dared not let the Numinator get close. She sprang to her feet, slipping on the smooth surface, and ran for her life.

'Stop, Maelys Nifferlin,' cried the Numinator, 'or it will go worse for you.'

The stiletto was upraised, ready to throw. Maelys swerved from side to side, to make herself a more difficult target, then raced on, expecting to feel the blade sear into her flesh. It did not, and after a minute she glanced back. The Numinator was jogging after her, but she was not a young woman and was being left behind. Maelys's boots were making a racket, though.

She took them off and stuffed her socks into them. Her bare feet glistened faintly but the Numinator might not see them from a distance. Veering to her left, Maelys ran silently and randomly until she could no longer see the faintest glimmer of her enemy. She slowed to a fast walk, fretting. Would the Numinator continue after her, or go for Emberr?

She would go after him, of course, and the stiletto was not a defensive weapon. Maelys tried to remember what the Numinator had said after learning about Emberr. Not much, though it was clear she knew who he was. Emberr had never been out of the Nightland, though, so why had the Numinator come after him in such haste? Only two reasons came to mind: to revenge herself on his mother by killing him, or to eliminate him because he posed some threat to her.

She stopped, shivering and rubbing her arms; the soles

of her feet were tingling on the cold floor; she felt exquisitely sensitive all over, and she remembered every detail of his face and figure as clearly as if he stood before her now.

Emberr was in deadly danger, but how was she to find him? Previously he had scented her; he had spoken into her mind, then she had answered and he had heard her voice. Could she open herself to him the same way?

Emberr? she said softly.

There was no answer. Perhaps he was asleep. It could be the middle of the night here; there was no way of telling. Or she might be too far away.

Emberr?

What if the Numinator could also pick up her call? Maelys couldn't allow herself to think about that. She had to find him first and hope that, together, they could get him out of here. What had he said – that he couldn't leave *unless a woman took his place.*

Maelys had a wicked thought; so shocking that she immediately shied away from it. No, she had to consider it, for Emberr would never be safe while the Numinator was free. Could she trap her here forever and allow Emberr to go free in her place?

It was a terrible thing to do to anyone but, Maelys reminded herself, the Numinator was a monster who had ruined thousands of lives through her failed bloodline project. And she had come here to kill Emberr. It was a fitting exchange. It would be justice.

Emberr? She put all her passion, her loneliness and desperation into the call.

Maelys? Have you really come back?

The tingling washed across her body again, and Maelys felt her nipples harden. *I had to see you again.*

Where are you? I can't smell your scent at all. Walk about; wave your arms in the air.

She did so, feeling flushed and faint at the thought of him finding her by her scent. Her knees were trembling;

she wanted to lie down, but she had to warn him, protect him, free him.

I don't know where I am. Emberr, you're in terrible danger. You're being hunted by the Numinator, and she's a powerful mancer.

Is she the woman who has come to free me and take my place?

I think she's your mother's enemy. She carries a poisoned stiletto and I'm scared she wants to kill you.

The Numinator? he said thoughtfully, not sounding concerned at all. *Does that mean 'The Numinous One'?*

'I don't know what numinous means,' Maelys said aloud, frustrated that he was ignoring the danger. Yet after spending his entire life in the Nightland, all alone, how could he understand the evils of the real world? How could he understand the malice, bitterness and rage that drove some people until they became inhuman monsters, incapable of feeling for their fellow men and women?

It's to do with a divine power or spirit . . .

'Not another one!' Maelys exclaimed, thinking about the God-Emperor.

Does she act like a divinity?

'No. She dwells in the frozen south and talks to no one save her faithful Whelm.'

Perhaps the title is meant to inspire fear and keep people at a distance. Ah, I'm picking up your scent. He sighed dreamily. *Maelys, Maelys. I know where you are. Would you turn to your right?*

She did so.

A little further.

She complied, and Emberr said, *Come to me, my love. Quiet now*, and he was gone.

My love! He called me his love. Maelys's eyes flooded; she swayed on her feet, quite overcome.

Again she felt that rush of air and was reminded that the Nightland could have a myriad of unknown dangers. She wiped her eyes and told herself to stop being a stupid romantic girl. To save Emberr, she had to keep all her wits about her; she had to be as tough as the Numinator herself. But not as hard. Never as hard.

She went forwards as she had done last time, walking blindly into the darkest recesses of the Nightland but this time trusting Emberr completely. She knew instinctively that he would never deceive or trick her. Knew with absolute surety that he was *the one*.

That shocked her, and Maelys had to stop for a moment to rub her hands on the cold floor and press them to her inflamed face. Her girlish passion for Nish, and her brief affection for Colm, she now knew to be mere infatuations born out of the romantic daydreams she'd indulged herself with through all the terrible years after Nifferlin Manor had been torn down and her clan lost. With Nish and Colm, though, she'd always had doubts; now she had none. This was the real thing – Emberr would be the love of her life.

Her face was still burning. Cooling her hands again, she rubbed them over her cheeks and throat, trying to regain some semblance of self-control. She felt as though she was boiling inside, and her tingling skin had become so sensitive that every movement was exquisite torment.

On Maelys went, step by slow step, in such a fever that she had no idea how far she had gone, or how long she had been walking. It must have been hours, though, for her empty stomach was grumbling and she felt faint from hunger before she finally saw the yellow lights of Emberr's cottage windows in the distance, then the door opening and the silhouette of a tall man blocking out the light shining from within.

Her self-control vanished and, letting out a glad cry of 'Emberr!', she ran to him, able to think of nothing but flinging herself into his arms. She did not think for an instant that he might have tricked her or lain some enchantment on her, to trap her here so he could go free. She trusted him utterly.

He was at the gate when she reached it, and he was dressed, as before, in just a knee-length kilt.

He swung open the gate of weathered grey wood. 'Maelys, my love, I have never stopped thinking about you. Every moment you were gone I prayed that you would come back, though I never expected you would manage it where my own mother, with all her mighty Arts, could not.'

She looked up at him and hesitated, suddenly feeling shy. She had no idea what to say or do. 'I – I –'

'I don't know the words either,' Emberr said, smiling down at her, 'but sometimes, words aren't needed.' He frowned at a private thought, quivered as if going through some internal struggle, then dismissed it and opened his arms.

She did not hesitate now. Maelys threw her arms around him and pressed her cheek against his bare chest, and he felt so right, so *safe*, that for a few seconds the Numinator went completely out of her mind.

'You're shivering,' said Emberr. 'Are you cold, my love?'

'I'm not cold . . . but I am hungry.'

'Come inside.'

Taking her by the hand, he led her up the steps and closed the door behind her. He took her through a small entrance hall into a room with thick rugs on the floor and a fire flickering in a grate. The Nightland flames gave forth little heat, but they were very cheery.

'There *is* something the matter, though, isn't there, Maelys?'

It came flooding back and she had to tell him, had to reveal that she'd betrayed his trust, no matter what happened once she had. 'The Numinator,' she gasped. 'It's my fault, Emberr. She forced me to tell; she used some spell. I couldn't resist it.'

'Then how can you be blamed?'

'But I've betrayed you to your mother's enemy. She's coming to kill you.'

'I don't think so, Maelys.'

Why wouldn't he listen? 'Emberr, please.'

'She cannot harm me here. I'm well protected.'

'Are you sure? I'm really afraid . . .'

'I'm very sure. My cottage cannot be found unless I will it; it was made that way. You're perfectly safe.'

Maelys felt it too – the moment the door had closed behind her, the threat of the Numinator had faded away. She sat on a cushion and watched him go back and forth, preparing titbits for her. He handed her the platter and sat opposite, watching her while she ate. Maelys had no idea what she was eating, and after taking several morsels she laid the platter aside and went to his arms again, letting out a little sigh.

'I feel all hot and inflamed inside.' She'd never felt this way before. 'And ever since I came through the portal, my skin has been tingling so much that I can hardly bear the way my clothes rub against me.'

'Then you must take your clothes off, Maelys.'

She did not hesitate, though she did feel rather shy at revealing herself. When they were piled on a chair he looked her up and down, at the white chthonic flames still shimmering faintly all over her, and gave her an enigmatic smile. 'You truly are the woman who will free me. Come.'

And she went to him.

Maelys lay in a daze afterwards, then drifted into a blissful sleep, cradled in his arms. She had never felt so warm, so safe, so fulfilled.

She woke slowly, not knowing whether mere minutes had passed, or hours, but with a feeling that something wasn't right. She felt chilly, and alone again, though Emberr was still with her, sound asleep. The fire in the grate had gone out and the room was cold. She disengaged herself, careful not to wake him, stood up, and the back of her neck prickled. The Numinator was out there some-where – how could she have been so bewitched as to put

500

her out of mind just because Emberr said they were safe? How could he be sure his cottage was hidden from her? He'd never met her; never left the Nightland, while her mighty Arts had once controlled a whole world.

Maelys looked down at him lovingly. His skin was so fine and pale, and the lines of chthonic fire that had been flickering on her skin now moved in ghostly patterns all over him. He seemed so contented and peaceful that she couldn't bear to wake him, but he was in terrible danger. She went to the front door, eased it open and looked out. And jumped.

The Numinator was not far from the gate, standing with her head cocked to one side, staring at the cottage, though Maelys did not think she could see it. The stiletto was still in her hand and yellow fumes were writhing up from its hilt. Heart crashing in her chest, Maelys tried to ease the door closed, but at the movement the Numinator's head shot around and she saw her; saw everything. By opening the door, Maelys must have broken Emberr's enchantment and revealed his cottage.

She leapt backwards, slammed the door and tried to lock it, but there was no lock or bolt. She ran to Emberr, shook him and hissed into his ear, 'Quick! The Numinator is here; she knows where you live. I'm sorry; I'm sorry!'

Maelys ran back, clothes in hand, and put her back against the door. She was trying to scramble into her pants when a blow on the front door forced it open and sent her skidding across the floor.

The Numinator stepped in, and there was a peculiar light in her eyes, an inner glow that Maelys could not quite reconcile with the satisfaction of imminent revenge. She got up, gathered her fallen garments and backed down the hall to where she and Emberr had lain together. The Numinator followed her in. She glanced at Maelys, then at Emberr who lay naked on the rugs with his back to her, dimly illuminated by the white fire on his skin. The Numinator took a deep, shuddering breath; the stiletto hung loosely from her hand as if forgotten. What was going on?

Maelys dressed hastily, her face flaming. The Numinator walked around Emberr, studying him in a way that made Maelys smoulder. How dare she look at *her* man so! The Numinator crouched to look at his face, then gasped and rocked back on her heels, the stiletto rolling across the floor towards the fireplace. Maelys watched it all the way, wondering if she could dive on it before the Numinator realised what she was doing. She was too far away, but if she edged along the wall a bit . . .

'So like!' the Numinator whispered. 'He is so very, very like.' She stood up and her stern face was ablaze with an incandescent joy that stripped decades off her and revealed a trace of the stern beauty she had been long ago.

'Like who?' said Maelys, not understanding.

'Rulke, of course. *My* Rulke; my precious, only love, who died in my arms. He was bigger, of course, and darker, but in other respects – oh, Rulke, Rulke!' A tear winked in her left eye but the Numinator dashed it away. 'He's gone forever, but now, out of two hundred and twenty years of failure I see a new and better way – *the perfect way*. And Emberr has been here all this time, preserved in youth by the Nightland, never ageing, waiting for me to come. If only I had known of him before.'

Chills radiated out from the centre of Maelys's back. This didn't make sense, but whatever the Numinator had in mind for Emberr, it wasn't good; Maelys could feel the little hairs on her arms and legs standing on end. 'He was waiting for his mother to return, but she could not. Why not, if she was so powerful that she could create this place, and maintain it for all this time?'

'I know who his mother was,' said the Numinator through her teeth. 'I can see her in his face. It can only be Yalkara!'

'Yalkara?' said Maelys. 'The Charon from the Histories?'

'The same. She pretended to treat me kindly after Rulke was killed, but I now know that she was my enemy – she stole Rulke's body and took it back to the void! Yalkara, who claimed all down a thousand ages that she hated Rulke, and that their clans had been enemies since time began. And now,' she said savagely, 'I learn that she *mated* with him while he was in the Nightland. Mated with *my* Rulke, and created this beautiful child here.'

Rage shook her; she slammed her clenched fists against her sides, and for a second her eyes rolled madly, but the age-old self-control reasserted itself and she went on, 'But she failed, and now Emberr is mine – to fulfil my long-held purpose, and revenge myself on her at the same time.'

What could she mean? Maelys couldn't think; couldn't work it out. All she knew was that Emberr was in danger, and she could not allow it.

'Oh, life is sweet!' said the Numinator. 'Life is very sweet. Together he and I are going to create a new species of humanity – one with *all* the strengths and *none* of the weaknesses of Charon, Faellem, Aachim or old humans.'

Was she mad? It certainly sounded insane. 'Rulke is dead, Numinator.'

'But I have his son.'

The Numinator thrust Maelys out of the way, and again she felt that she was utterly insignificant, even worthless. Only then did the obvious strike her – the Numinator wasn't planning to kill Emberr at all, but to *mate* with him to fulfil her age-old plan, whatever it was. But if the Numinator had been Rulke's lover too, she had to be hundreds of years old, since he had been dead for two hundred and twenty years. This was sick; disgusting; depraved. Maelys wanted to claw her face to shreds, but the Numinator had the poisoned stiletto. Maelys had to be careful, wait for an opportunity, then strike ruthlessly.

The Numinator went to her knees again, reached out to Emberr and gently stroked the hair off his brow. 'So like,' she repeated, 'though softer; gentler. Rulke had a hard life and he had to be as adamant to survive.' She touched his cheek with her fingertips. 'You're cold, Emberr, so very, very cold.'

She flicked her fingers at the fire and it sprang to life, then took Emberr's right hand in hers, rubbing it, but after a few seconds went so still that she seemed turned to stone. Worms crawled up Maelys's backbone. What was the matter?

A shudder racked the Numinator; she felt Emberr's throat; pushed up one eyelid with a finger; laid her ear against his bare chest, on which the last trails of chthonic fire were slowly winking out, like a life.

'No!' Maelys whispered. 'Emberr?'

What could the matter be? She went slowly towards him. Her muscles had gone stiff; she could barely force them to move, and it felt as though every hair on her head was standing up, writhing in horror for what had happened here.

'Dead!' the Numinator shrieked, letting his head fall with a thump.

Maelys wanted to strike her down for treating him so rudely. He couldn't be dead, he was just deeply asleep. She tried to push the Numinator out of the way and was slapped across the face so hard that it knocked her sideways.

Maelys snapped; she threw herself at the Numinator, clawing at her face. She had to get to Emberr. He couldn't be dead; he was just cold from lying on the floor, and if she could only hold him in her arms the way he'd held her, she knew she could make him better again.

The Numinator thrust her back against the wall, holding her away with the Art. 'You murdering little bitch!' she said, biting off every word and spitting it in Maelys's face. 'You did this deliberately, just to thwart me.'

'I love him,' Maelys whispered. 'You came here to kill him, and now you blame *me*?'

'Kill him!' cried the Numinator. 'I came to test him.'

That didn't make sense either. 'W-what for?'

'Fertility, of course. I didn't know who he was, but since he'd been in the Nightland all this time, there was a faint possibility he was Rulke's . . . though I never dreamt it could have been with another Charon – with *her*!'

'Why not?' Maelys said dazedly.

'Rulke and Yalkara hated each other. And on Aachan, most Charon had proven tragically sterile. They were becoming extinct. But I thought, just maybe, here . . .'

She picked up the stiletto, squeezed a yellow drop of what Maelys had thought to be poison onto a small white disc, and bent over Emberr's middle. Shortly she rose, holding the disc carefully. The yellow drop went white, then colourless, then in an instant changed to a brilliant carmine. Again that racking shudder from the Numinator, and the quivering indrawn breath.

'Fertile – massively so.' A tear formed in the corner of her eye. 'And you robbed me. You killed him.' She stood up straight, forced the emotion down and became the icily controlled Numinator once more.

Maelys pushed past her and went to Emberr. He was really cold now and his open eyes were glassy. She put her head on his bare chest and felt nothing: no rise and fall, no heartbeat. He *was* dead. She slumped to the floor, dazed, numb, lost.

She couldn't take it in, much less that the Numinator should believe she'd murdered him. She crouched over his body. How could it be? He'd been awake after they'd finished making love. He'd held her in his arms, rocking her tenderly to sleep. He'd spoken to her, though she'd been so drowsy she couldn't remember what he'd said.

The Numinator sprang at her, the stiletto upraised and her wrist wreathed in yellow fumes. Maelys saw her coming but couldn't focus; couldn't react; too late she tried to swerve out of the way but the stiletto caught her in the fleshy part of the left shoulder. It was so sharp that she barely felt it pierce her until the yellow fluid began to burn, spreading in a red-hot line down her arm. Sweat burst out on her forehead and the soles of her feet; she slipped and fell down.

The Numinator stood over her, her face a frozen mask, then bent and raised the knife again, as if to stab Maelys in the neck. She tried to scramble out of the way but her sweaty palms kept slipping on the floor.

At the moment the shining, hollow point of the ice stiletto was about to tear through her throat, the Numinator twitched it aside and bent over Emberr again, studying his naked body in a calculating way.

'What if a child should come of their union?' she mused, even more controlled. Pushing Maelys against the wall, the Numinator felt her belly. 'It's the right time of the month, I see, and it is clear that she was a virgin, so there can be no doubt any child would be his. Ahh, but the potion is inimical to new life!'

She sprang at Maelys, threw her onto her back, squatted over her and thrust the point of the stiletto into her shoulder wound. Maelys screamed; she couldn't help it this time.

The Numinator put her lips to the hilt of the ice stiletto and began to suck and spit the yellow, fuming potion onto the floor, where it fizzed like water on a hotplate. Maelys's bright red blood began to ooze, thread-like, up through the hollow stiletto into its hilt, followed by blood that was a murky yellow-brown. When the oozing blood turned red again the Numinator wrenched the stiletto out of the wound and stabbed it into Maelys's inner arm, near the elbow.

She sucked the potion from there as well until red blood reappeared, then did the same at Maelys's wrist and the back of her hand, before casting the stiletto aside. It shattered on the floor, making a small puddle of icy blood there.

The Numinator wiped blood off her lips, smiled and extended her hand to Maelys. 'Come. We are going home now.'

'I have no home,' Maelys managed to gasp.

'My home is your home. We have nine months to get to know each other.'

FORTY-SIX

The next two days were a nightmare of mud, mosquitoes, rain, exhaustion and diarrhoea so bad that Nish felt his bowels were dissolving, then more mud, and food which grew steadily worse with every meal. A third of his men had dysentery and he'd had to leave another thirty-five at the previous camp, for they were too ill to walk. The militia numbered just over five hundred now, counting Boobelar's drunken and abusive eighty, but at the current rate Nish would be lucky to have two hundred and fifty capable of fighting by the time they reached the pass. If they ever did.

They waded through mud, ate in mud, even slept in it. The remaining bags of flour and nut meal were threaded with black and green mould like smelly old cheeses; the haunches of meat were covered in a layer of grey slime and smelled worse each day; the onions and garlic were sprouting from their centres yet rotting on the outsides, and what was left of their other food was also on the turn.

Though they'd been on short rations since the seventh day, three-quarters of their supplies were gone. Nish now faced the terrifying prospect of engaging the enemy with only two or three days' food left, and still they hadn't reached Blisterbone. He felt that they were crawling up a monstrous quagmire-coated treadmill, to nowhere. In his worst moments, he doubted that their guide had ever crossed The Spine.

It was the most inhospitable place in the world, and he now understood why it had protected Gendrigore for so long. His only consolation was that his father's army would be struggling too, for the southern climb was even steeper and more rugged and, churned by the hard boots of thousands of soldiers, their track would become an even deeper wallow.

The only man untroubled by the conditions was Curr, whose wiry legs drove him ever upward, even after everyone else had collapsed. Despite his earlier words he was often well ahead, scouting, and sometimes Nish did not see him for a day, though he always returned as the cooks were dishing up the evening's ghastly meal. With his light weight and flat feet Curr skated over the mud wallows into which everyone else plunged to their thighs, and his leathery skin, which was always plastered with mud, resisted the attacks of all but the most aggressive mosquitoes.

But finally they were only a league from their destination; when the clouds cleared Nish could see the snow-capped peaks of The Spine, and made out a dip between them that was the pass. On its left flank stood an ominous white peak, shaped like an over-curving thorn.

'Time to camp,' said Nish, for his bowels were bubbling and he was desperate for relief, however temporary. 'If we start before dawn tomorrow and go hard in the moonlight we can reach the pass just after sunrise.'

Curr came sliding down the slope, so covered with mud lumps that he looked like a skinny, warty toad. More bad news, Nish felt sure.

'Where have you been?' he snapped, for Curr had disappeared before they had broken camp that morning and, as usual, hadn't bothered to tell him.

The guide skidded to a stop, his chest heaving. The column came to a halt behind Nish and he heard them flopping to the ground. No soldier wasted a moment in standing where he could sit, or sitting when he could lie flat on his back in the mire. There was no sound save for mud plopping to the ground all around Curr. His eyes were red and his reek was worse than ever.

He took a deep breath, met Nish's eyes, and said, 'The enemy is at the pass. We'll have to turn back.'

'You saw them?' Nish said stupidly. Curr was an experienced scout. Of course he'd seen them.

Pain jagged through his bowels. Nish ran awkwardly behind a tree and got there just in time. No one took any notice; most of the militia were suffering just as badly. He hobbled out again. 'Where are they, Curr?'

Curr grinned. No matter how bad the food, he ate it with gusto and never suffered for it. 'Must've just topped the pass. Saw three of them among the rocks, climbin' up to the lookout where they can see down. Two more standin' guard.'

'But they didn't see you?'

'Made sure of that.' Curr scratched his backside, dislodging a mud lump the size of a flounder. 'Crawled up along the lee side of a fallen log.'

'Leaving a trail they can't possibly miss as soon as they search the area.'

'Covered it with fallen leaves. Not a fool, Nish.'

'So we can't attack the pass. We'll have to go back and find a place we can defend.'

Nish knew it was hopeless. The enemy's scouts would soon find them and, with so many men, quickly overwhelm them. He was leading the militia to certain death, and he would die with them.

Unless Father turns up at the very end, he thought bitterly, striding over their corpses to take me back, just as he did last time. And the time before, when beautiful Irisis – No! He wasn't going down that path again. Father never gives up, and this time I've walked right into his trap, as he knew I would from the moment he discovered

I was in Gendrigore. He allowed his armies and fleets to be seen so I would rush off like the precipitate fool I am, right into the trap.

Once more he saw himself, arse-up over the rock with Boobelar whaling the life out of him with the flat of his sword. Fool! Failure! But this time Nish wasn't going to give way to his nagging self-doubt. He had been a great leader once and he could be again, as soon as he exorcised this particular demon.

'Or . . . you could go up the back way,' said Curr with a cunning sideways glance at Nish, but then shook his head. 'No, forget it; can't be done.'

Nish believed him. A thousand years of history could hardly be wrong, and if retreating meant a slow death, attacking the pass was the quick and brutal version.

'What are you suggesting, Curr?'

The guide began shaping mud with his fingers, mounding it into a peak-studded, precipice-bounded mountain chain to represent this section of The Spine. He sharpened its cliffs and ridges with a filthy fingernail, pared them even steeper with the point of his knife, and finally made a notch in The Spine to represent Blisterbone Pass.

'Just here,' said Curr, pointing to a tiny bowl high on the left, or eastern, side of the white-thorn mountain looming high above the pass. The bowl was encircled by knife-edged ridges running up to The Spine. 'Told you at the beginnin', didn't I? There's a second pass – Liver-Leech.' He made an insignificant nick in The Chain above the bowl. 'It's never used; too steep and dangerous, but desperate men might cross there and circle round the mountain to take Blisterbone from the south. Enemy won't be expecting that.'

'How do you know?' said Nish.

'No one knows about the other pass.'

'You know about it. And Barquine also mentioned it, as I recall, so Father's scouts will, too.'

Curr shrugged. 'No one has used it in hundreds of years.'

'Father thinks of everything. He'll make sure it's guarded.'

'Don't matter to me. Just thought I'd mention it, seein' as how yer desperate to get there first. Men I saw are just an advance guard. Move quick and you can take Blister-bone before the army arrives.'

'How long will this path take?' said Nish.

'Leave at dawn, you can attack at dawn day after termorrer.'

Nish bent over the mud map, but it was too small to tell him anything.

'It's the only way. If you retreat, they'll soon come after you, and you'll die.'

Nish did not like it. From the mud map, they would have to make a forced march up an exposed ridge to cross at Liver-Leech Pass, and if they were seen they would be cruelly exposed, trapped between the advance guard and Jal-Nish's army. But if they retreated now, their situation was nearly as bad. At least this way they had a tiny, desperate chance – assuming they were led by a military genius, rather than a man who'd had his arse whaled by a subordinate and hadn't found the courage to do anything about it.

The next morning, Nish's tiny hope was fading as he led the militia around the white-thorn mountain, walking in single file below the crest of the curving ridge so they would not be seen. Logic told him that the attack was doomed. If his little militia could have held Blisterbone Pass against an army of thousands, his father's advance guard could hold it against the militia, and then the main army would attack them from the rear.

What if he divided the militia and attacked the pass from both sides at once? Unfortunately, there was no way to coordinate two forces separated by the width of a mountain.

He stopped for a breather, perching on a rock and

studying the black sky. It had stopped raining a while back but the respite was only temporary. And what if Curr was wrong about Liver-Leech Pass?

'Is something the matter, Nish?' said Hoshi, coming up and laying an arm across his shoulder.

'No,' he lied. 'Why?'

'You seem very downcast today.'

'And you keep tearing at your hair,' said Gi, who had come with him. 'Like you are now.'

Nish, who hadn't realised he'd been doing it, lowered his hand onto the hilt of Vivimord's sabre. 'Curr said it was seven days' march from Wily's Clearing to Blisterbone Pass, and we've taken ten already. I'm beginning to wonder if he's ever been across The Spine; and if it takes a lot longer to cross by the higher pass . . .'

Hoshi looked at Gi, she nodded, and he said, 'There's another explanation.'

'What's that?' said Nish.

'That Curr deliberately led us astray.'

'He was sent by Barquine, and I trust him.'

'How do you know Barquine sent him?' said Gi.

Nish cursed inwardly. No one carried papers in Gendrigore, and there had been no way to check Curr's word without sending a messenger all the way back to Barquine, which would have taken a week at least. There hadn't been time. 'I – I don't suppose I do, though he did say he would send a guide.'

'Maybe Curr killed the guide. And he's always off on his own.'

'Scouts usually are,' said Nish. 'I'm in unknown country, Gi; I've got to trust my guide. I don't know this land, and neither do you.'

'Boobelar does,' said Hoshi. 'I heard Huwld, the cook's boy with the red hair, saying so.'

Worse and worse. Lately Boobelar had spent his nights drinking the hallucinogenic sap tapped from the scarlet-leaved nif trees, until he raved like a madman and had to be tied up for his own safety. Every night Nish hoped the soldier would fall over a cliff. He would be useless in a fight and was affecting everyone's morale, save for the eighty he'd brought with him, whose greed for plunder outweighed reason.

Nish knew there was going to be a confrontation the moment he spoke to the fellow, but he couldn't put it off any longer. Boobelar was bigger and stronger and, even in his cups, faster, and Nish was afraid of him. That wasn't the real problem, though. Nish felt sure that he was the better swordsman; he'd certainly taken down bigger opponents in the past, but Boobelar's humiliation of him lay in the back of Nish's mind all the time, undermining him the way his father always had. Well, he would just have to overcome it; and if he could not, his troubles would soon be over.

'How does Huwld know?' said Nish.

'Boobelar is his uncle,' said Hoshi, 'and he went over The Spine years ago, looking for gold.'

'Did he find any?'

'He came back months later with nothing, starving and in a fever.'

'No wonder he's so bitter. Well, I'd better talk to him. Fall out for ten minutes.'

The word was passed back and the exhausted troops dropped in their tracks. 'Fall out, I said,' Nish muttered. 'Not *down*. Or over the bloody cliff.'

Gi grinned, winked at Hoshi and they began to follow him down.

'Have a break,' Nish said, easing the sabre in its sheath. 'I don't need looking after.'

'Of course not,' said Gi. 'But we're coming anyway.'

He was glad to have their support when he reached Boobelar's squad, which was lying down forty or fifty paces from the rest of the militia.

'Wadder you wan',' slurred the captain, squatting bolt upright on a jutting rock like a man impaled on a spike.

His eyes were like rivers of blood issuing from muddy ferret holes; his nose was running and his lips were red from nif sap.

He pushed himself up, staggered, and the wine skin swung around in a loop on the thong which held it to his wrist, striking him in the chest. He looked down at it stupidly, tried to take a swig, discovered it was empty, hurled it away and lurched towards Nish. To the left, one of Boobelar's men had his pants down and was waggling his backside at Nish. Everyone roared with laughter. Nish flushed.

'Whadder ya want, purple-arse?' said Boobelar.

Nish's bruises had faded to greeny-yellow, but he felt the insult nonetheless. 'I heard you've been over The Spine before.'

'So what?' Boobelar grinned.

'I thought you might know the way.'

'Not as well as Curr –' He broke off and the bleeding eyes fixed on Nish. 'Whadder ya sayin'?'

His men were on their feet, staring at each other. Nish hadn't wanted to arouse their fears, which could only make morale worse, but it might be too late for that.

'I just like to check these things,' he said hastily. 'A prudent captain –'

Boobelar's fist came out of nowhere, slamming into Nish's nose so hard that he felt it break. He went down on his back, his head ringing and his eyes watering so badly that he couldn't see. He rubbed the wetness away, momentarily unable to get up. His face was covered in blood and it was flooding from his nose.

Boobelar was standing over him, swaying like a sapling in a gale. He booted Nish in the ribs. 'Curr's gone, hasn't he?'

Nish, spitting out blood, couldn't answer. This was it; he had to take Boobelar now.

'Curr's led us into a trap, then run like the dog he is – Curr the Cur,' bellowed Boobelar. He wiped his oozing nose on his sleeve, leaving a silvery trail there and a

514

muddy smear across his face. 'There'll be no plunder for any of us, boys, *and – it's – all – his – fault!'*

He raised his boot to smash Nish's face in. Nish couldn't roll out of the way in time, and was trying to get his hands up when Hoshi threw himself at Boobelar and shouldered him out of the way.

Gi heaved Nish up and put his hand on the hilt of his sabre. 'Only you can stop this, Nish,' she said in his ear.

Nish knew it. He'd put it off too long through self-doubt, but Boobelar had to be crushed, right away. He steadied himself and waited while the crazed drunk came at him, but did not draw his sabre. In wartime, attacking a senior officer was a capital offence, but capital punishment wasn't the Gendrigorean way, and if Nish cut him down in cold blood the whole militia might walk.

Boobelar, despite the nif sap, or perhaps because of it, was incredibly fast. He was on Nish before he had time to weave away, fists going one-two into his belly, and when Nish doubled over, wheezing and breathless, a knee coming for his groin. Nish couldn't pull back in time; he lurched forwards and the knee caught him in the belly instead.

Completely winded, all he could do was throw his arms around the bigger man and hang on like a punch-drunk boxer. He tried to knee Boobelar but he twisted sideways. Nish attempted to head-butt him under the chin, no more successfully. If he let go, Boobelar would knock him down; the captain's fists were pummelling his sore ribs.

Now laughing like a drain, Boobelar caught hold of Nish, trying to turn him over and pull his pants down. Nish struggled furiously and broke free. He wasn't going to suffer that humiliation again.

He swung hard and hit Boobelar in the mouth, breaking teeth and knocking him off his feet, but Boobelar didn't let go and Nish went down with him. Boobelar landed on his back and Nish twisted free; Boobelar bounced to his feet.

Nish rolled out of the way, sprang up and punched Boobelar in the left eye. Boobelar reeled back, then raised his arms, knotted his clenched fists into a club and swung it down at Nish's head with enough force to drive it half-way down his spine. Nish managed to get his head out of the way but the blow nearly broke his left collarbone and shoulder, and his arm began to go numb.

As the captain staggered, off-balance from the force of his swing, Nish back-pedalled away. His flooding nose had left a huge bloodstain on Boobelar's front. His head was ringing; the captain separated into two then the images slowly rejoined, but began to separate again. Nish knew he could not stay on his feet much longer.

He groped for his sabre. His bloody fingers slipped on the hilt, he took a firm grip and dragged it out as Boobelar rushed him, fists flailing. Unfortunately the tip of the blade snagged on its sheath, for the sabre was considerably longer than any blade Nish was used to, and he hadn't drawn it far enough.

Boobelar got in another blow to the jaw that knocked Nish sideways, rattling his teeth, then drew his knife. 'This time I'm gonna have yer balls for earrings.'

Nish just managed to stay on his feet; he jerked the sabre all the way out and, when the two images became one again, with the deftest of little jabs he cut Boobelar's belt on either side of his hips.

The captain did not realise his pants were falling down until they were halfway to his knees, and the grimy sight beneath was not one Nish wanted to remember. Boobelar caught his pants with his left hand and tried to heave them up, while hacking at Nish with his knife.

Nish wove backwards. Boobelar came after him, stumbled over his pants and fell to his knees. Nish swayed to the left and whacked him hard on his hairy backside with the flat of the sabre, counting the strokes aloud.

'One, two, three, and one for luck!'

A massed cheer went up behind him but Nish couldn't turn to see who it was, for Boobelar, incoherent with fury, had stepped out of his pants and caught the sword one of his men had tossed to him. He threw himself at Nish, knife in one hand, sword in the other.

Nish could have killed him then; he should have, but he wanted to bring him to trial the Gendrigorean way, to end it once and for all. He reversed the sabre and, the moment the captain came within reach of the long blade, swung the back of it at his head, just above the ear.

Boobelar crashed down and did not move. It was over.

Nish was seeing double again, and Boobelar's men were rising, drawing their rusty swords and home-made spears. Behind him he heard people shouting, and feet pounding down towards him, but whoever they were, they would not be in time to interfere. If he hesitated now, he was dead.

Forcing himself up to his full, meagre height, he advanced on Boobelar's men, the shiny sabre upright. They stopped but did not back away. The pain in his broken nose was ferocious, the double vision coming and going, but he had to fight it, and them, and everything. I will not be beaten, Nish kept telling himself. If I fail now, Gendrigore is lost and so is the war. I've got to impose my authority no matter the cost. I can't afford the least hesitation; even a stagger could bring me down.

Forcing the pain away, and holding himself rigid, he advanced, carving an arc through the air with his sabre; it was a beautiful, elegant stroke that made his opponents look like farm labourers. He took another step, lunged with the sabre, twisted and drew back. Boobelar's men swayed backwards away from the demonstration, for Nish's stroke, had he been within reach, would have sliced open an opponent's belly and hooked out his entrails.

The double vision was getting worse; he couldn't last much longer. 'Lay down your weapons!' he said, struggling to put on the commanding voice that had once come naturally to him. 'Swear to me, and me alone, or die by my hand.'

'You and whose army,' said a squat, burly man.

'Nish's army,' came Gi's high voice from behind, and another rousing cheer. 'Us!'

It helped. Nish managed to force his double vision back into a single image and concentrated as hard as he could. Boobelar's troops did not want to swear to him – they wanted to rush him and hack him to pieces, and if one among them dared, the rest would follow. Which would it be? Nish fixed his eye on the burly fellow, who was built like a blacksmith and carried a well-maintained broadsword.

'Who wants to die first?' Nish said.

'You do,' said the burly fellow, and came at him.

With his brawn, and that sword, he would be a formidable opponent, assuming he had any fighting skills. Nish had to take him first and hope the others didn't attack at the same time, from behind.

He advanced on the smith, step by slow step, with every stride demonstrating another from his repertoire of strokes. The smith raised the broadsword like a man about to chop wood and Nish felt a trace of hope. The fellow evidently knew no sword play and would be an easy target, if his blow could be evaded. But if he hit, the heavy broadsword would have enough power behind it to cut him in two. Nish stopped.

The smith grinned, a trifle nervously, evidently thinking Nish was afraid. He was terrified but he could not afford to show any hesitation, any fear. The smith advanced a step and Nish matched it, hoping the man would crack and run, though it didn't look as though he was going to.

'Cut the little turd in two, Lenn,' shouted a giant of a man carrying a woodsman's axe.

'Smack his skinny arse good,' yelled another.

Now the smith was only three steps away, almost within reach. Nish, hoping he would not have to kill the fellow, went forwards a half step and practised the gutting stroke again. It would have been a beautiful blow, had he not trodden on a round stone which made his left knee twist painfully.

Instantly, and with phenomenal speed, the smith leapt and swung his broadsword down and across in a sweeping curve that was near impossible to avoid. Nish couldn't block it, for it would have shattered his sabre. Nor could he weave out of the way or reverse direction in time. All that was left to him was to use his forward momentum, dive under the swing and hope to get his back and legs low enough.

He hit the ground on his belly, head and shoulders and chest between the smith's legs, clinging desperately to the sabre; if it jarred out of his hands he was finished. He just held on to it. The smith tried to stop his swing but the weight of the broadsword carried it on.

Nish's vision was blurring, bloody bubbles were shooting from each nostril, and he didn't think he would be able to get up. Still flat on the ground, he blindly swung the sabre in both hands up over his head and back as far as it would go, praying that he could aim true. It went up through the smith's lower back and came out the middle of his chest, and he was dead before he slammed into the rocks.

Nish forced himself to hands and knees, came to his feet, swaying, jerked the sabre out and held it up. 'Anyone else want to try me?'

A child with a toy sword could have cut him down, but Boobelar's men had their mouths hanging open, cowed and awed by his sword play. Nish held the pose for a moment, then hastily swung the sabre tip to the ground and leaned on it to prevent himself from falling down.

'I never knew you were a master swordsman,' said Hoshi quietly.

Nish wasn't; merely a well-trained and very experienced fighter who had been far luckier than he deserved, but he wasn't going to admit that to anyone. In the coming battle, his reputation was going to need all the help it could get.

'Throw the body over the side,' he said. 'Get two of my most reliable men and bind Boobelar securely. Guard him day and night until he can be tried the Gendrigorean way. If he gives any more trouble, heave him over the side.' His eyes met the eyes of Boobelar's most loyal troops. 'And anyone else who supports him.'

It was over, and even if Nish's troops felt no differently about him, Nish did. It was his first real victory on the long road to overthrowing his father.

They resumed the march until dusk, only an hour away, dragging Boobelar on a litter, since they could hardly leave him behind. That evening the camp was tense and silent, for everyone knew what the fight had been about. And maybe Boobelar had been right. For the first time, Curr did not appear when dinner was served.

Hoshi woke Nish before dawn the next morning. 'You should have killed Boobelar.'

'What's the matter now? What's he done?'

'Someone freed him and he's fled in the night with forty of his men – and most of our supplies.'

FORTY-SEVEN

The Numinator wrenched Maelys to her feet and dragged her down the hall without another glance at Emberr, as though his death, the most shattering loss of Maelys's life, no longer mattered. Maelys couldn't wonder about that – she was numb with despair.

The Numinator had her hand on the latch of the outer door when it was gently pushed from the other side. She leapt backwards, landing as softly as a cat, and drew a small triangular blade. Her other hand went over Maelys's mouth.

'That's pointless, and you know it,' said a deep, somewhat rasping voice. 'You can't keep me out, nor can you fight me here, for this place is mine and I maintain every part of it.' The hand fell away. 'Stand back.' A tall, statuesque woman entered.

'Bel?' said Maelys, for there was a hint of Bel in her now. Had Bel come to save her? Maelys hardly cared; nothing seemed to matter any more, not even her own family.

The tall woman's eyes took in Maelys, and the Numinator behind her, and she nodded stiffly, as if she knew her.

'Yalkara!' said the Numinator coldly.

Yalkara? Maelys was in the presence of a legend, probably the most powerful and dangerous woman in all the

Histories. Her heart was thumping like a great drum. Of course Yalkara hadn't come here for *her*; she'd come for Emberr – her son.

'Granddaughter,' said Yalkara.

Maelys stared at the Numinator. 'She's your *grandmother?*'

'You don't seem pleased to see me,' said Yalkara.

'You stole Rulke's body and took it to the void,' said the Numinator.

'That would have been his wish. Besides, you did not complain at the time.'

'I was sick with grief.'

'And you have been brooding about him ever since. You always were obsessive.'

'You were going back to the void as well; and to extinction. Why are you still here?'

'You know why. My people went, and I would have gone with them, had I not previously given birth to a child – here in the Nightland.'

'You never said.'

'I dared not reveal my secret, not to anyone, for my son was in deadly danger. Where is he?' said Yalkara.

Maelys jerked one hand down the hall, shivering in terror. What would Yalkara do when she discovered that her son was dead? The Charon had been the mightiest of all the human species, and the most barbaric. They believed in vengeance, she recalled; to the utmost degree.

'Go before me, both of you,' said Yalkara. 'Keep your hands where I can see them.'

'You don't trust your own granddaughter?'

'I know what you're like.'

To Maelys's surprise, the Numinator headed back to the room where Emberr's body lay. Maelys could not bear it. She could not bear to see him again; nor could she bear to leave him.

The Numinator let go of Maelys's arm and she went backwards until she came up against the wall. Yalkara entered slowly, her face tight with anticipation. She scanned the gloomy room, saw Emberr lying there as though asleep, and sighed.

'Beloved son,' she said softly, as if apologising for her failure. 'The past two hundred and twenty years since I conceived you have been the best of my life, and the worst.' The Numinator let out a hiss through clenched teeth. 'The best because I had a child at last. And the worst – because I conceived you here, while the Nightland was under prohibition, I had to bear you here, alone, then leave you. You were *of* the Nightland, and without the prohibition being broken you could not leave it.'

The Numinator quivered, but did not speak.

Maelys had to tell Yalkara. She opened her mouth to say, 'He's dead. My Emberr is dead,' but could not choke the words out.

'I could not tell anyone about it, least of all the father,' Yalkara went on. 'As Rulke escaped for the final time, all unknowing that he had a son, the Nightland was collapsing into a singularity. Even then, I could not break the prohibition and get *you* out. Instead, I spent my strength and my Art on the mightiest work of my long life – reversing the collapse of the Nightland and rebuilding it to shelter, protect and nourish your body and your mind for as long as it took, until I could find a way to return for you.'

The Numinator was making little stabs with the small blade, but Yalkara paid her no heed. She went to her knees beside Emberr. 'I'm sorry. I thought it would take a few years at most. I never thought that building the Nightland, and maintaining it, would take so much from me that I could not return. After I took your father's body back to the void, and saw my people to extinction, I spent all my days, for two hundred and twenty years, trying to find a way back. But there was none – until recently, when –'

'His father was Rulke,' the Numinator burst out. *'You mated with Rulke! Right here!'*

Yalkara stalked across to her. 'Who I have mated with

is my business. I knew Rulke three thousand years before you were born.'

'You hated each other! There was a feud between your clans, because of a terrible wrong done in ancient times.'

Maelys looked from one woman to the other. 'What terrible wrong?'

'I don't have to explain anything to either of you,' Yalkara said indifferently, and turned back. 'Emberr? Wake now.'

'Rulke was mine!' the Numinator hissed, her eyes as hard as the point of her knife. 'For all time.'

'I mated with him here before he ever met you,' said Yalkara.

'He was mine, before and after. Now and forever. Past, present and future.'

Yalkara shook her head in amazement. 'You're out of your mind.' She turned to her son again. 'Emberr?'

She knew something was wrong now. Yalkara went across as slowly as if she were a pallbearer at an emperor's funeral, crouched beside him and touched his bare chest. For a second her aloofness cracked; she let out a hissing breath, then lifted him with one hand under his knees and another behind his head to prevent it from flopping. Her jaw tightened but she was as controlled as the Numinator had been hysterical. Yalkara, evidently, was not one to display her grief to inferiors.

'It is a mother's duty to protect her children, and I failed you,' she said quietly. 'I did everything I could and it wasn't enough. Beloved Emberr, this is the end for you, for me, and for all the Charon. But before I go, I will exact a dreadful retribution for your slaying.'

She laid him down again, ever so gently, then came to her feet and the look in her eyes was awful. 'Who did this?' she said in a voice deliberately remote, and as cold as the central ice cap of Noom. 'Which of you slew my son? Or were you in league?'

'She killed him,' said the Numinator. 'Her name is Maelys of Nifferlin and I was taking her back for punishment –'

'I know Maelys. I would not have thought she had it in her to do such a deed. Well, girl?' said Yalkara. 'Did you kill my son?'

'I loved him the moment I saw him,' Maelys whispered, for it would have felt wrong to speak in normal tones beside his cold body. 'And Emberr loved me.'

'Explain!'

'When I first came here he called me, directly into my mind, and I went to him. I was never afraid. I knew I was safe –'

'He would never have harmed you,' said Yalkara, bending over Emberr again. 'He was a gentle soul, my son, unlike his father – *unlike me*! Answer the question – did you kill him?'

Beside Maelys, the Numinator's knuckles were white on the hilt of her knife and her throat was quivering. She was building up to something.

'I loved him,' Maelys wept. 'Of course I didn't kill –' But then something awful occurred to her.

'How did he die?' said Yalkara.

'I don't know –'

'But?' said Yalkara.

'I still had a trace of chthonic fire on me, from the Numinator's portal. And . . . after we lay together it was gone from me, and all over his skin.'

Yalkara's olive skin went a muddy colour, all the blood draining from her face. 'Did I doom my son,' she said to herself, 'by bringing the fire of damnation to Santhenar?'

'It didn't harm me,' said Maelys, bewildered, aching with her loss, and suffused with horror that she might have unwittingly brought Emberr's doom upon him. 'Or the Numinator.'

'Nor I,' said Yalkara, staring at her son. 'Nor any other person. But Emberr was engendered in the Nightland, a place remote from the laws which govern the real, physical worlds, and the Nightland would always be a part of him. The chthonic flame is a force like no other, one that can slide between the many dimensions of space and time as easily as you slide between the sheets of your bed. It is one of the few natural forces that can punch a portal through the Nightland, and for the same reason it was inimical to him, and so he died.' She turned to Maelys. 'How did he die?'

'I didn't know he had, at first. We were lying in each other's arms and I just thought he was cold; the fire had gone out.'

'But Emberr died content?' Yalkara gripped Maelys's shoulders and stared into her eyes.

'We were delirious with our love for each other. It was meant to be.'

'Was it the first time for you as well?' Maelys nodded stiffly, feeling her cheeks burning again. The Numinator went very still.

Yalkara wiped her eyes and crouched beside her son, examining him carefully. 'From the blood on his thighs it would appear so, but there is no end to the duplicity of scheming young women. I must be sure –'

Without warning, the Numinator sprang at her, raising the knife high as if to stab her grandmother in the back. She landed like a cat and was bringing the blade down when Maelys shrieked, 'Yalkara, look out.'

Yalkara whirled in a rising spiral, faster than the eye could follow, and her stiff right arm struck the Numinator across the chest so hard that she was lifted off her feet and flung backwards, to crash into the wall. The triangular knife went flying and Yalkara scooped it up. The Numinator slumped to the floor, groaning.

'You have Charon blood in you, granddaughter, but that is not the same as *being* Charon.'

Maelys was darting for the door when Yalkara's voice rang out. 'Hold!'

Maelys froze, for not even in battle had she seen anyone move as swiftly as Yalkara had – the Charon were a race apart and she had no hope of escaping her.

'On the floor!' rapped Yalkara. 'Take down your trousers.'

'What?' Maelys whispered, shocked witless, for Yalkara still had the knife in her hand. 'What are you going to do to me?'

'I'm going to make sure of you,' Yalkara said grimly.

Maelys shrank away. 'Please, no. I didn't mean to hurt him. He was everything to me.'

'Stupid girl! I'm not going to kill you. What would be the point of that?'

'What, then?' she bleated.

'I'm going to examine you intimately, of course, to make sure you *were* a virgin. There might be a child.'

Pain sheared through Maelys's chest – not Yalkara as well. Ever since her mother and aunts had sent her after Nish, no one had ever cared about her for herself. Her family *and* Jal-Nish wanted the child she could give them – the only grandchild of the God-Emperor. The Numinator and Yalkara both wanted the offspring of the last Charon. I'm just a worthless body, she thought, an *incubator*.

She lay on the cold floor, completely numb, while Yalkara completed her mortifying examination and stood up.

'You *were* a virgin. Should a child come of this union, it will be mine, and I will take it with me back to the void.'

'No,' Maelys whimpered. She was too young; she didn't want to have a baby, all alone, but if that came to pass no one else was having anything to do with it. No one!

'A child should have a mother,' said Yalkara, 'but, puny little thing that you are, you wouldn't survive an hour in the void. It's a pity, but there it is. Besides, you may bear many more children, but I never will. I am the sole survivor of the Charon. I'm sure you understand.'

Her arrogance cut right through Maelys's grief, and it was only with the utmost effort that she bit her tongue and maintained her self-control. She wanted to scream at Yalkara. No, she wanted to punch her teeth down her neck.

Don't give way, she told herself. Pretend to be meek, and compliant. Let them all underestimate you, but never give in until you've beaten them all. *Never* give in.

Yalkara studied her, head to one side. 'There's something about you. Something odd.' She pulled on the chain around Maelys's neck and heaved the taphloid out from between her breasts.

'What is this?' Yalkara said, studying it.

'Father gave it to me when I was a little girl, to suppress my aura and stop my gift from developing.'

'What gift?' Yalkara said idly.

Maelys explained about the family talent for detecting Jal-Nish's wisp-watchers and his other spying devices, and the nature of her own tiny gift, including what she'd seen in the Pit of Possibilities.

'So you have a latent talent for the Art,' said Yalkara, 'but it was never developed in the vital years when you were young, and now it's too late to master it.'

Maelys knew that already and was resigned to it. 'My aunts said the taphloid contained a secret that could help me in the future.'

'You certainly *need* protecting.' Yalkara opened the taphloid, and momentarily Maelys saw little dials spinning, though not ones she remembered seeing previously.

The Numinator groaned and tried to sit up.

'Not least from her,' Yalkara added quietly, 'and I must do what I can.' She closed the taphloid, wrapped one long finger around it and pressed it against her own forehead. For an instant Maelys felt so dizzy that she could barely stand up.

Yalkara caught Maelys's arm with her left hand, steadied her, then touched the taphloid to her forehead with her right hand. The dizziness passed but Maelys felt a sharp pain lance through her head from front to back, so fiercely barbed that she had to close her eyes.

Help!

The hoarse, whispery cry seemed to come from an

impossible distance. Maelys cocked her head, listening, but it wasn't repeated.

Yalkara thrust the taphloid, which was now uncomfortably warm, back into Maelys's cleavage and took her arm. 'Come!'

Maelys locked her knees and tried to hold on. She couldn't leave Emberr lying there all alone, *dead*. It wasn't right, or decent. She had to take care of him and prepare his body the way the dead had always been prepared at Nifferlin – gently, carefully, respectfully.

Yalkara jerked so hard that Maelys stumbled.

'No!' she wailed, but Yalkara would not desist. The Numinator followed, silently, the door of Emberr's little cottage banged, and the cottage vanished. Maelys wept all the way back to the portal, and was left to contemplate the irony, bitterest of all, of her lie to Jal-Nish about being pregnant coming true after all.

FORTY-EIGHT

Yalkara thrust Maelys in the back and she stumbled out
of the portal into the eyrie at the top of the Tower of a
Thousand Steps, and into utter devastation.

Its steepled roof, now shattered, lay open to the ele-
ments, and in the grey daylight that washed all colour from
the bleak icescape she made out a low, snow-clad range to
her left. To the right was the scarred and crevassed surface of the Kara Agel, the Frozen Sea. Below her, the moat
which had once protected the tower with shifting patterns
of water and berg was a seething morass of brown sludge
filled with floating bodies, bobbing ice coffins, drifting
pages from the bloodline registers, and all the other detri-
tus of the Numinator's failed project.

The circular eyrie, formerly so elegantly spare, was
littered with the bodies of human prisoners and Whelm,
bleeding onto heaps of smashed ice, along with broken weapons and greenly malodorous, unhuman corpses speckled
with chthonic fire. Some thirty prisoners crouched behind
a barricade across the top of the stairs, hurling chunks of
ice, and bodies, at a band of Whelm clustered on the steps
below. The Numinator's dish-shaped fire bowl was overturned and the spilled chthonic fire had eaten a pond-sized
hole in the floor.

Huge, freezing drops splashed onto Maelys's head. She looked up, received an icy deluge in the face, then stumbled aside as a barrel-sized chunk of rotten ice came crashing down. Only one splinter of the ice steeple remained; the rest had collapsed into broken stubs like the teeth of a rock-eating giant.

'What – what's happened?' she said, shivering as the icy water ran down her legs. Maelys couldn't take it in – in the brief time she'd been gone, the Numinator's two-hundred-year-old empire had been toppled.

The Numinator limped through the portal and her face hardened as she surveyed the ruin of her eyrie. She splashed to the ice barricade, looked down and the Whelm cried out, as one.

'Aiieeee! The Master has returned. Hail the Numinator, hail.'

They began to thump their weapons on the steps. *Hail, hail!* Maelys smelt their strong, oily onion odour.

Yalkara stalked out, her red Charon eyes fixed on Maelys, who edged away towards the fire-licked pond.

'Chthonic fire burns ice, that's what's happened,' said a blood-covered man brandishing an odd, jagged sword with a Whelm's ragged scalp stuck halfway along the blade. She recognised Flydd's voice, though not his face, which was so bruised and swollen that he could barely see.

'Xervish?' said Maelys.

'Where have you been?' he said coldly.

'I – I –' How could she explain the way she and Emberr had fallen for each other, or what they had done together, or how he had died? She couldn't bear to speak of it. 'I'm sorry.'

'Maelys met Emberr – my son with Rulke, the son he never knew he had – when you went to the Nightland,' said Yalkara baldly. 'They fell under each other's spell and he called her back.'

'That's not true!' cried Maelys. 'I followed the Numinator there because she had a poisoned knife; I was afraid she was going to kill him.'

'Why would I kill the one person I've been trying to create since Rulke's death?' said the Numinator in astonishment. 'The hollow knife contained a potion to test his fertility.'

'And he *was* fertile?' said Yalkara.

'Extremely.'

Yalkara, iron-faced, turned back to Flydd. 'Maelys and Emberr lay with one another, but chthonic fire on her killed him, and if she's pregnant the child comes to the void with me.'

'Any child is mine!' hissed the Numinator.

Yalkara went into a crouch, her fingers formed into blades. The Numinator whirled and scooped a handful of white fire from the pond.

'I wouldn't,' Yalkara said icily. 'I brought chthonic fire to the Three Worlds, and I can make it do what I want.'

'If only you dared!' The Numinator shook her flame-covered fist in Yalkara's face. 'I've waited two centuries to bring you down.'

Maelys clutched at her taphloid, feeling the painful thudding of her heart. If two such bitter enemies fought to the death, nothing on Noom would survive it.

A very tall, strongly built man with frost-grey eyes limped forwards, staring hungrily. '*You're* the Numinator? No wonder you hid yourself up here and never allowed me to see your face, since I'm the one person who could identify you, *Maigraith.*'

'Maigraith!' cried Flydd.

Who is Maigraith? Maelys thought. She knew the name from the Histories but could not remember which tale it came from.

The Numinator stiffened. 'I no longer use that name, Yggur. It died when Rulke was slain. I am the Numinator now.'

Yggur was another legend. Maelys knew he had fought on Flydd's side during the war, and took heart from it.

'Numinator, then,' said Yggur.

'I owe you nothing,' said the Numinator. 'I never cared for you when we were together; you never met my needs.' She allowed the excess flame to drip from her fingers into the pond. Yalkara slowly came upright.

'And Rulke did,' said Yggur stiffly. 'That's what it's all about, isn't it?' He swept an outstretched arm around the eyrie. 'He's been dead all this time but you can't let him go.'

'Why would I want to?' said the Numinator. 'He was everything to me, yet after he was slain, Yalkara, *his life-long enemy*, stole his body and took it back to the void.' She couldn't maintain her self-control now; her anguish showed fleetingly.

'Why were you lifelong enemies with Rulke?' Yggur asked Yalkara. 'I've always wondered about that.'

'Some ancient feud, long forgotten,' she said dismissively.

Maelys didn't believe her; Yalkara was hiding something.

Flydd turned to the Numinator. 'What is the purpose behind your bloodline project?

'The Charon were cursed and going to extinction,' said the Numinator. 'I had nothing left of Rulke.'

'You were pregnant to him,' Yggur exclaimed.

'A child wasn't enough. I could not allow Rulke's genius to be lost.'

'And so began your downfall, and the ruin of Santhenar.'

'The war ruined Santhenar; I did not start it.'

'But you prolonged it indefinitely. Or at least the scrutators did, and you controlled them. The war should have been won in the first ten years, when the lyrinx were still few; and weak. Because of you it lasted a hundred and fifty years.'

'My project took precedence. The moment I discovered I was with child, I thought of nothing save mating my offspring with another *triune's,* to create a new human species with all of the Charon's strengths and none of their weaknesses. A memorial to Rulke.'

'What's a triune?' asked Maelys.

No one answered.

'I was there, remember?' said Yggur, smouldering. 'At the end of the Age of the Mirror, after Llian told his Great Tale of those times, you wanted to mate Karan and Llian's firstborn child with yours.'

'It was fitting,' said the Numinator, her eyes glinting. 'Our children were an almost perfect match.'

'Why?' said Maelys. Again, no one answered.

'She was your friend,' cried Yggur in a fury, 'and it was obscene! You manipulated everyone weaker than you, as you were manipulated by Faelamor as a child. Karan refused you outright, but you would not give up your twisted plan.'

'You know nothing about the matter,' she said, standing very still.

'On the contrary – after Karan's and Llian's deaths, I took the trouble to learn how she came to be driven to that terrible crime. All she wanted was to live a normal life with her family at Gothryme Manor, and in all the Histories no one deserved it more. But you would not allow it. You pestered her, harassed her, and when she continued to refuse you, you kidnapped Karan's firstborn, Sulien, when she was just fourteen, and gave her to your thuggish son, Rulken.'

'I had promised her to him,' said the Numinator, as though that were justification enough.

'You had no right!' Yggur thundered. 'But Karan stole her daughter back then hid all her children, so you destroyed Llian's name as a Teller. You made him out to be Llian the Liar and had his *Tale of the Mirror*, the greatest and most truthful of all the Great Tales, banned, then rewritten by the scrutators.'

Flydd's head whipped around. Maelys had never seen him look so outraged. 'You used *us* to turn a Great Tale into a lie?'

The Numinator did not reply and Yggur went on. 'Finally Karan could take no more. You drove her insane and, in that madness, she killed Llian and her children, and herself.'

'Oh!' whispered Maelys, cold with shock and barely able to take it in. The day was already too full, with love, with dreadful revelations, and with untimely and undeserved death. 'How?'

'One day, at dawn,' said Yggur, 'she hurled them from the top of the ruined city-tower of Shazmak, where they had been hiding from you, into the terrible flood of the mighty river Garr, which no one has ever survived. I questioned the witnesses, Idlis and Yetchah, two Whelm who had once served me.'

'I also questioned them,' said the Numinator. 'Karan killed her family just to thwart me.' She bit off each word. 'She always resented me.'

'I knew Karan well,' said Yggur. 'She was the best friend anyone could have had, and you destroyed her.'

'I wish I'd known her,' Maelys said softly. She felt a closer kinship with Karan, dead two hundred years, than with anyone here, for they were both linked by the Numinator's monstrous scheme. If she was prepared to destroy a friend to get what she wanted, what would she do to Maelys?

'I only wanted *one* of her children,' said the Numinator. 'She had three.'

It was impossible to come to terms with such a wicked act, or with the Numinator's justifying it as though it was her right. And now she was doing it again, she and Yalkara fighting over the fruit of Maelys's body like dogs over a corpse. I will never let it happen, she thought. I'll fight the whole world for what is mine.

The taphloid burned between her breasts. *Help!* The Numinator cocked her head as if she had heard the cry as well, but her face froze and she turned away.

Help! There it was again, stronger this time, and fleetingly Maelys had a vision of booted feet squelching through

535

calf-deep mud. Who could it be? The taphloid cooled and something began to spin inside it, shaking it like a spinning top, before slowly running down.

'So that's what all this is about,' Flydd was saying. 'Karan thwarted you, so you took revenge on the world by creating the Council of Scrutators.'

'It had nothing to do with revenge, Flydd,' Yggur said wearily. 'Maigraith and I were lovers once, and I know her better than anyone.'

'You never knew me at all,' she snapped. 'That was your problem.'

'Aye,' he said, 'though in my seven years as your prisoner I've worked out what you were up to down below.'

'With the bloodline registers?' Flydd squinted at Yggur through swollen eyelids.

'Precisely,' said Yggur. 'When Karan thwarted you, *Numinator*, it only stiffened your resolve to find another way to achieve your goal, didn't it?'

She did not reply. Maelys watched her out of the corner of her eye, but could not tell what she might be thinking. More rotten ice fell, peppering them with fire-webbed fragments, though none touched Yalkara.

'You devoted yourself to the mastery of your Arts over many years, Numinator,' said Yggur, 'until a time came when the guiding Council of Santhenar grew weak. You crushed it and set up your own, the Council of Scrutators.'

'Why?' Colm ground out.

Maelys hadn't noticed him in the shadows to her right. She gave him a tentative smile, but he returned a look of such cold fury that she flinched. *Thief*, he mouthed. He must have found out about Flydd taking the mimemule, and Colm was not a forgiving man.

'I'm beginning to understand,' said Flydd. 'Maigraith – the Numinator – and Karan were incredibly rare people. They were both *triune* – they bore the blood of three of the four human species – and it gave them unique but very different talents.'

'And by breeding their children together,' said Yggur, 'the Numinator hoped to create *quartine* children; ones having the blood of all four human kinds. If any quartines survived, and weren't cursed by the madness that is the fate of most *triune*, they might become the foundation of a new human species, one greater than all the others put together. That was the Numinator's goal, as an eternal memorial to Rulke, and she has never given it up.'

Was the Numinator one of the mad ones, Maelys wondered. If so, it was a most particular, directed and obsessive kind of madness, completely lacking in empathy for others.

'No species crafted by a mere human could ever equal *our* kind,' sneered Yalkara.

'Yet your kind will be extinct when you die,' snapped the Numinator.

'I don't understand why you needed the scrutators,' said Maelys.

The Numinator did not reply.

'What happened to your child, Numinator?' Maelys persisted. She had to know. 'Why didn't you –?'

'She had twins,' said Yggur. 'Illiel and –'

'No one else tells *my* story,' grated the Numinator. 'I bore twin sons from Rulke's seed. Illiel came first and I named him for my Faellem father, Galgilliel. Illiel was small and golden-skinned, very Faellem in appearance, and of course I did not take to him.'

'Why not?' said Maelys.

'Maigraith was brought up by Faelamor, and held in her thrall all her life,' said Yggur, 'and she has always resented her Faellem heritage. You need look no further to understand why she's the way she is –'

The Numinator flicked her fingers at Yggur and he doubled over, struggling for breath. 'But next,' she continued as though he had not interrupted, 'after three days of the most awful labour, came Rulken.' Her stern, sad face lit up in memory. 'He was big and dark and strong, the image of his father, and from birth I taught him that he was the chosen son of a chosen people.'

'He was a spoiled, angry brute,' said Yggur, thin-lipped.

'Karan robbed him of what was his by right – her daughter!' the Numinator said, then faltered. 'But the curse of the Charon continued in him. Rulken spread his seed widely but died young and only ever produced one child; unfortunately, Gilhaelith proved unsuitable.'

'Gilhaelith?' frowned Yggur. 'The tetrarch we knew, who died – turned to crystal – at the end of the war?'

'Tetrarch is another word for *quartine*,' said the Numinator. 'Gilhaelith took that title to mock my failure. He was flawed; the curse was in him too.'

'So you were forced to turn to Illiel,' said Yggur, 'the son you'd scorned and sent back to live with his own kind.'

'What *kind*?' said Flydd.

'Not all of the Faellem returned to Tallallame at the end of the Time of the Mirror,' said Yggur. 'Some remained where they had lived for thousands of years, in the endless cold forests of the south.'

'Really?' said Flydd. 'How come the scrutators didn't know that?'

'I kept it from you,' said the Numinator. 'I already knew their bloodlines.'

'Illiel was a quiet, scholarly man, devoted to his mancery, though he never employed it on any useful task,' said the Numinator. 'He refused me, and with all the Faellem arrayed behind him I dared not try to take him back. He had only one child, a daughter, Liel, but he hid her from me and by the time I tracked her down it was too late.'

'You mean she was too old to bear children,' said Yggur, 'even if you could have found a suitable *triune* mate.'

'How come you were still fertile after thousands of years,' Maelys said to Yalkara, 'yet the Numinator's granddaughter was not, after, what, fifty years? It doesn't make sense.'

'We Charon are not as other species,' Yalkara said

imperiously. 'We might only be fertile once in five hundred years, and then only with the right mate. But once we know it,' she said with a chilly glance at the Numinator, 'no force in the universe can keep us apart.'

'But you did not give up,' Yggur continued to the Numinator as though the exchange had not taken place.

'I never give up,' said the Numinator. 'I was continuing the breeding project that Rulke began long ago, in a last attempt to save something of his kind. I owed it to him to complete it.'

'There was one other way to create a *quartine*,' said Yggur, evidently thinking aloud. 'Though it would be agonisingly difficult. The Charon, Faellem and Aachim rarely interbred with old humans, but it had happened from time to time and those *blendings* had many descendants. Few would be suitable, yet if you could assemble a bloodline registry covering everyone on Santhenar, you might, with immense labour, identify which blendings to breed together, and rebreed their *triune* offspring. It could take hundreds of years to produce the perfect *quartines* you needed, but you had infinite patience as well as long life.'

'Do you mean that the sole purpose of the scrutators,' cried Maelys, 'was to compile the bloodline registers for the Numinator? But . . . thousands of people must have suffered and died at their hands.'

'Tens of thousands,' said Flydd harshly, clearly mortified at how he had been used, 'and hundreds of thousands more died in the senselessly prolonged war. And I played a part in it. I thought I was doing the right thing, aiding the war, yet all my life I've been a pawn in a greater game –'

'It was no game. It was the noblest purpose of all,' said the Numinator, 'though none of *you* would have the vision to understand it.'

'There's not a drop of nobility in you, *Numinator*,' cried Maelys. 'You're evil; sick!'

Yellow light shot from the Numinator's hand and would have burned her eyes out had not Yggur deflected it with his right bracelet. It fizzed; his wrist sizzled; smoke rose from it and he thrust it into the shin-deep ice slurry on the floor, grimly enduring the pain. 'Maelys, be quiet!'

'So that's what all the monstrosities in jars are, down below,' said Colm, shaking his head. 'And the inhuman creatures in the ice coffins – *failed breedings*.'

'And the breeding factories were yours as well,' Flydd said, sparks flying from his eyes. 'They were set up so enough children would be born to replace everyone killed in the war, but that never rang true to me. The women in the breeding factories never mated with the same man twice, and that was your doing too.' His voice rose; he was shaking. 'Everything the scrutators did was a lie!'

'The flaws in your character are gaping, Flydd,' said Colm. 'You scrutators ruthlessly used everyone else, yet you can't bear to discover that *you* were duped.'

'It was the most far-reaching scheme of all time,' said the Numinator matter-of-factly. 'The bloodline registers had revealed a host of *blendings*; the breeding factories were my way of screening out those few worthy candidates from thousands of useless ones. *They* were fodder for the war, while those who showed promise were sent to me.'

'Where you callously bred them to produce the monstrosities down below,' said Flydd. 'So what went wrong, Numinator? You'd thought of everything; you'd perfected your plan over a hundred and fifty years. Why did it fail?'

'I was so close,' said the Numinator, tight-mouthed. She wrapped her arms around herself, rocking back and forth on the balls of her feet. 'Twenty-five years ago I finally saw born two perfect *triune* children, and all I had to do was wait until they grew old enough –'

'Then mate them like cattle in the barn!' Maelys burst out.

'I would not have treated *them* so crudely,' said the Numinator. 'They were worthy; they were precious and I did not want to damage them in any way. I planned to bring them together at the critical time, and then their off-spring – their perfect, *quartine* children – would be mine. I came so close. Ten years ago the girl was within weeks of bringing forth her first child when . . . when . . .' Her face crumpled and she covered it with her hands.

'When the war with the lyrinx ended,' said Yggur, 'and brilliant, foolish Tiaan, who had never come to terms with her own childhood in a breeding factory, destroyed every node on Santhenar.'

'A bitter blizzard swept across Noom that night, and it raged for weeks,' whispered the Numinator, shivering as though it was blowing through her eyrie now. 'I could not use my Art; I was lucky to survive. Had it not been for my loyal Whelm I would have frozen to death.'

'They were *my* loyal Whelm, once,' said Yggur, staring over the barricade at the silent gathering on the stairs. 'Though their oaths proved hollow when a *better* master came along.'

'They were Rulke's first of all,' said the Numinator, 'and once he escaped the Nightland their oath to him took precedence. Besides, they could have no better master than I, and they knew it.' She paused, then continued, her eyes wide in the horror of her memories. 'After the blizzard passed, I discovered that the hundreds of useful *blendings* I had so painstakingly gathered from the corners of the globe, the handful of worthy *triunes*, and my perfect pair with their unborn *quartine*, had frozen to death. I had lost everything.'

'Yet you did not give up,' said Yggur. Was that a trace of admiration in his voice? Surely he wasn't falling under her spell? 'You never despaired.'

'I despaired many times,' said the Numinator, 'but how could I give up? I began from scratch, though it was far harder this time, with no scrutators to do my work for me, and little power –'

'Until you enticed me here,' said Yggur, 'knowing that my mancery came from an older Art, independent of the nodes and not destroyed when they were lost. Your Whelm bound me with these bracelets, to tap my power for yourself.' He held up his wrists. The bracelets were somewhat corroded now, but still looked strong.

'I would have done anything,' said the Numinator. 'My memorial had to be completed, whatever the cost.'

'It never will be,' said Flydd. 'This ends here, now.'

He sprang towards her, and Yggur did too, but she wove between them, tapping Yggur's left bracelet as she passed, and a dazzling flash lit up the tower top. He fell to his knees, shaking his wrist; Maelys smelt burnt skin and charred flesh.

When she could see clearly again, the Numinator had scrambled over the ice barricade and the Whelm were closing around her, concealing her from view. Jag-swords up, they went backwards *en masse*, around the turn of the stairs.

'She took an awful lot of power that time,' said Yggur through bared teeth. His left arm had developed an uncontrollable tremor and he had to cling to the side of the empty fire bowl. 'She'll be back. Flydd, make the bloody portal and get us out of here!'

'I'm still suffering from the last one. Besides, we have one more matter to deal with.' Flydd's eyes met Yalkara's.

'My son is dead,' she said, 'but if a child comes of his union with Maelys, I will have it.'

'You won't!' cried Maelys despairingly.

'The Numinator's determination pales before mine,' said Yalkara. 'My power is almost spent but, when I return, I will have the child. Until then, Maelys is under my protection.'

She made a sign over Maelys's head and her aura sprang out, deep blue with a carmine border. The taphloid's innards spun; the aura faded.

'Your protection won't matter to Jal-Nish,' Maelys burst out.

'What's he got to do with it?' Yalkara said.

'I – I told him I was pregnant with Nish's child; it was the only way to save my family, for Jal-Nish wants a grandchild more than anything.'

'Yet you were a virgin when you lay with my son,' said Yalkara. 'Explain.'

Why hadn't she kept her mouth shut? Maelys would have given anything to avoid repeating her mortifying lie, but there was no way out of it. 'I nursed Nish when he was injured. Back at Mistmurk Mountain, I told Jal-Nish that I had gathered Nish's spilled seed and placed it within me, so as to get with his child, but that wasn't true.'

'You lied to the God-Emperor?' said Yalkara. 'Are you very bold, or incredibly stupid? The latter, I think; assuming you're telling the truth now.'

'I am,' Maelys said desperately, staring at the hard faces around her, and none harder than her former friends, Colm and Flydd. 'You've got to believe me this time . . .'

'How can I believe anything you say, even the story you *fed me* about Emberr? I think that, knowing his secret vulnerability, you carried chthonic fire back to the Nightland to kill him.'

'I loved him!' Maelys wailed, feeling every pillar of her life crumbling around her.

'Another lie?' said Yalkara, granite-faced.

'Everyone tells lies sometimes,' said Maelys. 'I –'

'But they don't boast about it to their enemies. You're a fool, Maelys Nifferlin, and that's unforgivable in the mother of *my* grandchild.'

'I didn't boast,' wept Maelys. 'I was just trying to explain.'

Yalkara cut her off. 'The Numinator is coming back, armed with a mighty power. Flydd, we need the portal *now*.'

Flydd put his hand into the pocket of his coat and began fiddling with something there. 'I'll try, though I don't know where to go. Portals can only open in a few special locations, but I can't think of any that would be safe from Jal-Nish.'

'I know a couple of lands we might try,' said Yggur, 'though they're at the furthest corners of his empire.'

'I'll jump to *any* corner of the empire, as long as it's warm. The very marrow of my bones has frozen.'

'I'll conjure up an image –' began Yggur. 'Maelys, is something wrong?'

HELP! HELP! HELP! HELP! HELP! She fell to her knees in the slush, holding her head, as the painful cry went on and on. It was vaguely familiar now. Pictures began to form in her mind.

'Feet, squelching through knee-deep mud,' she wheezed. 'Forest covered in vines and ferns; beautiful birds with tails like rainbow-coloured umbrellas. Hot! Sweating.'

'Hot sounds good,' said Flydd.

'A tall mountain shaped like a white, curved thorn or horn,' said Maelys.

'I know it!' cried Yggur. 'Far to the tropical north, Lauralin ends in a stubby peninsula called Gendrigore. No boat can land on its wild shores; the only way in is via a jungle track over a high pass guarded by a horn-shaped peak of white rock. We could hide in Gendrigore forever.'

HELP! HELP! HELP!

Could it be who she thought it was? It didn't seem right, for *she* never panicked, never seemed out of control. 'I think it's Tulitine,' whispered Maelys. 'Calling for help.'

'Who is Tulitine?' said Yalkara.

Maelys explained.

'You mentioned her when we first met,' said Flydd thoughtfully. 'If the Defiance have gone to Gendrigore, Nish might be there too. Can you locate this place, Yggur?'

'I believe I can pull the image from her mind and give it to you.' He took Maelys's wrist.

'Hold the taphloid to your forehead, Maelys,' said Yalkara. 'Hurry! I don't know where the Numinator has found such power, but it's growing fast. Soon she'll be stronger than all of us.'

Maelys didn't like the way Yalkara said *us*. She could never be one of us.

'The Whelm are coming!' rapped Flangers, on watch at the barricade. 'And the Numinator is carrying Zofloc's fire flask – it's as bright as the moon.'

Maelys pressed the taphloid against her head and concentrated on the white-thorn peak.

'Got it,' grunted Flydd, scooping up chthonic fire from the pit in the floor. The other hand was still in his pocket.

'Gather around,' Yggur said quietly to the prisoners. 'Get ready to jump the second it opens.'

With a roar, at least twenty Whelm stormed the barricade, boosting each other up and over, then the Numinator came soaring high above it, holding the flask of distilled white fire in her right hand. Maelys could feel the peril radiating from it. If only Flydd had left it alone. But if he had, she would never have met Emberr.

And Emberr would still be alive. If only she hadn't gone back to him.

The Numinator landed a few spans away, sliding in a curve like an ice skater. 'Hold! Be still!' she rapped, shaking the flask, whose brilliance swelled until it was dazzling. 'I have enough distilled flame to raze the entire Island of Noom. Maelys, come with me.'

'Don't move,' said Yalkara, shielding her eyes. 'Flydd, make the portal.'

Flydd whipped his fist from his pocket, held it high, then brought it together with the hand holding the chthonic flame. This time a whirling, cocoon-like portal exploded into being, pointing north.

'Get in!' he cried, and the prisoners ran for its puckered entrance. A shrill wind whistled down its wormhole, briefly interrupted as each person sprang in and was fired away like peas down a pea shooter.

The Whelm moved to stop them but the Numinator raised her free hand. 'The prisoners may go,' she said with a fixed smile. 'Why should I feed useless mouths? You, too, Flydd and Yggur. The lot of you may go, *save Maelys.*'

'If I have to stay,' gasped Maelys, finding it hard to breathe, 'at least give me something in return – to help them fight the God-Emperor.'

The Numinator frowned, then nodded. 'Everything has a price, even you. Beg your boon, and if it's within my power I will provide it.'

'Tell them where to look for the antithesis to Jal-Nish's Profane Tears.'

'You asked me that before,' said the Numinator. 'I do not know, though . . . all knowledge collected by the God-Emperor's spies passes through Gatherer. Look within the tears.'

'Thanks!' Maelys muttered. They'd come all this way and lost so much, for nothing. Perhaps the antithesis did not exist, and there would be nothing with which to fight the God-Emperor.

The Numinator inclined her head, as if Maelys's thanks had been genuine. She wasn't looking at her, though. She was staring at Yalkara, defying her enemy to take her on.

Yalkara stood with her arms folded across her breast, waiting, but for what?

The Numinator sniffed the air and looked around sharply. 'What's that in your hand, Flydd?'

'A little focus, to help me create the portal,' he said, too hastily.

She raised the roiling flask. 'You may be able to hold ordinary chthonic fire, Flydd, but were I to smash this flask, its contents would sear the flesh from your standing bones, then eat the bones as well. *Show me what's in your hand.*'

He opened his hand to reveal the dirty little ball of wood. 'It's just a mimemule . . .'

'Ahhh!' sighed the Numinator, as if a precious secret had been revealed. 'But there is no such thing as *just a mimemule*. There is only *one* mimemule, and that is it.'

'How can you tell?' said Maelys.

'It is the mimemule Faelamor brought to Santhenar from Tallallame when she came here, thousands of years ago. I would know it anywhere.'

Yalkara stepped forward and stood next to Maelys, studying the dirty wooden ball. Maelys shrank away and Yalkara smiled grimly. The last of the prisoners had passed through the portal now; it began making a soft *thrum-thrumming*. Colm, Chissmoul and Flangers stood beside the entrance; the Whelm were arrayed in a semi-circle behind the Numinator with the sorcerer Zofloc standing before them.

Yggur gestured. Flangers and Chissmoul jumped in, though Colm remained to the side, fists clenched around the black hilt of a jag-sword.

'*My* mimemule,' he grated. 'It was left to Karan, and after she murdered her family my branch of the clan inherited all that remained. I am the sole heir; the mimemule is mine.'

'I don't care who lays claim to it,' said the Numinator, though there was a strange, feverish light in her eyes which hadn't been there before. 'Hold it up so I can see.'

He did so and she stared at it for a full minute. 'And you've used it, what, seven times?'

'Only three times,' said Flydd. 'Once to open the portal from Dunnet, once down below, and now.'

'I also used it,' said Maelys, 'when I killed the flappeter. And you made our furs with it, Xervish.'

'I read seven times,' said the Numinator. 'Five times recently, and twice a long time ago.'

And Rulke's virtual construct had also been used before, Maelys remembered. By whom?

'Where did you find it?' said the Numinator.

'In Faelamor's treasure cave in Dunnet,' said Flydd. 'Just as it is told in the *Tale of the Mirror*.'

The feverish light grew. The Numinator's eyes reflected the chthonic flame as though it burned inside her. What had the mimemule told her, and why did it matter so much?

'I spent ages in that cave during the Time of the Mirror,' she said. 'I know it well. Karan refused to claim her treasure and, despite the perpetual illusion, the cave was soon looted. I went there after her death but nothing remained.'

'The mimemule wasn't with the box that had contained the treasures,' said Maelys. 'I found it buried in the dirt.'

'Well, it wasn't there when I came,' said the Numinator. 'I dug up the floor of the cavern to make sure.'

'Someone took the mimemule and later replaced it,' said Flydd. 'So what?'

'It is one of the most precious artefacts of all,' said the Numinator. 'Why take it, then travel all that way to bring it back?'

Flydd shrugged. 'To leave it for its rightful owner?'

'Me!' Colm hissed.

'Go through, Colm,' snarled Flydd.

Colm's jaw knotted and for one terrible moment Maelys thought he was going to cut Flydd down, then he whirled and jumped into the portal.

'I think I'll take a little trip to Dunnet.' The Numinator held out her hand for the mimemule. 'Come, Maelys.' The flask of chthonic fire shook ever so slightly; the Whelm were tense as wire.

'Now, Flydd!' Yalkara roared.

Her left arm snaked around Maelys's waist, lifted her effortlessly and threw her into the portal. As Yalkara dived after her, the wind tumbled them away, head over heels.

The Numinator swung the flask at them but Flydd and Yggur jumped in together. The portal began to close and she couldn't get to it in time. In furious silence she hurled the flask at the side wall of her eyrie, where it burst, spraying distilled fire everywhere. She drew power from the white fire, clapped her hands and vanished, and the Whelm with her.

As Maelys was fired along the portal, the Tower of a Thousand Steps exploded into a million shards of chthonic-fire-riven ice which were blasted up in a churning mushroom cloud. Fire-ice began to fall onto the Island of Noom and the frozen surface of the Kara Agel.

And Maelys could tell that it was going to feed on the ice, and grow and spread, until white fire had consumed every speck in the Antarctic realm of Santhenar.

FORTY-NINE

Gi winced every time she looked at Nish, for his whole face was swollen and the black bruising had spread up beneath both eyes and halfway across his right cheek. He was squatting in the mud with his commanders, Hoshi, Gi, Clech and Forzel, eating handfuls of raw, mouldy grain, for Boobelar's worst followers had fled in the night with all the good food. He had about four hundred and fifty men left, of which a hundred were so ill with dysentery that they could barely walk and certainly couldn't fight.

They were eating the grain raw because they dared not light a cooking fire this close to the pass, even if they could have made the saturated wood burn. They still had a few haunches of meat but it was so foul that eating it raw would have been a death sentence.

'We've got food enough for one more meal,' he said quietly, 'but I'm not sure what to do. If Curr *has* betrayed us, attacking via Liver-Leech Pass will put us between the jaws of Father's pincers. Yet if we retreat, the enemy can surge down and sweep us off the sides of the mountain. Whatever we do, it's bound –'

'Don't say it,' said Gi with an anxious glance at the miserable troops, who were huddled further down the slope. 'If you don't say it, it won't have as much force. If we retreat, we've lost. But if we continue the attack there's a faint chance we might succeed, and . . . if I have to die, I'm not going to die running away.'

Nish's stomach churned from the worst breakfast he'd had since escaping from his father's prison; it fumed in his belly like quicklime. Might they succeed? He thought it most unlikely, but Gi was right; attack was their only hope. 'Let's put it to the vote, shall we?'

'Let's not,' said Clech, the fisherman. He rubbed his lantern jaw with fingers scarred from his fishing lines, and his gentle eyes met Nish's. 'You're our commander; we trust you. Give the order and we'll follow it, whatever it is.'

Nish didn't think he had ever been that trusting, and he'd known more bad commanders than good ones, yet his militia were fighting for their country and their families, and nothing could better stiffen the backbone and fortify the quaking heart. He hoped *he* wouldn't betray their trust. No, he told himself, I won't, no matter what.

'All right; we attack.'

He sent the ill troops down in a staggering line, sure that he would never see any of them again. The able-bodied, all three hundred and forty-seven of them, headed up the razor-edged roof of the world, crossed the ravine at a natural rock arch and climbed along the left-hand ridge of a valley shaped like a steeply tilted oval bowl, in the incessant, teeming rain. The rain was cool at this height, which was a pleasant change. The humidity wasn't as stifling but his clothes still chafed with every movement. Above them towered the ominous white-thorn peak, pointing to the heavens like a warning finger.

'Are you sure this is only the wet season?' Nish grumbled. 'It feels like the *really wet* season to me.'

'When the *really wet* season gets here, you'll know it,' said Forzel, rubbing at a mark on his hand. He always looked his best, and even here his clothes appeared to have been freshly washed. 'The rain beats down so hard that it drives the hairs back into your skull and out your chin. In the *really wet* season, even women and children have whiskers.'

Nish smiled; Forzel was always talking nonsense.

'It's a wonder The Spine hasn't washed away,' said Hoshi.

'The faster it falls down, the faster the stone giants in the cracks of the world push it up again,' said Forzel. 'Careful where you sit down; you might get a pointy rock right up the –'

'What's that?' hissed Nish. He'd caught a faint flicker-flash from the lower side of the bowl.

'It's the *turn back* signal,' said Gi, sheltering her eyes from the rain.

'It could be a trap,' said Hoshi.

'Anything could be a trap,' said Nish, 'but I've a feeling this isn't. We're going down – this way.'

They descended a stony, moss-covered slope then crept into the rainforest covering the floor of the valley, heading towards a small oval clearing. He left the militia well above it and continued alone. The sodden ground squelched with every movement, like a sponge made of peat.

At the upper side of the clearing he stopped, alert for a trap. Nothing moved; nothing seemed suspicious, though an army could have been hidden in the forest below him and he would never know it.

He took a deep breath, which hurt his broken nose abominably, walked out into the open, and waited. Shortly a woman stopped at the lower edge and stood with her arms folded, watching him. She seemed familiar so he went closer. From a distance she could have been Tulitine's daughter, for she had the same tall, slender figure; rather more upright, though, and much younger. Not yet fifty.

'Who are you?' Nish said as he approached, for the likeness was uncanny. 'Are you Tulitine's daughter?'

She laughed, and it was like Tulitine's laughter, too, though lacking the hoarseness of the old woman's voice. 'My children are long dead. I am Tulitine.'

Nish gaped. 'It's a very fine illusion.'

'It's no illusion. I used the Regression Spell to turn back my age. Once it wears off I'll pay dearly, but for the moment I'm forty-five again – younger than you look, incidentally.'

Nish touched his swollen face. He had never heard of the Regression Spell; nor had he been aware that Tulitine could use the mancer's Art. 'How did you catch us?'

'I used another charm, of unrelenting stamina. Because of my heritage I see well in the dark –'

'What heritage?' Tulitine herself was an enigma enclosed within a paradox.

She went on as though he hadn't spoken. 'I've walked day and night for four days, without stopping. You must turn back, Nish. Whatever happened to your clearsight?'

'It hasn't been much in evidence since Vivimord took me to Gendrigore, but it was never reliable.'

'I've often wondered why your wits seemed so dull.'

Nish wasn't offended. She'd always had an acid tongue but he didn't think she meant it. But then, maybe she did. And maybe she was right.

Tulitine lifted his scarred hand, studying the restored skin there, which had grown steadily darker over the past weeks. 'I didn't notice this when I dressed your hand a month ago.'

He explained about the cursed flame, and Vivimord's blood dripping onto his hand.

'And you did that, even though Flydd tried to stop you? You're a fool punished by his folly. The blood formed a bond between you and Vivimord, and with it he fashioned an enchantment that still dulls your wits, even now he's gone. I'm not sure I can remove it completely.'

Her cool fingers tapped a lengthy pattern on his brow; she whispered something; he felt a sharp pain behind his eyes and the enchantment faded. The pain of his broken nose also eased a little.

'Who are you, Tulitine?' he said as they climbed to the

top of the clearing, slipping on the wet grass. 'Are you one of the great mages of ancient times, hidden for centuries?'

She shook her head. 'I was hidden for a long time, but for my own protection.'

'Who would want to harm you?'

'We have more important things to talk about, Nish. I know a spell or two, not because I have a great gift for the Art – I don't – but because I was taught by the best, for my protection. I've lived a humble life, and I never wanted to excel at anything save healing. I had a calling for that – it was my way of making good.'

It was an odd thing to say. 'Why? Had you done something terrible?'

'Not *I!*' They were at the top of the clearing now. She preceded him into the gloom under the trees, then turned to face him. 'And I was greatly loved,' she said as if in afterthought, 'which was worth more to me than a hundred lives of the mighty.'

'I don't understand,' said Nish. 'Where did –?'

'There's no time for this,' she said urgently. 'I learned four days ago that Curr was a traitor. He led you astray, delayed you so the enemy could reach the pass first. Blisterbone is strongly garrisoned and you could not take it with five times the troops you have. You must retreat all the way to the lowlands, not stopping day or night, or you won't survive.'

'We've got no food, and they'll cut us off before we can get down to our track.'

'There's still a chance,' said Tulitine. 'They don't know you're here.'

'They must. Curr has been gone for ages.'

'I know, for the birds spoke to me, and the wind in the trees, that he was set on betrayal. I followed him; came upon him in the dark so silently that he didn't know I was there.' Her unclouded eyes were bright in the dripping shade. 'I broke my solemn healer's oath, cut him down from behind and wrung the truth out of him before he died. He had not yet given you away. The cur will do no more betraying – and I no more healing. I am no longer worthy. Call your troops.' She turned away, head bowed and looking her age again.

Nish whistled; shortly Gi and Hoshi appeared. 'Curr's betrayed us. Retreat to the track we came up, and keep low.'

Gi and Hoshi ran, but the militia had just reached the clearing when an army horn echoed back and forth across the bowl-shaped valley. Another joined it from the lower rim. And Nish's force did not carry horns. His marrow went cold.

'They must have spotted you from the lookout above the pass,' said Tulitine.

'And they'll be quick down the ridges.' Nish suppressed the panic, trying to think. 'We may be able to get out the lower end of the valley before they close it off, if we run.'

'I don't know this valley.'

'The river cuts through a cliff-bound ravine with a natural arch across it. We can scramble through the ravine beside the water. Come on.'

Before they had skirted the clearing, however, Nish could see hundreds of soldiers moving down both ridges, making no effort to conceal themselves. The enemy must have been watching them for hours.

'They're moving faster than we are,' said Gi, heaving one boot out of calf-deep mud. 'They'll be at the stone bridge before we're halfway.'

Nish called a halt, watching his father's men moving around the edges of the bowl as if they owned the world. Gi was right. They couldn't get out through the ravine, nor over the ridges, and the top of the valley ended in an unclimbable cliff running all the way up to the white-thorn mountain. There was nowhere to go.

'Raise a surrender flag, Gi. One single life lost in a hopeless cause is too many.' Nish had trouble meeting her clear young eyes, for she was going to die; all his cheerful, friendly soldiers were. When Jal-Nish made an example of Gendrigore, everyone would die, save Nish.

Gi ran back to give the orders. Tulitine seemed even younger now; the faint wrinkles that had been at the corners of her eyes half an hour ago were gone, and her skin was smoother and paler, as if she'd lived her life indoors.

'The Regression Spell is still *younging* me,' she said with a faraway smile, 'though it doesn't have far to run now.'

'And then?'

'I'll reach a certain age, about thirty-five, and maintain it for a week, perhaps even a month, after which I'll slowly and painfully revert. Everything has a price, and the Regression Spell has a particularly cruel one.' She shuddered and clenched her small fists. 'It's no use; there's only one way to avert the catastrophe –'

Nish began to speak but she gestured him to silence.

'Which I helped to create by speaking in riddles, to avoid breaking my healer's oath and facing up to what had to be done. I must call on the one person I loathe more than any other – the one I swore *never* to turn to, no matter how bitter my circumstances.'

'Who's that?' said Nish, the skin of his back crawling.

'My terrible grandmother!'

She turned around several times, eyes closed, her beautiful face turned up to the drenching rain until it cascaded off her cheeks and chin. Her lips moved. More soldiers were lining up along the ridges, waiting for something, or *someone*. Jal-Nish?

'I can't see *her* at all,' Tulitine burst out. 'She's cut me off. Why would she do that?'

Nish's faint hope sank again, until he took in the emphasis in her words. 'Who can you see?'

'It – it feels like Maelys.'

'Maelys!' She was still alive, and that mattered, not just because she might be carrying his child. He understood her so much better now, and what drove her to do all she had done. 'Why would you see Maelys, of all people?'

'I cannot say. I haven't used this spell in ninety years – near half my lifetime. *And it wasn't answered that time, either,*' she said under her breath. 'What should I do? I'm at a loss. I'll call her. At least if we all die here, someone will know what's happened to us.'

Tulitine stood still for several minutes, her lips moving. More soldiers appeared on the ridges every minute.

The air crackled; a miniature bolt of lightning fizzed above their heads. Nish jumped; Hoshi let out a squeal; Tulitine broke off her murmuring.

A yellow sausage exploded into being twenty or thirty paces away in the clearing, expanded hugely and a puckered sphincter formed in its end. *Rrrrippp.* A hurricane of freezing air burst forth, hurling everyone off their feet; mist eddies spun in all directions like miniature tornadoes; bodies were ejected from the sphincter one by one – people wearing thick, fleecy clothes and furs covered in a layer of frost.

Nish had landed on his back in the mud and felt the tip of his nose and the lobes of his ears go numb, then the mud began to freeze around him. He looked up to the most astonishing sight – snow settling over the rainforest as a myriad of frost-covered people skidded down the wet slope, clutching swords and spears made from crystalline ice. They were looking back fearfully at the place where the portal had opened, but it could no longer be seen.

About thirty-five people had come through, half men and half women, and most had unnaturally pale skin, as if they had not seen the sun in many years. His gaze swung across their faces and he started.

'Xervish?' Flydd looked much as Nish had last seen him, except that his face was even more bruised and swollen than Nish's own. 'What are you doing here?'

'I should ask you the same question, but at least I know where we are,' for he recognised the white-thorn mountain. Flydd gestured at a very tall, well-built man who was climbing to his feet, frost melting off him.

It was a long time since Nish had shed tears of joy, but now he felt his eyes prickling at the sight of his old friend. Yggur had been one of the greatest mancers of all, and he hadn't aged a day in ten years. Surely with Yggur and Flydd they could find a way out of the trap. 'Well met; oh, well met! Tulitine, it's *Yggur*! Where did you come from?'

Flydd answered. 'The Island of Noom, in the Frozen Sea, and the Numinator's Tower of a Thousand Steps. And we didn't get what we went there for, since I'm sure you're about to ask.'

'I couldn't care less,' said Nish, his heart singing. 'Open the portal again and get us out of here.'

FIFTY

Maelys, thrown out of the portal onto a grassy slope in
a deluge, went sliding down on her back in the middle of a freezing cloud and splashed into a dip full of water,
which froze all around her. She tried to sit up but was stuck
fast.

There were hundreds of armed men above her, a rustic mud-drenched army dressed in homespun. She jerked
upright and broke free, for the ice was melting again. The
frost dissolved and suddenly she was sweltering in her
heavy clothing.

She threw off her furs, and all around her the rescued
prisoners were doing the same, their ice weapons melting on the saturated ground. Maelys looked up and Nish
was just five paces away, staring at her. He looked as if
he'd been hit in the face with a brick, but she was glad
to see him. Behind him stood a tall woman who looked
rather like Tulitine, save that she was at least forty years
too young, and very beautiful.

'Is this the help you were looking for?' said Nish to
Tulitine.

The woman who looked like Tulitine shook her head.
Maelys scanned the people who had come from the portal.
Neither Yalkara nor the Numinator were among them and,

for the first time since going back to the Nightland, she dared to hope that she might get away from her enemies.

'It's wonderful to see you, of course,' Nish said to Flydd and Yggur, grinning all over his face, 'but surely you didn't *plan* to hurl yourself into Father's trap.'

Flydd slowly rotated, his boots sinking into the muddy grass, as he took in the enemy army lined up along the ridges. His mouth opened and closed. Maelys, following his gaze, felt her stomach cramp. She'd hoped too soon.

'Well done, Yggur,' Flydd said hoarsely. 'You've excelled yourself this time.'

'You made the bloody portal!' Yggur laughed, though there was no mirth in it. 'How Jal-Nish will crow. All his enemies in one bag, and we climbed into it willingly.'

Maelys closed her eyes. Surely this was her punishment for all the wrongs she'd done, the lies she'd told, the little deceits she'd employed to get her way over the past months. Oh Emberr, Emberr, why did I go back?

'It was close, though,' said Nish. 'Had our guide not betrayed us we would have beaten them to the pass, and Father would have had the fight of a lifetime prising us out. We might even have turned him back; another victory on the long road to casting him off his throne.'

'I'll call again,' said Tulitine, turning her face up to the rain.

Maelys couldn't take her eyes off her. It could not be Tulitine, yet it was.

'Surrender!' boomed an amplified voice from the higher ridge, and Maelys jumped. 'My name is General Klarm. I am commander of the God-Emperor's forces here. Surrender and I give you my word that you will not be harmed. Fight on and you will be slain to the last man and woman, all save Cryl-Nish Hlar and Maelys Nifferlin.'

'I thought he died on Mistmurk Mountain,' said Maelys.

'Evidently Jal-Nish saved his miserable skin.' Flydd turned to Yggur. 'I told you Klarm went over to the enemy,' he said bitterly. 'Listen to him crow, the puffed up little runt.'

'You'll soon topple Jal-Nish from his post as the God of Liars, Flydd.' Colm rose from the grass, dripping mud and glowering. 'Klarm twice told you that he did not take Jal-Nish's side until after he'd won.'

'And you believed him?' cried Flydd.

'I did. I believed you, too, fool that I am, and you betrayed me in the hour of my greatest need. Klarm is an honourable man and I intend to surrender to him.'

'He'll shoot you down like a dog,' Flydd hissed.

'What have I got to lose? You treated me worse than I would ever treat a dog.'

'Colm, no!' cried Maelys.

He spat in her direction, raised his hands and shouted, 'My name is Colm. I surrender.' He walked slowly across the clearing in the direction of Klarm's voice. Maelys put her head in her hands, sure they would shoot Colm down.

'Your surrender is accepted, Colm of Gothryme. Stand well to one side,' called Klarm. 'Flydd, Yggur, my old friends, you cannot escape.'

'Make another portal, Flydd,' Yggur whispered.

'I used all my white fire for the last one.'

'Try the damn mimemule.'

'Without power, I don't know how to make it work.'

Yggur cursed. 'Once Klarm comes down, what say we wrest his knoblaggie from him, crack off these bracelets with it and reopen the portal?'

'As if he won't have thought of that,' Flydd said sourly.

Tulitine was standing face-up to the sky, her lips moving ceaselessly. 'Why won't you come, grandmother?'

'Because you're no use to her,' said Yggur brutally. 'A Regression Spell may have temporarily given you back your youth, but it cannot allow an old woman to bear children, and they're the only thing the Numinator is interested in.'

'The Numinator is your *grandmother*?' cried Maelys. 'Then you must be the only child of –'

'It is I, Liel, daughter of your firstborn, Illiel,' called Tuli-tine. 'I am the only kin you have – does that mean nothing to you?'

'Look out!' yelled Nish.

A hissing sound, like a boiling kettle, grew ever louder, and a platform the size of Rulke's Nightland bed scooted down the ridge and came skimming across the treetops towards them. A number of tall men stood at the back and sides, clad in white armour – Jal-Nish's Imperial Guard. Before them stood the God-Emperor, wearing his platinum half-mask again; the humming tears were looped around his neck on their chain. At his right hand was a handsome dwarf clad in a red and black military uniform, General Klarm. His mane of hair was sheared off in a flat plane across the top of his head, as if it had been burned away.

The air-sled began to shudder violently as it passed over the point where the portal had opened, and Jal-Nish set it down hastily on the grass. Along the ridges, the soldiers trained their arrows at the militia, and particularly at Flydd and Yggur.

Maelys, feeling as if every arrow was aimed at her, instinctively moved closer to Nish.

'I know how you feel.' He put his left arm around her shoulders as though they were old friends and the past had been forgotten, and Maelys felt strangely warmed by the gesture. How she needed a friend.

Nish raised his voice and spoke to his militia. 'My friends, you did everything I asked of you, but we've been beaten by a stronger foe. Your service is over. Run or stay, as you wish. Some of you may break through.'

There was not a trace of the despair he must be feeling – Nish sounded like the great leader from the tales she'd read as a child, and it gave her hope where she'd had none.

No one moved. 'This is just like the last time,' he said to Flydd and Yggur. 'My every encounter with Father repeats what has happened before, then takes it one step further.'

The previous bitterness was also gone; Nish seemed to have reached an acceptance of his fate, which was more than Maelys could do.

'Mutiny in your ranks, Cryl-Nish?' said the God-Emperor, referring to Nish's black and blue face. 'Flydd.' He nodded stiffly. '*Yggur* – what a pleasure it is to see *you* again after so many years. Where have you been hiding?'

Yggur held up the bracelets. 'I fell into the hands of the Numinator and she hobbled me.'

'It's as well I only recently learned of her existence,' said Jal-Nish. 'How did she hide her realm from Gatherer?'

'You'd have to ask her that,' said Yggur.

'Oh, I will.' The God-Emperor's gaze fell on Maelys and her insides turned to ice, for she knew what he was going to say. 'Not showing yet, I see.'

'There are signs, Grandfather, of my child,' she lied. 'It's only three months, but there are unmistakable signs.'

'My healers will check them with the utmost thoroughness.' On recognising Flangers and Chissmoul, who were holding hands, he smiled grimly. 'Minor fugitives from olden times, but revenge will be tasty nonetheless. Guards, take them.'

The guards had just stepped off the air-sled when the air went storm-cloud black beneath it, thunder rolled and the air-sled was thrown spans into the air. Klarm tumbled head over heels to the left but landed on his feet like a circus acrobat. Jal-Nish, taken by surprise, slammed into the ground on his good arm and shoulder and the tears went flying. He snatched at them but they rolled out of reach down the slope, connected by their chain, making ominous crackling sounds and charring the grass in twin, steaming paths.

Yggur was about to spring for them but Klarm had his knoblaggie out in the twitch of an eyelid, pointing its brassy end at Yggur's heart. 'You remember this, I'm sure.'

Yggur remained in his crouch for a few seconds, then raised his hands and stood up, and the chance was lost.

Klarm gathered up the tears by their chain, holding them well away from himself.

The air-sled turned over twice and thudded side-on into the ground, bending its frame like a banana. A black mushroom grew behind it – evidently the phenomenon that had thrown it into the air – and Yalkara pushed through its striated stalk.

Maelys moved behind Nish but not before Yalkara saw her. The Imperial Guard lifted the God-Emperor to his feet; he clutched his shoulder with his other hand, winced, then Klarm placed the tears around his neck and Jal-Nish limped across to Yalkara. She was almost a head taller, and inclined her head to look down her nose at him. In other circumstances, Maelys might have cheered.

'Who are you?' Jal-Nish said, unsuccessfully attempting to project the God-Emperor's air of power and invulnerability, though it was evident he was discomfited by her. 'I know all the great powers of this world, and you're not one of them.'

'You didn't know the Numinator existed,' Nish pointed out.

The exposed half of Jal-Nish's face twitched in annoyance. 'She would not have survived had she not siphoned power from Yggur.'

Yalkara said, staccato, 'I am Charon! I am Yalkara! I am not of this world, though I dwelt here for a long time. Indeed, I am not of *any* world. I was birthed in the void, and to the void do I return when my business is done.' Her gaze touched briefly on Maelys.

Maelys turned away; she could not meet Yalkara's eyes. To her left, the air was rippling in front of a tree on the edge of the clearing, twenty paces away. What now?

A faint outline formed there, a slender, female shape, not tall but very upright and stiff. It faded into air again, but Maelys knew the Numinator had come for her.

Yggur was looking in the same direction, probing the burned skin under his bracelets and wincing. He'd seen as well, and Maelys was pleased that he knew. Yggur alone had not judged her, but could he protect her?

Jal-Nish plunged his good hand into Gatherer as if he were checking the truth of what Yalkara had said. 'From the moment I set eyes on you, I knew you had to be from *beyond*. Indeed, when I recently discovered the Nightland had been restored, Reaper told me that no one on Santhenar had the power to do so. You restored it, didn't you?'

'I did,' said Yalkara.

'To attack Santhenar and take it for your own.' His voice had a triumphant ring. 'I read that threat months ago; I told Nish about it before he escaped from prison.'

'What a puffed-up little emperor you are,' she said contemptuously. 'I rebuilt the Nightland for one purpose only – to protect the son I conceived there with my enemy, Rulke, two centuries ago. Alas, being birthed in the Nightland, Emberr could never leave, and now he is dead. Once I have recovered his body I will allow the Nightland to decay into the nothingness it came from, and Santhenar will never see me again.'

Jal-Nish withdrew his hand from Gatherer, studied it – it shook a little – and hastily thrust it back in. The song of the tears resumed. 'You speak truth,' he said.

'I would not bother to lie to an insignificant worm like you.'

Jal-Nish flushed. 'You did not protect your son very well.'

'So says a man who has lost a daughter and three sons . . .'

Suddenly Yalkara's cheeks went as hard as sheets of metal, as though something terrible had occurred to her. 'Oh, irony most bitter!' she whispered.

Jal-Nish and Klarm looked at one another. Klarm shrugged.

'All that time I spent trapped in the void, trying to free Emberr from the Nightland,' she said softly. 'Maintaining it was draining all my strength and I knew it must soon fail; and he would die. I had to get Emberr out, but I could not force a portal through the Nightland's defences.'

'Why didn't you use the chthonic flame?' said Flydd.

'I dared not; not to go *there*. It could have killed Emberr, and alerted . . . *others* to the Nightland's existence. But when the nodes were destroyed, and Jal-Nish concentrated the world's power in his tears, an opportunity came.'

'Really?' said the God-Emperor. He did not look pleased to hear it. 'Pray go on. Tell me everything.'

'I saw an old mancer running for his life, hiding in ditches and living off voles and wood grubs.'

Flydd's head jerked up and he stared at Yalkara. Jal-Nish chuckled.

'He had once been one of the great,' she went on, 'and with a suitable source of power he might be great again. I influenced him – it wasn't hard; his mind lay wide open – to take refuge on top of Mistmurk Mountain. I'd once made portals from its obelisk, so it would be easiest to recreate one there, and power was available from the cursed flame. The mountain's seeping vapours would assist me to get into his mind and make him think my plan was his own.'

'What took you so long?' said Yggur.

'Flydd proved more stubborn than I'd expected. It's hard to influence anyone from the void, very hard; it took me years, but by that time he was close to the end of his life and no longer had the strength to make a portal. He was soon going to die, and my last chance to save Emberr would die with him.'

'But then Nish and Maelys came,' said Flydd. 'Maelys pressured me to take renewal, and you struck.'

'I entered your mind during renewal, when your will was weakest. I taught you the great portal spell and showed you how to use the abyssal flame to do what I could not: open a two-part portal: one part to bring me from the void to Mistmurk, and the other to take me to the Nightland.'

'Ah,' said Flydd. 'I wondered why there were two linked spirals.'

'But the renewal went wrong. You lost your memories and your Art with them and, in trying to help you regain it, I unwittingly allowed you access to *my* memories.'

'Ah,' said Flydd.

'When Vivimord blocked you from opening the portal, you looked deeper. You saw the hidden chthonic flame, the last thing I would have allowed near the Nightland, *or Emberr*, and you opened the portal with it. But that flame is far too powerful; it created the two-part portal in an instant and, before I was ready, Vivimord seized my portal and fled with it, leaving me stuck in the void.'

'He directed the portal here to Gendrigore,' said Nish. 'With me, to set up the Defiance anew.'

'But you got away from him,' said Flydd. 'We'd all like to hear that tale.'

'You can relate it in my torture chambers,' said Jal-Nish, though he made no move to enforce the threat.

Maelys eyed the God-Emperor uneasily. Why didn't he attack? Because he loved to toy with his victims, of course. He had them at his mercy; he could draw out the moment for as long as he liked.

'Flydd went to the Nightland and I was terrified for my son,' said Yalkara, ignoring Jal-Nish, 'but I managed to divert him away from Emberr towards Rulke's virtual construct. If Flydd used it to escape, I might still find a way into the Nightland. It never occurred to me that Maelys was the real danger, for I could barely see her – the taphloid concealed her from me.'

'Poor Emberr,' said Maelys aloud, remembering their first meeting.

'He had been locked into the age of a young man for more than two hundred years, and he was desperately lonely. Emberr was a *romantic!*' Yalkara said it as though it was a weakness. 'He yearned for the love of a good woman. I had shaped him thus, for he could only escape by trapping a young woman to take his place and passing his Nightland essence to her. I never thought he would be so weak as to put his feelings for another above his own needs.'

'I'm sure no other Charon was ever so weak,' said Maelys.

'If we had been, we would not have survived. Emberr scented you, and drew you to him, but instead of trapping you and escaping, as I'd taught him to do, he fell for you, and you for him. When the opportunity came, and the Numinator made her portal to the Nightland, Maelys went back to Emberr, lay with him, *and killed him.*'

Hundreds of heads, including the entire militia, turned Maelys's way, staring at her in horror and disgust. The God-Emperor's fingers sank, black-nailed and claw-like, into Reaper and she knew it was the end, for her and her family.

'She lay with him, then killed him?' Jal-Nish grated. 'The callous little bitch.'

'*And* killed him, I said,' Yalkara went on, very softly. 'Again, unwittingly. In a bitter irony of truly cosmic proportions, Maelys's skin bore traces of the chthonic flame she'd leapt through to enter the portal, and when they lay together it passed to him. It could not harm her, but it was deadly to Emberr.'

'Why so?' said Jal-Nish, his voice rather high-pitched. 'I don't see the irony.'

'You never could,' sneered Flydd, as if he had nothing to lose. 'It's one of your greatest failings, *God-Emperor.*'

The rain stopped suddenly. Yalkara spoke more softly yet. 'Chthonic fire does not exist only in our physical world. It can, or at least it once *could*, inhabit any of the eleven dimensions of space and time. That is why it's so useful for making portals, and why it was inimical to Emberr. Because he was partly *of* the Nightland, the chthonic fire began to unmake him inside. His love had betrayed him.'

Maelys ground her fists into her eyes to keep back the

tears, but as she did so, she remembered Emberr looking down at the white fire shimmering on her skin. Bestowing that enigmatic smile on her, he'd said, *You truly are the woman who will free me.* Had he known what the fire was? Had he lain with her, knowing that it would kill him, rather than obey his mother's imperative to trap her in his place? He must have, and it was the noblest sacrifice of all. Nothing could stop Maelys's tears now.

'I was sure the Nightland had been rebuilt by some beast from the void,' said Jal-Nish, and now the tremor was reflected in his voice, 'to attack beautiful Santhenar. I used Gatherer to peer into the void's darkest recesses –'

'You did what?' cried Yalkara.

Jal-Nish began to pace back and forth in agitation. 'I – I could not do any harm by looking.'

'The inhabitants of the void hate creeping, sneaking spies far more than they hate intruders, little emperor. You could see no more than the vaguest threat, and a meaningless one, since threats are everywhere in the void. But you, *and Santhenar,* out of all the billions of worlds in the universe, will have been located by at least one of the creatures that roam the void – the one that sees everything in it. When did you discover the Nightland? Quick!'

'After Flydd opened the portal there from Mistmurk Mountain, over a month ago,' said Jal-Nish. 'But I could not follow –'

'*You* could not break into the Nightland even if you expended all the power of the Profane Tears. But *it* will have seen what you were looking at,' she said relentlessly. '*It* cannot come straight here, for the Three Worlds are protected from the void, but *it* will have noted everything you were spying on.'

'The Nightland forms a weakness in the barrier that protects us from the void, and the desperate creatures that inhabit it,' explained Yggur, running his fingers around the left bracelet, then the right, then the left again.

'For one who knows how,' said Yalkara, 'the Nightland

might be used as a bridge across which to attack Santhe-nar. And there *is* one in the void, the very same all-seeing being, who *does* know how to make such a bridge – indeed, you could say that it *is* a bridge. At least, it *was*.'

Maelys looked from Yalkara to Yggur to Jal-Nish. Just when she thought she knew what was going on a new complication confused everything. This future had definitely not been in her vision in the Pit of Possibilities.

'Who?' whispered Jal-Nish, agitatedly stroking Gatherer, then Reaper, but finding no comfort in either. 'Or what?'

'The shiver-shifter; the ethereal absolute; the shadow of a flame. The Stilkeen.'

FIFTY-ONE

'What the blazes is a stilkeen?' said Jal-Nish.

'Not *a* stilkeen. *The* Stilkeen,' said Yalkara.

'What is *the* Stilkeen?' Jal-Nish snapped.

'A being above time, beyond place. The Stilkeen has a great hunger – seldom satisfied – for the life forces of sentient creatures from the material worlds that it can no longer reach. And once you revealed the Nightland, and Flydd opened it with chthonic fire, the Stilkeen will not have rested until it found a way inside.'

'Is that what killed your son?'

'Chthonic fire killed my son; the white fire I hid in the deepest roots of Thuntunnimoe long ago, because it was too dangerous to use.'

'Perhaps the Stilkeen put her up to it,' said Jal-Nish silkily, nodding at Maelys.

Maelys wiped her eyes and saw his simmering fury. Somehow, Jal-Nish *knew* she'd lied to him.

'Emberr was hidden from the Stilkeen by a spell to which only he held the key,' said Yalkara, 'but everyone else who entered the Nightland would have been in peril.'

'Why was Emberr hidden?' said Yggur, still stroking his bracelets. 'You didn't know Jal-Nish had revealed the Nightland. Indeed, why *would* your son be in danger, in the most secure prison ever built? This tale doesn't add up. There's something you're not telling us, Yalkara.'

The downpour resumed, harder than ever. 'The Stilkeen may have been close by while you and I and the Numinator were there,' Yalkara said, ignoring Yggur's question and looking fixedly at Maelys. 'Even while you lay with my son.'

'I didn't see anything,' said Maelys. Yalkara's gaze seemed to look into her, as if to see if she were bearing Emberr's child. And what if she was? She felt a darker, deeper terror. 'What does the Stilkeen look like?'

'It can take on any aspect. A flake of skin on the floor, a curtain moving in the wind, a flea in your armpit.'

Maelys instinctively scratched herself then, remembering the slurchie that had grown in her belly after she'd eaten contaminated meat, an even greater horror occurred to her. What if it had crept inside her while she and Emberr had made love, or when they'd lain in each other's arms?

'The Stilkeen might be among us now,' Yalkara went on. 'Maelys, or the Numinator, could have brought it back to Santhenar. It would be weak, for in its present state the real worlds are painful to it, but if it is here it's got to be forced out. The tears, *God-Emperor!*' She held out her hand.

Jal-Nish backed away. 'As if I'd fall for that one.' His guards closed around him; Klarm pointed the knoblaggie at Yalkara.

'Imbecile!' hissed Yalkara. 'You can't even touch the menace your folly has brought upon this world.'

'I'm not afraid of some beast from the void.'

'The Stilkeen is no beast. It's a *being!*'

'A – a deity?' Jal-Nish said haltingly.

Her lip curled. 'If it helps you to think of it that way, false God-Emperor. How are you enjoying *this* irony?'

He said nothing, and she went on, '*Give – me – the – tears.*'

'Gatherer and Reaper are the basis of my power,' said Jal-Nish, shaking his head. 'The tears have made me what I am.'

'An empty, self-titled God-Emperor, no more than a

small man's boast, ruling through terror because it's the only authority you'll ever have.'

'It's all I need to crush you!' Jal-Nish snarled, thrusting his good hand into Reaper.

Behind Yalkara, a red pinpoint exploded flames in all directions, throwing mud and smouldering grass high in the air. Maelys was punched backwards against Nish, her head cracking into his chin. His arms caught her, his breath was loud in her ear as some *thing* swelled to its full, enormous size.

No flea in her armpit, this – in its present aspect it stood head and shoulders above Yggur. It had a broad, flattened head, from the sides of which bony plates flared out and back like a multi-winged helmet; its small yellow eyes were covered in clear membranes that swept slowly from side to side; it had a split nose and a gaping, thick-lipped mouth clustered with needle teeth. Its long clawed fingers were webbed; a broad frilled membrane flared out from the backs of its long arms all the way across its shoulders, and it carried a meteoritic iron caduceus – a spear entwined by serpents – the height of a small tree.

The Stilkeen turned this way and that, its clawed, webbed feet tearing up grass, earth and chunks of rock. The muscles shivered all the way down its massive left leg; the left foot clenched and unclenched; dull red flames flickered on its chest and throat.

Why, it's suffering, Maelys realised. The Stilkeen is in terrible pain. This was small comfort, because pain would make it even more savage.

'Where – is – white-ice-fire?' it said in a thick, reverberating voice, the words barely audible over the furnace-rush of air in and out of its quivering throat. 'Who – stole – my – white-ice-fire?'

Its head rotated in a full circle on its massive neck and kept turning, staring at each of them one after another. Maelys noticed that Yalkara had subtly *shifted* her appearance to look smaller, younger, softer, weaker. Why was she hiding? Or *what* was she hiding?

Then Maelys saw that faint wavering outline again. The Numinator. Coming closer.

The Stilkeen's eyes fixed on Jal-Nish, who had his hand deep inside Reaper and was trying to choke out a spell, though he kept mispronouncing the words.

'You!' said the Stilkeen. 'Thief? Where – white-ice-fire?'

'I d-don't know what you're talking about,' Jal-Nish thrust Reaper out at it and began the spell anew.

Yalkara shifted her weight slightly, as if preparing to spring. When she struck the Numinator down in Emberr's cottage, she had been inhumanly fast.

The Imperial Guard swung their weapons from the Stilkeen to her, but Jal-Nish's spell failed as the Stilkeen wrung its hands together. With red flashes bursting from the tops of their skulls and their smoking eyes sliding out of their sockets, the guards fell dead. Klarm was hurled down the slope, clinging to his knoblaggie, then slowly rolled over, breathing steam from his nostrils. The archers on the ridge fired but their arrows exploded in mid-air.

'You – thief!' The Stilkeen caught Jal-Nish with one arm, tossed him high and whirled under him, the frilled membrane spinning out like a wing and lifting it off the ground, then caught him in mid-air.

'Stilkeen claims – God-Emperor – and . . . world.' Each word was like the throbbing of air sucked into a furnace, then it hurled the caduceus straight down so hard that it blasted grass and earth away, and penetrated half a span into solid rock. Its shaft glowed white-hot; the eyes of the entwined serpents were like red coals. Maelys could feel the heat beating on her cheeks.

'Hostage,' rumbled the Stilkeen. 'For – white-ice-fire.'

It shivered with pain, then spun faster and faster until it and Jal-Nish were just a blur. Suddenly the tears flew out and landed fizzing and shrilling at Klarm's feet.

'Klarm, my one honourable lieutenant,' came Jal-Nish's fading voice. 'Guard the tears; maintain my realm until I return.' In a reverse explosion of black flame streaking in to a point, they were gone.

Yalkara threw herself at the tears but was too late – Klarm had already taken them.

'Oh, I see it now,' came the Numinator's voice from just a few steps away.

Her outline became an image hovering on a disc above the grass, though the Numinator maintained a slight transparency. She wasn't taking any risks; wasn't fully appearing until she was ready – for what?

'I see it all now,' she went on, and the bitter edge to her voice was even stronger than it had been in her tower. 'Everything fits; the terrible story is complete.'

'Terrible indeed,' said Tulitine. 'And no one would know better than you, grandmother.'

The Numinator turned her way, started visibly at seeing a youthful woman where, evidently, she had expected a crone, then turned away without acknowledging her granddaughter. Maelys was shocked, and it brought home, as forcefully as anything she'd seen in the past days, just how inhuman the Numinator had become.

'Perhaps you'll enlighten us, Numinator,' said Yggur, again stroking his corroded bracelets. 'Though I don't see how it can be worse than your awful tale.'

'Oh, it's worse – Yalkara's crime began all the tales of the Three Worlds, including my own. I know about the Stilkeen and its loss; Rulke told me. It was the most beautiful and enigmatic being in all the void, one whose constantly changing form, indeed its very existence, was its art and craft; and its Art. It could roam across all of the eleven dimensions of space and time, even the ones rolled up to infinitesimal coils; and for millions of years it did – until someone stole its soul-core at the only moment when it was vulnerable – as it *shifted* to cross from one set of dimensions to another.

'That awful sacrilege *severed* the Stilkeen's body from the higher parts of its being and left what you just saw – its physical self – trapped in our universe, while its spirit aspects were lost in dimensions it could no longer reach. The Stilkeen suffered the most terrible pain and grief for the loss of its other aspects, that it might never join with again. It might never become *whole* again.'

The Numinator's eyes met Yalkara's, challenging her.

'I found chthonic fire hidden in the core of an exploded comet,' said Yalkara arrogantly. 'No one –'

'You knew what white-ice-fire was,' said the Numinator, 'and what it meant to the Stilkeen – its soul-core; the force that bound its physical and spiritual aspects together. Rulke warned you not to touch the chthonic fire, but you stole it anyway, for it was a treasure beyond any price – it offered an escape from the void that you dwindling, *insufficient* Charon had been looking for all your lives.'

'And why shouldn't I take it?' Yalkara flashed. 'In the void, life was a constant battle: survival or extinction. I chose life for my kind.'

'You gave them life – escape to the Three Worlds – and began a thousand tales that echo to this day; but in another, deeper irony, you robbed them of their future.'

Yalkara drew a sharp breath, and seemed to dwindle. She could not meet the Numinator's eyes. 'We did not know it then.'

'On Aachan, something had rendered almost all the Charon sterile,' the Numinator explained. 'No one knew why; they thought the tragedy was due to Aachan itself, for on Santhenar, Rulke and Kandor did father children. But the problem wasn't Aachan, was it, Yalkara? It was the stolen chthonic fire, which existed in many dimensions and could never be truly contained. That's why, when you worked it out, you brought the white fire to Santhenar and hid it where no one would ever find it. You did not tell the other Charon what you'd done to them, though, did you?'

'I could not,' said Yalkara in a bleached voice. 'It would have destroyed them.'

The Numinator, who looked completely solid now,

stepped down off her hovering disc onto the grass. 'It would have destroyed *you* in their eyes, and you could not bear that, for you'd always been hailed as one of the greatest. The Charon would become extinct because you'd stolen the fire, but no Charon must ever know what you'd done.'

'And no one would have known, had you not tried to take control of Flydd's mind, Yalkara,' said Yggur, 'and unwittingly allowed him into yours, where he saw the hidden fire.'

'I had no choice. I had to get Emberr out of the Nightland before . . .'

'The Stilkeen found it,' said Yggur. 'No wonder you left Emberr there, terrified of its revenge.'

'It wasn't the Stilkeen I was worried about. I'd *hidden* the Nightland from it.'

'What then?' Yggur grated. 'Please tell me that you haven't done something even worse.'

'No; everything springs from my first folly,' said Yalkara with bowed head. 'When I took the white fire, the Stilkeen's severed spirit-aspects, or *revenants*, fell into another dimension, a netherworld, and brought it to life. Flydd calls it the shadow realm, and it's the place where the dead from many worlds go. There the lost revenants roam like mischievous spirits, giving the dead a kind of life for their own amusement, and tempting living necromancers and corrupt mages –'

'Like Vivimord,' said Maelys, remembering his threats.

'The revenants grow ever more desperate to rejoin with Stilkeen. I could not hide the Nightland from *them* much longer. I had to get Emberr out before they found it.'

Maelys had an unpleasant thought. 'I pushed dead Phrune into the column of chthonic fire on Mistmurk Mountain. His body fell down the shaft but five wraiths came up, looking just like him, and they were all laughing at me. Have I done something bad?'

Yalkara froze. 'The white fire would have burned his dead flesh away, reducing him to his corrupt essence – those

577

wraiths, and they would be drawn inexorably to the shadow realm. Once they reached it, Stilkeen's revenants would soon have detected the tang of the chthonic flame on them. By now the revenants must know that the white-ice-fire – the one force that can rejoin their severed selves to the Stilkeen – has been found. They can't know where – Phrune can't tell them that – but they'll be struggling to break out of the shadow realm and find the flame.'

'Then give it to them!' cried Maelys. 'The damned stuff has caused nothing but trouble since you stole it.'

'It doesn't work like that.'

'Why not?' she shrieked.

'The Stilkeen will want . . . repayment.'

'Good!' Maelys said vengefully.

'Repayment from everyone who has ever used the flame,' said Yalkara, 'or defiled it by touching it; or has even seen it.'

'Seen it?'

'The Stilkeen is – was, and will be again – a higher being. Even setting eyes upon its soul-core is a monstrous sacrilege, one you'll *all* have to pay for.'

'*But not you?*' What was Yalkara planning?

'Everything you'd done was coming undone,' said the Numinator, 'so you planned to take Emberr and run back to the void, leaving Santhenar to the mercy of Stilkeen and its revenants.'

'Survival or extinction!' exclaimed Yalkara. 'Us or them. It always comes down to that in the end.'

'Not this time!' cried the Numinator. 'Your folly destroyed the only thing you cared about, and you're not getting what's left of him.'

The two women sprang at Maelys in the same moment, but Yggur cast off the bracelets which he had corroded to nothing, whipped her aside and, with a finger-flick, called the Numinator's hover-disc into Maelys's place. Yalkara and the Numinator collided with it in mid-air. The Numinator went transparent again; Yalkara too; light streaked all around them and they vanished as completely as the Stilkeen had done.

Yggur set Maelys on her feet on the grass, but did not let go of her. She could feel the power in his fingers – power such as he hadn't had in seven years.

'What do we do now?' said Flydd. 'This changes everything.'

'It changes nothing!' said Klarm. 'The greater beings may lie and cheat and play with the fate of worlds, but a simple man can only hold to his oath.' He shot a steely glance at Flydd, then settled the tears carefully around his neck. 'We have a common enemy now – the Stilkeen. We cannot afford to be divided, and none of you can fight the tears, or use them, so the God-Emperor's realm must prevail for the good of Santhenar. Surrender and I will do what I can for you.'

'Even with the fate of the world at stake, we're not such fools as that,' grated Flydd.

'Then you leave me no choice. I'm sorry Flydd, Yggur. You were good friends, but Santhenar must come first. It's war to the death, for all save Colm, Nish and any offspring he may have.' Klarm stepped up onto the crumpled air-raft. The song of the tears rose and fell, the air-raft lifted and wavered off through the rain.

Flydd looked at the ragged, filthy militia, then Jal-Nish's spit-polished troops on the ridges, surrounding them on all sides. 'Give your orders, Nish.'

Nish was staring at the red-hot caduceus, and the cracks radiating out from the rock. The grass had burned away for two spans in all directions.

'I wouldn't listen,' he whispered. 'I'm the biggest fool in the world.'

'What are you talking about?' Flydd said impatiently.

'On the day my ten years in prison were up, Father warned me that Santhenar was in danger from the void, but I refused to believe him. I was sure he was trying to manipulate me.

'And I did it again when he came to Mistmurk Mountain. He told me that he wanted to atone for all the terrible wrongs he had done. Father begged me for help, and no one can ever know what it cost him – proud, closed-off man that he is – to humble himself before a son who had always disappointed him. I refused him and called him a liar, both times. And both times he was telling the truth.'

'Jal-Nish is the God of Liars,' said Flydd, 'and the price liars pay is that no one believes them when they are telling the truth.'

'Oh yes,' yelled Colm. 'Oh yes, Flydd. How you're going to rue *your* lies.'

'Run to your new master,' snarled Flydd, hand on the hilt of his jag-sword. 'Run for your very life, and enjoy the price he pays you, while you can.'

Colm went without looking back. Will Klarm give him Gothryme, Maelys wondered, and will it be worth it? Or will it, as Ketila told him before she died, be far too late, as everything else has been too late for him?

'Father begged me for forgiveness,' said Nish, 'and I rejected him. He wanted my help to atone yet I, who seek redemption for my own failings, callously denied it to him. What kind of a man am I, to play god and refuse Father what he needed most?'

'You're human and fallible, like all of us,' said Flydd.

'Too fallible. I have made a terrible error of judgment. If I *had* believed Father,' said Nish, 'we wouldn't be here now. None of this would have happened. The chthonic fire would never have been found, and our world wouldn't be under threat. He *is* a monster, but I'm a fool.'

Maelys remembered the white fire spreading across all the southern ice around Noom, and shivered.

'The tears will take years to master,' said Yggur. 'Assuming Klarm can use them at all. He can't defend the world from the Stilkeen, or the revenants. To save Santhenar we've got to defeat Klarm first. Nish, are you all right?'

Nish shook his head, dazedly. 'I should be glad my

father is gone, never to be seen again. Why am I not?'

'Flesh is flesh and blood is blood,' said Flydd. 'The strongest bond of all.'

'The one I never appreciated until it was gone.'

Tulitine put an arm around him. 'Remember what I said about Vivimord after his trial at the Maelstrom of Justice and Retribution?'

'With powerful mancers, one must always see the body,' said Nish.

'The future is unwritten. Anything can happen.'

The horn sounded on the ridge, and Klarm's voice rang out. 'This is your last chance to surrender.'

Most of the prisoners followed Colm, though a few remained. No one spoke, and not a single man or woman of the militia moved, not even, to Nish's surprise, the few remaining of Boobelar's detachment.

'Very well,' said Klarm regretfully. 'You've made your choice. Imperial Militia, show them no quarter. Charge!'

THE END

OF BOOK TWO

The story concludes in book three of

THE SONG OF THE TEARS TRILOGY

THE DESTINY OF THE DEAD

GLOSSARY

Aachan: One of the Three Worlds, the original world of the Aachim and, after its conquest by The Hundred, the Charon. It was recently rendered uninhabitable by massive, and mysterious, volcanic eruptions, and some tens of thousands of Aachim fled to Santhenar through a portal, in a fleet of constructs.

Aachim: The human species native to Aachan; they are a long-lived, clever people, great artisans and engineers, but melancholy and prone to hubris. Many were brought as slaves to Santhenar in ancient times, but later the Aachim flourished, until they were betrayed by Rulke in the Clysm, after which they withdrew from the world to their hidden mountain cities (see also Aachan).

Aftersickness: Sickness that people suffer after using the Secret Art or a native gift or talent.

Antithesis: The one object (or power or force) that can break the power of the Profane Tears and bring down the God-Emperor.

Blending: A child of the union between two of the four different human species – Charon, Faellem, Aachim and old human. Blendings are rare, and often deranged, but can have remarkable talents.

Bladder-bat: A flesh-formed aerial attack beast. An internal bladder can be inflated with floater-gas, enabling it to lift heavy objects.

Calendar: Santhenar's year is roughly 395.7 days and contains twelve months, each of thirty-three days.

Charon: One of the four human species, once the master people of the world of Aachan where, mysteriously, the Charon were practically sterile, and though they had enormously long life, few children were born, until the race was almost extinct. At the end of the Time of the Mirror, the few survivors went back to the void, to go to their extinction with dignity.

Chissmoul: A thapter (flying construct) pilot during the lyrinx war, shy but known for her reckless verve.

Clanker: An armoured war cart which moved via pairs of mechanical legs and was powered by the field. All were rendered useless by the destruction of the nodes at the end of the war.

Clysm: A series of wars between the Charon and the Aachim beginning around 1500 years ago, resulting in the almost total devastation of Santhenar.

Colm: Once the heir to Gothryme, he lost both clan and heritage during the war and resents it deeply. He accompanied Maelys to Mistmurk Mountain and nurtures an affection for her. During the war, when Colm was just a boy, he helped Nish, and Nish promised to come back one day and help Colm regain his heritage. Colm is bitter that Nish forgot his promise, even though Nish was powerless in prison.

Compulsion: A form of the Secret Art; a way of forcing someone to do something against their will.

Construct: A war machine at least partly powered by the Secret Art, invented by Rulke in the Nightland. His construct was capable of creating portals, though the constructs later modelled on his by the Aachim were not. All were rendered useless by the destruction of the nodes at the end of the war.

Council of Santhenar: An alliance of powerful mancers. The Council helped to create the Nightland and cast Rulke into it, but was later overthrown by the Numinator.

Crandor: A rich, tropical land on the north-eastern side of Lauralin.

Cryl-Nish Hlar: Generally known as Nish, he started out badly but grew to become one of the greatest heroes of the lyrinx war, though at the end of it he was cast into prison for rebelling against his father, Jal-Nish. He was freed by Maelys a few months ago and has been on the run ever since. At the end of the war Nish vowed to overthrow his father and relieve the suffering of the people of Santhenar, but Nish has not been able to keep his promise, for he is stricken with self-doubt and afraid that he will take the same corrupt path as his father. He has always been tempted by power and what it can bring. And Nish never got over the death of his beloved Irisis, slain on his father's orders; Jal-Nish offers to bring her back from the dead and, though Nish knows this is impossible, he is unbearably tempted.

Cursed Flame: A mysterious flame in the caverns below the Charon obelisk on Mistmurk Mountain. It has somewhat ambiguous healing properties.

Defiance, the: The Deliverer's supporters and army, initially controlled by Monkshart.

Deliverer, the: The one person (or so the common folk believe) who can overthrow the God-Emperor.

Dry Sea: Formerly the Sea of Perion, it dried up in ancient times but began to flood at the end of the lyrinx war a decade ago and is now the Sea of Perion again.

Dunnet: A small, secluded land within Elludore Forest, once Faelamor's hideout.

Elludore: A large forested land, north and west of Thurkad on Meldorin Island.

Faelamor: Leader of the Faellem species who came to Santhenar soon after Rulke, to keep watch on the Charon and maintain the balance between the worlds. She was Maigraith's liege and kept her in thrall for most of her life. Faelamor took most of her people back to their world, Tallallame, at the end of the Time of the Mirror, and there they self-immolated.

Faellem: The human species who once inhabited the world of Tallallame. They were a small, dour people, forbidden to use machines and magical devices, but were masters of disguise and illusion.

Flangers: A soldier and hero in the lyrinx wars, he is stricken by guilt for following orders and shooting down a Council thapter, and desperate to atone.

Flappeter: A large flying creature flesh-formed by Jal-Nish, it has a pair of feather-rotors growing from the middle of its back. Flappeters are controlled by bonded riders, using enchanted amulets, and any harm to either flappeter or rider causes harm to the other.

Flesh-forming: A branch of the Secret Art invented by the lyrinx but now used by Jal-Nish.

Garr, Garrflood: The largest and wildest river in Meldorin. It arises to the west of Shazmak and runs to the Sea of Thurkad east of Sith.

Gate: A structure powered by the Secret Art, which permits people to move instantly from one place to another. Also called a portal.

Ghâshâd: The ancient, mortal enemies of the Aachim, they were a race born to serve unquestioningly. They were corrupted and swore allegiance to Rulke in ancient times, but when he was imprisoned in the Nightland they took a new name, Whelm, and served Yggur for a time. When Rulke escaped, they became Ghâshâd again, but upon his death swore to take no master ever after.

Ghorr: The corrupt former Chief Scrutator of the Council of Scrutators, and Flydd's bitter enemy, now dead.

Gilhaelith: An eccentric, amoral geomancer and tetrarch, he died by self-crystallisation at the end of the lyrinx war.

God-Emperor: The title assumed by Jal-Nish Hlar sometime after he took control of the world with the Profane Tears.

Gothryme: An impoverished manor near Tolryme in Bannador, on Meldorin Island. In the Time of the Mirror it belonged to Karan. Colm is the nominal heir but his family fled during the war and now it is occupied by people in the favour of the God-Emperor.

Great Library: Founded at Zile by the Zain in the time of the Empire of Zur, it lasted for thousands of years but disappeared from the Histories during the lyrinx war.

Great Tales: The greatest stories from the Histories of Santhenar. A tale can only become a Great Tale by the unanimous decision of the master chroniclers. In four thousand years only twenty-three Great Tales were made, the twenty-third being acclaimed by many as the greatest – Llian of Chanthed's *Tale of the Mirror*. More tales were written during the lyrinx war but they don't have the same force, as they were written as propaganda at the Chief Scrutator's behest.

Histories, the: The vast collection of records that chronicle more than four thousand years of history on Santhenar. The culture of Santhenar is interwoven with and inseparable from the Histories, and the most vital longing anyone can have is to be mentioned in them. Families and clans also keep their personal Histories.

Human species: There were four distinct human species: the Aachim of Aachan, the Faellem of Tallallame, the old humans of Santhenar, and the Charon who came out of the void. All but old humans could be very long-lived. Matings between the different species rarely produced children (see Blending).

Irisis Stirm: A heroine of the lyrinx war, and Nish's lover at the end of the war, she gave her life to try to save Nish from his father's vengeance.

Jal-Nish Hlar: Nish's father. He suffered massive injuries from a lyrinx attack during the war and begged to be allowed to die, but Nish and Irisis saved his life. Now hideously maimed and unable to repair himself even with the power of the tears, he controls the world as God-Emperor and plays malicious games with his enemies, though he has a secret fear that the world is under threat, once again, from the void. At the end of Book One he pleaded with Nish for help to atone for all his wrongs, but Nish, thinking Jal-Nish was playing another malicious game, repudiated him, and only realised too late that Jal-Nish was genuine.

Karan: During the Time of the Mirror, two centuries and more ago, she was a young woman of the house of Fyrn, but with blood of the Aachim from her father, Galliad, and old human and Faellem blood from her mother. This made her *triune*, though she did not know it. A sensitive whose home was Gothryme, Karan was the heroine of the *Tale of the Mirror* and wedded Llian at the end of it. She is now reviled as Karan Kin-Slayer, for killing Llian and her children, then herself, though no one can understand why.

Klarm: The former Dwarf Scrutator is a great mancer and a handsome, cheerful, brave man. He was one of Flydd's greatest allies during the lyrinx war.

Lauralin: The continent east of the Sea of Thurkad.

League: About 5000 paces, three miles or five kilometres.

Llian: An ostracised Zain, he was a master chronicler, a teller of the Great Tales, and one of the heroes of the *Tale of the Mirror*, which he wrote and which became the twenty-third Great Tale. He is now reviled as Llian the Liar, the master chronicler who dared to corrupt the histories and write a Great Tale that wasn't true.

Lyrinx: Massive winged humanoids, some of whom are

great mancers, who escaped from the void to Santhenar at the end of the Time of the Mirror. See also Lyrinx War.

Lyrinx War: The 150-year-long war between the winged lyrinx and the peoples of Santhenar, which ended ten years ago when the lyrinx were defeated and were given the alien-infested world of Tallallame for their own.

Maelys Nifferlin: A shy, demure girl of nineteen, one of the last of her clan, who was compelled by her mother and aunts to rescue Nish and get pregnant to him, so as to restore the clan. She did rescue Nish, and accompanied him on many adventures, though he, still obsessed with his beloved Irisis, repudiated her tentative advances and Maelys was so mortified that she was not game to try again.

Maigraith: An orphan brought up and trained by Faelamor, she was a master of the Secret Art. She became Yggur's lover, briefly, and at the end of the Time of the Mirror she fell for Rulke and became pregnant to him not long before he died.

Malien: An Aachim, and once one of their leaders, she was an ally of Flydd and Yggur during the lyrinx war but has not been seen since it ended.

Mancer: A wizard or sorcerer; someone who is a master of the Secret Art.

Mendark: A great mancer from the Time of the Mirror, he took renewal on many occasions but was killed at the end of the Time of the Mirror.

Monkshart: The name taken by Jal-Nish's former ally and friend, Vivimord, after renouncing his allegiance. He is a charismatic zealot and mancer, but corrupt. He is trying to use the Deliverer to bring down the God-Emperor because he believes that for any man to take such a title is blasphemy.

Nightland: A place, distant from the world of reality, where Rulke was kept prisoner for a thousand years. Tensor made a gate into the Nightland to revenge himself on Rulke, but only succeeded in letting him out, and shortly the Nightland collapsed into nothingness, or so it was believed.

Nish: See Cryl-Nish Hlar.

Numinator, the: A mysterious figure who dwells at the Tower of a Thousand Steps, on the Island of Noom in the frozen south, and secretly controlled the Council of Scrutators.

Nylatl: A small but vicious armoured beast created by lyrinx flesh-forming as a weapon in the war.

Old human: The original human species on Santhenar and by far the most numerous.

Phrune: Monkshart's acolyte, healer and perhaps lover; a sadistic killer whom Maelys slew at the Cursed Flame.

Portal: See Gate.

Profane Tears: Two tear-shaped globes, called Gatherer and Reaper, with the appearance of roiling quicksilver, created by the implosion of a node of power thirteen years ago and stolen by Jal-Nish. When all the nodes were destroyed at the end of the war, the tears gave him the power to control the world. Gatherer coordinates all Jal-Nish's spies and spying devices; Reaper punishes and destroys.

Quartine: see Tetrarch.

Rulke: A Charon and the greatest of The Hundred. In ancient times Rulke was imprisoned in the Nightland until a way could be found to banish him back to Aachan. When Tensor opened a gate into the Nightland, Rulke was able to escape into Santhenar, but he was later killed by Tensor.

Santhenar, Santh: The least of the Three Worlds, home of the old human peoples.

Secret Art: The use of magical or sorcerous powers (mancing). An art that very few can use and then only after considerable training. The Art was greatly weakened ten years ago, after Tiaan destroyed all the nodes of power, thus concentrating virtually all mancery in Jal-Nish's sorcerous Profane Tears.

Shadow Realm: The uncanny place through which Flydd hopes to pass, to escape Jal-Nish.

Shazmak: The forgotten city of the Aachim, in the mountains west of Bannador. It was sacked by the Ghâshâd after they were woken from their long years as Whelm.

Span: The distance spanned by the stretched arms of a tall man. About six feet, or slightly less than two metres.

Spying Devices: The God-Emperor has many spying devices, such as wisp-watchers, loop listeners and snoop-sniffers, all relaying information back to the tear, Gatherer.

Talent: A native skill or gift, usually honed by extensive training.

Tallallame: One of the Three Worlds, once the world of the Faellem. A beautiful, mountainous world covered in forest but now, in a cosmic irony, infested by alien creatures from the void.

Taphloid: An egg-sized device made from yellow metal, given to Maelys by her father to suppress the aura created by her talent; it has other, as yet unknown, properties.

Teller: One who has mastered the ritual telling of the tales that form part of the Histories of Santhenar.

Tensor: The proud, flawed leader of the Aachim for thousands of years, he let Rulke out of the Nightland. Tensor was killed at the end of the Tale of the Mirror.

Tetrarch: a person bearing the blood of all four human species. Also called quartine.

Thapter: A flying construct.

The Hundred: The one hundred surviving Charon who escaped from the void, led by Rulke, then took Aachan from the Aachim and held them in thrall for thousands of years.

Three Worlds: Santhenar, Aachan and Tallallame.

Thurkad: Once the greatest city on Santhenar, it was occupied and partly destroyed by the lyrinx.

Tiaan: A troubled heroine first heard of towards the end of the lyrinx war. She destroyed all the nodes of power at the end of the war, taking most of the world's Arts with them, and has not been seen since.

Time of the Mirror: The interval spanned by the *Tale of the Mirror*, roughly 224 to 220 years ago.

Triune: A double blending – one with the blood of all Three Worlds, three different human species. They are extremely rare but may have remarkable abilities. Karan and Maigraith were triune.

Tulitine: A mysterious old woman, healer and perhaps seer, who helped to bring together the Defiance.

Void, the: The spaces between the Three Worlds. A Darwinian place where life is more brutal and fleeting than anywhere. The void teems with the most exotic life imaginable, for nothing survives there without remaking itself constantly.

Vivimord: See Monkshart.

Whelm: See Ghâshâd.

Xervish Flydd: A former scrutator (spymaster and master inquisitor) on the Council of Scrutators, he was subsequently stripped of his position but helped to overthrow the corrupt scrutators and led the final struggle against the lyrinx which led to their defeat. Forced to flee at the end of the war, he spent nine years trapped by infirmity at the top of Mistmurk Mountain. There Maelys pressured him to take renewal so he could help them fight Jal-Nish and search for the antithesis to the tears, but the renewal went wrong.

Yalkara: The Demon Queen, the 'Mistress of Deceits'. She took the surviving, sterile Charon back to the void, to extinction, at the end of the Tale of the Mirror.

Yggur: A great and powerful mancer and sworn enemy of Mendark, whose long life and great gifts have always been a mystery; he was a reluctant ally of Flydd during the latter stages of the war but has not been seen since.

Ian Irvine was born in Bathurst, Australia, in 1950, and educated at Chevalier College and the University of Sydney, where he took a PhD in marine science.

After working as an environmental project manager, Ian set up his own consulting firm in 1986, carrying out studies for clients in Australia and overseas. He has worked in many countries in the Asia-Pacific region. An expert in marine pollution, Ian has developed some of Australia's national guidelines for the protection of the oceanic environment.

The international success of Ian Irvine's debut fantasy series, *The View from the Mirror*, immediately established him as one of the most popular new authors in the fantasy genre. He is now a full-time writer and lives in the mountains of northern New South Wales, Australia, with his family.

Ian Irvine has his own website at www.ian-irvine.com and can be contacted at Ianirvine@ozemail.com.au

Find out more about Ian Irvine and other Orbit authors by registering for the free monthly newsletter at www.orbitbooks.net